THE PORTABLE HENRY JAMES

The Viking Portable Library

Each Portable Library volume is made up of representative works of a favorite modern or classic author, or is a comprehensive anthology on a special subject. The format is designed for compactness and for pleasurable reading. The books average about 700 pages in length. Each is intended to fill a need not hitherto met by any single book. Each is edited by an authority distinguished in his field, who adds a thoroughgoing introductory essay and other helpful material. Most "Portables" are available both in durable cloth and in stiff paper covers.

****

THE PORTABLE

HENRY JAMES

EDITED, AND WITH AN INTRODUCTION, BY

MORTON DAUWEN ZABEL

*

Revised in 1968 by Lyall H. P. Powers,
University of Michigan

NEW YORK

THE VIKING PRESS

****

COPYRIGHT 1951, 1956, 1968

BY THE VIKING PRESS, INC.

PUBLISHED IN AUGUST 1951

PUBLISHED ON THE SAME DAY IN THE DOMINION

OF CANADA BY THE MACMILLAN COMPANY

OF CANADA LIMITED

TENTH PRINTING MARCH 1967

REVISED EDITION ISSUED IN SEPTEMBER 1968

Grateful acknowledgment is made to the following for permission to reprint selections: Charles Scribner's Sons, New York, for "Four Meetings" from Volume XVI of *The Novels and Tales of Henry James,* copyright 1909 by Charles Scribner's Sons, 1937 by Henry James; "The Pupil" from Volume XI of *The Novels and Tales of Henry James,* copyright 1908 by Charles Scribner's Sons, 1936 by Henry James; "The Turn of the Screw" from Volume XII of *The Novels and Tales of Henry James* (New York Edition), copyright 1908 by Charles Scribner's Sons; "The Beast in the Jungle" from *The Better Sort,* copyright 1903 by Charles Scribner's Sons, 1931 by Henry James; letters from *The Letters of Henry James,* copyright 1920 by Charles Scribner's Sons, 1948 by William James; "The Sense of Glory" from *A Small Boy and Others,* copyright 1913 by Charles Scribner's Sons, 1941 by Henry James; "The End of the Civil War" from *Notes of a Son and Brother,* copyright 1914 by Charles Scribner's Sons, 1942 by Henry James; "The Banquet of Initiation" from *The Middle Years,* copyright 1917, 1945 by Charles Scribner's Sons; Harper & Brothers, New York, for "New York Revisited" and "The Voice of Concord" from *The American Scene,* copyright 1907 by Henry James, 1935 by Henry James; Oxford University Press, Inc., New York, for the excerpt from *The Notebooks of Henry James,* edited by F. O. Matthiessen and Kenneth B. Murdock, copyright 1947 by Oxford University Press, Inc.; John Farquharson, London, for "The Art of Fiction," "Criticism," the excerpt from *Hawthorne,* "Honoré de Balzac," "Gustave Flaubert," "The After-Season in Rome," "Occasional Paris," and "London."

LIBRARY OF CONGRESS CATALOG CARD NUMBER: 51–12143

PRINTED IN U.S.A. BY THE COLONIAL PRESS INC.

CONTENTS

PART IV: PORTRAITS OF PLACES:
FOUR CITIES

PART V: PASSAGES OF AUTOBIOGRAPHY
AND A JOURNAL

PART VI: LETTERS

CONTENTS

BIBLIOGRAPHY

INTRODUCTION

I

Henry James once spoke of how "the private history of any sincere work . . . looms with its own completeness." In another place he wrote that "the figures in any picture, the agents in any drama, are interesting only in proportion as they feel their respective situations. . . . Their being finely aware—as Hamlet and Lear, say, are finely aware—*makes* absolutely the intensity of their adventure, gives the maximum of sense to what befalls them."

On both occasions James was defining principles for the art to which he devoted his entire life—the art of fiction. But it is safe to say that he also spoke with conscious reference to himself, to his own adventure in the eventful age he witnessed and his own way of turning it to account. The world of readers and critics was slow to admit the intensity of that adventure or to recognize the "maximum of sense" James gave it. His private history was not of the kind that "looms large" with the dramatic capacities in action or passion that have made a whole host of modern writers—from Goethe, Byron, and Dostoevski to Rimbaud, Yeats, Lawrence, and Lorca —vivid figures in the mythology of the human spirit. Outwardly viewed, his career was unspectacular. It was the art and mind by which he enriched it that made it a great life and that continue to make James one of the most interesting figures in the drama of the past century.

Henry James was born on April 15, 1843, in Washington Place in New York City. Fifty years earlier his Irish grandfather had come to America where he established himself in trade in several cities of New York state, prospered handsomely, married three times, and when he died in 1832 left a fortune of three million dollars to his children. By his third wife he had a son called Henry, who rebelled against assuming the family business and devoted himself instead to the study of religion, philosophy, and humanity. This son married at the age of thirty, and four sons and a daughter were born to him and his wife, the oldest son being called William after his grandfather, the second Henry, after his father. In 1843 these two infants were taken across the Atlantic by their parents to spend part of a year in France and England, but the family returned to America and during the next ten years the children received their early schooling in New York and Albany. They were back in Europe in 1855 for three years, and again in 1859 for one. There Henry James went to schools in Switzerland, France, England, and Germany and discovered his passion for books and writing. Back in Newport in 1860 he tried studying painting, gave it up, attended the Harvard Law School briefly, gave it up, lived with his family in Cambridge, began to meet literary men like Charles Eliot Norton, James Russell Lowell, and William Dean Howells, resolved to become a writer, began his public career with a review in the *North American* in 1864 and a story in the *Atlantic Monthly* in 1865, and in another ten years had his first book of tales ready for publication.

Meanwhile his love of travel took him to Europe on his first adult journey in 1869 and on two further trips during the following six years. He studied the French theater at the Comédie Française; he put himself to school among the literary circles of Paris and London, forming friendships with Turgenev, Flaubert, Renan, Zola, Daudet, George Eliot, Ruskin, Morris, Tennyson, Browning, Gladstone, Morley, and other public figures in both countries; he explored Italy, Germany, France, and England. By 1876 he had established himself permanently in London, and he continued to live there and in Sussex for the rest of his life. His books —novels, tales, critical essays, accounts of travel—appeared in increasing numbers year by year. Success came early, and at least twice—with *Daisy Miller* in 1879 and *The Portrait of a Lady* in 1881—he knew public celebrity; but gradually his novels fell into public and critical disfavor. For five years, from 1890 to 1895, he devoted himself to making a success in the theater, but this effort ended in failure. He resumed the writing of fiction; produced a long series of books of increasing subtlety and originality; cultivated a great host of friends; revisited America after an absence of twenty-one years in 1904 and rediscovered his native land as a famous man; revised his major fictions for a handsome collected edition; again tried writing for the theater, again unsuccessfully; came back to America in 1910 with his dying brother William; returned to England; witnessed the outbreak of war in 1914 with shock and anguish; wrote a series of memoirs of his early years; tried to resume the writing of novels; became a British citizen in 1915 as a sign of loyalty to his adopted country; was taken ill in his seventy-third year; received England's Order of Merit on his deathbed; and died in February 1916.

It was a life which, apart from deep family affections, many devoted friendships, many travels, a few high moments of public celebrity and several of uncomfortable notoriety, was a record of little except incessant labor at the desk, many books read and many written, and finally a quiet death in the fullness of years. It was committed to a difficult and increasingly thankless kind of work, and in spite of James's extreme respect for his calling, his almost sacerdotal conception of the literary vocation, he was frequently beset by fears that his efforts had come to nothing. More than once he felt that he had "entered upon evil days," that his finest work had "reduced the desire, and the demand, of [his] productions to zero," that he was "condemned apparently to eternal silence." What he called the "complete failure" of the sumptuous New York Edition of his fiction left him, toward the end of his life, "high and dry"— "at my age . . . and after my long career, utterly, insurmountably, unsaleable"—and he called that crowning monument of his labors "a sort of miniature Ozymandias of Egypt ('look on my *works*, ye mighty, and despair!')." He wrote his failure to win popular approval into a remarkable series of tales—"The Author of Beltraffio," "The Lesson of the Master," "The Death of the Lion," "The Middle Years," "The Next Time," and half a dozen others—which picture art as a tyrannical taskmaster who breaks his devotees when they are frail, tests them cruelly when they are strong, or grants them at best a secret victory which the world appears bound to condemn or ignore. It was with something like the defiance of a proud desperation that he told William Dean Howells, at one particularly bleak moment in his fortunes, that "some day all my buried prose will kick off its various tombstones at once."

We have seen his prophecy justified. When the hundredth anniversary of James's birth arrived in 1943 it saw his fame sweeping into the full tide of a revival that has raised him to a position of supremacy among the novelists of the English-speaking world and given him a rank in the highest company of modern writers. The decade of the nineteen-forties and the years of crisis just preceding it witnessed a crowded procession of centenaries—anniversaries of artists and thinkers who helped to shape a momentous century in the life of Western man. Hardy, Zola, and Nietzsche, Swinburne, Pater, and Butler, Mallarmé, Verlaine, and Anatole France, Cézanne and Renoir, Americans like Mark Twain, Howells, Henry Adams, William James, Bierce, and Lanier—in a time of danger and catastrophe the date of each of them sounded its knell on a darkening age and provided its occasion for revaluing the legacy, heartening or dubious, they left to their inheritors. None of them met a more dramatic recognition than Henry James. As if by a stroke of ironic justice, his own worst fears for his future were dispelled at a time that brought ignominy to much of the civilization he had most valued. "During our current afflictions," said one English tribute, "he has found a greater body of readers than ever before, who discover in him a mirror of the civilized enjoyments now in abeyance, a guardian of the values that war repudiates."

It was an axiom of the aesthetes of the nineties that nature imitates art. James's work makes us believe that history does so also. A great share of the history of his age now appears to find its permanent image in his pages. His books have become a standing example of what he meant when he told H. G. Wells in 1915 that literature *"makes* life, makes interest, makes importance . . . and I know no substitute whatever for the force and beauty of its process." Our present interest in James derives partly, no doubt, from the distrust of history and action that has been bred by the political and moral disorder into which the world has fallen, by the prolonged crisis and sense of disintegrating traditions in which we have come to live. We see in him, by a species of retrospective logic, what men have always seen in their image-makers and heroes of form—what Santayana meant when he said, defining Proust's achievement, that "Life as it flows is so much time wasted, and that nothing can ever be recovered or truly possessed save under the form of eternity, which is also . . . the form of art."

The revival of James has bred its excesses of cult and sanctimony. They come partly from a natural pride—notably an American pride—in reclaiming the books that were for many years disputed or rejected by critics of many schools and prejudices: by realists, by patriots, by skeptics of culture, by reformers of society, by proletarians, all of whom combined to make the public forget that James had his faithful if limited audience through fifty years; that his tales and novels were printed in magazines on a scale that has become incredible in our own boasted age of literary freedom and experiment; that he met positive defeat only once —in his efforts to become a successful dramatist—and turned even that drastic disappointment to the advantage of his real work in fiction; and that his fellow writers had granted him the title of "Master." His critics preferred to charge him with most of the sins in the literary and American calendars—with repudiating his birthright, with being a snob, with falling indecisively between two cultures and finding himself at home in neither, with evading a full commitment to life, with accepting only the values of privilege and aristocracy, with excluding a great share of human misery and injustice from serious consideration. He was accused of being the "culmination of the superficial type," a man

who "doesn't find things out" and so produces "tales of
nothingness"; of being "a fat, wistful remittance man
with a passion for elegance"; of having "never succeeded in coming to grips with life"; of creating "the
impassioned formalism of an art without content"; of
"magnificent pretensions, petty performances!—the fruits
of an irresponsible imagination, of a deranged sense of
values, of a mind working in the void, uncorrected by
any clear consciousness of human cause and effect";
even, finally, of being "simply not interesting: he is
only intelligent; he has no mystery in him, no secret;
no Figure in the Carpet." [1]

This long bill of particulars includes some arguments
with which every serious reader of James must eventually deal, but the verdict is now, on the whole, a very
different one. As early as 1918 one of James's most perceptive followers had made bold to call him "the most
intelligent man of his generation," and today critics of
resolute astuteness and of radically different standards
attest his distinction. "Henry James *is* a great artist, in
spite of everything," says one of them; "his work is
incomplete as his experience was; but it is in no respect
second-rate, and he can be judged only in the company
of the greatest." Another, asking only that he be permitted to define the novel in a way "neither difficult
nor illegitimate," has said he would "be inclined to consider James as the greatest novelist in English, as he is
certainly one of the five or six greatest writers of any
variety to be produced in North America." A third has
called James "a man who, if he had never written a
novel, would be considered the first of short-story writ-

[1] The critics quoted are H. G. Wells (in *Boon*, 1915), Bur-
ton Rascoe, Somerset Maugham, J. Middleton Murry, Van
Wyck Brooks (in *The Pilgrimage of Henry James*, 1925), and
André Gide.

ers, and if he had never written a short story, the
noblest of letter writers, and if he had never written
anything would by his talk alone be known as a great
man." A fourth has flatly asked, "What achievement
in the art of fiction—fiction as a completely serious art
addressed to the adult mind—can we point to in English as surpassing his?" [1]

When controversy, enthusiasm, personal legend, and
historic occasion combine in the rediscovery of a writer
and make of it a significant episode in the history of
taste, it is clear that he constitutes what James himself
would have called a "special type"—that he was marked
by circumstances as well as genius to play a significant
role in the drama of culture. James held a high opinion
of the artist's right to such a role. "To do something
great" of which "the world shall hear" was one of his
earliest ambitions. Once, in the earlier days of his conquest of England, he was a guest of Lord Rosebery and
his Rothschild wife amid the splendors of Mentmore.
"I have retired from the glittering scene, to meditate
by my bedroom fire on the fleeting character of earthly
possessions," he wrote home to his mother in America.
"Tomorrow I return to London and to my personal occupation, always doubly valued after 48 hours among
ces gens-ci, whose chief effect upon me is to sharpen
my desire to distinguish myself by personal achievement, of however limited a character." The desire for
fame and power, that "sense of glory" which had struck
him in boyhood like a revelation in the Galerie d'Apollon
in the Louvre, possessed him even though he felt the

[1] The critics quoted here are T. S. Eliot in *The Little Review,* August 1918; Edmund Wilson in *The Triple Thinkers*
(1938); Yvor Winters in *Maule's Curse* (1939); Cyril Con-
nolly in *Horizon,* May 1943; F. R. Leavis in *The Great Tradition* (1948).

peril it entailed. He would certainly have agreed with what one of his contemporaries, Gerard Manley Hopkins, then wholly unknown to literature, once wrote in a letter to Robert Bridges: that "fame, the being known, though in itself one of the most dangerous things to man, is nevertheless the true and appointed air, element, and setting of genius and its works. What are works of art for? to educate, to be standards. Education is meant for the many, standards are for public use. To produce then is of little use unless what we produce is known, if known widely known, the wider known the better, for it is by being known it works, it influences, it does its duty, it does good. We must then try to be known, aim at it, take means to it."

What James aimed at in his art, what means he took to provide a standard for the use and education of men, what tests and scruples he met in the effort, and by what means his purposes were finally vindicated—all this makes his career one of the dramatic chapters in modern literature, and permits him to loom large in a way that has become a lesson in the persistence and integrity of the writer's vocation. But because James was a man who, contrary to a still-surviving derogation, did not live or work unaware of his role in history, it has become something more.

II

James published his first tale in 1865, when he was twenty-two years old. That date, in the career of an American, acts as an initial signal. The Civil War had just ended. The American nation, like James himself, stood at the threshold of a new age. Her literature had already passed through its successive formative phases. Each of them had found a man, some of them several men, to voice its deciding impulse. Bradford, Mather, Edwards, and Franklin, Jefferson, Irving, Cooper, Emerson, and Whitman brought the republic by clearly defined stages—colonial, religious, revolutionary; frontier, pioneer, and nationalist—to the moment when several talents possessed of a vision more original and searching than any of these crowned the progress of the American spirit with what serious maturity in any ordained course inevitably entails: a moral challenge, a check to self-esteem, a warning to the will, a vision of the tragedy implicit in pride and success. The American mind, rooted in its hereditary conscience, had never escaped its hauntings by darker powers, its stirrings of ancestral guilt, what Howells was presently to call "the slavery implicated in our liberty." Poe had recently imaged them unmistakably. But an enormous confidence in the American destiny allayed them until Hawthorne, Melville, and, in her Amherst seclusion, Emily Dickinson gave them their classic and prophetic definition. The Civil War came as if to certify their presence. An hour of judgment sounded. It called for a new order of intelligence in American life, a critical intelligence; and neither the victory of 1865 nor the prosperity that followed it in the North could disguise the summons.

No writer more than the novelist is so likely to prove, once his work is finished, that he was born at precisely the right moment to become the artist he was intended to be. Stendhal, Balzac, Dickens, Tolstoi, Proust, and Thomas Mann all illustrate the opportunity with which history favors the prose chronicler beyond any other type of artist. The literary novice of 1865 could hardly remain unaware of his special opportunity, particularly when, as in Henry James's case, he saw the end—both triumphant and tragic—of a great national conflict in which a mischance of health had prevented him from taking an active part and whose meaning he was made to feel with a special personal intensity. Already in 1865 James had declared his opposition to Walt Whitman's kind of visionary emotion, but he shared with Whitman the non-participant's sense of the crisis that befell the American nation in the spring of that year.

This is to say that several distinct tasks—two great tasks especially—presented themselves to the young writer of 1865 who was able to see their urgency. One was the problem of defining the point at which America had arrived in her venture of nationhood and of determining her relation to the rival civilization of Europe— a problem which, in spite of the fact that almost every serious American writer had already addressed himself to it, still remained unsettled in the balance-books of history. The other was the re-creation of the art of fiction as a form of critical intelligence by rescuing it from the debris of tradition and the compromises of popularity, and by raising it to the dignity of moral power which novelists like Balzac, Turgenev, and Flaubert had already won for it in Europe, but which only Hawthorne and George Eliot had reached in the novel of the English-speaking world. James saw, with the full insight of his youthful acumen, these two great opportunities at his disposal. He saw he had a major theme to treat, and he saw that a new kind of art was needed to treat it adequately; and he took these as the special tokens of his vocation in literature.

His subject was made inescapable by the family into which he was born. His Irish grandfather had provided the wealth that endowed his heirs with the privileges of comfort, travel, and social affluence. His father, another adventurer but in religion and philosophic speculation instead of trade, had converted those assets to the service of thought and imagination. The James home was a breeding place of curiosity, ideas, and bookish pleasures. Emerson was a familiar guest there—"the divinely pompous rose of the philosophic garden," the elder James called him—and the air was a stir of enthusiasms. Idealism, transcendentalism, and democratic emancipation bred the new faith in humanity whose guides were Emerson and Fourier, and a creative freedom in religion whose prophets were Sandeman and Swedenborg. What a later American,[1] echoing Emerson, has ascribed to the American character as "a heightened sensitivity to the promises of life" was the native emotion of the James home. Man was to be redeemed by society. Society was to be redeemed by a rebirth of moral confidence and a faith in "possibilities." Such ideas implanted in both William and Henry James a religious conviction which, persisting beyond rationality or agnosticism, was to fix its stamp on their ultimate conceptions of science and of art.

But another emotion, balancing and complicating the ardor of emancipation, dominated the family. It was the spell of the past, the call ot Europe. "I saw my parents homesick, as I conceived, for the ancient order," Henry James said many years later, "and distressed and inconvenienced by many of the more immediate features of the modern, as the modern pressed about us, and since their theory of our better living was from an early time that we should renew the question of the ancient on the very first possibility I simply grew greater in the faith that somehow to manage that would constitute success in life. I never found myself deterred from this fond view, which was implied in every question I asked, every answer I got, and every plan I formed." In her early essay on James, Rebecca West has said that the essential thing about him was that "he was an American;

[1] F. Scott Fitzgerald.

and that meant, for his type and generation, that he could never feel at home until he was in exile." James himself said it better when he wrote, "It's a complex fate being an American," and better still when he declared it was his function as an artist to be a man "on whom nothing is lost." It was the decree of the elder Henry James that his children should experience their complete fate as Americans by knowing the share Europe played in their lives. By taking his family abroad he enforced the instinct of tradition and cultural complexity in his sons, and he prepared Henry James for the subject that was to tax him throughout his life.

James's Europe, first in boyhood but presently in early manhood, was what Europe is bound to be at some point in the life of every American with any of the emotion or imagination of history in his constitution. It was the "threshold of expectation," the "gate of admirations," a "scene for the reverential spirit." It was "this dear old Europe," a world "immemorial, complex, accumulated"; and he came to it as a "passionate pilgrim," an "heir of all the ages." There he feasted on his "banquet of initiation," experienced "the sense of glory," "looked at history as a still-felt past and a complacently personal future, at society, manners, types, characters, possibilities and prodigies and mysteries of fifty sorts." There he learned that glory meant "ever so many things at once, not only beauty and art and supreme design, but history and fame and power, the world in fine raised to the richest and noblest expression." But though he brought to Europe a good share of his traditional American innocence, he also brought a shrewd curiosity and a divided sympathy. "I still love my country," he wrote his mother in 1869 from his "wondrous England," and that love, tough-rooted and ineradicable, soon defined an attitude that was to assert itself as radical. It

set in motion a debate, a drama of contrasts and oppositions, that was never to subside wholly, either in his
mind or in the tales he created.

What he really had carried to Europe, along with his
native exhilaration and the reverence he had been bred
in in his father's house, was another emotion of which
the Jameses—father, William, Henry, Alice—were all
to become aware in their lives. Henry named it many
years later, in 1896, in a letter to a friend. "I have the
imagination of disaster—and see life indeed as ferocious
and sinister." It was a presentiment that had already
visited his father, as it was to visit his brother and sister, in the form of panic seizure and crises of emotional
illness. In Henry himself it remained controlled by a
strong and vigorous imagination, but it remained none
the less radical to his nature; and it soon added the
force of a tragic vision to his excited responses to the
scene of Europe.

We hear much about the dialectic intelligence in
modern literature. It has come to be regarded as a primary clue to all serious art, a symptom of genuine morality. It is a kind of intelligence of which James is a major
exponent in our literature. He was schooled in it by his
earliest experiences and education. It suffuses all of his
work, serves as fulcrum to his insights and judgments,
and plays its part continuously in the oppositions—
America and Europe, innocence and experience, glory
and disaster, illusion and reality—which are the basic
terms of his drama of morality and culture.

Its workings in his fiction have been variously defined.
One critic, Yvor Winters, has defined them with particular relevance: James's fiction argues that "there is a
moral sense, a sense of decency, inherent in human
character at its best; that this sense of decency, being
only a sense, exists precariously, and may become con-

fused and even hysterical in a crisis; that it may be enriched and cultivated through association with certain environments; that such association may, also, be carried so far as to extinguish the moral sense." And further: that "the moral sense as James conceives it is essentially or at least appears to James most clearly in American character; that it can be cultivated by association with European civilization and manners; that it may be weakened or in some other manner betrayed by an excess of such association." [1]

This is not to say that the American character supplies the invariable norm of virtue or decency in James's tales. The American he pictures in Europe may be innocent, worshipful, honest, or idealistic—may be Daisy Miller, Isabel Archer, Christopher Newman, Milly Theale, Maggie Verver—and thus fall victim through the very fault of his innocence to duplicity or intrigue in the older culture. He may also become perverted by some moral weakness, or by wealth, self-indulgence, and the corruption of cynicism, and thus a doer of evil —Roderick Hudson, Madame Merle, Gilbert Osmond, Charlotte Stant. He may save himself there like Lambert Strether or lose himself like Hudson and Osmond. He will in any case be tested by a complexity he is never likely to have known in his native element; and the test will measure not only his own capacities for intelligence and moral dignity but also the America he came from.

Equally he will act as a test of the culture he encounters, for James's Europe shows a hostility of forces equal to that shown by America or by the two worlds when they meet in conflict. If the America James knew

[1] Yvor Winters, "Maule's Well, or Henry James and the Relation of Morals to Manners," in *Maule's Curse* (1938), p. 169.

in youth gave him a standard of soundness and honesty (*The American, The Europeans, Washington Square*), it could also be crude, simple-minded, predatory, and half-barbaric (*Watch and Ward, Confidence, The Bostonians*); and if the America he rediscovered late in life revealed unsuspected capacities of energy, inventiveness, and social amenity (*The American Scene*), it also warned him of a corruption through wealth and power that could debase its victims and make Europe in turn assume the virtues of spiritual dignity and maturity ("The Jolly Corner," "A Round of Visits," *The Ivory Tower*). But when the Jamesian drama shifts to England and offers a drama exclusively European, as it does in *The Princess Casamassima, The Tragic Muse, What Maisie Knew, The Awkward Age, The Spoils of Poynton,* and *The Sacred Fount,* it may depict the forces of morality and culture not as stabilized by tradition but as even more dangerous in their workings, their pregnancy of evil and treachery, than in the younger and simpler society. There the idealist, the artist, the innocent, or the child may encounter an immanence of disaster even more "ferocious and sinister" than America offers, by reason of the cynicism which time and privilege have bred.

Henry James was incapable of his sister Alice's scathing criticism of European society and politics, as he was incapable of his brother William's robust confidence in the American future. But he fully sensed the evil in what he called "the increasing dehumanization of society"; he knew what threat existed in the "black depths" and "enormous misery" of "the people"; he dreaded the advance of the "grossly materialistic"; and he spoke partly for himself when he made the heroine of *The Princess Casamassima,* his most ambitious drama of modern politics, describe English society as "the old régime again, bristling with every iniquity and every abuse, over which the French Revolution passed like a whirlwind; or perhaps even more a reproduction of Roman society in its decadence, gouty, apoplectic, depraved, gorged and clogged with wealth and spoils, selfishness and scepticism, and waiting for the onset of the barbarians."

James's argument, however rooted in the antithetical values of America and Europe, was never capable of simplicity. He was too deeply implicated in his own divided loyalties to permit it to become so. He was " 'between' countries," as Edna Kenton has rightly said: "There lay his subject and his relation to it, and there was his home"; and "Life is a struggle, wherever we are." But another loyalty claimed him too, another law of moral justice that forbade the rigidities of bias or the simplifications of prejudice. It was the principle of his art, with its standards of detachment, critical lucidity, and mind—that "quality of mind" which he defined as art's crowning virtue because it embodies the fullest possible measure of critical and moral sympathy, "unprejudiced and imperative," and thus insures a value higher than either passion or dogmatism. "I have not the least hesitation," he wrote his brother William in 1888, "in saying that I aspire to write in such a way that it would be impossible to an outsider to say whether I am at a given moment an American writing about England or an Englishman writing about America (dealing as I do with both countries), and so far from being ashamed of such an ambiguity I should be exceedingly proud of it, for it would be highly civilized."

III

The worth of an art "civilized" in James's sense was not a matter of common acceptance when James wrote those sentences, and it is ceasing to be so in various quarters today. Literature, like life itself, is again being reclaimed by prejudice and force. Having passed through a great period of experiment and sophistication, it is once more called upon to declare positions, judgments, decisions; to revert to crudity or didacticism in order to serve the uses of social justice; to become partisan, political, or *engagé*. That demand continues to support the argument that James's work is a symptom of the casuistry, ambiguity, and equivocation that have undermined society and incurred its disasters. Thus the long-standing complaints about "a mind working in the void, uncorrected by any clear consciousness of human cause and effect," "an art without content," an inability "to come to grips with life."

They are complaints which, lodged against a minor part of his work, have a certain relevance, but they cannot stand against the weight and solidity of his whole achievement. James must be read, and read in his entirety; read not with the demand that he be another Tolstoi, Dostoevski, or Melville, or even a Balzac or Dickens, but because he had his own unique contribution to make to the art of fiction and made it in a way that proves him as much a moral historian as any of these, even when he fell short of their final range and eloquence.

It may be allowed that the lengths of subtlety, analysis, and density to which James carried his craft can, if we do not follow him far enough, obscure the laws on which he based it. A factor of contrivance or calculation does figure in his workmanship. The ideas or "germs" for his tales, which he compiled in his notebooks—those germs which illustrate the "odd law which somehow always makes the minimum of valid suggestion serve the man of imagination better than the maximum" —sometimes take on the appearance of theorems in moral algebra or exercises in dramatic calculus. Occasionally his stories—slighter tales like "The Solution," "The Real Right Thing," and "The Great Condition"; intricate parables like "The Figure in the Carpet"; elaborate studies in social morality like *The Tragic Muse* and *The Awkward Age;* dramas of obsession or hallucination like *The Other House* and *The Sacred Fount*—will show a virtuosity that results in sheer intellection or a disembodiment of sensibility. Most of James's plays for the theater, lacking his narrative and stylistic body, expose their skeletons of pure contrivance and lapse into theatrical formulae. H. G. Wells, hostile as a social and scientific realist to James's art, complained that James's exhaustive analysis of motives becomes "psychologizing" rather than genuine psychology; but even some of James's greatest admirers have found in the novels of his final period—*The Ambassadors, The Golden Bowl, The Sense of the Past*—an "unhealthy vitality of undernourishment and etiolation," a failure in the "sense of human solidarity," an excess of expression over "what is actually felt." Is *The Ambassadors,* for instance, what James himself and a large body of recent readers consider it, "the best 'all round'" of his novels, or is F. R. Leavis justified in thinking it "to be not only *not* one of his great books, but to be a bad one"? Is *The Awkward Age,* as Leavis insists, "one of James's major achievements," or does it, as Edmund Wilson believes, combine "a lifeless trickery of logic with the equivocal subjectivity of a nightmare"? James was always fascinated by the difference between "a given appearance and a taken meaning," and obviously this difference, pushed far enough, can produce a disproportion between fact and illusion, substance and ratiocination, manners and morals, which is likely to end in casuistry and moral enigma.

These are the serious grounds of Jamesian criticism. What seems clear to the present writer is that James established his certain mastery in the books of his so-called "middle period." That great sequence begins with the concise perfection of *Washington Square,* continues through *The Portrait of a Lady* (possibly the touchstone of his entire achievement, with its shapeliness and movement as of fine music and its superbly controlled sympathy and justice) and his two masterpieces of social drama, *The Bostonians* and *The Princess Casamassima,* and is rounded out by the brilliant *nouvelles* of the nineties, to reach its climax in such searching studies of human and ethical values as *What Maisie Knew* and *The Spoils of Poynton.*

Yet given James's gifts and purpose, it is impossible to expect him to have rested with the achievements of those astonishing twenty years. The momentum of his vision was incapable of stopping at that point. He had earned his right to carry his art into the poetic and metaphysical risks of his final period, particularly when that period produced the rich qualities of *The Wings of the Dove* (whatever the dramatic frailty of its nebulous heroine, certainly his highest point in delicacy of moral criticism), the profound ethical reverberation of *The Golden Bowl,* and that phenomenal revival of his powers as a critic of society, *The Ivory Tower. The Ambassadors* may show too arbitrary a schematization; *The Outcry* and *The Sense of the Past* may err in the direction of abstraction; but the final phase of James's work brought the modern novel into a greater sense of its moral and imaginative possibilities than any other work of the early twentieth century. And in spite of his increasing addiction to obsessive themes and subjective treatment, the vigorous recuperation of realism in *The Ivory Tower* shows how genuinely he was sustained to the end of his life by the principles he adopted in early maturity and how these gave him a creative longevity, a persistence in imaginative invention, that is virtually unique in the history of fiction.

Those principles animate his work as a critic; they are condensed in his most famous essay, "The Art of Fiction." James was not a formal critic, and it is doubtless true that he wrote brilliant criticism without being a "great" critic. He never formulated an organic aesthetic; he did not investigate classical literature, not even English and French; he had little skill in the theory and appreciation of poetry. R. P. Blackmur has said that he never arrived at "a relation to the whole body of literature" such as we find in Johnson, Coleridge, Sainte-Beuve, Arnold, and Eliot. Instead he worked empirically, pursuing consistently only his special interests in fiction and drama. But within these limits he showed an integrity of interest that was tireless, and he produced the most coherent study of a chosen craft by a practicing craftsman that we have in English. His essays rival Baudelaire's in their continuous relevance to actual creation and to the origins of such creation in the artist's mind and sensibility.

His emphasis is often on devices, on what he called "doing," at that time a major problem in his craft. Thus the attention he gave to the "grammar" of fiction—to such matters as "the point of view," "scene" and "dramatizing" ("Dramatize! dramatize!"), plotting and motivation, *ficelles* and *disponibles,* problems of inclusion and exclusion, form and structure, distancing and perspective, structure and selection. This may appear to be an exaggeration of method for method's sake. But James's practice always proves more than his theory, and there he succeeds in proving that technique of any valid kind is always an instrument of values. He never lets us forget what his primary values are, for they emerge from his books—from their complex craftsmanship, their subtleties and ironies, their wit and ambiguities—bearing the short and simple names he insisted on giving them. One is "truth"; the other is "life."

Truth was, for James, the basic law of realism. It means honesty, first of all, but it also means justice to the writer's material. It takes precedence over conscious morality. It is the single test of all genuinely valid morality. He defined it in an early essay: "When once a work of fiction may be classed as a novel, its foremost claim to merit, and indeed the measure of its merit, is its *truth*—its truth to something, however questionable that thing may be in point of morals or of taste." The something to which it refers is wide, various, and illimitable; it is, in fact, life itself—not Whitman's life of enraptured abstraction; not Zola's life in its raw and "unprejudiced identity," a phenomenon for scientific dissection; not the life lyrically idealized by Emerson and the naturalistic mystics. It is life "felt," "realized," "penetrated," "understood." In one of his prefaces James said that there is "no more nutritive or suggestive truth" than that of "the perfect dependence of the 'moral' sense of a work of art on the amount of felt life concerned in producing it." And when he said that "just in proportion as he is sentient and restless, just in proportion as he reacts and reciprocates and penetrates, is the critic a valuable instrument," he formulated a law that applies as much to the novelist as to the critic.

To lend himself, to project himself and steep himself, to feel and feel till he understands and to understand so well that he can say, to have perception at the pitch of passion and expression as embracing as the air, to be infinitely curious and incorrigibly patient, and yet plastic and inflammable and determinable, stooping to conquer and serving to direct—these are fine chances for an active mind, chances to add the idea of independent beauty to the conception of success.

These are the elements that make art great—feeling, passion, curiosity, patience; above all, understanding. They are the only basis of a valid realism. They tell us why James, in Paris in the seventies, believed *l'art pour l'art* to be an "absurdity" and naturalism a "treacherous ideal." They alone, incorruptibly exercised, can make of the novel "a living thing, all one and continuous, like any other organism"; give it the "air of reality," "solidity of specification," "illusion of life." They are "the beginning and the end of the art of the novelist"—"his inspiration, his despair, his reward, his torment, his delight."

When, in the summer of 1889, James was asked to participate in a summer school on the novel in Massachusetts, he sent his doctrine from England to "the nymphs and swains who propose to converse about it under the great trees at Deerfield," and he put it in his most generous and inspired terms.

Oh, do something from your point of view; an ounce of example is worth a ton of generalities; do something with the great art and the great form; do something with life. Any point of view is interesting that is a direct impression of life. You each have an impression coloured by your individual conditions; make that into a picture, a picture framed by your own personal wisdom, your glimpse of the American world. The field is vast for freedom, for study, for observation, for satire, for truth. . . . I have only two little words

for the matter remotely approaching to rule or doctrine; one
is life and the other freedom.

The two words are our best clues to everything James
said as a critic or achieved as an artist. He made them
imperative as principles among his disciples and fellow
craftsmen. Conrad, for one, was only speaking the
Jamesian language when he said that the artist "cannot be faithful to any one of the temporary formulas
of his craft." All of these will "abandon him—even on
the very threshold of the temple—to the stammerings
of his conscience and to the outspoken consciousness
of the difficulties of his work," leaving him to descend
"within himself, and in that lonely region of stress and
strife, if he be deserving and fortunate, [to find] the
terms of his appeal."

IV

James staked his appeal on the "quality of mind" he
sought to make his art embody, but quality of mind is
only another name for the quality of the life art gives
us when it achieves its essential purpose. Merely to live
is not enough. Strether's words to little Bilham in *The
Ambassadors*—"Live all you can; it's a mistake not to.
It doesn't so much matter what you do in particular,
so long as you have your life. . . . Live!"—can, if
taken too literally, be mistaken as the whole moral
teaching of James's work. The exhortation strikes one
of his deepest convictions, but it was never intended
as an argument for self-sufficient living or for the cults
of personality and experience which, whether among
optimists or aesthetes, became popular doctrines of
James's age. Strether himself qualified his advice when
he said, "What it comes to is that it's not, that it's never,

a happiness at all, to *take*. The only safe thing is to give. It's what plays you least false."

The essence of mediocrity for James was selfishness, as the essence of baseness was treachery and the essence of failure a denial of the spiritual quality of life—of the wisdom that comes through suffering or privation, the fulfillment that comes through generosity and love. To deny these is to face at last the real "beast in the jungle" and to meet the worst of damnations, which is negation. Isabel Archer, in *The Portrait of a Lady*, voiced another of James's deepest convictions. She first came to Europe with the theory that one "should move in a realm of light, of natural wisdom, of happy impulse, of inspiration fully chronic," and with "a fixed determination to regard the world as a place of brightness, of free expansion, of irresistible action." Yet she also brought a bolder sense of the human fate. One of her suitors, Lord Warburton, on being rejected by her, views her assertion that she "can't escape unhappiness" with skepticism and accuses her of fostering a romantic view of misery. "I'm not bent on a life of misery," Isabel answers. "I've always been intensely determined to be happy, and I've often believed I should be. . . . But it comes over me every now and then that I can never be happy in any extraordinary way; not by turning away, by separating myself." "By separating yourself from what?" he asks. "From life," she answers. "From the usual chances and dangers, from what most people know and suffer."

The ideal of consciousness she implies was the basis of James's morality as an artist. It has been called his religion. He refused to make it a means merely of spiritual luxury or happy self-extension. He shows it to be a much harder thing than that. It is a principle of realization, of self-knowledge, of moral limitation and recognition. And this is what permitted him to make it a principle of sanity and of tragedy. When he named Hamlet and Lear as examples of the kind of living that endows life with intensity and gives it a maximum of sense, he took his examples from tragic drama. By doing so he assented to the classical doctrine that it is the denials and privations of life that must be made to enrich it; its capacity for tragedy that gives it its final value. Yeats was one poet who agreed with him: "Hamlet and Lear are gay."

When James, in 1910, wrote his essay "Is There a Life After Death?" he gave his belief in "the unlimited vision of being" the appealing accents of a Platonic idea. Death offers the possibility of "a renewal of the interest, the appreciation, the passion, the large and consecrated consciousness" of life itself. But when he wrote closer to the actual conditions of living he found a stricter language. He used it in the magnificent letter he sent his old Cambridge friend Grace Norton in 1883, at a time when she was passing through an ordeal of suffering:

I am determined not to speak to you except with the voice of stoicism. I don't know *why* we live—the gift of life comes to us from I don't know what source or for what purpose; but I believe we can go on living for the reason that (always of course up to a certain point) life is the most valuable thing we know anything about, and it is therefore presumptively a great mistake to surrender it while there is any yet left in the cup. In other words consciousness is an illimitable power, and though at times it may seem to be all consciousness of misery, yet in the way it propagates itself from wave to wave, so that we never cease to feel, and though at moments we appear to, try to, pray to, there is something that holds one in one's place, makes it a standpoint in the universe which it is probably good not to forsake. . . . Only don't, I beseech you, *generalize* too much in these sympathies and tendernesses—remember that every life is a special problem which is not yours but another's, and content yourself with the terrible algebra of your own. Don't melt too much into the universe, but be as solid and dense and fixed as you can. We all live together, and those of us who love and know, live so most. We help each other— even unconsciously, each in our own effort, we lighten the effort of others, we contribute to the sum of success, make it possible for others to live. Sorrow comes in great waves. . . . It wears us, uses us, but we wear it and use it in return; and it is blind, whereas we after a manner see.

What James here phrased as a precept of experience he made the guiding principle of his vision as an artist. He had already recognized it as such early in his career, in 1874, when he first discovered the wisdom of Turgenev. Turgenev crystallized a reading of life James had already traced in his chosen models of seriousness in the craft of fiction—Hawthorne, George Eliot, Balzac— but he gave it a quality of "charm," of spiritual force, which lent a particular intensity to James's statement of it:

Life *is*, in fact, a battle. On this point optimists and pessimists agree. Evil is insolent and strong; beauty enchanting but rare; goodness very apt to be weak; folly very apt to be defiant; wickedness to carry the day; imbeciles to be in great places, people of sense in small, and mankind generally, unhappy. But the world as it stands is no illusion, no phantasm, no evil dream of a night; we wake up to it again for ever and ever; we can neither forget it nor deny it nor dispense with it. We can welcome experience as it comes, and give it what it demands, in exchange for something which it is idle to pause to call much or little so long as it contributes to swell the volume of consciousness. In this there is mingled pain and delight, but over the mysterious mixture there hovers a visible rule, that bids us learn to will and seek to understand.

James carried his conviction of that rule into the great scene of his age—carried it out of the simpler world of his youth in America into the *Imperium* of pride and vanity which he made the special stage of his complex drama of cultures and moralities. There he traced the rule in all its conditions of humor and pathos, success and hardship, virtue and evil; and to its workings he brought a wit, compassion, and inexhaustible moral curiosity which not only give his work its depth and richness of imagination but establish its authority as a historical document that comes close to being unique of its kind in English fiction. No one who reads James seriously today is likely to miss the bearing of his insight and prophetic vision on the present circumstances of our lives. As much as Balzac or Stendhal, Tolstoi or Proust, he saw his age in the perspective of the future. He seized his special opportunity as a citizen of two worlds to create a classic drama of their rivalries and oppositions; but before he had finished his work he also achieved an art that transcends the international drama and becomes capable of analyzing the forces in men or societies which the moral vision defines as comedy or tragedy.

To his task he brought a large fund of the faith, idealism, and capacity for confidence that was natural to his American generation; but the realism of vision that accompanied these, while it kept him from remaining an idealist, enforced in his character something of much greater importance to a novelist: a sense of the inescapable value of life and a responsibility, equally inescapable, to its moral necessities. It was these instincts that permitted him to show in his books what T. S. Eliot, in one of the most famous remarks ever made about James, once called "his mastery over, his baffling escape from, Ideas"—"a mind so fine that no idea could violate it." His personal character, as we come to know it through his work, exemplifies what his art embodies as a principle. His last secretary, Theodora Bosanquet, speaking as an intimate witness, has said that it became a passion with James "not to exercise any tyrannical power over other people"; that his "Utopia was an anarchy where nobody would be responsible for any other human being but only for his own civilized character." That passion is what finally gives James the terms of his appeal. It ensures both his authority as an artist and his responsible seriousness as an intelligence. In taking as his supreme ambition the achievement of an art fully civilized, he assumed the difficult task of reconciling knowledge with beauty, of holding "in a single thought reality and justice." That is why his work has reasserted its value for us in a tragic and ominous time, and that is why, the prospects for justice and intelligence being what they are in the modern world, it must remain valuable to the future.

HENRY JAMES: A CHRONOLOGY

WITH A LIST OF HIS PRINCIPAL WORKS ON THEIR FIRST PUBLICATION IN BOOK FORM

1793   William James, grandfather (1775-1832), comes from Ireland to the United States. Settles in Albany; conducts tobacco, salt, express, and land businesses in Albany, Utica, Syracuse, and New York City, thus laying the basis of the family fortune of three million dollars—with John Jacob Astor's and Stephen Van Rensselaer's, one of the three largest fortunes in the state.

1811   Henry James, fourth son of the ten children (seven sons and three daughters) of William James and his third wife, Catherine Barber, born in Albany. Educated at Union College, Schenectady, and Princeton Theological Seminary, he declined to assume the family business in order to study philosophy and religion and to become a follower of Sandeman, Emerson, Fourier, and Swedenborg.

1840   Henry James, Sr., marries Mary Robertson Walsh.

1842   William James, son of the above, born in New York City.

1843   April 15: HENRY JAMES, their second son, born at 2 Washington Place, New York City.

1843-44   Mr. and Mrs. James go to Europe, taking their two infant sons with them, and making extended sojourns in Paris and at Windsor, near London.

1845   Garth Wilkinson James, their third son, born (dies 1883).

1846   Robertson James, their fourth son, born (dies 1910).

1848   Alice James, their daughter, born.

1845-55   Family lives in New York City and Albany. H.J. and other children educated by governesses and in day schools in both cities.

1855-58   Family travels and lives in Switzerland (Geneva), England (London), France (Paris, Boulogne-sur-Mer). H.J. attends schools in Geneva, Paris (Institution Fezandié), and Boulogne. Begins youthful writing (Henry James, Sr., to Mrs. James, Boulogne, October 15, 1857: "Harry is not so fond of study, properly so-called, as of reading. He is a devourer of libraries, and an immense writer of novels and dramas.")

1858   Family returns to America; lives at Newport, Rhode Island.

1859   Family returns to Europe. H.J. studies at Geneva (Institution Rochette) and in Bonn, Germany. Friendship with John LaFarge and Thomas Sergeant Perry.

1860   They return to Newport. H.J. studies art in the studio of William Morris Hunt there. Translates Alfred de Musset's *Lorenzaccio* and Mérimée's *La Vénus d'Ille*.

1861   Receives injury—"a horrid even if an obscure hurt"—while helping extinguish a fire at Newport. Goes through a period of ill health. The brothers Wilkinson and Robertson James join the Union Army of the Civil War.

1862-63   H.J. studies law at Harvard Law School but abandons it.

1864   Family moves from Newport to Boston (Ashburton Place). H.J. begins friendships with Charles Eliot Norton, James Russell Lowell, William Dean Howells. Begins reviewing books in October for *The North American Review*.

1865   His first tale, "The Story of a Year," appears in March issue of *The Atlantic Monthly*. Begins reviewing books for E. L. Godkin's new magazine *The Nation*.

1866   Family settles in Cambridge, Massachusetts.

1869   H.J. makes first adult trip to Europe: England, France, Switzerland, Italy.

1870   Hears while in England of the death in America of Mary ("Minny") Temple, beloved cousin of the Jameses, later to be commemorated in a number of H.J.'s heroines, notably Milly Theale in *The Wings of the Dove*. Returns to Cambridge home.

1871   *Watch and Ward*, his first novel, serialized in *The Atlantic Monthly*.

1872   Goes to Europe with sister Alice and Aunt Katherine Walsh, traveling in Switzerland, Italy, Bavaria.

1872-74   Travels in England, Holland, Belgium, Germany, Switzerland; lives in Paris, Rome, Florence. Writes reviews and travel articles for *The Nation, The North American Review, The Galaxy, The Atlantic, The Independent.* Studies French theater in Paris.

1874-75   Spends winter in New York. Continues writing for above magazines and presently for *The New York Tribune, Scribner's Monthly, Lippincott's,* and other journals.

1875   First book: *A Passionate Pilgrim and Other Tales* ("The Last of the Valerii," "Eugene Pickering," "The Madonna of the Future," "The Romance of Certain Old Clothes," "Madame de Mauves"). *Transatlantic Sketches* (essays of travel in England, Switzerland, France, Italy, Germany, Holland, Belgium).

1876   *Roderick Hudson,* his first novel to appear in book form. Spends year in France, meeting Turgenev, Flaubert, Edmond de Goncourt, Renan, Maupassant, Daudet, Zola in Paris. Begins living in London (Bolton Street) in December, and meeting the literary and political leaders of England: Tennyson, Browning, Ruskin, George Eliot, Lewes, Leslie Stephen, William Morris, Herbert Spencer, Gladstone, Morley, and others.

1877   Revisits Paris; winters in Rome. *The American* (novel).

1878   Visits Scotland. *Watch and Ward* published in book form. First book of criticism: *French Poets and Novelists* (essays on Musset, Gautier, Baudelaire, Balzac, George Sand, Flaubert, Turgenev, Mérimée, and "The Théâtre Français"). *The Europeans* (novel).

1879   Travels in Italy; spends three months in Paris. *Daisy Miller,* his first tale to gain international celebrity. *An International Episode; "Four Meetings"* (tales). *Hawthorne* (critical biography in the English Men of Letters series). *The Madonna of the Future and Other Tales* (earlier tales collected, with "Longstaff's Marriage," "The Diary of a Man of Fifty," and "Benvolio" added). Continues his "siege" of English life and society, dining out 107 times in a single winter.

1880   *Confidence* (novel). Travels in Italy.

1881   *Washington Square* (novel; later reprinted with "The Pension Beaurepas" and "A Bundle of Letters"). *The Portrait of a Lady* (novel). Returns to the United States, visiting New York, Boston, Cambridge, Washington.

1882   Mother dies in Cambridge in February. H.J. writes dramatization of *Daisy Miller,* later rejected in both New York and London. Returns to England in May; visits France in autumn. Father dies in Cambridge in December. H.J. returns briefly to America.

1883   Returns to England. First collected edition of novels and tales published in 14 volumes in London. *The Siege of London* (with "The Pension Beaurepas" and "The Point of View"). *Portraits of Places* (essays of travel in Italy, France, England, United States, Canada).

1884   Visits Paris. *Tales of Three Cities* ("The Impressions of a Cousin," "Lady Barbarina," "A New England Winter"). Sojourns in Italy.

1885   *A Little Tour of France* (essays of travel in France). *Stories Revived* (collected in three volumes, with "The Author of 'Beltraffio,'" "Pandora," "The Path of Duty," "A Light Man," "A Day of Days," "Georgina's Reasons," "A Landscape Painter," "Rose-Agathe," "Poor Richard," "Master Eustace," "A Most Extraordinary Case" added to stories from earlier books). Sister Alice, now an invalid, comes to live in England, in London, Bournemouth, Leamington. Friendship with Robert Louis Stevenson begins.

1886   *The Bostonians* (novel). *The Princess Casamassima* (novel). Takes flat in De Vere Mansions (later De Vere Gardens), Kensington, London.

1887   Long sojourn in Italy.

1888   *Partial Portraits* (critical essays on Emerson, George Eliot, Trollope, Stevenson, Constance Fenimore Woolson, Daudet, Maupassant, Turgenev, George du Maurier, and "The Art of Fiction"). *The Aspern Papers* (with "Louisa Pallant" and "The Modern Warning"). *The Reverberator* (short novel). Travels in Switzerland, northern Italy, France. Returns to London.

1889   *A London Life* (with "The Patagonia," "The Liar," "Mrs. Temperley").

1890   *The Tragic Muse* (novel). Revisits Italy. Determines seriously to write plays.

1891   A dramatization of *The American* produced in provinces and London by Edward Compton.

1892   *The Lesson of the Master* (with "The Marriages," "The Pupil," "Brooksmith," "The Solution," "Sir Edmund Orme"). Alice James dies at Campden Hill, London, in March. H.J. summers in Italy. Continues writing plays.

1893   *The Private Life* (with "Lord Beaupré" and "The Visits"). *The Wheel of Time* (with "Collaboration" and "Owen Wingrave"). *The Real Thing and Other Tales* ("Sir Dominick Ferrand," "Nona Vincent," "The Chaperon," "Greville Fane"). *Picture and Text* (essays on artists: Edwin Austin Abbey, Charles S. Reinhart, Alfred Parsons, John S. Sargent, Daumier; and "After the Play"). *Essays in London and Elsewhere* (on London, James Russell Lowell, Frances Anne Kemble, Flaubert, Loti, the Goncourts, Browning, Ibsen, Mrs. Humphry Ward, "Criticism"). Visits Paris and Switzerland. Writes the play *Guy Domville*.

1894   *Theatricals* (two unproduced comedies for the theater: "Tenants" and "Disengaged").

1894-95 Contributes "The Death of the Lion," "The Coxon Fund," and "The Next Time" to *The Yellow Book*.

1895   January 5: *Guy Domville* produced at St. James's Theatre, London, by George Alexander; disastrous first night at which H.J. is jeered at the final curtain; it runs a month. *Theatri-*

cals: Second Series (two more unproduced comedies: "The Album" and "The Reprobate"). *Terminations* (tales: "The Death of the Lion," "The Coxon Fund," "The Middle Years," "The Altar of the Dead").

1896   *Embarrassments* (tales: "The Figure in the Carpet," "Glasses," "The Next Time," "The Way It Came"). *The Other House* (novel). Spends summer at Playden, near Rye, in Sussex; autumn in the "Old Vicarage" at Rye, where he discovers Lamb House and takes a lease on it.

1897   *The Spoils of Poynton* (novel). *What Maisie Knew* (novel).

1898   *The Two Magics* ("The Turn of the Screw" and "Covering End"). *In the Cage* (short novel). Begins living in Lamb House, Rye.

1899   *The Awkward Age* (novel). Summers in Italy.

1900   *The Soft Side* (tales: "The Great Good Place," " 'Europe,' " "Paste," "The Real Right Thing," "The Great Condition," "The Tree of Knowledge," "The Abasement of the North-mores," "The Given Case," "John Delavoy," "The Third Person," "Maud-Evelyn," "Miss Gunton of Poughkeepsie").

1901   *The Sacred Fount* (novel).

1902   *The Wings of the Dove* (novel).

1903   *The Ambassadors* (novel). *William Wetmore Story and His Friends* (memoir). *The Better Sort* (tales: "Broken Wings," "The Beldonald Holbein," "The Two Faces," "The Tone of Time," "The Special Type," "Mrs. Medwin," "Flicker-bridge," "The Story in It," "The Beast in the Jungle," "The Birthplace," "The Papers").

1904   *The Golden Bowl* (novel). September: returns to the United States for the first time since 1883; spends autumn with William James and family at Chocorua, New Hampshire, and in Cambridge; revisits New York.

1905   Travels in the United States, south to Florida, west across continent to California, lecturing on "The Lesson of Balzac" and "The Question of Our Speech." Returns to England and Lamb House in August. *English Hours* (old and new essays of travel in England).

1906   Lamb House: begins revising his fiction and writing the critical prefaces for the definitive collection (New York Edition), which begins to appear in 1907.

1907   *The American Scene* (essays of travel in the United States). Resumes writing plays after 12 years: *The High Bid* (three acts) and *The Saloon* (one act, based on "Owen Win-grave").

1908   *The High Bid* produced in Edinburgh, March 26, by Forbes-Robertson and Gertrude Elliott (again in London, February 18, 1909). Writes play *The Other House. Views and Reviews* (early critical essays and reviews of the years 1865-91 now collected by LeRoy Phillips).

1909   *Julia Bride* (short novel). *Italian Hours* (collected essays of travel in Italy). Writes play *The Outcry*. Long nervous illness.

1910   Continued illness. Goes with William James, now ill, to Nauheim, Germany; then back to Lamb House and thence with Mr. and Mrs. W.J. to New Hampshire, where W.J. dies on August 26. *The Finer Grain* (tales: "The Velvet Glove," "Mora Montravers," "A Round of Visits," "Crapy Cornelia," "The Bench of Desolation").

1911   Honorary degree from Harvard. Returns to England and Lamb House. *The Outcry* (novel). *The Saloon* produced January 17 by Gertrude Kingston in London.

1912   Takes flat at 21 Carlyle Mansions, Cheyne Walk, Chelsea, London. Receives honorary degree from Oxford (*fecundissimus et facundissimus scriptor*).

1913   *A Small Boy and Others* (first autobiographical memoir).

1914   *Notes on Novelists with Some Other Notes* (essays on Stevenson, Zola, Flaubert, Balzac, George Sand, D'Annunzio, Dumas, Browning, "The New Novel," etc.). *Notes of a Son and Brother* (second autobiographical memoir). Outbreak of war in Europe. H.J., greatly disturbed, begins war work, visits hospitals, writes for war charities, aids Belgian refugees, works for American ambulance corps.

1915   July 26: H.J. naturalized a British subject. December 2: his last illness, a stroke, followed by pneumonia, begins ("So here it is at last, the distinguished thing!").

1916   Awarded Order of Merit by King George V. February 28: dies in Chelsea, aged 72 years, 10 months. Funeral service in Chelsea Old Church, London; ashes interred in family plot in cemetery at Cambridge, Mass.

1917   *The Ivory Tower* (novel, unfinished). *The Sense of the Past* (novel, unfinished). *The Middle Years* (third autobiographical memoir, unfinished).

1918   *Within the Rim* (wartime papers written in England). *Gabrielle de Bergerac* (early tale of 1869, now published as book).

1919   *A Landscape Painter* (four early tales of 1866-68 now re-collected by Albert Mordell: "A Landscape Painter," "Poor Richard," "A Day of Days," "A Most Extraordinary Case"). *Travelling Companions* (seven early tales of 1868-74, never published by James in book form, now collected from magazines by Albert Mordell: "Travelling Companions," "The Sweetheart of M. Briseux," "Professor Fargo," "At Isella," "Guest's Confession," "Adina," "DeGrey: A Romance").

1920   *The Letters of Henry James*, selected and edited by Percy Lubbock. *Master Eustace* (five early tales of 1869-78, now re-collected by Albert Mordell: "Master Eustace," "Longstaff's Marriage," "Théodolinde," "A Light Man," "Benvolio").

1921   *Notes and Reviews* (early contributions to *The North American Review* and *The Nation*, 1864-86, collected by Pierre de Chaignon la Rose).

1921-23   *The Novels and Stories of Henry James* (collected edition in 35 volumes, London).

1930   *A Bibliography of the Writings of Henry James,* by LeRoy
        Phillips (a revision and enlargement of the first edition,
        which appeared in 1906).

1934   *The Art of the Novel* (the critical prefaces collected from
        the New York Edition of 1907-1909, with a preface by Rich-
        ard P. Blackmur).

1947   *The Notebooks of Henry James,* edited by F. O. Matthiessen
        and Kenneth B. Murdock.

1948   *The Scenic Art: Notes on Acting and the Drama, 1872-1901,*
        edited by Allan Wade.

1949   *The Complete Plays of Henry James,* edited by Leon Edel
        [contains the long plays: "Daisy Miller" (1882), "The
        American" (1890), "Tenants" (1890), "Disengaged" (1892),
        "The Album" (1891), "The Reprobate" (1891), "Guy
        Domville" (1893), "The Other House" (1908); and the
        shorter plays and dramatic sketches: "Pyramus and Thisbe"
        (1869), "Still Waters" (1871), "A Change of Heart"
        (1872), "Summersoft" (1895), "The High Bid" (1907),
        the project of "The Chaperon" (1893, 1907), "The Saloon"
        (1908), "The Outcry" (1909), and a monologue written
        for Ruth Draper (1913), together with lengthy biographi-
        cal and textual notes by Leon Edel].

1950   *Eight Uncollected Tales of Henry James,* edited by Edna
        Kenton (early tales of 1865-76 never collected by James in
        book form: "The Story of a Year," "My Friend Bingham,"
        "The Story of a Masterpiece," "A Problem," "Osborne's
        Revenge," "Gabrielle de Bergerac," "Crawford's Consist-
        ency," "The Ghostly Rental"). With *Travelling Companions*
        (see 1919) this volume completes the book publication of
        the 15 early tales not collected from magazines by James.

NOTE AND ACKNOWLEDGMENTS

The aim of this book is to show as fully as space permits the scope
and variety of Henry James's writings from his earliest work in the
1860s to the last year of his life. The examples cover fifty years, from
1865 to 1915, and represent selections from twenty of his books. My
choices are based on a total reading of the work published by James
or his editors in book form, and on a copious reading of the still uncollected contributions he made to magazines, newspapers, and books
during his lifetime. No experienced reader of James need be told the
acute problems an editor encounters when he attempts to represent in
a limited space an author of such bulk and diversity. For every inclusion there must be a score of omissions that appeal insistently to be
included; and no one knows better than the present editor how many
favorite items have had to be excluded or how final decisions are
bound to remain personal and arbitrary. While it has been impossible

to include one of James's full-length novels—these being in most cases now procurable in recent reprint editions—his work is shown in all its other major kinds: short stories, longer tales or *nouvelles*, essays and reviews in literary criticism and biography, travel writings, excerpts from his three autobiographical memoirs, one of the longest and most important personal journals from his notebooks, and his letters. A particular point has been made of showing James's *range*—range of production from early to late, range of themes, range of stylistic development and artistry. Room has not been found for any of his plays or dramatic criticisms (though the essay on Paris offers a glimpse of the latter in its paragraphs on Sarah Bernhardt and the Comédie Française), his random articles on art, or the prefaces for the New York Edition of his fiction; but to these more specialized sides of his work the reader will soon be led.

I have tried to strike something of a balance between familiar or celebrated writings, for which some readers will inevitably look, and those less familiar. Four of the eight tales, for instance, are recognized Jamesian classics; the other four will, I hope, suggest the riches that exist among the lesser-known stories. There was a strong temptation to include more of the uncollected work that still exists only in the files of newspapers and periodicals—book reviews, critical essays, travel and political reports from Europe, art notices, etc.—but this wish has been necessarily curbed. (I leave the student to explore these writings with the help of LeRoy Phillips's invaluable *Bibliography of the Writings of Henry James* in its revised edition of 1930.) The majority of the selections—including, of course, all the fiction—are printed complete. Where excerpts from long books or essays have been unavoidable, these are indicated in the editor's notes, and care has been taken to make such excerpts as self-contained as possible. The Bibliography gives suggestions for the further reading of James's work, as well as a selective account of biography and criticism on James.

I wish to thank a number of Jamesians whose advice has been helpful: first and particularly, Mr. Leon Edel, who has generously offered his expert knowledge of the biography and writings of Henry James in checking and amending the Chronology, Bibliography, and notes, and in making other valuable suggestions about the contents. I have also had the advantage of discussing my selections with other students of James—F. W. Dupee, the late F. O. Matthiessen, Philip Rahv, Lionel Trilling, Edmund Wilson, and Napier Wilt. All of them gave me valuable suggestions, and while their choices inevitably differed widely and could not all be included, I have profited greatly by their advice and trust that something survives of the recommendations of each of them.

A Note on the Texts: The spelling and punctuation in James's books show many changes and inconsistencies over a space of fifty years, and they also vary between the English and American editions. The sources of the present texts are indicated in the editor's notes. Those of the non-fiction are first editions unless otherwise noted. Spellings have been made as consistent as possible within individual items but not in the book as a whole; thus such variants as *connection—connexion, realize —realise, enquire—inquire, today—to-day, humor—humour, unmistakable—unmistakeable,* etc., have been allowed to stand. The three tales and three *nouvelles* are taken from the New York Edition of 1907-1909 and follow that text as James revised and supervised it. One liberty has been taken in the items printed in Parts III, IV, and V: titles of books or whole works, variously printed by James, have been set in italics; titles of shorter works and pictures have been set in Roman type inside quotation marks. The letters in Part VI preserve the inconsistent orthography and punctuation which Percy Lubbock followed in his edition of *The Letters of Henry James* (New York: Scribner, 1920). Acknowledgment to publishers and holders of copyright appears on the copyright page.   M.D.Z.

One remarkable discovery about James's fiction should be mentioned. In its first American edition by Harper and Brothers, 1903, two chapters of the novel *The Ambassadors*—xxviii and xxix—were accidentally reversed and have so persisted in all subsequent American editions, including the New York Edition (Scribner, 1907-1909). They were correctly printed in the London edition by Methuen, 1903, and in later English editions. This discovery was made by Robert E. Young in the quarterly *American Literature*, xxii, pp. 246-53 (November 1950), and was further discussed by Leon Edel and Mr. Young in that journal, xxiii, pp. 128-30 (March 1951); xxiii, pp. 487-90 (January 1952); and xxiv, pp. 370-72 (November 1952); and in *Notes and Queries*, New Series, II, pp. 37-38 (January 1, 1955). It is planned that future American editions of *The Ambassadors* by Harper and Brothers will restore these two chapters to their proper sequence.

January 15, 1956

M.D.Z.

ADDENDA, 1968

In this revised edition the bibliography is brought up to date and, more important, the *nouvelle* "The Turn of the Screw" is included. To make room for this popular and substantial story, two of the tales and a shorter *nouvelle* have been dropped from the table of contents. These changes follow a suggestion made by the editor of the first edition, Morton Dauwen Zabel, shortly before his death. The present editor has adhered as closely as possible to Zabel's taste and critical discernment. Although the headnotes to the first two sections had to be modified, chiefly to account for the revised contents of the volume, the rest of Zabel's text remains unchanged.

The most important additions to the Bibliography are the New York Edition of the *Novels and Tales,* lately reissued; *The Complete Tales of Henry James,* ed. Leon Edel; the second and third volumes of Mr. Edel's definitive biography; and the *Bibliography of Henry James* compiled by Mr. Edel and Dan H. Laurence. Chief among the new books on James's work are Dorothea Krook's brilliant *The Ordeal of Consciousness,* Frederick C. Crews' *The Tragedy of Manners,* Richard Poirier's *The Comic Sense of Henry James,* Joseph Ward's *The Imagination of Disaster,* and Oscar Cargill's *The Novels of Henry James* (which is much more than the handbook originally promised). Critical essays on James continue to proliferate and one cannot begin to list them here. An excellent selection of "classic" essays on James is Mr. Edel's *A Collection of Critical Essays* for the Prentice-Hall series;

and a collection of essays devoted to a dozen of James's major novels, ed. Lyall H. Powers, is to be published in 1968 by the Michigan State University Press. For a complete list of recent works on James, see "Supplement, 1968" which follows Morton Zabel's Bibliography at the end of the present volume.

Lyall H. Powers

I

THREE TALES

From his first published tale, "A Tragedy of Error" in *The Continental Monthly* for February 1864, to his final collection of fiction, *The Finer Grain* in 1910, Henry James wrote, in addition to his twenty book-length novels, about 106 shorter works in fiction. They range in length from fairly brief stories to the longer tales or *nouvelles* which became for him a favored form of fiction. In their subject matter these tales cover the entire range of James's themes and preoccupations: his moral drama, his "international subject," his criticism of culture and society, his explorations of character and situation, his studies of writers and artists, his fantasy and "ghostly" themes, his comedy and tragedy. They relate continuously to the full-scale treatment he gave these subjects in his novels, and the finest rank with the most powerful and original work he achieved.

The three tales that follow, chosen out of many possibilities for inclusion, show something of James's scope and maturing artistry in the shorter forms of fiction. Although the latest of them was written in 1892, about the midpoint of his career, they indicate the development in style and treatment which makes a continuous drama of his growth as an artist. "Four Meetings" (1877) is one of his earliest and most felicitous versions of the international theme, and a flawless example of his art in depicting the pathos of privation. "Greville Fane" (1892) presents the theme of the literary life

39

which he made peculiarly his own, in a style marked by the epigrammatic brilliance that was favored in the nineties; it is one of his wittiest pieces of writing. That theme and style become more explicit in a key story, "The Real Thing" (1892), which is one of his keenest parables of the conflict between art and life, and is thus to be coupled with such tales as "The Aspern Papers," "The Author of 'Beltraffio,'" "The Lesson of the Master," "The Death of the Lion," "The Next Time," "The Middle Years," and "The Figure in the Carpet."

"Four Meetings" first appeared in *Scribner's Monthly* for November 1877, and was first published in book form in *Daisy Miller: A Study, and Other Tales* in 1879. "Greville Fane" first appeared in the *Illustrated London News* of September 17 and 24, 1892, and "The Real Thing" in *Black and White* for April 16, 1892; and both these stories—whose first magazine appearance has been discovered by Mr. Allan Wade—were collected in *The Real Thing and Other Tales* in 1893. All three of these tales were revised for the New York Edition of James's *Novels and Tales,* 1907-1909, and the texts here printed were taken from it. For suggestions on the further reading of James's stories and tales, the reader is referred to the Bibliography.

—L.H.P.

*

FOUR MEETINGS

I saw her but four times, though I remember them
vividly; she made her impression on me. I thought her
very pretty and very interesting—a touching specimen
of a type with which I had had other and perhaps less
charming associations. I'm sorry to hear of her death,
and yet when I think of it why *should* I be? The last
time I saw her she was certainly not—! But it will be
of interest to take our meetings in order.

I

The first was in the country, at a small tea-party,
one snowy night some seventeen years ago. My friend
Latouche, going to spend Christmas with his mother,
had insisted on my company, and the good lady had
given in our honour the entertainment of which I speak.
To me it was really full of savour—it had all the right
marks: I had never been in the depths of New England
at that season. It had been snowing all day and the drifts
were knee-high. I wondered how the ladies had made
their way to the house; but I inferred that just those
general rigours rendered any assembly offering the attraction of two gentlemen from New York worth a desperate effort.

Mrs. Latouche in the course of the evening asked me

if I "didn't want to" show the photographs to some of
the young ladies. The photographs were in a couple
of great portfolios, and had been brought home by her
son, who, like myself, was lately returned from Europe.
I looked round and was struck with the fact that most
of the young ladies were provided with an object of
interest more absorbing than the most vivid sun-picture.
But there was a person alone near the mantelshelf who
looked round the room with a small vague smile, a discreet, a disguised yearning, which seemed somehow at
odds with her isolation. I looked at her a moment and
then chose. "I should like to show them to that young
lady."

"Oh yes," said Mrs. Latouche, "she's just the person.
She doesn't care for flirting—I'll speak to her." I replied
that if she didn't care for flirting she wasn't perhaps just
the person; but Mrs. Latouche had already, with a few
steps, appealed to her participation. "She's delighted,"
my hostess came back to report; "and she's just the
person—so quiet and so bright." And she told me the
young lady was by name Miss Caroline Spencer—with
which she introduced me.

Miss Caroline Spencer was not quite a beauty, but
was none the less, in her small odd way, formed to
please. Close upon thirty, by every presumption, she
was made almost like a little girl and had the complexion of a child. She had also the prettiest head, on which
her hair was arranged as nearly as possible like the hair
of a Greek bust, though indeed it was to be doubted if
she had ever seen a Greek bust. She was "artistic," I
suspected, so far as the polar influences of North Verona
could allow for such yearnings or could minister to them.
Her eyes were perhaps just too round and too inveterately surprised, but her lips had a certain mild decision
and her teeth, when she showed them, were charming.

About her neck she wore what ladies call, I believe, a "ruche" fastened with a very small pin of pink coral, and in her hand she carried a fan made of plaited straw and adorned with pink ribbon. She wore a scanty black silk dress. She spoke with slow soft neatness, even without smiles showing the prettiness of her teeth, and she seemed extremely pleased, in fact quite fluttered, at the prospect of my demonstrations. These went forward very smoothly after I had moved the portfolios out of their corner and placed a couple of chairs near a lamp. The photographs were usually things I knew—large views of Switzerland, Italy and Spain, landscapes, reproductions of famous buildings, pictures and statues. I said what I could for them, and my companion, looking at them as I held them up, sat perfectly still, her straw fan raised to her under-lip and gently, yet, as I could feel, almost excitedly, rubbing it. Occasionally, as I laid one of the pictures down, she said without confidence, which would have been too much: "Have you seen that place?" I usually answered that I had seen it several times—I had been a great traveller, though I was somehow particularly admonished not to swagger— and then I felt her look at me askance for a moment with her pretty eyes. I had asked her at the outset whether she had been to Europe; to this she had answered "No, no, no"—almost as much below her breath as if the image of such an event scarce, for solemnity, brooked phrasing. But after that, though she never took her eyes off the pictures, she said so little that I feared she was at last bored. Accordingly when we had finished one portfolio I offered, if she desired it, to desist. I rather guessed the exhibition really held her, but her reticence puzzled me and I wanted to make her speak. I turned round to judge better and then saw a faint flush in each of her cheeks. She kept waving her little fan to and fro.

Instead of looking at me she fixed her eyes on the remainder of the collection, which leaned, in its receptacle, against the table.

"Won't you show me that?" she quavered, drawing the long breath of a person launched and afloat but conscious of rocking a little.

"With pleasure," I answered, "if you're really not tired."

"Oh I'm not tired a bit. I'm just fascinated." With which as I took up the other portfolio she laid her hand on it, rubbing it softly. "And have you been here too?"

On my opening the portfolio it appeared I had indeed been there. One of the first photographs was a large view of the Castle of Chillon by the Lake of Geneva. "Here," I said, "I've been many a time. Isn't it beautiful?" And I pointed to the perfect reflexion of the rugged rocks and pointed towers in the clear still water. She didn't say "Oh enchanting!" and push it away to see the next picture. She looked a while and then asked if it weren't where Bonnivard, about whom Byron wrote, had been confined. I assented, trying to quote Byron's verses, but not quite bringing it off.

She fanned herself a moment and then repeated the lines correctly, in a soft flat voice but with charming conviction. By the time she had finished, she was nevertheless blushing. I complimented her and assured her she was perfectly equipped for visiting Switzerland and Italy. She looked at me askance again, to see if I might be serious, and I added that if she wished to recognise Byron's descriptions she must go abroad speedily—Europe was getting sadly dis-Byronised. "How soon must I go?" she thereupon enquired.

"Oh I'll give you ten years."

"Well, I guess I can go in *that* time," she answered as if measuring her words.

"Then you'll enjoy it immensely," I said; "you'll find it of the highest interest." Just then I came upon a photograph of some nook in a foreign city which I had been very fond of and which recalled tender memories. I discoursed (as I suppose) with considerable spirit; my companion sat listening breathless.

"Have you been *very* long over there?" she asked some time after I had ceased.

"Well, it mounts up, put all the times together."

"And have you travelled everywhere?"

"I've travelled a good deal. I'm very fond of it and happily have been able."

Again she turned on me her slow shy scrutiny. "Do you know the foreign languages?"

"After a fashion."

"Is it hard to speak them?"

"I don't imagine you'd find it so," I gallantly answered.

"Oh I shouldn't want to speak—I should only want to listen." Then on a pause she added: "They say the French theatre's so beautiful."

"Ah the best in the world."

"Did you go there very often?"

"When I was first in Paris I went every night."

"Every night!" And she opened her clear eyes very wide. "That to me is"—and her expression hovered—"as if you tell me a fairy-tale." A few minutes later she put to me: "And which country do you prefer?"

"There's one I love beyond any. I think you'd do the same."

Her gaze rested as on a dim revelation and then she breathed "Italy?"

"Italy," I answered softly too; and for a moment we communed over it. She looked as pretty as if instead of showing her photographs I had been making love to her.

To increase the resemblance she turned off blushing. It made a pause which she broke at last by saying: "That's the place which—in particular—I thought of going to."

"Oh that's the place—that's the place!" I laughed.

She looked at two or three more views in silence. "They say it's not very dear."

"As some other countries? Well, one gets back there one's money. That's not the least of the charms."

"But it's *all* very expensive, isn't it?"

"Europe, you mean?"

"Going there and travelling. That has been the trouble. I've very little money. I teach, you know," said Miss Caroline Spencer.

"Oh of course one must have money," I allowed; "but one can manage with a moderate amount judiciously spent."

"I think I should manage. I've saved and saved up, and I'm always adding a little to it. It's all for that." She paused a moment, and then went on with suppressed eagerness, as if telling me the story were a rare, but possibly an impure satisfaction. "You see it hasn't been only the money—it has been everything. Everything has acted against it. I've waited and waited. It has been my castle in the air. I'm almost afraid to talk about it. Two or three times it has come a little nearer, and then I've talked about it and it has melted away. I've talked about it too much," she said hypocritically—for I saw such talk was now a small tremulous ecstasy. "There's a lady who's a great friend of mine—she doesn't want to go, but I'm always at her about it. I think I must tire her dreadfully. She told me just the other day she didn't know what would become of me. She guessed I'd go crazy if I didn't sail, and yet certainly I'd go crazy if I did."

"Well," I laughed, "you haven't sailed up to now—so I suppose you *are* crazy."

She took everything with the same seriousness. "Well, I guess I must be. It seems as if I couldn't think of anything else—and I don't require photographs to work me up! I'm always right *on* it. It kills any interest in things nearer home—things I ought to attend to. That's a kind of craziness."

"Well then the cure for it's just to go," I smiled—"I mean the cure for this kind. Of course you may have the other kind worse," I added—"the kind you get over there."

"Well, I've a faith that I'll go *some* time all right!" she quite elatedly cried. "I've a relative right there on the spot," she went on, "and I guess he'll know how to control me." I expressed the hope that he would, and I forget whether we turned over more photographs; but when I asked her if she had always lived just where I found her, "Oh no sir," she quite eagerly replied; "I've spent twenty-two months and a half in Boston." I met it with the inevitable joke that in this case foreign lands might prove a disappointment to her, but I quite failed to alarm her. "I know more about them than you might think"—her earnestness resisted even that. "I mean by reading—for I've really read considerable. In fact I guess I've prepared my mind about as much as you *can* —in advance. I've not only read Byron—I've read histories and guide-books and articles and lots of things. I know I shall rave about everything."

" 'Everything' is saying much, but I understand your case," I returned. "You've the great American disease, and you've got it 'bad'—the appetite, morbid and monstrous, for colour and form, for the picturesque and the romantic at any price. I don't know whether we come into the world with it—with the germs implanted and antecedent to experience; rather perhaps we catch it early, almost before developed consciousness—we *feel,* as we look about, that we're going (to save our souls, or at least our senses) to be thrown back on it hard. We're like travellers in the desert—deprived of water and subject to the terrible mirage, the torment of illusion, of the thirst-fever. They hear the plash of fountains, they see green gardens and orchards that are hundreds of miles away. So we with *our* thirst—except that with us it's *more* wonderful: we have before us the beautiful old things we've never seen at all, and when we do at last see them—if we're lucky!—we simply recognise them. What experience does is merely to confirm and consecrate our confident dream."

She listened with her rounded eyes. "The way you express it's too lovely, and I'm sure it will be just like that. I've dreamt of everything—I'll know it all!"

"I'm afraid," I pretended for harmless comedy, "that you've wasted a great deal of time."

"Oh yes, that has been my great wickedness!" The people about us had begun to scatter; they were taking their leave. She got up and put out her hand to me, timidly, but as if quite shining and throbbing.

"I'm going back there—one *has* to," I said as I shook hands with her. "I shall look out for you."

Yes, she fairly glittered with her fever of excited faith. "Well, I'll tell you if I'm disappointed." And she left me, fluttering all expressively her little straw fan.

II

A few months after this I crossed the sea eastward again and some three years elapsed. I had been living in Paris and, toward the end of October, went from that city to the Havre, to meet a pair of relatives who had written me they were about to arrive there. On reaching the

Havre I found the steamer already docked—I was two
or three hours late. I repaired directly to the hotel,
where my travellers were duly established. My sister
had gone to bed, exhausted and disabled by her voyage;
she was the unsteadiest of sailors and her sufferings on
this occasion had been extreme. She desired for the moment undisturbed rest and was able to see me but five
minutes—long enough for us to agree to stop over, re-
storatively, till the morrow. My brother-in-law, anxious
about his wife, was unwilling to leave her room; but
she insisted on my taking him a walk for aid to recovery
of his spirits and his land-legs.

The early autumn day was warm and charming, and
our stroll through the bright-coloured busy streets of
the old French seaport beguiling enough. We walked
along the sunny noisy quays and then turned into a
wide pleasant street which lay half in sun and half in
shade—a French provincial street that resembled an old
water-colour drawing: tall grey steep-roofed red-gabled
many-storied houses; green shutters on windows and
old scroll-work above them; flower-pots in balconies and
white-capped women in doorways. We walked in the
shade; all this stretched away on the sunny side of the
vista and made a picture. We looked at it as we passed
along; then suddenly my companion stopped—pressing
my arm and staring. I followed his gaze and saw that we
had paused just before reaching a café where, under an
awning, several tables and chairs were disposed upon
the pavement. The windows were open behind; half
a dozen plants in tubs were ranged beside the door; the
pavement was besprinkled with clean bran. It was a
dear little quiet old-world café; inside, in the comparative dusk, I saw a stout handsome woman, who had
pink ribbons in her cap, perched up with a mirror behind her back and smiling at some one placed out of

sight. This, to be exact, I noted afterwards; what I
first observed was a lady seated alone, outside, at one
of the little marble-topped tables. My brother-in-law
had stopped to look at her. Something had been put
before her, but she only leaned back, motionless and
with her hands folded, looking down the street and
away from us. I saw her but in diminished profile;
nevertheless I was sure I knew on the spot that we must
already have met.

"The little lady of the steamer!" my companion cried.

"Was she on your steamer?" I asked with interest.

"From morning till night. She was never sick. She
used to sit perpetually at the side of the vessel with her
hands crossed that way, looking at the eastward horizon."

"And are you going to speak to her?"

"I don't know her. I never made acquaintance with
her. I wasn't in form to make up to ladies. But I used
to watch her and—I don't know why—to be interested
in her. She's a dear little Yankee woman. I've an idea
she's a school-mistress taking a holiday—for which her
scholars have made up a purse."

She had now turned her face a little more into profile,
looking at the steep grey house-fronts opposite. On this
I decided. "I shall speak to her myself."

"I wouldn't—she's very shy," said my brother-in-law.

"My dear fellow, I know her. I once showed her
photographs at a tea-party." With which I went up to
her, making her, as she turned to look at me, leave me
in no doubt of her identity. Miss Caroline Spencer had
achieved her dream. But she was less quick to recognise
me and showed a slight bewilderment. I pushed a chair
to the table and sat down. "Well," I said, "I hope you're
not disappointed!"

She stared, blushing a little—then gave a small jump

and placed me. "It was you who showed me the photographs—at North Verona."

"Yes, it was I. This happens very charmingly, for isn't it quite proper for me to give you a formal reception here—the official welcome? I talked to you so much about Europe."

"You didn't say too much. I'm so intensely happy!" she declared.

Very happy indeed she looked. There was no sign of her being older; she was as gravely, decently, demurely pretty as before. If she had struck me then as a thin-stemmed, mild-hued flower of Puritanism it may be imagined whether in her present situation this clear bloom was less appealing. Beside her an old gentleman was drinking absinthe; behind her the *dame de comptoir* in the pink ribbons called "Alcibiade, Alcibiade!" to the long-aproned waiter. I explained to Miss Spencer that the gentleman with me had lately been her shipmate, and my brother-in-law came up and was introduced to her. But she looked at him as if she had never so much as seen him, and I remembered he had told me her eyes were always fixed on the eastward horizon. She had evidently not noticed him, and, still timidly smiling, made no attempt whatever to pretend the contrary. I stayed with her on the little terrace of the café while he went back to the hotel and to his wife. I remarked to my friend that this meeting of ours at the first hour of her landing partook, among all chances, of the miraculous, but that I was delighted to be there and receive her first impressions.

"Oh I can't tell you," she said—"I feel so much in a dream. I've been sitting here an hour and I don't want to move. Everything's so delicious and romantic. I don't know whether the coffee has gone to my head—it's *so* unlike the coffee of my dead past."

"Really," I made answer, "if you're so pleased with this poor prosaic Havre you'll have no admiration left for better things. Don't spend your appreciation all the first day—remember it's your intellectual letter of credit. Remember all the beautiful places and things that are waiting for you. Remember that lovely Italy we talked about."

"I'm not afraid of running short," she said gaily, still looking at the opposite houses. "I could sit here all day —just saying to myself that here I am at last. It's so dark and strange—so old and different."

"By the way then," I asked, "how come you to be encamped in this odd place? Haven't you gone to one of the inns?" For I was half-amused, half-alarmed at the good conscience with which this delicately pretty woman had stationed herself in conspicuous isolation on the edge of the sidewalk.

"My cousin brought me here and—a little while ago —left me," she returned. "You know I told you I had a relation over here. He's still here—a real cousin. Well," she pursued with unclouded candour, "he met me at the steamer this morning."

It was absurd—and the case moreover none of my business; but I felt somehow disconcerted. "It was hardly worth his while to meet you if he was to desert you so soon."

"Oh he has only left me for half an hour," said Caroline Spencer. "He has gone to get my money."

I continued to wonder. "Where *is* your money?"

She appeared seldom to laugh, but she laughed for the joy of this. "It makes me feel very fine to tell you! It's in circular notes."

"And where are your circular notes?"

"In my cousin's pocket."

This statement was uttered with such clearness of

candour that—I can hardly say why—it gave me a sensible chill. I couldn't at all at the moment have justified my lapse from ease, for I knew nothing of Miss Spencer's cousin. Since he stood in that relation to her—dear respectable little person—the presumption was in his favour. But I found myself wincing at the thought that half an hour after her landing her scanty funds should have passed into his hands. "Is he to travel with you?" I asked.

"Only as far as Paris. He's an art-student in Paris—I've always thought that so splendid. I wrote to him that I was coming, but I never expected him to come off to the ship. I supposed he'd only just meet me at the train in Paris. It's very kind of him. But he *is*," said Caroline Spencer, "very kind—and very bright."

I felt at once a strange eagerness to see this bright kind cousin who was an art-student. "He's gone to the banker's?" I enquired.

"Yes, to the banker's. He took me to an hotel—such a queer quaint cunning little place, with a court in the middle and a gallery all round, and a lovely landlady in such a beautifully fluted cap and such a perfectly fitting dress! After a while we came out to walk to the banker's, for I hadn't any French money. But I was very dizzy from the motion of the vessel and I thought I had better sit down. He found this place for me here—then he went off to the banker's himself. I'm to wait here till he comes back."

Her story was wholly lucid and my impression perfectly wanton, but it passed through my mind that the gentleman would never come back. I settled myself in a chair beside my friend and determined to await the event. She was lost in the vision and the imagination of everything near us and about us—she observed, she recognised and admired, with a touching intensity. She

noticed everything that was brought before us by the
movement of the street—the peculiarities of costume,
the shapes of vehicles, the big Norman horses, the fat
priests, the shaven poodles. We talked of these things,
and there was something charming in her freshness of
perception and the way her book-nourished fancy sal-
lied forth for the revel.

"And when your cousin comes back what are you
going to do?" I went on.

For this she had, a little oddly, to think. "We don't
quite know."

"When do you go to Paris? If you go by the four
o'clock train I may have the pleasure of making the
journey with you."

"I don't think we shall do that." So far she was prepared. "My cousin thinks I had better stay here a few
days."

"Oh!" said I—and for five minutes had nothing to
add. I was wondering what our absentee was, in vulgar
parlance, "up to." I looked up and down the street, but
saw nothing that looked like a bright and kind American
art-student. At last I took the liberty of observing that
the Havre was hardly a place to choose as one of the
æsthetic stations of a European tour. It was a place
of convenience, nothing more; a place of transit, through
which transit should be rapid. I recommended her to
go to Paris by the afternoon train and meanwhile to
amuse herself by driving to the ancient fortress at the
mouth of the harbour—that remarkable circular structure which bore the name of Francis the First and figured a sort of small Castle of Saint Angelo. (I might
really have foreknown that it was to be demolished.)

She listened with much interest—then for a moment
looked grave. "My cousin told me that when he returned he should have something particular to say to

me, and that we could do nothing or decide nothing till
I should have heard it. But I'll make him tell me right
off, and then we'll go to the ancient fortress. Francis
the First, did you say? Why, that's lovely. There's no
hurry to get to Paris; there's plenty of time."

She smiled with her softly severe little lips as she
spoke those last words, yet, looking at her with a purpose, I made out in her eyes, I thought, a tiny gleam
of apprehension. "Don't tell me," I said, "that this
wretched man's going to give you bad news!"

She coloured as if convicted of a hidden perversity,
but she was soaring too high to drop. "Well I guess it's
a *little* bad, but I don't believe it's *very* bad. At any rate
I must listen to it."

I usurped an unscrupulous authority. "Look here;
you didn't come to Europe to listen—you came to *see!*"
But now I was sure her cousin would come back; since
he had something disagreeable to say to her he'd infallibly turn up. We sat a while longer and I asked her
about her plans of travel. She had them on her fingers'
ends and told over the names as solemnly as a daughter
of another faith might have told over the beads of a
rosary: from Paris to Dijon and to Avignon, from Avignon to Marseilles and the Cornice road; thence to
Genoa, to Spezia, to Pisa, to Florence, to Rome. It apparently had never occurred to her that there could be
the least incommodity in her travelling alone; and since
she was unprovided with a companion I of course civilly
abstained from disturbing her sense of security.

At last her cousin came back. I saw him turn toward
us out of a side-street, and from the moment my eyes
rested on him I knew he could but be the bright, if not
the kind, American art-student. He wore a slouch hat
and a rusty black velvet jacket, such as I had often encountered in the Rue Bonaparte. His shirt-collar dis-

played a stretch of throat that at a distance wasn't strikingly statuesque. He was tall and lean, he had red hair and freckles. These items I had time to take in while he approached the café, staring at me with natural surprise from under his romantic brim. When he came up to us I immediately introduced myself as an old acquaintance of Miss Spencer's, a character she serenely permitted me to claim. He looked at me hard with a pair of small sharp eyes, then he gave me a solemn wave, in the "European" fashion, of his rather rusty sombrero.

"You weren't on the ship?" he asked.

"No, I wasn't on the ship. I've been in Europe these several years."

He bowed once more, portentously, and motioned me to be seated again. I sat down, but only for the purpose of observing him an instant—I saw it was time I should return to my sister. Miss Spencer's European protector was, by my measure, a very queer quantity. Nature hadn't shaped him for a Raphaelesque or Byronic attire, and his velvet doublet and exhibited though not columnar throat weren't in harmony with his facial attributes. His hair was cropped close to his head; his ears were large and ill-adjusted to the same. He had a lackadaisical carriage and a sentimental droop which were peculiarly at variance with his keen conscious strange-coloured eyes—of a brown that was almost red. Perhaps I was prejudiced, but I thought his eyes too shifty. He said nothing for some time; he leaned his hands on his stick and looked up and down the street. Then at last, slowly lifting the stick and pointing with it, "That's a very nice bit," he dropped with a certain flatness. He had his head to one side—he narrowed his ugly lids. I followed the direction of his stick; the object it in-

dicated was a red cloth hung out of an old window.
"Nice bit of colour," he continued; and without moving his head transferred his half-closed gaze to me.
"Composes well. Fine old tone. Make a nice thing." He
spoke in a charmless vulgar voice.

"I see you've a great deal of eye," I replied. "Your
cousin tells me you're studying art." He looked at me in
the same way, without answering, and I went on with
deliberate urbanity: "I suppose you're at the studio of
one of those great men." Still on this he continued to
fix me, and then he named one of the greatest of that
day; which led me to ask him if he liked his master.

"Do you understand French?" he returned.

"Some kinds."

He kept his little eyes on me; with which he remarked: "Je suis fou de la peinture!"

"Oh I understand that kind!" I replied. Our companion laid her hand on his arm with a small pleased and
fluttered movement; it was delightful to be among people who were on such easy terms with foreign tongues.
I got up to take leave and asked her where, in Paris, I
might have the honour of waiting on her. To what hotel would she go?

She turned to her cousin enquiringly and he favoured
me again with his little languid leer. "Do you know the
Hôtel des Princes?"

"I know where it is."

"Well, that's the shop."

"I congratulate you," I said to Miss Spencer. "I believe it's the best inn in the world; but, in case I should
still have a moment to call on you here, where are you
lodged?"

"Oh it's such a pretty name," she returned gleefully.
"À la Belle Normande."

"I guess I know my way round!" her kinsman threw in; and as I left them he gave me with his swaggering head-cover a great flourish that was like the wave of a banner over a conquered field.

III

My relative, as it proved, was not sufficiently restored to leave the place by the afternoon train; so that as the autumn dusk began to fall I found myself at liberty to call at the establishment named to me by my friends. I must confess that I had spent much of the interval in wondering what the disagreeable thing was that the less attractive of these had been telling the other. The *auberge* of the Belle Normande proved an hostelry in a shady by-street, where it gave me satisfaction to think Miss Spencer must have encountered local colour in abundance. There was a crooked little court, where much of the hospitality of the house was carried on; there was a staircase climbing to bedrooms on the outer side of the wall; there was a small trickling fountain with a stucco statuette set in the midst of it; there was a little boy in a white cap and apron cleaning copper vessels at a conspicuous kitchen door; there was a chattering landlady, neatly laced, arranging apricots and grapes into an artistic pyramid upon a pink plate. I looked about, and on a green bench outside of an open door labelled Salle-à-Manger, I distinguished Caroline Spencer. No sooner had I looked at her than I was sure something had happened since the morning. Supported by the back of her bench, with her hands clasped in her lap, she kept her eyes on the other side of the court, where the landlady manipulated the apricots.

But I saw that, poor dear, she wasn't thinking of apricots or even of landladies. She was staring absently, thoughtfully; on a nearer view I could have certified she had been crying. I had seated myself beside her before she was aware; then, when she had done so, she simply turned round without surprise and showed me her sad face. Something very bad indeed had happened; she was completely changed, and I immediately charged her with it. "Your cousin has been giving you bad news. You've had a horrid time."

For a moment she said nothing, and I supposed her afraid to speak lest her tears should again rise. Then it came to me that even in the few hours since my leaving her she had shed them all—which made her now intensely, stoically composed. "My poor cousin has been having one," she replied at last. "He has had great worries. His news was bad." Then after a dismally conscious wait: "He was in dreadful want of money."

"In want of yours, you mean?"

"Of any he could get—honourably of course. Mine *is* all—well, that's available."

Ah it was as if I had been sure from the first! "And he has taken it from you?"

Again she hung fire, but her face meanwhile was pleading. "I gave him what I had."

I recall the accent of those words as the most angelic human sound I had ever listened to—which is exactly why I jumped up almost with a sense of personal outrage. "Gracious goodness, madam, do you call that his getting it 'honourably'?"

I had gone too far—she coloured to her eyes. "We won't speak of it."

"We *must* speak of it," I declared as I dropped beside her again. "I'm your friend—upon my word I'm your protector; it seems to me you need one. What's the matter with this extraordinary person?"

She was perfectly able to say. "He's just badly in debt."

"No doubt he is! But what's the special propriety of your—in such tearing haste!—paying for that?"

"Well, he has told me all his story. I *feel* for him so much."

"So do I, if you come to that! But I hope," I roundly added, "he'll give you straight back your money."

As to this she was prompt. "Certainly he will—as soon as ever he can."

"And when the deuce will that be?"

Her lucidity maintained itself. "When he has finished his great picture."

It took me full in the face. "My dear young lady, damn his great picture! Where is this voracious man?"

It was as if she must let me feel a moment that I did push her!—though indeed, as appeared, he was just where he'd naturally be. "He's having his dinner."

I turned about and looked through the open door into the salle-à-manger. There, sure enough, alone at the end of a long table, was the object of my friend's compassion—the bright, the kind young art-student. He was dining too attentively to notice me at first, but in the act of setting down a well-emptied wineglass he caught sight of my air of observation. He paused in his repast and, with his head on one side and his meagre jaws slowly moving, fixedly returned my gaze. Then the landlady came brushing lightly by with her pyramid of apricots.

"And that nice little plate of fruit is for him?" I wailed.

Miss Spencer glanced at it tenderly. "They seem to arrange everything so nicely!" she simply sighed.

I felt helpless and irritated. "Come now, really," I said; "do you think it right, do you think it decent, that that long strong fellow should collar your funds?" She looked away from me—I was evidently giving her pain.

The case was hopeless; the long strong fellow had "interested" her.

"Pardon me if I speak of him so unceremoniously," I said. "But you're really too generous, and he hasn't, clearly, the rudiments of delicacy. He made his debts himself—he ought to pay them himself."

"He has been foolish," she obstinately said—"of course I know that. He has told me everything. We had a long talk this morning—the poor fellow threw himself on my charity. He has signed notes to a large amount."

"The more fool he!"

"He's in real distress—and it's not only himself. It's his poor young wife."

"Ah he has a poor young wife?"

"I didn't know—but he made a clean breast of it. He married two years since—secretly."

"Why secretly?"

My informant took precautions as if she feared listeners. Then with low impressiveness: "She was a Countess!"

"Are you very sure of that?"

"She has written me the most beautiful letter."

"Asking you—whom she has never seen—for money?"

"Asking me for confidence and sympathy"—Miss Spencer spoke now with spirit. "She has been cruelly treated by her family—in consequence of what she has done for him. My cousin has told me every particular, and she appeals to me in her own lovely way in the letter, which I've here in my pocket. It's such a wonderful old-world romance," said my prodigious friend. "She was a beautiful young widow—her first husband was a Count, tremendously high-born, but really most wicked, with whom she hadn't been happy and whose death had left her ruined after he had deceived her in all sorts of

ways. My poor cousin, meeting her in that situation and
perhaps a little too recklessly pitying her and charmed
with her, found her, don't you see?"—Caroline's appeal
on this head was amazing!—"but too ready to trust a
better man after all she had been through. Only when
her 'people,' as he says—and I do like the word!—understood she *would* have him, poor gifted young American art-student though he simply was, because she just
adored him, her great-aunt, the old Marquise, from
whom she had expectations of wealth which she could
yet sacrifice for her love, utterly cast her off and
wouldn't so much as speak to her, much less to *him*, in
their dreadful haughtiness and pride. They *can* be
haughty over here, it seems," she ineffably developed—
"there's no mistake about that! It's like something in
some famous old book. The family, my cousin's wife's,"
she by this time almost complacently wound up, "are of
the oldest Provençal noblesse."

I listened half-bewildered. The poor woman positively
found it so interesting to be swindled by a flower of that
stock—if stock or flower or solitary grain of truth was
really concerned in the matter—as practically to have
lost the sense of what the forfeiture of her hoard meant
for her. "My dear young lady," I groaned, "you don't
want to be stripped of every dollar for such a rigmarole!"

She asserted, at this, her dignity—much as a small
pink shorn lamb might have done. "It isn't a rigmarole,
and I shan't be stripped. I shan't live any worse than I
have lived, don't you see? And I'll come back before
long to stay with them. The Countess—he still gives her,
he says, her title, as they do to noble widows, that is to
'dowagers,' don't you know? in England—insists on a
visit from me *some* time. So I guess for *that* I can start

afresh—and meanwhile I'll have recovered my money."

It was all too heart-breaking. "You're going home then at once?"

I felt the faint tremor of voice she heroically tried to stifle. "I've nothing left for a tour."

"You gave it *all* up?"

"I've kept enough to take me back."

I uttered, I think, a positive howl, and at this juncture the hero of the situation, the happy proprietor of my little friend's sacred savings and of the infatuated *grande dame* just sketched for me, reappeared with the clear consciousness of a repast bravely earned and consistently enjoyed. He stood on the threshold an instant, extracting the stone from a plump apricot he had fondly retained; then he put the apricot into his mouth and, while he let it gratefully dissolve there, stood looking at us with his long legs apart and his hands thrust into the pockets of his velvet coat. My companion got up, giving him a thin glance that I caught in its passage and which expressed at once resignation and fascination— the last dregs of her sacrifice and with it an anguish of upliftedness. Ugly vulgar pretentious dishonest as I thought him, and destitute of every grace of plausibility, he had yet appealed successfully to her eager and tender imagination. I was deeply disgusted, but I had no warrant to interfere, and at any rate felt that it would be vain. He waved his hand meanwhile with a breadth of appreciation. "Nice old court. Nice mellow old place. Nice crooked old staircase. Several pretty things."

Decidedly I couldn't stand it, and without responding I gave my hand to my friend. She looked at me an instant with her little white face and rounded eyes, and as she showed her pretty teeth I suppose she meant to smile. "Don't be sorry for me," she sublimely pleaded;

"I'm very sure I shall see something of this dear old Europe yet."

I refused however to take literal leave of her—I should find a moment to come back next morning. Her awful kinsman, who had put on his sombrero again, flourished it off at me by way of a bow—on which I hurried away.

On the morrow early I did return, and in the court of the inn met the landlady, more loosely laced than in the evening. On my asking for Miss Spencer, "*Partie*, monsieur," the good woman said. "She went away last night at ten o'clock, with her—her—not her husband, eh?—in fine her Monsieur. They went down to the American ship." I turned off—I felt the tears in my eyes. The poor girl had been some thirteen hours in Europe.

IV

I myself, more fortunate, continued to sacrifice to opportunity as I myself met it. During this period—of some five years—I lost my friend Latouche, who died of a malarious fever during a tour in the Levant. One of the first things I did on my return to America was to go up to North Verona on a consolatory visit to his poor mother. I found her in deep affliction and sat with her the whole of the morning that followed my arrival—I had come in late at night—listening to her tearful descant and singing the praises of my friend. We talked of nothing else, and our conversation ended only with the arrival of a quick little woman who drove herself up to the door in a "carry-all" and whom I saw toss the reins to the horse's back with the briskness of a startled sleeper throwing off the bedclothes. She jumped out of the carry-all and she jumped into the room. She proved to be the minister's wife and the great town-gossip, and she had evidently, in the latter capacity, a choice morsel to communicate. I was as sure of this as I was that poor Mrs. Latouche was not absolutely too bereaved to listen to her. It seemed to me discreet to retire, and I described myself as anxious for a walk before dinner.

"And by the way," I added, "if you'll tell me where my old friend Miss Spencer lives, I think I'll call on her."

The minister's wife immediately responded. Miss Spencer lived in the fourth house beyond the Baptist church; the Baptist church was the one on the right, with that queer green thing over the door; they called it a portico, but it looked more like an old-fashioned bedstead swung in the air. "Yes, do look up poor Caroline," Mrs. Latouche further enjoined. "It will refresh her to see a strange face."

"I should think she had had enough of strange faces!" cried the minister's wife.

"To see, I mean, a charming visitor"—Mrs. Latouche amended her phrase.

"I should think she had had enough of charming visitors!" her companion returned. "But *you* don't mean to stay ten years," she added with significant eyes on me.

"Has she a visitor of that sort?" I asked in my ignorance.

"You'll make out the sort!" said the minister's wife. "She's easily seen; she generally sits in the front yard. Only take care what you say to her, and be very sure you're polite."

"Ah she's so sensitive?"

The minister's wife jumped up and dropped me a curtsey—a most sarcastic curtsey. "That's what she is, if you please. 'Madame la Comtesse!' "

And pronouncing these titular words with the most

scathing accent, the little woman seemed fairly to laugh in the face of the lady they designated. I stood staring, wondering, remembering.

"Oh I shall be very polite!" I cried; and, grasping my hat and stick, I went on my way.

I found Miss Spencer's residence without difficulty. The Baptist church was easily identified, and the small dwelling near it, of a rusty white, with a large central chimney-stack and a Virginia creeper, seemed naturally and properly the abode of a withdrawn old maid with a taste for striking effects inexpensively obtained. As I approached I slackened my pace, for I had heard that some one was always sitting in the front yard, and I wished to reconnoitre. I looked cautiously over the low white fence that separated the small garden-space from the unpaved street, but I descried nothing in the shape of a Comtesse. A small straight path led up to the crooked door-step, on either side of which was a little grass-plot fringed with currant-bushes. In the middle of the grass, right and left, was a large quince-tree, full of antiquity and contortions, and beneath one of the quince-trees were placed a small table and a couple of light chairs. On the table lay a piece of unfinished embroidery and two or three books in bright-coloured paper covers. I went in at the gate and paused halfway along the path, scanning the place for some further token of its occupant, before whom—I could hardly have said why—I hesitated abruptly to present myself. Then I saw the poor little house to be of the shabbiest and felt a sudden doubt of my right to penetrate, since curiosity had been my motive and curiosity here failed of confidence. While I demurred a figure appeared in the open doorway and stood there looking at me. I immediately recognised Miss Spencer, but she faced me as if we had never met. Gently, but gravely and timidly,

I advanced to the door-step, where I spoke with an attempt at friendly banter.

"I waited for you over there to come back, but you never came."

"Waited where, sir?" she quavered, her innocent eyes rounding themselves as of old. She was much older; she looked tired and wasted.

"Well," I said, "I waited at the old French port."

She stared harder, then recognised me, smiling, flushing, clasping her two hands together. "I remember you now—I remember that day." But she stood there, neither coming out nor asking me to come in. She was embarrassed.

I too felt a little awkward while I poked at the path with my stick. "I kept looking out for you year after year."

"You mean in Europe?" she ruefully breathed.

"In Europe of course! Here apparently you're easy enough to find."

She leaned her hand against the unpainted door-post and her head fell a little to one side. She looked at me thus without speaking, and I caught the expression visible in women's eyes when tears are rising. Suddenly she stepped out on the cracked slab of stone before her threshold and closed the door. Then her strained smile prevailed and I saw her teeth were as pretty as ever. But there had been tears too. "Have you been there ever since?" she lowered her voice to ask.

"Until three weeks ago. And you—you never came back?"

Still shining at me as she could, she put her hand behind her and reopened the door. "I'm not very polite," she said. "Won't you come in?"

"I'm afraid I incommode you."

"Oh no!"—she wouldn't hear of it now. And she

pushed back the door with a sign that I should enter.

I followed her in. She led the way to a small room on the left of the narrow hall, which I supposed to be her parlour, though it was at the back of the house, and we passed the closed door of another apartment which apparently enjoyed a view of the quince-trees. This one looked out upon a small wood-shed and two clucking hens. But I thought it pretty until I saw its elegance to be of the most frugal kind; after which, presently, I thought it prettier still, for I had never seen faded chintz and old mezzotint engravings, framed in varnished autumn leaves, disposed with so touching a grace. Miss Spencer sat down on a very small section of the sofa, her hands tightly clasped in her lap. She looked ten years older, and I needn't now have felt called to insist on the facts of her person. But I still thought them interesting, and at any rate I was moved by them. She was peculiarly agitated. I tried to appear not to notice it; but suddenly, in the most inconsequent fashion—it was an irresistible echo of our concentrated passage in the old French port—I said to her: "I do incommode you. Again you're in distress."

She raised her two hands to her face and for a moment kept it buried in them. Then taking them away, "It's because you remind me," she said.

"I remind you, you mean, of that miserable day at the Havre?"

She wonderfully shook her head. "It wasn't miserable. It was delightful."

Ah was it? my manner of receiving this must have commented. "I never was so shocked as when, on going back to your inn the next morning, I found you had wretchedly retreated."

She waited an instant, after which she said: "Please let us not speak of that."

"Did you come straight back here?" I nevertheless went on.

"I was back here just thirty days after my first start."

"And here you've remained ever since?"

"Every minute of the time."

I took it in; I didn't know what to say, and what I presently said had almost the sound of mockery. "When then are you going to make that tour?" It might be practically aggressive; but there was something that irritated me in her depths of resignation, and I wished to extort from her some expression of impatience.

She attached her eyes a moment to a small sun-spot on the carpet; then she got up and lowered the window-blind a little to obliterate it. I waited, watching her with interest—as if she had still something more to give me. Well, presently, in answer to my last question, she gave it. "Never!"

"I hope at least your cousin repaid you that money," I said.

At this again she looked away from me. "I don't care for it now."

"You don't care for your money?"

"For ever going to Europe."

"Do you mean you wouldn't go if you could?"

"I can't—I can't," said Caroline Spencer. "It's all over. Everything's different. I never think of it."

"The scoundrel never repaid you then!" I cried.

"Please, please—!" she began.

But she had stopped—she was looking toward the door. There had been a rustle and a sound of steps in the hall.

I also looked toward the door, which was open and now admitted another person—a lady who paused just within the threshold. Behind her came a young man. The lady looked at me with a good deal of fixedness—

long enough for me to rise to a vivid impression of herself. Then she turned to Caroline Spencer and, with a
smile and a strong foreign accent, "*Pardon, ma chère!* I
didn't know you had company," she said. "The gentleman came in so quietly." With which she again gave
me the benefit of her attention. She was very strange,
yet I was at once sure I had seen her before. Afterwards
I rather put it that I had only seen ladies remarkably
like her. But I had seen them very far away from North
Verona, and it was the oddest of all things to meet one
of them in that frame. To what quite other scene did the
sight of her transport me? To some dusky landing before a shabby Parisian *quatrième*—to an open door
revealing a greasy ante-chamber and to Madame leaning
over the banisters while she holds a faded wrapper
together and bawls down to the portress to bring up
her coffee. My friend's guest was a very large lady, of
middle age, with a plump dead-white face and hair
drawn back *à la chinoise*. She had a small penetrating
eye and what is called in French *le sourire agréable*. She
wore an old pink cashmere dressing-gown covered with
white embroideries, and, like the figure in my momentary vision, she confined it in front with a bare and
rounded arm and a plump and deeply-dimpled hand.

"It's only to spick about my café," she said to her
hostess with her *sourire agréable*. "I should like it served
in the garden under the leetle tree."

The young man behind her had now stepped into the
room, where he also stood revealed, though with rather
less of a challenge. He was a gentleman of few inches
but a vague importance, perhaps the leading man of
the world of North Verona. He had a small pointed
nose and a small pointed chin; also, as I observed, the
most diminutive feet and a manner of no point at all.
He looked at me foolishly and with his mouth open.

"You shall have your coffee," said Miss Spencer as if an army of cooks had been engaged in the preparation of it.

"C'est bien!" said her massive inmate. "Find your bouk"—and this personage turned to the gaping youth.

He gaped now at each quarter of the room. "My grammar, d' ye mean?"

The large lady however could but face her friend's visitor while persistently engaged with a certain laxity in the flow of her wrapper. "Find your bouk," she more absently repeated.

"My poetry, d' ye mean?" said the young man, who also couldn't take his eyes off me.

"Never mind your bouk"—his companion reconsidered. "To-day we'll just talk. We'll make some conversation. But we mustn't interrupt Mademoiselle's. Come, come"—and she moved off a step. "Under the leetle tree," she added for the benefit of Mademoiselle. After which she gave me a thin salutation, jerked a measured "Monsieur!" and swept away again with her swain following.

I looked at Miss Spencer, whose eyes never moved from the carpet, and I spoke, I fear, without grace. "Who in the world's that?"

"The Comtesse—that *was:* my *cousine* as they call it in French."

"And who's the young man?"

"The Countess's pupil, Mr. Mixter." This description of the tie uniting the two persons who had just quitted us must certainly have upset my gravity; for I recall the marked increase of my friend's own as she continued to explain. "She gives lessons in French and music, the simpler sorts—"

"The simpler sorts of French?" I fear I broke in.

But she was still impenetrable, and in fact had now an

intonation that put me vulgarly in the wrong. "She has had the worst reverses—with no one to look to. She's prepared for any exertion—and she takes her misfortunes with gaiety."

"Ah well," I returned—no doubt a little ruefully, "that's all I myself am pretending to do. If she's determined to be a burden to nobody, nothing could be more right and proper."

My hostess looked vaguely, though I thought quite wearily enough, about: she met this proposition in no other way. "I must go and get the coffee," she simply said.

"Has the lady many pupils?" I none the less persisted.

"She has only Mr. Mixter. She gives him all her time." It might have set me off again, but something in my whole impression of my friend's sensibility urged me to keep strictly decent. "He pays very well," she at all events inscrutably went on. "He's not very bright—as a pupil; but he's very rich and he's very kind. He has a buggy—with a back, and he takes the Countess to drive."

"For good long spells I hope," I couldn't help interjecting—even at the cost of her so taking it that she had still to avoid my eyes. "Well, the country's beautiful for miles," I went on. And then as she was turning away: "You're going for the Countess's coffee?"

"If you'll excuse me a few moments."

"Is there no one else to do it?"

She seemed to wonder who there should be. "I keep no servants."

"Then can't I help?" After which, as she but looked at me, I bettered it. "Can't she wait on herself?"

Miss Spencer had a slow headshake—as if that too had been a strange idea. "She isn't used to *manual* labour."

The discrimination was a treat, but I cultivated decorum. "I see—and you *are*." But at the same time I couldn't abjure curiosity. "Before you go, at any rate, please tell me this: who *is* this wonderful lady?"

"I told you just who in France—that extraordinary day. She's the wife of my cousin, whom you saw there."

"The lady disowned by her family in consequence of her marriage?"

"Yes; they've never seen her again. They've completely broken with her."

"And where's her husband?"

"My poor cousin's dead."

I pulled up, but only a moment. "And where's your money?"

The poor thing flinched—I kept her on the rack. "I don't know," she woefully said.

I scarce know what it didn't prompt me to—but I went step by step. "On her husband's death this lady at once came to you?"

It was as if she had had too often to describe it. "Yes, she arrived one day."

"How long ago?"

"Two years and four months."

"And has been here ever since?"

"Ever since."

I took it all in. "And how does she like it?"

"Well, not *very* much," said Miss Spencer divinely.

That too I took in. "And how do *you*—?"

She laid her face in her two hands an instant as she had done ten minutes before. Then, quickly, she went to get the Countess's coffee.

Left alone in the little parlour I found myself divided between the perfection of my disgust and a contrary wish to see, to learn more. At the end of a few minutes the young man in attendance on the lady in question reappeared as for a fresh gape at me. He was inordinately grave—to be dressed in such parti-coloured flannels; and he produced with no great confidence on his own side the message with which he had been charged. "She wants to know if you won't come right out."

"Who wants to know?"

"The Countess. That French lady."

"She has asked you to bring me?"

"Yes sir," said the young man feebly—for I may claim to have surpassed him in stature and weight.

I went out with him, and we found his instructress seated under one of the small quince-trees in front of the house; where she was engaged in drawing a fine needle with a very fat hand through a piece of embroidery not remarkable for freshness. She pointed graciously to the chair beside her and I sat down. Mr. Mixter glanced about him and then accommodated himself on the grass at her feet; whence he gazed upward more gapingly than ever and as if convinced that between us something wonderful would now occur.

"I'm sure you spick French," said the Countess, whose eyes were singularly protuberant as she played over me her agreeable smile.

"I do, madam—*tant bien que mal,*" I replied, I fear, more dryly.

"Ah voilà!" she cried as with delight. "I knew it as soon as I looked at you. You've been in my poor dear country."

"A considerable time."

"You love it then, *mon pays de France?*"

"Oh it's an old affection." But I wasn't exuberant.

"And you know Paris well?"

"Yes, *sans me vanter,* madam, I think I really do."

And with a certain conscious purpose I let my eyes meet her own.

She presently, hereupon, moved her own and glanced down at Mr. Mixter. "What are we talking about?" she demanded of her attentive pupil.

He pulled his knees up, plucked at the grass, stared, blushed a little. "You're talking French," said Mr. Mixter.

"*La belle découverte!*" mocked the Countess. "It's going on ten months," she explained to me, "since I took him in hand. Don't put yourself out not to say he's *la bêtise même*," she added in fine style. "He won't in the least understand you."

A moment's consideration of Mr. Mixter, awkwardly sporting at our feet, quite assured me that he wouldn't. "I hope your other pupils do you more honour," I then remarked to my entertainer.

"I have no others. They don't know what French— or what anything else—is in this place; they don't want to know. You may therefore imagine the pleasure it is to me to meet a person who speaks it like yourself." I could but reply that my own pleasure wasn't less, and she continued to draw the stitches through her embroidery with an elegant curl of her little finger. Every few moments she put her eyes, near-sightedly, closer to her work—this as if for elegance too. She inspired me with no more confidence than her late husband, if husband he was, had done, years before, on the occasion with which this one so detestably matched: she was coarse, common, affected, dishonest—no more a Countess than I was a Caliph. She had an assurance— based clearly on experience; but this couldn't have been the experience of "race." Whatever it was indeed it did now, in a yearning fashion, flare out of her. "Talk to me of Paris, *mon beau Paris* that I'd give my eyes to see. The very name of it *me fait languir*. How long since you were there?"

"A couple of months ago."

"*Vous avez de la chance!* Tell me something about it. What were they doing? Oh for an hour of the Boulevard!"

"They were doing about what they're always doing—amusing themselves a good deal."

"At the theatres, *hein?*" sighed the Countess. "At the cafés-concerts? *sous ce beau ciel*—at the little tables before the doors? *Quelle existence!* You know I'm a Parisienne, monsieur," she added, "to my finger-tips."

"Miss Spencer was mistaken then," I ventured to return, "in telling me you're a Provençale."

She stared a moment, then put her nose to her embroidery, which struck me as having acquired even while we sat a dingier and more desultory air. "Ah I'm a Provençale by birth, but a Parisienne by—inclination." After which she pursued: "And by the saddest events of my life—as well as by some of the happiest, hélas!"

"In other words by a varied experience!" I now at last smiled.

She questioned me over it with her hard little salient eyes. "Oh experience!—I could talk of that, no doubt, if I wished. *On en a de toutes les sortes*—and I never dreamed that mine, for example, would ever have *this* in store for me." And she indicated with her large bare elbow and with a jerk of her head all surrounding objects; the little white house, the pair of quince-trees, the rickety paling, even the rapt Mr. Mixter.

I took them all bravely in. "Ah if you mean you're decidedly in exile—!"

"You may imagine what it is. These two years of my *épreuve—elles m'en ont données, des heures, des heures!* One gets used to things"—and she raised her shoulders to the highest shrug ever accomplished at North Verona; "so that I sometimes think I've got used to this. But there are some things that are always beginning again. For example my coffee."

I so far again lent myself. "Do you always have coffee at this hour?"

Her eyebrows went up as high as her shoulders had done. "At what hour would you propose to me to have it? I must have my little cup after breakfast."

"Ah you breakfast at this hour?"

"At mid-day—*comme cela se fait.* Here they breakfast at a quarter past seven. That 'quarter past' is charming!"

"But you were telling me about your coffee," I observed sympathetically.

"My *cousine* can't believe in it; she can't understand it. C'est une fille charmante, but that little cup of black coffee with a drop of '*fine,*' served at this hour—they exceed her comprehension. So I have to break the ice each day, and it takes the coffee the time you see to arrive. And when it does arrive, monsieur—! If I don't press it on *you*—though monsieur here sometimes joins me!—it's because you've drunk it on the Boulevard."

I resented extremely so critical a view of my poor friend's exertions, but I said nothing at all—the only way to be sure of my civility. I dropped my eyes on Mr. Mixter, who, sitting cross-legged and nursing his knees, watched my companion's foreign graces with an interest that familiarity had apparently done little to restrict. She became aware, naturally, of my mystified view of him and faced the question with all her boldness. "He adores me, you know," she murmured with her nose again in her tapestry—"he dreams of becoming *mon amoureux.* Yes, *il me fait une cour acharnée*—such as you see him. That's what we've come to. He has read some French novel—it took him six months. But ever since that he has thought himself a hero and me—such as I am, monsieur—*je ne sais quelle dévergondée!*"

Mr. Mixter may have inferred that he was to that extent the object of our reference; but of the manner in which he was handled he must have had small suspicion—preoccupied as he was, as to my companion, with the ecstasy of contemplation. Our hostess moreover at this moment came out of the house, bearing a coffee-pot and three cups on a neat little tray. I took from her eyes, as she approached us, a brief but intense appeal—the mute expression as I felt, conveyed in the hardest little look she had yet addressed me, of her longing to know what, as a man of the world in general and of the French world in particular, I thought of these allied forces now so encamped on the stricken field of her life. I could only "act" however, as they said at North Verona, quite impenetrably—only make no answering sign. I couldn't intimate, much less could I frankly utter, my inward sense of the Countess's probable past, with its measure of her virtue, value and accomplishments, and of the limits of the consideration to which she could properly pretend. I couldn't give my friend a hint of how I myself personally "saw" her interesting pensioner—whether as the runaway wife of a too-jealous hair-dresser or of a too-morose pastry-cook, say; whether as a very small bourgeoise, in fine, who had vitiated her case beyond patching up, or even as some character, of the nomadic sort, less edifying still. I couldn't let in, by the jog of a shutter, as it were, a hard informing ray and then, washing my hands of the business, turn my back for ever. I could on the contrary but save the situation, my own at least, for the moment, by pulling myself together with a master hand and appearing to ignore everything but that the dreadful person between us *was* a "grande dame." This effort was possible indeed but as a retreat in good order and with all the forms of courtesy. If I couldn't speak, still less could I stay, and I think I must, in spite of everything, have turned black with disgust to see Caroline Spencer stand there like a waiting-maid. I therefore won't answer for the shade of success that may have attended my saying to the Countess, on my feet and as to leave her: "You expect to remain some time in these *parages?*"

What passed between us, as from face to face, while she looked up at me, *that* at least our companion may have caught, that at least may have sown, for the aftertime, some seed of revelation. The Countess repeated her terrible shrug. "Who knows? I don't see my way—! It isn't an existence, but when one's in misery—! *Chère belle,*" she added as an appeal to Miss Spencer, "you've gone and forgotten the *'fine'!*"

I detained that lady as, after considering a moment in silence the small array, she was about to turn off in quest of this article. I held out my hand in silence—I had to go. Her wan set little face, severely mild and with the question of a moment before now quite cold in it, spoke of extreme fatigue, but also of something else strange and conceived—whether a desperate patience still, or at last some other desperation, being more than I can say. What was clearest on the whole was that she was glad I was going. Mr. Mixter had risen to his feet and was pouring out the Countess's coffee. As I went back past the Baptist church I could feel how right my poor friend had been in her conviction at the other, the still intenser, the now historic crisis, that she should still see something of that dear old Europe.

1877

*

GREVILLE FANE

Coming in to dress for dinner I found a telegram: "Mrs. Stormer dying; can you give us half a column for tomorrow evening? Let her down easily, but not too easily." I was late; I was in a hurry; I had very little time to think; but at a venture I despatched a reply: "Will do what I can." It was not till I had dressed and was rolling away to dinner that, in the hansom, I bethought myself of the difficulty of the condition attached. The difficulty was not of course in letting her down easily but in qualifying that indulgence. "So I simply won't qualify it," I said. I didn't admire but liked her, and had known her so long that I almost felt heartless in sitting down at such an hour to a feast of indifference. I must have seemed abstracted, for the early years of my acquaintance with her came back to me. I spoke of her to the lady I had taken down, but the lady I had taken down had never heard of Greville Fane. I tried my other neighbour, who pronounced her books "too vile." I had never thought them very good, but I should let her down more easily than that.

I came away early, for the express purpose of driving to ask about her. The journey took time, for she lived in the northwest district, in the neighbourhood of Primrose Hill. My apprehension that I should be too late was justified in a fuller sense than I had attached to it—I had only feared that the house would be shut up. There were lights in the windows, and the temperate tinkle of my bell brought a servant immediately to the door; but poor Mrs. Stormer had passed into a state in which the resonance of no earthly knocker was to be feared. A lady hovering behind the servant came forward into the hall when she heard my voice. I recognised Lady Luard, but she had mistaken me for the doctor.

"Pardon my appearing at such an hour," I said; "it was the first possible moment after I heard."

"It's all over," Lady Luard replied. "Dearest mamma!"

She stood there under the lamp with her eyes on me; she was very tall, very stiff, very cold, and always looked as if these things, and some others beside, in her dress, in her manner and even in her name, were an implication that she was very admirable. I had never been able to follow the argument, but that's a detail. I expressed briefly and frankly what I felt, while the little mottled maidservant flattened herself against the wall of the narrow passage and tried to look detached without looking indifferent. It was not a moment to make a visit, and I was on the point of retreating when Lady Luard arrested me with a queer casual drawling "Would you —a—would you perhaps be *writing* something?" I felt for the instant like an infamous interviewer, which I wasn't. But I pleaded guilty to this intention, on which she returned: "I'm so very glad—but I think my brother would like to see you." I detested her brother, but it wasn't an occasion to act this out; so I suffered myself to be inducted, to my surprise, into a small back room which I immediately recognised as the scene, during the later years, of Mrs. Stormer's imperturbable industry. Her table was there, the battered and blotted accessory to innumerable literary lapses, with its contracted space for the arms (she wrote only from the elbow down) and the confusion of scrappy scribbled sheets which had already become literary remains. Leolin was also there, smoking a cigarette before the fire and looking impudent even in his grief, sincere as it well might have been.

To meet him, to greet him, I had to make a sharp effort; for the air he wore to me as he stood before me was quite that of his mother's murderer. She lay silent for ever upstairs—as dead as an unsuccessful book, and his swaggering erectness was a kind of symbol of his having killed her. I wondered if he had already, with his sister, been calculating what they could get for the poor papers on the table; but I hadn't long to wait to learn, since in reply to the few words of sympathy I addressed him he puffed out: "It's miserable, miserable, yes; but she has left three books complete." His words had the oddest effect; they converted the cramped little room into a seat of trade and made the "book" wonderfully feasible. He would certainly get all that could be got for the three. Lady Luard explained to me that her husband had been with them, but had had to go down to the House. To her brother she mentioned that I was going to write something, and to me again made it clear that she hoped I would "do mamma justice." She added that she didn't think this had ever been done. She said to her brother: "Don't you think there are some things he ought thoroughly to understand?" and on his instantly exclaiming "Oh thoroughly, thoroughly!" went on rather austerely: "I mean about mamma's birth."

"Yes and her connexions," Leolin added.

I professed every willingness, and for five minutes I listened; but it would be too much to say I clearly understood. I don't even now, but it's not important. My vision was of other matters than those they put before me, and while they desired there should be no mistake about their ancestors I became keener and keener about themselves. I got away as soon as possible and walked home through the great dusky empty London—the best of all conditions for thought. By the time I reached my door my little article was practically composed—ready to be transferred on the morrow from the polished plate of fancy. I believe it attracted some notice, was thought "graceful" and was said to be by some one else. I had to be pointed without being lively, and it took some doing. But what I said was much less interesting than what I thought—especially during the half-hour I spent in my armchair by the fire, smoking the cigar I always light before going to bed. I went to sleep there, I believe; but I continued to moralise about Greville Fane. I'm reluctant to lose that retrospect altogether, and this is a dim little memory of it, a document not to "serve." The dear woman had written a hundred stories, but none so curious as her own.

When first I knew her she had published half a dozen fictions, and I believe I had also perpetrated a novel. She was more than a dozen years my elder, but a person who always acknowledged her comparative state. It wasn't so very long ago, but in London, amid the big waves of the present, even a near horizon gets hidden. I met her at some dinner and took her down, rather flattered at offering my arm to a celebrity. She didn't look like one, with her matronly mild inanimate face, but I supposed her greatness would come out in her conversation. I gave it all the opportunities I could, but was nevertheless not disappointed when I found her only a dull kind woman. This was why I liked her—she rested me so from literature. To myself literature was an irritation, a torment; but Greville Fane slumbered in the intellectual part of it even as a cat on a hearthrug or a Creole in a hammock. She wasn't a woman of genius, but her faculty was so special, so much a gift out of hand, that

I've often wondered why she fell below that distinction. This was doubtless because the transaction, in her case, had remained incomplete; genius always pays for the gift, feels the debt, and she was placidly unconscious of a call. She could invent stories by the yard, but couldn't write a page of English. She went down to her grave without suspecting that though she had contributed volumes to the diversion of her contemporaries she hadn't contributed a sentence to the language. This hadn't prevented bushels of criticism from being heaped on her head; she was worth a couple of columns any day to the weekly papers, in which it was shown that her pictures of life were dreadful but her style superior. She asked me to come and see her and I complied. She lived then in Montpellier Square; which helped me to see how dissociated her imagination was from her character.

An industrious widow, devoted to her daily stint, to meeting the butcher and baker and making a home for her son and daughter, from the moment she took her pen in her hand she became a creature of passion. She thought the English novel deplorably wanting in that element, and the task she had cut out for herself was to supply the deficiency. Passion in high life was the general formula of this work, for her imagination was at home only in the most exalted circles. She adored in truth the aristocracy, and they constituted for her the romance of the world or what is more to the point, the prime material of fiction. Their beauty and luxury, their loves and revenges, their temptations and surrenders, their immoralities and diamonds were as familiar to her as the blots on her writing-table. She was not a belated producer of the old fashionable novel, but, with a cleverness and a modernness of her own, had freshened up the fly-blown tinsel. She turned off plots by the hundred and—so far as her flying quill could convey her—was perpetually going abroad. Her types, her illustrations, her tone were nothing if not cosmopolitan. She recognised nothing less provincial than European society, and her fine folk knew each other and made love to each other from Doncaster to Bucharest. She had an idea that she resembled Balzac, and her favourite historical characters were Lucien de Rubempré and the Vidame de Pamiers. I must add that when I once asked her who the latter personage was she was unable to tell me. She was very brave and healthy and cheerful, very abundant and innocent and wicked. She was expert and vulgar and snobbish, and never so intensely British as when she was particularly foreign.

This combination of qualities had brought her early success, and I remember having heard with wonder and envy of what she "got," in those days, for a novel. The revelation gave me a pang: it was such a proof that, practising a totally different style, I should never make my fortune. And yet when, as I knew her better she told me her real tariff and I saw how rumour had quadrupled it, I liked her enough to be sorry. After a while I discovered too that if she got less it was not that I was to get any more. My failure never had what Mrs. Stormer would have called the banality of being relative—it was always admirably absolute. She lived at ease however in those days—ease is exactly the word, though she produced three novels a year. She scorned me when I spoke of difficulty—it was the only thing that made her angry. If I hinted at the grand licking into shape that a work of art required she thought it a pretension and a *pose*. She never recognised the "torment of form"; the furthest she went was to introduce into one of her books (in satire her hand was heavy) a young poet who was always talking about it. I couldn't quite understand

her irritation on this score, for she had nothing at stake
in the matter. She had a shrewd perception that form,
in prose at least, never recommended any one to the
public we were condemned to address; according to
which she lost nothing (her private humiliation not
counted) by having none to show. She made no pretence
of producing works of art, but had comfortable tea-
drinking hours in which she freely confessed herself
a common pastrycook, dealing in such tarts and pud-
dings as would bring customers to the shop. She put in
plenty of sugar and of cochineal, or whatever it is that
gives these articles a rich and attractive colour. She had
a calm independence of observation and opportunity
which constituted an inexpugnable strength and would
enable her to go on indefinitely. It's only real success
that wanes, it's only solid things that melt. Greville Fane's
ignorance of life was a resource still more unfailing than
the most approved receipt. On her saying once that the
day would come when she should have written herself
out I answered: "Ah you open straight into fairyland,
and the fairies love you and *they* never change. Fairyland's always there; it always was from the beginning
of time and always will be to the end. They've given
you the key and you can always open the door. With
me it's different; I try, in my clumsy way, to be in some
direct relation to life." "Oh bother your direct relation
to life!" she used to reply, for she was always annoyed
by the phrase—which wouldn't in the least prevent her
using it as a note of elegance. With no more prejudices
than an old sausage-mill, she would give forth again
with patient punctuality any poor verbal scrap that had
been dropped into her. I cheered her with saying that
the dark day, at the end, would be for the "likes" of
me; since, proceeding in our small way by experience
and study—priggish we!—we depended not on a reve-

lation but on a little tiresome process. Attention depended on occasion, and where should we be when occasion failed?

One day she told me that as the novelist's life was so delightful and, during the good years at least, such a comfortable support—she had these staggering optimisms—she meant to train up her boy to follow it. She took the ingenious view that it was a profession like another and that therefore everything was to be gained by beginning young and serving an apprenticeship. Moreover the education would be less expensive than any other special course, inasmuch as she could herself administer it. She didn't profess to keep a school, but she could at least teach her own child. It wasn't that she had such a gift, but—she confessed to me as if she were afraid I should laugh at her—that *he* had. I didn't laugh at her for that, because I thought the boy sharp— I had seen him sundry times. He was well-grown and good-looking and unabashed, and both he and his sister made me wonder about their defunct papa, concerning whom the little I knew was that he had been a country vicar and brother to a small squire. I explained them to myself by suppositions and imputations possibly unjust to the departed; so little were they—superficially at least—the children of their mother. There used to be on an easel in her drawing-room an enlarged photograph of her husband, done by some horrible posthumous "process" and draped, as to its florid frame, with a silken scarf which testified to the candour of Greville Fane's bad taste. It made him look like an unsuccessful tragedian, but it wasn't a thing to trust. He may have been a successful comedian. Of the two children the girl was the elder, and struck me in all her younger years as singularly colourless. She was only long, very long, like an undecipherable letter. It wasn't till Mrs. Stormer

came back from a protracted residence abroad that Ethel
(which was this young lady's name) began to produce
the effect, large and stiff and afterwards eminent in her,
of a certain kind of resolution, something as public and
important as if a meeting and a chairman had passed it.
She gave one to understand she meant to do all she
could for herself. She was long-necked and near-sighted
and striking, and I thought I had never seen sweet
seventeen in a form so hard and high and dry. She was
cold and affected and ambitious, and she carried an eye-
glass with a long handle, which she put up whenever
she wanted not to see. She had come out, as the phrase
is, immensely; and yet I felt as if she were surrounded
with a spiked iron railing. What she meant to do for
herself was to marry, and it was the only thing, I think,
that she meant to do for any one else; yet who would
be inspired to clamber over that bristling barrier? What
flower of tenderness or of intimacy would such an adventurer conceive as his reward?

This was for Sir Baldwin Luard to say; but he naturally never confided me the secret. He was a joyless
jokeless young man, with the air of having other secrets
as well, and a determination to get on politically that
was indicated by his never having been known to commit himself—as regards any proposition whatever—
beyond an unchallengeable "Oh!" His wife and he must
have conversed mainly in prim ejaculations, but they
understood sufficiently that they were kindred spirits.
I remember being angry with Greville Fane when she
announced these nuptials to me as magnificent; I remember asking her what splendour there was in the
union of the daughter of a woman of genius with an
irredeemable mediocrity. "Oh he has immense ability,"
she said; but she blushed for the maternal fib. What she
meant was that though Sir Baldwin's estates were not

vast—he had a dreary house in South Kensington and a still drearier "Hall" somewhere in Essex, which was let—the connexion was a "smarter" one than a child of hers could have aspired to form. In spite of the social bravery of her novels she took a very humble and dingy view of herself, so that of all her productions "my daughter Lady Luard" was quite the one she was proudest of. That personage thought our authoress vulgar and was distressed and perplexed by the frequent freedoms of her pen, but had a complicated attitude for this indirect connexion with literature. So far as it was lucrative her ladyship approved of it and could compound with the inferiority of the pursuit by practical justice to some of its advantages. I had reason to know—my reason was simply that poor Mrs. Stormer told me—how she suffered the inky fingers to press an occasional banknote into her palm. On the other hand she deplored the "peculiar style" to which Greville Fane had devoted herself, and wondered where a spectator with the advantage of so ladylike a daughter could have picked up such views about the best society. "She might know better, with Leolin and me," Lady Luard had been heard to remark; but it appeared that some of Greville Fane's superstitions were incurable. She didn't live in Lady Luard's society, and the best wasn't good enough for her—she must improve on it so prodigiously.

I could see this necessity increase in her during the years she spent abroad, when I had glimpses of her in the shifting sojourns that lay in the path of my annual ramble. She betook herself from Germany to Switzerland and from Switzerland to Italy; she favoured cheap places and set up her desk in the smaller capitals. I took a look at her whenever I could, and I always asked how Leolin was getting on. She gave me beautiful accounts of him, and, occasion favouring, the boy was produced

for my advantage. I had entered from the first into the
joke of his career—I pretended to regard him as a consecrated child. It had been a joke for Mrs. Stormer at first,
but the youth himself had been shrewd enough to make
the matter serious. If his parent accepted the principle
that the intending novelist can't begin too early to see
life, Leolin wasn't interested in hanging back from the
application of it. He was eager to qualify himself and
took to cigarettes at ten on the highest literary grounds.
His fond mother gazed at him with extravagant envy
and, like Desdemona, wished heaven had made *her* such
a man. She explained to me more than once that in her
profession she had found her sex a dreadful drawback.
She loved the story of Madame George Sand's early
rebellion against this hindrance, and believed that if she
had worn trousers she could have written as well as that
lady. Leolin had for the career at least the qualification
of trousers, and as he grew older he recognised its importance by laying in ever so many pair. He grew up
thus in gorgeous apparel, which was his way of inter-
preting his mother's system. Whenever I met her, accordingly, I found her still under the impression that
she was carrying this system out and that the sacrifices
made him were bearing heavy fruit. She was giving him
experience, she was giving him impressions, she was
putting a *gagne-pain* into his hand. It was another name
for spoiling him with the best conscience in the world.
The queerest pictures come back to me of this period
of the good lady's life and of the extraordinarily virtuous muddled bewildering tenor of it. She had an idea
she was seeing foreign manners as well as her petticoats
would allow; but in reality she wasn't seeing anything,
least of all, fortunately, how much she was laughed at.
She drove her whimsical pen at Dresden and at Florence—she produced in all places and at all times the

same romantic and ridiculous fictions. She carried about her box of properties, tumbling out promptly the familiar tarnished old puppets. She believed in them when others couldn't, and as they were like nothing that was to be seen under the sun it was impossible to prove by comparison that they were wrong. You can't compare birds and fishes; you could only feel that, as Greville Fane's characters had the fine plumage of the former species, human beings must be of the latter.

It would have been droll if it hadn't been so exemplary to see her tracing the loves of the duchesses beside the innocent cribs of her children. The immoral and the maternal lived together, in her diligent days, on the most comfortable terms, and she stopped curling the moustaches of her Guardsmen to pat the heads of her babes. She was haunted by solemn spinsters who came to tea from Continental pensions, and by unsophisticated Americans who told her she was just loved in *their* country. "I had rather be just paid there," she usually replied; for this tribute of transatlantic opinion was the only thing that galled her. The Americans went away thinking her coarse; though as the author of so many beautiful love-stories she was disappointing to most of these pilgrims, who hadn't expected to find a shy stout ruddy lady in a cap like a crumbled pyramid. She wrote about the affections and the impossibility of controlling them, but she talked of the price of pension and the convenience of an English chemist. She devoted much thought and many thousands of francs to the education of her daughter, who spent three years at a very superior school at Dresden, receiving wonderful instruction in sciences, arts and tongues, and who, taking a different line from Leolin, was to be brought up wholly as a *femme du monde*. The girl was musical and philological; she went in for several languages and learned enough about them to be inspired with a great contempt for her mother's artless accents. Greville Fane's French and Italian were droll; the imitative faculty had been denied her, and she had an unequalled gift, especially pen in hand, of squeezing big mistakes into small opportunities. She knew it but didn't care; correctness was the virtue in the world that, like her heroes and heroines, she valued least. Ethel, who had noted in her pages some remarkable lapses, undertook at one time to revise her proofs; but I remember her telling me a year after the girl had left school that this function had been very briefly exercised. "She can't read me," said Mrs. Stormer; "I offend her taste. She tells me that at Dresden—at school—I was never allowed." The good lady seemed surprised at this, having the best conscience in the world about her lucubrations. She had never meant to fly in the face of anything, and considered that she grovelled before the Rhadamanthus of the English literary tribunal, the celebrated and awful Young Person. I assured her, as a joke, that she was frightfully indecent—she had in fact that element of truth as little as any other—my purpose being solely to prevent her guessing that her daughter had dropped her not because she was immoral but because she was vulgar. I used to figure her children closeted together and putting it to each other with a gaze of dismay: "Why should she *be* so—and so *fearfully* so—when she has the advantage of our society? Shouldn't *we* have taught her better?" Then I imagined their recognising with a blush and a shrug that she was unteachable, irreformable. Indeed she was, poor lady, but it's never fair to read by the light of taste things essentially not written in it. Greville Fane kept through all her riot of absurdity a witless confidence that should have been as safe from criticism as a stutter or a squint.

She didn't make her son ashamed of the profession to which he was destined, however; she only made him ashamed of the way she herself exercised it. But he bore his humiliation much better than his sister, being ready to assume he should one day restore the balance. A canny and far-seeing youth, with appetites and aspirations, he hadn't a scruple in his composition. His mother's theory of the happy knack he could pick up deprived him of the wholesome discipline required to prevent young idlers from becoming cads. He enjoyed on foreign soil a casual tutor and the common snatch or two of a Swiss school, but addressed himself to no consecutive study nor to any prospect of a university or a degree. It may be imagined with what zeal, as the years went on, he entered into the pleasantry of there being no manual so important to him as the massive book of life. It was an expensive volume to peruse, but Mrs. Stormer was willing to lay out a sum in what she would have called her *premiers frais*. Ethel disapproved—she found this education irregular for an English gentleman. Her voice was for Eton and Oxford or for any public school—she would have resigned herself to one of the scrubbier—with the army to follow. But Leolin never was afraid of his sister, and they visibly disliked, though they sometimes agreed to assist, each other. They could combine to work the oracle—to keep their mother at her desk.

When she reappeared in England, telling me she had "secured" all the Continent could give her, Leolin was a broad-shouldered red-faced young man with an immense wardrobe and an extraordinary assurance of manner. She was fondly, quite aggressively certain she had taken the right course with him, and addicted to boasting of all he knew and had seen. He was now quite ready to embark on the family profession, to commence

author, as they used to say, and a little while later she
told me he had started. He had written something tremendously clever which was coming out in the *Cheapside*. I believe it came out; I had no time to look for it;
I never heard anything about it. I took for granted that
if this contribution had passed through his mother's
hands it would virtually rather illustrate *her* fine facility,
and it was interesting to consider the poor lady's future
in the light of her having to write her son's novels as
well as her own. This wasn't the way she looked at it
herself—she took the charming ground that he'd help
her to write hers. She used to assure me he supplied
passages of the greatest value to these last—all sorts of
telling technical things, happy touches about hunting
and yachting and cigars and wine, about City slang and
the way men talk at clubs—that she couldn't be expected to get very straight. It was all so much practice
for him and so much alleviation for herself. I was unable
to identify such pages, for I had long since ceased to
"keep up" with Greville Fane; but I could quite believe
at least that the wine-question had been put by Leolin's good offices on a better footing, for the dear woman
used to mix her drinks—she was perpetually serving
the most splendid suppers—in the queerest fashion. I
could see him quite ripe to embrace regularly that care.
It occurred to me indeed, when she settled in England
again, that she might by a shrewd use of both her children be able to rejuvenate her style. Ethel had come
back to wreak her native, her social yearning, and if she
couldn't take her mother into company would at least
go into it herself. Silently, stiffly, almost grimly, this
young lady reared her head, clenched her long teeth,
squared her lean elbows and found her way up the staircases she had marked. The only communication she ever
made, the only effusion of confidence with which she

ever honoured me, was when she said "I don't want to know the people mamma knows, I mean to know others." I took due note of the remark, for I wasn't one of the "others." I couldn't trace therefore the steps and stages of her climb; I could only admire it at a distance and congratulate her mother in due course on the results. The results, the gradual, the final, the wonderful, were that Ethel went to "big" parties and got people to take her. Some of them were people she had met abroad, and others people the people she had met abroad had met. They ministered alike to Miss Ethel's convenience, and I wondered how she extracted so many favours without the expenditure of a smile. Her smile was the dimmest thing in nature, diluted, unsweetened, inexpensive lemonade, and she had arrived precociously at social wisdom, recognising that if she was neither pretty enough nor rich enough nor clever enough, she could at least, in her muscular youth, be rude enough. Therefore, so placed to give her parent tips, to let her know what really occurred in the mansions of the great, to supply her with local colour, with *data* to work from, she promoted the driving of the well-worn quill, over the brave old battered blotting book, to a still lustier measure and precisely at the moment when most was to depend on this labour. But if she became a great critic it appeared that the labourer herself was constitutionally inapt for the lesson. It was late in the day for Greville Fane to learn, and I heard nothing of her having developed a new manner. She was to have had only one manner, as Leolin would have said, from start to finish.

She was weary and spent at last, but confided to me that she couldn't afford to pause. She continued to speak of her son's work as the great hope of their future—she had saved no money—though the young man wore to my sense an air more and more professional if you like,

but less and less literary. There was at the end of a couple of years something rare in the impudence of his playing of his part in the comedy. When I wondered how
she could play hers it was to feel afresh the fatuity of
her fondness, which was proof, I believed—I indeed
saw to the end—against any interference of reason.
She loved the young impostor with a simple blind benighted love, and of all the heroes of romance who had
passed before her eyes he was by far the brightest. He
was at any rate the most real—she could touch him, pay
for him, suffer for him, worship him. He made her
think of her princes and dukes, and when she wished to
fix these figures in her mind's eye she thought of her
boy. She had often told me she was herself carried away
by her creations, and she was certainly carried away by
Leolin. He vivified—by what romantically might have
been at least—the whole question of youth and passion. She held, not unjustly, that the sincere novelist
should feel the whole flood of life; she acknowledged
with regret that she hadn't had time to feel it herself,
and the lapse in her history was in a manner made up
by the sight of its rush through this magnificent young
man. She exhorted him, I suppose, to encourage the
rush; she wrung her own flaccid little sponge into the
torrent. What passed between them in her pedagogic
hours was naturally a blank to me, but I gathered that
she mainly impressed on him that the great thing was to
live, because that gave you material. He asked nothing
better; he collected material, and the recipe served as a
universal pretext. You had only to look at him to see
that, with his rings and breastpins, his crossbarred jackets, his early *embonpoint*, his eyes that looked like
imitation jewels, his various indications of a dense full-
blown temperament, his idea of life was singularly vulgar; but he was so far auspicious as that his response to

his mother's expectations was in a high degree practical. If she had imposed a profession on him from his tenderest years it was exactly a profession that he followed. The two were not quite the same, inasmuch as the one he had adopted was simply to live at her expense; but at least she couldn't say he hadn't taken a line. If she insisted on believing in him he offered himself to the sacrifice. My impression is that her secret dream was that he should have a *liaison* with a countess, and he persuaded her without difficulty that he had one. I don't know what countesses are capable of, but I've a clear notion of what Leolin was.

He didn't persuade his sister, who despised him—she wished to work her mother in her own way; so that I asked myself why the girl's judgment of him didn't make me like her better. It was because it didn't save her after all from the mute agreement with him to go halves. There were moments when I couldn't help looking hard into his atrocious young eyes, challenging him to confess his fantastic fraud and give it up. Not a little tacit conversation passed between us in this way, but he had always the best of the business. If I said: "Oh come now, with *me* you needn't keep it up; plead guilty and I'll let you off," he wore the most ingenuous, the most candid expression, in the depths of which I could read: "Ah yes, I know it exasperates you—that's just why I do it." He took the line of earnest enquiry, talked about Balzac and Flaubert, asked me if I thought Dickens *did* exaggerate and Thackeray *ought* to be called a pessimist. Once he came to see me, at his mother's suggestion he declared, on purpose to ask me how far, in my opinion, in the English novel, one really might venture to "go." He wasn't resigned to the usual pruderies, the worship of childish twaddle; he suffered already from too much bread and butter. He struck out the brilliant idea that nobody knew how far we might go, since nobody had ever tried. Did I think *he* might safely try— would it injure his mother if he did? He would rather disgrace himself by his timidities than injure his mother, but certainly some one ought to try. Wouldn't *I* try— couldn't I be prevailed upon to look at it as a duty? Surely the ultimate point ought to be fixed—he was worried, haunted by the question. He patronised me unblushingly, made me feel a foolish amateur, a helpless novice, inquired into my habits of work and conveyed to me that I was utterly *vieux jeu* and hadn't had the advantage of an early training. I hadn't been brought up from the egg, I knew nothing of life—didn't go at it on *his* system. He had dipped into French feuilletons and picked up plenty of phrases, and he made a much better show in talk than his poor mother, who never had time to read anything and could only be showy with her pen. If I didn't kick him downstairs it was because he would have landed on her at the bottom.

When she went to live at Primrose Hill I called there and found her wasted and wan. It had visibly dropped, the elation caused the year before by Ethel's marriage; the foam on the cup had subsided and there was bitterness in the draught. She had had to take a cheaper house—and now had to work still harder to pay even for that. Sir Baldwin was obliged to be close; his charges were fearful, and the dream of her living with her daughter—a vision she had never mentioned to me— must be renounced. "I'd have helped them with things, and could have lived perfectly in one room," she said; "I'd have paid for everything, and—after all—I'm some one, ain't I? But I don't fit in, and Ethel tells me these are tiresome people she *must* receive. I can help them from here, no doubt, better than from there. She told me once, you know, what she thinks of my picture of life. 'Mamma, your picture of life's preposterous!' No doubt it is, but she's vexed with me for letting my prices go down; and I had to write three novels to pay for all her marriage cost me. I did it very well—I mean the outfit and the wedding; but that's why I'm here. At any rate she doesn't want a dingy old woman at Blicket. I should give the place an atmosphere of literary prestige, but literary prestige is only the eminence of no-bodies. Besides, she knows what to think of my glory—she knows I'm glorious only at Peckham and Hackney. She doesn't want her friends to ask if I've never known nice people. She can't tell them I've never been in society. She tried to teach me better once, but I couldn't catch on. It would seem too as if Peckham and Hackney had had enough of me; for (don't tell any one) I've had to take less for my last than I ever took for any-thing." I asked her how little this had been, not from curiosity, but in order to upbraid her, more disinter-estedly than Lady Luard had done, for such concessions. She answered "I'm ashamed to tell you" and then began to cry.

I had never seen her break down and I was propor-tionately moved; she sobbed like a frightened child over the extinction of her vogue and the exhaustion of her vein. Her little workroom seemed indeed a barren place to grow flowers for the market, and I wondered in the after years (for she continued to produce and publish) by what desperate and heroic process she dragged them out of the soil. I remember asking her on that occasion what had become of Leolin and how much longer she intended to allow him to amuse himself at her cost. She retorted with spirit, wiping her eyes, that he was down at Brighton hard at work—he was in the midst of a novel—and that he *felt* life so, in all its misery and mystery, that it was cruel to speak of such experiences as a pleasure. "He goes beneath the surface," she said, "and he *forces* himself to look at things from which he'd rather turn away. Do you call that amusing yourself? You should see his face sometimes! And he does it for me as much as for himself. He tells me everything— he comes home to me with his *trouvailles*. We're artists together, and to the artist all things are pure. I've often heard you say so yourself." The novel Leolin was engaged in at Brighton never saw the light, but a friend of mine and of Mrs. Stormer's who was staying there happened to mention to me later that he had seen the young apprentice to fiction driving, in a dog-cart, a young lady with a very pink face. When I suggested that she was perhaps a woman of title with whom he was conscientiously flirting my informant replied: "She is indeed, but do you know what her title is?" He pronounced it—it was familiar and descriptive—but I won't reproduce it here. I don't know whether Leolin mentioned it to his mother: she would have needed all the purity of the artist to forgive him. I hated so to come across him that in the very last years I went rarely to see her, though I knew she had come pretty well to the end of her rope. I didn't want her to tell me she had fairly to give her books away; I didn't want to see her old and abandoned and derided; I didn't want, in a word, to see her terribly cry. She still, however, kept it up amazingly, and every few months, at my club, I saw three new volumes, in green, in crimson, in blue, on the booktable that groaned with light literature. Once I met her at the Academy soirée, where you meet people you thought were dead, and she vouchsafed the information, as if she owed it to me in candour, that Leolin had been obliged to recognise the insuperable difficulties of the question of *form*—he was so fastidious; but that she had now arrived at a definite understanding with him (it was such a comfort!)

that *she* would do the form if he would bring home the substance. That was now his employ—he foraged for her in the great world at a salary. "He's my 'devil,' don't you see? as if I were a great lawyer: he gets up the case and I argue it." She mentioned further that in addition to his salary he was paid by the piece: he got so much for a striking character, so much for a pretty name, so much for a plot, so much for an incident, and had so much promised him if he would invent a new crime.

"He *has* invented one," I said, "and he's paid every day of his life."

"What is it?" she asked, looking hard at the picture of the year, "Baby's Tub," near which we happened to be standing.

I hesitated a moment. "I myself will write a little story about it, and then you'll see."

But she never saw; she had never seen anything, and she passed away with her fine blindness unimpaired. Her son published every scrap of scribbled paper that could be extracted from her table-drawers, and his sister quarrelled with him mortally about the proceeds, which showed her only to have wanted a pretext, for they can't have been great. I don't know what Leolin lives on unless on a queer lady many years older than himself, whom he lately married. The last time I met him he said to me with his infuriating smile: "Don't you think we can go a little further still—just a little?" *He* really—with me at least—goes too far.

1892

*

THE REAL THING

I

When the porter's wife, who used to answer the house-bell, announced "A gentleman and a lady, sir," I had, as I often had in those days—the wish being father to the thought—an immediate vision of sitters. Sitters my visitors in this case proved to be; but not in the sense I should have preferred. There was nothing at first however to indicate that they mightn't have come for a portrait. The gentleman, a man of fifty, very high and very straight, with a moustache slightly grizzled and a dark grey walking-coat admirably fitted, both of which I noted professionally—I don't mean as a barber or yet as a tailor—would have struck me as a celebrity if celebrities often were striking. It was a truth of which I had for some time been conscious that a figure with a good deal of frontage was, as one might say, almost never a public institution. A glance at the lady helped to remind me of this paradoxical law: she also looked too distinguished to be a "personality." Moreover one would scarcely come across two variations together.

Neither of the pair immediately spoke—they only prolonged the preliminary gaze suggesting that each wished to give the other a chance. They were visibly shy; they stood there letting me take them in—which, as I afterwards perceived, was the most practical thing they could have done. In this way their embarrassment served their cause. I had seen people painfully reluctant to mention that they desired anything so gross as to be represented on canvas; but the scruples of my new friends appeared almost insurmountable. Yet the gentleman might have said "I should like a portrait of my wife, and the lady might have said "I should like a portrait of my husband." Perhaps they weren't husband and wife—this naturally would make the matter more delicate. Perhaps they wished to be done together— in which case they ought to have brought a third person to break the news.

"We come from Mr. Rivet," the lady finally said with a dim smile that had the effect of a moist sponge passed over a "sunk" piece of painting, as well as of a vague allusion to vanished beauty. She was as tall and straight, in her degree, as her companion, and with ten years less to carry. She looked as sad as a woman could look whose face was not charged with expression; that is her tinted oval mask showed waste as an exposed surface shows friction. The hand of time had played over her freely, but to an effect of elimination. She was slim and stiff, and so well-dressed, in dark blue cloth, with lappets and pockets and buttons, that it was clear she employed the same tailor as her husband. The couple had an indefinable air of prosperous thrift —they evidently got a good deal of luxury for their money. If I was to be one of their luxuries it would behoove me to consider my terms.

"Ah Claude Rivet recommended me?" I echoed; and I added that it was very kind of him, though I could reflect that, as he only painted landscape, this wasn't a sacrifice.

The lady looked very hard at the gentleman, and the gentleman looked round the room. Then staring at the floor a moment and stroking his moustache, he rested his pleasant eyes on me with the remark: "He said you were the right one."

"I try to be, when people want to sit."

"Yes, we should like to," said the lady anxiously.

"Do you mean together?"

My visitors exchanged a glance. "If you could do anything with *me* I suppose it would be double," the gentleman stammered.

"Oh yes, there's naturally a higher charge for two figures than for one."

"We should like to make it pay," the husband confessed.

"That's very good of you," I returned, appreciating so unwonted a sympathy—for I supposed he meant pay the artist.

A sense of strangeness seemed to dawn on the lady. "We mean for the illustrations—Mr. Rivet said you might put one in."

"Put in—an illustration?" I was equally confused.

"Sketch her off, you know," said the gentleman, colouring.

It was only then that I understood the service Claude Rivet had rendered me; he had told them how I worked in black-and-white, for magazines, for story-books, for sketches of contemporary life, and consequently had copious employment for models. These things were true, but it was not less true—I may confess it now; whether because the aspiration was to lead to everything or to nothing I leave the reader to guess—that I couldn't get the honours, to say nothing of the emoluments, of a great painter of portraits out of my head. My "illustrations" were my pot-boilers; I looked to a different branch of art—far and away the most interesting it had always seemed to me—to perpetuate my fame. There was no shame in looking to it also to make my fortune; but that fortune was by so much further from being made from the moment my visitors wished to be "done" for nothing. I was disappointed; for in the pictorial sense I had immediately *seen* them. I had seized their type—I had already settled what I would do with it. Something that wouldn't absolutely have pleased them, I afterwards reflected.

"Ah you're—you're—a?" I began as soon as I had mastered my surprise. I couldn't bring out the dingy word "models": it seemed so little to fit the case.

"We haven't had much practice," said the lady.

"We've got to *do* something, and we've thought that an artist in your line might perhaps make something of us," her husband threw off. He further mentioned that they didn't know many artists and that they had gone first, on the off-chance— he painted views of course, but sometimes put in figures; perhaps I remembered—to Mr. Rivet, whom they had met a few years before at a place in Norfolk where he was sketching.

"We used to sketch a little ourselves," the lady hinted.

"It's very awkward, but we absolutely *must* do something," her husband went on.

"Of course we're not so *very* young," she admitted with a wan smile.

With the remark that I might as well know something more about them the husband had handed me a card extracted from a neat new pocket-book—their appurtenances were all of the freshest—and inscribed with the words "Major Monarch." Impressive as these words were they didn't carry my knowledge much further; but my visitor presently added: "I've left the army and we've had the misfortune to lose our money. In fact our means are dreadfully small."

"It's awfully trying—a regular strain," said Mrs. Monarch.

They evidently wished to be discreet—to take care not to swagger because they were gentlefolk. I felt them willing to recognise this as something of a draw-back, at the same time that I guessed at an underlying sense—their consolation in adversity—that they *had* their points. They certainly had; but these advantages struck me as preponderantly social; such for instance as would help to make a drawing-room look well. However, a drawing-room was always, or ought to be, a picture.

In consequence of his wife's allusion to their age Major Monarch observed: "Naturally it's more for the figure that we thought of going in. We can still hold ourselves up." On the instant I saw that the figure was indeed their strong point. His "naturally" didn't sound vain, but it lighted up the question. "*She* has the best one," he continued, nodding at his wife with a pleasant after-dinner absence of circumlocution. I could only reply, as if we were in fact sitting over our wine, that this didn't prevent his own from being very good; which led him in turn to make answer: "We thought that if you ever have to do people like us we might be something like it. *She* particularly—for a lady in a book, you know."

I was so amused by them that, to get more of it, I did my best to take their point of view; and though it was an embarrassment to find myself appraising physically, as if they were animals on hire or useful blacks, a pair whom I should have expected to meet only in one of the relations in which criticism is tacit, I looked at Mrs. Monarch judicially enough to be able to exclaim after a moment with conviction: "Oh yes, a lady in a book!" She was singularly like a bad illustration.

"We'll stand up, if you like," said the Major; and he raised himself before me with a really grand air.

I could take his measure at a glance—he was six feet two and a perfect gentleman. It would have paid any club in process of formation and in want of a stamp to engage him at a salary to stand in the principal window. What struck me at once was that in coming to me they had rather missed their vocation; they could surely have been turned to better account for advertising purposes. I couldn't of course see the thing in detail, but I could see them make somebody's fortune—I don't mean their own. There was something in them for a waistcoat-maker, an hotel-keeper or a soap-vendor. I could imagine "We always use it" pinned on their bosoms with the greatest effect; I had a vision of the brilliancy with which they would launch a table d'hôte.

Mrs. Monarch sat still, not from pride but from shyness, and presently her husband said to her: "Get up, my dear, and show how smart you are." She obeyed, but she had no need to get up to show it. She walked to the end of the studio and then came back blushing, her fluttered eyes on the partner of her appeal. I was reminded of an incident I had accidentally had a glimpse of in Paris—being with a friend there, a dramatist about to produce a play, when an actress came to him to ask to be entrusted with a part. She went through her paces before him, walked up and down as Mrs. Monarch was doing. Mrs. Monarch did it quite as well, but I abstained from applauding. It was very odd to see such people apply for such poor pay. She looked as if she had ten thousand a year. Her husband had used the word that described her: she was in the London current jargon essentially and typically "smart." Her figure was, in the same order of ideas, conspicuously and irreproachably "good." For a woman of her age her waist was surprisingly small; her elbow moreover had the orthodox crook. She held her head at the conventional angle, but why did she come to *me*? She ought to have tried on jackets at a big shop. I feared my visitors were not only destitute but "artistic"—which would be a great complication. When she sat down again I thanked her, observing that what a draughtsman most valued in his model was the faculty of keeping quiet.

"Oh *she* can keep quiet," said Major Monarch. Then he added jocosely: "I've always kept her quiet."

"I'm not a nasty fidget, am I?" It was going to wring tears from me, I felt, the way she hid her head, ostrich-like, in the other broad bosom.

The owner of this expanse addressed his answer to me. "Perhaps it isn't out of place to mention—because we ought to be quite business-like, oughtn't we?—that when I married her she was known as the Beautiful Statue."

"Oh dear!" said Mrs. Monarch ruefully.

"Of course I should want a certain amount of expression," I rejoined.

"Of *course!*"—and I had never heard such unanimity.

"And then I suppose you know that you'll get awfully tired."

"Oh we *never* get tired!" they eagerly cried.

"Have you had any kind of practice?"

They hesitated—they looked at each other. "We've been photographed—*immensely*," said Mrs. Monarch.

"She means the fellows have asked us themselves," added the Major.

"I see—because you're so good-looking."

"I don't know what they thought, but they were always after us."

"We always got our photographs for nothing," smiled Mrs. Monarch.

"We might have brought some, my dear," her husband remarked.

"I'm not sure we have any left. We've given quanti-ties away," she explained to me.

"With our autographs and that sort of thing," said the Major.

"Are they to be got in the shops?" I enquired as a harmless pleasantry.

"Oh yes, *hers*—they used to be."

"Not now," said Mrs. Monarch with her eyes on the floor.

II

I could fancy the "sort of thing" they put on the presen-tation copies of their photographs, and I was sure they wrote a beautiful hand. It was odd how quickly I was sure of everything that concerned them. If they were now so poor as to have to earn shillings and pence they could never have had much of a margin. Their good looks had been their capital, and they had good-humour-edly made the most of the career that this resource marked out for them. It was in their faces, the blank-ness, the deep intellectual repose of the twenty years of country-house visiting that had given them pleasant intonations. I could see the sunny drawing-rooms, sprin-kled with periodicals she didn't read, in which Mrs. Monarch had continuously sat; I could see the wet shrubberies in which she had walked, equipped to ad-miration for either exercise. I could see the rich covers the Major had helped to shoot and the wonderful gar-ments in which, late at night, he repaired to the smok-ing-room to talk about them. I could imagine their leg-gings and waterproofs, their knowing tweeds and rugs, their rolls of sticks and cases of tackle and neat umbrellas; and I could evoke the exact appearance of their servants and the compact variety of their luggage on the platforms of country stations.

They gave small tips, but they were liked; they didn't do anything themselves, but they were welcome. They looked so well everywhere; they gratified the general relish for stature, complexion and "form." They knew it without fatuity or vulgarity, and they respected themselves in consequence. They weren't superficial; they were thorough and kept themselves up—it had been their line. People with such a taste for activity had to have some line. I could feel how even in a dull house they could have been counted on for the joy of life. At present something had happened—it didn't matter what, their little income had grown less, it had grown least—and they had to do something for pocket-money. Their friends could like them, I made out, without liking to support them. There was something about them that represented credit—their clothes, their manners, their type; but if credit is a large empty pocket in which an occasional chink reverberates, the chink at least must be audible. What they wanted of me was to help to make it so. Fortunately they had no children—I soon divined that. They would also perhaps wish our relations to be kept secret: this was why it was "for the figure"—the reproduction of the face would betray them.

I liked them—I felt, quite as their friends must have done—they were so simple; and I had no objection to them if they would suit. But somehow with all their perfections I didn't easily believe in them. After all they were amateurs, and the ruling passion of my life was the detestation of the amateur. Combined with this was another perversity—an innate preference for the represented subject over the real one: the defect of the real

one was so apt to be a lack of representation. I like things
that appeared; then one was sure. Whether they *were*
or not was a subordinate and almost always a profitless
question. There were other considerations, the first of
which was that I already had two or three recruits in
use, notably a young person with big feet, in alpaca,
from Kilburn, who for a couple of years had come to
me regularly for my illustrations and with whom I was
still—perhaps ignobly—satisfied. I frankly explained to
my visitors how the case stood, but they had taken more
precautions than I supposed. They had reasoned out
their opportunity, for Claude Rivet had told them of
the projected *édition de luxe* of one of the writers of our
day—the rarest of the novelists—who, long neglected
by the multitudinous vulgar and dearly prized by the
attentive (need I mention Philip Vincent?) had had the
happy fortune of seeing, late in life, the dawn and then
the full light of a higher criticism; an estimate in which
on the part of the public there was something really of
expiation. The edition preparing, planned by a publisher
of taste, was practically an act of high reparation; the
wood-cuts with which it was to be enriched were the
homage of English art to one of the most independent
representatives of English letters. Major and Mrs. Monarch confessed to me they had hoped I might be able
to work *them* into my branch of the enterprise. They
knew I was to do the first of the books, "Rutland Ramsay," but I had to make clear to them that my participation in the rest of the affair—this first book was to be a
test—must depend on the satisfaction I should give. If
this should be limited my employers would drop me
with scarce common forms. It was therefore a crisis for
me, and naturally I was making special preparations,
looking about for new people, should they be necessary,

and securing the best types. I admitted however that I should like to settle down to two or three good models who would do for everything.

"Should we have often to—a—put on special clothes?" Mrs. Monarch timidly demanded.

"Dear yes—that's half the business."

"And should we be expected to supply our own costumes?"

"Oh no; I've got a lot of things. A painter's models put on—or put off—anything he likes."

"And you mean—a—the same?"

"The same?"

Mrs. Monarch looked at her husband again.

"Oh she was just wondering," he explained, "if the costumes are in *general* use." I had to confess that they were, and I mentioned further that some of them—I had a lot of genuine greasy last-century things—had served their time, a hundred years ago, on living world-stained men and women; on figures not perhaps so far removed, in that vanished world, from *their* type, the Monarchs', *quoi!* of a breeched and bewigged age. "We'll put on anything that *fits*," said the Major.

"Oh I arrange that—they fit in the pictures."

"I'm afraid I should do better for the modern books. I'd come as you like," said Mrs. Monarch.

"She has got a lot of clothes at home: they might do for contemporary life," her husband continued.

"Oh I can fancy scenes in which you'd be quite natural." And indeed I could see the slipshod rearrangements of stale properties—the stories I tried to produce pictures for without the exasperation of reading them—whose sandy tracts the good lady might help to people. But I had to return to the fact that for this sort of work —the daily mechanical grind—I was already equipped: the people I was working with were fully adequate.

"We only thought we might be more like *some* characters," said Mrs. Monarch mildly, getting up.

Her husband also rose; he stood looking at me with a dim wistfulness that was touching in so fine a man. "Wouldn't it be rather a pull sometimes to have—a—to have—?" He hung fire; he wanted me to help him by phrasing what he meant. But I couldn't—I didn't know. So he brought it out awkwardly: "The *real* thing; a gentleman, you know, or a lady." I was quite ready to give a general assent—I admitted that there was a great deal in that. This encouraged Major Monarch to say, following up his appeal with an unacted gulp: "It's awfully hard—we've tried everything." The gulp was communicative; it proved too much for his wife. Before I knew it Mrs. Monarch had dropped again upon a divan and burst into tears. Her husband sat down beside her, holding one of her hands; whereupon she quickly dried her eyes with the other, while I felt embarrassed as she looked up at me. "There isn't a confounded job I haven't applied for—waited for—prayed for. You can fancy we'd be pretty bad first. Secretaryships and that sort of thing? You might as well ask for a peerage. I'd be *anything*—I'm strong; a messenger or a coalheaver. I'd put on a gold-laced cap and open carriage-doors in front of the haberdasher's; I'd hang about a station to carry portmanteaux; I'd be a postman. But they won't *look* at you; there are thousands as good as yourself already on the ground. *Gentlemen*, poor beggars, who've drunk their wine, who've kept their hunters!"

I was as reassu. ng as I knew how to be, and my visitors were presently on their feet again while, for the experiment, we agreed on an hour. We were discussing it when the door opened and Miss Churm came in with a wet umbrella. Miss Churm had to take the omnibus to Maida Vale and then walk half a mile. She looked a trifle blowsy and slightly splashed. I scarcely ever saw her come in without thinking afresh how odd it was that, being so little in herself, she should yet be so much in others. She was a meagre little Miss Churm, but was such an ample heroine of romance. She was only a freckled cockney, but she could represent everything, from a fine lady to a shepherdess; she had the faculty as she might have had a fine voice or long hair. She couldn't spell and she loved beer, but she had two or three "points," and practice, and a knack, and mother-wit, and a whimsical sensibility, and a love of the theatre, and seven sisters, and not an ounce of respect, especially for the *h*. The first thing my visitors saw was that her umbrella was wet, and in their spotless perfection they visibly winced at it. The rain had come on since their arrival.

"I'm all in a soak; there *was* a mess of people in the 'bus. I wish you lived near a stytion," said Miss Churm. I requested her to get ready as quickly as possible, and she passed into the room in which she always changed her dress. But before going out she asked me what she was to get into this time.

"It's the Russian princess, don't you know?" I answered; "the one with the 'golden eyes,' in black velvet, for the long thing in the *Cheapside*."

"Golden eyes? I *say!*" cried Miss Churm, while my companions watched her with intensity as she withdrew. She always arranged herself, when she was late, before I could turn round; and I kept my visitors a little on purpose, so that they might get an idea, from seeing her, what would be expected of themselves. I mentioned that she was quite my notion of an excellent model—she was really very clever.

"Do you think she looks like a Russian princess?" Major Monarch asked with lurking alarm.

"When I make her, yes."

"Oh if you have to *make* her—!" he reasoned, not without point.

"That's the most you can ask. There are so many who are not makeable."

"Well now, *here's* a lady"—and with a persuasive smile he passed his arm into his wife's—"who's already made!"

"Oh I'm not a Russian princess," Mrs. Monarch protested a little coldly. I could see she had known some and didn't like them. There at once was a complication of a kind I never had to fear with Miss Churm.

This young lady came back in black velvet—the gown was rather rusty and very low on her lean shoulders—and with a Japanese fan in her red hands. I reminded her that in the scene I was doing she had to look over some one's head. "I forget whose it is; but it doesn't matter. Just look over a head."

"I'd rather look over a stove," said Miss Churm; and she took her station near the fire. She fell into position, settled herself into a tall attitude, gave a certain backward inclination to her head and a certain forward droop to her fan, and looked, at least to my prejudiced sense, distinguished and charming, foreign and dangerous. We left her looking so while I went downstairs with Major and Mrs. Monarch.

"I believe I could come about as near it as that," said Mrs. Monarch.

"Oh you think she's shabby, but you must allow for the alchemy of art."

However, they went off with an evident increase of comfort founded on their demonstrable advantage in being the real thing. I could fancy them shuddering over Miss Churm. She was very droll about them when I went back, for I told her what they wanted.

"Well, if *she* can sit I'll tyke to book-keeping," said my model.

"She's very ladylike," I replied as an innocent form of aggravation.

"So much the worse for *you*. That means she can't turn round."

"She'll do for the fashionable novels."

"Oh yes, she'll *do* for them!" my model humorously declared. "Ain't they bad enough without her?" I had often sociably denounced them to Miss Churm.

III

It was for the elucidation of a mystery in one of these works that I first tried Mrs. Monarch. Her husband came with her, to be useful if necessary—it was sufficiently clear that as a general thing he would prefer to come with her. At first I wondered if this were for "propriety's" sake—if he were going to be jealous and meddling. The idea was too tiresome, and if it had been confirmed it would speedily have brought our acquaintance to a close. But I soon saw there was nothing in it and that if he accompanied Mrs. Monarch it was—in addition to the chance of being wanted—simply because he had nothing else to do. When they were separate his occupation was gone and they never *had* been separate. I judged rightly that in their awkward situation their close union was their main comfort and that this union had no weak spot. It was a real marriage, an encouragement to the hesitating, a nut for pessimists to crack. Their address was humble—I remember afterwards thinking it had been the only thing about them that was really professional—and I could fancy the lamentable lodgings in which the Major would have been left alone. He could sit there more or less grimly with his wife—he couldn't sit there anyhow without her.

He had too much tact to try and make himself agree-able when he couldn't be useful; so when I was too absorbed in my work to talk he simply sat and waited. But I liked to hear him talk—it made my work, when not interrupting it, less mechanical, less special. To listen to him was to combine the excitement of going out with the economy of staying at home. There was only one hindrance—that I seemed not to know any of the people this brilliant couple had known. I think he wondered extremely, during the term of our intercourse, whom the deuce I *did* know. He hadn't a stray sixpence of an idea to fumble for, so we didn't spin it very fine; we confined ourselves to questions of leather and even of liquor—saddlers and breeches-makers and how to get excellent claret cheap—and matters like "good trains" and the habits of small game. His lore on these last sub-jects was astonishing—he managed to interweave the station-master with the ornithologist. When he couldn't talk about greater things he could talk cheerfully about smaller, and since I couldn't accompany him into remi-niscences of the fashionable world he could lower the conversation without a visible effort to my level.

So earnest a desire to please was touching in a man who could so easily have knocked one down. He looked after the fire and had an opinion on the draught of the stove without my asking him, and I could see that he thought many of my arrangements not half knowing. I remember telling him that if I were only rich I'd offer him a salary to come and teach me how to live. Some-times he gave a random sigh of which the essence might have been: "Give me even such a bare old barrack as *this*, and I'd do something with it!" When I wanted to use him he came alone; which was an illustration of the superior courage of women. His wife could bear her solitary second floor, and she was in general more dis-

creet; showing by various small reserves that she was
alive to the propriety of keeping our relations markedly
professional—not letting them slide into sociability. She
wished it to remain clear that she and the Major were
employed, not cultivated, and if she approved of me as
a superior, who could be kept in his place, she never
thought me quite good enough for an equal.

She sat with great intensity, giving the whole of her
mind to it, and was capable of remaining for an hour
almost as motionless as before a photographer's lens. I
could see she had been photographed often, but somehow the very habit that made her good for that purpose unfitted her for mine. At first I was extremely
pleased with her ladylike air, and it was a satisfaction,
on coming to follow her lines, to see how good they
were and how far they could lead the pencil. But after a
little skirmishing I began to find her too insurmountably
stiff; do what I would with it my drawing looked like a
photograph or a copy of a photograph. Her figure had
no variety of expression—she herself had no sense of
variety. You may say that this was my business and was
only a question of placing her. Yet I placed her in every
conceivable position and she managed to obliterate their
differences. She was always a lady certainly, and into
the bargain was always the same lady. She was the real
thing, but always the same thing. There were moments
when I rather writhed under the serenity of her confidence that she *was* the real thing. All her dealings with
me and all her husband's were an implication that this
was lucky for *me*. Meanwhile I found myself trying to
invent types that approached her own, instead of making her own transform itself—in the clever way that was
not impossible for instance to poor Miss Churm. Arrange
as I would and take the precautions I would, she always

came out, in my pictures, too tall—landing me in the dilemma of having represented a fascinating woman as seven feet high, which (out of respect perhaps to my own very much scantier inches) was far from my idea of such a personage.

The case was worse with the Major—nothing I could do would keep *him* down, so that he became useful only for the representation of brawny giants. I adored variety and range, I cherished human accidents, the illustrative note; I wanted to characterise closely, and the thing in the world I most hated was the danger of being ridden by a type. I had quarrelled with some of my friends about it; I had parted company with them for maintaining that one *had* to be, and that if the type was beautiful—witness Raphael and Leonardo—the servitude was only a gain. I was neither Leonardo nor Raphael—I might only be a presumptuous young modern searcher; but I held that everything was to be sacrificed sooner than character. When they claimed that the obsessional form could easily *be* character I retorted, perhaps superficially, "Whose?" It couldn't be everybody's—it might end in being nobody's.

After I had drawn Mrs. Monarch a dozen times I felt surer even than before that the value of such a model as Miss Churm resided precisely in the fact that she had no positive stamp, combined of course with the other fact that what she did have was a curious and inexplicable talent for imitation. Her usual appearance was like a curtain which she could draw up at request for a capital performance. This performance was simply suggestive; but it was a word to the wise—it was vivid and pretty. Sometimes even I thought it, though she was plain herself, too insipidly pretty; I made it a reproach to her that the figures drawn from her were

monotonously (*bêtement,* as we used to say) graceful.
Nothing made her more angry; it was so much her pride
to feel she could sit for characters that had nothing in
common with each other. She would accuse me at such
moments of taking away her "reputytion."

It suffered a certain shrinkage, this queer quantity,
from the repeated visits of my new friends. Miss Churm
was greatly in demand, never in want of employment,
so I had no scruple in putting her off occasionally, to
try them more at my ease. It was certainly amusing at
first to do the real thing—it was amusing to do Major
Monarch's trousers. They *were* the real thing, even if
he did come out colossal. It was amusing to do his wife's
back hair—it was so mathematically neat—and the particular "smart" tension of her tight stays. She lent herself especially to positions in which the face was somewhat averted or blurred; she abounded in ladylike back
views and *profils perdus.* When she stood erect she took
naturally one of the attitudes in which court-painters
represent queens and princesses; so that I found myself
wondering whether, to draw out this accomplishment,
I couldn't get the editor of the *Cheapside* to publish a
really royal romance, "A Tale of Buckingham Palace."
Sometimes however the real thing and the make-believe
came into contact; by which I mean that Miss Churm,
keeping an appointment or coming to make one on days
when I had much work in hand, encountered her invidious rivals. The encounter was not on their part,
for they noticed her no more than if she had been the
housemaid; not from intentional loftiness, but simply
because as yet, professionally, they didn't know how to
fraternise, as I could imagine they would have liked—or
at least that the Major would. They couldn't talk about
the omnibus—they always walked; and they didn't
know what else to try—she wasn't interested in good

trains or cheap claret. Besides, they must have felt—in
the air—that she was amused at them, secretly derisive
of their ever knowing how. She wasn't a person to con-
ceal the limits of her faith if she had had a chance to
show them. On the other hand Mrs. Monarch didn't
think her tidy; for why else did she take pains to say to
me—it was going out of the way, for Mrs. Monarch—
that she didn't like dirty women?

One day when my young lady happened to be present with my other sitters—she even dropped in, when
it was convenient, for a chat—I asked her to be so good
as to lend a hand in getting tea, a service with which
she was familiar and which was one of a class that, living as I did in a small way, with slender domestic resources, I often appealed to my models to render. They
liked to lay hands on my property, to break the sitting,
and sometimes the china—it made them feel Bohemian. The next time I saw Miss Churm after this incident she surprised me greatly by making a scene about
it—she accused me of having wished to humiliate her.
She hadn't resented the outrage at the time, but had
seemed obliging and amused, enjoying the comedy of
asking Mrs. Monarch, who sat vague and silent,
whether she would have cream and sugar, and putting
an exaggerated simper into the question. She had tried
intonations—as if she too wished to pass for the real
thing—till I was afraid my other visitors would take
offence.

Oh they were determined not to do this, and their
touching patience was the measure of their great need.
They would sit by the hour, uncomplaining, till I was
ready to use them; they would come back on the chance
of being wanted and would walk away cheerfully if it
failed. I used to go to the door with them to see in what
magnificent order they retreated. I tried to find other

employment for them—I introduced them to several
artists. But they didn't "take," for reasons I could appreciate, and I became rather anxiously aware that after
such disappointments they fell back upon me with a
heavier weight. They did me the honour to think me
most *their* form. They weren't romantic enough for the
painters, and in those days there were few serious work-
ers in black-and-white. Besides, they had an eye to the
great job I had mentioned to them—they had secretly
set their hearts on supplying the right essence for my
pictorial vindication of our fine novelist. They knew that
for this undertaking I should want no costume-effects,
none of the frippery of past ages—that it was a case in
which everything would be contemporary and satirical
and presumably genteel. If I could work them into it
their future would be assured, for the labour would of
course be long and the occupation steady.

One day Mrs. Monarch came without her husband—
she explained his absence by his having had to go to the
City. While she sat there in her usual relaxed majesty
there came at the door a knock which I immediately
recognised as the subdued appeal of a model out of
work. It was followed by the entrance of a young man
whom I at once saw to be a foreigner and who proved
in fact an Italian acquainted with no English word but
my name, which he uttered in a way that made it seem
to include all others. I hadn't then visited his country,
nor was I proficient in his tongue; but as he was not so
meanly constituted—what Italian is?—as to depend
only on that member for expression he conveyed to me,
in familiar but graceful mimicry, that he was in search
of exactly the employment in which the lady before me
was engaged. I was not struck with him at first, and
while I continued to draw I dropped few signs of interest
or encouragement. He stood his ground however—not

importunately, but with a dumb dog-like fidelity in his
eyes that amounted to innocent impudence, the manner
of a devoted servant—he might have been in the house
for years—unjustly suspected. Suddenly it struck me
that this very attitude and expression made a picture;
whereupon I told him to sit down and wait till I should
be free. There was another picture in the way he obeyed
me, and I observed as I worked that there were others
still in the way he looked wonderingly, with his head
thrown back, about the high studio. He might have been
crossing himself in Saint Peter's. Before I finished I said
to myself "The fellow's a bankrupt orange-monger, but
a treasure."

When Mrs. Monarch withdrew he passed across the
room like a flash to open the door for her, standing there
with the rapt pure gaze of the young Dante spellbound
by the young Beatrice. As I never insisted, in such situations, on the blankness of the British domestic, I reflected that he had the making of a servant—and I
needed one, but couldn't pay him to be only that—as
well as of a model; in short I resolved to adopt my
bright adventurer if he would agree to officiate in the
double capacity. He jumped at my offer, and in the
event my rashness—for I had really known nothing
about him—wasn't brought home to me. He proved a
sympathetic though a desultory ministrant, and had in a
wonderful degree the *sentiment de la pose*. It was un-
cultivated, instinctive, a part of the happy instinct that
had guided him to my door and helped him to spell
out my name on the card nailed to it. He had had no
other introduction to me than a guess, from the shape of
my high north window, seen outside, that my place was
a studio and that as a studio it would contain an artist.
He had wandered to England in search of fortune, like
other itinerants, and had embarked, with a partner

and a small green hand-cart, on the sale of penny ices. The ices had melted away and the partner had dissolved in their train. My young man wore tight yellow trousers with reddish stripes and his name was Oronte. He was sallow but fair, and when I put him into some old clothes of my own he looked like an Englishman. He was as good as Miss Churm, who could look, when requested, like an Italian.

IV

I thought Mrs. Monarch's face slightly convulsed when, on her coming back with her husband, she found Oronte installed. It was strange to have to recognise in a scrap of a lazzarone a competitor to her magnificent Major. It was she who scented danger first, for the Major was anecdotically unconscious. But Oronte gave us tea, with a hundred eager confusions—he had never been concerned in so queer a process—and I think she thought better of me for having at last an "establishment." They saw a couple of drawings that I had made of the establishment, and Mrs. Monarch hinted that it never would have struck her he had sat for them. "Now the drawings you make from *us*, they look exactly like us," she reminded me, smiling in triumph; and I recognised that this was indeed just their defect. When I drew the Monarchs I couldn't anyhow get away from them—get into the character I wanted to represent; and I hadn't the least desire my model should be discoverable in my picture. Miss Churm never was, and Mrs. Monarch thought I hid her, very properly, because she was vulgar; whereas if she was lost it was only as the dead who go to heaven are lost—in the gain of an angel the more.

By this time I had got a certain start with "Rutland Ramsay," the first novel in the great projected series;

that is I had produced a dozen drawings, several with the help of the Major and his wife, and I had sent them in for approval. My understanding with the publishers, as I have already hinted, had been that I was to be left to do my work, in this particular case, as I liked, with the whole book committed to me; but my connexion with the rest of the series was only contingent. There were moments when, frankly, it *was* a comfort to have the real thing under one's hand; for there were characters in "Rutland Ramsay" that were very much like it. There were people presumably as erect as the Major and women of as good a fashion as Mrs. Monarch. There was a great deal of country-house life— treated, it is true, in a fine fanciful ironical generalised way—and there was a considerable implication of knickerbockers and kilts. There were certain things I had to settle at the outset; such things for instance as the exact appearance of the hero and the particular bloom and figure of the heroine. The author of course gave me a lead, but there was a margin for interpretation. I took the Monarchs into my confidence, I told them frankly what I was about, I mentioned my embarrassments and alternatives. "Oh take *him!*" Mrs. Monarch murmured sweetly, looking at her husband; and "What could you want better than my wife?" the Major enquired with the comfortable candour that now prevailed between us.

I wasn't obliged to answer these remarks—I was only obliged to place my sitters. I wasn't easy in mind, and I postponed a little timidly perhaps the solving of my question. The book was a large canvas, the other figures were numerous, and I worked off at first some of the episodes in which the hero and the heroine were not concerned. When once I had set *them* up I should have to stick to them—I couldn't make my young man seven feet high in one place and five feet nine in another. I inclined on the whole to the latter measurement, though the Major more than once reminded me that *he* looked about as young as any one. It was indeed quite possible to arrange him, for the figure, so that it would have been difficult to detect his age. After the spontaneous Oronte had been with me a month, and after I had given him to understand several times over that his native exuberance would presently constitute an insurmountable barrier to our further intercourse, I waked to a sense of his heroic capacity. He was only five feet seven, but the remaining inches were latent. I tried him almost secretly at first, for I was really rather afraid of the judgement my other models would pass on such a choice. If they regarded Miss Churm as little better than a snare what would they think of the representation by a person so little the real thing as an Italian street-vendor of a protagonist formed by a public school?

If I went a little in fear of them it wasn't because they bullied me, because they had got an oppressive foothold, but because in their really pathetic decorum and mysteriously permanent newness they counted on me so intensely. I was therefore very glad when Jack Hawley came home: he was always of such good counsel. He painted badly himself, but there was no one like him for putting his finger on the place. He had been absent from England for a year; he had been somewhere—I don't remember where—to get a fresh eye. I was in a good deal of dread of any such organ, but we were old friends; he had been away for months and a sense of emptiness was creeping into my life. I hadn't dodged a missile for a year.

He came back with a fresh eye, but with the same old

black velvet blouse, and the first evening he spent in
my studio we smoked cigarettes till the small hours.
He had done no work himself, he had only got the eye;
so the field was clear for the production of my little
things. He wanted to see what I had produced for the
Cheapside, but he was disappointed in the exhibition.
That at least seemed the meaning of two or three comprehensive groans which, as he lounged on my big
divan, his leg folded under him, looking at my latest
drawings, issued from his lips with the smoke of the
cigarette.

"What's the matter with you?" I asked.

"What's the matter with *you?*"

"Nothing save that I'm mystified."

"You are indeed. You're quite off the hinge. What's
the meaning of this new fad?" And he tossed me, with
visible irreverence, a drawing in which I happened to
have depicted both my elegant models. I asked if he
didn't think it good, and he replied that it struck him as
execrable, given the sort of thing I had always represented myself to him as wishing to arrive at; but I let
that pass—I was so anxious to see exactly what he
meant. The two figures in the picture looked colossal,
but I supposed this was *not* what he meant, inasmuch
as, for aught he knew to the contrary, I might have been
trying for some such effect. I maintained that I was
working exactly in the same way as when he last had
done me the honour to tell me I might do something
some day. "Well, there's a screw loose somewhere," he
answered; "wait a bit and I'll discover it." I depended
upon him to do so: where else was the fresh eye? But he
produced at last nothing more luminous than "I don't
know—I don't like your types." This was lame for a
critic who had never consented to discuss with me any-

thing but the question of execution, the direction of strokes and the mystery of values.

"In the drawings you've been looking at I think my types are very handsome."

"Oh they won't do!"

"I've been working with new models."

"I see you have. *They* won't do."

"Are you very sure of that?"

"Absolutely—they're stupid."

"You mean *I* am—for I ought to get round that."

"You *can't*—with such people. Who are they?"

I told him, so far as was necessary, and he concluded heartlessly: "Ce sont des gens qu'il faut mettre à la porte."

"You've never seen them; they're awfully good"—I flew to their defence.

"Not seen them? Why all this recent work of yours drops to pieces with them. It's all I want to see of them."

"No one else has said anything against it—the *Cheapside* people are pleased."

"Every one else is an ass, and the *Cheapside* people the biggest asses of all. Come, don't pretend at this time of day to have pretty illusions about the public, especially about publishers and editors. It's not for *such* animals you work—it's for those who know, *coloro che sanno;* so keep straight for *me* if you can't keep straight for yourself. There was a certain sort of thing you used to try for—and a very good thing it was. But this twaddle isn't *in* it." When I talked with Hawley later about "Rutland Ramsay" and its possible successors he declared that I must get back into my boat again or I should go to the bottom. His voice in short was the voice of warning.

I noted the warning, but I didn't turn my friends out

of doors. They bored me a good deal; but the very fact
that they bored me admonished me not to sacrifice
them—if there was anything to be done with them—
simply to irritation. As I look back at this phase they
seem to me to have pervaded my life not a little. I have
a vision of them as most of the time in my studio, seated
against the wall on an old velvet bench to be out of the
way, and resembling the while a pair of patient cour-
tiers in a royal ante-chamber. I'm convinced that during
the coldest weeks of the winter they held their ground
because it saved them fire. Their newness was losing
its gloss, and it was impossible not to feel them objects
of charity. Whenever Miss Churm arrived they went
away, and after I was fairly launched in "Rutland Ramsay" Miss Churm arrived pretty often. They managed to
express to me tacitly that they supposed I wanted her
for the low life of the book, and I let them suppose it,
since they had attempted to study the work—it was
lying about the studio—without discovering that it
dealt only with the highest circles. They had dipped
into the most brilliant of our novelists without decipher-
ing many passages. I still took an hour from them, now
and again, in spite of Jack Hawley's warning: it would
be time enough to dismiss them, if dismissal should be
necessary, when the rigour of the season was over. Hawley had made their acquaintance—he had met them
at my fireside—and thought them a ridiculous pair.
Learning that he was a painter they tried to approach
him, to show him too that they were the real thing; but
he looked at them, across the big room, as if they were
miles away: they were a compendium of everything he
most objected to in the social system of his country.
Such people as that, all convention and patent-leather,
with ejaculations that stopped conversation, had no business in a studio. A studio was a place to learn to see,

and how could you see through a pair of feather-beds?

The main inconvenience I suffered at their hands was that at first I was shy of letting it break upon them that my artful little servant had begun to sit to me for "Rutland Ramsay." They knew I had been odd enough— they were prepared by this time to allow oddity to artists—to pick a foreign vagabond out of the streets when I might have had a person with whiskers and credentials; but it was some time before they learned how high I rated his accomplishments. They found him in an attitude more than once, but they never doubted I was doing him as an organ-grinder. There were several things they never guessed, and one of them was that for a striking scene in the novel, in which a footman briefly figured, it occurred to me to make use of Major Monarch as the menial. I kept putting this off, I didn't like to ask him to don the livery—besides the difficulty of finding a livery to fit him. At last, one day late in the winter, when I was at work on the despised Oronte, who caught one's idea on the wing, and was in the glow of feeling myself go very straight, they came in, the Major and his wife, with their society laugh about nothing (there was less and less to laugh at); came in like country-callers —they always reminded me of that—who have walked across the park after church and are presently persuaded to stay to luncheon. Luncheon was over, but they could stay to tea—I knew they wanted it. The fit was on me, however, and I couldn't let my ardour cool and my work wait, with the fading daylight, while my model prepared it. So I asked Mrs. Monarch if she would mind laying it out—a request which for an instant brought all the blood to her face. Her eyes were on her husband's for a second, and some mute telegraphy passed between them. Their folly was over the next instant; his cheerful shrewdness put an end to it. So far from pitying their wounded pride, I must add, I was moved to give it as complete a lesson as I could. They bustled about together and got out the cups and saucers and made the kettle boil. I know they felt as if they were waiting on my servant, and when the tea was prepared I said: "He'll have a cup, please—he's tired." Mrs. Monarch brought him one where he stood, and he took it from her as if he had been a gentleman at a party squeezing a crush-hat with an elbow.

Then it came over me that she had made a great effort for me—made it with a kind of nobleness—and that I owed her a compensation. Each time I saw her after this I wondered what the compensation could be. I couldn't go on doing the wrong thing to oblige them. Oh it *was* the wrong thing, the stamp of the work for which they sat—Hawley was not the only person to say it now. I sent in a large number of the drawings I had made for "Rutland Ramsay," and I received a warning that was more to the point than Hawley's. The artistic adviser of the house for which I was working was of opinion that many of my illustrations were not what had been looked for. Most of these illustrations were the subjects in which the Monarchs had figured. Without going into the question of what *had* been looked for, I had to face the fact that at this rate I shouldn't get the other books to do. I hurled myself in despair on Miss Churm—I put her through all her paces. I not only adopted Oronte publicly as my hero, but one morning when the Major looked in to see if I didn't require him to finish a *Cheapside* figure for which he had begun to sit the week before, I told him I had changed my mind —I'd do the drawing from my man. At this my visitor turned pale and stood looking at me. "Is *he* your idea of an English gentleman?" he asked.

I was disappointed, I was nervous, I wanted to get

on with my work; so I replied with irritation: "Oh my dear Major—I can't be ruined for *you!*"

It was a horrid speech, but he stood another moment —after which, without a word, he quitted the studio. I drew a long breath, for I said to myself that I shouldn't see him again. I hadn't told him definitely that I was in danger of having my work rejected, but I was vexed at his not having felt the catastrophe in the air, read with me the moral of our fruitless collaboration, the lesson that in the deceptive atmosphere of art even the highest respectability may fail of being plastic.

I didn't owe my friends money, but I did see them again. They reappeared together three days later, and, given all the other facts, there was something tragic in that one. It was a clear proof they could find nothing else in life to do. They had threshed the matter out in a dismal conference—they had digested the bad news that they were not in for the series. If they weren't useful to me even for the *Cheapside* their function seemed difficult to determine, and I could only judge at first that they had come, forgivingly, decorously, to take a last leave. This made me rejoice in secret that I had little leisure for a scene; for I had placed both my other models in position together and I was pegging away at a drawing from which I hoped to derive glory. It had been suggested by the passage in which Rutland Ramsay, drawing up a chair to Artemisia's piano-stool, says extraordinary things to her while she ostensibly fingers out a difficult piece of music. I had done Miss Churm at the piano before—it was an attitude in which she knew how to take on an absolutely poetic grace. I wished the two figures to "compose" together with intensity, and my little Italian had entered perfectly into my conception. The pair were vividly before me, the piano had been pulled out; it was a charming show of blended youth and murmured love, which I had only to catch and keep. My visitors stood and looked at it, and I was friendly to them over my shoulder.

They made no response, but I was used to silent company and went on with my work, only a little disconcerted—even though exhilarated by the sense that *this* was at least the ideal thing—at not having got rid of them after all. Presently I heard Mrs. Monarch's sweet voice beside or rather above me: "I wish her hair were a little better done." I looked up and she was staring with a strange fixedness at Miss Churm, whose back was turned to her. "Do you mind my just touching it?" she went on—a question which made me spring up for an instant as with the instinctive fear that she might do the young lady a harm. But she quieted me with a glance I shall never forget—I confess I should like to have been able to paint *that*—and went for a moment to my model. She spoke to her softly, laying a hand on her shoulder and bending over her; and as the girl, understanding, gratefully assented, she disposed her rough curls, with a few quick passes, in such a way as to make Miss Churm's head twice as charming. It was one of the most heroic personal services I've ever seen rendered. Then Mrs. Monarch turned away with a low sigh and, looking about her as if for something to do, stooped to the floor with a noble humility and picked up a dirty rag that had dropped out of my paint-box.

The Major meanwhile had also been looking for something to do, and, wandering to the other end of the studio, saw before him my breakfast-things neglected, unremoved. "I say, can't I be useful *here*?" he called out to me with an irrepressible quaver. I assented with a laugh that I fear was awkward, and for the next ten minutes, while I worked, I heard the light clatter of china and the tinkle of spoons and glass. Mrs. Monarch assisted her husband—they washed up my crockery, they put it away. They wandered off into my little scullery, and I afterwards found that they had cleaned my knives and that my slender stock of plate had an unprecedented surface. When it came over me, the latent eloquence of what they were doing, I confess that my drawing was blurred for a moment—the picture swam. They had accepted their failure, but they couldn't accept their fate. They had bowed their heads in bewilderment to the perverse and cruel law in virtue of which the real thing could be so much less precious than the unreal; but they didn't want to starve. If my servants were my models, then my models might be my servants. They would reverse the parts—the others would sit for the ladies and gentlemen and *they* would do the work. They would still be in the studio—it was an intense dumb appeal to me not to turn them out. "Take us on," they wanted to say—"we'll do *anything*."

My pencil dropped from my hand; my sitting was spoiled and I got rid of my sitters, who were also evidently rather mystified and awestruck. Then, alone with the Major and his wife I had a most uncomfortable moment. He put their prayer into a single sentence: "I say, you know—just let *us* do for you, can't you?" I couldn't —it was dreadful to see them emptying my slops; but I pretended I could, to oblige them, for about a week. Then I gave them a sum of money to go away, and I never saw them again. I obtained the remaining books, but my friend Hawley repeats that Major and Mrs. Monarch did me a permanent harm, got me into false ways. If it be true I'm content to have paid the price—for the memory.

1892

THREE NOUVELLES

James was increasingly attracted to what he called "the loved *nouvelle* form," a story length in which "the general sense of the expansive, the explosive principle in one's material" might be "adroitly allowed to flush and colour and animate the disputed value, but with its other appetites and treacheries, its characteristic space-hunger and space-cunning, kept down." He could there devote his shrewdest faculties "to the only compactness that has a charm, to the only spareness that has a force, to the only simplicity that has a grace—those, in each order, that produce the *rich* effect." R. P. Blackmur recognized it as "perhaps James's favorite form . . . a small reflector capable of illuminating or mirroring a great deal of material."

While James never specified the length of the *nouvelle*, one judges the category would include fairly concise examples like "The Pupil," "The Beast in the Jungle," and "The Bench of Desolation" as well as tales of virtual book length such as *Daisy Miller*, "The Aspern Papers," "The Turn of the Screw," and *In the Cage*. The three examples printed here are, in any event, among James's finest: they are concerned with three of his radical subjects and illustrate important developments in his narrative technique.

135

In "The Pupil" (1891) he treats the theme of moral confusion or treachery in modern society, heightening the effect of evil (as he was also to do in *What Maisie Knew* and *The Awkward Age*) by focusing on the victimized child, and thus suggesting a combination of moral sophistication and vulnerability. In the compelling appeal that binds young Morgan to his tutor (the naïve and morally confused Pemberton, from whose point of view the action is narrated) there is a subtlety of psychological suggestion that touches the secret spring of tragic emotion. . . . Similarly, the horror of "The Turn of the Screw" (1898) arises from the involvement of little Miles and Flora in unspeakable evil. At the same time they are victimized by the stifling overprotectiveness of the well-intentioned governess, and James thus explores another favorite theme: the maleficence of an excess of virtue (as in Daisy Miller's excessive "self-reliance," and Maggie Verver's excessive unselfishness in *The Golden Bowl*). "The Turn of the Screw" is not only his most famous ghost story; it is also a penetrating psychological study of the young governess—the sole authority for the bewildering and awful "facts" of the story. . . . "The Beast in the Jungle" (1903), unquestionably a masterpiece, dramatizes the destructive fear of life that derives from benighted selfishness. The tragic irony of the story is effectively understated in Marcher's recognition that he was "the man of his time, *the man,* to whom nothing on earth was to have happened": his selfishness brings death to May and condemns himself to a lifeless existence.

In these three stories we find brilliant examples of James's development in the technique of restricted point of view, which makes possible their richly contributive dramatic irony. The insufficient ken of Pemberton, the selfish blindness of Marcher, and the romantically clouded vision of the governess provide the controlling point of view in the respective stories; but the very untrustworthiness of these "narrative authorities" becomes a central dramatic feature. Their "view" of the action exposes themselves, and thus they are characterized reflexively. In so far as the subject of their respective stories is their inadequate vision, the strategy of allowing that vision to focus the action is a superbly appropriate narrative device. Technique and subject matter merge, and the medium is the message, as who should say. "The Beast in the Jungle" offers the clearest example of this strategy, but the other stories obviously anticipate its culmination in *The Ambassadors,* which James understandably regarded as "quite the best, 'all round,' of my productions."

"The Pupil" was first printed in *Longman's Magazine* in March and April 1891, and in book form in *The Lesson of the Master and Other Tales* in 1892. "The Turn of the Screw" was first published in *Collier's Weekly,* January 27 to April 2, 1898, and in book form in *The Two Magics* (with "Covering End") later that year. "The Beast in the Jungle" was first published in James's book of tales *The Better Sort* in 1903. The present texts of all three tales are taken from the New York Edition. Again the reader is referred to the Bibliography in this book for other recommended titles among James's longer tales and *nouvelles.*

—L.H.P.

THE PUPIL

I

The poor young man hesitated and procrastinated: it cost him such an effort to broach the subject of terms, to speak of money to a person who spoke only of feelings and, as it were, of the aristocracy. Yet he was unwilling to take leave, treating his engagement as settled, without some more conventional glance in that direction than he could find an opening for in the manner of the large affable lady who sat there drawing a pair of soiled *gants de Suède* through a fat jewelled hand and, at once pressing and gliding, repeated over and over everything but the thing he would have liked to hear. He would have

liked to hear the figure of his salary; but just as he was
nervously about to sound that note the little boy came
back—the little boy Mrs. Moreen had sent out of the
room to fetch her fan. He came back without the fan,
only with the casual observation that he couldn't find it.
As he dropped this cynical confession he looked straight
and hard at the candidate for the honour of taking his
education in hand. This personage reflected somewhat
grimly that the first thing he should have to teach his
little charge would be to appear to address himself to
his mother when he spoke to her—especially not to make
her such an improper answer as that.

When Mrs. Moreen bethought herself of this pretext
for getting rid of their companion Pemberton supposed
it was precisely to approach the delicate subject of his
remuneration. But it had been only to say some things
about her son that it was better a boy of eleven shouldn't
catch. They were extravagantly to his advantage save
when she lowered her voice to sigh, tapping her left side
familiarly, "And all overclouded by *this,* you know; all
at the mercy of a weakness—!" Pemberton gathered that
the weakness was in the region of the heart. He had
known the poor child was not robust: this was the basis
on which he had been invited to treat, through an English lady, an Oxford acquaintance, then at Nice, who
happened to know both his needs and those of the amiable American family looking out for something really
superior in the way of a resident tutor.

The young man's impression of his prospective pupil,
who had come into the room as if to see for himself the
moment Pemberton was admitted, was not quite the soft
solicitation the visitor had taken for granted. Morgan
Moreen was somehow sickly without being "delicate,"
and that he looked intelligent—it is true Pemberton
would have enjoyed his being stupid—only added to

the suggestion that, as with his big mouth and big ears
he really couldn't be called pretty, he might too utterly
fail to please. Pemberton was modest, was even timid;
and the chance that his small scholar would prove cleverer than himself had quite figured, to his anxiety,
among the dangers of an untried experiment. He reflected, however, that these were risks one had to run
when one accepted a position, as it was called, in a private family; when as yet one's university honours had,
pecuniarily speaking, remained barren. At any rate when
Mrs. Moreen got up as to intimate that, since it was
understood he would enter upon his duties within the
week she would let him off now, he succeeded, in spite
of the presence of the child, in squeezing out a phrase
about the rate of payment. It was not the fault of the
conscious smile which seemed a reference to the lady's
expensive identity, it was not the fault of this demonstration, which had, in a sort, both vagueness and point, if
the allusion didn't sound rather vulgar. This was exactly
because she became still more gracious to reply: "Oh
I can assure you that all that will be quite regular."

Pemberton only wondered, while he took up his hat,
what "all that" was to amount to—people had such different ideas. Mrs. Moreen's words, however, seemed to
commit the family to a pledge definite enough to elicit
from the child a strange little comment in the shape of
the mocking foreign ejaculation "Oh la-la!"

Pemberton, in some confusion, glanced at him as he
walked slowly to the window with his back turned, his
hands in his pockets and the air in his elderly shoulders
of a boy who didn't play. The young man wondered
if he should be able to teach him to play, though his
mother had said it would never do and that this was
why school was impossible. Mrs. Moreen exhibited no
discomfiture; she only continued blandly: "Mr. Moreen

will be delighted to meet your wishes. As I told you, he has been called to London for a week. As soon as he comes back you shall have it out with him."

This was so frank and friendly that the young man could only reply, laughing as his hostess laughed: "Oh I don't imagine we shall have much of a battle."

"They'll give you anything you like," the boy remarked unexpectedly, returning from the window. "We don't mind what anything costs—we live awfully well."

"My darling, you're too quaint!" his mother exclaimed, putting out to caress him a practised but ineffectual hand. He slipped out of it, but looked with intelligent innocent eyes at Pemberton, who had already had time to notice that from one moment to the other his small satiric face seemed to change its time of life. At this moment it was infantine, yet it appeared also to be under the influence of curious intuitions and knowledges. Pemberton rather disliked precocity and was disappointed to find gleams of it in a disciple not yet in his teens. Nevertheless he divined on the spot that Morgan wouldn't prove a bore. He would prove on the contrary a source of agitation. This idea held the young man, in spite of a certain repulsion.

"You pompous little person! We're not extravagant!" Mrs. Moreen gaily protested, making another unsuccessful attempt to draw the boy to her side. "You must know what to expect," she went on to Pemberton.

"The less you expect the better!" her companion interposed. "But we *are* people of fashion."

"Only so far as *you* make us so!" Mrs. Moreen tenderly mocked. "Well then, on Friday—don't tell me you're superstitious—and mind you don't fail us. Then you'll see us all. I'm so sorry the girls are out. I guess you'll like the girls. And, you know, I've another son, quite different from this one."

"He tries to imitate me," Morgan said to their friend.

"He tries? Why he's twenty years old!" cried Mrs. Moreen.

"You're very witty," Pemberton remarked to the child —a proposition his mother echoed with enthusiasm, declaring Morgan's sallies to be the delight of the house.

The boy paid no heed to this; he only enquired abruptly of the visitor, who was surprised afterwards that he hadn't struck him as offensively forward: "Do you *want* very much to come?"

"Can you doubt it after such a description of what I shall hear?" Pemberton replied. Yet he didn't want to come at all; he was coming because he had to go somewhere, thanks to the collapse of his fortune at the end of a year abroad spent on the system of putting his scant patrimony into a single full wave of experience. He had had his full wave but couldn't pay the score at his inn. Moreover he had caught in the boy's eyes the glimpse of a far-off appeal.

"Well, I'll do the best I can for you," said Morgan; with which he turned away again. He passed out of one of the long windows; Pemberton saw him go and lean on the parapet of the terrace. He remained there while the young man took leave of his mother, who, on Pemberton's looking as if he expected a farewell from him, interposed with: "Leave him, leave him; he's so strange!" Pemberton supposed her to fear something he might say. "He's a genius—you'll love him," she added. "He's much the most interesting person in the family." And before he could invent some civility to oppose to this she wound up with: "But we're all good, you know!"

"He's a genius—you'll love him!" were words that recurred to our aspirant before the Friday, suggesting among many things that geniuses were not invariably loveable. However, it was all the better if there was an element that would make tutorship absorbing: he had perhaps taken too much for granted it would only disgust him. As he left the villa after his interview he looked up at the balcony and saw the child leaning over it. "We shall have great larks!" he called up.

Morgan hung fire a moment and then gaily returned: "By the time you come back I shall have thought of something witty!"

This made Pemberton say to himself "After all he's rather nice."

II

On the Friday he saw them all, as Mrs. Moreen had promised, for her husband had come back and the girls and the other son were at home. Mr. Moreen had a white moustache, a confiding manner and, in his buttonhole, the ribbon of a foreign order—bestowed, as Pemberton eventually learned, for services. For what services he never clearly ascertained: this was a point—one of a larger number—that Mr. Moreen's manner never confided. What it emphatically did confide was that he was even more a man of the world than you might first make out. Ulick, the firstborn, was in visible training for the same profession—under the disadvantage as yet, however, of a buttonhole but feebly floral and a moustache with no pretensions to type. The girls had hair and figures and manners and small fat feet, but had never been out alone. As for Mrs. Moreen, Pemberton saw on a nearer view that her elegance was intermittent and her parts didn't always match. Her husband, as she had promised, met with enthusiasm Pemberton's ideas in regard to a salary. The young man had endeavoured to keep these stammerings modest, and Mr. Moreen made it no secret that *he* found them wanting in "style." He further mentioned that he aspired to be intimate

with his children, to be their best friend, and that he
was always looking out for them. That was what he
went off for, to London and other places—to look out;
and this vigilance was the theory of life, as well as the
real occupation, of the whole family. They all looked
out, for they were very frank on the subject of its being
necessary. They desired it to be understood that they
were earnest people, and also that their fortune, though
quite adequate for earnest people, required the most
careful administration. Mr. Moreen, as the parent bird,
sought sustenance for the nest. Ulick invoked support
mainly at the club, where Pemberton guessed that it was
usually served on green cloth. The girls used to do up
their hair and their frocks themselves, and our young
man felt appealed to to be glad, in regard to Morgan's
education, that, though it must naturally be of the best,
it didn't cost too much. After a little he *was* glad, for-
getting at times his own needs in the interest inspired
by the child's character and culture and the pleasure of
making easy terms for him.

During the first weeks of their acquaintance Morgan
had been as puzzling as a page in an unknown language
—altogether different from the obvious little Anglo-
Saxons who had misrepresented childhood to Pemberton. Indeed the whole mystic volume in which the boy
had been amateurishly bound demanded some practice
in translation. Today, after a considerable interval, there
is something phantasmagoric, like a prismatic reflexion
or a serial novel, in Pemberton's memory of the queerness of the Moreens. If it were not for a few tangible
tokens—a lock of Morgan's hair cut by his own hand,
and the half-dozen letters received from him when they
were disjoined—the whole episode and the figures peo-
pling it would seem too inconsequent for anything but
dreamland. Their supreme quaintness was their success

—as it appeared to him for a while at the time; since he had never seen a family so brilliantly equipped for failure. Wasn't it success to have kept him so hatefully long? Wasn't it success to have drawn him in that first morning at déjeuner, the Friday he came—it was enough to *make* one superstitious—so that he utterly committed himself, and this not by calculation or on a signal, but from a happy instinct which made them, like a band of gipsies, work so neatly together? They amused him as much as if they had really been a band of gipsies. He was still young and had not seen much of the world —his English years had been properly arid; therefore the reversed conventions of the Moreens—for they had *their* desperate properties—struck him as topsy-turvy. He had encountered nothing like them at Oxford; still less had any such note been struck to his younger American ear during the four years at Yale in which he had richly supposed himself to be reacting against a Puritan strain. The reaction of the Moreens, at any rate, went ever so much further. He had thought himself very sharp that first day in hitting them all off in his mind with the "cosmopolite" label. Later it seemed feeble and colourless—confessedly helplessly provisional.

He yet when he first applied it felt a glow of joy—for an instructor he was still empirical—rise from the apprehension that living with them would really be to see life. Their sociable strangeness was an imitation of that— their chatter of tongues, their gaiety and good humour, their infinite dawdling (they were always getting themselves up, but it took for ever, and Pemberton had once found Mr. Moreen shaving in the drawing-room), their French, their Italian and, cropping up in the foreign fluencies, their cold tough slices of American. They lived on maccaroni and coffee—they had these articles prepared in perfection—but they knew recipes for a hun-

dred other dishes. They overflowed with music and
song, were always humming and catching each other
up, and had a sort of professional acquaintance with
Continental cities. They talked of "good places" as if
they had been pickpockets or strolling players. They had
at Nice a villa, a carriage, a piano and a banjo, and they
went to official parties. They were a perfect calendar of
the "days" of their friends, which Pemberton knew
them, when they were indisposed, to get out of bed
to go to, and which made the week larger than life when
Mrs. Moreen talked of them with Paula and Amy. Their
initiations gave their new inmate at first an almost dazzling sense of culture. Mrs. Moreen had translated something at some former period—an author whom it made
Pemberton feel *borné* never to have heard of. They
could imitate Venetian and sing Neapolitan, and when
they wanted to say something very particular communicated with each other in an ingenious dialect of their
own, an elastic spoken cipher which Pemberton at first
took for some *patois* of one of their countries, but which
he "caught on to" as he would not have grasped provincial development of Spanish or German.

"It's the family language—Ultramoreen," Morgan
explained to him drolly enough; but the boy rarely con-
descended to use it himself, though he dealt in colloquial Latin as if he had been a little prelate.

Among all the "days" with which Mrs. Moreen's
memory was taxed she managed to squeeze in one of her
own, which her friends sometimes forgot. But the house
drew a frequented air from the number of fine people
who were freely named there and from several mysterious men with foreign titles and English clothes whom
Morgan called the Princes and who, on sofas with the
girls, talked French very loud—though sometimes with
some oddity of accent—as if to show they were saying

nothing improper. Pemberton wondered how the Princes could ever propose in that tone and so publicly: he took for granted cynically that this was what was desired of them. Then he recognised that even for the chance of such an advantage Mrs. Moreen would never allow Paula and Amy to receive alone. These young ladies were not at all timid, but it was just the safeguards that made them so candidly free. It was a houseful of Bohemians who wanted tremendously to be Philistines.

In one respect, however, certainly, they achieved no rigour—they were wonderfully amiable and ecstatic about Morgan. It was a genuine tenderness, an artless admiration, equally strong in each. They even praised his beauty, which was small, and were as afraid of him as if they felt him of finer clay. They spoke of him as a little angel and a prodigy—they touched on his want of health with long, vague faces. Pemberton feared at first an extravagance that might make him hate the boy, but before this happened he had become extravagant himself. Later, when he had grown rather to hate the others, it was a bribe to patience for him that they were at any rate nice about Morgan, going on tiptoe if they fancied he was showing symptoms, and even giving up somebody's "day" to procure him a pleasure. Mixed with this too was the oddest wish to make him independent, as if they had felt themselves not good enough for him. They passed him over to the new members of their circle very much as if wishing to force some charity of adoption on so free an agent and get rid of their own charge. They were delighted when they saw Morgan take so to his kind playfellow, and could think of no higher praise for the young man. It was strange how they contrived to reconcile the appearance, and indeed the essential fact, of adoring the child with their eagerness to wash their hands of him. Did they want to get rid of him before he should find them out? Pemberton was finding them out month by month. The boy's fond family, however this might be, turned their backs with exaggerated delicacy, as if to avoid the reproach of interfering. Seeing in time how little he had in common with them—it was by *them* he first observed it; they proclaimed it with complete humility—his companion was moved to speculate on the mysteries of transmission, the far jumps of heredity. Where his detachment from most of the things they represented had come from was more than an observer could say—it certainly had burrowed under two or three generations.

As for Pemberton's own estimate of his pupil, it was a good while before he got the point of view, so little had he been prepared for it by the smug young barbarians to whom the tradition of tutorship, as hitherto revealed to him, had been adjusted. Morgan was scrappy and surprising, deficient in many properties supposed common to the *genus* and abounding in others that were the portion only of the supernaturally clever. One day his friend made a great stride: it cleared up the question to perceive that Morgan *was* supernaturally clever and that, though the formula was temporarily meagre, this would be the only assumption on which one could successfully deal with him. He had the general quality of a child for whom life had not been simplified by school, a kind of homebred sensibility which might have been bad for himself but was charming for others, and a whole range of refinement and perception—little musical vibrations as taking as picked-up airs—begotten by wandering about Europe at the tail of his migratory tribe. This might not have been an education to recommend in advance, but its results with so special a subject were as appreciable as the marks on a piece of fine procelain.

There was at the same time in him a small strain of stoicism, doubtless the fruit of having had to begin early to bear pain, which counted for pluck and made it of less consequence that he might have been thought at school rather a polyglot little beast. Pemberton indeed quickly found himself rejoicing that school was out of the question: in any million of boys it was probably good for all but one, and Morgan was that millionth. It would have made him comparative and superior—it might have made him really require kicking. Pemberton would try to be school himself—a bigger seminary than five hundred grazing donkeys, so that, winning no prizes, the boy would remain unconscious and irresponsible and amusing—amusing, because, though life was already intense in his childish nature, freshness still made there a strong draught for jokes. It turned out that even in the still air of Morgan's various disabilities jokes flourished greatly. He was a pale lean acute undeveloped little cosmopolite, who liked intellectual gymnastics and who also, as regards the behaviour of mankind, had noticed more things than you might suppose, but who nevertheless had his proper playroom of superstitions, where he smashed a dozen toys a day.

III

At Nice once, toward evening, as the pair rested in the open air after a walk, and looked over the sea at the pink western lights, he said suddenly to his comrade: "Do you like it, you know—being with us all in this intimate way?"

"My dear fellow, why should I stay if I didn't?"

"How do I know you'll stay? I'm almost sure you won't, very long."

"I hope you don't mean to dismiss me," said Pemberton.

Morgan debated, looking at the sunset. "I think if I did right I ought to."

"Well, I know I'm supposed to instruct you in virtue; but in that case don't do right."

"You're very young—fortunately," Morgan went on, turning to him again.

"Oh yes, compared with you!"

"Therefore it won't matter so much if you do lose a lot of time."

"That's the way to look at it," said Pemberton accommodatingly.

They were silent a minute; after which the boy asked: "Do you like my father and my mother very much?"

"Dear me, yes. Charming people."

Morgan received this with another silence; then unexpectedly, familiarly, but at the same time affectionately, he remarked: "You're a jolly old humbug!"

For a particular reason the words made our young man change colour. The boy noticed in an instant that he had turned red, whereupon he turned red himself and pupil and master exchanged a longish glance in which there was a consciousness of many more things than are usually touched upon, even tacitly, in such a relation. It produced for Pemberton an embarrassment; it raised in a shadowy form a question—this was the first glimpse of it—destined to play a singular and, as he imagined, owing to the altogether peculiar conditions, an unprecedented part in his intercourse with his little companion. Later, when he found himself talking with the youngster in a way in which few youngsters could ever have been talked with, he thought of that clumsy moment on the bench at Nice as the dawn of an understanding that had broadened. What had added to the clumsiness then was that he thought it his duty to declare to Morgan that he might abuse him, Pemberton, as much as he liked, but must never abuse his parents. To this Morgan had the easy retort that he hadn't dreamed of abusing them; which appeared to be true: it put Pemberton in the wrong.

"Then why am I a humbug for saying *I* think them charming?" the young man asked, conscious of a certain rashness.

"Well—they're not your parents."

"They love you better than anything in the world— never forget that," said Pemberton.

"Is that why you like them so much?"

"They're very kind to me," Pemberton replied evasively.

"You *are* a humbug!" laughed Morgan, passing an arm into his tutor's. He leaned against him looking off at the sea again and swinging his long thin legs.

"Don't kick my shins," said Pemberton while he reflected "Hang it, I can't complain of them to the child!'

"There's another reason too," Morgan went on, keeping his legs still.

"Another reason for what?"

"Besides their not being your parents."

"I don't understand you," said Pemberton.

"Well, you will before long. All right!"

He did understand fully before long, but he made a fight even with himself before he confessed it. He thought it the oddest thing to have a struggle with the child about. He wondered he didn't hate the hope of the Moreens for bringing the struggle on. But by the time it began any such sentiment for that scion was closed to him. Morgan was a special case, and to know him was to accept him on his own odd terms. Pemberton had spent his aversion to special cases before arriving at knowledge. When at last he did arrive his quandary was great. Against every interest he had attached himself.

They would have to meet things together. Before they
went home that evening at Nice the boy had said, cling-
ing to his arm:

"Well, at any rate you'll hang on to the last."

"To the last?"

"Till you're fairly beaten."

"*You* ought to be fairly beaten!" cried the young man,
drawing him closer.

IV

A year after he had come to live with them Mr. and
Mrs. Moreen suddenly gave up the villa at Nice. Pemberton had got used to suddenness, having seen it practised on a considerable scale during two jerky little tours
—one in Switzerland the first summer, and the other
late in the winter, when they all ran down to Florence
and then, at the end of ten days, liking it much less than
they had intended, straggled back in mysterious depression. They had returned to Nice "for ever," as they said;
but this didn't prevent their squeezing, one rainy muggy
May night, into a second-class railway-carriage—you
could never tell by which class they would travel—
where Pemberton helped them to stow away a wonderful collection of bundles and bags. The explanation of
this manœuvre was that they had determined to spend
the summer "in some bracing place"; but in Paris they
dropped into a small furnished apartment—a fourth
floor in a third-rate avenue, where there was a smell on
the staircase and the *portier* was hateful—and passed
the next four months in blank indigence.

The better part of this baffled sojourn was for the
preceptor and his pupil, who, visiting the Invalides and
Notre Dame, the Conciergerie and all the museums,
took a hundred remunerative rambles. They learned to
know their Paris, which was useful, for they came back

another year for a longer stay, the general character
of which in Pemberton's memory to-day mixes pitiably
and confusedly with that of the first. He sees Morgan's
shabby knickerbockers—the everlasting pair that didn't
match his blouse and that as he grew longer could only
grow faded. He remembers the particular holes in his
three or four pair of coloured stockings.

Morgan was dear to his mother, but he never was
better dressed than was absolutely necessary—partly,
no doubt, by his own fault, for he was as indifferent to
his appearance as a German philosopher. "My dear fellow, you *are* coming to pieces," Pemberton would say
to him in sceptical remonstrance; to which the child
would reply, looking at him serenely up and down: "My
dear fellow, so are you! I don't want to cast you in the
shade." Pemberton could have no rejoinder for this—
the assertion so closely represented the fact. If however
the deficiencies of his own wardrobe were a chapter by
themselves he didn't like his little charge to look too
poor. Later he used to say "Well, if we're poor, why,
after all, shouldn't we look it?" and he consoled himself
with thinking there was something rather elderly and
gentlemanly in Morgan's disrepair—it differed from the
untidiness of the urchin who plays and spoils his things.
He could trace perfectly the degrees by which, in proportion as her little son confined himself to his tutor for
society, Mrs. Moreen shrewdly forbore to renew his
garments. She did nothing that didn't show, neglected
him because he escaped notice, and then, as he illustrated this clever policy, discouraged at home his public
appearances. Her position was logical enough—those
members of her family who did show had to be showy.

During this period and several others Pemberton was
quite aware of how he and his comrade might strike
people; wandering languidly through the Jardin des

Plantes as if they had nowhere to go, sitting on the winter days in the galleries of the Louvre, so splendidly ironical to the homeless, as if for the advantage of the *calorifère*. They joked about it sometimes: it was the sort of joke that was perfectly within the boy's compass. They figured themselves as part of the vast vague hand-to-mouth multitude of the enormous city and pretended they were proud of their position in it—it showed them "such a lot of life" and made them conscious of a demo-cratic brotherhood. If Pemberton couldn't feel a sym-pathy in destitution with his small companion—for after all Morgan's fond parents would never have let him really suffer—the boy would at least feel it with him, so it came to the same thing. He used sometimes to won-der what people would think they were—to fancy they were looked askance at, as if it might be a suspected case of kidnapping. Morgan wouldn't be taken for a young patrician with a preceptor—he wasn't smart enough; though he might pass for his companion's sickly little brother. Now and then he had a five-franc piece, and except once, when they bought a couple of lovely neckties, one of which he made Pemberton accept, they laid it out scientifically in old books. This was sure to be a great day, always spent on the quays, in a rummage of the dusty boxes that garnish the parapets. Such occa-sions helped them to live, for their books ran low very soon after the beginning of their acquaintance. Pember-ton had a good many in England, but he was obliged to write to a friend and ask him kindly to get some fel-low to give him something for them.

If they had to relinquish that summer the advantage of the bracing climate the young man couldn't but sus-pect this failure of the cup when at their very lips to have been the effect of a rude jostle of his own. This had represented his first blow-out, as he called it, with his patrons; his first successful attempt—though there was little other success about it—to bring them to a consideration of his impossible position. As the ostensible eve of a costly journey the moment had struck him as favourable to an earnest protest, the presentation of an ultimatum. Ridiculous as it sounded, he had never yet been able to compass an uninterrupted private interview with the elder pair or with either of them singly. They were always flanked by their elder children, and poor Pemberton usually had his own little charge at his side. He was conscious of its being a house in which the surface of one's delicacy got rather smudged; nevertheless he had preserved the bloom of his scruple against announcing to Mr. and Mrs. Moreen with publicity that he shouldn't be able to go on longer without a little money. He was still simple enough to suppose Ulick and Paula and Amy might not know that since his arrival he had only had a hundred and forty francs; and he was magnanimous enough to wish not to compromise their parents in their eyes. Mr. Moreen now listened to him, as he listened to every one and to every thing, like a man of the world, and seemed to appeal to him—though not of course too grossly—to try and be a little more of one himself. Pemberton recognised in fact the importance of the character—from the advantage it gave Mr. Moreen. He was not even confused or embarrassed, whereas the young man in his service was more so than there was any reason for. Neither was he surprised—at least any more than a gentleman had to be who freely confessed himself a little shocked—though not perhaps strictly at Pemberton.

"We must go into this, mustn't we, dear?" he said to his wife. He assured his young friend that the matter should have his very best attention; and he melted into space as elusively as if, at the door, he were taking an inevitable but deprecatory precedence. When, the next moment, Pemberton found himself alone with Mrs. Moreen it was to hear her say "I see, I see"—stroking the roundness of her chin and looking as if she were only hesitating between a dozen easy remedies. If they didn't make their push Mr. Moreen could at least disappear for several days. During his absence his wife took up the subject again spontaneously, but her contribution to it was merely that she had thought all the while they were getting on so beautifully. Pemberton's reply to this revelation was that unless they immediately put down something on account he would leave them on the spot and for ever. He knew she would wonder how he would get away, and for a moment expected her to enquire. She didn't, for which he was almost grateful to her, so little was he in a position to tell.

"You won't, you *know* you won't—you're too interested," she said. "You *are* interested, you know you are, you dear kind man!" She laughed with almost condemnatory archness, as if it were a reproach—though she wouldn't insist; and flirted a soiled pocket-handkerchief at him.

Pemberton's mind was fully made up to take his step the following week. This would give him time to get an answer to a letter he had dispatched to England. If he did in the event nothing of the sort—that is if he stayed another year and then went away only for three months —it was not merely because before the answer to his letter came (most unsatisfactory when it did arrive) Mr. Moreen generously counted out to him, and again with the sacrifice to "form" of a marked man of the world, three hundred francs in elegant ringing gold. He was irritated to find that Mrs. Moreen was right, that he couldn't at the pinch bear to leave the child. This stood out clearer for the very reason that, the night

of his desperate appeal to his patrons, he had seen fully
for the first time where he was. Wasn't it another proof
of the success with which those patrons practised their
arts that they had managed to avert for so long the
illuminating flash? It descended on our friend with a
breadth of effect which perhaps would have struck
a spectator as comical, after he had returned to his little
servile room, which looked into a close court where
a bare dirty opposite wall took, with the sound of shrill
clatter, the reflexion of lighted back windows. He had
simply given himself away to a band of adventurers.
The idea, the word itself, wore a romantic horror for
him—he had always lived on such safe lines. Later it
assumed a more interesting, almost a soothing, sense:
it pointed a moral, and Pemberton could enjoy a moral.
The Moreens were adventurers not merely because they
didn't pay their debts, because they lived on society,
but because their whole view of life, dim and confused
and instinctive, like that of clever colour-blind animals,
was speculative and rapacious and mean. Oh they were
"respectable," and that only made them more *immondes!*
The young man's analysis, while he brooded, put it at
last very simply—they were adventurers because they
were toadies and snobs. That was the completest account of them—it was the law of their being. Even
when this truth became vivid to their ingenious inmate
he remained unconscious of how much his mind had
been prepared for it by the extraordinary little boy who
had now become such a complication in his life. Much
less could he then calculate on the information he was
still to owe the extraordinary little boy.

v

But it was during the ensuing time that the real problem
came up—the problem of how far it was excusable to

discuss the turpitude of parents with a child of twelve, of thirteen, of fourteen. Absolutely inexcusable and quite impossible it of course at first appeared; and indeed the question didn't press for some time after Pemberton had received his three hundred francs. They produced a temporary lull, a relief from the sharpest pressure. The young man frugally amended his wardrobe and even had a few francs in his pocket. He thought the Moreens looked at him as if he were almost too smart, as if they ought to take care not to spoil him. If Mr. Moreen hadn't been such a man of the world he would perhaps have spoken of the freedom of such neckties on the part of a subordinate. But Mr. Moreen was always enough a man of the world to let things pass—he had certainly shown that. It was singular how Pemberton guessed that Morgan, though saying nothing about it, knew something had happened. But three hundred francs, especially when one owed money, couldn't last for ever; and when the treasure was gone—the boy knew when it had failed—Morgan did break ground. The party had returned to Nice at the beginning of the winter, but not to the charming villa. They went to an hotel, where they stayed three months, and then moved to another establishment, explaining that they had left the first because, after waiting and waiting, they couldn't get the rooms they wanted. These apartments, the rooms they wanted, were generally very splendid; but fortunately they never *could* get them—fortunately, I mean, for Pemberton, who reflected always that if they had got them there would have been a still scanter educational fund. What Morgan said at last was said suddenly, irrelevantly, when the moment came, in the middle of a lesson, and consisted of the apparently unfeeling words: "You ought to *filer*, you know—you really ought."

Pemberton stared. He had learnt enough French slang from Morgan to know that to *filer* meant to cut sticks. "Ah my dear fellow, don't turn me off!"

Morgan pulled a Greek lexicon toward him—he used a Greek-German—to look out a word, instead of asking it of Pemberton. "You can't go on like this, you know."

"Like what, my boy?"

"You know they don't pay you up," said Morgan, blushing and turning his leaves.

"Don't pay me?" Pemberton stared again and feigned amazement. "What on earth put that into your head?"

"It has been there a long time," the boy replied rummaging his book.

Pemberton was silent, then he went on: "I say, what are you hunting for? They pay me beautifully."

"I'm hunting for the Greek for awful whopper," Morgan dropped.

"Find that rather for gross impertinence and disabuse your mind. What do I want of money?"

"Oh that's another question!"

Pemberton wavered—he was drawn in different ways. The severely correct thing would have been to tell the boy that such a matter was none of his business and bid him go on with his lines. But they were really too intimate for that; it was not the way he was in the habit of treating him; there had been no reason it should be. On the other hand Morgan had quite lighted on the truth—he really shouldn't be able to keep it up much longer; therefore why not let him know one's real motive for forsaking him? At the same time it wasn't decent to abuse to one's pupil the family of one's pupil; it was better to misrepresent than to do that. So in reply to his comrade's last exclamation he just declared, to dismiss the subject, that he had received several payments.

"I say—I say!" the boy ejaculated, laughing.

"That's all right," Pemberton insisted. "Give me your written rendering."

Morgan pushed a copybook across the table, and he began to read the page, but with something running in his head that made it no sense. Looking up after a minute or two he found the child's eyes fixed on him and felt in them something strange. Then Morgan said: "I'm not afraid of the stern reality."

"I haven't yet seen the thing you *are* afraid of—I'll do you that justice!"

This came out with a jump—it was perfectly true—and evidently gave Morgan pleasure. "I've thought of it a long time," he presently resumed.

"Well, don't think of it any more."

The boy appeared to comply, and they had a comfortable and even an amusing hour. They had a theory that they were very thorough, and yet they seemed always to be in the amusing part of lessons, the intervals between the dull dark tunnels, where there were waysides and jolly views. Yet the morning was brought to a violent end by Morgan's suddenly leaning his arms on the table, burying his head in them and bursting into tears: at which Pemberton was the more startled that, as it then came over him, it was the first time he had ever seen the boy cry and that the impression was consequently quite awful.

The next day, after much thought, he took a decision and, believing it to be just, immediately acted on it. He cornered Mr. and Mrs. Moreen again and let them know that if on the spot they didn't pay him all they owed him he wouldn't only leave their house but would tell Morgan exactly what had brought him to it.

"Oh you *haven't* told him?" cried Mrs. Moreen with a pacifying hand on her well-dressed bosom.

"Without warning you? For what do you take me?" the young man returned.

Mr. and Mrs. Moreen looked at each other; he could see that they appreciated, as tending to their security, his superstition of delicacy, and yet that there was a certain alarm in their relief. "My dear fellow," Mr. Moreen demanded, "what use *can* you have, leading the quiet life we all do, for such a lot of money?"—a question to which Pemberton made no answer, occupied as he was in noting that what passed in the mind of his patrons was something like: "Oh then, if we've felt that the child, dear little angel, has judged us and how he regards us, and we haven't been betrayed, he must have guessed—and in short it's *general!*" an inference that rather stirred up Mr. and Mrs. Moreen, as Pemberton had desired it should. At the same time, if he had supposed his threat would do something towards bringing them round, he was disappointed to find them taking for granted—how vulgar their perception *had* been!— that he had already given them away. There was a mystic uneasiness in their parental breasts, and that had been the inferior sense of it. None the less, however, his threat did touch them; for if they had escaped it was only to meet a new danger. Mr. Moreen appealed to him, on every precedent, as a man of the world; but his wife had recourse, for the first time since his domestication with them, to a fine *hauteur*, reminding him that a devoted mother, with her child, had arts that protected her against gross misrepresentation.

"I should misrepresent you grossly if I accused you of common honesty!" our friend replied; but as he closed the door behind him sharply, thinking he had not done himself much good, while Mr. Moreen lighted another cigarette, he heard his hostess shout after him more touchingly:

"Oh you do, you *do*, put the knife to one's throat!"

The next morning, very early, she came to his room. He recognised her knock, but had no hope she brought him money; as to which he was wrong, for she had fifty francs in her hand. She squeezed forward in her dressing-gown, and he received her in his own, between his bath-tub and his bed. He had been tolerably schooled by this time to the "foreign ways" of his hosts. Mrs. Moreen was ardent, and when she was ardent she didn't care what she did; so she now sat down on his bed, his clothes being on the chairs, and, in her preoccupation, forgot, as she glanced round, to be ashamed of giving him such a horrid room. What Mrs. Moreen's ardour now bore upon was the design of persuading him that in the first place she was very good-natured to bring him fifty francs, and that in the second, if he would only see it, he was really too absurd to expect to be *paid*. Wasn't he paid enough without perpetual money—wasn't he paid by the comfortable luxurious home he enjoyed with them all, without a care, an anxiety, a solitary want? Wasn't he sure of his position, and wasn't that everything to a young man like him, quite unknown, with singularly little to show, the ground of whose exorbitant pretensions it had never been easy to discover? Wasn't he paid above all by the sweet relation he had established with Morgan—quite ideal as from master to pupil—and by the simple privilege of knowing and living with so amazingly gifted a child; than whom really (and she meant literally what she said) there was no better company in Europe? Mrs. Moreen herself took to appealing to him as a man of the world; she said "Voyons, mon cher," and "My dear man, look here now"; and urged him to be reasonable, putting it before him that it was truly a chance for him. She spoke as if, according as he *should* be reasonable, he would prove himself worthy to be her son's tutor and of the extraordinary confidence they had placed in him.

After all, Pemberton reflected, it was only a difference of theory and the theory didn't matter much. They had hitherto gone on that of remunerated, as now they would go on that of gratuitous, service; but why should they have so many words about it? Mrs. Moreen at all events continued to be convincing; sitting there with her fifty francs she talked and reiterated as women reiterate, and bored and irritated him, while he leaned against the wall with his hands in the pockets of his wrapper, drawing it together round his legs and looking over the head of his visitor at the grey negations of his window. She wound up with saying: "You see I bring you a definite proposal."

"A definite proposal?"

"To make our relations regular, as it were—to put them on a comfortable footing."

"I see—it's a system," said Pemberton. "A kind of organised blackmail."

Mrs. Moreen bounded up, which was exactly what he wanted. "What do you mean by that?"

"You practise on one's fears—one's fears about the child if one should go away."

"And pray what would happen to him in that event?" she demanded with majesty.

"Why he'd be alone with *you*."

"And pray with whom *should* a child be but with those whom he loves most?"

"If you think that, why don't you dismiss me?"

"Do you pretend he loves you more than he loves *us*?" cried Mrs. Moreen.

"I think he ought to. I make sacrifices for him. Though I've heard of those *you* make I don't see them."

Mrs. Moreen stared a moment; then with emotion she grasped her inmate's hand. "*Will* you make it—the sacrifice?"

He burst out laughing. "I'll see. I'll do what I can. I'll stay a little longer. Your calculation's just—I *do* hate intensely to give him up; I'm fond of him and he thoroughly interests me, in spite of the inconvenience I suffer. You know my situation perfectly. I haven't a penny in the world and, occupied as you see me with Morgan, am unable to earn money."

Mrs. Moreen tapped her undressed arm with her folded bank-note. "Can't you write articles? Can't you translate as *I* do?"

"I don't know about translating; it's wretchedly paid."

"I'm glad to earn what I can," said Mrs. Moreen with prodigious virtue.

"You ought to tell me who you do it for." Pemberton paused a moment, and she said nothing; so he added: "I've tried to turn off some little sketches, but the magazines won't have them—they're declined with thanks."

"You see then you're not such a phœnix," his visitor pointedly smiled—"to pretend to abilities you're sacrificing for our sake."

"I haven't time to do things properly," he ruefully went on. Then as it came over him that he was almost abjectly good-natured to give these explanations he added: "If I stay on longer it must be on one condition—that Morgan shall know distinctly on what footing I am."

Mrs. Moreen demurred. "Surely you don't want to show off to a child?"

"To show *you* off, do you mean?"

Again she cast about, but this time it was to produce a still finer flower. "And *you* talk of blackmail!"

"You can easily prevent it," said Pemberton.

"And *you* talk of practising on fears!" she bravely pushed on.

"Yes, there's no doubt I'm a great scoundrel."

His patroness met his eyes—it was clear she was in straits. Then she thrust out her money at him. "Mr. Moreen desired me to give you this on account."

"I'm much obliged to Mr. Moreen, but we *have* no account."

"You won't take it?"

"That leaves me more free," said Pemberton.

"To poison my darling's mind?" groaned Mrs. Moreen.

"Oh your darling's mind—!" the young man laughed.

She fixed him a moment, and he thought she was going to break out tormentedly, pleadingly: "For God's sake, tell me what *is* in it!" But she checked this impulse —another was stronger. She pocketed the money—the crudity of the alternative was comical—and swept out of the room with the desperate concession: "You may tell him any horror you like!"

VI

A couple of days after this, during which he had failed to profit by so free a permission, he had been for a quarter of an hour walking with his charge in silence when the boy became sociable again with the remark: "I'll tell you how I know it; I know it through Zénobie."

"Zénobie? Who in the world is *she?*"

"A nurse I used to have—ever so many years ago. A charming woman. I liked her awfully, and she liked me."

"There's no accounting for tastes. What is it you know through her?"

"Why what their idea is. She went away because they

didn't fork out. She did like me awfully, and she stayed two years. She told me all about it—that at last she could never get her wages. As soon as they saw how much she liked me they stopped giving her anything. They thought she'd stay for nothing—just *because*, don't you know?" And Morgan had a queer little conscious lucid look. "She did stay ever so long—as long as she could. She was only a poor girl. She used to send money to her mother. At last she couldn't afford it any longer, and went away in a fearful rage one night—I mean of course in a rage against *them*. She cried over me tremendously, she hugged me nearly to death. She told me all about it," the boy repeated. "She told me it was their idea. So I guessed, ever so long ago, that they have had the same idea with you."

"Zénobie was very sharp," said Pemberton. "And she made you so."

"Oh that wasn't Zénobie; that was nature. And experience!" Morgan laughed.

"Well, Zénobie was a part of your experience."

"Certainly I was a part of hers, poor dear!" the boy wisely sighed. "And I'm part of yours."

"A very important part. But I don't see how you know I've been treated like Zénobie."

"Do you take me for the biggest dunce you've known?" Morgan asked. "Haven't I been conscious of what we've been through together?"

"What we've been through?"

"Our privations—our dark days."

"Oh our days have been bright enough."

Morgan went on in silence for a moment. Then he said: "My dear chap, you're a hero!"

"Well, you're another!" Pemberton retorted.

"No I'm not, but I ain't a baby. I won't stand it any longer. You must get some occupation that pays. I'm

ashamed, I'm ashamed!" quavered the boy with a ring
of passion, like some high silver note from a small cathedral chorister, that deeply touched his friend.

"We ought to go off and live somewhere together,"
the young man said.

"I'll go like a shot if you'll take me."

"I'd get some work that would keep us both afloat,"
Pemberton continued.

"So would I. Why shouldn't *I* work? I ain't such a
beastly little muff as *that* comes to."

"The difficulty is that your parents wouldn't hear of
it. They'd never part with you; they worship the ground
you tread on. Don't you see the proof of it?" Pemberton
developed. "They don't dislike me; they wish me no
harm; they're very amiable people; but they're perfectly
ready to expose me to any awkwardness in life for your
sake."

The silence in which Morgan received his fond sophis-
try struck Pemberton somehow as expressive. After a
moment the child repeated: "You *are* a hero!" Then he
added: "They leave me with you altogether. You've all
the responsibility. They put me off on you from morning
till night. Why then should they object to my taking up
with you completely? I'd help you."

"They're not particularly keen about my being helped,
and they delight in thinking of you as *theirs*. They're
tremendously proud of you."

"I'm not proud of *them*. But you know that," Morgan
returned.

"Except for the little matter we speak of they're
charming people," said Pemberton, not taking up the
point made for his intelligence, but wondering greatly
at the boy's own, and especially at this fresh reminder
of something he had been conscious of from the first—
the strangest thing in his friend's large little composition,

a temper, a sensibility, even a private ideal, which made
him as privately disown the stuff his people were made of.
Morgan had in secret a small loftiness which made
him acute about betrayed meanness; as well as a critical
sense for the manners immediately surrounding him that
was quite without precedent in a juvenile nature, especially when one noted that it had not made this nature
"old-fashioned," as the word is of children—quaint or
wizened or offensive. It was as if he had been a little
gentleman and had paid the penalty by discovering that
he was the only such person in his family. This comparison didn't make him vain, but it could make him melancholy and a trifle austere. While Pemberton guessed at
these dim young things, shadows of shadows, he was
partly drawn on and partly checked, as for a scruple,
by the charm of attempting to sound the little cool shal-
lows that were so quickly growing deeper. When he
tried to figure to himself the morning twilight of childhood, so as to deal with it safely, he saw it was never
fixed, never arrested, that ignorance, at the instant he
touched it, was already flushing faintly into knowledge,
that there was nothing that at a given moment you could
say an intelligent child didn't know. It seemed to him
that he himself knew too much to imagine Morgan's
simplicity and too little to disembroil his tangle.

The boy paid no heed to his last remark; he only went
on: "I'd have spoken to them about their idea, as I call
it, long ago, if I hadn't been sure what they'd say."

"And what would they say?"

"Just what they said about what poor Zénobie told
me—that it was a horrid dreadful story, that they had
paid her every penny they owed her."

"Well, perhaps they had," said Pemberton.

"Perhaps they've paid you!"

"Let us pretend they have, and *n'en parlons plus*."

"They accused her of lying and cheating"—Morgan stuck to historic truth. "That's why I don't want to speak to them."

"Lest they should accuse me too?" To this Morgan made no answer, and his companion, looking down at him—the boy turned away his eyes, which had filled —saw that he couldn't have trusted himself to utter. "You're right. Don't worry them," Pemberton pursued. "Except for that, they *are* charming people."

"Except for *their* lying and *their* cheating?"

"I say—I say!" cried Pemberton, imitating a little tone of the lad's which was itself an imitation.

"We must be frank, at the last; we *must* come to an understanding," said Morgan with the importance of the small boy who lets himself think he is arranging great affairs—almost playing at shipwreck or at Indians. "I know all about everything."

"I dare say your father has his reasons," Pemberton replied, but too vaguely, as he was aware.

"For lying and cheating?"

"For saving and managing and turning his means to the best account. He has plenty to do with his money. You're an expensive family."

"Yes, I'm very expensive," Morgan concurred in a manner that made his preceptor burst out laughing.

"He's saving for *you*," said Pemberton. "They think of you in everything they do."

"He might, while he's about it, save a little—" The boy paused, and his friend waited to hear what. Then Morgan brought out oddly: "A little reputation."

"Oh there's plenty of that. That's all right!"

"Enough of it for the people they know, no doubt. The people they know are awful."

"Do you mean the princes? We mustn't abuse the princes."

"Why not? They haven't married Paula—they haven't married Amy. They only clean out Ulick."

"You *do* know everything!" Pemberton declared.

"No I don't after all. I don't know what they live on, or how they live, or *why* they live! What have they got and how did they get it? Are they rich, are they poor, or have they a *modeste aisance*? Why are they always chiveying me about—living one year like ambassadors and the next like paupers? Who are they, anyway, and what are they? I've thought of all that—I've thought of a lot of things. They're so beastly worldly. That's what I hate most—oh I've *seen* it! All they care about is to make an appearance and to pass for something or other. What the dickens do they want to pass for? What *do* they, Mr. Pemberton?"

"You pause for a reply," said Pemberton, treating the question as a joke, yet wondering too and greatly struck with his mate's intense if imperfect vision. "I haven't the least idea."

"And what good does it do? Haven't I seen the way people treat them—the 'nice' people, the ones they want to know? They'll take anything from them—they'll lie down and be trampled on. The nice ones hate that—they just sicken them. You're the only really nice person we know."

"Are you sure? They don't lie down for me!"

"Well, you shan't lie down for them. You've got to go —that's what you've got to do," said Morgan.

"And what will become of you?"

"Oh I'm growing up. I shall get off before long. I'll see you later."

"You had better let me finish you," Pemberton urged. lending himself to the child's strange superiority.

Morgan stopped in their walk, looking up at him. He had to look up much less than a couple of years before

—he had grown, in his loose leanness, so long and high. "Finish me?" he echoed.

"There are such a lot of jolly things we can do together yet. I want to turn you out—I want you to do me credit."

Morgan continued to look at him. "To give you credit —do you mean?"

"My dear fellow, you're too clever to live."

"That's just what I'm afraid you think. No, no; it isn't fair—I can't endure it. We'll separate next week. The sooner it's over the sooner to sleep."

"If I hear of anything—any other chance—I promise to go," Pemberton said.

Morgan consented to consider this. "But you'll be honest," he demanded; "you won't pretend you haven't heard?"

"I'm much more likely to pretend I have."

"But what can you hear of, this way, stuck in a hole with us? You ought to be on the spot, to go to England —you ought to go to America."

"One would think you were *my* tutor!" said Pemberton.

Morgan walked on and after a little had begun again: "Well, now that you know I know and that we look at the facts and keep nothing back—it's much more comfortable, isn't it?"

"My dear boy, it's so amusing, so interesting, that it will surely be quite impossible for me to forego such hours as these."

This made Morgan stop once more. "You *do* keep something back. Oh you're not straight—*I* am!"

"How am I not straight?"

"Oh you've got your idea!"

"My idea?"

"Why that I probably shan't make old—make older
—bones, and that you can stick it out till I'm removed."

"You *are* too clever to live!" Pemberton repeated.

"I call it a mean idea," Morgan pursued. "But I shall
punish you by the way I hang on."

"Look out or I'll poison you!" Pemberton laughed.

"I'm stronger and better every year. Haven't you
noticed that there hasn't been a doctor near me since
you came?"

"*I'm* your doctor," said the young man, taking his arm
and drawing him tenderly on again.

Morgan proceeded and after a few steps gave a sigh
of mingled weariness and relief. "Ah now that we look
at the facts it's all right!"

VII

They looked at the facts a good deal after this; and one
of the first consequences of their doing so was that Pemberton stuck it out, in his friend's parlance, for the purpose. Morgan made the facts so vivid and so droll, and
at the same time so bald and so ugly, that there was
fascination in talking them over with him, just as there
would have been heartlessness in leaving him alone with
them. Now that the pair had such perceptions in common it was useless for them to pretend they didn't judge
such people; but the very judgement and the exchange
of perceptions created another tie. Morgan had never
been so interesting as now that he himself was made
plainer by the sidelight of these confidences. What came
out in it most was the small fine passion of his pride.
He had plenty of that, Pemberton felt—so much that
one might perhaps wisely wish for it some early bruises.
He would have liked his people to have a spirit and
had waked up to the sense of their perpetually eating

humble-pie. His mother would consume any amount, and his father would consume even more than his mother. He had a theory that Ulick had wriggled out of an "affair" at Nice: there had once been a flurry at home, a regular panic, after which they all went to bed and took medicine, not to be accounted for on any other supposition. Morgan had a romantic imagination, fed by poetry and history, and he would have liked those who "bore his name"—as he used to say to Pemberton with the humour that made his queer delicacies manly—to carry themselves with an air. But their one idea was to get in with people who didn't want them and to take snubs as if they were honourable scars. Why people didn't want them more he didn't know—that was people's own affair; after all they weren't superficially repulsive, they were a hundred times cleverer than most of the dreary grandees, the "poor swells" they rushed about Europe to catch up with. "After all they *are* amusing—they are!" he used to pronounce with the wisdom of the ages. To which Pemberton always replied: "Amusing—the great Moreen troupe? Why they're altogether delightful; and if it weren't for the hitch that you and I (feeble performers!) make in the *ensemble* they'd carry everything before them."

What the boy couldn't get over was the fact that this particular blight seemed, in a tradition of self-respect, so undeserved and so arbitrary. No doubt people had a right to take the line they liked; but why should *his* people have liked the line of pushing and toadying and lying and cheating? What had their forefathers—all decent folk, so far as he knew—done to them, or what had *he* done to them? Who had poisoned their blood with the fifth-rate social ideal, the fixed idea of making smart acquaintances and getting into the *monde chic,* especially when it was foredoomed to failure and exposure? They showed so what they were after; that was what made the people they wanted not want *them*. And never a wince for dignity, never a throb of shame at looking each other in the face, never any independence or resentment or disgust. If his father or his brother would only knock some one down once or twice a year! Clever as they were they never guessed the impression they made. They were good-natured, yes—as good-natured as Jews at the doors of clothing-shops! But was that the model one wanted one's family to follow? Morgan had dim memories of an old grandfather, the maternal, in New York, whom he had been taken across the ocean at the age of five to see: a gentleman with a high neck-cloth and a good deal of pronunciation, who wore a dress-coat in the morning, which made 'one wonder what he wore in the evening, and had, or was supposed to have, "property" and something to do with the Bible Society. It couldn't have been but that *he* was a good type. Pemberton himself remembered Mrs. Clancy, a widowed sister of Mr. Moreen's, who was as irritating as a moral tale and had paid a fortnight's visit to the family at Nice shortly after he came to live with them. She was "pure and refined," as Amy said over the banjo, and had the air of not knowing what they meant when they talked, and of keeping something rather important back. Pemberton judged that what she kept back was an approval of many of their ways; therefore it was to be supposed that she too was of a good type, and that Mr. and Mrs. Moreen and Ulick and Paula and Amy might easily have been of a better one if they would.

But that they wouldn't was more and more perceptible from day to day. They continued to "chivey," as Morgan called it, and in due time became aware of a variety of reasons for proceeding to Venice. They mentioned a great many of them—they were always strikingly frank and had the brightest friendly chatter, at the late foreign breakfast in especial, before the ladies had made up their faces, when they leaned their arms on the table, had something to follow the *demi-tasse,* and, in the heat of familiar discussion as to what they "really ought" to do, fell inevitably into the languages in which they could *tutoyer.* Even Pemberton liked them then; he could endure even Ulick when he heard him give his little flat voice for the "sweet sea-city." That was what made him have a sneaking kindness for them—that they were so out of the workaday world and kept him so out of it. The summer had waned when, with cries of ecstasy, they all passed out on the balcony that overhung the Grand Canal. The sunsets then were splendid and the Dorringtons had arrived. The Dorringtons were the only reason they hadn't talked of at breakfast; but the reasons they didn't talk of at breakfast always came out in the end. The Dorringtons on the other hand came out very little; or else when they did they stayed—as was natural—for hours, during which periods Mrs. Moreen and the girls sometimes called at their hotel (to see if they had returned) as many as three times running. The gondola was for the ladies, as in Venice too there were "days," which Mrs. Moreen knew in their order an hour after she arrived. She immediately took one herself, to which the Dorringtons never came, though on a certain occasion when Pemberton and his pupil were together at Saint Mark's—where, taking the best walks they had ever had and haunting a hundred churches, they spent a great deal of time—they saw the old lord turn up with Mr. Moreen and Ulick, who showed him the dim basilica as if it belonged to them. Pemberton noted how much less, among its curiosities, Lord Dorrington carried himself as a man of the world; wondering too whether, for such services, his companions took a fee from him. The

autumn at any rate waned, the Dorringtons departed,
and Lord Verschoyle, the eldest son, had proposed neither for Amy nor for Paula.

One sad November day, while the wind roared round
the old palace and the rain lashed the lagoon, Pemberton, for exercise and even somewhat for warmth—the
Moreens were horribly frugal about fires; it was a cause
of suffering to their inmate—walked up and down the
big bare *sala* with his pupil. The scagliola floor was cold,
the high battered casements shook in the storm, and the
stately decay of the place was unrelieved by a particle
of furniture. Pemberton's spirits were low, and it came
over him that the fortune of the Moreens was now even
lower. A blast of desolation, a portent of disgrace and
disaster, seemed to draw through the comfortless hall.
Mr. Moreen and Ulick were in the Piazza, looking out
for something, strolling drearily, in mackintoshes, under
the arcades; but still, in spite of mackintoshes, unmistakeable men of the world. Paula and Amy were in bed—it
might have been thought they were staying there to
keep warm. Pemberton looked askance at the boy at his
side, to see to what extent he was conscious of these
dark omens. But Morgan, luckily for him, was now mainly
conscious of growing taller and stronger and indeed of
being in his fifteenth year. This fact was intensely interesting to him and the basis of a private theory—which,
however, he had imparted to his tutor—that in a little
while he should stand on his own feet. He considered
that the situation would change—that in short he
should be "finished," grown up, producible in the world
of affairs and ready to prove himself of sterling ability.
Sharply as he was capable at times of analysing, as he
called it, his life, there were happy hours when he remained, as he also called it—and as the name, really,
of their right ideal—"jolly" superficial; the proof of

which was his fundamental assumption that he should presently go to Oxford, to Pemberton's college, and aided and abetted by Pemberton, do the most wonderful things. It depressed the young man to see how little in such a project he took account of ways and means: in other connexions he mostly kept to the measure. Pemberton tried to imagine the Moreens at Oxford and fortunately failed; yet unless they were to adopt it as a residence there would be no *modus vivendi* for Morgan. How could he live without an allowance, and where was the allowance to come from? He, Pemberton, might live on Morgan; but how could Morgan live on *him?* What was to become of him anyhow? Somehow the fact that he was a big boy now, with better prospects of health, made the question of his future more difficult. So long as he was markedly frail the great consideration he inspired seemed enough of an answer to it. But at the bottom of Pemberton's heart was the recognition of his probably being strong enough to live and not yet strong enough to struggle or to thrive. Morgan himself at any rate was in the first flush of the rosiest consciousness of adolescence, so that the beating of the tempest seemed to him after all but the voice of life and the challenge of fate. He had on his shabby little overcoat, with the collar up, but was enjoying his walk.

It was interrupted at last by the appearance of his mother at the end of the *sala*. She beckoned him to come to her, and while Pemberton saw him, complaisant, pass down the long vista and over the damp false marble, he wondered what was in the air. Mrs. Moreen said a word to the boy and made him go into the room she had quitted. Then, having closed the door after him, she directed her steps swiftly to Pemberton. There *was* something in the air, but his wildest flight of fancy wouldn't have suggested what it proved to be. She

signified that she had made a pretext to get Morgan out
of the way, and then she enquired—without hesitation
—if the young man could favour her with the loan of
three louis. While, before bursting into a laugh, he
stared at her with surprise, she declared that she was
awfully pressed for the money; she was desperate for
it—it would save her life.

"Dear lady, *c'est trop fort!*" Pemberton laughed in the
manner and with the borrowed grace of idiom that
marked the best colloquial, the best anecdotic, moments
of his friends themselves. "Where in the world do you
suppose I should get three louis, *du train dont vous
allez?*"

"I thought you worked—wrote things. Don't they
pay you?"

"Not a penny."

"Are you such a fool as to work for nothing?"

"You ought surely to know that."

Mrs. Moreen stared, then she coloured a little. Pemberton saw she had quite forgotten the terms—if
"terms" they could be called—that he had ended by
accepting from herself; they had burdened her memory
as little as her conscience. "Oh yes, I see what you mean
—you've been very nice about that; but why drag it in
so often?" She had been perfectly urbane with him ever
since the rough scene of explanation in his room the
morning he made her accept *his* "terms"—the necessity
of his making his case known to Morgan. She had felt no
resentment after seeing there was no danger Morgan
would take the matter up with her. Indeed, attributing
this immunity to the good taste of his influence with the
boy, she had once said to Pemberton "My dear fellow,
it's an immense comfort you're a gentleman." She repeated this in substance now. "Of course you're a gentleman—that's a bother the less!" Pemberton reminded

her that he had not "dragged in" anything that wasn't already in as much as his foot was in his shoe; and she also repeated her prayer that, somewhere and somehow, he would find her sixty francs. He took the liberty of hinting that if he could find them it wouldn't be to lend them to *her*—as to which he consciously did himself injustice, knowing that if he had them he would certainly put them at her disposal. He accused himself, at bottom and not unveraciously, of a fantastic, a demoralised sympathy with her. If misery made strange bed-fellows it also made strange sympathies. It was moreover a part of the abasement of living with such people that one had to make vulgar retorts, quite out of one's own tradition of good manners. "Morgan, Morgan, to what pass have I come for you?" he groaned while Mrs. Moreen floated voluminously down the *sala* again to liberate the boy, wailing as she went that everything was too odious.

Before their young friend was liberated there came a thump at the door communicating with the staircase, followed by the apparition of a dripping youth who poked in his head. Pemberton recognised him as the bearer of a telegram and recognised the telegram as addressed to himself. Morgan came back as, after glancing at the signature—that of a relative in London—he was reading the words: "Found jolly job for you, engagement to coach opulent youth on own terms. Come at once." The answer happily was paid and the messenger waited. Morgan, who had drawn near, waited too and looked hard at Pemberton; and Pemberton, after a moment, having met his look, handed him the telegram. It was really by wise looks—they knew each other so well now —that, while the telegraph-boy, in his waterproof cape, made a great puddle on the floor, the thing was settled between them. Pemberton wrote the answer with a pencil against the frescoed wall, and the messenger departed. When he had gone the young man explained himself.

"I'll make a tremendous charge; I'll earn a lot of money in a short time, and we'll live on it."

"Well, I hope the opulent youth will be a dismal dunce—he probably will," Morgan parenthesised—"and keep you a long time a-hammering of it in."

"Of course the longer he keeps me the more we shall have for our old age."

"But suppose *they* don't pay you!" Morgan awfully suggested.

"Oh there are not two such—!" But Pemberton pulled up; he had been on the point of using too invidious a term. Instead of this he said "Two such fatalities."

Morgan flushed—the tears came to his eyes. "*Dites toujours* two such rascally crews!" Then in a different tone he added: "Happy opulent youth!"

"Not if he's a dismal dunce."

"Oh they're happier then. But you can't have everything, can you?" the boy smiled.

Pemberton held him fast, hands on his shoulders—he had never loved him so. "What will become of *you*, what will you do?" He thought of Mrs. Moreen, desperate for sixty francs.

"I shall become an *homme fait*." And then as if he recognised all the bearings of Pemberton's allusion: "I shall get on with them better when you're not here."

"Ah don't say that—it sounds as if I set you against them!"

"You do—the sight of you. It's all right; you know what I mean. I shall be beautiful. I'll take their affairs in hand; I'll marry my sisters."

"You'll marry yourself!" joked Pemberton; as high, rather tense pleasantry would evidently be the right, or the safest, tone for their separation.

It was, however, not purely in this strain that Morgan suddenly asked: "But I say—how will you get to your jolly job? You'll have to telegraph to the opulent youth for money to come on."

Pemberton bethought himself. "They won't like that, will they?"

"Oh look out for them!"

Then Pemberton brought out his remedy. "I'll go to the American Consul; I'll borrow some money of him—just for the few days, on the strength of the telegram."

Morgan was hilarious. "Show him the telegram—then collar the money and stay!"

Pemberton entered into the joke sufficiently to reply that for Morgan he was really capable of that; but the boy, growing more serious, and to prove he hadn't meant what he said, not only hurried him off to the Consulate—since he was to start that evening, as he had wired to his friend—but made sure of their affair by going with him. They splashed through the tortuous perforations and over the humpbacked bridges, and they passed through the Piazza, where they saw Mr. Moreen and Ulick go into a jeweller's shop. The Consul proved accommodating—Pemberton said it wasn't the letter, but Morgan's grand air—and on their way back they went into Saint Mark's for a hushed ten minutes. Later they took up and kept up the fun of it to the very end; and it seemed to Pemberton a part of that fun that Mrs. Moreen, who was very angry when he had announced her his intention, should charge him, grotesquely and vulgarly and in reference to the loan she had vainly endeavoured to effect, with bolting lest they should "get something out" of him. On the other hand he had to do Mr. Moreen and Ulick the justice to recognise that when on coming in *they* heard the cruel news they took it like perfect men of the world.

VIII

When he got at work with the opulent youth, who was to be taken in hand for Balliol, he found himself unable to say if this aspirant had really such poor parts or if the appearance were only begotten of his own long association with an intensely living little mind. From Morgan he heard half a dozen times: the boy wrote charming young letters, a patchwork of tongues, with indulgent postscripts in the family Volapuk and, in little squares and rounds and crannies of the text, the drollest illustrations—letters that he was divided between the impulse to show his present charge as a vain, a wasted incentive, and the sense of something in them that publicity would profane. The opulent youth went up in due course and failed to pass; but it seemed to add to the presumption that brilliancy was not expected of him all at once that his parents, condoning the lapse, which they goodnaturedly treated as little as possible as if it were Pemberton's, should have sounded the rally again, begged the young coach to renew the siege.

The young coach was now in a position to lend Mrs. Moreen three louis, and he sent her a post-office order even for a larger amount. In return for his favour he received a frantic scribbled line from her: "Implore you to come back instantly—Morgan dreadfully ill." They were on the rebound, once more in Paris—often as Pemberton had seen them depressed he had never seen them crushed—and communication was therefore rapid. He wrote to the boy to ascertain the state of his health, but awaited the answer in vain. He accordingly, after three days, took an abrupt leave of the opulent youth and, crossing the Channel, alighted at the small hotel, in the quarter of the Champs Élysées, of which Mrs. Moreen had given him the address. A deep if dumb dissatisfaction with this lady and her companions bore him company: they couldn't be vulgarly honest, but they could live at hotels, in velvety *entresols,* amid a smell of burnt pastilles, surrounded by the most expensive city in Europe. When he had left them in Venice it was with an irrepressible suspicion that something was going to happen; but the only thing that could have taken place was again their masterly retreat. "How is he? where is he?" he asked of Mrs. Moreen; but before she could speak these questions were answered by the pressure round his neck of a pair of arms, in shrunken sleeves, which still were perfectly capable of an effusive young foreign squeeze.

"Dreadfully ill—I don't see it!" the young man cried. And then to Morgan: "Why on earth didn't you relieve me? Why didn't you answer my letter?"

Mrs. Moreen declared that when she wrote he was very bad, and Pemberton learned at the same time from the boy that he had answered every letter he had received. This led to the clear inference that Pemberton's note had been kept from him so that the game to be practised should not be interfered with. Mrs. Moreen was prepared to see the fact exposed, as Pemberton saw the moment he faced her that she was prepared for a good many other things. She was prepared above all to maintain that she had acted from a sense of duty, that she was enchanted she had got him over, whatever they might say, and that it was useless of him to pretend he didn't know in all his bones that his place at such a time was with Morgan. He had taken the boy away from them and now had no right to abandon him. He had created for himself the gravest responsibilities and must at least abide by what he had done.

"Taken him away from you?" Pemberton exclaimed indignantly.

"Do it—do it for pity's sake; that's just what I want. I can't stand *this*—and such scenes. They're awful frauds—poor dears!" These words broke from Morgan, who had intermitted his embrace, in a key which made Pemberton turn quickly to him and see that he had suddenly seated himself, was breathing in great pain and was very pale.

"*Now* do you say he's not in a state, my precious pet?" shouted his mother, dropping on her knees before him with clasped hands, but touching him no more than if he had been a gilded idol. "It will pass—it's only for an instant; but don't say such dreadful things!"

"I'm all right—all right," Morgan panted to Pemberton, whom he sat looking up at with a strange smile, his hands resting on either side of the sofa.

"Now do you pretend I've been dishonest, that I've deceived?" Mrs. Moreen flashed at Pemberton as she got up.

"It isn't *he* says it, it's I!" the boy returned, apparently easier but sinking back against the wall; while his restored friend, who had sat down beside him, took his hand and bent over him.

"Darling child, one does what one can; there are so many things to consider," urged Mrs. Moreen. "It's his *place*—his only place. You see *you* think it is now."

"Take me away—take me away," Morgan went on, smiling to Pemberton with his white face.

"Where shall I take you, and how—oh *how*, my boy?" the young man stammered, thinking of the rude way in which his friends in London held that, for his convenience, with no assurance of prompt return, he had thrown them over; of the just resentment with which they would already have called in a successor, and of the scant help to finding fresh employment that resided for him in the grossness of his having failed to pass his pupil.

"Oh we'll settle that. You used to talk about it," said Morgan. "If we can only go all the rest's a detail."

"Talk about it as much as you like, but don't think you can attempt it. Mr. Moreen would never consent— it would be so *very* hand-to-mouth," Pemberton's hostess beautifully explained to him. Then to Morgan she made it clearer: "It would destroy our peace, it would break our hearts. Now that he's back it will be all the same again. You'll have your life, your work and your freedom, and we'll all be happy as we used to be. You'll bloom and grow perfectly well, and we won't have any more silly experiments, will we? They're too absurd. It's Mr. Pemberton's place—every one in his place. You in yours, your papa in his, me in mine— *n'est-ce pas, chéri?* We'll all forget how foolish we've been and have lovely times."

She continued to talk and to surge vaguely about the little draped stuffy salon while Pemberton sat with the boy, whose colour gradually came back; and she mixed up her reasons, hinting that there were going to be changes, that the other children might scatter (who knew?—Paula had her ideas) and that then it might be fancied how much the poor old parent-birds would want the little nestling. Morgan looked at Pemberton, who wouldn't let him move; and Pemberton knew exactly how he felt at hearing himself called a little nestling. He admitted that he had had one or two bad days, but he protested afresh against the wrong of his mother's having made them the ground of an appeal to poor Pemberton. Poor Pemberton could laugh now,

apart from the comicality of Mrs. Moreen's mustering
so much philosophy for her defence—she seemed to
shake it out of her agitated petticoats, which knocked
over the light gilt chairs—so little did their young companion, *marked*, unmistakeably marked at the best,
strike him as qualified to repudiate any advantage.

He himself was in for it at any rate. He should have
Morgan on his hands again indefinitely; though indeed
he saw the lad had a private theory to produce which
would be intended to smooth this down. He was obliged
to him for it in advance; but the suggested amend-
ment didn't keep his heart rather from sinking, any
more than it prevented him from accepting the prospect
on the spot, with some confidence moreover that he
should do even better if he could have a little supper.
Mrs. Moreen threw out more hints about the changes
that were to be looked for, but she was such a mixture
of smiles and shudders—she confessed she was very
nervous—that he couldn't tell if she were in high feather
or only in hysterics. If the family was really at last going to pieces why shouldn't she recognise the necessity
of pitching Morgan into some sort of lifeboat? This presumption was fostered by the fact that they were established in luxurious quarters in the capital of pleasure;
that was exactly where they naturally *would* be established in view of going to pieces. Moreover didn't she
mention that Mr. Moreen and the others were enjoying
themselves at the opera with Mr. Granger, and wasn't
that also precisely where one would look for them on
the eve of a smash? Pemberton gathered that Mr.
Granger was a rich vacant American—a big bill with a
flourishy heading and no items; so that one of Paula's
"ideas" was probably that this time she hadn't missed
fire—by which straight shot indeed she would have
shattered the general cohesion. And if the cohesion was

to crumble what would become of poor Pemberton? He
felt quite enough bound up with them to figure to his
alarm as a dislodged block in the edifice.

It was Morgan who eventually asked if no supper had
been ordered for him; sitting with him below, later, at
the dim delayed meal, in the presence of a great deal of
corded green plush, a plate of ornamental biscuit and an
aloofness marked on the part of the waiter. Mrs. Moreen
had explained that they had been obliged to secure a
room for the visitor out of the house; and Morgan's consolation—he offered it while Pemberton reflected on the
nastiness of luke-warm sauces—proved to be, largely,
that this circumstance would facilitate their escape. He
talked of their escape—recurring to it often afterwards
—as if they were making up a "boy's book" together.
But he likewise expressed his sense that there was something in the air, that the Moreens couldn't keep it up
much longer. In point of fact, as Pemberton was to see,
they kept it up for five or six months. All the while,
however, Morgan's contention was designed to cheer
him. Mr. Moreen and Ulick, whom he had met the day
after his return, accepted that return like perfect men
of the world. If Paula and Amy treated it even with less
formality an allowance was to be made for them, inasmuch as Mr. Granger hadn't come to the opera after all.
He had only placed his box at their service, with a bouquet for each of the party; there was even one apiece,
embittering the thought of his profusion, for Mr. Moreen
and Ulick. "They're all like that," was Morgan's comment; "at the very last, just when we think we've landed
them they're back in the deep sea!"

Morgan's comments in these days were more and
more free; they even included a large recognition of
the extraordinary tenderness with which he had been
treated while Pemberton was away. Oh yes, they

couldn't do enough to be nice to him, to show him they
had him on their mind and make up for his loss. That
was just what made the whole thing so sad and caused
him to rejoice after all in Pemberton's return—he had
to keep thinking of their affection less, had less sense of
obligation. Pemberton laughed out at this last reason,
and Morgan blushed and said "Well, dash it, you know
what I mean." Pemberton knew perfectly what he
meant; but there were a good many things that—dash
it too!—it didn't make any clearer. This episode of his
second sojourn in Paris stretched itself out wearily, with
their resumed readings and wanderings and maunder-
ings, their potterings on the quays, their hauntings of
the museums, their occasional lingerings in the Palais
Royal when the first sharp weather came on and there
was a comfort in warm emanations, before Chevet's wonderful succulent window. Morgan wanted to hear all
about the opulent youth—he took an immense interest
in him. Some of the details of his opulence—Pemberton could spare him none of them—evidently fed the
boy's appreciation of all his friend had given up to come
back to him; but in addition to the greater reciprocity
established by that heroism he had always his little
brooding theory, in which there was a frivolous gaiety
too, that their long probation was drawing to a close.
Morgan's conviction that the Moreens couldn't go on
much longer kept pace with the unexpended impetus
with which, from month to month, they did go on.
Three weeks after Pemberton had rejoined them they
went on to another hotel, a dingier one than the first;
but Morgan rejoiced that his tutor had at least still
not sacrificed the advantage of a room outside. He clung
to the romantic utility of this when the day, or rather
the night, should arrive for their escape.

For the first time, in this complicated connexion, our

friend felt his collar gall him. It was, as he had said to
Mrs. Moreen in Venice, *trop fort*—everything was *trop
fort*. He could neither really throw off his blighting burden nor find in it the benefit of a pacified conscience or
of a rewarded affection. He had spent all the money ac-
cruing to him in England, and he saw his youth going
and that he was getting nothing back for it. It was all
very well of Morgan to count it for reparation that he
should now settle on him permanently—there was an
irritating flaw in such a view. He saw what the boy had
in his mind; the conception that as his friend had had
the generosity to come back he must show his gratitude by giving him his life. But the poor friend didn't
desire the gift—what could he do with Morgan's dreadful little life? Of course at the same time that Pemberton
was irritated he remembered the reason, which was very
honourable to Morgan and which dwelt simply in his
making one so forget that he was no more than a patched
urchin. If one dealt with him on a different basis one's
misadventures were one's own fault. So Pemberton
waited in a queer confusion of yearning and alarm for
the catastrophe which was held to hang over the house
of Moreen, of which he certainly at moments felt the
symptoms brush his cheek and as to which he wondered much in what form it would find its liveliest effect.

Perhaps it would take the form of sudden dispersal—
a frightened *sauve qui peut,* a scuttling into selfish corners. Certainly they were less elastic than of yore; they
were evidently looking for something they didn't find.
The Dorringtons hadn't re-appeared, the princes had
scattered; wasn't that the beginning of the end? Mrs.
Moreen had lost her reckoning of the famous "days";
her social calendar was blurred—it had turned its face
to the wall. Pemberton suspected that the great, the
cruel discomfiture had been the unspeakable behaviour

of Mr. Granger, who seemed not to know what he
wanted, or, what was much worse, what *they* wanted.
He kept sending flowers, as if to bestrew the path of his
retreat, which was never the path of a return. Flowers
were all very well, but—Pemberton could complete the
proposition. It was now positively conspicuous that in
the long run the Moreens were a social failure; so that
the young man was almost grateful the run had not been
short. Mr. Moreen indeed was still occasionally able to
get away on business and, what was more surprising,
was likewise able to get back. Ulick had no club, but
you couldn't have discovered it from his appearance,
which was as much as ever that of a person looking at
life from the window of such an institution; therefore
Pemberton was doubly surprised at an answer he once
heard him make his mother in the desperate tone of a
man familiar with the worst privations. Her question
Pemberton had not quite caught; it appeared to be an
appeal for a suggestion as to whom they might get to
take Amy. "Let the Devil take her!" Ulick snapped; so
that Pemberton could see that they had not only lost
their amiability but had ceased to believe in themselves.
He could also see that if Mrs. Moreen was trying to get
people to take her children she might be regarded as
closing the hatches for the storm. But Morgan would be
the last she would part with.

One winter afternoon—it was a Sunday—he and the
boy walked far together in the Bois de Boulogne. The
evening was so splendid, the cold lemon-coloured sunset so clear, the stream of carriages and pedestrians so
amusing and the fascination of Paris so great, that they
stayed out later than usual and became aware that they
should have to hurry home to arrive in time for dinner.
They hurried accordingly, arm-in-arm, good-humoured
and hungry, agreeing that there was nothing like Paris

after all and that after everything too that had come and gone they were not yet sated with innocent pleasures. When they reached the hotel they found that, though scandalously late, they were in time for all the dinner they were likely to sit down to. Confusion reigned in the apartments of the Moreens—very shabby ones this time, but the best in the house—and before the interrupted service of the table, with objects displaced almost as if there had been a scuffle and a great wine-stain from an overturned bottle, Pemberton couldn't blink the fact that there had been a scene of the last proprietary firmness. The storm had come—they were all seeking refuge. The hatches were down, Paula and Amy were invisible—they had never tried the most casual art upon Pemberton, but he felt they had enough of an eye to him not to wish to meet him as young ladies whose frocks had been confiscated—and Ulick appeared to have jumped overboard. The host and his staff, in a word, had ceased to "go on" at the pace of their guests, and the air of embarrassed detention, thanks to a pile of gaping trunks in the passage, was strangely commingled with the air of indignant withdrawal.

When Morgan took all this in—and he took it in very quickly—he coloured to the roots of his hair. He had walked from his infancy among difficulties and dangers, but he had never seen a public exposure. Pemberton noticed in a second glance at him that the tears had rushed into his eyes and that they were tears of a new and untasted bitterness. He wondered an instant, for the boy's sake, whether he might successfully pretend not to understand. Not successfully, he felt, as Mr. and Mrs. Moreen, dinnerless by their extinguished hearth, rose before him in their little dishonoured salon, casting about with glassy eyes for the nearest port in such a storm. They were not prostrate but were horribly white, and Mrs. Moreen had evidently been crying. Pemberton quickly learned however that her grief was not for the loss of her dinner, much as she usually enjoyed it, but the fruit of a blow that struck even deeper, as she made all haste to explain. He would see for himself, so far as that went, how the great change had come, the dreadful bolt had fallen, and how they would now all have to turn themselves about. Therefore cruel as it was to them to part with their darling she must look to him to carry a little further the influence he had so fortunately acquired with the boy—to induce his young charge to follow him into some modest retreat. They depended on him—that was the fact—to take their delightful child temporarily under his protection: it would leave Mr. Moreen and herself so much more free to give the proper attention (too little, alas! had been given) to the readjustment of their affairs.

"We trust you—we feel we *can*," said Mrs. Moreen, slowly rubbing her plump white hands and looking with compunction hard at Morgan, whose chin, not to take liberties, her husband stroked with a tentative paternal forefinger.

"Oh yes—we feel that we *can*. We trust Mr. Pemberton fully, Morgan," Mr. Moreen pursued.

Pemberton wondered again if he might pretend not to understand; but everything good gave way to the intensity of Morgan's understanding. "Do you mean he may take me to live with him for ever and ever?" cried the boy. "May take me away, away, anywhere he likes?"

"For ever and ever? *Comme vous-y-allez!*" Mr. Moreen laughed indulgently. "For as long as Mr. Pemberton may be so good."

"We've struggled, we've suffered," his wife went on;

"but you've made him so your own that we've already been through the worst of the sacrifice."

Morgan had turned away from his father—he stood looking at Pemberton with a light in his face. His sense of shame for their common humiliated state had dropped; the case had another side—the thing was to clutch at *that*. He had a moment of boyish joy, scarcely mitigated by the reflexion that with this unexpected consecration of his hope—too sudden and too violent; the turn taken was away from a *good* boy's book—the "escape" was left on their hands. The boyish joy was there an instant, and Pemberton was almost scared at the rush of gratitude and affection that broke through his first abasement. When he stammered "My dear fellow, what do you say to *that*?" how could one not say something enthusiastic? But there was more need for courage at something else that immediately followed and that made the lad sit down quickly on the nearest chair. He had turned quite livid and had raised his hand to his left side. They were all three looking at him, but Mrs. Moreen suddenly bounded forward. "Ah his darling little heart!" she broke out; and this time, on her knees before him and without respect for the idol, she caught him ardently in her arms. "You walked him too far, you hurried him too fast!" she hurled over her shoulder at Pemberton. Her son made no protest, and the next instant, still holding him, she sprang up with her face convulsed and with the terrified cry "Help, help! he's going, he's gone!" Pemberton saw with equal horror, by Morgan's own stricken face, that he was beyond their wildest recall. He pulled him half out of his mother's hands, and for a moment, while they held him together, they looked all their dismay into each other's eyes. "He couldn't stand it with his weak organ," said

Pemberton—"the shock, the whole scene, the violent emotion."

"But I thought he *wanted* to go to you!" wailed Mrs. Moreen.

"I *told* you he didn't, my dear," her husband made answer. Mr. Moreen was trembling all over and was in his way as deeply affected as his wife. But after the very first he took his bereavement as a man of the world.

1891

What kind of story is it?

* Do the ghosts truly appear or are they hallucinations?

THE TURN OF THE SCREW

The story had held us, round the fire, sufficiently breathless, but except the obvious remark that it was gruesome, as on Christmas Eve in an old house a strange tale should essentially be, I remember no comment uttered till somebody happened to note it as the only case he had met in which such a visitation had fallen on a child. The case, I may mention, was that of an apparition in just such an old house as had gathered us for the occasion—an appearance, of a dreadful kind, to a little boy sleeping in the room with his mother and waking her up in the terror of it; waking her not to dissipate his dread and soothe him to sleep again, but to encounter also herself, before she had succeeded in doing so, the same sight that had shocked him. It was this observation that drew from Douglas—not immediately, but later in the evening—a reply that had the interesting consequence to which I call attention. Some one else told a story not particularly effective, which I saw he was not following. This I took for a sign that he had himself something to produce and that we should only have to wait. We waited in fact till two nights later; but that same evening, before we scattered, he brought out what was in his mind.

"I quite agree—in regard to Griffin's ghost, or whatever it was—that its appearing first to the little boy, at so tender an age, adds a particular touch. But it's not the first occurrence of its charming kind that I know to have been concerned with a child. If the child gives the effect another turn of the screw, what do you say to two children—?"

"We say of course," somebody exclaimed, "that two children give two turns! Also that we want to hear about them."

I can see Douglas there before the fire, to which he had got up to present his back, looking down at this converser with his hands in his pockets. "Nobody but me, till now, has ever heard. It's quite too horrible." This was naturally declared by several voices to give the thing the utmost price, and our friend, with quiet art, prepared his triumph by turning his eyes over the rest of us and going on: "It's beyond everything. Nothing at all that I know touches it."

"For sheer terror?" I remember asking.

He seemed to say it wasn't so simple as that; to be really at a loss how to qualify it. He passed his hand over his eyes, made a little wincing grimace. "For dreadful—dreadfulness!"

"Oh how delicious!" cried one of the women.

He took no notice of her; he looked at me, but as if, instead of me, he saw what he spoke of. "For general uncanny ugliness and horror and pain."

"Well then," I said, "just sit right down and begin."

He turned round to the fire, gave a kick to a log,

watched it an instant. Then as he faced us again: "I can't begin. I shall have to send to town." There was a unanimous groan at this, and much reproach; after which, in his preoccupied way, he explained. "The story's written. It's in a locked drawer—it has not been out for years. I could write to my man and enclose the key; he could send down the packet as he finds it." It was to me in particular that he appeared to propound this—appeared almost to appeal for aid not to hesitate. He had broken a thickness of ice, the formation of many a winter; had had his reasons for a long silence. The others resented postponement, but it was just his scruples that charmed me. I adjured him to write by the first post and to agree with us for an early hearing; then I asked him if the experience in question had been his own. To this his answer was prompt. "Oh thank God, no!"

"And is the record yours? You took the thing down?"

"Nothing but the impression. I took that _here_"—he tapped his heart. "I've never lost it."

"Then your manuscript—?"

"Is in old faded ink and in the most beautiful hand." He hung fire again. "A woman's. She has been dead these twenty years. She sent me the pages in question before she died." They were all listening now, and of course there was somebody to be arch, or at any rate to draw the inference. But if he put the inference by without a smile it was also without irritation. "She was a most charming person, but she was ten years older than I. She was my sister's governess," he quietly said. "She was the most agreeable woman I've ever known in her position; she'd have been worthy of any whatever. It was long ago, and this episode was long before. I was at Trinity, and I found her at home on my coming down the second summer. I was much there that year—it was a beautiful one; and we had, in her off-hours, some strolls and talks in the garden—talks in which she struck me as awfully clever and nice. Oh yes; don't grin: I liked her extremely and am glad to this day to think she liked me too. If she hadn't she wouldn't have told me. She had never told any one. It wasn't simply that she said so, but that I knew she hadn't. I was sure; I could see. You'll easily judge why when you hear."

"Because the thing had been such a scare?"

He continued to fix me. "You'll easily judge," he repeated: "*you* will."

I fixed him too. "I see. She was in love."

He laughed for the first time. "You *are* acute. Yes, she was in love. That is she *had* been. That came out—she couldn't tell her story without its coming out. I saw it, and she saw it; but neither of us spoke of it. I remember the time and the place—the corner of the lawn, the shade of the great beeches and the long hot summer afternoon. It wasn't a scene for a shudder; but oh—!" He quitted the fire and dropped back into his chair.

"You'll receive the packet Thursday morning?" I said.

"Probably not till the second post."

"Well then; after dinner—"

"You'll all meet me here?" He looked us round again. "Isn't anybody going?" It was almost the tone of hope.

"Everybody will stay!"

"*I* will—and *I* will!" cried the ladies whose departure had been fixed. Mrs. Griffin, however, expressed the need for a little more light. "Who was it she was in love with?"

"The story will tell," I took upon myself to reply.

"Oh I can't wait for the story!"

"The story *won't* tell," said Douglas; "not in any literal vulgar way."

"More's the pity then. That's the only way I ever understand."

"Won't *you* tell, Douglas?" somebody else enquired.

He sprang to his feet again. "Yes—to-morrow. Now I must go to bed. Good-night." And, quickly catching up a candlestick, he left us slightly bewildered. From our end of the great brown hall we heard his step on the stair; whereupon Mrs. Griffin spoke. "Well, if I don't know who she was in love with I know who *he* was."

"She was ten years older," said her husband.

"*Raison de plus*—at that age! But it's rather nice, his long reticence."

"Forty years!" Griffin put in.

"With this outbreak at last."

"The outbreak," I returned, "will make a tremendous occasion of Thursday night"; and every one so agreed with me that in the light of it we lost all attention for everything else. The last story, however incomplete and like the mere opening of a serial, had been told; we handshook and "candlestuck," as somebody said, and went to bed.

I knew the next day that a letter containing the key had, by the first post, gone off to his London apartments; but in spite of—or perhaps just on account of— the eventual diffusion of this knowledge we quite let him alone till after dinner, till such an hour of the evening in fact as might best accord with the kind of emotion on which our hopes were fixed. Then he became as communicative as we could desire, and indeed gave us his best reason for being so. We had it from him again before the fire in the hall, as we had had our mild wonders of the previous night. It appeared that the narrative he had promised to read us really required for a proper intelligence a few words of prologue. Let me say here distinctly, to have done with it, that this narrative, from an exact transcript of my own made much later, is what I shall presently give. Poor Douglas, before his death—when it was in sight—committed to me the manuscript that reached him on the third of these days and that, on the same spot, with immense effect, he began to read to our hushed little circle on the night of the fourth. The departing ladies who had said they would stay didn't, of course, thank heaven, stay: they departed, in consequence of arrangements made, in a rage of curiosity, as they professed, produced by the touches with which he had already worked us up. But that only made his little final auditory more compact and select, kept it, round the hearth, subject to a common thrill.

The first of these touches conveyed that the written statement took up the tale at a point after it had, in a manner, begun. The fact to be in possession of was therefore that his old friend, the youngest of several daughters of a poor country parson, had at the age of twenty, on taking service for the first time in the schoolroom, come up to London, in trepidation, to answer in person an advertisement that had already placed her in brief correspondence with the advertiser. This person proved, on her presenting herself for judgment at a house in Harley Street that impressed her as vast and imposing—this prospective patron proved a gentleman, a bachelor in the prime of life, such a figure as had never risen, save in a dream or an old novel, before a fluttered anxious girl out of Hampshire vicarage. One could easily fix his type; it never, happily, dies out. He was handsome and bold and pleasant, off-hand and gay and kind. He struck her, inevitably, as gallant and splendid, but what took her most of all and gave her the courage she afterwards showed was that he put the whole thing to her as a favour, an obligation he should gratefully incur. She figured him as rich, but as fearfully extravagant—saw him all in a glow of high fashion, of good looks, of expensive habits, of charming ways with women. He had for his town residence a big house filled with the spoils of travel and the trophies of the chase; but it was to his country home, an old family place in Essex, that he wished her immediately to proceed.

He had been left, by the death of his parents in India, guardian to a small nephew and a small niece, children of a younger, a military brother whom he had lost two years before. These children were, by the strangest of chances for a man in his position—a lone man without the right sort of experience or a grain of patience—very heavy on his hands. It had all been a great worry and, on his own part doubtless, a series of blunders, but he immensely pitied the poor chicks and had done all he could; had in particular sent them down to his other house, the proper place for them being of course the country, and kept them there from the first with the best people he could find to look after them, parting even with his own servants to wait on them and going down himself, whenever he might, to see how they were doing. The awkward thing was that they had practically no other relations and that his own affairs took up all his time. He had put them in possession of Bly, which was healthy and secure, and had placed at the head of their little establishment—but belowstairs only—an excellent woman, Mrs. Grose, whom he was sure his visitor would like and who had formerly been maid to his mother. She was now housekeeper and was also acting for the time as superintendent to the little girl, of whom, without children of her own, she was by good luck extremely fond. There were plenty of people to help, but of course the young lady who

should go down as governess would be in supreme
authority. She would also have, in holidays, to look after the small boy, who had been for a term at school—
young as he was to be sent, but what else could be
done?—and who, as the holidays were about to begin,
would be back from one day to the other. There had
been for the two children at first a young lady whom
they had had the misfortune to lose. She had done for
them quite beautifully—she was a most respectable
person—till her death, the great awkwardness of which
had, precisely, left no alternative but the school for little Miles. Mrs. Grose, since then, in the way of manners and things, had done as she could for Flora; and
there were, further, a cook, a housemaid, a dairywoman,
an old pony, an old groom and an old gardener, all likewise thoroughly respectable.

So far had Douglas presented his picture when some
one put a question. "And what did the former governess die of? Of so much respectability?"

Our friend's answer was prompt. "That will come
out. I don't anticipate."

"Pardon me—I thought that was just what you *are*
doing."

"In her successor's place," I suggested, "I should
have wished to learn if the office brought with it—"

"Necessary danger to life?" Douglas completed my
thought. "She did wish to learn, and she did learn. You
shall hear to-morrow what she learnt. Meanwhile of
course the prospect struck her as slightly grim. She was
young, untried, nervous: it was a vision of serious duties
and little company, of really great loneliness. She hesitated—took a couple of days to consult and consider.
But the salary offered much exceeded her modest
measure, and on a second interview she faced the music, she engaged." And Douglas, with this, made a

pause that, for the benefit of the company, moved me to throw in—

"The moral of which was of course the seduction exercised by the splendid young man. She succumbed to it."

He got up and, as he had done the night before, went to the fire, gave a stir to a log with his foot, then stood a moment with his back to us. "She saw him only twice."

"Yes, but that's just the beauty of her passion."

A little to my surprise, on this, Douglas turned round to me. "It *was* the beauty of it. There were others," he went on, "who hadn't succumbed. He told her frankly all his difficulty—that for several applicants the conditions had been prohibitive. They were somehow simply afraid. It sounded dull—it sounded strange; and all the more so because of his main condition."

"Which was—?"

"That she should never trouble him—but never, never: neither appeal nor complain nor write about anything; only meet all questions herself, receive all moneys from his solicitor, take the whole thing over and let him alone. She promised to do this, and she mentioned to me that when, for a moment, disburdened, delighted, he held her hand, thanking her for the sacrifice, she already felt rewarded."

"But was that all her reward?" one of the ladies asked.

"She never saw him again."

"Oh!" said the lady; which, as our friend immediately again left us, was the only other word of importance contributed to the subject till, the next night, by the corner of the hearth, in the best chair, he opened the faded red cover of a thin old-fashioned gilt-edged album. The whole thing took indeed more nights than one, but on the first occasion the same lady put another question. "What's your title?"

"I haven't one."

"Oh *I* have!" I said. But Douglas, without heeding me, had begun to read with a fine clearness that was like a rendering to the ear of the beauty of his author's hand.

The tale begins

I

I remember the whole beginning as a succession of flights and drops, a little see-saw of the right throbs and the wrong. After rising, in town, to meet his appeal I had at all events a couple of very bad days—found all my doubts bristle again, felt indeed sure I had made a mistake. In this state of mind I spent the long hours of bumping, swinging coach that carried me to the stopping-place at which I was to be met by a vehicle from the house. This convenience, I was told, had been ordered, and I found, toward the close of the June afternoon, a commodious fly in waiting for me. Driving at that hour, on a lovely day, through a country the summer sweetness of which served as a friendly welcome, my fortitude revived and, as we turned into the avenue, took a flight that was probably but a proof of the point to which it had sunk. I suppose I had expected, or had dreaded, something so dreary that what greeted me was a good surprise. I remember as a thoroughly pleasant impression the broad clear front, its open windows and fresh curtains and the pair of maids looking out; I remember the lawn and the bright flowers and the crunch of my wheels on the gravel and the clustered tree-tops over which the rooks circled and cawed in the golden sky. The scene had a greatness that made it a different affair from my own scant home, and there immediately appeared at the door, with a little girl in

her hand, a civil person who dropped me as decent a
curtsey as if I had been the mistress or a distinguished
visitor. I had received in Harley Street a narrower notion of the place, and that, as I recalled it, made me
think the proprietor still more of a gentleman, suggested
that what I was to enjoy might be a matter beyond his
promise.

I had no drop again till the next day, for I was carried triumphantly through the following hours by my
introduction to the younger of my pupils. The little girl
who accompanied Mrs. Grose affected me on the spot
as a creature too charming not to make it a great fortune to have to do with her. She was the most beautiful
child I had ever seen, and I afterwards wondered why
my employer hadn't made more of a point to me of this.
I slept little that night—I was too much excited; and
this astonished me too, I recollect, remained with me,
adding to my sense of the liberality with which I was
treated. The large impressive room, one of the best in
the house, the great state bed, as I almost felt it, the
figured full draperies, the long glasses in which, for the
first time, I could see myself from head to foot, all struck
me—like the wonderful appeal of my small charge—as
so many things thrown in. It was thrown in as well, from
the first moment, that I should get on with Mrs. Grose in
a relation over which, on my way, in the coach, I fear I
had rather brooded. The one appearance indeed that
in this early outlook might have made me shrink again
was that of her being so inordinately glad to see me. I
felt within half an hour that she was so glad—stout
simple plain clean wholesome woman—as to be positively on her guard against showing it too much. I wondered even then a little why she should wish *not* to
show it, and that, with reflexion, with suspicion, might
of course have made me uneasy.

first is suspicion

But it was a comfort that there could be no uneasiness in a connexion with anything so beatific as the radiant image of my little girl, the vision of whose angelic beauty had probably more than anything else to do with the restlessness that, before morning, made me several times rise and wander about my room to take in the whole picture and prospect; to watch from my open window the faint summer dawn, to look at such stretches of the rest of the house as I could catch, and to listen, while in the fading dusk the first birds began to twitter, for the possible recurrence of a sound or two, less natural and not without but within, that I had fancied I heard. There had been a moment when I believed I recognised, faint and far, the cry of a child; there had been another when I found myself just consciously starting as at the passage, before my door, of a light footstep. But these fancies were not marked enough not to be thrown off, and it is only in the light, or the gloom, I should rather say, of other and subsequent matters that they now come back to me. To watch, teach, "form" little Flora would too evidently be the making of a happy and useful life. It had been agreed between us downstairs that after this first occasion I should have her as a matter of course at night, her small white bed being already arranged, to that end, in my room. What I had undertaken was the whole care of her, and she had remained just this last time with Mrs. Grose only as an effect of our consideration for my inevitable strangeness and her natural timidity. In spite of this timidity— which the child herself, in the oddest way in the world, had been perfectly frank and brave about, allowing it, without a sign of uncomfortable consciousness, with the deep sweet serenity indeed of one of Raphael's holy infants, to be discussed, to be imputed to her and to determine us—I felt quite sure she would presently like me. It was part of what I already liked Mrs. Grose herself for, the pleasure I could see her feel in my admiration and wonder as I sat at supper with four tall candles and with my pupil, in a high chair and a bib, brightly facing me between them over bread and milk. There were naturally things that in Flora's presence could pass between us only as prodigious and gratified looks, obscure and round-about allusions.

"And the little boy—does he look like her? Is he too so very remarkable?"

One wouldn't, it was already conveyed between us, too grossly flatter a child. "Oh Miss, *most* remarkable. If you think well of this one!"—and she stood there with a plate in her hand, beaming at our companion, who looked from one of us to the other with placid heavenly eyes that contained nothing to check us.

"Yes; if I do—?"

"You *will* be carried away by the little gentleman!"

"Well, that, I think, is what I came for—to be carried away. I'm afraid, however," I remember feeling the impulse to add, "I'm rather easily carried away. I was carried away in London!"

I can still see Mrs. Grose's broad face as she took this in. "In Harley Street?"

"In Harley Street."

"Well, Miss, you're not the first—and you won't be the last."

"Oh I've no pretensions," I could laugh, "to being the only one. My other pupil, at any rate, as I understand, comes back to-morrow?"

"Not to-morrow—Friday, Miss. He arrives, as you did, by the coach, under care of the guard, and is to be met by the same carriage."

I forthwith wanted to know if the proper as well as the pleasant and friendly thing wouldn't therefore be that on the arrival of the public conveyance I should await him with his little sister; a proposition to which Mrs. Grose assented so heartily that I somehow took her manner as a kind of comforting pledge—never falsified, thank heaven!—that we should on every question be quite at one. Oh she was glad I was there!

What I felt the next day was, I suppose, nothing that could be fairly called a reaction from the cheer of my arrival; it was probably at the most only a slight oppression produced by a fuller measure of the scale, as I walked round them, gazed up at them, took them in, of my new circumstances. They had, as it were, an extent and mass for which I had not been prepared and in the presence of which I found myself, freshly, a little scared not less than a little proud. Regular lessons, in this agitation, certainly suffered some wrong; I reflected that my first duty was, by the gentlest arts I could contrive, to win the child into the sense of knowing me. I spent the day with her out of doors; I arranged with her, to her great satisfaction, that it should be she, she only, who might show me the place. She showed it step by step and room by room and secret by secret, with droll delightful childish talk about it and with the result, in half an hour, of our becoming tremendous friends. Young as she was I was struck, throughout our little tour, with her confidence and courage, with the way, in empty chambers and dull corridors, on crooked staircases that made me pause and even on the summit of an old machicolated square tower that made me dizzy, her morning music, her disposition to tell me so many more things than she asked, rang out and led me on. I have not seen Bly since the day I left it, and I dare say that to my present older and more informed eyes it would show a very reduced importance. But as my little conductress, with her hair of gold and her frock of blue, danced before me round corners and pattered down passages, I had the view of a castle of romance inhabited by a rosy sprite, such a place as would somehow, for diversion of the young idea, take all colour out of story-books and fairy-tales. Wasn't it just a story-book over which I had fallen a-doze and a-dream? No; it was a big ugly antique but convenient house, embodying a few features of a building still older, half-displaced and half-utilised, in which I had the fancy of our being almost as lost as a handful of passengers in a great drifting ship. Well, I was strangely at the helm!

II

This came home to me when, two days later, I drove over with Flora to meet, as Mrs. Grose said, the little gentleman; and all the more for an incident that, presenting itself the second evening, had deeply disconcerted me. The first day had been, on the whole, as I have expressed, reassuring; but I was to see it wind up to a change of note. The postbag that evening—it came late—contained a letter for me which, however, in the hand of my employer, I found to be composed but of a few words enclosing another, addressed to himself, with a seal still unbroken. "This, I recognise, is from the head-master, and the head-master's an awful bore. Read him, please; deal with him; but mind you don't report. Not a word. I'm off!" I broke the seal with a great effort —so great a one that I was a long time coming to it; took the unopened missive at last up to my room and only attacked it just before going to bed. I had better have let it wait till morning, for it gave me a second sleepless night. With no counsel to take, the next day, I was full of distress; and it finally got so the better of me that I determined to open myself at least to Mrs. Grose.

"What does it mean? The child's dismissed his school."

She gave me a look that I remarked at the moment; then, visibly, with a quick blankness, seemed to try to take it back. "But aren't they all—?"

"Sent home—yes. But only for the holidays. Miles may never go back at all."

Consciously, under my attention, she reddened. "They won't take him?"

"They absolutely decline."

At this she raised her eyes, which she had turned from me; I saw them fill with good tears. "What has he done?"

I cast about; then I judged best simply to hand her my document—which, however, had the effect of making her, without taking it, simply put her hands behind her. She shook her head sadly. "Such things are not for me, Miss."

My counsellor couldn't read! I winced at my mistake, which I attenuated as I could, and opened the letter again to repeat it to her; then, faltering in the act and folding it up once more, I put it back in my pocket. "Is he really *bad?*"

The tears were still in her eyes. "Do the gentlemen say so?"

"They go into no particulars. They simply express their regret that it should be impossible to keep him. That can have but one meaning." Mrs. Grose listened with dumb emotion; she forbore to ask me what this meaning might be; so that, presently, to put the thing with some coherence and with the mere aid of her presence to my own mind, I went on: "That he's an injury to the others."

At this, with one of the quick turns of simple folk,

she suddenly flamed up. "Master Miles!—*him* an injury?"

There was such a flood of good faith in it that, though I had not yet seen the child, my very fears made me jump to the absurdity of the idea. I found myself, to meet my friend the better, offering it, on the spot, sarcastically. "To his poor little innocent mates!"

"It's too dreadful," cried Mrs. Grose, "to say such cruel things! Why he's scarce ten years old."—

"Yes, yes; it would be incredible."

She was evidently grateful for such a profession. "See him, Miss, first. *Then* believe it!" I felt forthwith a new impatience to see him; it was the beginning of a curiosity that, all the next hours, was to deepen almost to pain. Mrs. Grose was aware, I could judge, of what she had produced in me, and she followed it up with assurance. "You might as well believe it of the little lady. Bless her," she added the next moment—"*look* at her!"

I turned and saw that Flora, whom, ten minutes before, I had established in the schoolroom with a sheet of white paper, a pencil and a copy of nice "round O's," now presented herself to view at the open door. She expressed in her little way an extraordinary detachment from disagreeable duties, looking at me, however, with a great childish light that seemed to offer it as a mere result of the affection she had conceived for my person, which had rendered necessary that she should follow me. I needed nothing more than this to feel the full force of Mrs. Grose's comparison, and, catching my pupil in my arms, covered her with kisses in which there was a sob of atonement.

None the less, the rest of the day, I watched for further occasion to approach my colleague, especially as, toward evening, I began to fancy she rather sought to avoid me. I overtook her, I remember, on the staircase;

we went down together and at the bottom I detained her, holding her there with a hand on her arm. "I take what you said to me at noon as a declaration that *you've* never known him to be bad."

She threw back her head; she had clearly by this time, and very honestly, adopted an attitude. "Oh never known him—I don't pretend *that!*"

I was upset again. "Then you *have* known him—?"

"Yes indeed, Miss, thank God!"

On reflexion I accepted this. "You mean that a boy who never is—?"

"Is no boy for *me!*"

I held her tighter. "You like them with the spirit to be naughty?" Then, keeping pace with her answer, "So do I!" I eagerly brought out. "But not to the degree to contaminate—"

"To contaminate?"—my big word left her at a loss.

I explained it. "To corrupt."

She stared, taking my meaning in; but it produced in her an odd laugh. "Are you afraid he'll corrupt *you?*" She put the question with such a fine bold humour that with a laugh, a little silly doubtless, to match her own, I gave way for the time to the apprehension of ridicule.

But the next day, as the hour for my drive approached, I cropped up in another place. "What was the lady who was here before?"

"The last governess? She was also young and pretty —almost as young and almost as pretty, Miss, even as you."

"Ah then I hope her youth and her beauty helped her!" I recollect throwing off. "He seems to like us young and pretty!"

"Oh he *did*," Mrs. Grose assented: "it was the way he liked every one!" She had no sooner spoken indeed than she caught herself up. "I mean that's *his* way—the master's."

I was struck. "But of whom did you speak first?"

She looked blank, but she coloured. "Why of *him*."

"Of the master?"

"Of who else?"

There was so obviously no one else that the next moment I had lost my impression of her having accidentally said more than she meant; and I merely asked what I wanted to know. "Did *she* see anything in the boy—?"

"That wasn't right? She never told me."

I had a scruple, but I overcame it. "Was she careful—particular?"

Mrs. Grose appeared to try to be conscientious. "About some things—yes."

"But not about all?"

Again she considered. "Well, Miss—she's gone. I won't tell tales."

"I quite understand your feeling," I hastened to reply; but I thought it after an instant not opposed to this concession to pursue: "Did she die here?"

"No—she went off."

I don't know what there was in this brevity of Mrs. Grose's that struck me as ambiguous. "Went off to die?" Mrs. Grose looked straight out of the window, but I felt that, hypothetically, I had a right to know what young persons engaged for Bly were expected to do. "She was taken ill, you mean, and went home?"

"She was not taken ill, so far as appeared, in this house. She left it, at the end of the year, to go home, as she said, for a short holiday, to which the time she had put in had certainly given her a right. We had then a young woman—a nursemaid who had stayed on and who was a good girl and clever; and *she* took the children altogether for the interval. But our young lady never came back, and at the very moment I was ex-

interdict: to prohibit or forbid, esp. by official sanction. A prohibition.

pecting her I heard from the master that she was dead."

I turned this over. "But of what?"

"He never told me! But please, Miss," said Mrs. Grose, "I must get to my work."

III

Her thus turning her back on me was fortunately not, for my just preoccupations, a snub that could check the growth of our mutual esteem. We met, after I had brought little Miles, more intimately than ever on the ground of my stupefaction, my general emotion: so monstrous was I then ready to pronounce it that such a child as had now been revealed to me should be under an interdict. I was a little late on the scene of his arrival, and I felt, as he stood wistfully looking out for me before the door of the inn at which the coach had put him down, that I had seen him on the instant, without and within, in the great glow of freshness, the same positive fragrance of purity, in which I had from the first moment seen his little sister. He was incredibly beautiful, and Mrs. Grose had put her finger on it: everything but a sort of passion of tenderness for him was swept away by his presence. What I then and there took him to my heart for was something divine that I have never found to the same degree in any child—his indescribable little air of knowing nothing in the world but love. It would have been impossible to carry a bad name with a greater sweetness of innocence, and by the time I had got back to Bly with him I remained merely bewildered —so far, that is, as I was not outraged—by the sense of the horrible letter locked up in one of the drawers of my room. As soon as I could compass a private word with Mrs. Grose I declared to her that it was grotesque.

She promptly understood me. "You mean the cruel charge—?"

"It doesn't live an instant. My dear woman, *look* at him!"

She smiled at my pretension to have discovered his charm. "I assure you, Miss, I do nothing else! What will you say then?" she immediately added.

"In answer to the letter?" I had made up my mind. "Nothing at all."

"And to his uncle?"

I was incisive. "Nothing at all."

"And to the boy himself?"

I was wonderful. "Nothing at all."

She gave with her apron a great wipe to her mouth. "Then I'll stand by you. We'll see it out."

"We'll see it out!" I ardently echoed, giving her my hand to make it a vow.

She held me there a moment, then whisked up her apron again with her detached hand. "Would you mind, Miss, if I used the freedom—"

"To kiss me? No!" I took the good creature in my arms and after we had embraced like sisters felt still more fortified and indignant.

This at all events was for the time: a time so full that as I recall the way it went it reminds me of all the art I now need to make it a little distinct. What I look back at with amazement is the situation I accepted. I had undertaken, with my companion, to see it out, and I was under a charm apparently that could smooth away the extent and the far and difficult connexions of such an effort. I was lifted aloft on a great wave of infatuation and pity. I found it simple, in my ignorance, my confusion and perhaps my conceit, to assume that I could deal with a boy whose education for the world was all on the point of beginning. I am unable even to remember at this day what proposal I framed for the end of his holidays and the resumption of his studies. Lessons with me indeed, that charming summer, we all had a theory that he was to have; but I now feel that for weeks the lessons must have been rather my own. I learnt something—at first certainly—that had not been one of the teachings of my small smothered life; learnt to be amused, and even amusing, and not to think for the morrow. It was the first time, in a manner, that I had known space and air and freedom, all the music of summer and all the mystery of nature. And then there was consideration—and consideration was sweet. Oh it was a trap—not designed but deep—to my imagination, to my delicacy, perhaps to my vanity; to whatever in me was most excitable. The best way to picture it all is to say that I was off my guard. They gave me so little trouble—they were of a gentleness so extraordinary. I used to speculate—but even this with a dim disconnectedness—as to how the rough future (for all futures are rough!) would handle them and might bruise them. They had the bloom of health and happiness; and yet, as if I had been in charge of a pair of little grandees, of princes of the blood, for whom everything, to be right, would have to be fenced about and ordered and arranged, the only form that in my fancy the after-years could take for them was that of a romantic, a really royal extension of the garden and the park. It may be of course above all that what suddenly broke into this gives the previous time a charm of stillness—that hush in which something gathers or crouches. The change was actually like the spring of a beast.

In the first weeks the days were long; they often, at their finest, gave me what I used to call my own hour, the hour when, for my pupils, tea-time and bed-time having come and gone, I had before my final retirement a small interval alone. Much as I liked my companions this hour was the thing in the day I liked most; and I liked it best of all when, as the light faded—or rather, I should say, the day lingered and the last calls of the last birds sounded, in a flushed sky, from the old trees—I could take a turn into the grounds and enjoy, almost with a sense of property that amused and flattered me, the beauty and dignity of the place. It was a pleasure at these moments to feel myself tranquil and justified; doubtless perhaps also to reflect that by my discretion, my quiet good sense and general high propriety, I was giving pleasure—if he ever thought of it!—to the person to whose pressure I had yielded. What I was doing was what he had earnestly hoped and directly asked of me, and that I *could*, after all, do it proved even a greater joy than I had expected. I dare say I fancied myself in short a remarkable young woman and took comfort in the faith that this would more publicly appear. Well, I needed to be remarkable to offer a front to the remarkable things that presently gave their first sign.

It was plump, one afternoon, in the middle of my very hour: the children were tucked away and I had come out for my stroll. One of the thoughts that, as I don't in the least shrink now from noting, used to be with me in these wanderings was that it would be as charming as a charming story suddenly to meet some one. Some one would appear there at the turn of a path and would stand before me and smile and approve. I didn't ask more than that—I only asked that he should *know*; and the only way to be sure he knew would be to see it, and the kind light of it, in his handsome face. That was exactly present to me—by which I mean the face was—when, on the first of these occasions, at the end of a long June day, I stopped short

on emerging from one of the plantations and coming
into view of the house. What arrested me on the spot
—and with a shock much greater than any vision had
allowed for—was the sense that my imagination had,
in a flash, turned real. He did stand there!—but high
up, beyond the lawn and at the very top of the tower
to which, on that first morning, little Flora had conducted me. This tower was one of a pair—square incongruous crenellated structures—that were distinguished, for some reason, though I could see little difference, as the new and the old. They flanked opposite
ends of the house and were probably architectural absurdities, redeemed in a measure indeed by not being
wholly disengaged nor of a height too pretentious,
dating, in their gingerbread antiquity, from a romantic
revival that was already a respectable past. I admired
them, had fancies about them, for we could all profit
in a degree, especially when they loomed through the
dusk, by the grandeur of their actual battlements; yet
it was not at such an elevation that the figure I had so
often invoked seemed most in place.

It produced in me, this figure, in the clear twilight,
I remember, two distinct gasps of emotion, which were,
sharply, the shock of my first and that of my second surprise. My second was a violent perception of the mistake of my first: the man who met my eyes was not the
person I had precipitately supposed. There came to me
thus a bewilderment of vision of which, after these
years, there is no living view that I can hope to give.
An unknown man in a lonely place is a permitted object of fear to a young woman privately bred; and the
figure that faced me was—a few more seconds assured
me—as little any one else I knew as it was the image
that had been in my mind. I had not seen it in Harley
Street—I had not seen it anywhere. The place more-

over, in the strangest way in the world, had on the instant and by the very fact of its appearance become a solitude. To me at least, making my statement here with a deliberation with which I have never made it, the whole feeling of the moment returns. It was as if, while I took in what I did take in, all the rest of the scene had been stricken with death. I can hear again, as I write, the intense hush in which the sounds of evening dropped. The rooks stopped cawing in the golden sky and the friendly hour lost for the unspeakable minute all its voice. But there was no other change in nature, unless indeed it were a change that I saw with a stranger sharpness. The gold was still in the sky, the clearness in the air, and the man who looked at me over the battlements was as definite as a picture in a frame. That's how I thought, with extraordinary quickness, of each person he might have been and that he wasn't. We were confronted across our distance quite long enough for me to ask myself with intensity who then he was and to feel, as an effect of my inability to say, a wonder that in a few seconds more became intense.

The great question, or one of these, is afterwards, I know, with regard to certain matters, the question of how long they have lasted. Well, this matter of mine, think what you will of it, lasted while I caught at a dozen possibilities, none of which made a difference for the better, that I could see, in there having been in the house—and for how long, above all?—a person of whom I was in ignorance. It lasted while I just bridled a little with the sense of how my office seemed to require that there should be no such ignorance and no such person. It lasted while this visitant, at all events —and there was a touch of the strange freedom, as I remember, in the sign of familiarity of his wearing no hat—seemed to fix me, from his position, with just the question, just the scrutiny through the fading light, that his own presence provoked. We were too far apart to call to each other, but there was a moment at which, at shorter range, some challenge between us, breaking the hush, would have been the right result of our straight mutual stare. He was in one of the angles, the one away from the house, very erect, as it struck me, and with both hands on the ledge. So I saw him as I see the letters I form on this page; then, exactly, after a minute, as if to add to the spectacle, he slowly changed his place—passed, looking at me hard all the while, to the opposite corner of the platform. Yes, it was intense to me that during this transit he never took his eyes from me, and I can see at this moment the way his hand, as he went, moved from one of the crenellations to the next. He stopped at the other corner, but less long, and even as he turned away still markedly fixed me. He turned away; that was all I knew.

It was not that I didn't wait, on this occasion, for more, since I was as deeply rooted as shaken. Was there a "secret" at Bly—a mystery of Udolpho or an insane, an unmentionable relative kept in unsuspected confinement? I can't say how long I turned it over, or how long, in a confusion of curiosity and dread, I remained where I had had my collision; I only recall that when I re-entered the house darkness had quite closed in. Agitation, in the interval, certainly had held me and driven me, for I must, in circling about the place, have walked three miles; but I was to be later on so much more overwhelmed that this mere dawn of alarm was a comparatively human chill. The most singular part of

it in fact—singular as the rest had been—was the part
I became, in the hall, aware of in meeting Mrs. Grose.
This picture comes back to me in the general train—
the impression, as I received it on my return, of the
wide white panelled space, bright in the lamplight and
with its portraits and red carpet, and of the good surprised look of my friend, which immediately told me
she had missed me. It came to me straightway, under
her contact, that, with plain heartiness, mere relieved
anxiety at my appearance, she knew nothing whatever
that could bear upon the incident I had there ready
for her. I had not suspected in advance that her comfortable face would pull me up, and I somehow measured the importance of what I had seen by my thus
finding myself hesitate to mention it. Scarce anything in
the whole history seems to me so odd as this fact that
my real beginning of fear was one, as I may say, with
the instinct of sparing my companion. On the spot, accordingly, in the pleasant hall and with her eyes on me,
I, for a reason that I couldn't then have phrased,
achieved an inward revolution—offered a vague pretext for my lateness and, with the plea of the beauty of
the night and of the heavy dew and wet feet, went
as soon as possible to my room.

Here it was another affair; here, for many days after,
it was a queer affair enough. There were hours,
from day to day—or at least there were moments,
snatched even from clear duties—when I had to shut
myself up to think. It wasn't so much yet that I was
more nervous than I could bear to be as that I was remarkably afraid of becoming so; for the truth I had
now to turn over was simply and clearly the truth that
I could arrive at no account whatever of the visitor
with whom I had been so inexplicably and yet, as it
seemed to me, so intimately concerned. It took me little

time to see that I might easily sound, without forms of enquiry and without exciting remark, any domestic complication. The shock I had suffered must have sharpened all my senses; I felt sure, at the end of three days and as the result of mere closer attention, that I had not been practised upon by the servants nor made the object of any "game." Of whatever it was that I knew nothing was known around me. There was but one sane inference: some one had taken a liberty rather monstrous. That was what, repeatedly, I dipped into my room and locked the door to say to myself. We had been, collectively, subject to an intrusion; some unscrupulous traveller, curious in old houses, had made his way in unobserved, enjoyed the prospect from the best point of view and then stolen out as he came. If he had given me such a bold hard stare, that was but a part of his indiscretion. The good thing, after all, was that we should surely see no more of him.

This was not so good a thing, I admit, as not to leave me to judge that what, essentially, made nothing else much signify was simply my charming work. My charming work was just my life with Miles and Flora, and through nothing could I so like it as through feeling that to throw myself into it was to throw myself out of my trouble. The attraction of my small charges was a constant joy, leading me to wonder afresh at the vanity of my original fears, the distaste I had begun by entertaining for the probable grey prose of my office. There was to be no grey prose, it appeared, and no long grind; so how could work not be charming that presented itself as daily beauty? It was all the romance of the nursery and the poetry of the schoolroom. I don't mean by this of course that we studied only fiction and verse; I mean that I can express no otherwise the sort of interest my companions inspired. How can I describe that except by saying that instead of growing deadly used to them—and it's a marvel for a governess: I call the sisterhood to witness!—I made constant fresh discoveries. There was one direction, assuredly, in which these discoveries stopped: deep obscurity continued to cover the region of the boy's conduct at school. It had been promptly given me, I have noted, to face that mystery without a pang. Perhaps even it would be nearer the truth to say that—without a word—he himself had cleared it up. He had made the whole charge absurd. My conclusion bloomed there with the real rose-flush of his innocence: he was only too fine and fair for the little horrid unclean school-world, and he had paid a price for it. I reflected acutely that the sense of such individual differences, such superiorities of quality, always, on the part of the majority—which could include even stupid sordid head-masters—turns infallibly to the vindictive.

Both the children had a gentleness—it was their only fault, and it never made Miles a muff—that kept them (how shall I express it?) almost impersonal and certainly quite unpunishable. They were like those cherubs of the anecdote who had—morally at any rate —nothing to whack! I remember feeling with Miles in especial as if he had had, as it were, nothing to call even an infinitesimal history. We expect of a small child scant enough "antecedents," but there was in this beautiful little boy something extraordinarily sensitive, yet extraordinarily happy, that, more than in any creature of his age I have seen, struck me as beginning anew each day. He had never for a second suffered. I took this as a direct disproof of his having really been chastised. If he had been wicked he would have "caught" it, and I should have caught it by the rebound—I should have found the trace, should have felt the wound and the dishonour. I could reconstitute nothing at all, and he was therefore an angel. He never spoke of his school, never mentioned a comrade or a master; and I, for my part, was quite too much disgusted to allude to them. Of course I was under the spell, and the wonderful part is that, even at the time, I perfectly knew I was. But I gave myself up to it; it was an antidote to any pain, and I had more pains than one. I was in receipt in these days of disturbing letters from home, where things were not going well. But with this joy of my children what things in the world mattered? That was the question I used to put to my scrappy retirements. I was dazzled by their loveliness.

There was a Sunday—to get on—when it rained with such force and for so many hours that there could be no procession to church; in consequence of which, as the day declined, I had arranged with Mrs. Grose that, should the evening show improvement, we would attend together the late service. The rain happily stopped, and I prepared for our walk, which, through the park and by the good road to the village, would be a matter of twenty minutes. Coming downstairs to meet my colleague in the hall, I remembered a pair of gloves that had required three stitches and that had received them —with a publicity perhaps not edifying—while I sat with the children at their tea, served on Sundays, by exception, in that cold clean temple of mahogany and brass, the "grown-up" dining-room. The gloves had been dropped there, and I turned in to recover them. The day was grey enough, but the afternoon light still lingered, and it enabled me, on crossing the threshold, not only to recognise, on a chair near the wide window, then closed, the articles I wanted, but to become aware of a person on the other side of the window and looking straight in. One step into the room had sufficed; my vision was instantaneous; it was all there. The person looking staight in was the person who had already appeared to me. He appeared thus again with I won't say greater distinctness, for that was impossible, but with a nearness that represented a forward stride in our intercourse and made me, as I met him, catch my breath and turn cold. He was the same—he was the same, and seen, this time, as he had been seen before, from the waist up, the window, though the dining-room was on the ground floor, not going down to the terrace on which he stood. His face was close to the glass, yet the effect of this better view was, strangely, just to show me how intense the former had been. He remained but a few seconds—long enough to convince me he also saw and recognised; but it was as if I had been looking at him for years and had known him always. Something, however, happened this time that had not happened before; his stare into my face, through the glass and across the room, was as deep and hard as then, but it quitted me for a moment during which I could still watch it, see it fix successively several other things. On the spot there came to me the added shock of a certitude that it was not for me he had come. He had come for some one else.

The flash of this knowledge—for it was knowledge in the midst of dread—produced in me the most extraordinary effect, starting, as I stood there, a sudden vibration of duty and courage. I say courage because I was beyond all doubt already far gone. I bounded straight out of the door again, reached that of the house, got in an instant upon the drive and, passing along the terrace as fast as I could rush, turned a corner and came full in sight. But it was in sight of nothing now—my visitor had vanished. I stopped, almost dropped, with the real relief of this; but I took in the whole scene—I gave him time to reappear. I call it time, but how long was it? I can't speak to the purpose to-day of the duration of these things. That kind of measure must have left me: they couldn't have lasted as they actually appeared to me to last. The terrace and the whole place, the lawn and the garden beyond it, all I could see of the park, were empty with a great emptiness. There were shrubberies and big trees, but I remember the clear assurance I felt that none of them concealed him. He was there or was not there: not there if I didn't see him. I got hold of this; then, instinctively, instead of returning as I had come, went to the window. It was confusedly present to me that I ought to place myself where he had stood. I did so; I applied my face to the pane and looked, as he had looked, into the room. As if, at this moment, to show me exactly what his range had been, Mrs. Grose, as I had done for himself just before, came in from the hall. With this I had the full image of a repetition of what had already occurred. She saw me as I had seen my own visitant; she pulled up short as I had done; I gave her something of the shock that I had received. She turned white, and this made me ask myself if I had blanched as much. She stared, in short, and retreated just on *my* lines, and I knew she had then passed out and come round to me and that I should presently meet her. I remained where I was, and while I waited I thought of more things than one. But there's only one I take space to mention. I wondered why *she* should be scared.

Oh she let me know as soon as, round the corner of the house, she loomed again into view. "What in the name of goodness is the matter—?" She was now flushed and out of breath.

I said nothing till she came quite near. "With me?" I must have made a wonderful face. "Do I show it?"

"You're as white as a sheet. You look awful."

I considered; I could meet on this, without scruple, any degree of innocence. My need to respect the bloom of Mrs. Grose's had dropped, without a rustle, from my shoulders, and if I wavered for the instant it was not with what I kept back. I put out my hand to her and she took it; I held her hard a little, liking to feel her close to me. There was a kind of support in the shy heave of her surprise. "You came for me for church, of course, but I can't go."

"Has anything happened?"

"Yes. You must know now. Did I look very queer?"

"Through this window? Dreadful!"

"Well," I said, "I've been frightened." Mrs. Grose's eyes expressed plainly that *she* had no wish to be, yet also that she knew too well her place not to be ready to share with me any marked inconvenience. Oh it was quite settled that she *must* share! "Just what you saw from the dining-room a minute ago was the effect of that. What *I* saw—just before—was much worse."

Her hand tightened. "What was it?"

"An extraordinary man. Looking in."

"What extraordinary man?"

"I haven't the least idea."

Mrs. Grose gazed round us in vain. "Then where is he gone?"

"I know still less."

"Have you seen him before?"

"Yes—once. On the old tower."

She could only look at me harder. "Do you mean he's a stranger?"

"Oh very much!"

"Yet you didn't tell me?"

"No—for reasons. But now that you've guessed—"

Mrs. Grose's round eyes encountered this charge. "Ah I haven't guessed!" she said very simply. "How can I if *you* don't imagine?"

"I don't in the very least."

"You've seen him nowhere but on the tower?"

"And on this spot just now."

Mrs. Grose looked round again. "What was he doing on the tower?"

"Only standing there and looking down at me."

She thought a minute. "Was he a gentleman?"

I found I had no need to think. "No." She gazed in deeper wonder. "No."

"Then nobody about the place? Nobody from the village?"

"Nobody—nobody. I didn't tell you, but I made sure."

She breathed a vague relief: this was, oddly, so much to the good. It only went indeed a little way. "But if he isn't a gentleman—"

"What *is* he? He's a horror."

"A horror?"

"He's—God help me if I know *what* he is!"

Mrs. Grose looked round once more; she fixed her eyes on the duskier distance and then, pulling herself together, turned to me with full inconsequence. "It's time we should be at church."

"Oh I'm not fit for church!"

"Won't it do you good?"

"It won't do *them*—!" I nodded at the house.

"The children?"

"I can't leave them now."

"You're afraid—?"

I spoke boldly. "I'm afraid of *him*."

Mrs. Grose's large face showed me, at this, for the first time, the far-away faint glimmer of a consciousness more acute: I somehow made out in it the delayed dawn of an idea I myself had not given her and that was as yet quite obscure to me. It comes back to me that I thought instantly of this as something I could get from her; and I felt it to be connected with the desire she presently showed to know more. "When was it—on the tower?"

"About the middle of the month. At this same hour."

"Almost at dark," said Mrs. Grose.

"Oh no, not nearly. I saw him as I see you."

"Then how did he get in?"

"And how did he get out?" I laughed. "I had no opportunity to ask him! This evening, you see," I pursued, "he has not been able to get in."

"He only peeps?"

"I hope it will be confined to that!" She had now let go my hand; she turned away a little. I waited an instant; then I brought out: "Go to church. Good-bye. I must watch."

Slowly she faced me again. "Do you fear for them?"

We met in another long look. "Don't *you*?" Instead of answering she came nearer to the window and, for a minute, applied her face to the glass. "You see how he could see," I meanwhile went on.

She didn't move. "How long was he here?"

"Till I came out. I came to meet him."

Mrs. Grose at last turned round, and there was still more in her face. "*I* couldn't have come out."

"Neither could I!" I laughed again. "But I did come. I've my duty."

"So have I mine," she replied; after which she added: "What's he like?"

"I've been dying to tell you. But he's like nobody."

"Nobody?" she echoed.

"He has no hat." Then seeing in her face that she already, in this, with a deeper dismay, found a touch of picture, I quickly added stroke to stroke. "He has red hair, very red, close-curling, and a pale face, long in shape, with straight good features and little rather queer whiskers that are as red as his hair. His eyebrows are somehow darker; they look particularly arched and as if they might move a good deal. His eyes are sharp, strange—awfully; but I only know clearly that they're rather small and very fixed. His mouth's wide, and his lips are thin, and except for his little whiskers he's quite clean-shaven. He gives me a sort of sense of looking like an actor."

"An actor!" It was impossible to resemble one less, at least, than Mrs. Grose at that moment.

"I've never seen one, but so I suppose them. He's tall, active, erect," I continued, "but never—no, never! —a gentleman."

My companion's face had blanched as I went on; her round eyes started and her mild mouth gaped. "A gentleman?" she gasped, confounded, stupefied: "a gentleman *he*?"

"You know him then?"

She visibly tried to hold herself. "But he *is* handsome?"

I saw the way to help her. "Remarkably!"

"And dressed—?"

"In somebody's clothes. They're smart, but they're not his own."

She broke into a breathless affirmative groan.

"They're the master's!"

I caught it up. "You *do* know him?"

She faltered but a second. "Quint!" she cried.

"Quint?"

"Peter Quint—his own man, his valet, when he was here!"

"When the master was?"

Gaping still, but meeting me, she pieced it all together. "He never wore his hat, but he did wear— well, there were waistcoats missed! They were both here—last year. Then the master went, and Quint was alone."

I followed, but halting a little. "Alone?"

"Alone with *us.*" Then as from a deeper depth, "In charge," she added.

"And what became of him?"

She hung fire so long that I was still more mystified. "He went too," she brought out at last.

"Went where?"

Her expression, at this, became extraordinary. "God knows where! He died."

"Died?" I almost shrieked.

She seemed fairly to square herself, plant herself more firmly to express the wonder of it. "Yes. Mr. Quint's dead."

VI

It took of course more than that particular passage to place us together in presence of what we had now to live with as we could, my dreadful liability to impressions of the order so vividly exemplified, and my companion's knowledge henceforth—a knowledge half consternation and half compassion—of that liability. There had been this evening, after the revelation that left me for an hour so prostrate—there had been for either of us no attendance on any service but a little service of tears and vows, of prayers and promises, a climax to the series of mutual challenges and pledges that had straightway ensued on our retreating together to the schoolroom and shutting ourselves up there to have everything out. The result of our having everything out was simply to reduce our situation to the last rigour of its elements. She herself had seen nothing, not the shadow of a shadow, and nobody in the house but the governess was in the governess's plight; yet she accepted without directly impugning my sanity the truth as I gave it to her, and ended by showing me on this ground an awestricken tenderness, a deference to my more than questionable privilege, of which the very breath has remained with me as that of the sweetest of human charities.

What was settled between us accordingly that night was that we thought we might bear things together; and I was not even sure that in spite of her exemption it was she who had the best of the burden. I knew at this hour, I think, as well as I knew later, what I was capable of meeting to shelter my pupils; but it took me some time to be wholly sure of what my honest comrade was prepared for to keep terms with so stiff an agreement. I was queer company enough—quite as queer as the company I received; but as I trace over what we went through I see how much common ground we must have found in the one idea that, by good fortune, *could* steady us. It was the idea, the second movement, that led me straight out, as I may say, of the inner chamber of my dread. I could take the air in the court, at least, and there Mrs. Grose could join me. Perfectly can I recall now the particular way strength came to me before we separated for the night. We had gone over and over every feature of what I had seen.

"He was looking for some one else, you say—some

portentous:

one who was not you?"

"He was looking for little Miles." A portentous clearness now possessed me. "*That's* whom he was looking for."

"But how do you know?"

"I know, I know, I know!" My exaltation grew. "And
you know, my dear!"

She didn't deny this, but I required, I felt, not even
so much telling as that. She took it up again in a moment. "What if *he* should see him?"

"Little Miles? That's what he wants!"

She looked immensely scared again. "The child?"

"Heaven forbid! The man. He wants to appear to
them." That he might was an awful conception, and
yet somehow I could keep it at bay; which moreover,
as we lingered there, was what I succeeded in practically proving. I had an absolute certainty that I should
see again what I had already seen, but something within me said that by offering myself bravely as the sole
subject of such experience, by accepting, by inviting,
by surmounting it all, I should serve as an expiatory
victim and guard the tranquillity of the rest of the
household. The children in especial I should thus
fence about and absolutely save. I recall one of the last
things I said that night to Mrs. Grose.

"It does strike me that my pupils have never mentioned—!"

She looked at me hard as I musingly pulled up. "His
having been here and the time they were with him?"

"The time they were with him, and his name, his presence, his history, in any way. They've never alluded
to it."

"Oh the little lady doesn't remember. She never
heard or knew."

"The circumstances of his death?" I thought with

some intensity. "Perhaps not. But Miles would remember—Miles would know."

"Ah don't try him!" broke from Mrs. Grose.

I returned her the look she had given me. "Don't be afraid." I continued to think. "It *is* rather odd."

"That he has never spoken of him?"

"Never by the least reference. And you tell me they were 'great friends.'"

"Oh it wasn't *him!*" Mrs. Grose with emphasis declared. "It was Quint's own fancy. To play with him, I mean—to spoil him." She paused a moment; then she added: "Quint was much too free."

This gave me, straight from my vision of his face—*such* a face!—a sudden sickness of disgust. "Too free with *my* boy?"

"Too free with every one!"

I forbore for the moment to analyse this description further than by the reflexion that a part of it applied to several of the members of the household, of the half-dozen maids and men who were still of our small colony. But there was everything, for our apprehension, in the lucky fact that no discomfortable legend, no perturbation of scullions, had ever, within any one's memory, attached to the kind old place. It had neither bad name nor ill fame, and Mrs. Grose, most apparently, only desired to cling to me and to quake in silence. I even put her, the very last thing of all, to the test. It was when, at midnight, she had her hand on the schoolroom door to take leave. "I *have* it from you then—for it's of great importance—that he was definitely and admittedly bad?"

"Oh not admittedly. *I* knew it—but the master didn't."

"And you never told him?"

"Well, he didn't like tale-bearing—he hated complaints. He was terribly short with anything of that kind, and if people were all right to *him*—"

"He wouldn't be bothered with more?" This squared well enough with my impression of him: he was not a trouble-loving gentleman, nor so very particular perhaps about some of the company he himself kept. All the same, I pressed my informant. "I promise you *I* would have told!"

She felt my discrimination. "I dare say I was wrong. But really I was afraid."

"Afraid of what?"

"Of things that man could do. Quint was so clever —he was so deep."

I took this in still more than I probably showed. "You weren't afraid of anything else? Not of his effect—?"

"His effect?" she repeated with a face of anguish and waiting while I faltered.

"On innocent little precious lives. They were in your charge."

"No, they weren't in mine!" she roundly and distressfully returned. "The master believed in him and placed him here because he was supposed not to be quite in health and the country air so good for him. So he had everything to say. Yes"—she let me have it— "even about *them*."

"Them—that creature?" I had to smother a kind of howl. "And you could bear it?"

"No. I couldn't—and I can't now!" And the poor woman burst into tears.

A rigid control, from the next day, was, as I have said, to follow them; yet how often and how passionately, for a week, we came back together to the subject! Much as we had discussed it that Sunday night, I was, in the immediate later hours in especial—for it may be imagined whether I slept—still haunted with

the shadow of something she had not told me. I myself had kept back nothing, but there was a word Mrs.
Grose had kept back. I was sure moreover by morning that this was not from a failure of frankness, but because on every side there were fears. It seems to me indeed, in raking it all over, that by the time the morrow's sun was high I had restlessly read into the facts
before us almost all the meaning they were to receive
from subsequent and more cruel occurrences. What they
gave me above all was just the sinister figure of the living man—the dead one would keep a while!—and of
the months he had continuously passed at Bly, which,
added up, made a formidable stretch. The limit of this
evil time had arrived only when, on the dawn of a
winter's morning, Peter Quint was found, by a labourer
going to early work, stone dead on the road from the
village: a catastrophe explained—superficially at least
—by a visible wound to his head; such a wound as
might have been produced (and as, on the final evidence, *had* been) by a fatal slip, in the dark and after
leaving the public-house, on the steepish icy slope, a
wrong path altogether, at the bottom of which he lay.
The icy slope, the turn mistaken at night and in liquor,
accounted for much—practically, in the end and after
the inquest and boundless chatter, for everything; but
there had been matters in his life, strange passages and
perils, secret disorders, vices more than suspected, that
would have accounted for a good deal more.

I scarce know how to put my story into words that
shall be a credible picture of my state of mind; but I
was in these days literally able to find a joy in the extraordinary flight of heroism the occasion demanded of
me. I now saw that I had been asked for a service admirable and difficult; and there would be a greatness
in letting it be seen—oh in the right quarter!—that I

could succeed where many another girl might have
failed. It was an immense help to me—I confess I rather
applaud myself as I look back!—that I saw my response
so strongly and so simply. I was there to protect and
defend the little creatures in the world the most bereaved and the most loveable, the appeal of whose helplessness had suddenly become only too explicit, a deep
constant ache of one's own engaged affection. We were
cut off, really, together; we were united in our danger.
They had nothing but me, and I—well, I had *them*.
It was in short a magnificent chance. This chance presented itself to me in an image richly material. I was a
screen—I was to stand before them. The more I saw
the less they would. I began to watch them in a stifled
suspense, a disguised tension, that might well, had it
continued too long, have turned to something like
madness. What saved me, as I now see, was that it
turned to another matter altogether. It didn't last as
suspense—it was superseded by horrible proofs. Proofs,
I say, yes—from the moment I really took hold.

This moment dated from an afternoon hour that I
happened to spend in the grounds with the younger of
my pupils alone. We had left Miles indoors, on the red
cushion of a deep window-seat; he had wished to finish
a book, and I had been glad to encourage a purpose
so laudable in a young man whose only defect was a
certain ingenuity of restlessness. His sister, on the contrary, had been alert to come out, and I strolled with
her half an hour, seeking the shade, for the sun was still
high and the day exceptionally warm. I was aware afresh
with her, as we went, of how, like her brother, she contrived—it was the charming thing in both children—
to let me alone without appearing to drop me and to
accompany me without appearing to oppress. They were
never importunate and yet never listless. My attention

to them all really went to seeing them amuse themselves immensely without me: this was a spectacle
they seemed actively to prepare and that employed me
as an active admirer. I walked in a world of their invention—they had no occasion whatever to draw upon
mine; so that my time was taken only with being for
them some remarkable person or thing that the game
of the moment required and that was merely, thanks to
my superior, my exalted stamp, a happy and highly distinguished sinecure. I forget what I was on the present
occasion; I only remember that I was something very
important and very quiet and that Flora was playing
very hard. We were on the edge of the lake, and, as
we had lately begun geography, the lake was the Sea
of Azof.

Suddenly, amid these elements, I became aware that
on the other side of the Sea of Azof we had an interested
spectator. The way this knowledge gathered in me was
the strangest thing in the world—the strangest, that is,
except the very much stranger in which it quickly
merged itself. I had sat down with a piece of work—for
I was something or other that could sit—on the old stone
bench which overlooked the pond; and in this position
I began to take in with certitude and yet without direct
vision the presence, a good way off, of a third person.
The old trees, the thick shrubbery, made a great and
pleasant shade, but it was all suffused with the
brightness of the hot still hour. There was no ambiguity
in anything; none whatever at least in the conviction
I from one moment to another found myself forming as
to what I should see straight before me and across
the lake as a consequence of raising my eyes. They were
attached at this juncture to the stitching in which I was
engaged, and I can feel once more the spasm of my
effort not to move them till I should so have steadied

myself as to be able to make up my mind what to do. There was an alien object in view—a figure whose right of presence I instantly and passionately questioned. I recollect counting over perfectly the possibilities, reminding myself that nothing was more natural for instance than the appearance of one of the men about the place, or even of a messenger, a postman or a tradesman's boy, from the village. That reminder had as little effect on my practical certitude as I was conscious—still even without looking—of its having upon the character and attitude of our visitor. Nothing was more natural than that these things should be the other things they absolutely were not.

Of the positive identity of the apparition I would assure myself as soon as the small clock of my courage should have ticked out the right second; meanwhile, with an effort that was already sharp enough, I transferred my eyes straight to little Flora, who, at the moment, was about ten yards away. My heart had stood still for an instant with the wonder and terror of the question whether she too would see; and I held my breath while I waited for what a cry from her, what some sudden innocent sign either of interest or of alarm, would tell me. I waited, but nothing came; then in the first place—and there is something more dire in this, I feel, than in anything I have to relate—I was determined by a sense that within a minute all spontaneous sounds from her had dropped; and in the second by the circumstance that also within the minute she had, in her play, turned her back to the water. This was her attitude when I at last looked at her—looked with the confirmed conviction that we were still, together, under direct personal notice. She had picked up a small flat piece of wood which happened to have in it a little hole that had evidently suggested to her the idea of sticking in another fragment that might figure as a mast and make the thing a boat. This second morsel, as I watched her, she was very markedly and intently attempting to tighten in its place. My apprehension of what she was doing sustained me so that after some seconds I felt I was ready for more. Then I again shifted my eyes—I faced what I had to face.

VII

I got hold of Mrs. Grose as soon after this as I could; and I can give no intelligible account of how I fought out the interval. Yet I still hear myself cry as I fairly threw myself into her arms: "They *know*—it's too monstrous: they know, they know!"

"And what on earth—?" I felt her incredulity as she held me.

"Why all that *we* know—and heaven knows what more besides!" Then as she released me I made it out to her, made it out perhaps only now with full coherency even to myself. "Two hours ago, in the garden" —I could scarce articulate—"Flora *saw!*"

Mrs. Grose took it as she might have taken a blow in the stomach. "She has told you?" she panted.

"Not a word—that's the horror. She kept it to herself! The child of eight, *that* child!" Unutterable still for me was the stupefaction of it.

Mrs. Grose of course could only gape the wider. "Then how do you know?"

"I was there—I saw with my eyes: saw she was perfectly aware."

"Do you mean aware of *him?*"

"No—of *her*." I was conscious as I spoke that I looked prodigious things, for I got the slow reflexion of them in my companion's face. "Another person—this time; but a figure of quite as unmistakeable horror and evil: a woman in black, pale and dreadful—with such an air also, and such a face!—on the other side of the lake. I was there with the child—quiet for the hour; and in the midst of it she came."

"Came how—from where?"

"From where they come from! She just appeared and stood there—but not so near."

"And without coming nearer?"

"Oh for the effect and the feeling she might have been as close as you!"

My friend, with an odd impulse, fell back a step. "Was she some one you've never seen?"

"Never. But some one the child has. Some one *you* have." Then to show how I had thought it all out: "My predecessor—the one who died."

"Miss Jessel?"

"Miss Jessel. You don't believe me?" I pressed.

She turned right and left in her distress. "How can you be sure?"

This drew from me, in the state of my nerves, a flash of impatience. "Then ask Flora—*she's* sure!" But I had no sooner spoken than I caught myself up. "No, for God's sake *don't!* She'll say she isn't—she'll lie!"

Mrs. Grose was not too bewildered instinctively to protest. "Ah how *can* you?"

"Because I'm clear. Flora doesn't want me to know."

"It's only then to spare you."

"No, no—there are depths, depths! The more I go over it the more I see in it, and the more I see in it the more I fear. I don't know what I *don't* see, what I *don't* fear!"

Mrs. Grose tried to keep up with me. "You mean you're afraid of seeing her again?"

"Oh no; that's nothing—now!" Then I explained. "It's of *not* seeing her."

But my companion only looked wan. "I don't understand."

"Why, it's that the child may keep it up—and that the child assuredly *will*—without my knowing it."

At the image of this possibility Mrs. Grose for a moment collapsed, yet presently to pull herself together again as from the positive force of the sense of what, should we yield an inch, there would really be to give way to. "Dear, dear—we must keep our heads! And after all, if she doesn't mind it—!" She even tried a grim joke. "Perhaps she likes it!"

"Like *such* things—a scrap of an infant!"

"Isn't it just a proof of her blest innocence?" my friend bravely enquired.

She brought me, for the instant, almost round. "Oh we must clutch at *that*—we must cling to it! If it isn't a proof of what you say, it's a proof of—God knows what! For the woman's a horror of horrors."

Mrs. Grose, at this, fixed her eyes a minute on the ground; then at last raising them, "Tell me how you know," she said.

"Then you admit it's what she was?" I cried.

"Tell me how you know," my friend simply repeated.

"Know? By seeing her! By the way she looked."

"At you, do you mean—so wickedly?"

"Dear me, no—I could have borne that. She gave me never a glance. She only fixed the child."

Mrs. Grose tried to see it. "Fixed her?"

"Ah with such awful eyes!"

She stared at mine as if they might really have resembled them. "Do you mean of dislike?"

"God help us, no. Of something much worse."

"Worse than dislike?"—this left her indeed at a loss.

"With a determination—indescribable. With a kind of fury of intention."

I made her turn pale. "Intention?"

"To get hold of her." Mrs. Grose—her eyes just lingering on mine—gave a shudder and walked to the window; and while she stood there looking out I completed my statement. "*That's* what Flora knows."

After a little she turned round. "The person was in black, you say?"

"In mourning—rather poor, almost shabby. But—yes —with extraordinary beauty." I now recognised to what I had at last, stroke by stroke, brought the victim of my confidence, for she quite visibly weighed this. "Oh handsome—very, very," I insisted; "wonderfully handsome. But infamous."

She slowly came back to me. "Miss Jessel—*was* infamous." She once more took my hand in both her own, holding it as tight as if to fortify me against the increase of alarm I might draw from this disclosure. "They were both infamous," she finally said.

So for a little we faced it once more together; and I found absolutely a degree of help in seeing it now so straight. "I appreciate," I said, "the great decency of your not having hitherto spoken; but the time has certainly come to give me the whole thing." She appeared to assent to this, but still only in silence; seeing which I went on: "I must have it now. Of what did she die? Come, there was something between them."

"There was everything."

"In spite of the difference—?"

"Oh of their rank, their condition"—she brought it woefully out. "*She* was a lady."

I turned it over; I again saw. "Yes—she was a lady."

"And he so dreadfully below," said Mrs. Grose.

I felt that I doubtless needn't press too hard, in such

company, on the place of a servant in the scale; but
there was nothing to prevent an acceptance of my companion's own measure of my predecessor's abasement.
There was a way to deal with that, and I dealt; the
more readily for my full vision—on the evidence—of
our employer's late clever good-looking "own" man;
impudent, assured, spoiled, depraved. "The fellow was
a hound."

Mrs. Grose considered as if it were perhaps a little
a case for a sense of shades. "I've never seen one like
him. He did what he wished."

"With *her?*"

"With them all."

It was as if now in my friend's own eyes Miss Jessel
had again appeared. I seemed at any rate for an instant
to trace their evocation of her as distinctly as I had seen
her by the pond; and I brought out with decision: "It
must have been also what *she* wished!"

Mrs. Grose's face signified that it had been indeed,
but she said at the same time: "Poor woman—she paid
for it!"

"Then you do know what she died of?" I asked.

"No—I know nothing. I wanted not to know; I was
glad enough I didn't; and I thanked heaven she was
well out of this!"

"Yet you had then your idea—"

"Of her real reason for leaving? Oh yes—as to that.
She couldn't have stayed. Fancy it here—for a gover-
ness! And afterwards I imagined—and I still imagine.
And what I imagine is dreadful."

"Not so dreadful as what *I* do," I replied; on which
I must have shown her—as I was indeed but too conscious—a front of miserable defeat. It brought out again
all her compassion for me, and at the renewed touch of
her kindness my power to resist broke down. I burst, as

I had the other time made her burst, into tears; she took
me to her motherly breast, where my lamentation overflowed. "I don't do it!" I sobbed in despair; "I don't
save or shield them! It's far worse than I dreamed.
They're lost!"

VIII

What I had said to Mrs. Grose was true enough: there
were in the matter I had put before her depths and possibilities that I lacked resolution to sound; so that when
we met once more in the wonder of it we were of a
common mind about the duty of resistance to extravagant fancies. We were to keep our heads if we should
keep nothing else—difficult indeed as that might be
in the face of all that, in our prodigious experience,
seemed least to be questioned. Late that night, while
the house slept, we had another talk in my room; when
she went all the way with me as to its being beyond
doubt that I had seen exactly what I had seen. I found
that to keep her thoroughly in the grip of this I had
only to ask her how, if I had "made it up," I came to
be able to give, of each of the persons appearing to me,
a picture disclosing, to the last detail, their special
marks—a portrait on the exhibition of which she had
instantly recognised and named them. She wished, of
course—small blame to her!—to sink the whole subject; and I was quick to assure her that my own interest
in it had now violently taken the form of a search for
the way to escape from it. I closed with her cordially
on the article of the likelihood that with recurrence—
for recurrence we took for granted—I should get used
to my danger; distinctly professing that my personal
exposure had suddenly become the least of my dis-

comforts. It was my new suspicion that was intolerable; and yet even to this complication the later hours of the day had brought a little ease.

On leaving her, after my first outbreak, I had of course returned to my pupils, associating the right remedy for my dismay with that sense of their charm which I had already recognised as a resource I could positively cultivate and which had never failed me yet. I had simply, in other words, plunged afresh into Flora's special society and there become aware—it was almost a luxury!—that she could put her little conscious hand straight upon the spot that ached. She had looked at me in sweet speculation and then had accused me to my face of having "cried." I had supposed the ugly signs of it brushed away; but I could literally—for the time at all events—rejoice, under this fathomless charity, that they had not entirely disappeared. To gaze into the depths of blue of the child's eyes and pronounce their loveliness a trick of premature cunning was to be guilty of a cynicism in preference to which I naturally preferred to abjure my judgement and, so far as might be, my agitation. I couldn't abjure for merely wanting to, but I could repeat to Mrs. Grose—as I did there, over and over, in the small hours—that with our small friends' voices in the air, their pressure on one's heart and their fragrant faces against one's cheek, everything fell to the ground but their incapacity and their beauty. It was a pity that, somehow, to settle this once for all, I had equally to re-enumerate the signs of subtlety that, in the afternoon, by the lake, had made a miracle of my show of self-possession. It was a pity to be obliged to re-investigate the certitude of the moment itself and repeat how it had come to me as a revelation that the inconceivable communion I then surprised must have been for both parties a matter of habit. It was a pity I should have had to quaver out again the reasons for my not having, in my delusion, so much as questioned that the little girl saw our visitant even as I actually saw Mrs. Grose herself, and that she wanted, by just so much as she did thus see, to make me suppose she didn't, and at the same time, without showing anything, arrive at a guess as to whether I myself did! It was a pity I needed to recapitulate the portentous little activities by which she sought to divert my attention—the perceptible increase of movement, the greater intensity of play, the singing, the gabbling of nonsense and the invitation to romp.

Yet if I had not indulged, to prove there was nothing in it, in this review, I should have missed the two or three dim elements of comfort that still remained to me. I shouldn't for instance have been able to asseverate to my friend that I was certain—which was so much to the good—that *I* at least had not betrayed myself. I shouldn't have been prompted, by stress of need, by desperation of mind—I scarce know what to call it— to invoke such further aid to intelligence as might spring from pushing my colleague fairly to the wall. She had told me, bit by bit, under pressure, a great deal; but a small shifty spot on the wrong side of it all still sometimes brushed my brow like the wing of a bat; and I remember how on this occasion—for the sleeping house and the concentration alike of our danger and our watch seemed to help—I felt the importance of giving the last jerk to the curtain. "I don't believe anything so horrible," I recollect saying; "no, let us put it definitely, my dear, that I don't. But if I did, you know, there's a thing I should require now, just without sparing you the least bit more—oh not a scrap, come!— to get out of you. What was it you had in mind when, in our distress, before Miles came back, over the letter from his school, you said, under my insistence, that you didn't pretend for him he hadn't literally *ever* been 'bad'? He was *not*, truly, 'ever,' in these weeks that I myself have lived with him and so closely watched him; he has been an imperturbable little prodigy of delightful loveable goodness. Therefore you might perfectly have made the claim for him if you had not, as it happened, seen an exception to take. What was your exception, and to what passage in your personal observation of him did you refer?"

It was a straight question enough, but levity was not our note, and in any case I had before the grey dawn admonished us to separate got my answer. What my friend had had in mind proved immensely to the purpose. It was neither more nor less than the particular fact that for a period of several months Quint and the boy had been perpetually together. It was indeed the very appropriate item of evidence of her having ventured to criticise the propriety, to hint at the incongruity, of so close an alliance, and even to go so far on the subject as a frank overture to Miss Jessel would take her. Miss Jessel had, with a very high manner about it, requested her to mind her business, and the good woman had on this directly approached little Miles. What she had said to him, since I pressed, was that *she* liked to see young gentlemen not forget their station.

I pressed again, of course, the closer for that. "You reminded him that Quint was only a base menial?"

"As you might say! And it was his answer, for one thing, that was bad."

"And for another thing?" I waited. "He repeated your words to Quint?"

"No, not that. It's just what he *wouldn't*!" she could still impress on me. "I was sure, at any rate," she added, "that he didn't. But he denied certain occasions."

"What occasions?"

"When they had been about together quite as if Quint were his tutor—and a very grand one—and Miss Jessel only for the little lady. When he had gone off with the fellow, I mean, and spent hours with him."

"He then prevaricated about it—he said he hadn't?" Her assent was clear enough to cause me to add in a moment: "I see. He lied."

"Oh!" Mrs. Grose mumbled. This was a suggestion that it didn't matter; which indeed she backed up by a further remark. "You see, after all, Miss Jessel didn't mind. She didn't forbid him."

I considered. "Did he put that to you as a justification?"

At this she dropped again. "No, he never spoke of it."

"Never mentioned her in connexion with Quint?"

She saw, visibly flushing, where I was coming out. "Well, he didn't show anything. He denied," she repeated; "he denied."

Lord, how I pressed her now! "So that you could see he knew what was between the two wretches?"

"I don't know—I don't know!" the poor woman wailed.

"You do know, you dear thing," I replied; "only you haven't my dreadful boldness of mind, and you keep back, out of timidity and modesty and delicacy, even the impression that in the past, when you had, without my aid, to flounder about in silence, most of all made you miserable. But I shall get it out of you yet! There was something in the boy that suggested to you," I continued, "his covering and concealing their relation."

"Oh he couldn't prevent—"

"Your learning the truth? I dare say! But, heavens," I fell, with vehemence, a-thinking, "what it shows that they must, to that extent, have succeeded in making of him!"

"Ah nothing that's not nice *now!*" Mrs. Grose lugubriously pleaded.

"I don't wonder you looked queer," I persisted, "when I mentioned to you the letter from his school!"

"I doubt if I looked as queer as you!" she retorted with homely force. "And if he was so bad then as that comes to, how is he such an angel now?"

"Yes indeed—and if he was a fiend at school! How, how, how? Well," I said in my torment, "you must put it to me again, though I shall not be able to tell you for some days. Only put it to me again!" I cried in a way that made my friend stare. "There are directions in which I mustn't for the present let myself go." Meanwhile I returned to her first example—the one to which she had just previously referred—of the boy's happy capacity for an occasional slip. "If Quint—on your remonstrance at the time you speak of—was a base menial, one of the things Miles said to you, I find myself guessing, was that you were another." Again her admission was so adequate that I continued: "And you forgave him that?"

"Wouldn't *you?*"

"Oh yes!" And we exchanged there, in the stillness, a sound of the oddest amusement. Then I went on: "At all events, while he was with the man—"

"Miss Flora was with the woman. It suited them all!"

It suited me too, I felt, only too well; by which I mean that it suited exactly the particular deadly view I was in the very act of forbidding myself to entertain. But I so far succeeded in checking the expression of this view that I will throw, just here, no further light on it than may be offered by the mention of my final observation to Mrs. Grose. "His having lied and been impudent are, I confess, less engaging specimens than I had hoped to have from you of the outbreak in him of the little natural man. Still," I mused, "they must do, for they make me feel more than ever that I must watch."

It made me blush, the next minute, to see in my friend's face how much more unreservedly she had forgiven him than her anecdote struck me as pointing out to my own tenderness any way to do. This was marked when, at the schoolroom door, she quitted me. "Surely you don't accuse *him*—"

"Of carrying on an intercourse that he conceals from me? Ah remember that, until further evidence, I now accuse nobody." Then before shutting her out to go by another passage to her own place, "I must just wait," I wound up.

IX

I waited and waited, and the days took as they elapsed something from my consternation. A very few of them, in fact, passing, in constant sight of my pupils, without a fresh incident, sufficed to give to grievous fancies and even to odious memories a kind of brush of the sponge. I have spoken of the surrender to their extraordinary childish grace as a thing I could actively promote in myself, and it may be imagined if I neglected now to apply at this source for whatever balm it would yield. Stranger than I can express, certainly, was the effort to struggle against my new lights. It would doubtless have been a greater tension still, however, had it not been so frequently successful. I used to wonder how my little charges could help guessing that I thought strange things about them; and the circumstance that these things only made them more interesting was not by itself a direct aid to keeping them in the dark. I trembled lest they should see that they *were* so immensely more interesting. Putting things at the worst, at all events, as in meditation I so often did, any clouding of their innocence could only be—blameless and foredoomed as they were—a reason the more for taking risks. There were moments when I knew myself to catch them up by an irresistible impulse and press them to my heart. As soon as I had done so I used to wonder—"What will they think of that? Doesn't it betray too much?" It would have been easy to get into a sad wild tangle about how much I might betray; but the real account, I feel, of the hours of peace I could still enjoy was that the immediate charm of my companions was a beguilement still effective even under the shadow of the possibility that it was studied. For if it occurred to me that I might occasionally excite suspicion by the little outbreaks of my sharper passion for them, so too I remember asking if I mightn't see a queerness in the traceable increase of their own demonstrations.

They were at this period extravagantly and preternaturally fond of me; which, after all, I could reflect, was no more than a graceful response in children perpetually bowed down over and hugged. The homage of which they were so lavish succeeded in truth for my nerves quite as well as if I never appeared to myself, as I may say, literally to catch them at a purpose in it. They had never, I think, wanted to do so many things for their poor protectress; I mean—though they got their lessons better and better, which was naturally what would please her most—in the way of diverting, entertaining, surprising her; reading her passages, telling her stories, acting her charades, pouncing out at her, in disguises, as animals and historical characters, and above all astonishing her by the "pieces" they had secretly got by heart and could interminably recite. I should never get to the bottom—were I to let myself go even now—of the prodigious private commentary, all under still more private correction, with which I in these days overscored their full hours. They had shown me from the first a facility for everything, a general faculty which, taking a fresh start, achieved remarkable flights. They got their little tasks as if they loved them; they indulged, from the mere exuberance of the gift, in the most unimposed little miracles of memory. They not only popped out at me as tigers and as Romans, but as Shakespeareans, astronomers and navigators. This was so singularly the case that it had presumably much to do with the fact as to which, at the present day, I am at a loss for a different explanation: I allude to my unnatural composure on the subject of another school for Miles. What I remember is that I was content for the time not to open the question, and that contentment must have sprung from the sense of his perpetually striking show of cleverness. He was too clever for a bad governess, for a parson's daughter, to spoil; and the strangest if not the brightest thread in the pensive embroidery I just spoke of was the impression I might have got, if I had dared to work it out, that he was under some influence operating in his small intellectual life as a tremendous incitement.

If it was easy to reflect, however, that such a boy could postpone school, it was at least as marked that for such a boy to have been "kicked out" by a schoolmaster was a mystification without end. Let me add that in their company now—and I was careful almost never to be out of it—I could follow no scent very far. We lived in a cloud of music and affection and success and private theatricals. The musical sense in each of

the children was of the quickest, but the elder in especial had a marvellous knack of catching and repeating.
The schoolroom piano broke into all gruesome fancies;
and when that failed there were confabulations in
corners, with a sequel of one of them going out in the
highest spirits in order to "come in" as something new.
I had had brothers myself, and it was no revelation to
me that little girls could be slavish idolaters of little
boys. What surpassed everything was that there was a
little boy in the world who could have for the inferior
age, sex and intelligence so fine a consideration. They
were extraordinarily at one, and to say that they never
either quarrelled or complained is to make the note of
praise coarse for their quality of sweetness. Sometimes
perhaps indeed (when I dropped into coarseness) I
came across traces of little understandings between
them by which one of them should keep me occupied
while the other slipped away. There is a naïf side, I suppose, in all diplomacy; but if my pupils practised upon
me it was surely with the minimum of grossness. It was
all in the other quarter that, after a lull, the grossness
broke out.

I find that I really hang back; but I must take my
horrid plunge. In going on with the record of what was
hideous at Bly I not only challenge the most liberal
faith—for which I little care; but (and this is another
matter) I renew what I myself suffered, I again push
my dreadful way through it to the end. There came
suddenly an hour after which, as I look back, the business seems to me to have been all pure suffering; but I
have at least reached the heart of it, and the straightest
road out is doubtless to advance. One evening—with
nothing to lead up or prepare it—I felt the cold touch
of the impression that had breathed on me the night of
my arrival and which, much lighter then as I have

mentioned, I should probably have made little of in memory had my subsequent sojourn been less agitated. I had not gone to bed; I sat reading by a couple of candles. There was a roomful of old books at Bly—last-century fiction some of it, which, to the extent of a distinctly deprecated renown, but never to so much as that of a stray specimen, had reached the sequestered home and appealed to the unavowed curiosity of my youth. I remember that the book I had in my hand was Fielding's "Amelia"; also that I was wholly awake. I recall further both a general conviction that it was horribly late and a particular objection to looking at my watch. I figure finally that the white curtain draping, in the fashion of those days, the head of Flora's little bed, shrouded, as I had assured myself long before, the perfection of childish rest. I recollect in short that thought I was deeply interested in my author I found myself, at the turn of a page and with his spell all scattered, looking straight up from him and hard at the door of my room. There was a moment during which I listened, reminded of the faint sense I had had, the first night, of there being something undefinably astir in the house, and noted the soft breath of the open casement just move the half-drawn blind. Then, with all the marks of a deliberation that must have seemed magnificent had there been any one to admire it, I laid down my book, rose to my feet and, taking a candle, went straight out of the room and, from the passage, on which my light made little impression, noiselessly closed and locked the door.

I can say now neither what determined nor what guided me, but I went straight along the lobby, holding my cradle high, till I came within sight of the tall window that presided over the great turn of the staircase. At this point I precipitately found myself aware of three things. They were practically simultaneous, yet they had flashes of succession. My candle, under a bold flourish, went out, and I perceived, by the uncovered window, that the yielding dusk of earliest morning rendered it unnecessary. Without it, the next instant, I knew that there was a figure on the stair. I speak of sequences, but I required no lapse of seconds to stiffen myself for a third encounter with Quint. The apparition had reached the landing half-way up and was therefore on the spot nearest the window, where, at sight of me, it stopped short and fixed me exactly as it had fixed me from the tower and from the garden. He knew me as well as I knew him; and so, in the cold faint twilight, with a glimmer in the high glass and another on the polish of the oak stair below, we faced each other in our common intensity. He was absolutely, on this occasion, a living detestable dangerous presence. But that was not the wonder of wonders; I reserve this distinction for quite another circumstance: the circumstance that dread had unmistakeably quitted me and that there was nothing in me unable to meet and measure him.

I had plenty of anguish after that extraordinary moment, but I had, thank God, no terror. And he knew I hadn't—I found myself at the end of an instant magnificently aware of this. I felt, in a fierce rigour of confidence, that if I stood my ground a minute I should cease —for the time at least—to have him to reckon with; and during the minute, accordingly, the thing was as human and hideous as a real interview: hideous just because it *was* human, as human as to have met alone, in the small hours, in a sleeping house, some enemy, some adventurer, some criminal. It was the dead silence of our long gaze at such close quarters that gave the whole horror, huge as it was, its only note of the unnatural.

If I had met a murderer in such a place and at such an
hour we still at least would have spoken. Something
would have passed, in life, between us; if nothing had
passed one of us would have moved. The moment was
so prolonged that it would have taken but little more
to make me doubt if even *I* were in life. I can't express
what followed it save by saying that the silence itself—
which was indeed in a manner an attestation of my
strength—became the element into which I saw the
figure disappear; in which I definitely saw it turn, as I
might have seen the low wretch to which it had once belonged turn on receipt of an order, and pass, with my
eyes on the villainous back that no hunch could have
more disfigured, straight down the staircase and into
the darkness in which the next bend was lost.

x

I remained a while at the top of the stair, but with the
effect presently of understanding that when my visitor
had gone, he had gone; then I returned to my room. The
foremost thing I saw there by the light of the candle I
had left burning was that Flora's little bed was empty;
and on this I caught my breath with all the terror that,
five minutes before, I had been able to resist. I dashed
at the place in which I had left her lying and over
which—for the small silk counterpane and the sheets
were disarranged—the white curtains had been de-
ceivingly pulled forward; then my step, to my unutterable relief, produced an answering sound: I noticed
an agitation of the window-blind, and the child, duck-
ing down, emerged rosily from the other side of it. She
stood there in so much of her candour and so little of
her night-gown, with pink bare feet and the golden

glow of her curls. She looked intensely grave, and I
had never had such a sense of losing an advantage acquired (the thrill of which had just been so prodigious) as on my consciousness that she addressed me
with a reproach—"You naughty: where *have* you been?"
Instead of challenging her own irregularity I found myself arraigned and explaining. She herself explained,
for that matter, with the loveliest eagerest simplicity.
She had known suddenly, as she lay there, that I was
out of the room, and had jumped up to see what had
become of me. I had dropped, with the joy of her reappearance, back into my chair—feeling then, and then
only, a little faint; and she had pattered straight over
to me, thrown herself upon my knee, given herself to
be held with the flame of the candle full in the wonderful little face that was still flushed with sleep. I remember closing my eyes an instant, yieldingly, consciously,
as before the excess of something beautiful that shone
out of the blue of her own. "You were looking for me
out of the window?" I said. "You thought I might be
walking in the grounds?"

"Well, you know, I thought some one was"—she
never blanched as she smiled out that at me.

Oh how I looked at her now! "And did you see any
one?"

"Ah *no!*" she returned almost (with the full privilege
of childish inconsequence) resentfully, though with a
long sweetness in her little drawl of the negative.

At that moment, in the state of my nerves, I absolutely believed she lied; and if I once more closed my
eyes it was before the dazzle of the three or four possible ways in which I might take this up. One of these
for a moment tempted me with such singular force
that, to resist it, I must have gripped my little girl with
a spasm that, wonderfully, she submitted to with-

out a cry or a sign of fright. Why not break out at her
on the spot and have it all over?—give it to her straight
in her lovely little lighted face? "You see, you see, you
know that you do and that you already quite suspect I
believe it; therefore why not frankly confess it to me,
so that we may at least live with it together and learn
perhaps, in the strangeness of our fate, where we are
and what it means?" This solicitation dropped, alas, as
it came: if I could immediately have succumbed to it I
might have spared myself—well, you'll see what. Instead of succumbing I sprang again to my feet, looked
at her bed and took a helpless middle way. "Why did
you pull the curtain over the place to make me think
you were still there?"

Flora luminously considered; after which, with her
little divine smile: "Because I don't like to frighten
you!"

"But if I had, by your idea, gone out—?"

She absolutely declined to be puzzled; she turned
her eyes to the flame of the candle as if the question
were as irrelevant, or at any rate as impersonal, as Mrs.
Marcet or nine-times-nine. "Oh but you know," she
quite adequately answered, "that you might come back,
you dear, and that you *have!*" And after a little, when
she had got into bed, I had, a long time, by almost sitting on her for the retention of her hand, to show how
I recognised the pertinence of my return.

You may imagine the general complexion, from that
moment, of my nights. I repeatedly sat up till I didn't
know when; I selected moments when my room-mate
unmistakeably slept, and, stealing out, took noiseless
turns in the passage. I even pushed as far as to where I
had last met Quint. But I never met him there again,
and I may as well say at once that I on no other occasion
saw him in the house. I just missed, on the staircase,

nevertheless, a different adventure. Looking down it from the top I once recognised the presence of a woman seated on one of the lower steps with her back presented to me, her body half-bowed and her head, in an attitude of woe, in her hands. I had been there but an instant, however, when she vanished without looking round at me. I knew, for all that, exactly what dreadful face she had to show; and I wondered whether, if instead of being above I had been below, I should have had the same nerve for going up that I had lately shown Quint. Well, there continued to be plenty of call for nerve. On the eleventh night after my lastest encounter with that gentleman—they were all numbered now—I had an alarm that perilously skirted it and that indeed, from the particular quality of its unexpectedness, proved quite my sharpest shock. It was precisely the first night during this series that, weary with vigils, I had conceived I might again without laxity lay myself down at my old hour. I slept immediately and, as I afterwards knew, till about one o'clock; but when I woke it was to sit straight up, as completely roused as if a hand had shaken me. I had left a light burning, but it was now out, and I felt an instant certainty that Flora had extinguished it. This brought me to my feet and straight, in the darkness, to her bed, which I found she had left. A glance at the window enlightened me further, and the striking of a match completed the picture.

The child had again got up—this time blowing out the taper, and had again, for some purpose of observation or response, squeezed in behind the blind and was peering out into the night. That she now saw—as she had not, I had satisfied myself, the previous time—was proved to me by the fact that she was disturbed neither by my re-illumination nor by the haste I made to get into slippers and into a wrap. Hidden, protected, absorbed, she evidently rested on the sill—the casement opened forward—and gave herself up. There was a great still moon to help her, and this fact had counted in my quick decision. She was face to face with the apparition we had met at the lake, and could now communicate with it as she had not then been able to do. What I, on my side, had to care for was, without disturbing her, to reach, from the corridor, some other window turned to the same quarter. I got to the door without her hearing me; I got out of it, closed it and listened, from the other side, for some sound from her. While I stood in the passage I had my eyes on her brother's door, which was but ten steps off and which, indescribably, produced in me a renewal of the strange impulse that I lately spoke of as my temptation. What if I should go straight in and march to *his* window?—what if, by risking to his boyish bewilderment a revelation of my motive, I should throw across the rest of the mystery the long halter of my boldness?

This thought held me sufficiently to make me cross to his threshold and pause again. I preturnaturally listened; I figured to myself what might portentously be; I wondered if his bed were also empty and he also secretly at watch. It was a deep soundless minute, at the end of which my impulse failed. He was quiet; he might be innocent; the risk was hideous; I turned away. There was a figure in the grounds—a figure prowling for a sight, the visitor with whom Flora was engaged; but it wasn't the visitor most concerned with my boy. I hesitated afresh, but on other grounds and only a few seconds; then I had made my choice. There were empty rooms enough at Bly, and it was only a question of choosing the right one. The right one suddenly presented itself to me as the lower one—though high above the gardens—in the solid corner of the house that I have spoken of as the old tower. This was a large square chamber, arranged with some state as a bedroom, the extravagant size of which made it so inconvenient that it had not for years, though kept by Mrs. Grose in exemplary order, been occupied. I had often admired it and I knew my way about in it; I had only, after just faltering at the first chill gloom of its disuse, to pass across it and unbolt in all quietness one of the shutters. Achieving this transit I uncovered the glass without a sound and, applying my face to the pane, was able, the darkness without being much less than within, to see that I commanded the right direction. Then I saw something more. The moon made the night extraordinarily penetrable and showed me on the lawn a person, diminished by distance, who stood there motionless and as if fascinated, looking up to where I had appeared—looking, that is, not so much straight at me as at something that was apparently above me. There was clearly another person above me—there was a person on the tower; but the presence on the lawn was not in the least what I had conceived and had confidently hurried to meet. The presence on the lawn—I felt sick as I made it out—was poor little Miles himself.

XI

It was not till late next day that I spoke to Mrs. Grose; the rigour with which I kept my pupils in sight making it often difficult to meet her privately: the more as we each felt the importance of not provoking—on the part of the servants quite as much as on that of the children—any suspicion of a secret flurry or of a discussion of mysteries. I drew a great security in this

particular from her mere smooth aspect. There was
nothing in her fresh face to pass on to others the least
of my horrible confidences. She believed me, I was
sure, absolutely: if she hadn't I don't know what would
have become of me, for I couldn't have borne the
strain alone. But she was a magnificent monument to
the blessing of a want of imagination, and if she could
see in our little charges nothing but their beauty and
amiability, their happiness and cleverness, she had no
direct communication with the sources of my trouble.
If they had been at all visibly blighted or battered she
would doubtless have grown, on tracing it back, haggard enough to match them; as matters stood, however, I could feel her, when she surveyed them with
her large white arms folded and the habit of serenity in
all her look, thank the Lord's mercy that if they were
ruined the pieces would still serve. Flights of fancy
gave place, in her mind, to a steady fireside glow, and
I had already begun to perceive how, with the development of the conviction that—as time went on without a public accident—our young things could, after
all, look out for themselves, she addressed her greatest
solicitude to the sad case presented by their deputy-
guardian. That, for myself, was a sound simplification:
I could engage that, to the world, my face should tell
no tales, but it would have been, in the conditions, an
immense added worry to find myself anxious about
hers.

At the hour I now speak of she had joined me, under pressure, on the terrace, where, with the lapse of
the season, the afternoon sun was now agreeable; and
we sat there together while before us and at a distance, yet within call if we wished, the children strolled
to and fro in one of their most manageable moods. They
moved slowly, in unison, below us, over the lawn, the

boy, as they went, reading aloud from a story-book and passing his arm round his sister to keep her quite in touch. Mrs. Grose watched them with positive placidity; then I caught the suppressed intellectual creak with which she conscientiously turned to take from me a view of the back of the tapestry. I had made her a receptacle of lurid things, but there was an odd recognition of my superiority—my accomplishments and my function—in her patience under my pain. She offered her mind to my disclosures as, had I wished to mix a witch's broth and proposed it with assurance, she would have held out a large clean saucepan. This had become thoroughly her attitude by the time that, in my recital of the events of the night, I reached the point of what Miles had said to me when, after seeing him, at such a monstrous hour, almost on the very spot where he happened now to be, I had gone down to bring him in; choosing then, at the window, with a concentrated need of not alarming the house, rather that method than any noisier process. I had left her meanwhile in little doubt of my small hope of representing with success even to her actual sympathy my sense of the real splendour of the little inspiration with which, after I had got him into the house, the boy met my final articulate challenge. As soon as I appeared in the moonlight on the terrace he had come to me as straight as possible; on which I had taken his hand without a word and led him, through the dark spaces, up the staircase where Quint had so hungrily hovered for him, along the lobby where I had listened and trembled, and so to his forsaken room.

Not a sound, on the way, had passed between us, and I had wondered—oh *how* I had wondered!—if he were groping about in his dreadful little mind for something plausible and not too grotesque. It would tax his invention certainly, and I felt, this time, over his real embarrassment, a curious thrill of triumph. It was a sharp trap for any game hitherto successful. He could play no longer at perfect propriety, nor could he pretend to it; so how the deuce would he get out of the scrape? There beat in me indeed, with the passionate throb of this question, an equal dumb appeal as to how the deuce *I* should. I was confronted at last, as never yet, with all the risk attached even now to sounding my own horrid note. I remember in fact that as we pushed into his little chamber, where the bed had not been slept in at all and the window, uncovered to the moonlight, made the place so clear that there was no need of striking a match—I remember how I suddenly dropped, sank upon the edge of the bed from the force of the idea that he must know how he really, as they say, "had" me. He could do what he liked, with all his cleverness to help him, so long as I should continue to defer to the old tradition of the criminality of those caretakers of the young who minister to superstitions and fears. He "had" me indeed, and in a cleft stick; for who would ever absolve me, who would consent that I should go unhung, if, by the faintest tremor of an overture, I were the first to introduce into our perfect intercourse an element so dire? No, no: it was useless to attempt to convey to Mrs. Grose, just as it is scarcely less so to attempt to suggest here, how, during our short stiff brush there in the dark, he fairly shook me with admiration. I was of course thoroughly kind and merciful; never, never yet had I placed on his small shoulders hands of such tenderness as those with which, while I rested against the bed, I held him there well under fire. I had no alternative but, in form at least, to put it to him.

"You must tell me now—and all the truth. What did

you go out for? What were you doing there?"

I can still see his wonderful smile, the whites of his beautiful eyes and the uncovering of his clear teeth, shine to me in the dusk. "If I tell you why, will you understand?" My heart, at this, leaped into my mouth. *Would* he tell me why? I found no sound on my lips to press it, and I was aware of answering only with a vague repeated grimacing nod. He was gentleness itself, and while I wagged my head at him he stood there more than ever a little fairy prince. It was his brightness indeed that gave me a respite. Would it be so great if he were really going to tell me? "Well," he said at last, "just exactly in order that you should do this."

"Do what?"

"Think me—for a change—*bad!*" I shall never forget the sweetness and gaiety with which he brought out the word, nor how, on top of it, he bent forward and kissed me. It was practically the end of everything. I met his kiss and I had to make, while I folded him for a minute in my arms, the most stupendous effort not to cry. He had given exactly the account of himself that permitted least my going behind it, and it was only with the effect of confirming my acceptance of it that, as I presently glanced about the room, I could say—

"Then you didn't undress at all?"

He fairly glittered in the gloom. "Not at all. I sat up and read."

"And when did you go down?"

"At midnight. When I'm bad I *am* bad!"

"I see, I see—it's charming. But how could you be sure I should know it?"

"Oh I arranged that with Flora." His answers rang out with a readiness! "She was to get up and look out."

"Which is what she did do." It was I who fell into the trap!

"So she disturbed you, and, to see what she was looking at, you also looked—you saw."

"While you," I concurred, "caught your death in the night air!"

He literally bloomed so from this exploit that he could afford radiantly to assent. "How otherwise should I have been bad enough?" he asked. Then, after another embrace, the incident and our interview closed on my recognition of all the reserves of goodness that, for his joke, he had been able to draw upon.

XII

The particular impression I had received proved in the morning light, I repeat, not quite successfully presentable to Mrs. Grose, though I re-enforced it with the mention of still another remark that he had made before we separated. "It all lies in half a dozen words," I said to her, "words that really settle the matter. 'Think, you know, what I *might* do!' He threw that off to show me how good he is. He knows down to the ground what he 'might do.' That's what he gave them a taste of at school."

"Lord, you do change!" cried my friend.

"I don't change—I simply make it out. The four, depend upon it, perpetually meet. If on either of these last nights you had been with either child you'd clearly have understood. The more I've watched and waited the more I've felt that if there were nothing else to make it sure it would be made so by the systematic silence of each. *Never*, by a slip of the tongue, have they so much as alluded to either of their old friends, any more than Miles has alluded to his expulsion. Oh yes, we may sit here and look at them, and they may show off to us there to their fill; but even while they pretend to be lost in their fairy-tale they're steeped in their vision of the dead restored to them. He's not reading to her," I declared; "they're talking of *them*—they're talking horrors! I go on, I know, as if I were crazy; and it's a wonder I'm not. What I've seen would have made *you* so; but it has only made me more lucid, made me get hold of still other things."

My lucidity must have seemed awful, but the charming creatures who were victims of it, passing and repassing in their interlocked sweetness, gave my colleague something to hold on by; and I felt how tight she held as, without stirring in the breath of my passion, she covered them still with her eyes. "Of what other things have you got hold?"

"Why of the very things that have delighted, fascinated and yet, at bottom, as I now so strangely see, mystified and troubled me. Their more than earthly beauty, their absolutely unnatural goodness. It's a game," I went on; "it's a policy and a fraud!"

"On the part of little darlings—?"

"As yet mere lovely babies? Yes, mad as that seems!" The very act of bringing it out really helped me to trace it—follow it all up and piece it all together. "They haven't been good—they've only been absent. It has been easy to live with them because they're simply leading a life of their own. They're not mine—they're not ours. They're his and they're hers!"

"Quint's and that woman's?"

"Quint's and that woman's. They want to get to them."

Oh how, at this, poor Mrs. Grose appeared to study them! "But for what?"

"For the love of all the evil that, in those dreadful days, the pair put into them. And to ply them with that evil still, to keep up the work of demons, is what brings the others back."

"Laws!" said my friend under her breath. The exclamation was homely, but it revealed a real acceptance of my further proof of what, in the bad time—for there had been a worse even than this!—must have occurred. There could have been no such justification for me as the plain assent of her experience to whatever depth of depravity I found credible in our brace of scoundrels. It was in obvious submission of memory that she brought out after a moment. "They *were* rascals! But what can they now do?" she pursued.

"Do?" I echoed so loud that Miles and Flora, as they passed at their distance, paused an instant in their walk and looked at us. "Don't they do enough?" I demanded in a lower tone, while the children, having smiled and nodded and kissed hands to us, resumed their exhibition. We were held by it a minute; then I answered: "They can destroy them!" At this my companion did turn, but the appeal she launched was a silent one, the effect of which was to make me more explicit. "They don't know as yet quite how—but they're trying hard. They're seen only across, as it were, and beyond—in strange places and on high places, the top of towers, the roof of houses, the outside of windows, the further edge of pools; but there's a deep design, on either side, to shorten the distance and overcome the obstacle: so the success of the tempters is only a question of time. They've only to keep to their suggestions of danger."

"For the children to come?"

"And perish in the attempt!" Mrs. Grose slowly got up, and I scrupulously added: "Unless, of course, we can prevent!"

Standing there before me while I kept my seat she visibly turned things over. "Their uncle must do the preventing. He must take them away."

"And who's to make him?"

She had been scanning the distance, but she now dropped on me a foolish face. "You, Miss."

"By writing to him that his house is poisoned and his little nephew and niece mad?"

"But if they *are*, Miss?"

"And if I am myself, you mean? That's charming news to be sent him by a person enjoying his confidence and whose prime undertaking was to give him no worry."

Mrs. Grose considered, following the children again. "Yes, he do hate worry. That was the great reason—"

"Why those fiends took him in so long? No doubt, though his indifference must have been awful. As I'm not a fiend, at any rate, I shouldn't take him in."

My companion, after an instant and for all answer, sat down again and grasped my arm. "Make him at any rate come to you."

I stared. "To *me*?" I had a sudden fear of what she might do. " 'Him'?"

"He ought to *be* here—he ought to help."

I quickly rose and I think I must have shown her a queerer face than ever yet. "You see me asking him for a visit?" No, with her eyes on my face she evidently couldn't. Instead of it even—as a woman reads another —she could see what I myself saw: his derision, his amusement, his contempt for the breakdown of my resignation at being left alone and for the fine machinery I had set in motion to attract his attention to my slighted charms. She didn't know—no one knew—how proud I had been to serve him and to stick to our terms; yet she none the less took the measure, I think,

of the warning I now gave her. "If you should so lose
your head as to appeal to him for me—"

She was really frightened. "Yes, Miss?"

"I would leave, on the spot, both him and you."

XIII

It was all very well to join them, but speaking to them
proved quite as much as ever an effort beyond my
strength—offered, in close quarters, difficulties as insurmountable as before. This situation continued a
month, and with new aggravations and particular notes,
the note above all, sharper and sharper, of the small
ironic consciousness on the part of my pupils. It was
not, I am as sure to-day as I was sure then, my mere
infernal imagination: it was absolutely traceable that
they were aware of my predicament and that this
strange relation made, in a manner, for a long time, the
air in which we moved. I don't mean that they had
their tongues in their cheeks or did anything vulgar,
for that was not one of their dangers: I do mean, on
the other hand, that the element of the unnamed and
untouched became, between us, greater than any other,
and that so much avoidance couldn't have been made
successful without a great deal of tacit arrangement. It
was as if, at moments, we were perpetually coming into
sight of subjects before which we must stop short, turning suddenly out of alleys that we perceived to be
blind, closing with a little bang that made us look at
each other—for, like all bangs, it was something louder
than we had intended—the doors we had indiscreetly
opened. All roads lead to Rome, and there were times
when it might have struck us that almost every branch
of study or subject of conversation skirted forbidden

ground. Forbidden ground was the question of the return of the dead in general and of whatever, in especial, might survive, for memory, of the friends little
children had lost. There were days when I could have
sworn that one of them had, with a small invisible
nudge, said to the other: "She thinks she'll do it this
time—but she *won't!*" To "do it" would have been to
indulge for instance—and for once in a way—in some
direct reference to the lady who had prepared them
for my discipline. They had a delightful endless appetite for passages in my own history to which I had again
and again treated them; they were in possession of
everything that had ever happened to me, had had,
with every circumstance, the story of my smallest adventures and of those of my brothers and sisters and of
the cat and the dog at home, as well as many particulars of the whimsical bent of my father, of the furniture
and arrangement of our house and of the conversation of the old women of our village. There were things
enough, taking one with another, to chatter about, if
one went very fast and knew by instinct when to go
round. They pulled with an art of their own the strings
of my invention and my memory; and nothing else perhaps, when I thought of such occasions afterwards,
gave me so the suspicion of being watched from under
cover. It was in any case over *my* life, *my* past and *my*
friends alone that we could take anything like our ease;
a state of affairs that led them sometimes without the
least pertinence to break out into sociable reminders.
I was invited—with no visible connexion—to repeat
afresh Goody Gosling's celebrated *mot* or to confirm
the details already supplied as to the cleverness of the
vicarage pony.

It was partly at such junctures as these and partly at
quite different ones that, with the turn my matters had

now taken, my predicament, as I have called it, grew
most sensible. The fact that the days passed for me
without another encounter ought, it would have appeared, to have done something toward soothing my
nerves. Since the light brush, that second night on the
upper landing, of the presence of a woman at the foot
of the stair, I had seen nothing, whether in or out of
the house, that one had better not have seen. There
was many a corner round which I expected to come
upon Quint, and many a situation that, in a merely
sinister way, would have favoured the appearance of
Miss Jessel. The summer had turned, the summer had
gone; the autumn had dropped upon Bly and had
blown out half our lights. The place, with its grey sky
and withered garlands, its bared spaces and scattered
dead leaves, was like a theatre after the performance—
all strewn with crumpled playbills. There were exactly
states of the air, conditions of sound and of stillness, unspeakable impressions of the *kind* of ministering moment, that brought back to me, long enough to catch
it, the feeling of the medium in which, that June evening out of doors, I had had my first sight of Quint, and
in which too, at those other instants, I had, after seeing
him through the window, looked for him in vain in the
circle of shrubbery. I recognised the signs, the portents—I recognised the moment, the spot. But they
remained unaccompanied and empty, and I continued
unmolested; if unmolested one could call a young
woman whose sensibility had, in the most extraordinary
fashion, not declined but deepened. I had said in my
talk with Mrs. Grose on that horrid scene of Flora's by
the lake—and had perplexed her by so saying—that
it would from that moment distress me much more to
lose my power than to keep it. I had then expressed
what was vividly in my mind: the truth that, whether

the children really saw or not—since, that is, it was not yet definitely proved—I greatly preferred, as a safeguard, the fulness of my own exposure. I was ready to know the very worst that was to be known. What I had then had an ugly glimpse of was that my eyes might be sealed just while theirs were most opened. Well, my eyes *were* sealed, it appeared, at present— a consummation for which it seemed blasphemous not to thank God. There was, alas, a difficulty about that: I would have thanked him with all my soul had I not had in a proportionate measure this conviction of the secret of my pupils.

How can I retrace to-day the strange steps of my obsession? There were times of our being together when I would have been ready to swear that, literally, in my presence, but with my direct sense of it closed, they had visitors who were known and were welcome. Then it was that, had I not been deterred by the very chance that such an injury might prove greater than the injury to be averted, my exaltation would have broken out. "They're here, they're here, you little wretches," I would have cried, "and you can't deny it now!" The little wretches denied it with all the added volume of their sociability and their tenderness, just in the crystal depths of which—like the flash of a fish in a stream—the mockery of their advantage peeped up. The shock had in truth sunk into me still deeper than I knew on the night when, looking out either for Quint or for Miss Jessel under the stars, I had seen there the boy over whose rest I watched and who had immediately brought in with him—had straightway there turned on me—the lovely upward look with which, from the battlements above us, the hideous apparition of Quint had played. If it was a question of a scare my discovery on this occasion had scared me more than any other, and it was essentially in the scared state that I drew my actual conclusions. They harassed me so that sometimes, at odd moments, I shut myself up audibly to rehearse—it was at once a fantastic relief and a renewed despair—the manner in which I might come to the point. I approached it from one side and the other while, in my room, I flung myself about, but I always broke down in the monstrous utterance of names. As they died away on my lips I said to myself that I should indeed help them to represent something infamous if by pronouncing them I should violate as rare a little case of instinctive delicacy as any school-room probably had ever known. When I said to myself: "*They* have the manners to be silent, and you, trusted as you are, the baseness to speak!" I felt myself crimson and covered my face with my hands. After these secret scenes I chattered more than ever, going on volubly enough till one of our prodigious palpable hushes occurred—I can call them nothing else—the strange dizzy lift or swim (I try for terms!) into a stillness, a pause of all life, that had nothing to do with the more or less noise we at the moment might be engaged in making and that I could hear through any intensified mirth or quickened recitation or louder strum of the piano. Then it was that the others, the outsiders, were there. Though they were not angels they "passed," as the French say, causing me, while they stayed, to tremble with the fear of their addressing to their younger victims some yet more infernal message or more vivid image than they had thought good enough for myself.

What it was least possible to get rid of was the cruel idea that, whatever I had seen, Miles and Flora saw *more*—things terrible and unguessable and that sprang from dreadful passages of intercourse in the past. Such things naturally left on the surface, for the time, a chill that we vociferously denied we felt; and we had all three, with repetition, got into such splendid training that we went, each time, to mark the close of the incident, almost automatically through the very same movements. It was striking of the children at all events to kiss me inveterately with a wild irrelevance and never to fail—one or the other—of the precious question that had helped us through many a peril. "When do you think he *will* come? Don't you think we *ought* to write?"—there was nothing like that enquiry, we found by experience, for carrying off an awkwardness. "He" of course was their uncle in Harley Street; and we lived in much profusion of theory that he might at any moment arrive to mingle in our circle. It was impossible to have given less encouragement than he had administered to such a doctrine, but if we had not had the doctrine to fall back upon we should have deprived each other of some of our finest exhibitions. He never wrote to them—that may have been selfish, but it was a part of the flattery of his trust of myself; for the way in which a man pays his highest tribute to a woman is apt to be but by the more festal celebration of one of the sacred laws of his comfort. So I held that I carried out the spirit of the pledge given not to appeal to him when I let our young friends understand that their own letters were but charming literary exercises. They were too beautiful to be posted; I kept them myself; I have them all to this hour. This was a rule indeed which only added to the satiric effect of my being plied with the supposition that he might at any moment be among us. It was exactly as if our young friends knew how almost more awkward than anything else that might be for me. There appears to me moreover as I look back no note in all this more

extraordinary than the mere fact that, in spite of my
tension and of their triumph, I never lost patience with
them. Adorable they must in truth have been, I now
feel, since I didn't in these days hate them! Would
exasperation, however, if relief had longer been postponed, finally have betrayed me? It little matters, for
relief arrived. I call it relief though it was only the relief that a snap brings to a strain or the burst of a thunderstorm to a day of suffocation. It was at least change,
and it came with a rush.

XIV

Walking to church a certain Sunday morning, I had
little Miles at my side and his sister, in advance of us
and at Mrs. Grose's, well in sight. It was a crisp clear
day, the first of its order for some time; the night had
brought a touch of frost and the autumn air, bright
and sharp, made the church-bells almost gay. It was
an odd accident of thought that I should have happened at such a moment to be particularly and very
gratefully struck with the obedience of my little
charges. Why did they never resent my inexorable,
my perpetual society? Something or other had brought
nearer home to me that I had all but pinned the boy
to my shawl, and that in the way our companions were
marshalled before me I might have appeared to provide against some danger of rebellion. I was like a
gaoler with an eye to possible surprises and escapes.
But all this belonged—I mean their magnificent little
surrender—just to the special array of the facts that
were most abysmal. Turned out for Sunday by his uncle's tailor, who had had a free hand and a notion of
pretty waistcoats and of his grand little air, Miles's

whole title to independence, the rights of his sex and situation, were so stamped upon him that if he had suddenly struck for freedom I should have had nothing to say. I was by the strangest of chances wondering how I should meet him when the revolution unmistakeably occurred. I call it a revolution because I now see how, with the word he spoke, the curtain rose on the last act of my dreadful drama and the catastrophe was precipitated. "Look here, my dear, you know," he charmingly said, "when in the world, please, am I going back to school?"

Transcribed here the speech sounds harmless enough, particularly as uttered in the sweet, high, casual pipe with which, at all interlocutors, but above all at his eternal governess, he threw off intonations as if he were tossing roses. There was something in them that always made one "catch," and I caught at any rate now so effectually that I stopped as short as if one of the trees of the park had fallen across the road. There was something new, on the spot, between us, and he was perfectly aware I recognised it, though to enable me to do so he had no need to look a whit less candid and charming than usual. I could feel in him how he already, from my at first finding nothing to reply, perceived the advantage he had gained. I was so slow to find anything that he had plenty of time, after a minute, to continue with his suggestive but inconclusive smile: "You know, my dear, that for a fellow to be with a lady *always*—!" His "my dear" was constantly on his lips for me, and nothing could have expressed more the exact shade of the sentiment with which I desired to inspire my pupils than its fond familiarity. It was so respectfully easy.

But oh how I felt that at present I must pick my own phrases! I remember that, to gain time, I tried to laugh, and I seemed to see in the beautiful face with which he watched me how ugly and queer I looked. "And always with the same lady?" I returned.

He neither blenched nor winked. The whole thing was virtually out between us. "Ah of course she's a jolly 'perfect' lady; but after all I'm a fellow, don't you see? who's—well, getting on."

I lingered there with him an instant ever so kindly. "Yes, you're getting on." Oh but I felt helpless!

I have kept to this day the heartbreaking little idea of how he seemed to know that and to play with it. "And you can't say I've not been awfully good, can you?"

I laid my hand on his shoulder, for though I felt how much better it would have been to walk on I was not yet quite able. "No, I can't say that, Miles."

"Except just that one night, you know—!"

"That one night?" I couldn't look as straight as he.

"Why when I went down—went out of the house."

"Oh yes. But I forget what you did it for."

"You forget?"—he spoke with the sweet extravagance of childish reproach. "Why it was just to show you I could!"

"Oh yes—you could."

"And I can again."

I felt I might perhaps after all succeed in keeping my wits about me. "Certainly. But you won't."

"No, not *that* again. It was nothing."

"It was nothing," I said. "But we must go on."

He resumed our walk with me, passing his hand into my arm. "Then when *am* I going back?"

I wore, in turning it over, my most responsible air. "Were you very happy at school?"

He just considered. "Oh I'm happy enough anywhere!"

"Well then," I quavered, "if you're just as happy here—!"

"Ah but that isn't everything! Of course *you* know a lot—"

"But you hint that you know almost as much?" I risked as he paused.

"Not half I want to!" Miles honestly professed. "But it isn't so much that."

"What is it then?"

"Well—I want to see more life."

"I see; I see." We had arrived within sight of the church and of various persons, including several of the household of Bly, on their way to it and clustered about the door to see us go in. I quickened our step; I wanted to get there before the question between us opened up much further; I reflected hungrily that he would have for more than an hour to be silent; and I thought with envy of the comparative dusk of the pew and of the almost spiritual help of the hassock on which I might bend my knees. I seemed literally to be running a race with some confusion to which he was about to reduce me, but I felt he had got in first when, before we had even entered the churchyard, he threw out—

"I want my own sort!"

It literally made me bound forward. "There aren't many of your own sort, Miles!" I laughed. "Unless perhaps dear little Flora!"

"You really compare me to a baby girl?"

This found me singularly weak. "Don't you then *love* our sweet Flora?"

"If I didn't—and you too; if I didn't—!" he repeated as if retreating for a jump, yet leaving his thought so unfinished that, after we had come into the gate, another stop, which he imposed on me by the pressure of his arm, had become inevitable. Mrs. Grose and Flora had passed into the church, the other worshippers had followed and we were, for the minute, alone among the old thick graves. We had paused, on the path from the gate, by a low oblong table-like tomb.

"Yes, if you didn't—?"

He looked, while I waited, about at the graves. "Well, you know what!" But he didn't move, and he presently produced something that made me drop straight down on the stone slab as if suddenly to rest. "Does my uncle think what *you* think?"

I markedly rested. "How do you know what I think?"

"Ah well, of course I don't; for it strikes me you never tell me. But I mean does *he* know?"

"Know what, Miles?"

"Why the way I'm going on."

I recognised quickly enough that I could make, to this enquiry, no answer that wouldn't involve something of a sacrifice of my employer. Yet it struck me that we were all, at Bly, sufficiently sacrificed to make that venial. "I don't think your uncle much cares."

Miles, on this, stood looking at me. "Then don't you think he can be made to?"

"In what way?"

"Why by his coming down."

"But who'll get him to come down?"

"*I* will!" the boy said with extraordinary brightness and emphasis. He gave me another look charged with that expression and then marched off alone into church.

XV

The business was practically settled from the moment I never followed him. It was a pitiful surrender to agi-

tation, but my being aware of this had somehow no
power to restore me. I only sat there on my tomb and
read into what our young friend had said to me the
fulness of its meaning; by the time I had grasped the
whole of which I had also embraced, for absence, the
pretext that I was ashamed to offer my pupils and
the rest of the congregation such an example of delay.
What I said to myself above all was that Miles had got
something out of me and that the gage of it for him
would be just this awkward collapse. He had got out
of me that there was something I was much afraid of,
and that he should probably be able to make use of
my fear to gain, for his own purpose, more freedom.
My fear was of having to deal with the intolerable
question of the grounds of his dismissal from school,
since that was really but the question of the horrors
gathered behind. That his uncle should arrive to treat
with me of these things was a solution that, strictly
speaking, I ought now to have desired to bring on;
but I could so little face the ugliness and the pain of it
that I simply procrastinated and lived from hand to
mouth. The boy, to my deep discomposure, was immensely in the right, was in a position to say to me:
"Either you clear up with my guardian the mystery of
this interruption of my studies, or you cease to expect
me to lead with you a life that's so unnatural for a boy."
What was so unnatural for the particular boy I was
concerned with was this sudden revelation of a consciousness and a plan.

That was what really overcame me, what prevented
my going in. I walked round the church, hesitating,
hovering; I reflected that I had already, with him, hurt
myself beyond repair. Therefore I could patch up
nothing and it was too extreme an effort to squeeze
beside him into the pew: he would be so much more

sure than ever to pass his arm into mine and make me
sit there for an hour in close mute contact with his
commentary on our talk. For the first minute since his
arrival I wanted to get away from him. As I paused
beneath the high east window and listened to the
sounds of worship I was taken with an impulse that
might master me, I felt, and completely, should I give
it the least encouragement. I might easily put an end
to my ordeal by getting away altogether. Here was
my chance; there was no one to stop me; I could give
the whole thing up—turn my back and bolt. It was
only a question of hurrying again, for a few preparations, to the house which the attendance at church of
so many of the servants would practically have left un-
occupied. No one, in short, could blame me if I should
just drive desperately off. What was it to get away if
I should get away only till dinner? That would be in a
couple of hours, at the end of which—I had the acute
prevision—my little pupils would play at innocent wonder about my non-appearance in their train.

"What *did* you do, you naughty bad thing? Why in
the world, to worry us so—and take our thoughts off
too, don't you know?—did you desert us at the very
door?" I couldn't meet such questions nor, as they
asked them, their false little lovely eyes; yet it was all
so exactly what I should have to meet that, as the prospect grew sharp to me, I at last let myself go.

I got, so far as the immediate moment was concerned,
away; I came straight out of the churchyard and,
thinking hard, retraced my steps through the park. It
seemed to me that by the time I reached the house I
had made up my mind to cynical flight. The Sunday
stillness both of the approaches and of the interior, in
which I met no one, fairly stirred me with a sense of
opportunity. Were I to get off quickly this way I should

get off without a scene, without a word. My quickness
would have to be remarkable, however, and the question of a conveyance was the great one to settle. Tormented, in the hall, with difficulties and obstacles, I
remember sinking down at the foot of the staircase—
suddenly collapsing there on the lowest step and then,
with a revulsion, recalling that it was exactly where,
more than a month before, in the darkness of night and
just so bowed with evil things, I had seen the spectre
of the most horrible of women. At this I was able to
straighten myself; I went the rest of the way up; I
made, in my turmoil, for the schoolroom, where there
were objects belonging to me that I should have to
take. But I opened the door to find again, in a flash,
my eyes unsealed. In the presence of what I saw I
reeled straight back upon resistance.

Seated at my own table in the clear noonday light I
saw a person whom, without my previous experience,
I should have taken at the first blush for some housemaid who might have stayed at home to look after the
place and who, availing herself of rare relief from observation and of the schoolroom table and my pens,
ink and paper, had applied herself to the considerable
effort of a letter to her sweetheart. There was an effort
in the way that, while her arms rested on the table,
her hands, with evident weariness, supported her head;
but at the moment I took this in I had already become
aware that, in spite of my entrance, her attitude
strangely persisted. Then it was—with the very act
of its announcing itself—that her identity flared up in
a change of posture. She rose, not as if she had heard
me, but with an indescribable grand melancholy of indifference and detachment, and, within a dozen feet of
me, stood there as my vile predecessor. Dishonoured
and tragic, she was all before me; but even as I fixed

and, for memory, secured it, the awful image passed away. Dark as midnight in her black dress, her haggard beauty and her unutterable woe, she had looked at me long enough to appear to say that her right to sit at my table was as good as mine to sit at hers. While these instants lasted indeed I had the extraordinary chill of a feeling that it was I who was the intruder. It was as a wild protest against it that, actually addressing her— "You terrible miserable woman!"—I heard myself break into a sound that, by the open door, rang through the long passage and the empty house. She looked at me as if she heard me, but I had recovered myself and cleared the air. There was nothing in the room the next minute but the sunshine and the sense that I must stay.

XVI

I had so perfectly expected the return of the others to be marked by a demonstration that I was freshly upset at having to find them merely dumb and discreet about my desertion. Instead of gaily denouncing and caressing me they made no allusion to my having failed them, and I was left, for the time, on perceiving that she too said nothing, to study Mrs. Grose's odd face. I did this to such purpose that I made sure they had in some way bribed her to silence; a silence that, however, I would engage to break down on the first private opportunity. This opportunity came before tea: I secured five minutes with her in the housekeeper's room, where, in the twilight, amid a smell of lately-baked bread, but with the place all swept and garnished, I found her sitting in pained placidity before the fire. So I see her still, so I see her best: facing the flame from her straight chair in the dusky shining room, a large clean picture of the "put away"—of drawers closed and locked and rest without a remedy.

"Oh yes, they asked me to say nothing; and to please them—so long as they were there—of course I promised. But what had happened to you?"

"I only went with you for the walk," I said. "I had then to come back to meet a friend."

She showed her surprise. "A friend—*you*?"

"Oh yes, I've a couple!" I laughed. "But did the children give you a reason?"

"For not alluding to your leaving us? Yes; they said you'd like it better. *Do* you like it better?"

My face had made her rueful. "No, I like it worse!" But after an instant I added: "Did they say why I should like it better?"

"No; Master Miles only said 'We must do nothing but what she likes!'"

"I wish indeed he would! And what did Flora say?"

"Miss Flora was too sweet. She said 'Oh of course, of course!'—and I said the same."

I thought a moment. "You were too sweet too—I can hear you all. But none the less, between Miles and me, it's now all out."

"All out?" My companion stared. "But what, Miss?"

"Everything. It doesn't matter. I've made up my mind. I came home, my dear," I went on, "for a talk with Miss Jessel."

I had by this time formed the habit of having Mrs. Grose literally well in hand in advance of my sounding that note; so that even now, as she bravely blinked under the signal of my word, I could keep her comparatively firm. "A talk! Do you mean she spoke?"

"It came to that. I found her, on my return, in the schoolroom."

"And what did she say?" I can hear the good woman still, and the candour of her stupefaction.

"That she suffers the torments—!"

It was this, of a truth, that made her, as she filled out my picture, gape. "Do you mean," she faltered "—of the lost?"

"Of the lost. Of the damned. And that's why, to share them—" I faltered myself with the horror of it.

But my companion, with less imagination, kept me up. "To share them—?"

"She wants Flora." Mrs. Grose might, as I gave it to her, fairly have fallen away from me had I not been prepared. I still held her there, to show I was. "As I've told you, however, it doesn't matter."

"Because you've made up your mind? But to what?"

"To everything."

"And what do you call 'everything'?"

"Why to sending for their uncle."

"Oh Miss, in pity do," my friend broke out.

"Ah but I will, I *will!* I see it's the only way. What's 'out,' as I told you, with Miles is that if he thinks I'm afraid to—and has ideas of what he gains by that— he shall see he's mistaken. Yes, yes; his uncle shall have it here from me on the spot (and before the boy himself if necessary) that if I'm to be reproached with having done nothing again about more school—"

"Yes, Miss—" my companion pressed me.

"Well, there's that awful reason."

There were now clearly so many of these for my poor colleague that she was excusable for being vague. "But—a—which?"

"Why the letter from his old place."

"You'll show it to the master?"

"I ought to have done so on the instant."

"Oh no!" said Mrs. Grose with decision.

"I'll put it before him," I went on inexorably, "that I can't undertake to work the question on behalf of a child who has been expelled—"

"For we've never in the least known what!" Mrs. Grose declared.

"For wickedness. For what else—when he's so clever and beautiful and perfect? Is he stupid? Is he untidy? Is he infirm? Is he ill-natured? He's exquisite—so it can be only *that;* and that would open up the whole thing. After all," I said, "it's their uncle's fault. If he left here such people—!"

"He didn't really in the least know them. The fault's mine." She had turned quite pale.

"Well, you shan't suffer," I answered.

"The children shan't!" she emphatically returned.

I was silent a while; we looked at each other. "Then what am I to tell him?"

"You needn't tell him anything. *I'll* tell him."

I measured this. "Do you mean you'll write—?" Remembering she couldn't, I caught myself up. "How do you communicate?"

"I tell the bailiff. *He* writes."

"And should you like him to write our story?"

My question had a sarcastic force that I had not fully intended, and it made her after a moment inconsequently break down. The tears were again in her eyes. "Ah Miss, *you* write!"

"Well—to-night," I at last returned; and on this we separated.

XVII

I went so far, in the evening, as to make a beginning. The weather had changed back, a great wind was abroad, and beneath the lamp, in my room, with Flora at peace beside me, I sat for a long time before a blank sheet of paper and listened to the lash of the rain and the batter of the gusts. Finally I went out, taking a candle; I crossed the passage and listened a minute at Miles's door. What, under my endless obsession, I had been impelled to listen for was some betrayal of his not being at rest, and I presently caught one, but not in the form I had expected. His voice tinkled out. "I say, you there—come in." It was gaiety in the gloom!

I went in with my light and found him in bed, very wide awake but very much at his ease. "Well, what are *you* up to?" he asked with a grace of sociability in which it occurred to me that Mrs. Grose, had she been present, might have looked in vain for proof that anything was "out."

I stood over him with my candle. "How did you know I was there?"

"Why of course I heard you. Did you fancy you made no noise? You're like a troop of cavalry!" he beautifully laughed.

"Then you weren't asleep?"

"Not much! I lie awake and think."

I had put my candle, designedly, a short way off, and then, as he held out his friendly old hand to me, had sat down on the edge of his bed. "What is it," I asked, "that you think of?"

"What in the world, my dear, but *you?*"

"Ah the pride I take in your appreciation doesn't insist on that! I had so far rather you slept."

"Well, I think also, you know, of this queer business of ours."

I marked the coolness of his firm little hand. "Of what queer business, Miles?"

"Why the way you bring me up. And all the rest!"

I fairly held my breath a minute, and even from my glimmering taper there was light enough to show how he smiled up at me from his pillow. "What do you mean by all the rest?"

"Oh you know, you know!"

I could say nothing for a minute, though I felt as I held his hand and our eyes continued to meet that my silence had all the air of admitting his charge and that nothing in the whole world of reality was perhaps at that moment so fabulous as our actual relation. "Certainly you shall go back to school," I said, "if it be that that troubles you. But not to the old place—we must find another, a better. How could I know it did trouble you, this question, when you never told me so, never spoke of it at all?" His clear listening face, framed in its smooth whiteness, made him for the minute as appealing as some wistful patient in a children's hospital; and I would have given, as the resemblance came to me, all I possessed on earth really to be the nurse or the sister of charity who might have helped to cure him. Well, even as it was I perhaps might help! "Do you know you've never said a word to me about your school—I mean the old one; never mentioned it in any way?"

He seemed to wonder; he smiled with the same loveliness. But he clearly gained time; he waited, he called for guidance. "Haven't I?" It wasn't for *me* to help him—it was for the thing I had met!

Something in his tone and the expression of his face, as I got this from him, set my heart aching with such a pang as it had never yet known; so unutterably touching was it to see his little brain puzzled and his little resources taxed to play, under the spell laid on him, a part of innocence and consistency. "No, never—from the hour you came back. You've never mentioned to me one of your masters, one of your comrades, nor the

least little thing that ever happened to you at school.
Never, little Miles—no never—have you given me an
inkling of anything that *may* have happened there.
Therefore you can fancy how much I'm in the dark.
Until you came out, that way, this morning, you had
since the first hour I saw you scarce even made a reference to anything in your previous life. You seemed so
perfectly to accept the present." It was extraordinary
how my absolute conviction of his secret precocity—
or whatever I might call the poison of an influence that
I dared but half-phrase—made him, in spite of the faint
breath of his inward trouble, appear as accessible as an
older person, forced me to treat him as an intelligent
equal. "I thought you wanted to go on as you are."

It struck me that at this he just faintly coloured. He
gave, at any rate, like a convalescent slightly fatigued,
a languid shake of his head. "I don't—I don't. I want
to get away."

"You're tired of Bly?"

"Oh no, I like Bly."

"Well then—?"

"Oh *you* know what a boy wants!"

I felt I didn't know so well as Miles, and I took temporary refuge. "You want to go to your uncle?"

Again, at this, with his sweet ironic face, he made a
movement on the pillow. "Ah you can't get off with
that!"

I was silent a little, and it was I now, I think, who
changed colour. "My dear, I don't want to get off!"

"You can't even if you do. You can't, you can't!"—
he lay beautifully staring. "My uncle must come down
and you must completely settle things."

"If we do," I returned with some spirit, "you may be
sure it will be to take you quite away."

"Well, don't you understand that that's exactly what

I'm working for? You'll have to *tell* him—about the way you've let it all drop: you'll have to tell him a tremendous lot!"

The exultation with which he uttered this helped me somehow for the instant to meet him rather more. "And how much will *you*, Miles, have to tell him? There are things he'll ask you!"

He turned it over. "Very likely. But what things?"

"The things you've never told me. To make up his mind what to do with you. He can't send you back—"

"I don't want to go back!" he broke in. "I want a new field."

He said it with admirable serenity, with positive unimpeachable gaiety; and doubtless it was that very note that most evoked for me the poignancy, the unnatural childish tragedy, of his probable reappearance at the end of three months with all this bravado and still more dishonour. It overwhelmed me now that I should never be able to bear that, and it made me let myself go. I threw myself upon him and in the tenderness of my pity I embraced him. "Dear little Miles, dear little Miles—!"

My face was close to his, and he let me kiss him, simply taking it with indulgent good humour. "Well, old lady?"

"Is there nothing—nothing at all that you want to tell me?"

He turned off a little, facing round toward the wall and holding up his hand to look at as one had seen sick children look. "I've told you—I told you this morning."

Oh I was sorry for him! "That you just want me not to worry you?"

He looked round at me now as if in recognition of my understanding him; then ever so gently, "To let me alone," he replied.

There was even a strange little dignity in it, something that made me release him, yet, when I had slowly risen, linger beside him. God knows I never wished to harass him, but I felt that merely, at this, to turn my back on him was to abandon or, to put it more truly, lose him. "I've just begun a letter to your uncle," I said.

"Well then, finish it!"

I waited a minute. "What happened before?"

He gazed up at me again. "Before what?"

"Before you came back. And before you went away."

For some time he was silent, but he continued to meet my eyes. "What happened?"

It made me, the sound of the words, in which it seemed to me I caught for the very first time a small faint quaver of consenting consciousness—it made me drop on my knees beside the bed and seize once more the chance of possessing him. "Dear little Miles, dear little Miles, if you *knew* how I want to help you! It's only that, it's nothing but that, and I'd rather die than give you a pain or do you a wrong—I'd rather die than hurt a hair of you. Dear little Miles"—oh I brought it out now even if I *should* go too far—"I just want you to help me to save you!" But I knew in a moment after this that I had gone too far. The answer to my appeal was instantaneous, but it came in the form of an extraordinary blast and chill, a gust of frozen air and a shake of the room as great as if, in the wild wind, the casement had crashed in. The boy gave a loud high shriek which, lost in the rest of the shock of sound, might have seemed, indistinctly, though I was so close to him, a note either of jubilation or of terror. I jumped to my feet again and was conscious of darkness. So for a moment we remained, while I stared about me and saw the drawn curtains unstirred and the window still tight.

"Why the candle's out!" I then cried.

"It was I who blew it, dear!" said Miles.

XVIII

The next day, after lessons, Mrs. Grose found a moment to say to me quietly: "Have you written, Miss?"

"Yes—I've written." But I didn't add—for the hour —that my letter, sealed and directed, was still in my pocket. There would be time enough to send it before the messenger should go to the village. Meanwhile there had been on the part of my pupils no more brilliant, more exemplary morning. It was exactly as if they had both had at heart to gloss over any recent little friction. They performed the dizziest feats of arithmetic, soaring quite out of *my* feeble range, and perpetrated, in higher spirits than ever, geographical and historical jokes. It was conspicuous of course in Miles in particular that he appeared to wish to show how easily he could let me down. This child, to my memory, really lives in a setting of beauty and misery that no words can translate; there was a distinction all his own in every impulse he revealed; never was a small natural creature, to the uninformed eye all frankness and freedom, a more ingenious, a more extraordinary little gentleman. I had perpetually to guard against the wonder of contemplation into which my initiated view betrayed me; to check the irrelevant gaze and discouraged sigh in which I constantly both attacked and renounced the enigma of what such a little gentleman could have done that deserved a penalty. Say that, by the dark prodigy I knew, the imagination of all evil *had* been opened up to him: all the justice within me ached for the proof that it could ever have flowered into an act.

He had never at any rate been such a little gentleman as when, after our early dinner on this dreadful
day, he came round to me and asked if I shouldn't like
him for half an hour to play to me. David playing to
Saul could never have shown a finer sense of the occasion. It was literally a charming exhibition of tact, of
magnanimity, and quite tantamount to his saying out-
right: "The true knights we love to read about never
push an advantage too far. I know what you mean
now: you mean that—to be let alone yourself and not
followed up—you'll cease to worry and spy upon me,
won't keep me so close to you, will let me go and come.
Well, I 'come,' you see—but I don't go! There'll be
plenty of time for that. I do really delight in your society and I only want to show you that I contended for
a principle." It may be imagined whether I resisted this
appeal or failed to accompany him again, hand in hand,
to the schoolroom. He sat down at the old piano and
played as he had never played; and if there are those
who think he had better have been kicking a football I
can only say that I wholly agree with them. For at the
end of a time that under his influence I had quite ceased
to measure I started up with a strange sense of having
literally slept at my post. It was after luncheon, and by
the schoolroom fire, and yet I hadn't really in the least
slept; I had only done something much worse—I had
forgotten. Where all this time was Flora? When I put
the question to Miles he played on a minute before answering, and then could only say: "Why, my dear, how
do *I* know?"—breaking moreover into a happy laugh
which immediately after, as if it were a vocal accom-
paniment, he prolonged into incoherent extravagant
song.

I went straight to my room, but his sister was not
there; then, before going downstairs, I looked into sev-

eral others. As she was nowhere about she would surely
be with Mrs. Grose, whom in the comfort of that theory
I accordingly proceeded in quest of. I found her where
I had found her the evening before, but she met my
quick challenge with blank scared ignorance. She had
only supposed that, after the repast, I had carried off
both the children; as to which she was quite in her right,
for it was the very first time I had allowed the little girl
out of my sight without some special provision. Of
course now indeed she might be with the maids, so
that the immediate thing was to look for her without
an air of alarm. This we promptly arranged between us;
but when, ten minutes later and in pursuance of our
arrangement, we met in the hall, it was only to report
on either side that after guarded enquiries we had altogether failed to trace her. For a minute there, apart
from observation, we exchanged mute alarms, and I
could feel with what high interest my friend returned
me all those I had from the first given her.

"She'll be above," she presently said—"in one of the
rooms you haven't searched."

"No; she's at a distance." I had made up my mind.
"She has gone out."

Mrs. Grose stared. "Without a hat?"

I naturally also looked volumes. "Isn't that woman
always without one?"

"She's with *her?*"

"She's with *her!*" I declared. "We must find them."

My hand was on my friend's arm, but she failed for
the moment, confronted with such an account of the
matter, to respond to my pressure. She communed, on
the contrary, where she stood, with her uneasiness.
"And where's Master Miles?"

"Oh *he's* with Quint. They'll be in the schoolroom."

"Lord, Miss!" My view, I was myself aware—and

therefore I suppose my tone—had never yet reached so calm an assurance.

"The trick's played," I went on; "they've successfully worked their plan. He found the most divine little way to keep me quiet while she went off."

"'Divine'?" Mrs. Grose bewilderedly echoed.

"Infernal then!" I almost cheerfully rejoined. "He has provided for himself as well. But come!"

She had helplessly gloomed at the upper regions. "You leave him—?"

"So long with Quint? Yes—I don't mind that now."

She always ended at these moments by getting possession of my hand, and in this manner she could at present still stay me. But after gasping an instant at my sudden resignation, "Because of your letter?" she eagerly brought out.

I quickly, by way of answer, felt for my letter, drew it forth, held it up, and then, freeing myself, went and laid in on the great hall-table. "Luke will take it," I said as I came back. I reached the house-door and opened it; I was already on the steps.

My companion still demured: the storm of the night and the early morning had dropped, but the afternoon was damp and grey. I came down to the drive while she stood in the doorway. "You go with nothing on?"

"What do I care when the child has nothing? I can't wait to dress," I cried, "and if you must do so I leave you. Try meanwhile yourself upstairs."

"With *them*?" Oh on this the poor woman promptly joined me!

XIX

We went straight to the lake, as it was called at Bly, and I dare say rightly called, though it may have been a sheet of water less remarkable than my untravelled eyes supposed it. My acquaintance with sheets of water was small, and the pool of Bly, at all events on the few occasions of my consenting, under the protection of my pupils, to affront its surface in the old flat-bottomed boat moored there for our use, had impressed me both with its extent and its agitation. The usual place of embarkation was half a mile from the house, but I had an intimate conviction that, wherever Flora might be, she was not near home. She had not given me the slip for any small adventure, and, since the day of the very great one that I had shared with her by the pond, I had been aware, in our walks, of the quarter to which she most inclined. This was why I had now given to Mrs. Grose's steps so marked a direction—a direction making her, when she perceived it, oppose a resistance that showed me she was freshly mystified. "You're going to the water, Miss?—you think she's *in*—?"

"She may be, though the depth is, I believe, nowhere very great. But what I judge most likely is that she's on the spot from which, the other day, we saw together what I told you."

"When she pretended not to see—?"

"With that astounding self-possession! I've always been sure she wanted to go back alone. And now her brother has managed it for her."

Mrs. Grose still stood where she had stopped. "You suppose they really *talk* of them?"

I could meet this with an assurance! "They say things that, if we heard them, would simply appal us."

"And if she *is* there—?"

"Yes?"

"Then Miss Jessel is?"

"Beyond a doubt. You shall see."

"Oh thank you!" my friend cried, planted so firm that,

taking it in, I went straight on without her. By the time I reached the pool, however, she was close behind me, and I knew that, whatever, to her apprehension, might befall me, the exposure of sticking to me struck her as her least danger. She exhaled a moan of relief as we at last came in sight of the greater part of the water without a sight of the child. There was no trace of Flora on that nearer side of the bank where my observation of her had been most startling, and none on the opposite edge, where, save for a margin of some twenty yards, a thick copse came down to the pond. This expanse, oblong in shape, was so narrow compared to its length that, with its ends out of view, it might have been taken for a scant river. We looked at the empty stretch, and then I felt the suggestion in my friend's eyes. I knew what she meant and I replied with a negative headshake.

"No, no; wait! She has taken the boat."

My companion stared at the vacant mooring-place and then again across the lake. "Then where is it?"

"Our not seeing it is the strongest of proofs. She has used it to go over, and then has managed to hide it."

"All alone—that child?"

"She's not alone, and at such times she's not a child: she's an old, old woman." I scanned all the visible shore while Mrs. Grose took again, into the queer element I offered her, one of her plunges of submission; then I pointed out that the boat might perfectly be in a small refuge formed by one of the recesses of the pool, an indentation masked, for the hither side, by a projection of the bank and by a clump of trees growing close to the water.

"But if the boat's there, where on earth's *she*?" my colleague anxiously asked.

"That's exactly what we must learn." And I started to walk further.

"By going all the way round?"

"Certainly, far as it is. It will take us but ten minutes, yet it's far enough to have made the child prefer not to walk. She went straight over."

"Laws!" cried my friend again: the chain of my logic was ever too strong for her. It dragged her at my heels even now, and when we had got halfway round—a devious tiresome process, on ground much broken and by a path choked with overgrowth—I paused to give her breath. I sustained her with a grateful arm, assuring her that she might hugely help me; and this started us afresh, so that in the course of but few minutes more we reached a point from which we found the boat to be where I had supposed it. It had been intentionally left as much as possible out of sight and was tied to one of the stakes of a fence that came, just there, down to the brink and that had been an assistance to disembarking. I recognised, as I looked at the pair of short thick oars, quite safely drawn up, the prodigious character of the feat for a little girl; but I had by this time lived too long among wonders and had panted to too many livelier measures. There was a gate in the fence, through which we passed, and that brought us after a trifling interval more into the open. Then "There she is!" we both exclaimed at once.

Flora, a short way off, stood before us on the grass and smiled as if her performance had now become complete. The next thing she did, however, was to stoop straight down and pluck—quite as if it were all she was there for—a big ugly spray of withered fern. I at once felt sure she had just come out of the copse. She waited for us, not herself taking a step, and I was conscious of the rare solemnity with which we presently approached her. She smiled and smiled, and we met; but it was all done in a silence by this time flagrantly ominous. Mrs. Grose was the first to break the spell: she threw herself on her knees and, drawing the child to her breast, clasped in a long embrace the little tender yielding body. While this dumb convulsion lasted I could only watch it—which I did the more intently when I saw Flora's face peep at me over our companion's shoulder. It was serious now—the flicker had left it; but it strengthened the pang with which I at that moment envied Mrs. Grose the simplicity of *her* relation. Still, all this while, nothing more passed between us save that Flora had let her foolish fern again drop to the ground. What she and I had virtually said to each other was that pretexts were useless now. When Mrs. Gross finally got up she kept the child's hand, so that the two were still before me; and the singular reticence of our communion was even more marked in the frank look she addressed me. "I'll be hanged," it said, "if *I'll* speak!"

It was Flora who, gazing all over me in candid wonder, was the first. She was struck with our bareheaded aspect. "Why where are your things?"

"Where yours are, my dear!" I promptly returned.

She had already got back her gaiety and appeared to take this as an answer quite sufficient. "And where's Miles?" she went on.

There was something in the small valour of it that quite finished me: these three words from her were in a flash like the glitter of a drawn blade the jostle of the cup that my hand for weeks and weeks had held high and full to the brim and that now, even before speaking, I felt overflow in a deluge. "I'll tell you if you'll tell *me*—" I heard myself say, then heard the tremor in which it broke.

"Well, what?"

Mrs. Grose's suspense blazed at me, but it was too late now, and I brought the thing out handsomely. "Where, my pet, is Miss Jessel?"

XX

Just as in the churchyard with Miles, the whole thing was upon us. Much as I had made of the fact that this name had never once, between us, been sounded, the quick smitten glare with which the child's face now received it fairly likened my breach of the silence to the smash of a pane of glass. It added to the interposing cry, as if to stay the blow, that Mrs. Grose at the same instant uttered over my violence—the shriek of a creature scared, or rather wounded, which, in turn, within a few seconds, was completed by a gasp of my own. I seized my colleague's arm. "She's there, she's there!"

Miss Jessel stood before us on the opposite bank exactly as she had stood the other time, and I remember, strangely, as the first feeling now produced in me, my thrill of joy at having brought on a proof. She was there, so I was justified; she was there, so I was neither cruel nor mad. She was there for poor scared Mrs. Grose, but she was there most for Flora; and no moment of my monstrous time was perhaps so extraordinary as that in which I consciously threw out to her—with the sense that, pale and ravenous demon as she was, she would catch and understand it—an inarticulate message of gratitude. She rose erect on the spot my friend and I had lately quitted, and there wasn't in all the long reach of her desire an inch of her evil that fell short. This first vividness of vision and emotion were things of a few seconds, during which Mrs. Grose's dazed blink across to where I pointed struck me as showing that she too at last saw, just as it carried my own eyes precipitately to the child. The revelation then of the manner in which Flora was affected startled me in truth far more than it would have done to find her also merely agitated, for direct dismay was of course not what I had expected. Prepared and on her guard as our pursuit had actually made her, she would repress every betrayal; and I was therefore at once shaken by my first glimpse of the particular one for which I had not allowed. To see her, without a convulsion of her small pink face, not even feign to glance in the direction of the prodigy I announced, but only, instead of that, turn at *me* an expression of hard still gravity, an expression absolutely new and unprecedented and that appeared to read and accuse and judge me—this was a stroke that somehow converted the little girl herself into a figure portentous. I gaped at her coolness even though my certitude of her thoroughly seeing was never greater than at that instant, and then, in the immediate need to defend myself, I called her passionately to witness. "She's there, you little unhappy thing—there, there, *there*, and you know it as well as you know me!" I had said shortly before to Mrs. Grose that she was not at these times a child, but an old, old woman, and my description of her couldn't have been more strikingly confirmed than in the way in which, for all notice of this, she simply showed me, without an expressional concession or admission, a countenance of deeper and deeper, of indeed suddenly quite fixed reprobation. I was by this time—if I can put the whole thing at all together— more appalled at what I may properly call her manner than at anything else, though it was quite simultaneously that I became aware of having Mrs. Grose also, and very formidably, to reckon with. My elder companion, the next moment, at any rate, blotted out everything but her own flushed face and her loud shocked protest, a burst of high disapproval. "What a dreadful turn, to be sure, Miss! Where on earth do you see anything?"

I could only grasp her more quickly yet, for even while she spoke the hideous plain presence stood undimmed and undaunted. It had already lasted a minute, and it lasted while I continued, seizing my colleague, quite thrusting her at it and presenting her to it, to insist with my pointing hand. "You don't see her exactly as *we* see?—you mean to say you don't now—*now?* She's as big as a blazing fire! Only look, dearest woman, *look*—!" She looked, just as I did, and gave me, with her deep groan of negation, repulsion, compassion—the mixture with her pity of her relief at her exemption—a sense, touching to me even then, that she would have backed me up if she had been able. I might well have needed that, for with this hard blow of the proof that her eyes were hopelessly sealed I felt my own situation horribly crumble, I felt—I *saw*—my livid predecessor press, from her position, on my defeat, and I took the measure, more than all, of what I should have from this instant to deal with in the astounding little attitude of Flora. Into this attitude Mrs. Grose immediately and violently entered, breaking, even while there pierced through my sense of ruin a prodigious private triumph, into breathless reassurance.

"She isn't there, little lady, and nobody's there— and you never see nothing, my sweet! How can poor Miss Jessel—when poor Miss Jessel's dead and buried? *We* know, don't we, love?"—and she appealed, blundering in, to the child. "It's all a mere mistake and a worry and a joke—and we'll go home as fast as we can!"

Our companion, on this, had responded with a strange quick primness of propriety, and they were again, with Mrs. Grose on her feet, united, as it were, in shocked opposition to me. Flora continued to fix me with her small mask of disaffection, and even at that minute I prayed God to forgive me for seeming to see that, as she stood there holding tight to our friend's dress, her incomparable childish beauty had suddenly failed, had quite vanished. I've said it already—she was literally, she was hideously hard; she had turned common and almost ugly. "I don't know what you mean. I see nobody. I see nothing. I never *have*. I think you're cruel. I don't like you!" Then, after this deliverance, which might have been that of a vulgarly pert little girl in the street, she hugged Mrs. Grose more closely and buried in her skirts the dreadful little face. In this position she launched an almost furious wail. "Take me away, take me away—oh take me away from *her!*"

"From *me?*" I panted.

"From you—from you!" she cried.

Even Mrs. Grose looked across at me dismayed; while I had nothing to do but communicate again with the figure that, on the opposite bank, without a movement, as rigidly still as if catching, beyond the interval, our voices, was as vividly there for my disaster as it was not there for my service. The wretched child had spoken exactly as if she had got from some outside source each of her stabbing little words, and I could therefore, in the full despair of all I had to accept, but sadly shake my head at her. "If I had ever doubted all my doubt would at present have gone. I've been living with the miserable truth, and now it has only too much closed round me. Of course I've lost you: I've interfered, and you've seen, under *her* dictation"—with which I faced, over the pool again, our infernal witness—"the easy and perfect way to meet it. I've done my best, but I've lost you. Good-bye." For Mrs. Grose I had an imperative, an almost frantic "Go, go!" before which, in infinite distress, but mutely possessed of the little girl and clearly convinced, in spite of her blindness, that something awful had occurred and some collapse engulfed us, she retreated, by the way we had come, as fast as she could move.

Of what first happened when I was left alone I had no subsequent memory. I only knew that at the end of, I suppose, a quarter of an hour, an odorous dampness and roughness, chilling and piercing my trouble, had made me understand that I must have thrown myself, on my face, to the ground and given way to a wildness of grief. I must have lain there long and cried and wailed, for when I raised my head the day was almost done. I got up and looked a moment, through the twilight, at the grey pool and its blank haunted edge, and then I took, back to the house, my dreary and difficult course. When I reached the gate in the fence the boat, to my surprise, was gone, so that I had a fresh reflexion to make on Flora's extraordinary command of the situation. She passed that night, by the most tacit and, I should add, were not the word so grotesque a false note, the happiest of arrangements, with Mrs. Grose. I saw neither of them on my return, but on the other hand I saw, as by an ambiguous compensation, a great deal of Miles. I saw—I can use no other phrase—so much of him that it fairly measured more than it had ever measured. No evening I had passed at Bly was to have had the portentous quality of this one; in spite of which—and in spite also of the deeper depths of consternation that had opened beneath my feet—there was literally, in the ebbing actual, an extraordinarily sweet sadness. On reaching the house I had never so much as looked for the boy; I had simply gone straight to my room to change what I was wearing and to take in, at a glance, much material testimony to Flora's rupture. Her

portentous.

little belongings had all been removed. When later, by the schoolroom fire, I was served with tea by the usual maid, I indulged, on the article of my other pupil, in no enquiry whatever. He had his freedom now—he might have it to the end! Well, he did have it; and it consisted—in part at least—of his coming in at about eight o'clock and sitting down with me in silence. On the removal of the tea-things I had blown out the candles and drawn my chair closer: I was conscious of a mortal coldness and felt as if I should never again be warm. So when he appeared I was sitting in the glow with my thoughts. He paused a moment by the door as if to look at me; then—as if to share them—came to the other side of the hearth and sank into a chair. We sat there in absolute stillness; yet he wanted, I felt, to be with me.

XXI

Before a new day, in my room, had fully broken, my eyes opened to Mrs. Grose, who had come to my bedside with worse news. Flora was so markedly feverish that an illness was perhaps at hand; she had passed a night of extreme unrest, a night agitated above all by fears that had for their subject not in the least her former but wholly her present governess. It was not against the possible re-entrance of Miss Jessel on the scene that she protested—it was conspicuously and passionately against mine. I was at once on my feet, and with an immense deal to ask; the more that my friend had discernibly now girded her loins to meet me afresh. This I felt as soon as I had put to her the question of her sense of the child's sincerity as against my own. "She persists in denying to you that she saw, or has ever seen, anything?"

My visitor's trouble truly was great. "Ah Miss, it isn't a matter on which I can push her! Yet it isn't either, I must say, as if I much needed to. It has made her, every inch of her, quite old."

"Oh I see her perfectly from here. She resents, for all the world like some high little personage, the imputation on her truthfulness and, as it were, her respectability. 'Miss Jessel indeed—*she!*' Ah she's 'respectable,' the chit! The impression she gave me there yesterday was, I assure you, the very strangest of all: it was quite beyond any of the others. I *did* put my foot in it! She'll never speak to me again."

Hideous and obscure as it all was, it held Mrs. Grose briefly silent; then she granted my point with a frankness which, I made sure, had more behind it. "I think indeed, Miss, she never will. She do have a grand manner about it!"

"And that manner"—I summed it up—"is practically what's the matter with her now."

Oh that manner, I could see in my visitor's face, and not a little else besides! "She asks me every three minutes if I think you're coming in."

"I see—I see." I too, on my side, had so much more than worked it out. "Has she said to you since yesterday—except to repudiate her familiarity with anything so dreadful—a single other word about Miss Jessel?"

"Not one, Miss. And of course, you know," my friend added, "I took it from her by the lake that just then and there at least there *was* nobody."

"Rather! And naturally you take it from her still."

"I don't contradict her. What else can I do?"

"Nothing in the world! You've the cleverest little person to deal with. They've made them—their two friends, I mean—still cleverer even than nature did;

for it was wondrous material to play on! Flora has now her grievance, and she'll work it to the end."

"Yes, Miss; but to *what* end?"

"Why that of dealing with me to her uncle. She'll make me out to him the lowest creature—!"

I winced at the fair show of the scene in Mrs. Grose's face; she looked for a minute as if she sharply saw them together. "And him who thinks so well of you!"

"He has an odd way—it comes over me now," I laughed, "—of proving it! But that doesn't matter. What Flora wants of course is to get rid of me."

My companion bravely concurred. "Never again to so much as look at you."

"So that what you've come to me now for," I asked, "is to speed me on my way?" Before she had time to reply, however, I had her in check. "I've a better idea —the result of my reflexions. My going *would* seem the right thing, and on Sunday I was terribly near it. Yet that won't do. It's *you* who must go. You must take Flora."

My visitor, at this, did speculate. "But where in the world—?"

"Away from here. Away from *them*. Away, even most of all, now, from me. Straight to her uncle."

"Only to tell on you—?"

"No, not 'only'! To leave me, in addition, with my remedy."

She was still vague. "And what *is* your remedy?"

"Your loyalty, to begin with. And then Miles's."

She looked at me hard. "Do you think he—?"

"Won't, if he has the chance, turn on me? Yes, I venture still to think it. At all events I want to try. Get off with his sister as soon as possible and leave me with him alone." I was amazed, myself, at the spirit I had still in reserve, and therefore perhaps a trifle the more disconcerted at the way in which, in spite of this fine example of it, she hesitated. "There's one thing, of course," I went on: "they mustn't, before she goes, see each other for three seconds." Then it came over me that, in spite of Flora's presumable sequestration from the instant of her return from the pool, it might already be too late. "Do you mean," I anxiously asked, "that they *have* met?"

At this she quite flushed. "Ah, Miss, I'm not such a fool as that! If I've been obliged to leave her three or four times, it has been each time with one of the maids, and at present, though she's alone, she's locked in safe. And yet—and yet!" There were too many things.

"And yet what?"

"Well, are you so sure of the little gentleman?"

"I'm not sure of anything but *you*. But I have, since last evening, a new hope. I think he wants to give me an opening. I do believe that—poor little exquisite wretch!—he wants to speak. Last evening, in the fire-light and the silence, he sat with me for two hours as if it were just coming."

Mrs. Grose looked hard through the window at the grey gathering day. "And did it come?"

"No, though I waited and waited I confess it didn't, and it was without a breach of the silence, or so much as a faint allusion to his sister's condition and absence, that we at last kissed for good-night. All the same," I continued, "I can't, if her uncle sees her, consent to his seeing her brother without my having given the boy—and most of all because things have got so bad—a little more time."

My friend appeared on this ground more reluctant than I could quite understand. "What do you mean by more time?"

"Well, a day or two—really to bring it out. He'll then

be on *my* side—of which you see the importance. If nothing comes I shall only fail, and you at the worst have helped me by doing on your arrival in town whatever you may have found possible." So I put it before her, but she continued for a little so lost in other reasons that I came again to her aid. "Unless indeed," I wound up, "you really want *not* to go."

I could see it, in her face, at last clear itself: she put out her hand to me as a pledge. "I'll go—I'll go. I'll go this morning."

I wanted to be very just. "If you *should* wish still to wait I'd engage she shouldn't see me."

"No, no: it's the place itself. She must leave it." She held me a moment with heavy eyes, then brought out the rest. "Your idea's the right one. I myself, Miss—"

"Well?"

"I can't stay."

The look she gave me with it made me jump at possibilities. "You mean that, since yesterday, you *have* seen—?"

She shook her head with dignity. "I've *heard*—!"

"Heard?"

"From that child—horrors! There!" she sighed with tragic relief. "On my honour, Miss, she says things—!" But at this evocation she broke down; she dropped with a sudden cry upon my sofa and, as I had seen her do before, gave way to all the anguish of it.

It was quite in another manner that I for my part let myself go. "Oh thank God!"

She sprang up again at this, drying her eyes with a groan. " 'Thank God'?"

"It so justifies me!"

"It does that, Miss!"

I couldn't have desired more emphasis, but I just waited. "She's so horrible?"

I saw my colleague scarce knew how to put it. "Really shocking."

"And about me?"

"About you, Miss—since you must have it. It's beyond everything, for a young lady; and I can't think wherever she must have picked up—"

"The appalling language she applies to me? I can then!" I broke in with a laugh that was doubtless significant enough.

It only in truth left my friend still more grave. "Well, perhaps I ought to also—since I've heard some of it before! Yet I can't bear it," the poor woman went on while with the same movement she glanced, on my dressing-table, at the face of my watch. "But I must go back."

I kept her, however. "Ah if you can't bear it—!"

"How can I stop with her, you mean? Why just *for* that: to get her away. Far from this," she pursued, "far from *them*—"

"She may be different? She may be free?" I seized her almost with joy. "Then in spite of yesterday you *believe*—"

"In such doings?" Her simple description of them required, in the light of her expression, to be carried no further, and she gave me the whole thing as she had never done. "I believe."

Yes, it was a joy, and we were still shoulder to shoulder: if I might continue sure of that I should care but little what else happened. My support in the presence of disaster would be the same as it had been in my early need of confidence, and if my friend would answer for my honesty I would answer for all the rest. On the point of taking leave of her, none the less, I was to some extent embarrassed. "There's one thing of course —it occurs to me—to remember. My letter giving the alarm will have reached town before you."

I now felt still more how she had been beating about the bush and how weary at last it had made her. "Your letter won't have got there. Your letter never went."

"What then became of it?"

"Goodness knows! Master Miles—"

"Do you mean *he* took it?" I gasped.

She hung fire, but she overcame her reluctance. "I mean that I saw yesterday, when I came back with Miss Flora, that it wasn't where you had put it. Later in the evening I had the chance to question Luke, and he declared that he had neither noticed nor touched it." We could only exchange, on this, one of our deeper mutual soundings, and it was Mrs. Grose who first brought up the plumb with an almost elate "You see!"

"Yes, I see that if Miles took it instead he probably will have read it and destroyed it."

"And don't you see anything else?"

I faced her a moment with a sad smile. "It strikes me that by this time your eyes are open even wider than mine."

They proved to be so indeed, but she could still almost blush to show it. "I make out now what he must have done at school." And she gave, in her simple sharpness, an almost droll disillusioned nod. "He stole!"

I turned it over—I tried to be more judicial. "Well —perhaps."

She looked as if she found me unexpectedly calm. "He stole *letters!*"

She couldn't know my reasons for a calmness after all pretty shallow; so I showed them off as I might. "I hope then it was to more purpose than in this case! The note, at all events, that I put on the table yesterday," I pursued, "will have given him so scant an advantage— for it contained only the bare demand for an interview —that he's already much ashamed of having gone so far for so little, and that what he had on his mind last evening was precisely the need of confession." I seemed to myself for the instant to have mastered it, to see it all. "Leave us, leave us"—I was already, at the door, hurrying her off. "I'll get it out of him. He'll meet me. He'll confess. If he confesses he's saved. And if he's saved—"

"Then *you* are?" The dear woman kissed me on this, and I took her farewell. "I'll save you without him!" she cried as she went.

XXII

Yet it was when she had got off—and I missed her on the spot—that the great pinch really came. If I had counted on what it would give me to find myself alone with Miles I quickly recognised that it would give me at least a measure. No hour of my stay in fact was so assailed with apprehensions as that of my coming down to learn that the carriage containing Mrs. Grose and my younger pupil had already rolled out of the gates. Now I *was,* I said to myself, face to face with the elements, and for much of the rest of the day, while I fought my weakness, I could consider that I had been supremely rash. It was a tighter place still than I had yet turned round in; all the more that, for the first time, I could see in the aspect of others a confused reflexion of the crisis. What had happened naturally caused them all to stare; there was too little of the explained, throw out whatever we might, in the suddenness of my colleague's act. The maids and the men looked blank; the effect of which on my nerves was an aggravation until I saw the necessity of making it a positive aid. It was in short by just clutching the helm that I avoided total wreck; and I dare say that, to bear up at all, I became that morning very grand and very dry. I welcomed the consciousness that I was charged with much to do, and I caused it to be known as well that, left thus to myself, I was quite remarkably firm. I wandered with that manner, for the next hour or two, all over the place and looked, I have no doubt, as if I were ready for any onset. So, for the benefit of whom it might concern, I paraded with a sick heart.

The person it appeared least to concern proved to be, till dinner, little Miles himself. My perambulations had given me meanwhile no glimpse of him, but they had tended to make more public the change taking place in our relation as a consequence of his having at the piano, the day before, kept me, in Flora's interest, so beguiled and befooled. The stamp of publicity had of course been fully given by her confinement and departure, and the change itself was now ushered in by our non-observance of the regular custom of the schoolroom. He had already disappeared when, on my way down, I pushed open his door, and I learned below that he had breakfasted—in the presence of a couple of the maids—with Mrs. Grose and his sister. He had then gone out, as he said, for a stroll; than which nothing, I reflected, could better have expressed his frank view of the abrupt transformation of my office. What he would now permit this office to consist of was yet to be settled: there was at the least a queer relief—I mean for myself in especial—in the renouncement of one pretension. If so much had sprung to the surface I scarce put it too strongly in saying that what had perhaps sprung highest was the absurdity of our prolonging the fiction that I had anything more to teach him. It sufficiently stuck out that, by tacit little tricks in which even more than myself he carried out the care for my dignity, I had had to appeal to him to let me off straining to meet him on the ground of his true capacity. He had at any rate his freedom now; I was never to touch it again: as I had amply shown, moreover, when, on his joining me in the schoolroom the previous night, I uttered, in reference to the interval just concluded, neither challenge nor hint. I had too much, from this moment, my other ideas. Yet when he at last arrived the difficulty of applying them, the accumulations of my problem, were brought straight home to me by the beautiful little presence on which what had occurred had as yet, for the eye, dropped neither stain nor shadow.

To mark, for the house, the high state I cultivated I decreed that my meals with the boy should be served, as we called it, downstairs; so that I had been awaiting him in the ponderous pomp of the room outside the window of which I had had from Mrs. Grose, that first scared Sunday, my flash of something it would scarce have done to call light. Here at present I felt afresh— for I had felt it again and again—how my equilibrium depended on the success of my rigid will, the will to shut my eyes as tight as possible to the truth that what I had to deal with was, revoltingly, against nature. I could only get on at all by taking "nature" into my confidence and my account, by treating my monstrous ordeal as a push in a direction unusual, of course, and unpleasant, but demanding after all, for a fair front, only another turn of the screw of ordinary human virtue. No attempt, none the less, could well require more tact than just this attempt to supply, one's self, *all* the nature. How could I put even a little of that article into a suppression of reference to what had occurred? How on the other hand could I make a reference without a new plunge into the hideous obscure? Well, a sort of answer, after a time, had come to me, and it was so far confirmed as that I was met, incontestably, by the quickened vision of what was rare in my little companion. It was indeed as if he had found even now—as he had so often found at lessons—still some other delicate way to ease me off. Wasn't there light in the fact which, as we shared our solitude, broke out with a specious glitter it had never yet quite worn?—the fact that (opportunity aiding, precious opportunity which had now come) it would be preposterous, with a child so endowed, to forego the help one might wrest from absolute intelligence? What had his intelligence been given him for but to save him? Mightn't one, to reach his mind, risk the stretch of a stiff arm across his character? It was as if, when we were face to face in the dining-room, he had literally shown me the way. The roast mutton was on the table and I had dispensed with attendance. Miles, before he sat down, stood a moment with his hands in his pockets and looked at the joint, on which he seemed on the point of passing some humorous judgement. But what he presently produced was: "I say, my dear, is she really very awfully ill?"

"Little Flora? Not so bad but that she'll presently be better. London will set her up. Bly had ceased to agree with her. Come here and take your mutton."

He alertly obeyed me, carried the plate carefully to his seat and, when he was established, went on. "Did Bly disagree with her so terribly all at once?"

"Not so suddenly as you might think. One had seen it coming on."

"Then why didn't you get her off before?"

"Before what?"

"Before she became too ill to travel."

I found myself prompt. "She's *not* too ill to travel; she only might have become so if she had stayed. This was just the moment to seize. The journey will dissipate the influence"—oh I was grand!—"and carry it off."

"I see, I see"—Miles, for that matter, was grand too. He settled to his repast with the charming little "table manner" that, from the day of his arrival, had relieved me of all grossness of admonition. Whatever he had been expelled from school for, it wasn't for ugly feeding. He was irreproachable, as always, to-day; but was unmistakeably more conscious. He was discernibly trying to take for granted more things than he found, without assistance, quite easy; and he dropped into peaceful silence while he felt his situation. Our meal was of the briefest—mine a vain pretence, and I had the things immediately removed. While this was done Miles stood again with his hands in his little pockets and his back to me—stood and looked out of the wide window through which, that other day, I had seen what pulled me up. We continued silent while the maid was with us—as silent, it whimsically occurred to me, as some young couple who, on their wedding-journey, at the inn, fell shy in the presence of the waiter. He turned round only when the waiter had left us. "Well—so we're alone!"

XXIII

"Oh more or less." I imagine my smile was pale. "Not absolutely. We shouldn't like that!" I went on.

"No—I suppose we shouldn't. Of course we've the others."

"We've the others—we've indeed the others," I concurred.

"Yet even though we have them," he returned, still with his hands in his pockets and planted there in front of me, "they don't much count, do they?"

I made the best of it, but I felt wan. "It depends on what you call 'much'!"

"Yes"—with all accommodation—"everything depends!" On this, however, he faced to the window again and presently reached it with his vague restless cogitating step. He remained there a while with his forehead against the glass, in contemplation of the stupid shrubs I knew and the dull things of November. I had always my hypocrisy of "work," behind which I now gained the sofa. Steadying myself with it there as I had repeatedly done at those moments of torment that I have described as the moments of my knowing the children to be given to something from which I was barred, I sufficiently obeyed my habit of being prepared for the worst. But an extraordinary impression dropped on me as I extracted a meaning from the boy's embarrassed back—none other than the impression that I was not barred now. This inference grew in a few minutes to sharp intensity and seemed bound up with the direct perception that it was positively *he* who was. The frames and squares of the great window were a kind of image, for him, of a kind of failure. I felt that I saw him, in any case, shut in or shut out. He was admirable but not comfortable: I took it in with a throb of hope. Wasn't he looking through the haunted pane for something he couldn't see?—and wasn't it the first time in the whole business that he had known such a lapse? The first, the very first: I found it a splendid portent. It made him anxious, though he watched himself; he had been anxious all day and, even while in his usual sweet little manner he sat at table, had needed all his small strange genius to give it a gloss. When he at last turned round to meet me it was almost as if this genius had succumbed. "Well, I think I'm glad Bly agrees with *me!*"

"You'd certainly seem to have seen, these twenty-four hours, a good deal more of it than for some time before. I hope," I went on bravely, "that you've been enjoying yourself."

"Oh yes, I've been ever so far; all round about—miles and miles away. I've never been so free."

He had really a manner of his own, and I could only try to keep up with him. "Well, do you like it?"

He stood there smiling; then at last he put into two words—"Do *you*?"—more discrimination than I had ever heard two words contain. Before I had time to deal with that, however, he continued as if with the sense that this was an impertinence to be softened. "Nothing could be more charming than the way you take it, for of course if we're alone together now it's you that are alone most. But I hope," he threw in, "you don't particularly mind!"

"Having to do with you?" I asked. "My dear child, how can I help minding? Though I've renounced all claim to your company—you're so beyond me—I at least greatly enjoy it. What else should I stay on for?"

He looked at me more directly, and the expression of his face, graver now, struck me as the most beautiful I had ever found in it. "You stay on just for *that*?"

"Certainly. I stay on as your friend and from the tremendous interest I take in you till something can be done for you that may be more worth your while. That needn't surprise you." My voice trembled so that I felt it impossible to suppress the shake. "Don't you remember how I told you, when I came and sat on your bed the night of the storm, that there was nothing in the world I wouldn't do for you?"

"Yes, yes!" He, on his side, more and more visibly nervous, had a tone to master; but he was so much more successful than I that, laughing out through his gravity, he could pretend we were pleasantly jesting. "Only that, I think, was to get me to do something for *you!*"

"It was partly to get you to do something," I conceded. "But, you know, you didn't do it."

"Oh yes," he said with the brightest superficial eagerness, "you wanted me to tell you something."

"That's it. Out, straight out. What you have on your mind, you know."

"Ah then is *that* what you've stayed over for?"

He spoke with a gaiety through which I could still catch the finest little quiver of resentful passion; but I can't begin to express the effect upon me of an implication of surrender even so faint. It was as if what I had yearned for had come at last only to astonish me. "Well, yes—I may as well make a clean breast of it. It was precisely for that."

He waited so long that I supposed it for the purpose of repudiating the assumption on which my action had been founded; but what he finally said was: "Do you mean now—here?"

"There couldn't be a better place or time." He looked round him uneasily, and I had the rare—oh the queer! —impression of the very first symptom I had seen in him of the approach of immediate fear. It was as if he were suddenly afraid of me—which struck me indeed as perhaps the best thing to make him. Yet in the very pang of the effort I felt it vain to try sternness, and I heard myself the next instant so gentle as to be almost grotesque. "You want so to go out again?"

"Awfully!" He smiled at me heroically, and the touching little bravery of it was enhanced by his actually flushing with pain. He had picked up his hat, which he had brought in, and stood twirling it in a way that gave me, even as I was just nearly reaching port, a perverse horror of what I was doing. To do it in *any* way was an act of violence, for what did it consist of but the obtrusion of the idea of grossness and guilt on a small helpless creature who had been for me a revelation of the possibilities of beautiful intercourse? Wasn't it base to create for a being so exquisite a mere alien awkwardness? I suppose I now read into our situation a clearness it couldn't have had at the time, for I seem to see our poor eyes already lighted with some spark of a prevision of the anguish that was to come. So we circled about with terrors and scruples, fighters not daring to close. But it was for each other we feared! That kept us a little longer suspended and unbruised. "I'll tell you everything," Miles said—"I mean I'll tell you anything you like. You'll stay on with me, and we shall both be all right, and I *will* tell you— I *will*. But not now."

"Why not now?"

My insistence turned him from me and kept him once more at his window in a silence during which, between us, you might have heard a pin drop. Then he was before me again with the air of a person for whom, outside, some one who had frankly to be reckoned with was waiting. "I have to see Luke."

I had not yet reduced him to quite so vulgar a lie, and I felt proportionately ashamed. But, horrible as it was, his lies made up my truth. I achieved thoughtfully a few loops of my knitting. "Well then go to Luke, and I'll wait for what you promise. Only in return for that satisfy, before you leave me, one very much smaller request."

He looked as if he felt he had succeeded enough to be able still a little to bargain. "Very much smaller—?"

"Yes, a mere fraction of the whole. Tell me"—oh my work preoccupied me, and I was off-hand!—"if, yesterday afternoon, from the table in the hall, you took, you know, my letter."

My grasp of how he received this suffered for a minute from something that I can describe only as a fierce split of my attention—a stroke that at first, as I sprang straight up, reduced me to the mere blind movement of getting hold of him, drawing him close and, while I just fell for support against the nearest piece of furniture, instinctively keeping him with his back to the window. The appearance was full upon us that I had already had to deal with here: Peter Quint had come into view like a sentinel before a prison. The next thing I saw was that, from outside, he had reached the window, and then I knew that, close to the glass and glaring in through it, he offered once more to the room his white face of damnation. It represents but grossly what took place within me at the sight to say that on the second my decision was made; yet I believe that no woman so overwhelmed ever in so short a time recovered her command of the *act*. It came to me in the very horror of the immediate presence that the act would be, seeing and facing what I saw and faced, to keep the boy himself unaware. The inspiration—I can call it by no other name—was that I felt how voluntarily, how transcendently, I *might*. It was like fighting with a demon for a human soul, and when I had fairly so appraised it I saw how the human soul—held out, in the tremor of my hands, at arms' length—had a perfect dew of sweat on a lovely childish forehead. The face that was close to mine was as white as the face against the glass, and out of it presently came a sound, not low nor weak, but as if from much further away, that I drank like a waft of fragrance.

"Yes—I took it."

At this, with a moan of joy, I enfolded, I drew him close; and while I held him to my breast, where I could feel in the sudden fever of his little body the tremendous pulse of his little heart, I kept my eyes on the thing at the window and saw it move and shift its posture. I have likened it to a sentinel, but its slow wheel, for a moment, was rather the prowl of a baffled beast. My present quickened courage, however, was such that, not too much to let it through, I had to shade, as it were, my flame. Meanwhile the glare of the face was again at the window, the scoundrel fixed as if to watch and wait. It was the very confidence that I might now defy him, as well as the positive certitude, by this time, of the child's unconsciousness, that made me go on. "What did you take it for?"

"To see what you said about me."

"You opened the letter?"

"I opened it."

My eyes were now, as I held him off a little again, on Miles's own face, in which the collapse of mockery showed me how complete was the ravage of uneasiness. What was prodigious was that at last, by my success, his sense was sealed and his communication stopped: he knew that he was in presence, but knew not of what, and knew still less that I also was and that I did know. And what did this strain of trouble matter when my eyes went back to the window only to see that the air was clear again and—by my personal triumph—the influence quenched? There was nothing there. I felt that the cause was mine and that I should surely get *all*. "And you found nothing!"—I let my elation out.

He gave the most mournful, thoughtful little head-shake. "Nothing."

"Nothing, nothing!" I almost shouted in my joy.

"Nothing, nothing," he sadly repeated.

I kissed his forehead; it was drenched. "So what have you done with it?"

"I've burnt it."

"Burnt it?" It was now or never. "Is that what you did at school?"

Oh what this brought up! "At school?"

"Did you take letters?—or other things?"

"Other things?" He appeared now to be thinking of something far off and that reached him only through the pressure of his anxiety. Yet it did reach him. "Did I steal?"

I felt myself redden to the roots of my hair as well as wonder if it were more strange to put to a gentleman such a question or to see him take it with allowances that gave the very distance of his fall in the world. "Was it for that you mightn't go back?"

The only thing he felt was rather a dreary little surprise. "Did you know I mightn't go back?"

"I know everything."

He gave me at this the longest and strangest look. "Everything?"

"Everything. Therefore *did* you—?" But I couldn't say it again.

Miles could, very simply. "No. I didn't steal."

My face must have shown him I believed him utterly; yet my hands—but it was for pure tenderness—shook him as if to ask him why, if it was all for nothing, he had condemned me to months of torment. "What then did you do?"

He looked in vague pain all round the top of the room and drew his breath, two or three times over, as if with difficulty. He might have been standing at the bottom of the sea and raising his eyes to some faint green twilight. "Well—I said things."

"Only that?"

"They thought it was enough!"

"To turn you out for?"

Never, truly, had a person "turned out" shown so little to explain it as this little person! He appeared to weigh my question, but in a manner quite detached and almost helpless. "Well, I suppose I oughtn't."

"But to whom did you say them?"

He evidently tried to remember, but it dropped—he had lost it. "I don't know!"

He almost smiled at me in the desolation of his surrender, which was indeed practically, by this time, so complete that I ought to have left it there. But I was infatuated—I was blind with victory, though even then the very effect that was to have brought him so much nearer was already that of added separation. "Was it to every one?" I asked.

"No; it was only to—" But he gave a sick little headshake. "I don't remember their names."

"Were they then so many?"

"No—only a few. Those I liked."

Those he liked? I seemed to float not into clearness, but into a darker obscure, and within a minute there had come to me out of my very pity the appalling alarm of his being perhaps innocent. It was for the instant confounding and bottomless, for if he *were* innocent what then on earth was I? Paralysed, while it lasted, by the mere brush of the question, I let him go a little, so that, with a deep-drawn sigh, he turned away from me again; which, as he faced toward the clear window, I suffered, feeling that I had nothing now there to keep him from. "And did they repeat what you said?" I went on after a moment.

He was soon at some distance from me, still breathing hard and again with the air, though now without anger for it, of being confined against his will. Once more, as he had done before, he looked up at the dim day as if, of what had hitherto sustained him, nothing was left but an unspeakable anxiety. "Oh yes," he nevertheless replied—"they must have repeated them. To those *they* liked," he added.

There was somehow less of it than I had expected; but I turned it over. "And these things came round—?"

"To the masters? Oh yes!" he answered very simply. "But I didn't know they'd tell."

"The masters? They didn't—they've never told. That's why I ask you."

He turned to me again his little beautiful fevered face. "Yes, it was too bad."

"Too bad?"

"What I suppose I sometimes said. To write home."

I can't name the exquisite pathos of the contradiction given to such a speech by such a speaker; I only know that the next instant I heard myself throw off with homely force: "Stuff and nonsense!" But the next after that I must have sounded stern enough. "What *were* these things?"

My sternness was all for his judge, his executioner; yet it made him avert himself again, and that movement made *me*, with a single bound and an irrepressible cry, spring straight upon him. For there again, against the glass, as if to blight his confession and stay his answer, was the hideous author of our woe—the white face of damnation. I felt a sick swim at the drop of my victory and all the return of my battle, so that the wildness of my veritable leap only served as a great betrayal. I saw him, from the midst of my act, meet it with a divination, and on the perception that even now he only guessed, and that the window was still to his own eyes free, I let the impulse flame up to convert the climax of his dismay into the very proof of his liberation. "No more, no more, no more!" I shrieked to my visitant as I tried to press him against me.

"Is she *here*?" Miles panted as he caught with his sealed eyes the direction of my words. Then as his strange "she" staggered me and, with a gasp, I echoed it, "Miss Jessel, Miss Jessel!" he with sudden fury gave me back.

I seized, stupefied, his supposition—some sequel to what we had done to Flora, but this made me only want to show him that it was better still than that. "It's not Miss Jessel! But it's at the window—straight before us. It's *there*—the coward horror, there for the last time!"

At this, after a second in which his head made the movement of a baffled dog's on a scent and then gave a frantic little shake for air and light, he was at me in a white rage, bewildered, glaring vainly over the place and missing wholly, though it now, to my sense, filled the room like the taste of poison, the wide overwhelming presence. "It's *he*?"

I was so determined to have all my proof that I flashed into ice to challenge him. "Whom do you mean by 'he'?"

"Peter Quint—you devil!" His face gave again, round the room, its convulsed supplication. "*Where*?"

They are in my ears still, his supreme surrender of the name and his tribute to my devotion. "What does he matter now, my own?—what will he *ever* matter? *I* have you," I launched at the beast, "but he has lost you for ever!" Then for the demonstration of my work, "There, *there!*" I said to Miles.

But he had already jerked straight round, stared,

glared again, and seen but the quiet day. With the
stroke of the loss I was so proud of he uttered the cry
of a creature hurled over an abyss, and the grasp with
which I recovered him might have been that of catching him in his fall. I caught him, yes, I held him—it
may be imagined with what a passion; but at the end
of a minute I began to feel what it truly was that I
held. We were alone with the quiet day, and his little
heart, dispossessed, had stopped.

*

THE BEAST IN THE JUNGLE

I

What determined the speech that startled him in the
course of their encounter scarcely matters, being probably but some words spoken by himself quite without
intention—spoken as they lingered and slowly moved
together after their renewal of acquaintance. He had
been conveyed by friends an hour or two before to the
house at which she was staying; the party of visitors at
the other house, of whom he was one, and thanks to
whom it was his theory, as always, that he was lost in
the crowd, had been invited over to luncheon. There
had been after luncheon much dispersal, all in the interest of the original motive, a view of Weatherend
itself and the fine things, intrinsic features, pictures,
heirlooms, treasures of all the arts, that made the place
almost famous; and the great rooms were so numerous
that guests could wander at their will, hang back from
the principal group and in cases where they took such
matters with the last seriousness give themselves up to

mysterious appreciations and measurements. There were persons to be observed, singly or in couples, bending toward objects in out-of-the-way corners with their hands on their knees and their heads nodding quite as with the emphasis of an excited sense of smell. When they were two they either mingled their sounds of ecstasy or melted into silences of even deeper import, so that there were aspects of the occasion that gave it for Marcher much the air of the "look round," previous to a sale highly advertised, that excites or quenches, as may be, the dream of acquisition. The dream of acquisition at Weatherend would have had to be wild indeed, and John Marcher found himself, among such suggestions, disconcerted almost equally by the presence of those who knew too much and by that of those who knew nothing. The great rooms caused so much poetry and history to press upon him that he needed some straying apart to feel in a proper relation with them, though this impulse was not, as happened, like the gloating of some of his companions, to be compared to the movements of a dog sniffing a cupboard. It had an issue promptly enough in a direction that was not to have been calculated.

It led, briefly, in the course of the October afternoon, to his closer meeting with May Bartram, whose face, a reminder, yet not quite a remembrance, as they sat much separated at a very long table, had begun merely by troubling him rather pleasantly. It affected him as the sequel of something of which he had lost the beginning. He knew it, and for the time quite welcomed it, as a continuation, but didn't know what it continued, which was an interest or an amusement the greater as he was also somehow aware—yet without a direct sign from her—that the young woman herself hadn't lost the thread. She hadn't lost it, but she wouldn't give it back to him, he saw, without some putting forth of his hand for it; and he not only saw that, but saw several things more, things odd enough in the light of the fact at the moment some accident of grouping brought them face to face he was still merely fumbling with the idea that any contact between them in the past would have had no importance. If it had had no importance he scarcely knew why his actual impression of her should so seem to have so much; the answer to which, however, was that in such a life as they all appeared to be leading for the moment one could but take things as they came. He was satisfied, without in the least being able to say why, that this young lady might roughly have ranked in the house as a poor relation; satisfied also that she was not there on a brief visit, but was more or less a part of the establishment—almost a working, a remunerated part. Didn't she enjoy at periods a protection that she paid for by helping, among other services, to show the place and explain it, deal with the tiresome people, answer questions about the dates of the building, the styles of the furniture, the authorship of the pictures, the favourite haunts of the ghost? It wasn't that she looked as if you could have given her shillings—it was impossible to look less so. Yet when she finally drifted toward him, distinctly handsome, though ever so much older—older than when he had seen her before—it might have been as an effect of her guessing that he had, within the couple of hours, devoted more imagination to her than to all the others put together, and had thereby penetrated to a kind of truth that the others were too stupid for. She *was* there on harder terms than any one; she was there as a consequence of things suffered, one way and another, in the interval of years; and she remembered him very much as she was remembered—only a good deal better.

By the time they at last thus came to speech they were alone in one of the rooms—remarkable for a fine portrait over the chimney-place—out of which their friends had passed, and the charm of it was that even before they had spoken they had practically arranged with each other to stay behind for talk. The charm, happily, was in other things too—partly in there being scarce a spot at Weatherend without something to stay behind for. It was in the way the autumn day looked into the high windows as it waned; the way the red light, breaking at the close from under a low sombre sky, reached out in a long shaft and played over old wainscots, old tapestry, old gold, old colour. It was most of all perhaps in the way she came to him as if, since she had been turned on to deal with the simpler sort, he might, should he choose to keep the whole thing down, just take her mild attention for a part of her general business. As soon as he heard her voice, however, the gap was filled up and the missing link supplied; the slight irony he divined in her attitude lost its advantage. He almost jumped at it to get there before her. "I met you years and years ago in Rome. I remember all about it." She confessed to disappointment—she had been so sure he didn't; and to prove how well he did he began to pour forth the particular recollections that popped up as he called for them. Her face and her voice, all at his service now, worked the miracle—the impression operating like the torch of a lamplighter who touches into flame, one by one, a long row of gas-jets. Marcher flattered himself the illumination was brilliant, yet he was really still more pleased on her showing him, with amusement, that in his haste to make everything right he had got most things rather wrong. It hadn't been at Rome—it had been at Naples; and it hadn't been eight years before—it had been more nearly ten. She hadn't been,

either, with her uncle and aunt, but with her mother
and her brother; in addition to which it was not with
the Pembles *he* had been, but with the Boyers, coming
down in their company from Rome—a point on which
she insisted, a little to his confusion, and as to which she
had her evidence in hand. The Boyers she had known,
but didn't know the Pembles, though she had heard of
them, and it was the people he was with who had made
them acquainted. The incident of the thunderstorm that
had raged round them with such violence as to drive
them for refuge into an excavation—this incident had
not occurred at the Palace of the Cæsars, but at Pom-
peii, on an occasion when they had been present there at
an important find.

He accepted her amendments, he enjoyed her cor-
rections, though the moral of them was, she pointed
out, that he *really* didn't remember the least thing about
her; and he only felt it as a drawback that when all was
made strictly historic there didn't appear much of anything left. They lingered together still, she neglecting
her office—for from the moment he was so clever she
had no proper right to him—and both neglecting the
house, just waiting as to see if a memory or two more
wouldn't again breathe on them. It hadn't taken them
many minutes, after all, to put down on the table, like
the cards of a pack, those that constituted their respective hands; only what came out was that the pack was
unfortunately not perfect—that the past, invoked, invited, encouraged, could give them, naturally, no more
than it had. It had made them anciently meet—her at
twenty, him at twenty-five; but nothing was so strange,
they seemed to say to each other, as that, while so occupied, it hadn't done a little more for them. They
looked at each other as with the feeling of an occasion
missed; the present would have been so much better if

the other, in the far distance, in the foreign land, hadn't
been so stupidly meagre. There weren't apparently, all
counted, more than a dozen little old things that had
succeeded in coming to pass between them; trivialities
of youth, simplicities of freshness, stupidities of ignorance, small possible germs, but too deeply buried—too
deeply (didn't it seem?) to sprout after so many years.
Marcher could only feel he ought to have rendered her
some service—saved her from a capsized boat in the Bay
or at least recovered her dressing-bag, filched from her
cab in the streets of Naples by a lazzarone with a sti-
letto. Or it would have been nice if he could have been
taken with fever all alone at his hotel, and she could
have come to look after him, to write to his people, to
drive him out in convalescence. *Then* they would be in
possession of the something or other that their actual
show seemed to lack. It yet somehow presented itself,
this show, as too good to be spoiled; so that they were
reduced for a few minutes more to wondering a little
helplessly why—since they seemed to know a certain
number of the same people—their reunion had been so
long averted. They didn't use that name for it, but their
delay from minute to minute to join the others was a
kind of confession that they didn't quite want it to be
a failure. Their attempted supposition of reasons for
their not having met but showed how little they knew
of each other. There came in fact a moment when
Marcher felt a positive pang. It was vain to pretend she
was an old friend, for all the communities were wanting,
in spite of which it was as an old friend that he saw
she would have suited him. He had new ones enough—
was surrounded with them for instance on the stage of
the other house; as a new one he probably wouldn't
have so much as noticed her. He would have liked to

invent something, get her to make believe with him that some passage of a romantic or critical kind *had* originally occurred. He was really almost reaching out in imagination—as against time—for something that would do, and saying to himself that if it didn't come this sketch of a fresh start would show for quite awkwardly bungled. They would separate, and now for no second or no third chance. They would have tried and not succeeded. Then it was, just at the turn, as he afterwards made it out to himself, that, everything else failing, she herself decided to take up the case and, as it were, save the situation. He felt as soon as she spoke that she had been consciously keeping back what she said and hoping to get on without it; a scruple in her that immensely touched him when, by the end of three or four minutes more, he was able to measure it. What she brought out, at any rate, quite cleared the air and supplied the link —the link it was so odd he should frivolously have managed to lose.

"You know you told me something I've never forgotten and that again and again has made me think of you since; it was that tremendously hot day when we went to Sorrento, across the bay, for the breeze. What I allude to was what you said to me, on the way back, as we sat under the awning of the boat enjoying the cool. Have you forgotten?"

He had forgotten and was even more surprised than ashamed. But the great thing was that he saw in this no vulgar reminder of any "sweet" speech. The vanity of women had long memories, but she was making no claim on him of a compliment or a mistake. With another woman, a totally different one, he might have feared the recall possibly even of some imbecile "offer." So, in having to say that he had indeed forgotten, he was conscious rather of a loss than of a gain; he already saw an interest in the matter of her mention. "I try to think—but I give it up. Yet I remember the Sorrento day."

"I'm not very sure you do," May Bartram after a moment said; "and I'm not very sure I ought to want you to. It's dreadful to bring a person back at any time to what he was ten years before. If you've lived away from it," she smiled, "so much the better."

"Ah if *you* haven't why should I?" he asked.

"Lived away, you mean, from what I myself was?"

"From what *I* was. I was of course an ass," Marcher went on; "but I would rather know from you just the sort of ass I was than—from the moment you have something in your mind—not know anything."

Still, however, she hesitated. "But if you've completely ceased to be that sort—?"

"Why I can then all the more bear to know. Besides, perhaps I haven't."

"Perhaps. Yet if you haven't," she added, "I should suppose you'd remember. Not indeed that *I* in the least connect with my impression the invidious name you use. If I had only thought you foolish," she explained, "the thing I speak of wouldn't so have remained with me. It was about yourself." She waited as if it might come to him; but as, only meeting her eyes in wonder, he gave no sign, she burnt her ships. "Has it ever happened?"

Then it was that, while he continued to stare, a light broke for him and the blood slowly came to his face, which began to burn with recognition. "Do you mean I told you—?" But he faltered, lest what came to him shouldn't be right, lest he should only give himself away.

"It was something about yourself that it was natural one shouldn't forget—that is if one remembered you at all. That's why I ask you," she smiled, "if the thing you then spoke of has ever come to pass?"

Oh then he saw, but he was lost in wonder and found himself embarrassed. This, he also saw, made her sorry for him, as if her allusion had been a mistake. It took him but a moment, however, to feel it hadn't been, much as it had been a surprise. After the first little shock of it her knowledge on the contrary began, even if rather strangely, to taste sweet to him. She was the only other person in the world then who would have it, and she had had it all these years, while the fact of his having so breathed his secret had unaccountably faded from him. No wonder they couldn't have met as if nothing had happened. "I judge," he finally said, "that I know what you mean. Only I had strangely enough lost any sense of having taken you so far into my confidence."

"Is it because you've taken so many others as well?"

"I've taken nobody. Not a creature since then."

"So that I'm the only person who knows?"

"The only person in the world."

"Well," she quickly replied, "I myself have never spoken. I've never, never repeated of you what you told me." She looked at him so that he perfectly believed her. Their eyes met over it in such a way that he was without a doubt. "And I never will."

She spoke with an earnestness that, as if almost excessive, put him at ease about her possible derision. Somehow the whole question was a new luxury to him—that is from the moment she was in possession. If she didn't take the sarcastic view she clearly took the sympathetic, and that was what he had had, in all the long time, from no one whomsoever. What he felt was that he couldn't at present have begun to tell her, and yet could profit perhaps exquisitely by the accident of having done so of old. "Please don't then. We're just right as it is."

"Oh I am," she laughed, "if you are!" To which she added: "Then you do still feel in the same way?"

It was impossible he shouldn't take to himself that she was really interested, though it all kept coming as perfect surprise. He had thought of himself so long as abominably alone, and lo he wasn't alone a bit. He hadn't been, it appeared, for an hour—since those moments on the Sorrento boat. It was *she* who had been, he seemed to see as he looked at her—she who had been made so by the graceless fact of his lapse of fidelity. To tell her what he had told her—what had it been but to ask something of her? something that she had given, in her charity, without his having, by a remembrance, by a return of the spirit, failing another encounter, so much as thanked her. What he had asked of her had been simply at first not to laugh at him. She had beautifully not done so for ten years, and she was not doing so now. So he had endless gratitude to make up. Only for that he must see just how he had figured to her. "What, exactly, was the account I gave—?"

"Of the way you did feel? Well, it was very simple. You said you had had from your earliest time, as the deepest thing within you, the sense of being kept for something rare and strange, possibly prodigious and terrible, that was sooner or later to happen to you, that you had in your bones the foreboding and the conviction of, and that would perhaps overwhelm you."

"Do you call that very simple?" John Marcher asked.

She thought a moment. "It was perhaps because I seemed, as you spoke, to understand it."

"You do understand it?" he eagerly asked.

Again she kept her kind eyes on him. "You still have the belief?"

"Oh!" he exclaimed helplessly. There was too much to say.

"Whatever it's to be," she clearly made out, "it hasn't yet come."

He shook his head in complete surrender now. "It hasn't yet come. Only, you know, it isn't anything I'm to *do,* to achieve in the world, to be distinguished or admired for. I'm not such an ass as *that.* It would be much better, no doubt, if I were."

"It's to be something you're merely to suffer?"

"Well, say to wait for—to have to meet, to face, to see suddenly break out in my life; possibly destroying all further consciousness, possibly annihilating me; possibly, on the other hand, only altering everything, striking at the root of all my world and leaving me to the consequences, however they shape themselves."

She took this in, but the light in her eyes continued for him not to be that of mockery. "Isn't what you describe perhaps but the expectation—or at any rate the sense of danger, familiar to so many people—of falling in love?"

John Marcher wondered. "Did you ask me that before?"

"No—I wasn't so free-and-easy then. But it's what strikes me now."

"Of course," he said after a moment, "it strikes you. Of course it strikes *me.* Of course what's in store for me may be no more than that. The only thing is," he went on, "that I think if it had been that I should by this time know."

"Do you mean because you've *been* in love?" And then as he but looked at her in silence: "You've been in love, and it hasn't meant such a cataclysm, hasn't proved the great affair?"

"Here I am, you see. It hasn't been overwhelming."

"Then it hasn't been love," said May Bartram.

"Well, I at least thought it was. I took it for that—

I've taken it till now. It was agreeable, it was delightful, it was miserable," he explained. "But it wasn't strange. It wasn't what *my* affair's to be."

"You want something all to yourself—something that nobody else knows or *has* known?"

"It isn't a question of what I 'want'—God knows I don't want anything. It's only a question of the apprehension that haunts me—that I live with day by day."

He said this so lucidly and consistently that he could see it further impose itself. If she hadn't been interested before she'd have been interested now. "Is it a sense of coming violence?"

Evidently now too again he liked to talk of it. "I don't think of it as—when it does come—necessarily violent. I only think of it as natural and as of course above all unmistakeable. I think of it simply as *the* thing. *The* thing will of itself appear natural."

"Then how will it appear strange?"

Marcher bethought himself. "It won't—to *me*."

"To whom then?"

"Well," he replied, smiling at last, "say to you."

"Oh then I'm to be present?"

"Why you *are* present—since you know."

"I see." She turned it over. "But I mean at the catastrophe."

At this, for a minute, their lightness gave way to their gravity; it was as if the long look they exchanged held them together. "It will only depend on yourself—if you'll watch with me."

"Are you afraid?" she asked.

"Don't leave me *now*," he went on.

"Are you afraid?" she repeated.

"Do you think me simply out of my mind?" he pursued instead of answering. "Do I merely strike you as a harmless lunatic?"

"No," said May Bartram. "I understand you. I believe you."

"You mean you feel how my obsession—poor old thing!—may correspond to some possible reality?"

"To some possible reality."

"Then you *will* watch with me?"

She hesitated, then for the third time put her question. "Are you afraid?"

"Did I tell you I was—at Naples?"

"No, you said nothing about it."

"Then I don't know. And I should *like* to know," said John Marcher. "You'll tell me yourself whether you think so. If you'll watch with me you'll see."

"Very good then." They had been moving by this time across the room, and at the door, before passing out, they paused as for the full wind-up of their understanding. "I'll watch with you," said May Bartram.

II

The fact that she "knew"—knew and yet neither chaffed him nor betrayed him—had in a short time begun to constitute between them a goodly bond, which became more marked when, within the year that followed their afternoon at Weatherend, the opportunities for meeting multiplied. The event that thus promoted these occasions was the death of the ancient lady her great-aunt, under whose wing, since losing her mother, she had to such an extent found shelter, and who, though but the widowed mother of the new successor to the property, had succeeded—thanks to a high tone and a high temper—in not forfeiting the supreme position at the great house. The deposition of this personage arrived but with her death, which, followed by many changes, made in particular a difference for the young woman in whom Marcher's expert attention had recognised from the first a dependent with a pride that might ache though it didn't bristle. Nothing for a long time had made him easier than the thought that the aching must have been much soothed by Miss Bartram's now finding herself able to set up a small home in London. She had acquired property, to an amount that made that luxury just possible, under her aunt's extremely complicated will, and when the whole matter began to be straightened out, which indeed took time, she let him know that the happy issue was at last in view. He had seen her again before that day, both because she had more than once accompanied the ancient lady to town and because he had paid another visit to the friends who so conveniently made of Weatherend one of the charms of their own hospitality. These friends had taken him back there; he had achieved there again with Miss Bartram some quiet detachment; and he had in London succeeded in persuading her to more than one brief absence from her aunt. They went together, on these latter occasions, to the National Gallery and the South Kensington Museum, where, among vivid reminders, they talked of Italy at large—not now attempting to recover, as at first, the taste of their youth and their ignorance. That recovery, the first day at Weatherend, had served its purpose well, had given them quite enough; so that they were, to Marcher's sense, no longer hovering about the headwaters of their stream, but had felt their boat pushed sharply off and down the current.

They were literally afloat together; for our gentleman this was marked, quite as marked as that the fortunate cause of it was just the buried treasure of her knowledge. He had with his own hands dug up this little hoard, brought to light—that is to within reach of the dim day constituted by their discretions and privacies— the object of value the hiding-place of which he had, after putting it into the ground himself, so strangely, so long forgotten. The rare luck of his having again just stumbled on the spot made him indifferent to any other question; he would doubtless have devoted more time to the odd accident of his lapse of memory if he hadn't been moved to devote so much to the sweetness, the comfort, as he felt, for the future, that this accident itself had helped to keep fresh. It had never entered into his plan that any one should "know," and mainly for the reason that it wasn't in him to tell any one. That would have been impossible, for nothing but the amusement of a cold world would have waited on it. Since, however, a mysterious fate had opened his mouth betimes, in spite of him, he would count that a compensation and profit by it to the utmost. That the right person *should* know tempered the asperity of his secret more even than his shyness had permitted him to imagine; and May Bartram was clearly right, because—well, because there she was. Her knowledge simply settled it; he would have been sure enough by this time had she been wrong. There was that in his situation, no doubt, that disposed him too much to see her as a mere confidant, taking all her light for him from the fact—the fact only—of her interest in his predicament; from her mercy, sympathy, seriousness, her consent not to regard him as the funniest of the funny. Aware, in fine, that her price for him was just in her giving him this constant sense of his being admirably spared, he was careful to remember that she had also a life of her own, with things that might happen to *her*, things that in friendship one should likewise take account of. Something fairly remarkable came to pass with him, for that matter, in this connexion—something represented by a certain passage of his consciousness, in the suddenest way, from one extreme to the other.

He had thought himself, so long as nobody knew, the most disinterested person in the world, carrying his concentrated burden, his perpetual suspense, ever so quietly, holding his tongue about it, giving others no glimpse of it nor of its effect upon his life, asking of them no allowance and only making on his side all those that were asked. He hadn't disturbed people with the queerness of their having to know a haunted man, though he had had moments of rather special temptation on hearing them say they were forsooth "unsettled." If they were as unsettled as he was—he who had never been settled for an hour in his life—they would know what it meant. Yet it wasn't, all the same, for him to make them, and he listened to them civilly enough. This was why he had such good—though possibly such rather colourless—manners; this was why, above all, he could regard himself, in a greedy world, as decently—as in fact perhaps even a little sublimely—unselfish. Our point is accordingly that he valued this character quite sufficiently to measure his present danger of letting it lapse, against which he promised himself to be much on his guard. He was quite ready, none the less, to be selfish just a little, since surely no more charming occasion for it had come to him. "Just a little," in a word, was just as much as Miss Bartram, taking one day with another, would let him. He never would be in the least coercive, and would keep well before him the lines on which consideration for her—the very highest—ought to proceed. He would thoroughly establish the heads under which her affairs, her requirements, her peculiarities—he went so far as to give them the latitude of that name—would come into their intercourse. All this naturally was a sign of how much he took the intercourse itself for granted. There was nothing more to be done about *that*. It simply existed; had sprung into being with her first penetrating question to him in the autumn light there at Weather-end. The real form it should have taken on the basis that stood out large was the form of their marrying. But the devil in this was that the very basis itself put marrying out of the question. His conviction, his apprehension, his obsession, in short, wasn't a privilege he could invite a woman to share; and that consequence of it was precisely what was the matter with him. Something or other lay in wait for him, amid the twists and the turns of the months and the years, like a crouching beast in the jungle. It signified little whether the crouching beast were destined to slay him or to be slain. The definite point was the inevitable spring of the creature; and the definite lesson from that was that a man of feeling didn't cause himself to be accompanied by a lady on a tiger-hunt. Such was the image under which he had ended by figuring his life.

They had at first, none the less, in the scattered hours spent together, made no allusion to that view of it; which was a sign he was handsomely alert to give that he didn't expect, that he in fact didn't care, always to be talking about it. Such a feature in one's outlook was really like a hump on one's back. The difference it made every minute of the day existed quite independently of discussion. One discussed of course *like* a hunchback, for there was always, if nothing else, the hunchback face. That remained, and she was watching him; but people watched best, as a general thing, in silence, so that such would be predominantly the manner of their vigil. Yet he didn't want, at the same time, to be tense and solemn; tense and solemn was what he imagined he too much showed for with other people. The thing to be, with the one person who knew, was easy and natural—to make the reference rather than be seeming to avoid it, to avoid it rather than be seeming to make it, and to keep it, in any case, familiar, facetious even, rather than pedantic and portentous. Some such consideration as the latter was doubtless in his mind for instance when he wrote pleasantly to Miss Bartram that perhaps the great thing he had so long felt as in the lap of the gods was no more than this circumstance, which touched him so nearly, of her acquiring a house in London. It was the first allusion they had yet again made, needing any other hitherto so little; but when she replied, after having given him the news, that she was by no means satisfied with such a trifle as the climax to so special a suspense, she almost set him wondering if she hadn't even a larger conception of singularity for him than he had for himself. He was at all events destined to become aware little by little, as time went by, that she was all the while looking at his life, judging it, measuring it, in the light of the thing she knew, which grew to be at last, with the consecration of the years, never mentioned between them save as "the real truth" about him. That had always been his own form of reference to it, but she adopted the form so quietly that, looking back at the end of a period, he knew there was no moment at which it was traceable that she had, as he might say, got inside his idea, or exchanged the attitude of beautifully indulging for that of still more beautifully believing him.

It was always open to him to accuse her of seeing him but as the most harmless of maniacs, and this, in the long run—since it covered so much ground—was his easiest description of their friendship. He had a screw loose for her, but she liked him in spite of it and was practically, against the rest of the world, his kind wise keeper, unremunerated but fairly amused and, in the absence of other near ties, not disreputably occupied. The rest of the world of course thought him queer, but she, she only, knew how, and above all why, queer;

which was precisely what enabled her to dispose the concealing veil in the right folds. She took his gaiety from him—since it had to pass with them for gaiety—as she took everything else; but she certainly so far justified by her unerring touch his finer sense of the degree to which he had ended by convincing her. *She* at least never spoke of the secret of his life except as "the real truth about you," and she had in fact a wonderful way of making it seem, as such, the secret of her own life too. That was in fine how he so constantly felt her as allowing for him; he couldn't on the whole call it anything else. He allowed himself, but she, exactly, allowed still more; partly because, better placed for a sight of the matter, she traced his unhappy perversion through reaches of its course into which he could scarce follow it. He knew how he felt, but, besides knowing that, she knew how he *looked* as well; he knew each of the things of importance he was insidiously kept from doing, but she could add up the amount they made, understand how much, with a lighter weight on his spirit, he might have done, and thereby established how, clever as he was, he fell short. Above all she was in the secret of the difference between the forms he went through—those of his little office under Government, those of caring for his modest patrimony, for his library, for his garden in the country, for the people in London whose invitations he accepted and repaid—and the detachment that reigned beneath them and that made of all behaviour, all that could in the least be called behaviour, a long act of dissimulation. What it had come to was that he wore a mask painted with the social simper, out of the eyeholes of which there looked eyes of an expression not in the least matching the other features. This the stupid world, even after years, had never more than half-discovered. It was only May Bartram who had, and she

achieved, by an art indescribable, the feat of at once—
or perhaps it was only alternately—meeting the eyes
from in front and mingling her own vision, as from over
his shoulder, with their peep through the apertures.

So while they grew older together she did watch with
him, and so she let this association give shape and colour
to her own existence. Beneath *her* forms as well detachment had learned to sit, and behaviour had become for
her, in the social sense, a false account of herself. There
was but one account of her that would have been true
all the while and that she could give straight to nobody,
least of all to John Marcher. Her whole attitude was a
virtual statement, but the perception of that only seemed
called to take its place for him as one of the many things
necessarily crowded out of his consciousness. If she had
moreover, like himself, to make sacrifices to their real
truth, it was to be granted that her compensation might
have affected her as more prompt and more natural.
They had long periods, in this London time, during
which, when they were together, a stranger might have
listened to them without in the least pricking up his
ears; on the other hand the real truth was equally liable
at any moment to rise to the surface, and the auditor
would then have wondered indeed what they were talking about. They had from an early hour made up their
mind that society was, luckily, unintelligent, and the
margin allowed them by this had fairly become one of
their commonplaces. Yet there were still moments when
the situation turned almost fresh—usually under the
effect of some expression drawn from herself. Her expressions doubtless repeated themselves, but her intervals were generous. "What saves us, you know, is that
we answer so completely to so usual an appearance: that
of the man and woman whose friendship has become
such a daily habit—or almost—as to be at last indispen-

sable." That for instance was a remark she had frequently enough had occasion to make, though she had
given it at different times different developments. What
we are especially concerned with is the turn it happened
to take from her one afternoon when he had come to see
her in honour of her birthday. This anniversary had
fallen on a Sunday, at a season of thick fog and general
outward gloom; but he had brought her his customary
offering, having known her now long enough to have
established a hundred small traditions. It was one of his
proofs to himself, the present he made her on her birthday, that he hadn't sunk into real selfishness. It was
mostly nothing more than a small trinket, but it was
always fine of its kind, and he was regularly careful to
pay for it more than he thought he could afford. "Our
habit saves you at least, don't you see? because it makes
you, after all, for the vulgar, indistinguishable from other
men. What's the most inveterate mark of men in general? Why the capacity to spend endless time with dull
women—to spend it I won't say without being bored,
but without minding that they are, without being driven
off at a tangent by it; which comes to the same thing.
I'm your dull woman, a part of the daily bread for which
you pray at church. That covers your tracks more than
anything."

"And what covers yours?" asked Marcher, whom his
dull woman could mostly to this extent amuse. "I see of
course what you mean by your saving me, in this way
and that, so far as other people are concerned—I've seen
it all along. Only what is it that saves *you?* I often think,
you know, of that."

She looked as if she sometimes thought of that too,
but rather in a different way. "Where other people, you
mean, are concerned?"

"Well, you're really so in with me, you know—as a

sort of result of my being so in with yourself. I mean of my having such an immense regard for you, being so tremendously mindful of all you've done for me. I sometimes ask myself if it's quite fair. Fair I mean to have so involved and—since one may say it—interested you. I almost feel as if you hadn't really had time to do anything else."

"Anything else but be interested?" she asked. "Ah what else does one ever want to be? If I've been 'watching' with you, as we long ago agreed I was to do, watching's always in itself an absorption."

"Oh certainly," John Marcher said, "if you hadn't had your curiosity—! Only doesn't it sometimes come to you as time goes on that your curiosity isn't being particularly repaid?"

May Bartram had a pause. "Do you ask that, by any chance, because you feel at all that yours isn't? I mean because you have to wait so long."

Oh he understood what she meant! "For the thing to happen that never does happen? For the beast to jump out? No, I'm just where I was about it. It isn't a matter as to which I can *choose,* I can decide for a change. It isn't one as to which there *can* be a change. It's in the lap of the gods. One's in the hands of one's law—there one is. As to the form the law will take, the way it will operate, that's its own affair."

"Yes," Miss Bartram replied; "of course one's fate's coming, of course it *has* come in its own form and its own way, all the while. Only, you know, the form and the way in your case were to have been—well, something so exceptional and, as one may say, so particularly *your* own."

Something in this made him look at her with suspicion. "You say 'were to *have* been,' as if in your heart you had begun to doubt."

"Oh!" she vaguely protested.

"As if you believed," he went on, "that nothing will now take place."

She shook her head slowly but rather inscrutably. "You're far from my thought."

He continued to look at her. "What then is the matter with you?"

"Well," she said after another wait, "the matter with me is simply that I'm more sure than ever my curiosity, as you call it, will be but too well repaid."

They were frankly grave now; he had got up from his seat, had turned once more about the little drawing-room to which, year after year, he brought his inevitable topic; in which he had, as he might have said, tasted their intimate community with every sauce, where every object was as familiar to him as the things of his own house and the very carpets were worn with his fitful walk very much as the desks in old counting-houses are worn by the elbows of generations of clerks. The generations of his nervous moods had been at work there, and the place was the written history of his whole middle life. Under the impression of what his friend had just said he knew himself, for some reason, more aware of these things; which made him, after a moment, stop again before her. "Is it possibly that you've grown afraid?"

"Afraid?" He thought, as she repeated the word, that his question had made her, a little, change colour; so that, lest he should have touched on a truth, he explained very kindly: "You remember that that was what you asked me long ago—that first day at Weather-end."

"Oh yes, and you told me you didn't know—that I was to see for myself. We've said little about it since, even in so long a time."

"Precisely," Marcher interposed—"quite as if it were too delicate a matter for us to make free with. Quite as if we might find, on pressure, that I *am* afraid. For then," he said, "we shouldn't, should we? quite know what to do."

She had for the time no answer to this question. "There have been days when I thought you were. Only, of course," she added, "there have been days when we have thought almost anything."

"Everything. Oh!" Marcher softly groaned as with a gasp, half-spent, at the face, more uncovered just then than it had been for a long while, of the imagination always with them. It had always had its incalculable moments of glaring out, quite as with the very eyes of the very Beast, and, used as he was to them, they could still draw from him the tribute of a sigh that rose from the depths of his being. All they had thought, first and last, rolled over him; the past seemed to have been reduced to mere barren speculation. This in fact was what the place had just struck him as so full of—the simplification of everything but the state of suspense. That remained only by seeming to hang in the void surrounding it. Even his original fear, if fear it had been, had lost itself in the desert. "I judge, however," he continued, "that you see I'm not afraid now."

"What I see, as I make it out, is that you've achieved something almost unprecedented in the way of getting used to danger. Living with it so long and so closely you've lost your sense of it; you know it's there, but you're indifferent, and you cease even, as of old, to have to whistle in the dark. Considering what the danger is," May Bartram wound up, "I'm bound to say I don't think your attitude could well be surpassed."

John Marcher faintly smiled. "It's heroic?"

"Certainly—call it that."

It was what he would have liked indeed to call it. "I *am* then a man of courage?"

"That's what you were to show me."

He still, however, wondered. "But doesn't the man of courage know what he's afraid of—or *not* afraid of? I don't know *that*, you see. I don't focus it. I can't name it. I only know I'm exposed."

"Yes, but exposed—how shall I say?—so directly. So intimately. That's surely enough."

"Enough to make you feel then—as what we may call the end and the upshot of our watch—that I'm not afraid?"

"You're not afraid. But it isn't," she said, "the end of our watch. That is it isn't the end of yours. You've everything still to see."

"Then why haven't *you?*" he asked. He had had, all along, to-day, the sense of her keeping something back, and he still had it. As this was his first impression of that it quite made a date. The case was the more marked as she didn't at first answer; which in turn made him go on. "You know something I don't." Then his voice, for that of a man of courage, trembled a little. "You know what's to happen." Her silence, with the face she showed, was almost a confession—it made him sure. "You know, and you're afraid to tell me. It's so bad that you're afraid I'll find out."

All this might be true, for she did look as if, unexpectedly to her, he had crossed some mystic line that she had secretly drawn round her. Yet she might, after all, not have worried; and the real climax was that he himself, at all events, needn't. "You'll never find out."

III

It was all to have made, none the less, as I have said, a date; which came out in the fact that again and again,

even after long intervals, other things that passed between them wore in relation to this hour but the character of recalls and results. Its immediate effect had been
indeed rather to lighten insistence—almost to provoke
a reaction; as if their topic had dropped by its own
weight and as if moreover, for that matter, Marcher had
been visited by one of his occasional warnings against
egotism. He had kept up, he felt, and very decently on
the whole, his consciousness of the importance of not
being selfish, and it was true that he had never sinned in
that direction without promptly enough trying to press
the scales the other way. He often repaired his fault,
the season permitting, by inviting his friend to accompany him to the opera; and it not infrequently thus
happened that, to show he didn't wish her to have but
one sort of food for her mind, he was the cause of her
appearing there with him a dozen nights in the month.
It even happened that, seeing her home at such times,
he occasionally went in with her to finish, as he called it,
the evening, and, the better to make his point, sat down
to the frugal but always careful little supper that
awaited his pleasure. His point was made, he thought,
by his not eternally insisting with her on himself; made
for instance, at such hours, when it befell that, her piano
at hand and each of them familiar with it, they went
over passages of the opera together. It chanced to be
on one of these occasions, however, that he reminded
her of her not having answered a certain question he had
put to her during the talk that had taken place between
them on her last birthday. "What is it that saves *you*?"
—saved her, he meant, from that appearance of variation from the usual human type. If he had practically
escaped remark, as she pretended, by doing, in the most
important particular, what most men do—find the an-

swer to life in patching up an alliance of a sort with a woman no better than himself—how had she escaped it, and how could the alliance, such as it was, since they must suppose it had been more or less noticed, have failed to make her rather positively talked about?

"I never said," May Bartram replied, "that it hadn't made me a good deal talked about."

"Ah well then you're not 'saved.'"

"It hasn't been a question for me. If you've had your woman I've had," she said, "my man."

"And you mean that makes you all right?"

Oh it was always as if there were so much to say! "I don't know why it shouldn't make me—humanly, which is what we're speaking of—as right as it makes you."

"I see," Marcher returned. "'Humanly,' no doubt, as showing that you're living for something. Not, that is, just for me and my secret."

May Bartram smiled. "I don't pretend it exactly shows that I'm not living for you. It's my intimacy with you that's in question."

He laughed as he saw what she meant. "Yes, but since, as you say, I'm only, so far as people make out, ordinary, you're—aren't you?—no more than ordinary either. You help me to pass for a man like another. So if I *am*, as I understand you, you're not compromised. Is that it?"

She had another of her waits, but she spoke clearly enough. "That's it. It's all that concerns me—to help you to pass for a man like another."

He was careful to acknowledge the remark handsomely. "How kind, how beautiful, you are to me! How shall I ever repay you?"

She had her last grave pause, as if there might be a choice of ways. But she chose. "By going on as you are."

It was into this going on as he was that they relapsed, and really for so long a time that the day inevitably came for a further sounding of their depths. These depths, constantly bridged over by a structure firm enough in spite of its lightness and of its occasional oscillation in the somewhat vertiginous air, invited on occasion, in the interest of their nerves, a dropping of the plummet and a measurement of the abyss. A difference had been made moreover, once for all, by the fact that she had all the while not appeared to feel the need of rebutting his charge of an idea within her that she didn't dare to express—a charge uttered just before one of the fullest of their later discussions ended. It had come up for him then that she "knew" something and that what she knew was bad—too bad to tell him. When he had spoken of it as visibly so bad that she was afraid he might find it out, her reply had left the matter too equivocal to be let alone and yet, for Marcher's special sensibility, almost too formidable again to touch. He circled about it at a distance that alternately narrowed and widened and that still wasn't much affected by the consciousness in him that there was nothing she could "know," after all, any better than he did. She had no source of knowledge he hadn't equally—except of course that she might have finer nerves. That was what women had where they were interested; they made out things, where people were concerned, that the people often couldn't have made out for themselves. Their nerves, their sensibility, their imagination, were conductors and revealers, and the beauty of May Bartram was in particular that she had given herself so to his case. He felt in these days what, oddly enough, he had never felt before, the growth of a dread of losing her by some catastrophe—some catastrophe that yet wouldn't at all be *the* catastrophe: partly because she had almost of a sudden be-

gun to strike him as more useful to him than ever yet,
and partly by reason of an appearance of uncertainty
in her health, coincident and equally new. It was characteristic of the inner detachment he had hitherto so
successfully cultivated and to which our whole account
of him is a reference, it was characteristic that his complications, such as they were, had never yet seemed so
as at this crisis to thicken about him, even to the point
of making him ask himself if he were, by any chance,
of a truth, within sight or sound, within touch or
reach, within the immediate jurisdiction, of the thing
that waited.

When the day came, as come it had to, that his friend
confessed to him her fear of a deep disorder in her
blood, he felt somehow the shadow of a change and the
chill of a shock. He immediately began to imagine aggravations and disasters, and above all to think of her peril
as the direct menace for himself of personal privation.
This indeed gave him one of those partial recoveries
of equanimity that were agreeable to him—it showed
him that what was still first in his mind was the loss she
herself might suffer. "What if she should have to die
before knowing, before seeing—?" It would have been
brutal, in the early stages of her trouble, to put that
question to her; but it had immediately sounded for him
to his own concern, and the possibility was what most
made him sorry for her. If she did "know," moreover,
in the sense of her having had some—what should he
think?—mystical irresistible light, this would make the
matter not better, but worse, inasmuch as her original
adoption of his own curiosity had quite become the basis
of her life. She had been living to see what would *be* to
be seen, and it would quite lacerate her to have to give
up before the accomplishment of the vision. These reflexions, as I say, quickened his generosity; yet, make

them as he might, he saw himself, with the lapse of the period, more and more disconcerted. It lapsed for him with a strange steady sweep, and the oddest oddity was that it gave him, independently of the threat of much inconvenience, almost the only positive surprise his career, if career it could be called, had yet offered him. She kept the house as she had never done; he had to go to her to see her—she could meet him nowhere now, though there was scarce a corner of their loved old London in which she hadn't in the past, at one time or another, done so; and he found her always seated by her fire in the deep old-fashioned chair she was less and less able to leave. He had been struck one day, after an absence exceeding his usual measure, with her suddenly looking much older to him than he had ever thought of her being; then he recognised that the suddenness was all on his side—he had just simply and suddenly noticed. She looked older because inevitably, after so many years, she *was* old, or almost; which was of course true in still greater measure of her companion. If she was old, or almost, John Marcher assuredly was, and yet it was her showing of the lesson, not his own, that brought the truth home to him. His surprises began here; when once they had begun they multiplied; they came rather with a rush: it was as if, in the oddest way in the world, they had all been kept back, sown in a thick cluster, for the late afternoon of life, the time at which for people in general the unexpected has died out.

One of them was that he should have caught himself —for he *had* so done—*really* wondering if the great accident would take form now as nothing more than his being condemned to see this charming woman, this admirable friend, pass away from him. He had never so unreservedly qualified her as while confronted in thought with such a possibility; in spite of which there was small doubt for him that as an answer to his long riddle the mere effacement of even so fine a feature of his situation would be an abject anticlimax. It would represent, as connected with his past attitude, a drop of dignity under the shadow of which his existence could only become the most grotesque of failures. He had been far from holding it a failure—long as he had waited for the appearance that was to make it a success. He had waited for quite another thing, not for such a thing as that. The breath of his good faith came short, however, as he recognised how long he had waited, or how long at least his companion had. That she, at all events, might be recorded as having waited in vain—this affected him sharply, and all the more because of his at first having done little more than amuse himself with the idea. It grew more grave as the gravity of her condition grew, and the state of mind it produced in him, which he himself ended by watching as if it had been some definite disfigurement of his outer person, may pass for another of his surprises. This conjoined itself still with another, the really stupefying consciousness of a question that he would have allowed to shape itself had he dared. What did everything mean—what, that is, did *she* mean, she and her vain waiting and her probable death and the soundless admonition of it all—unless that, at this time of day, it was simply, it was overwhelmingly too late? He had never at any stage of his queer consciousness admitted the whisper of such a correction; he had never till within these last few months been so false to his conviction as not to hold that what was to come to him had time, whether *he* struck himself as having it or not. That at last, at last, he certainly hadn't it, to speak of, or had it but in the scantiest measure—such, soon enough, as things went with him, became the inference with which his old obsession had to reckon:

and this it was not helped to do by the more and more
confirmed appearance that the great vagueness casting
the long shadow in which he had lived had, to attest
itself, almost no margin left. Since it was in Time that he
was to have met his fate, so it was in Time that his fate
was to have acted; and as he waked up to the sense of
no longer being young, which was exactly the sense
of being stale, just as that, in turn, was the sense of being weak, he waked up to another matter beside. It all
hung together; they were subject, he and the great
vagueness, to an equal and indivisible law. When the
possibilities themselves had accordingly turned stale,
when the secret of the gods had grown faint, had perhaps even quite evaporated, that, and that only, was
failure. It wouldn't have been failure to be bankrupt,
dishonoured, pilloried, hanged; it was failure not to be
anything. And so, in the dark valley into which his path
had taken its unlooked-for twist, he wondered not a little
as he groped. He didn't care what awful crash might
overtake him, with what ignominy or what monstrosity
he might yet be associated—since he wasn't after all too
utterly old to suffer—if it would only be decently proportionate to the posture he had kept, all his life, in the
threatened presence of it. He had but one desire left—
that he shouldn't have been "sold."

IV

Then it was that, one afternoon, while the spring of the
year was young and new she met all in her own way his
frankest betrayal of these alarms. He had gone in late
to see her, but evening hadn't settled and she was presented to him in that long fresh light of waning April
days which affects us often with a sadness sharper than
the greyest hours of autumn. The week had been warm,
the spring was supposed to have begun early, and May

Bartram sat, for the first time in the year, without a fire; a fact that, to Marcher's sense, gave the scene of which she formed part a smooth and ultimate look, an air of knowing, in its immaculate order and cold meaningless cheer, that it would never see a fire again. Her own aspect—he could scarce have said why—intensified this note. Almost as white as wax, with the marks and signs in her face as numerous and as fine as if they had been etched by a needle, with soft white draperies relieved by a faded green scarf on the delicate tone of which the years had further refined, she was the picture of a serene and exquisite but impenetrable sphinx, whose head, or indeed all whose person, might have been powdered with silver. She was a sphinx, yet with her white petals and green fronds she might have been a lily too—only an artificial lily, wonderfully imitated and constantly kept, without dust or stain, though not exempt from a slight droop and a complexity of faint creases, under some clear glass bell. The perfection of household care, of high polish and finish, always reigned in her rooms, but they now looked most as if everything had been wound up, tucked in, put away, so that she might sit with folded hands and with nothing more to do. She was "out of it," to Marcher's vision; her work was over; she communicated with him as across some gulf or from some island of rest that she had already reached, and it made him feel strangely abandoned. Was it—or rather wasn't it—that if for so long she had been watching with him the answer to their question must have swum into her ken and taken on its name, so that her occupation was verily gone? He had as much as charged her with this in saying to her, many months before, that she even then knew something she was keeping from him. It was a point he had never since ventured to press, vaguely fearing as he did that it might become a difference, per-

haps a disagreement, between them. He had in this later
time turned nervous, which was what he in all the other
years had never been; and the oddity was that his nerv-
ousness should have waited till he had begun to doubt,
should have held off so long as he was sure. There was
something, it seemed to him, that the wrong word would
bring down on his head, something that would so at least
ease off his tension. But he wanted not to speak the
wrong word; that would make everything ugly. He
wanted the knowledge he lacked to drop on him, if drop
it could, by its own august weight. If she was to forsake
him it was surely for her to take leave. This was why
he didn't directly ask her again what she knew; but it
was also why, approaching the matter from another side,
he said to her in the course of his visit: "What do you
regard as the very worst that at this time of day *can*
happen to me?"

He had asked her that in the past often enough; they
had, with the odd irregular rhythm of their intensities
and avoidances, exchanged ideas about it and then had
seen the ideas washed away by cool intervals, washed
like figures traced in sea-sand. It had ever been the
mark of their talk that the oldest allusions in it required
but a little dismissal and reaction to come out again,
sounding for the hour as new. She could thus at present
meet his enquiry quite freshly and patiently. "Oh yes,
I've repeatedly thought, only it always seemed to me
of old that I couldn't quite make up my mind. I thought
of dreadful things, between which it was difficult to
choose; and so must you have done."

"Rather! I feel now as if I had scarce done anything
else. I appear to myself to have spent my life in thinking
of nothing *but* dreadful things. A great many of them
I've at different times named to you, but there were
others I couldn't name."

"They were too, too dreadful?"

"Too, too dreadful—some of them."

She looked at him a minute, and there came to him as he met it an inconsequent sense that her eyes, when one got their full clearness, were still as beautiful as they had been in youth, only beautiful with a strange cold light—a light that somehow was a part of the effect, if it wasn't rather a part of the cause, of the pale hard sweetness of the season and the hour. "And yet," she said at last, "there are horrors we've mentioned."

It deepened the strangeness to see her, as such a figure in such a picture, talk of "horrors," but she was to do in a few minutes something stranger yet—though even of this he was to take the full measure but afterwards—and the note of it already trembled. It was, for the matter of that, one of the signs that her eyes were having again the high flicker of their prime. He had to admit, however, what she said. "Oh yes, there were times when we did go far." He caught himself in the act of speaking as if it all were over. Well, he wished it were; and the consummation depended for him clearly more and more on his friend.

But she had now a soft smile. "Oh far—!"

It was oddly ironic. "Do you mean you're prepared to go further?"

She was frail and ancient and charming as she continued to look at him, yet it was rather as if she had lost the thread. "Do you consider that we went far?"

"Why I thought it the point you were just making—that we *had* looked most things in the face."

"Including each other?" She still smiled. "But you're quite right. We've had together great imaginations, often great fears; but some of them have been unspoken."

"Then the worst—we haven't faced that. I *could* face it, I believe, if I knew what you think it. I feel," he explained, "as if I had lost my power to conceive such things." And he wondered if he looked as blank as he sounded. "It's spent."

"Then why do you assume," she asked, "that mine isn't?"

"Because you've given me signs to the contrary. It isn't a question for you of conceiving, imagining, comparing. It isn't a question now of choosing." At last he came out with it. "You know something I don't. You've shown me that before."

These last words had affected her, he made out in a moment, exceedingly, and she spoke with firmness. "I've shown you, my dear, nothing."

He shook his head. "You can't hide it."

"Oh, oh!" May Bartram sounded over what she couldn't hide. It was almost a smothered groan.

"You admitted it months ago, when I spoke of it to you as of something you were afraid I should find out. Your answer was that I couldn't, that I wouldn't, and I don't pretend I have. But you had something therefore in mind, and I now see how it must have been, how it still is, the possibility that, of all possibilities, has settled itself for you as the worst. This," he went on, "is why I appeal to you. I'm only afraid of ignorance today—I'm not afraid of knowledge." And then as for a while she said nothing: "What makes me sure is that I see in your face and feel here, in this air and amid these appearances, that you're out of it. You've done. You've had your experience. You leave me to my fate."

Well, she listened, motionless and white in her chair, as on a decision to be made, so that her manner was fairly an avowal, though still, with a small fine inner stiffness, an imperfect surrender. "It *would* be the worst," she finally let herself say. "I mean the thing I've never said."

It hushed him a moment. "More monstrous than all the monstrosities we've named?"

"More monstrous. Isn't that what you sufficiently express," she asked, "in calling it the worst?"

Marcher thought. "Assuredly—if you mean, as I do, something that includes all the loss and all the shame that are thinkable."

"It would if it *should* happen," said May Bartram. "What we're speaking of, remember, is only my idea."

"It's your belief," Marcher returned. "That's enough for me. I feel your beliefs are right. Therefore if, having this one, you give me no more light on it, you abandon me."

"No, no!" she repeated. "I'm with you—don't you see?—still." And as to make it more vivid to him she rose from her chair—a movement she seldom risked in these days—and showed herself, all draped and all soft, in her fairness and slimness. "I haven't forsaken you."

It was really, in its effort against weakness, a generous assurance, and had the success of the impulse not, happily, been great, it would have touched him to pain more than to pleasure. But the cold charm in her eyes had spread, as she hovered before him, to all the rest of her person, so that it was for the minute almost a recovery of youth. He couldn't pity her for that; he could only take her as she showed—as capable even yet of helping him. It was as if, at the same time, her light might at any instant go out; wherefore he must make the most of it. There passed before him with intensity the three or four things he wanted most to know; but the question that came of itself to his lips really covered the others. "Then tell me if I shall consciously suffer."

She promptly shook her head. "Never!"

It confirmed the authority he imputed to her, and it

produced on him an extraordinary effect. "Well, what's better than that? Do you call that the worst?"

"You think nothing is better?" she asked.

She seemed to mean something so special that he again sharply wondered, though still with the dawn of a prospect of relief. "Why not, if one doesn't *know?*" After which, as their eyes, over his question, met in a silence, the dawn deepened and something to his purpose came prodigiously out of her very face. His own, as he took it in, suddenly flushed to the forehead, and he gasped with the force of a perception to which, on the instant, everything fitted. The sound of his gasp filled the air; then he became articulate. "I see—if I don't suffer!"

In her own look, however, was doubt. "You see what?"

"Why what you mean—what you've always meant."

She again shook her head. "What I mean isn't what I've always meant. It's different."

"It's something new?"

She hung back from it a little. "Something new. It's not what you think. I see what you think."

His divination drew breath then; only her correction might be wrong. "It isn't that I *am* a blockhead?" he asked between faintness and grimness. "It isn't that it's all a mistake?"

"A mistake?" she pityingly echoed. *That* possibility, for her, he saw, would be monstrous; and if she guaranteed him the immunity from pain it would accordingly not be what she had in mind. "Oh no," she declared; "it's nothing of that sort. You've been right."

Yet he couldn't help asking himself if she weren't, thus pressed, speaking but to save him. It seemed to him he should be most in a hole if his history should prove all a platitude. "Are you telling me the truth, so

that I shan't have been a bigger idiot than I can bear
to know? I *haven't* lived with a vain imagination, in the
most besotted illusion? I haven't waited but to see the
door shut in my face?"

She shook her head again. "However the case stands
that isn't the truth. Whatever the reality, it *is* a reality.
The door isn't shut. The door's open," said May Bartram.

"Then something's to come?"

She waited once again, always with her cold sweet
eyes on him. "It's never too late." She had, with her
gliding step, diminished the distance between them, and
she stood nearer to him, close to him, a minute, as if
still charged with the unspoken. Her movement might
have been for some finer emphasis of what she was at
once hesitating and deciding to say. He had been standing by the chimney-piece, fireless and sparely adorned,
a small perfect old French clock and two morsels of rosy
Dresden constituting all its furniture; and her hand
grasped the shelf while she kept him waiting, grasped
it a little as for support and encouragement. She only
kept him waiting, however; that is he only waited. It
had become suddenly, from her movement and attitude,
beautiful and vivid to him that she had something more
to give him; her wasted face delicately shone with it—
it glittered almost as with the white lustre of silver in
her expression. She was right, incontestably, for what
he saw in her face was the truth, and strangely, without
consequence, while their talk of it as dreadful was still
in the air, she appeared to present it as inordinately soft.
This, prompting bewilderment, made him but gape the
more gratefully for her revelation, so that they continued
for some minutes silent, her face shining at him, her
contact imponderably pressing, and his stare all kind but
all expectant. The end, none the less, was that what he

had expected failed to come to him. Something else took place instead, which seemed to consist at first in the mere closing of her eyes. She gave way at the same instant to a slow fine shudder, and though he remained staring—though he stared in fact but the harder—turned off and regained her chair. It was the end of what she had been intending, but it left him thinking only of that.

"Well, you don't say—?"

She had touched in her passage a bell near the chimney and had sunk back strangely pale. "I'm afraid I'm too ill."

"Too ill to tell me?" It sprang up sharp to him, and almost to his lips, the fear she might die without giving him light. He checked himself in time from so expressing his question, but she answered as if she had heard the words.

"Don't you know—now?"

" 'Now'—?" She had spoken as if some difference had been made within the moment. But her maid, quickly obedient to her bell, was already with them. "I know nothing." And he was afterwards to say to himself that he must have spoken with odious impatience, such an impatience as to show that, supremely disconcerted, he washed his hands of the whole question.

"Oh!" said May Bartram.

"Are you in pain?" he asked as the woman went to her.

"No," said May Bartram.

Her maid, who had put an arm round her as if to take her to her room, fixed on him eyes that appealingly contradicted her; in spite of which, however, he showed once more his mystification. "What then has happened?"

She was once more, with her companion's help, on her

feet, and, feeling withdrawal imposed on him, he had blankly found his hat and gloves and had reached the door. Yet he waited for her answer. "What *was* to," she said.

V

He came back the next day, but she was then unable to see him, and as it was literally the first time this had occurred in the long stretch of their acquaintance he turned away, defeated and sore, almost angry—or feeling at least that such a break in their custom was really the beginning of the end—and wandered alone with his thoughts, especially with the one he was least able to keep down. She was dying and he would lose her; she was dying and his life would end. He stopped in the Park, into which he had passed, and stared before him at his recurrent doubt. Away from her the doubt pressed again; in her presence he had believed her, but as he felt his forlornness he threw himself into the explanation that, nearest at hand, had most of a miserable warmth for him and least of a cold torment. She had deceived him to save him—to put him off with something in which he should be able to rest. What could the thing that was to happen to him be, after all, but just this thing that had begun to happen? Her dying, her death, his consequent solitude—*that* was what he had figured as the Beast in the Jungle, that was what had been in the lap of the gods. He had had her word for it as he left her—what else on earth could she have meant? It wasn't a thing of a monstrous order; not a fate rare and distinguished; not a stroke of fortune that overwhelmed and immortalised; it had only the stamp of the common doom. But poor Marcher at this hour judged the common doom sufficient. It would serve his turn, and even as the consummation of infinite waiting he would bend his pride to accept it. He sat down on a bench in the twilight. He hadn't been a fool. Something had *been,* as she had said, to come. Before he rose indeed it had quite struck him that the final fact really matched with the long avenue through which he had had to reach it. As sharing his suspense and as giving herself all, giving her life, to bring it to an end, she had come with him every step of the way. He had lived by her aid, and to leave her behind would be cruelly, damnably to miss her. What could be more overwhelming than that?

Well, he was to know within the week, for though she kept him a while at bay, left him restless and wretched during a series of days on each of which he asked about her only again to have to turn away, she ended his trial by receiving him where she had always received him. Yet she had been brought out at some hazard into the presence of so many of the things that were, consciously, vainly, half their past, and there was scant service left in the gentleness of her mere desire, all too visible, to check his obsession and wind up his long trouble. That was clearly what she wanted, the one thing more for her own peace while she could still put out her hand. He was so affected by her state that, once seated by her chair, he was moved to let everything go; it was she herself therefore who brought him back, took up again, before she dismissed him, her last word of the other time. She showed how she wished to leave their business in order. "I'm not sure you understood. You've nothing to wait for more. It *has* come."

Oh how he looked at her! "Really?"

"Really."

"The thing that, as you said, *was* to?"

"The thing that we began in our youth to watch for." Face to face with her once more he believed her; it was a claim to which he had so abjectly little to oppose. "You mean that it has come as a positive definite occurrence, with a name and a date?"

"Positive. Definite. I don't know about the 'name,' but oh with a date!"

He found himself again too helplessly at sea. "But come in the night—come and passed me by?"

May Bartram had her strange faint smile. "Oh no, it hasn't passed you by!"

"But if I haven't been aware of it and it hasn't touched me—?"

"Ah your not being aware of it"—and she seemed to hesitate an instant to deal with this—"your not being aware of it is the strangeness *in* the strangeness. It's the wonder *of* the wonder." She spoke as with the softness almost of a sick child, yet now at last, at the end of all, with the perfect straightness of a sibyl. She visibly knew that she knew, and the effect on him was of something co-ordinate, in its high character, with the law that had ruled him. It was the true voice of the law; so on her lips would the law itself have sounded. "It *has* touched you," she went on. "It has done its office. It has made you all its own."

"So utterly without my knowing it?"

"So utterly without your knowing it." His hand, as he leaned to her, was on the arm of her chair, and, dimly smiling always now, she placed her own on it. "It's enough if *I* know it."

"Oh!" he confusedly breathed, as she herself of late so often had done.

"What I long ago said is true. You'll never know now, and I think you ought to be content. You've *had* it," said May Bartram.

"But had what?"

"Why what was to have marked you out. The proof

of your law. It has acted. I'm too glad," she then bravely added, "to have been able to see what it's *not*."

He continued to attach his eyes to her, and with the sense that it was all beyond him, and that *she* was too, he would still have sharply challenged her hadn't he so felt it an abuse of her weakness to do more than take devoutly what she gave him, take it hushed as to a revelation. If he did speak, it was out of the foreknowledge of his loneliness to come. "If you're glad of what it's 'not' it might then have been worse?"

She turned her eyes away, she looked straight before her; with which after a moment: "Well, you know our fears."

He wondered. "It's something then we never feared?"

On this slowly she turned to him. "Did we ever dream, with all our dreams, that we should sit and talk of it thus?"

He tried for a little to make out that they had; but it was as if their dreams, numberless enough, were in solution in some thick cold mist through which thought lost itself. "It might have been that we couldn't talk?"

"Well"—she did her best for him—"not from this side. This, you see," she said, "is the *other* side."

"I think," poor Marcher returned, "that all sides are the same to me." Then, however, as she gently shook her head in correction: "We mightn't, as it were, have got across—?"

"To where we are—no. We're *here*"—she made her weak emphasis.

"And much good does it do us!" was her friend's frank comment.

"It does us the good it can. It does us the good that *it* isn't here. It's past. It's behind," said May Bartram. "Before—" but her voice dropped.

He had got up, not to tire her, but it was hard to

combat his yearning. She after all told him nothing but that his light had failed—which he knew well enough without her. "Before——?" he blankly echoed.

"Before, you see, it was always to *come*. That kept it present."

"Oh I don't care what comes now! Besides," Marcher added, "it seems to me I liked it better present, as you say, than I can like it absent with *your* absence."

"Oh mine!"—and her pale hands made light of it.

"With the absence of everything." He had a dreadful sense of standing there before her for—so far as anything but this proved, this bottomless drop was concerned—the last time of their life. It rested on him with a weight he felt he could scarce bear, and this weight it apparently was that still pressed out what remained in him of speakable protest. "I believe you; but I can't begin to pretend I understand. *Nothing*, for me, is past; nothing *will* pass till I pass myself, which I pray my stars may be as soon as possible. Say, however," he added, "that I've eaten my cake, as you contend, to the last crumb—how can the thing I've never felt at all be the thing I was marked out to feel?"

She met him perhaps less directly, but she met him unperturbed. "You take your 'feelings' for granted. You were to suffer your fate. That was not necessarily to know it."

"How in the world—when what is such knowledge but suffering?"

She looked up at him a while in silence. "No—you don't understand."

"I suffer," said John Marcher.

"Don't, dont!"

"How can I help at least *that?*"

"*Don't!*" May Bartram repeated.

She spoke it in a tone so special, in spite of her weakness, that he stared an instant—stared as if some light, hitherto hidden, had shimmered across his vision. Darkness again closed over it, but the gleam had already become for him an idea. "Because I haven't the right—?"

"Don't *know*—when you needn't," she mercifully urged. "You needn't—for we shouldn't."

"Shouldn't?" If he could but know what she meant!

"No—it's too much."

"Too much?" he still asked but, with a mystification that was the next moment of a sudden to give way. Her words, if they meant something, affected him in this light—the light also of her wasted face—as meaning *all*, and the sense of what knowledge had been for herself came over him with a rush which broke through into a question. "Is it of that then you're dying?"

She but watched him, gravely at first, as to see, with this, where he was, and she might have seen something or feared something that moved her sympathy. "I would live for you still—if I could." Her eyes closed for a little, as if, withdrawn into herself, she were for a last time trying. "But I can't!" she said as she raised them again to take leave of him.

She couldn't indeed, as but too promptly and sharply appeared, and he had no vision of her after this that was anything but darkness and doom. They had parted for ever in that strange talk; access to her chamber of pain, rigidly guarded, was almost wholly forbidden him; he was feeling now moreover, in the face of doctors, nurses, the two or three relatives attracted doubtless by the presumption of what she had to "leave," how few were the rights, as they were called in such cases, that he had to put forward, and how odd it might even seem that their intimacy shouldn't have given him more of them. The stupidest fourth cousin had more, even though she had been nothing in such a person's life.

She had been a feature of features in *his,* for what else was it to have been so indispensable? Strange beyond saying were the ways of existence, baffling for him the anomaly of his lack, as he felt it to be, of producible claim. A woman might have been, as it were, everything to him, and it might yet present him in no connexion that any one seemed held to recognise. If this was the case in these closing weeks it was the case more sharply on the occasion of the last offices rendered, in the great grey London cemetery, to what had been mortal, to what had been precious, in his friend. The concourse at her grave was not numerous, but he saw himself treated as scarce more nearly concerned with it than if there had been a thousand others. He was in short from this moment face to face with the fact that he was to profit extraordinarily little by the interest May Bartram had taken in him. He couldn't quite have said what he expected, but he hadn't surely expected this approach to a double privation. Not only had her interest failed him, but he seemed to feel himself unattended—and for a reason he couldn't seize—by the distinction, the dignity, the propriety, if nothing else, of the man markedly bereaved. It was as if in the view of society he had not *been* markedly bereaved, as if there still failed some sign or proof of it, and as if none the less his character could never be affirmed nor the deficiency ever made up. There were moments as the weeks went by when he would have liked, by some almost aggressive act, to take his stand on the intimacy of his loss, in order that it *might* be questioned and his retort, to the relief of his spirit, so recorded; but the moments of an irritation more helpless followed fast on these, the moments during which, turning things over with a good conscience but with a bare horizon, he found himself wondering if he oughtn't to have begun, so to speak, further back.

He found himself wondering indeed at many things, and this last speculation had others to keep it company. What could he have done, after all, in her lifetime, without giving them both, as it were, away? He couldn't have made known she was watching him, for that would have published the superstition of the Beast. This was what closed his mouth now—now that the Jungle had been threshed to vacancy and that the Beast had stolen away. It sounded too foolish and too flat; the difference for him in this particular, the extinction in his life of the element of suspense, was such as in fact to surprise him. He could scarce have said what the effect resembled; the abrupt cessation, the positive prohibition, of music perhaps, more than anything else, in some place all adjusted and all accustomed to sonority and to attention. If he could at any rate have conceived lifting the veil from his image at some moment of the past (what had he done, after all, if not lift it to *her*?) so to do this today, to talk to people at large of the Jungle cleared and confide to them that he now felt it as safe, would have been not only to see them listen as to a goodwife's tale, but really to hear himself tell one. What it presently came to in truth was that poor Marcher waded through his beaten grass, where no life stirred, where no breath sounded, where no evil eye seemed to gleam from a possible lair, very much as if vaguely looking for the Beast, and still more as if acutely missing it. He walked about in an existence that had grown strangely more spacious, and, stopping fitfully in places where the undergrowth of life struck him as closer, asked himself yearningly, wondered secretly and sorely, if it would have lurked here or there. It would have at all events *sprung;* what was at least complete was his belief in the truth itself of the assurance given him. The change from his old sense to his new was absolute and final: what was to happen *had* so absolutely and finally happened that he was as little able to know a fear for his future as to know a hope; so absent in short was any question of anything still to come. He was to live entirely with the other question, that of his unidentified past, that of his having to see his fortune impenetrably muffled and masked.

The torment of this vision became then his occupation; he couldn't perhaps have consented to live but for the possibility of guessing. She had told him, his friend, not to guess; she had forbidden him, so far as he might, to know, and she had even in a sort denied the power in him to learn: which were so many things, precisely, to deprive him of rest. It wasn't that he wanted, he argued for fairness, that anything past and done should repeat itself; it was only that he shouldn't, as an anticlimax, have been taken sleeping so sound as not to be able to win back by an effort of thought the lost stuff of consciousness. He declared to himself at moments that he would either win it back or have done with consciousness for ever; he made this idea his one motive in fine, made it so much his passion that none other, to compare with it, seemed ever to have touched him. The lost stuff of consciousness became thus for him as a strayed or stolen child to an unappeasable father; he hunted it up and down very much as if he were knocking at doors and enquiring of the police. This was the spirit in which, inevitably, he set himself to travel; he started on a journey that was to be as long as he could make it; it danced before him that, as the other side of the globe couldn't possibly have less to say to him, it might, by a possibility of suggestion, have more. Before he quitted London, however, he made a pilgrimage to May Bartram's grave, took his way to it through the endless avenues of the grim suburban metropolis, sought it out in the wilderness of tombs, and, though he had come but for the renewal of the act of farewell, found himself, when he had at last stood by it, beguiled into long intensities. He stood for an hour, powerless to turn away and yet powerless to penetrate the darkness of death; fixing with his eyes her inscribed name and date, beating his forehead against the fact of the secret they kept, drawing his breath, while he waited, as if some sense would in pity of him rise from the stones. He kneeled on the stones, however, in vain; they kept what they concealed; and if the face of the tomb did become a face for him it was because her two names became a pair of eyes that didn't know him. He gave them a last long look, but no palest light broke.

VI

He stayed away, after this, for a year; he visited the depths of Asia, spending himself on scenes of romantic interest, of superlative sanctity; but what was present to him everywhere was that for a man who had known what *he* had known the world was vulgar and vain. The state of mind in which he had lived for so many years shone out to him, in reflexion, as a light that coloured and refined, a light beside which the glow of the East was garish and cheap and thin. The terrible truth was that he had lost—with everything else—a distinction as well; the things he saw couldn't help being common when he had become common to look at them. He was simply now one of them himself—he was in the dust, without a peg for the sense of difference; and there were hours when, before the temples of gods and the sepulchres of kings, his spirit turned for nobleness of association to the barely discriminated slab in the London suburb. That had become for him, and more intensely with time and distance, his one witness of a past glory. It was all that was left to him for proof or pride, yet the past glories of Pharaohs were nothing to him as he thought of it. Small wonder then that he came back to it on the morrow of his return. He was drawn there this time as irresistibly as the other, yet with a confidence, almost, that was doubtless the effect of the many months that had elapsed. He had lived, in spite of himself, into his change of feeling, and in wandering over the earth had wandered, as might be said, from the circumference to the centre of his desert. He had settled to his safety and accepted perforce his extinction; figuring to himself, with some colour, in the likeness of certain little old men he remembered to have seen, of whom, all meagre and wizened as they might look, it was related that they had in their time fought twenty duels or been loved by ten princesses. They indeed had been wondrous for others while he was but wondrous for himself; which, however, was exactly the cause of his haste to renew the wonder by getting back, as he might put it, into his own presence. That had quickened his steps and checked his delay. If his visit was prompt it was because he had been separated so long from the part of himself that alone he now valued.

It's accordingly not false to say that he reached his goal with a certain elation and stood there again with a certain assurance. The creature beneath the sod *knew* of his rare experience, so that, strangely now, the place had lost for him its mere blankness of expression. It met him in mildness—not, as before, in mockery; it wore for him the air of conscious greeting that we find, after absence, in things that have closely belonged to us and which seem to confess of themselves to the connexion. The plot of ground, the graven tablet, the tended flowers affected him so as belonging to him that he resembled for the hour a contented landlord reviewing a piece of property. Whatever had happened—well, had happened. He had not come back this time with the vanity of that question, his former worrying "What, *what?*" now practically so spent. Yet he would none the less never again so cut himself off from the spot; he would come back to it every month, for if he did nothing else by its aid he at least held up his head. It thus grew for him, in the oddest way, a positive resource; he carried out his idea of periodical returns, which took their place at last among the most inveterate of his habits. What it all amounted to, oddly enough, was that in his finally so simplified world this garden of death gave him the few square feet of earth on which he could still most live. It was as if, being nothing anywhere else for any one, nothing even for himself, he were just everything here, and if not for a crowd of witnesses or indeed for any witness but John Marcher, then by clear right of the register that he could scan like an open page. The open page was the tomb of his friend, and *there* were the facts of the past, there the truth of his life, there the backward reaches in which he could lose himself. He did this from time to time with such effect that he seemed to wander through the old years with his hand in the arm of a companion who was, in the most extraordinary manner, his other, his younger self; and to wander, which was more extraordinary yet, round and round a third presence—not wandering she, but stationary, still, whose eyes, turning with his revolution, never ceased to follow him, and whose seat was his point, so to speak, of orientation. Thus in short he settled to live —feeding all on the sense that he once *had* lived, and dependent on it not alone for a support but for an identity.

It sufficed him in its way for months and the year elapsed; it would doubtless even have carried him further but for an accident, superficially slight, which moved him, quite in another direction, with a force beyond any of his impressions of Egypt or of India. It was a thing of the merest chance—the turn, as he afterwards felt, of a hair, though he was indeed to live to believe that if light hadn't come to him in this particular fashion it would still have come in another. He was to live to believe this, I say, though he was not to live, I may not less definitely mention, to do much else. We allow him at any rate the benefit of the conviction, struggling up for him at the end, that, whatever might have happened or not happened, he would have come round of himself to the light. The incident of an autumn day had put the match to the train laid from of old by his misery. With the light before him he knew that even of late his ache had only been smothered. It was strangely drugged, but it throbbed; at the touch it began to bleed. And the touch, in the event, was the face of a fellow mortal. This face, one grey afternoon when the leaves were thick in the alleys, looked into Marcher's own, at the cemetery, with an expression like the cut of a blade. He felt it, that is, so deep down that he winced at the steady thrust. The person who so mutely assaulted him was a figure he had noticed, on reaching his own goal, absorbed by a grave a short distance away, a grave apparently fresh, so that the emotion of the visitor would probably match it for frankness. This fact alone forbade further attention, though during the time he stayed he remained vaguely conscious of his neighbour, a middle-aged man apparently, in mourning, whose bowed back, among the clustered monuments and mortuary yews, was constantly presented. Marcher's theory that these were elements in contact with which he himself revived, had suffered, on this occasion, it may be granted, a marked, an excessive check. The autumn day was dire for him as none had recently been, and he rested with a heaviness he had not yet known on the low stone table that bore May Bartram's name. He rested without power to move, as if some spring in him, some spell vouchsafed, had suddenly been broken for ever. If he could have done that moment as he wanted he would simply have stretched himself on the slab that was ready to take him, treating it as a place prepared to receive his last sleep. What in all the wide world had he now to keep awake for? He stared before him with the question, and it was then that, as one of the cemetery walks passed near him, he caught the shock of the face.

His neighbour at the other grave had withdrawn, as he himself, with force enough in him, would have done by now, and was advancing along the path on his way to one of the gates. This brought him close, and his pace was slow, so that—and all the more as there was a kind of hunger in his look—the two men were for a minute directly confronted. Marcher knew him at once for one of the deeply stricken—a perception so sharp that nothing else in the picture comparatively lived, neither his dress, his age, nor his presumable character and class; nothing lived but the deep ravage of the features he showed. He *showed* them—that was the point; he was moved, as he passed, by some impulse that was either a signal for sympathy or, more possibly, a challenge to an opposed sorrow. He might already have been aware of our friend, might at some previous hour have noticed in him the smooth habit of the scene, with which the state of his own senses so scantly consorted, and might thereby have been stirred as by an overt discord. What Marcher was at all events conscious of was in the first place that the image of scarred passion presented to him was conscious too—of something that profaned the air; and in the second that, roused, startled, shocked, he was yet the next moment looking after it, as it went, with envy. The most extraordinary thing that had happened to him—though he had given that name to other matters as well—took place, after his immediate vague stare, as a consequence of this impression. The stranger passed, but the raw glare of his grief remained, making our friend wonder in pity what wrong, what wound it expressed, what injury not to be healed. What had the man *had,* to make him by the loss of it so bleed and yet live?

Something—and this reached him with a pang—that *he,* John Marcher, hadn't; the proof of which was precisely John Marcher's arid end. No passion had ever touched him, for this was what passion meant; he had survived and maundered and pined, but where had been *his* deep ravage? The extraordinary thing we speak of was the sudden rush of the result of this question. The sight that had just met his eyes named to him, as in letters of quick flame, something he had utterly, insanely missed, and what he had missed made these things a train of fire, made them mark themselves in an anguish of inward throbs. He had seen *outside* of his life, not learned it within, the way a woman was mourned when she had been loved for herself: such was the force of his conviction of the meaning of the stranger's face, which still flared for him as a smoky torch. It hadn't come to him, the knowledge, on the wings of experience; it had brushed him, jostled him, upset him, with the disrespect of chance, the insolence of accident. Now that the illumination had begun, however, it blazed to the zenith, and what he presently stood there gazing at was the sounded void of his life. He gazed, he drew breath, in pain; he turned in his dismay, and, turning, he had before him in sharper incision than ever the open page of his story. The name on the table smote him as the passage of his neighbour had done, and what it said

to him, full in the face, was that *she* was what he had
missed. This was the awful thought, the answer to all
the past, the vision at the dread clearness of which he
grew as cold as the stone beneath him. Everything fell
together, confessed, explained, overwhelmed; leaving
him most of all stupefied at the blindness he had cherished. The fate he had been marked for he had met
with a vengeance—he had emptied the cup to the lees;
he had been the man of his time, *the* man, to whom
nothing on earth was to have happened. That was the
rare stroke—that was his visitation. So he saw it, as we
say, in pale horror, while the pieces fitted and fitted. So
she had seen it while he didn't, and so she served at
this hour to drive the truth home. It was the truth, vivid
and monstrous, that all the while he had waited the
wait was itself his portion. This the companion of his
vigil had at a given moment made out, and she had then
offered him the chance to baffle his doom. One's doom,
however, was never baffled, and on the day she told
him his own had come down she had seen him but stupidly stare at the escape she offered him.

The escape would have been to love her; then, *then*
he would have lived. *She* had lived—who could say
now with what passion?—since she had loved him for
himself; whereas he had never thought of her (ah how
it hugely glared at him!) but in the chill of his egotism
and the light of her use. Her spoken words came back
to him—the chain stretched and stretched. The Beast
had lurked indeed, and the Beast, at its hour, had sprung;
it had sprung in that twilight of the cold April when,
pale, ill, wasted, but all beautiful, and perhaps even
then recoverable, she had risen from her chair to stand
before him and let him imaginably guess. It had sprung
as he didn't guess; it had sprung as she hopelessly
turned from him, and the mark, by the time he left her,

had fallen where it *was* to fall. He had justified his fear and achieved his fate; he had failed, with the last exactitude, of all he was to fail of; and a moan now rose to his lips as he remembered she had prayed he mightn't know. This horror of waking—*this* was knowledge, knowledge under the breath of which the very tears in his eyes seemed to freeze. Through them, none the less, he tried to fix it and hold it; he kept it there before him so that he might feel the pain. That at least, belated and bitter, had something of the taste of life. But the bitterness suddenly sickened him, and it was as if, horribly, he saw, in the truth, in the cruelty of his image, what had been appointed and done. He saw the Jungle of his life and saw the lurking Beast; then, while he looked, perceived it, as by a stir of the air, rise, huge and hideous, for the leap that was to settle him. His eyes darkened—it was close; and, instinctively turning, in his hallucination, to avoid it, he flung himself, face down, on the tomb.

1903

III

CRITICISM

*

EDITOR'S NOTE

James began his public career as a critic. His first published work was a review of Nassau W. Senior's *Essays on Fiction* in *The North American Review* of October 1864, when he was twenty-one. His reviews and critical articles appeared in increasing numbers during the next decade in *The Nation, The North American, The Atlantic Monthly,* and *The Independent.* In 1878 he put out his first book of critical studies, *French Poets and Novelists.* His work as critic became part of his literary profession; it appeared regularly in American and English periodicals over a space of fifty years, and reached a kind of climax in the critical prefaces he wrote for his own fiction in the New York Edition of 1907-1909. His last contribution to a magazine in his lifetime was an article he wrote for *The Nation* of July 8, 1915, commemorating its founding fifty years earlier and his own share in it. He is, among writers of fiction in English, the pre-eminent case of the critic as novelist and the novelist as critic.

The present selections cover this career from 1865 to 1915. The earliest examples I include are two reviews James wrote for *The Nation* in 1865: one of Whitman's *Drum Taps* in the issue of November 16, the other of Dickens' *Our Mutual Friend* in the issue of December 21. I include them not because they present the full critical case on either Whitman or Dickens, or even James's own full dealings with these two writers, but because they show two of the formidable forces in the literature of his early lifetime with which he had to break in order to decide his own purpose and aims in art. Whitman represented for him the expansive democratic emotion and visionary gusto in American poetry which he saw as directly opposed to his own critical temperament. Dickens stood for the capacious methods and popular sentiment in Victorian fiction from which James was convinced the novel must be rescued if it was to fulfill its destiny as a form of art and moral intelligence. Dickens was, of course, one of the authors James had most greedily devoured in childhood; and years later, when he came to write his memoirs, he remembered how much the England he first encountered was the England Dickens had made real to him. Whitman came to be treated with greater sympathy in later years: his *Calamus* was discussed with considerable indulgence when James wrote about it in an "American Letter" for the London journal *Literature* of April 16, 1898; and Mrs. Wharton, in her memoir, *A Backward Glance* (1934), tells how James read Whitman's poems aloud at Lenox in 1905 "in a mood of subdued ecstasy" that made the two "divergent intelligences" seem to "walk together like gods." (The occasion ended, however, with James flinging up his hands and crying out "with the old stammer and twinkle: 'Oh, yes, a great genius; undoubtedly a very great genius! Only one cannot help deploring his too-extensive acquaintance with the foreign languages.'") I believe, none the less, that the two reviews of 1865, for all their youthful severity, are documents of radical importance in James's intellectual history, and that they also show brilliantly his critical acumen at the age of twenty-two.

"The Art of Fiction," which heads these selections, is James's most famous essay in criticism and the keystone of his arch. It was written as a rejoinder to Walter Besant's lecture on behalf of popular and realistic standards in fiction delivered at the Royal Institution on April 25, 1884. James's riposte appeared in *Longman's Magazine* for September 1884, and in book form in a volume titled *The Art of Fiction* in Boston in 1885, where it was included along with Besant's essay. (Robert Louis Stevenson in turn contributed a demurrer on both Besant and James—"A Humble Remonstrance"—to *Longman's* for December 1884.) In 1888 James included the essay in his *Partial Portraits,* from which the present text is taken. The letter which I have titled "The Great Form" was sent to a summer school at Deerfield, Mass., in the summer of 1889, and repeats, this time specifically for an American audience, the central doctrine of "The Art of Fiction." The essay "Criticism" first appeared as "The Science of Criticism" in *The New Review* (London) for May 1891, and was included under its present title in James's book *Essays in London and Elsewhere* in 1893.

The four passages on Hawthorne, Turgenev (James spelled the name *Turgénieff*), Balzac, and Flaubert show James dealing with four great modern masters who strongly influenced his own conception and practice of his art and on all of whom he wrote numerous times. The discussion of *The Scarlet Letter* is taken from Chapter V of the book on *Hawthorne* (1879). The essay on Turgenev was written for the *Library of the World's Best Literature,* edited by Charles Dudley Warner (1897); here the reader should also consult the essays on Turgenev in *French Poets and Novelists* (1878) and in *Partial Portraits* (1888). The passage on Balzac is from one of James's later essays on the French master who attracted him most powerfully; it comes from a critical introduction he wrote for Balzac's novel *Deux Jeunes Mariées* when it appeared in London as *Two Young Brides* in 1902, and was included in his *Notes on Novelists* in 1914. The account of Flaubert's *Madame Bovary* is taken from an introduction James wrote for an English edition of the novel in 1902, and it was also included in *Notes on Novelists* in 1914.

The circumstances of the letters James wrote in 1915 to H. G. Wells, one of the younger novelists who had aroused his liveliest admiration but from whose standards and practice in fiction he was later to find himself estranged, are explained in the note I have prefixed to them. They show

James in a last rally of defense on behalf of his art and purposes in fiction, and are taken from *The Letters of Henry James* as edited by Percy Lubbock (1920).

*

THE ART OF FICTION

I should not have affixed so comprehensive a title to these few remarks, necessarily wanting in any completeness upon a subject the full consideration of which would carry us far, did I not seem to discover a pretext for my temerity in the interesting pamphlet lately published under this name by Mr. Walter Besant. Mr. Besant's lecture at the Royal Institution—the original form of his pamphlet—appears to indicate that many persons are interested in the art of fiction, and are not indifferent to such remarks, as those who practise it may attempt to make about it. I am therefore anxious not to lose the benefit of this favourable association, and to edge in a few words under cover of the attention which Mr. Besant is sure to have excited. There is something very encouraging in his having put into form certain of his ideas on the mystery of story-telling.

It is a proof of life and curiosity—curiosity on the part of the brotherhood of novelists as well as on the part of their readers. Only a short time ago it might have been supposed that the English novel was not what the French call *discutable*. It had no air of having a theory, a conviction, a consciousness of itself behind it—of being the expression of an artistic faith, the result of choice and comparison. I do not say it was necessarily the worse for that; it would take much more courage than

I possess to intimate that the form of the novel as Dickens and Thackeray (for instance) saw it had any taint of incompleteness. It was, however, *naïf* (if I may help myself out with another French word); and evidently if it be destined to suffer in any way for having lost its *naïveté* it has now an idea of making sure of the corresponding advantages. During the period I have alluded to there was a comfortable, good-humoured feeling abroad that a novel is a novel, as a pudding is a pudding, and that our only business with it could be to swallow it. But within a year or two, for some reason or other, there have been signs of returning animation— the era of discussion would appear to have been to a certain extent opened. Art lives upon discussion, upon experiment, upon curiosity, upon variety of attempt, upon the exchange of views and the comparison of standpoints; and there is a presumption that those times when no one has anything particular to say about it, and has no reason to give for practice or preference, though they may be times of honour, are not times of development—are times, possibly even, a little of dulness. The successful application of any art is a delightful spectacle, but the theory too is interesting; and though there is a great deal of the latter without the former I suspect there has never been a genuine success that has not had a latent core of conviction. Discussion, suggestion, formulation, these things are fertilizing when they are frank and sincere. Mr. Besant has set an excellent example in saying what he thinks, for his part, about the way in which fiction should be written, as well as about the way in which it should be published; for his view of the "art," carried on into an appendix, covers that too. Other labourers in the same field will doubtless take up the argument, they will give it the light of their experience, and the effect will surely be to make our interest in the

novel a little more what it had for some time threatened
to fail to be—a serious, active, inquiring interest, under
protection of which this delightful study may, in moments of confidence, venture to say a little more what
it thinks of itself.

It must take itself seriously for the public to take it so.
The old superstition about fiction being "wicked" has
doubtless died out in England; but the spirit of it lingers
in a certain oblique regard directed toward any story
which does not more or less admit that it is only a joke.
Even the most jocular novel feels in some degree the
weight of the proscription that was formerly directed
against literary levity: the jocularity does not always
succeed in passing for orthodoxy. It is still expected,
though perhaps people are ashamed to say it, that a
production which is after all only a "make-believe"
(for what else is a "story"?) shall be in some degree
apologetic—shall renounce the pretension of attempting
really to represent life. This, of course, any sensible,
wide-awake story declines to do, for it quickly perceives
that the tolerance granted to it on such a condition is
only an attempt to stifle it disguised in the form of generosity. The old evangelical hostility to the novel, which
was as explicit as it was narrow, and which regarded
it as little less favourable to our immortal part than a
stage-play, was in reality far less insulting. The only
reason for the existence of a novel is that it does attempt
to represent life. When it relinquishes this attempt, the
same attempt that we see on the canvas of the painter,
it will have arrived at a very strange pass. It is not expected of the picture that it will make itself humble
in order to be forgiven; and the analogy between the art
of the painter and the art of the novelist is, so far as I
am able to see, complete. Their inspiration is the same,
their process (allowing for the different quality of the

vehicle) is the same, their success is the same. They may learn from each other, they may explain and sustain each other. Their cause is the same, and the honour of one is the honour of another. The Mahometans think a picture an unholy thing, but it is a long time since any Christian did, and it is therefore the more odd that in the Christian mind the traces (dissimulated though they may be) of a suspicion of the sister art should linger to this day. The only effectual way to lay it to rest is to emphasize the analogy to which I just alluded—to insist on the fact that as the picture is reality, so the novel is history. That is the only general description (which does it justice) that we may give of the novel. But history also is allowed to represent life; it is not, any more than painting, expected to apologize. The subject-matter of fiction is stored up likewise in documents and records, and if it will not give itself away, as they say in California, it must speak with assurance, with the tone of the historian. Certain accomplished novelists have a habit of giving themselves away which must often bring tears to the eyes of people who take their fiction seriously. I was lately struck, in reading over many pages of Anthony Trollope, with his want of discretion in this particular. In a digression, a parenthesis or an aside, he concedes to the reader that he and this trusting friend are only "making believe." He admits that the events he narrates have not really happened, and that he can give his narrative any turn the reader may like best. Such a betrayal of a sacred office seems to me, I confess, a terrible crime; it is what I mean by the attitude of apology, and it shocks me every whit as much in Trollope as it would have shocked me in Gibbon or Macaulay. It implies that the novelist is less occupied in looking for the truth (the truth, of course I mean, that he assumes, the premises that we must grant him, whatever they may be) than the historian, and in doing so it deprives him at a stroke of all his standing-room. To represent and illustrate the past, the actions of men, is the task of either writer, and the only difference that I can see is, in proportion as he succeeds, to the honour of the novelist, consisting as it does in his having more-difficult in collecting his evidence, which is so far from being purely literary. It seems to me to give him a great character, the fact that he has at once so much in common with the philosopher and the painter; this double analogy is a magnificent heritage.

It is of all this evidently that Mr. Besant is full when he insists upon the fact that fiction is one of the *fine* arts, deserving in its turn of all the honours and emoluments that have hitherto been reserved for the successful profession of music, poetry, painting, architecture. It is impossible to insist too much on so important a truth, and the place that Mr. Besant demands for the work of the novelist may be represented, a trifle less abstractly, by saying that he demands not only that it shall be reputed artistic, but that it shall be reputed very artistic indeed. It is excellent that he should have struck this note, for his doing so indicates that there was need of it, that his proposition may be to many people a novelty. One rubs one's eyes at the thought; but the rest of Mr. Besant's essay confirms the revelation. I suspect in truth that it would be possible to confirm it still further, and that one would not be far wrong in saying that in addition to the people to whom it has never occurred that a novel ought to be artistic, there are a great many others who, if this principle were urged upon them, would be filled with an indefinable mistrust. They would find it difficult to explain their repugnance, but it would operate strongly to put them on their guard. "Art," in our Protestant communities, where so many things have got so strangely twisted about, is supposed in certain circles to have some vaguely injurious effect upon those who make it an important consideration, who let it weigh in the balance. It is assumed to be opposed in some mysterious manner to morality, to amusement, to instruction. When it is embodied in the work of the painter (the sculptor is another affair!) you know what it is: it stands there before you, in the honesty of pink and green and a gilt frame; you can see the worst of it at a glance, and you can be on your guard. But when it is introduced into literature it becomes more insidious —there is danger of its hurting you before you know it. Literature should be either instructive or amusing, and there is in many minds an impression that these artistic preoccupations, the search for form, contribute to neither end, interfere indeed with both. They are too frivolous to be edifying, and too serious to be diverting; and they are moreover priggish and paradoxical and superfluous. That, I think, represents the manner in which the latent thought of many people who read novels as an exercise in skipping would explain itself if it were to become articulate. They would argue, of course, that a novel ought to be "good," but they would interpret this term in a fashion of their own, which indeed would vary considerably from one critic to another. One would say that being good means representing virtuous and aspiring characters, placed in prominent positions; another would say that it depends on a "happy ending," on a distribution at the last of prizes, pensions, husbands, wives, babies, millions, appended paragraphs, and cheerful remarks. Another still would say that it means being full of incident and movement, so that we shall wish to jump ahead, to see who was the mysterious stranger, and if the stolen will was ever found, and shall not be distracted from this pleasure by any tiresome analysis or "description." But they would all agree that the "artistic" idea would spoil some of their fun. One would hold it accountable for all the description, another would see it revealed in the absence of sympathy. Its hostility to a happy ending would be evident, and it might even in some cases render any ending at all impossible. The "ending" of a novel is, for many persons, like that of a good dinner, a course of dessert and ices, and the artist in fiction is regarded as a sort of meddlesome doctor who forbids agreeable aftertastes. It is therefore true that this conception of Mr. Besant's of the novel as a superior form encounters not only a negative but a positive indifference. It matters little that as a work of art it should really be as little or as much of its essence to supply happy endings, sympathetic characters, and an objective tone, as if it were a work of mechanics: the association of ideas, however incongruous, might easily be too much for it if an eloquent voice were not sometimes raised to call attention to the fact that it is at once as free and as serious a branch of literature as any other.

Certainly this might sometimes be doubted in presence of the enormous number of works of fiction that appeal to the credulity of our generation, for it might easily seem that there could be no great character in a commodity so quickly and easily produced. It must be admitted that good novels are much compromised by bad ones, and that the field at large suffers discredit from overcrowding. I think, however, that this injury is only superficial, and that the superabundance of written fiction proves nothing against the principle itself. It has been vulgarized, like all other kinds of literature, like everything else to-day, and it has proved more than some kinds accessible to vulgarization. But there is as much difference as there ever was between a good novel and a bad one: the bad is swept with all the daubed canvases and spoiled marble into some unvisited limbo, or infinite rubbish-yard beneath the back-windows of the world, and the good subsists and emits its light and stimulates our desire for perfection. As I shall take the liberty of making but a single criticism of Mr. Besant, whose tone is so full of the love of his art, I may as well have done with it at once. He seems to me to mistake in attempting to say so definitely beforehand what sort of an affair the good novel will be. To indicate the danger of such an error as that has been the purpose of these few pages; to suggest that certain traditions on the subject, applied *a priori*, have already had much to answer for, and that the good health of an art which undertakes so immediately to reproduce life must demand that it be perfectly free. It lives upon exercise, and the very meaning of exercise is freedom. The only obligation to which in advance we may hold a novel, without incurring the accusation of being arbitrary, is that it be interesting. That general responsibility rests upon it, but it is the only one I can think of. The ways in which it is at liberty to accomplish this result (of interesting us) strike me as innumerable, and such as can only suffer from being marked out or fenced in by prescription. They are as various as the temperament of man, and they are successful in proportion as they reveal a particular mind, different from others. A novel is in its broadest definition a personal, a direct impression of life: that, to begin with, constitutes its value, which is greater or less according to the intensity of the impression. But there will be no intensity at all, and therefore no value, unless there is freedom to feel and say. The tracing of a line to be followed, of a tone to be taken, of a form to be filled out, is a limitation of that freedom and a suppression of the very thing that we are most curious about. The form, it seems to me, is to be appreciated after the fact: then the author's choice has been made, his standard has been indicated; then we can follow lines and directions and compare tones and resemblances. Then in a word we can enjoy one of the most charming of pleasures, we can estimate quality, we can apply the test of execution. The execution belongs to the author alone; it is what is most personal to him, and we measure him by that. The advantage, the luxury, as well as the torment and responsibility of the novelist, is that there is no limit to what he may attempt as an executant—no limit to his possible experiments, efforts, discoveries, successes. Here it is especially that he works, step by step, like his brother of the brush, of whom we may always say that he has painted his picture in a manner best known to himself. His manner is his secret, not necessarily a jealous one. He cannot disclose it as a general thing if he would; he would be at a loss to teach it to others. I say this with a due recollection of having insisted on the community of method of the artist who paints a picture and the artist who writes a novel. The painter *is* able to teach the rudiments of his practice, and it is possible, from the study of good work (granted the aptitude), both to learn how to paint and to learn how to write. Yet it remains true, without injury to the *rapprochement,* that the literary artist would be obliged to say to his pupil much more than the other, "Ah, well, you must do it as you can!" It is a question of degree, a matter of delicacy. If there are exact sciences, there are also exact arts, and the grammar of painting is so much more definite that it makes the difference.

I ought to add, however, that if Mr. Besant says at the beginning of his essay that the "laws of fiction may be laid down and taught with as much precision and exactness as the laws of harmony, perspective, and

proportion," he mitigates what might appear to be an
extravagance by applying his remark to "general" laws,
and by expressing most of these rules in a manner with
which it would certainly be unaccommodating to disagree. That the novelist must write from his experience,
that his "characters must be real and such as might be
met with in actual life"; that "a young lady brought up
in a quiet country village should avoid descriptions of
garrison life," and "a writer whose friends and personal
experiences belong to the lower middle-class should
carefully avoid introducing his characters into society";
that one should enter one's notes in a common-place
book; that one's figures should be clear in outline; that
making them clear by some trick of speech or of carriage is a bad method, and "describing them at length"
is a worse one; that English Fiction should have a "conscious moral purpose"; that "it is almost impossible to
estimate too highly the value of careful workmanship
—that is, of style"; that "the most important point of
all is the story," that "the story is everything": these
are principles with most of which it is surely impossible
not to sympathize. That remark about the lower middle-
class writer and his knowing his place is perhaps rather
chilling; but for the rest I should find it difficult to dissent from any one of these recommendations. At the
same time, I should find it difficult positively to assent
to them, with the exception, perhaps, of the injunction
as to entering one's notes in a common-place book. They
scarcely seem to me to have the quality that Mr. Besant
attributes to the rules of the novelist—the "precision
and exactness" of "the laws of harmony, perspective, and
proportion." They are suggestive, they are even inspiring, but they are not exact, though they are doubtless
as much so as the case admits of: which is a proof of
that liberty of interpretation for which I just contended.

For the value of these different injunctions—so beautiful and so vague—is wholly in the meaning one attaches to them. The characters, the situation, which strike one as real will be those that touch and interest one most, but the measure of reality is very difficult to fix. The reality of Don Quixote or of Mr. Micawber is a very delicate shade; it is a reality so coloured by the author's vision that, vivid as it may be, one would hesitate to propose it as a model: one would expose one's self to some very embarrassing questions on the part of a pupil. It goes without saying that you will not write a good novel unless you possess the sense of reality; but it will be difficult to give you a recipe for calling that sense into being. Humanity is immense, and reality has a myriad forms; the most one can affirm is that some of the flowers of fiction have the odour of it, and others have not; as for telling you in advance how your nosegay should be composed, that is another affair. It is equally excellent and inconclusive to say that one must write from experience; to our supposititious aspirant such a declaration might savour of mockery. What kind of experience is intended, and where does it begin and end? Experience is never limited, and it is never complete; it is an immense sensibility, a kind of huge spider-web of the finest silken threads suspended in the chamber of consciousness, and catching every air-borne particle in its tissue. It is the very atmosphere of the mind; and when the mind is imaginative—much more when it happens to be that of a man of genius—it takes to itself the faintest hints of life, it converts the very pulses of the air into revelations. The young lady living in a village has only to be a damsel upon whom nothing is lost to make it quite unfair (as it seems to me) to declare to her that she shall have nothing to say about the military. Greater miracles have been seen than that, imagination assisting, she should speak the truth about some of these gentlemen. I remember an English novelist, a woman of genius, telling me that she was much commended for the impression she had managed to give in one of her tales of the nature and way of life of the French Protestant youth. She had been asked where she learned so much about this recondite being, she had been congratulated on her peculiar opportunities. These opportunities consisted in her having once, in Paris, as she ascended a staircase, passed an open door where, in the household of a *pasteur*, some of the young Protestants were seated at table round a finished meal. The glimpse made a picture; it lasted only a moment, but that moment was experience. She had got her direct personal impression, and she turned out her type. She knew what youth was, and what Protestantism; she also had the advantage of having seen what it was to be French, so that she converted these ideas into a concrete image and produced a reality. Above all, however, she was blessed with the faculty which when you give it an inch takes an ell, and which for the artist is a much greater source of strength than any accident of residence or of place in the social scale. The power to guess the unseen from the seen, to trace the implication of things, to judge the whole piece by the pattern, the condition of feeling life in general so completely that you are well on your way to knowing any particular corner of it—this cluster of gifts may almost be said to constitute experience, and they occur in country and in town, and in the most differing stages of education. If experience consists of impressions, it may be said that impressions *are* experience, just as (have we not seen it?) they are the very air we breathe. Therefore, if I should certainly say to a novice, "Write from experience and experience only," I should feel that this was rather a tantalizing monition if I were not careful immediately to add, "Try to be one of the people on whom nothing is lost!"

I am far from intending by this to minimize the importance of exactness—of truth of detail. One can speak best from one's own taste, and I may therefore venture to say that the air of reality (solidity of specification) seems to me to be the supreme virtue of a novel—the merit on which all its other merits (including that conscious moral purpose of which Mr. Besant speaks) helplessly and submissively depend. If it be not there they are all as nothing, and if these be there, they owe their effect to the success with which the author has produced the illusion of life. The cultivation of this success, the study of this exquisite process, form, to my taste, the beginning and the end of the art of the novelist. They are his inspiration, his despair, his reward, his torment, his delight. It is here in very truth that he competes with life; it is here that he competes with his brother the painter in *his* attempt to render the look of things, the look that conveys their meaning, to catch the colour, the relief, the expression, the surface, the substance of the human spectacle. It is in regard to this that Mr. Besant is well inspired when he bids him take notes. He cannot possibly take too many, he cannot possibly take enough. All life solicits him, and to "render" the simplest surface, to produce the most momentary illusion, is a very complicated business. His case would be easier, and the rule would be more exact, if Mr. Besant had been able to tell him what notes to take. But this, I fear, he can never learn in any manual; it is the business of his life. He has to take a great many in order to select a few, he has to work them up as he can, and even the guides and philosophers who might have most to say to him must leave him alone when it comes to the application of precepts, as we leave the painter in communion with his palette. That his characters "must be clear in outline," as Mr. Besant says—he feels that down to his boots; but how he shall make them so is a secret between his good angel and himself. It would be absurdly simple if he could be taught that a great deal of "description" would make them so, or that on the contrary the absence of description and the cultivation of dialogue, or the absence of dialogue and the multiplication of "incident," would rescue him from his difficulties. Nothing, for instance, is more possible than that he be of a turn of mind for which this odd, literal opposition of description and dialogue, incident and description, has little meaning and light. People often talk of these things as if they had a kind of internecine distinctness, instead of melting into each other at every breath, and being intimately associated parts of one general effort of expression. I cannot imagine composition existing in a series of blocks, nor conceive, in any novel worth discussing at all, of a passage of description that is not in its intention narrative, a passage of dialogue that is not in its intention descriptive, a touch of truth of any sort that does not partake of the nature of incident, or an incident that derives its interest from any other source than the general and only source of the success of a work of art—that of being illustrative. A novel is a living thing, all one and continuous, like any other organism, and in proportion as it lives will it be found, I think, that in each of the parts there is something of each of the other parts. The critic who over the close texture of a finished work shall pretend to trace a geography of items will mark some frontiers as artificial, I fear, as any that have been known to history. There is an old-fashioned distinction between the novel of character and the novel of incident which must have cost many a smile to the intending fabulist who was keen about his work. It appears to me as little to the point as the equally celebrated distinction between the novel and the romance—to answer as little to any reality. There are bad novels and good novels, as there are bad pictures and good pictures; but that is the only distinction in which I see any meaning, and I can as little imagine speaking of a novel of character as I can imagine speaking of a picture of character. When one says picture one says of character, when one says novel one says of incident, and the terms may be transposed at will. What is character but the determination of incident? What is incident but the illustration of character? What is either a picture or a novel that is *not* of character? What else do we seek in it and find in it? It is an incident for a woman to stand up with her hand resting on a table and look out at you in a certain way; or if it be not an incident I think it will be hard to say what it is. At the same time it is an expression of character. If you say you don't see it (character in *that—allons donc!*), this is exactly what the artist who has reasons of his own for thinking he *does* see it undertakes to show you. When a young man makes up his mind that he has not faith enough after all to enter the church as he intended, that is an incident, though you may not hurry to the end of the chapter to see whether perhaps he doesn't change once more. I do not say that these are extraordinary or startling incidents. I do not pretend to estimate the degree of interest proceeding from them, for this will depend upon the skill of the painter. It sounds almost puerile to say that some incidents are intrinsically much more important than others, and I need not take this precaution after having professed my sympathy for the major ones in remarking that the only classification of the novel that I can understand is into that which has life and that which has it not.

The novel and the romance, the novel of incident and that of character—these clumsy separations appear to me to have been made by critics and readers for their own convenience, and to help them out of some of their occasional queer predicaments, but to have little reality or interest for the producer, from whose point of view it is of course that we are attempting to consider the art of fiction. The case is the same with another shadowy category which Mr. Besant apparently is disposed to set up—that of the "modern English novel"; unless indeed it be that in this matter he has fallen into an accidental confusion of standpoints. It is not quite clear whether he intends the remarks in which he alludes to it to be didactic or historical. It is as difficult to suppose a person intending to write a modern English as to suppose him writing an ancient English novel: that is a label which begs the question. One writes the novel, one paints the picture, of one's language and of one's time, and calling it modern English will not, alas! make the difficult task any easier. No more, unfortunately, will calling this or that work of one's fellow-artist a romance—unless it be, of course, simply for the pleasantness of the thing, as for instance when Hawthorne gave this heading to his story of *Blithedale*. The French, who have brought the theory of fiction to remarkable completeness, have but one name for the novel, and have not attempted smaller things in it, that I can see, for that. I can think of no obligation to which the "romancer" would not be held equally with the novelist; the standard of execution is equally high for each. Of course it is of execution that we are talking—that being the only point of a novel that is open to contention. This is perhaps too often lost sight of, only to produce interminable confusions and cross-purposes. We must grant the artist his subject, his idea, his *donnée:* our criticism is applied only to what he makes of it. Naturally I do not mean that we are bound to like it or find it interesting: in case we do not our course is perfectly simple—to let it alone. We may believe that of a certain idea even the most sincere novelist can make nothing at all, and the event may perfectly justify our belief; but the failure will have been a failure to execute, and it is in the execution that the fatal weakness is recorded. If we pretend to respect the artist at all, we must allow him his freedom of choice, in the face, in particular cases, of innumerable presumptions that the choice will not fructify. Art derives a considerable part of its beneficial exercise from flying in the face of presumptions, and some of the most interesting experiments of which it is capable are hidden in the bosom of common things. Gustave Flaubert has written a story about the devotion of a servant-girl to a parrot, and the production, highly-finished as it is, cannot on the whole be called a success. We are perfectly free to find it flat, but I think it might have been interesting; and I, for my part, am extremely glad he should have written it; it is a contribution to our knowledge of what can be done— or what cannot. Ivan Turgénieff has written a tale about a deaf and dumb serf and a lap-dog, and the thing is touching, loving, a little masterpiece. He struck the note of life where Gustave Flaubert missed it—he flew in the face of a presumption and achieved a victory.

Nothing, of course, will ever take the place of the good old fashion of "liking" a work of art or not liking it: the most improved criticism will not abolish that primitive, that ultimate test. I mention this to guard myself from the accusation of intimating that the idea, the subject, of a novel or a picture, does not matter. It matters, to my sense, in the highest degree, and if I might put up a prayer it would be that artists should select none but the richest. Some, as I have already hastened to admit, are much more remunerative than others, and it would be a world happily arranged in which persons intending to treat them should be exempt from confusions and mistakes. This fortunate condition will arrive only, I fear, on the same day that critics become purged from error. Meanwhile, I repeat, we do not judge the artist with fairness unless we say to him,

"Oh, I grant you your starting-point, because if I did not I should seem to prescribe to you, and heaven forbid I should take that responsibility. If I pretend to tell you what you must not take, you will call upon me to tell you then what you must take; in which case I shall be prettily caught. Moreover, it isn't till I have accepted your data that I can begin to measure you. I have the standard, the pitch; I have no right to tamper with your flute and then criticize your music. Of course I may not care for your idea at all; I may think it silly, or stale, or unclean; in which case I wash my hands of you altogether. I may content myself with believing that you will not have succeeded in being interesting, but I shall, of course, not attempt to demonstrate it, and you will be as indifferent to me as I am to you. I needn't remind you that there are all sorts of tastes: who can know it better? Some people, for excellent reasons, don't like to read about carpenters; others, for reasons even better, don't like to read about courtesans. Many object to Americans. Others (I believe they are mainly editors and publishers) won't look at Italians. Some readers don't like quiet subjects; others don't like bustling ones. Some enjoy a complete illusion, others the consciousness of large concessions. They choose their novels accordingly, and if they don't care about your idea they won't, *a fortiori*, care about your treatment."

So that it comes back very quickly, as I have said, to the liking: in spite of M. Zola, who reasons less power fully than he represents, and who will not reconcile himself to this absoluteness of taste, thinking that there are certain things that people ought to like, and that they can be made to like. I am quite at a loss to imagine anything (at any rate in this matter of fiction) that people *ought* to like or to dislike. Selection will be sure to take care of itself, for it has a constant motive behind it. That motive is simply experience. As people feel life, so they will feel the art that is most closely related to it. This closeness of relation is what we should never forget in talking of the effort of the novel. Many people speak of it as a factitious, artificial form, a product of ingenuity, the business of which is to alter and arrange the things that surround us, to translate them into conventional, traditional moulds. This, however, is a view of the matter which carries us but a very short way, condemns the art to an eternal repetition of a few familiar *clichés,* cuts short its development, and leads us straight up to a dead wall. Catching the very note and trick, the strange irregular rhythm of life, that is the attempt whose strenuous force keeps Fiction upon her feet. In proportion as in what she offers us we see life *without* rearrangement do we feel that we are touching the truth; in proportion as we see it *with* rearrangement do we feel that we are being put off with a substitute, a compromise and convention. It is not uncommon to hear an extraordinary assurance of remark in regard to this matter of rearranging, which is often spoken of as if it were the last word of art. Mr. Besant seems to me in danger of falling into the great error with his rather unguarded talk about "selection." Art is essentially selection, but it is a selection whose main care is to be

typical, to be inclusive. For many people art means rose-
coloured window-panes, and selection means picking
a bouquet for Mrs. Grundy. They will tell you glibly
that artistic considerations have nothing to do with the
disagreeable, with the ugly; they will rattle off shallow
commonplaces about the province of art and the limits
of art till you are moved to some wonder in return as to
the province and the limits of ignorance. It appears to
me that no one can ever have made a seriously artistic
attempt without becoming conscious of an immense
increase—a kind of revelation—of freedom. One perceives in that case—by the light of a heavenly ray—
that the province of art is all life, all feeling, all observation, all vision. As Mr. Besant so justly intimates, it is
all experience. That is a sufficient answer to those who
maintain that it must not touch the sad things of life, who
stick into its divine unconscious bosom little prohibitory
inscriptions on the end of sticks, such as we see in public
gardens—"It is forbidden to walk on the grass; it is forbidden to touch the flowers; it is not allowed to introduce dogs or to remain after dark; it is requested to keep
to the right." The young aspirant in the line of fiction
whom we continue to imagine will do nothing without
taste, for in that case his freedom would be of little use
to him; but the first advantage of his taste will be to
reveal to him the absurdity of the little sticks and tickets.
If he have taste, I must add, of course he will have ingenuity, and my disrespectful reference to that quality
just now was not meant to imply that it is useless in fiction. But it is only a secondary aid; the first is a capacity
for receiving straight impressions.

Mr. Besant has some remarks on the question of "the
story" which I shall not attempt to criticize, though they
seem to me to contain a singular ambiguity, because
I do not think I understand them. I cannot see what is

meant by talking as if there were a part of a novel which
is the story and part of it which for mystical reasons is
not—unless indeed the distinction be made in a sense
in which it is difficult to suppose that any one should
attempt to convey anything. "The story," if it represents
anything, represents the subject, the idea, the *donnée*
of the novel; and there is surely no "school"—Mr.
Besant speaks of a school—which urges that a novel
should be all treatment and no subject. There must assuredly be something to treat; every school is intimately
conscious of that. This sense of the story being the idea,
the starting-point, of the novel, is the only one that I
see in which it can be spoken of as something different
from its organic whole; and since in proportion as the
work is successful the idea permeates and penetrates it,
informs and animates it, so that every word and every
punctuation-point contribute directly to the expression,
in that proportion do we lose our sense of the story being
a blade which may be drawn more or less out of its
sheath. The story and the novel, the idea and the form,
are the needle and thread, and I never heard of a guild
of tailors who recommended the use of the thread without the needle, or the needle without the thread. Mr.
Besant is not the only critic who may be observed to
have spoken as if there were certain things in life which
constitute stories, and certain others which do not. I
find the same odd implication in an entertaining article
in the *Pall Mall Gazette*, devoted, as it happens, to Mr.
Besant's lecture. "The story is the thing!" says this graceful writer, as if with a tone of opposition to some other
idea. I should think it was, as every painter who, as the
time for "sending in" his picture looms in the distance,
finds himself still in quest of a subject—as every belated artist not fixed about his theme will heartily agree.
There are some subjects which speak to us and others

which do not, but he would be a clever man who should undertake to give a rule—an *index expurgatorius*—by which the story and the no-story should be known apart. It is impossible (to me at least) to imagine any such rule which shall not be altogether arbitrary. The writer in the *Pall Mall* opposes the delightful (as I suppose) novel of *Margot la Balafrée* to certain tales in which "Bostonian nymphs" appear to have "rejected English dukes for psychological reasons." I am not acquainted with the romance just designated, and can scarcely forgive the *Pall Mall* critic for not mentioning the name of the author, but the title appears to refer to a lady who may have received a scar in some heroic adventure. I am inconsolable at not being acquainted with this episode, but am utterly at a loss to see why it is a story when the rejection (or acceptance) of a duke is not, and why a reason, psychological or other, is not a subject when a cicatrix is. They are all particles of the multitudinous life with which the novel deals, and surely no dogma which pretends to make it lawful to touch the one and unlawful to touch the other will stand for a moment on its feet. It is the special picture that must stand or fall, according as it seem to possess truth or to lack it. Mr. Besant does not, to my sense, light up the subject by intimating that a story must, under penalty of not being a story, consist of "adventures." Why of adventures more than of green spectacles? He mentions a category of impossible things, and among them he places "fiction without adventure." Why without adventure, more than without matrimony, or celibacy, or parturition, or cholera, or hydropathy, or Jansenism? This seems to me to bring the novel back to the hapless little *rôle* of being an artificial, ingenious thing—bring it down from its large, free character of an immense and exquisite correspondence with life. And what *is* adventure, when it comes to that, and by what sign is the listening pupil to recognize it? It is an adventure—an immense one—for me to write this little article; and for a Bostonian nymph to reject an English duke is an adventure only less stirring, I should say, than for an English duke to be rejected by a Bostonian nymph. I see dramas within dramas in that, and innumerable points of view. A psychological reason is, to my imagination, an object adorably pictorial; to catch the tint of its complexion—I feel as if that idea might inspire one to Titianesque efforts. There are few things more exciting to me, in short, than a psychological reason, and yet, I protest, the novel seems to me the most magnificent form of art. I have just been reading, at the same time, the delightful story of *Treasure Island*, by Mr. Robert Louis Stevenson and, in a manner less consecutive, the last tale from M. Edmond de Goncourt, which is entitled *Chérie*. One of these works treats of murders, mysteries, islands of dreadful renown, hair-breadth escapes, miraculous coincidences and buried doubloons. The other treats of a little French girl who lived in a fine house in Paris, and died of wounded sensibility because no one would marry her. I call *Treasure Island* delightful, because it appears to me to have succeeded wonderfully in what it attempts; and I venture to bestow no epithet upon *Chérie*, which strikes me as having failed deplorably in what it attempts—that is in tracing the development of the moral consciousness of a child. But one of these productions strikes me as exactly as much of a novel as the other, and as having a "story" quite as much. The moral consciousness of a child is as much a part of life as the islands of the Spanish Main, and the one sort of geography seems to me to have those "surprises" of which Mr. Besant speaks quite as much as the other. For myself (since it comes back in the last resort, as I say, to the preference of the individual), the picture of the child's experience has the advantage that I can at successive steps (an immense luxury, near to the "sensual pleasure" of which Mr. Besant's critic in the *Pall Mall* speaks) say Yes or No, as it may be, to what the artist puts before me. I have been a child in fact, but I have been on a quest for a buried treasure only in supposition, and it is a simple accident that with M. de Goncourt I should have for the most part to say No. With George Eliot, when she painted that country with a far other intelligence, I always said Yes.

The most interesting part of Mr. Besant's lecture is unfortunately the briefest passage—his very cursory allusion to the "conscious moral purpose" of the novel. Here again it is not very clear whether he be recording a fact or laying down a principle; it is a great pity that in the latter case he should not have developed his idea. This branch of the subject is of immense importance, and Mr. Besant's few words point to considerations of the widest reach, not to be lightly disposed of. He will have treated the art of fiction but superficially who is not prepared to go every inch of the way that these considerations will carry him. It is for this reason that at the beginning of these remarks I was careful to notify the reader that my reflections on so large a theme have no pretension to be exhaustive. Like Mr. Besant, I have left the question of the morality of the novel till the last, and at the last I find I have used up my space. It is a question surrounded with difficulties, as witness the very first that meets us, in the form of a definite question, on the threshold. Vagueness, in such a discussion, is fatal, and what is the meaning of your morality and your conscious moral purpose? Will you not define your terms and explain how (a novel being a picture) a picture can be either moral or immoral? You wish to paint a moral picture or carve a moral statue: will you not tell us how you would set about it? We are discussing the Art of Fiction; questions of art are questions (in the widest sense) of execution; questions of morality are quite another affair, and will you not let us see how it is that you find it so easy to mix them up? These things are so clear to Mr. Besant that he has deduced from them a law which he sees embodied in English Fiction, and which is "a truly admirable thing and a great cause for congratulation." It is a great cause for congratulation indeed when such thorny problems become as smooth as silk. I may add that in so far as Mr. Besant perceives that in point of fact English Fiction has addressed itself preponderantly to these delicate questions he will appear to many people to have made a vain discovery. They will have been positively struck, on the contrary, with the moral timidity of the usual English novelist; with his (or with her) aversion to face the difficulties with which on every side the treatment of reality bristles. He is apt to be extremely shy (whereas the picture that Mr. Besant draws is a picture of boldness), and the sign of his work, for the most part, is a cautious silence on certain subjects. In the English novel (by which of course I mean the American as well), more than in any other, there is a traditional difference between that which people know and that which they agree to admit that they know, that which they see and that which they speak of, that which they feel to be a part of life and that which they allow to enter into literature. There is the great difference, in short, between what they talk of in conversation and what they talk of in print. The essence of moral energy is to survey the whole field, and I should directly reverse Mr. Besant's remark and say not that the English novel has a purpose, but that it has a diffidence. To what degree a purpose in a work of art is a source of corruption I shall not attempt to inquire; the one that seems to me least dangerous is the purpose of making a perfect work. As for our novel, I may say lastly on this score that as we find it in England to-day it strikes me as addressed in a large degree to "young people," and that this in itself constitutes a presumption that it will be rather shy. There are certain things which it is generally agreed not to discuss, not even to mention, before young people. That is very well, but the absence of discussion is not a symptom of the moral passion. The purpose of the English novel—"a truly admirable thing, and a great cause for congratulation"—strikes me therefore as rather negative.

There is one point at which the moral sense and the artistic sense lie very near together; that is in the light of the very obvious truth that the deepest quality of a work of art will always be the quality of the mind of the producer. In proportion as that intelligence is fine will the novel, the picture, the statue partake of the substance of beauty and truth. To be constituted of such elements is, to my vision, to have purpose enough. No good novel will ever proceed from a superficial mind; that seems to me an axiom which, for the artist in fiction, will cover all needful moral ground: if the youthful aspirant take it to heart it will illuminate for him many of the mysteries of "purpose." There are many other useful things that might be said to him, but I have come to the end of my article, and can only touch them as I pass. The critic in the *Pall Mall Gazette*, whom I have already quoted, draws attention to the danger, in speaking of the art of fiction, of generalizing. The danger that he has in mind is rather, I imagine, that of particularizing, for there are some comprehensive remarks which, in addition to those embodied in Mr. Besant's suggestive lecture, might without fear of misleading him be addressed to the ingenuous student. I should remind him first of the magnificence of the form that is open to him, which offers to sight so few restrictions and such innumerable opportunities. The other arts, in comparison, appear confined and hampered; the various conditions under which they are exercised are so rigid and definite. But the only condition that I can think of attaching to the composition of the novel is, as I have already said, that it be sincere. This freedom is a splendid privilege, and the first lesson of the young novelist is to learn to be worthy of it.

"Enjoy it as it deserves [I should say to him]; take possession of it, explore it to its utmost extent, publish it, rejoice in it. All life belongs to you, and do not listen either to those who would shut you up into corners of it and tell you that it is only here and there that art inhabits, or to those who would persuade you that this heavenly messenger wings her way outside of life altogether, breathing a superfine air, and turning away her head from the truth of things. There is no impression of life, no manner of seeing it and feeling it, to which the plan of the novelist may not offer a place; you have only to remember that talents so dissimilar as those of Alexandre Dumas and Jane Austen, Charles Dickens and Gustave Flaubert have worked in this field with equal glory. Do not think too much about optimism and pessimism; try and catch the colour of life itself. In France to-day we see a prodigious effort (that of Émile Zola, to whose solid and serious work no explorer of the capacity of the novel can allude without respect), we see an extraordinary effort vitiated by a spirit of pessimism on a narrow basis. M. Zola is magnificent, but he strikes an English reader as ignorant; he has an air of working in the dark; if he had as much light as energy, his results would be of the highest value. As for the aberrations of a shallow optimism, the ground (of English fiction especially) is strewn with their brittle particles as with broken glass. If you must indulge in conclusions, let them have the taste of a wide knowledge. Remember that your first duty is to be as complete as possible— to make as perfect a work. Be generous and delicate and pursue the prize."

1884. From *Partial Portraits* (1888).

"THE GREAT FORM"

[In the summer of 1889 there was held at Deerfield, Massachusetts, a summer school on "The Novel," to which Henry James, then in England, was invited to contribute. The appeal of the school's organizers told him that it was their object to discuss and resist "the materialism of our present tendencies" in this form of literature. Henry James, unable to attend the sessions, participated by letter; his message was then published in full in the *New York Tribune* of Sunday, August 4, 1889, and summarized in briefer form in *The Critic* (New York) of August 17, 1889. This letter was rediscovered by Mr. Leon Edel and published by him in the *Times Literary Supplement* (London) of July 29, 1939, with a note in which he remarks that the letter "is interesting, for it is a reiteration, in concise form, of the views set forth by James in his famous essay 'The Art of Fiction,' while being at the same time probably the most concrete advice he ever vouchsafed his countrymen on novel-writing." *Editor's note.*]

I am afraid I can do little more than thank you for your courteous invitation to be present at the sittings of your delightfully sounding school of romance, which ought to inherit happiness and honour from such a name. I am so very far away from you that I am afraid I can't participate very intelligently in your discussions, but I can only give them the furtherance of a dimly discriminating sympathy. I am not sure that I apprehend very well your apparent premise "the materialism of our present tendencies," and I suspect that this would require some clearing up before I should be able (if even then) to contribute any suggestive or helpful word. To tell the truth, I can't help thinking that we already talk too much about the novel, about and around it, in proportion to the quantity of it having any importance that we produce. What I should say to the nymphs and swains who propose to converse about it under the great trees at Deerfield is: "Oh, do something from your point of view; an ounce of example is worth a ton of generalities; do something with the great art and the great form; do something with life. Any point of view is interesting that is a direct impression of life. You each have an impression coloured by your individual conditions; make that into a picture, a picture framed by your own personal wisdom, your glimpse of the American world. The field is vast for freedom, for study, for observation, for satire, for truth." I don't think I really do know what you mean by "materializing tendencies" any more than I should by "spiritualizing" or "etherealizing." There are no tendencies worth anything but to see the actual or the imaginative, which is just as visible, and to paint it. I have only two little words for the matter remotely approaching to rule or doctrine; one is life and the other freedom. Tell the ladies and gentlemen, the ingenious inquirers, to consider life directly and closely, and not to be put off with mean and puerile falsities, and be conscientious about it. It is infinitely large, various and comprehensive. Every sort of mind will find what it looks for in it, whereby the novel becomes truly multifarious and illustrative. That is what I mean by liberty; give it its head and let it range. If it is in a bad way, and the English novel is, I think, nothing but absolute freedom can refresh it and restore its self-respect. Hence these raw brevities and please convey to your companions, my dear sir, the cordial good wishes of yours and theirs,

Henry James

1889

CRITICISM

If literary criticism may be said to flourish among us at all, it certainly flourishes immensely, for it flows through the periodical press like a river that has burst its dikes. The quantity of it is prodigious, and it is a commodity of which, however the demand may be estimated, the supply will be sure to be in any supposable extremity the last thing to fail us. What strikes the observer above all, in such an affluence, is the unexpected proportion the discourse uttered bears to the objects discoursed of —the paucity of examples, of illustrations and productions, and the deluge of doctrine suspended in the void; the profusion of talk and the contraction of experiment, of what one may call literary conduct. This, indeed, ceases to be an anomaly as soon as we look at the conditions of contemporary journalism. Then we see that these conditions have engendered the practice of "reviewing"—a practice that in general has nothing in common with the art of criticism. Periodical literature is a huge, open mouth which has to be fed—a vessel of immense capacity which has to be filled. It is like a regular train which starts at an advertised hour, but which is free to start only if every seat be occupied. The seats are many, the train is ponderously long, and hence the manufacture of dummies for the seasons when there are not passengers enough. A stuffed mannikin is thrust into the empty seat, where it makes a creditable figure till the end of the journey. It looks sufficiently like a passenger, and you know it is not one only when you perceive that it neither says anything nor gets out. The guard attends to it when the train is shunted, blows the cinders from its wooden face and gives a different crook to its elbow, so that it may serve for another run. In this way, in a well-conducted periodical, the blocks of *remplissage* are the dummies of criticism—the recurrent, regulated breakers in the tide of talk. They have a reason for being, and the situation is simpler when we perceive it. It helps to explain the disproportion I just mentioned, as well, in many a case, as the quality of the particular discourse. It helps us to understand that the "organs of public opinion" must be no less copious than punctual, that publicity must maintain its high standard, that ladies and gentlemen may turn an honest penny by the free expenditure of ink. It gives us a glimpse of the high figure presumably reached by all the honest pennies accumulated in the cause, and throws us quite into a glow over the march of civilization and the way we have organized our conveniences. From this point of view it might indeed go far towards making us enthusiastic about our age. What is more calculated to inspire us with a just complacency than the sight of a new and flourishing industry, a fine economy of production? The great business of reviewing has, in its roaring routine, many of the signs of blooming health, many of the features which beguile one into rendering an involuntary homage to successful enterprise.

Yet it is not to be denied that certain captious persons are to be met who are not carried away by the spectacle, who look at it much askance, who see but dimly whither it tends, and who find no aid to vision even in the great light (about itself, its spirit, and its purposes, among other things) that it might have been expected to diffuse. "Is there any such great light at all?" we may imagine the most restless of the sceptics to inquire, "and isn't the effect rather one of a certain kind of pretentious and unprofitable gloom?" The vulgarity, the crudity, the stupidity which this cherished combination of the offhand review and of our wonderful system of publicity have put into circulation on so vast a scale may be represented, in such a mood, as an unprecedented invention for darkening counsel. The bewildered spirit may ask itself, without speedy answer, What is the function in the life of man of such a periodicity of platitude and irrelevance? Such a spirit will wonder how the life of man survives it, and, above all, what is much more important, how literature resists it; whether, indeed, literature does resist it and is not speedily going down beneath it. The signs of this catastrophe will not in the case we suppose be found too subtle to be pointed out—the failure of distinction, the failure of style, the failure of knowledge, the failure of thought. The case is therefore one for recognizing with dismay that we are paying a tremendous price for the diffusion of penmanship and opportunity; that the multiplication of endowments for chatter may be as fatal as an infectious disease; that literature lives essentially, in the sacred depths of its being, upon example, upon perfection wrought; that, like other sensitive organisms, it is highly susceptible of demoralization, and that nothing is better calculated than irresponsible pedagogy to make it close its ears and lips. To be puerile and untutored about it is to deprive it of air and light, and the consequence of its keeping bad company is that it loses all heart. We may, of course, continue to talk about it long after it has bored itself to death, and there is every appearance that this is mainly the way in which our descendants will hear of it. They will, however, acquiesce in its extinction.

This, I am aware, is a dismal conviction, and I do not pretend to state the case gaily. The most I can say is that there are times and places in which it strikes one as less desperate than at others. One of the places is Paris, and one of the times is some comfortable occasion of being there. The custom of rough-and-ready reviewing is, among the French, much less rooted than with us, and the dignity of criticism is, to my perception, in consequence much higher. The art is felt to be one of the most difficult, the most delicate, the most occasional; and the material on which it is exercised is subject to selection, to restriction. That is, whether or no the French are always right as to what they do notice, they strike me as infallible as to what they don't. They publish hundreds of books which are never noticed at all, and yet they are much neater bookmakers than we. It is recognized that such volumes have nothing to say to the critical sense, that they do not belong to literature, and that the possession of the critical sense is exactly what makes it impossible to read them and dreary to discuss them—places them, as a part of critical experience, out of the question. The critical sense, in France, *ne se dérange pas,* as the phrase is, for so little.

No one would deny, on the other hand, that when it does set itself in motion it goes further than with us. It handles the subject in general with finer finger-tips. The bluntness of ours, as tactile implements addressed to an exquisite process, is still sometimes surprising, even after frequent exhibition. We blunder in and out of the affair as if it were a railway station—the easiest and most public of the arts. It is in reality the most complicated and the most particular. The critical sense is so far from frequent that it is absolutely rare, and the possession of the cluster of qualities that minister to it is one of the highest distinctions. It is a gift inestimably precious and beautiful; therefore, so far from thinking that it passes overmuch from hand to hand, one knows that one has only to stand by the counter an hour to see that business is done with baser coin. We have too many small schoolmasters; yet not only do I not question in literature the high utility of criticism, but I should be tempted to say that the part it plays may be the supremely beneficent one when it proceeds from deep sources, from the efficient combination of experience and perception. In this light one sees the critic as the real helper of the artist, a torch-bearing outrider, the interpreter, the brother. The more the tune is noted and the direction observed the more we shall enjoy the convenience of a critical literature. When one thinks of the outfit required for free work in this spirit, one is ready to pay almost any homage to the intelligence that has put it on; and when one considers the noble figure completely equipped—armed *cap-à-pie* in curiosity and sympathy—one falls in love with the apparition. It certainly represents the knight who has knelt through his long vigil and who has the piety of his office. For there is something sacrificial in his function, inasmuch as he offers himself as a general touchstone. To lend himself,

to project himself and steep himself, to feel and feel till
he understands, and to understand so well that he can
say, to have perception at the pitch of passion and expression as embracing as the air, to be infinitely curious
and incorrigibly patient, and yet plastic and inflammable
and determinable, stooping to conquer and serving to
direct—these are fine chances for an active mind,
chances to add the idea of independent beauty to the
conception of success. Just in proportion as he is sentient and restless, just in proportion as he reacts and
reciprocates and penetrates, is the critic a valuable
instrument; for in literature assuredly criticism *is* the
critic, just as art is the artist; it being assuredly the artist
who invented art and the critic who invented criticism,
and not the other way round.

And it is with the kinds of criticism exactly as it is
with the kinds of art—the best kind, the only kind
worth speaking of, is the kind that springs from the liveliest experience. There are a hundred labels and tickets,
in all this matter, that have been pasted on from the outside and appear to exist for the convenience of pass-
ers-by; but the critic who lives *in* the house, ranging
through its innumerable chambers, knows nothing about
the bills on the front. He only knows that the more impressions he has the more he is able to record, and that
the more he is saturated, poor fellow, the more he can
give out. His life, at this rate, is heroic, for it is immensely vicarious. He has to understand for others, to
answer for them; he is always under arms. He knows
that the whole honour of the matter, for him, besides
the success in his own eyes, depends upon his being
indefatigably supple, and that is a formidable order. Let
me not speak, however, as if his work were a conscious
grind, for the sense of effort is easily lost in the enthusiasm of curiosity. Any vocation has its hours of intensity

that is so closely connected with life. That of the critic, in literature, is connected doubly, for he deals with life at second-hand as well as at first; that is, he deals with the experience of others, which he resolves into his own, and not of those invented and selected others with whom the novelist makes comfortable terms, but with the uncompromising swarm of authors, the clamorous children of history. He has to make them as vivid and as free as the novelist makes *his* puppets, and yet he has, as the phrase is, to take them as they come. We must be easy with him if the picture, even when the aim has really been to penetrate, is sometimes confused, for there are baffling and there are thankless subjects; and we make everything up to him by the peculiar purity of our esteem when the portrait is really, like the happy portraits of the other art, a text preserved by translation.

1891. From *Essays in London and Elsewhere* (1893).

*

MR. WALT WHITMAN

It has been a melancholy task to read this book;[1] and it is a still more melancholy one to write about it. Perhaps since the day of Mr. Tupper's *Philosophy* there has been no more difficult reading of the poetic sort. It exhibits the effort of an essentially prosaic mind to lift itself, by a prolonged muscular strain, into poetry. Like hundreds of other good patriots, during the last four years, Mr. Walt Whitman has imagined that a cer-

[1] *Drum-Taps,* by Walt Whitman (1865).

tain amount of violent sympathy with the great deeds and sufferings of our soldiers, and of admiration for our national energy, together with a ready command of picturesque language, are sufficient inspiration for a poet. If this were the case, we had been a nation of poets. The constant developments of the war moved us continually to strong feeling and to strong expression of it. But in those cases in which these expressions were written out and printed with all due regard to prosody, they failed to make poetry, as any one may see by consulting now in cold blood the back volumes of the *Rebellion Record.*

Of course the city of Manhattan, as Mr. Whitman delights to call it, when regiments poured through it in the first months of the war, and its own sole god, to borrow the words of a real poet, ceased for a while to be the millionaire, was a noble spectacle, and a poetical statement to this effect is possible. *Of course* the tumult of a battle is grand, the results of a battle tragic, and the untimely deaths of young men a theme for elegies. But he is not a poet who merely reiterates these plain facts *ore rotundo.* He only sings them worthily who views them from a height. Every tragic event collects about it a number of persons who delight to dwell upon its superficial points—of minds which are bullied by the *accidents* of the affair. The temper of such minds seems to us to be the reverse of the poetic temper; for the poet, although he incidentally masters, grasps, and uses the superficial traits of his theme, is really a poet only in so far as he extracts its latent meaning and holds it up to common eyes. And yet from such minds most of our war-verses have come, and Mr. Whitman's utterances, much as the assertion may surprise his friends, are in this respect no exception to general fashion. They are an exception, however, in that they openly pretend to be something better; and this it is that makes them melancholy reading.

Mr. Whitman is very fond of blowing his own trumpet, and he has made very explicit claims for his books. "Shut not your doors," he exclaims at the outset—

Shut not your doors to me, proud libraries,
For that which was lacking among you all, yet needed most,
 I bring;
A book I have made for your dear sake, O soldiers,
And for you, O soul of man, and you, love of comrades;
The words of my book nothing, the life of it everything;
A book separate, not link'd with the rest, nor felt by the
 intellect;
But you will feel every word, O Libertad! arm'd Libertad!
It shall pass by the intellect to swim the sea, the air,
 With joy with you, O soul of man.

These are great pretensions, but it seems to us that the following are even greater:

From Paumanok starting, I fly like a bird,
Around and around to soar, to sing the idea of all;
To the north betaking myself, to sing there arctic songs,
To Kanada, 'till I absorb Kanada in myself—to Michigan
 then,
To Wisconsin, Iowa, Minnesota, to sing their songs (they
 are inimitable);
Then to Ohio and Indiana, to sing theirs—to Missouri and
 Kansas and Arkansas to sing theirs,
To Tennessee and Kentucky—to the Carolinas and Georgia,
 to sing theirs,
To Texas, and so along up toward California, to roam
 accepted everywhere;
To sing first (to the tap of the war-drum, if need be)
The idea of all—of the western world, one and inseparable,
And then the song of each member of these States.

Mr. Whitman's primary purpose is to celebrate the greatness of our armies; his secondary purpose is to celebrate the greatness of the city of New York. He pursues these objects through a hundred pages of matter which remind us irresistibly of the story of the college professor who, on a venturesome youth bringing him a theme done in blank verse, reminded him that it was not customary in writing prose to begin each line with a capital. The frequent capitals are the only marks of verse in Mr. Whitman's writings. There is, fortunately, but one attempt at rhyme. We say fortunately, for if the inequality of Mr. Whitman's lines were self-registering, as it would be in the case of an anticipated syllable at their close, the effect would be painful in the extreme. As the case stands, each line stands off by itself, in resolute independence of its companions, without a visible goal.

But if Mr. Whitman does not write verse, he does not write ordinary prose. The reader has seen that liberty is "libertad." In like manner, comrade is "camerado"; Americans are "Americanos"; a pavement is a "trottoir," and Mr. Whitman himself is a "chansonnier." If there is one thing that Mr. Whitman is not, it is this, for Béranger was a *chansonnier*. To appreciate the force of our conjunction, the reader should compare his military lyrics with Mr. Whitman's declamations. Our author's novelty, however, is not in his words, but in the form of his writing. As we have said, it begins for all the world like verse and turns out to be arrant prose. It is more like Mr. Tupper's proverbs than anything we have met.

But what if, in form, it *is* prose? it may be asked. Very good poetry has come out of prose before this. To this we would reply that it must first have gone into it. Prose, in order to be good poetry, must first be good prose. As a general principle, we know of no circumstance more likely to impugn a writer's earnestness than the adoption of an anomalous style. He must have something very original to say if none of the old vehicles will carry his thoughts. Of course he *may* be surprisingly original. Still, presumption is against him. If on examination the matter of his discourse proves very valuable, it justifies, or at any rate excuses, his literary innovation.

But if, on the other hand, it is of a common quality, with nothing new about it but its manners, the public will judge the writer harshly. The most that can be said of Mr. Whitman's vaticinations is, that, cast in a fluent and familiar manner, the average substance of them might escape unchallenged. But we have seen that Mr. Whitman prides himself especially on the substance— the life—of his poetry. It may be rough, it may be grim, it may be clumsy—such we take to be the author's argument—but it is sincere, it is sublime, it appeals to the soul of man, it is the voice of a people. He tells us, in the lines quoted, that the words of his book are nothing. To our perception they are everything, and very little at that.

A great deal of verse that is nothing but words has, during the war, been sympathetically sighed over and cut out of newspaper corners, because it has possessed a certain simple melody. But Mr. Whitman's verse, we are confident, would have failed even of this triumph, for the simple reason that no triumph, however small, is won but through the exercise of art, and that this volume is an offence against art. It is not enough to be grim and rough and careless; common sense is also necessary, for it is by common sense that we are judged. There exists in even the commonest minds, in literary matters, a certain precise instinct of conservatism, which is very shrewd in detecting wanton eccentricities.

To this instinct Mr. Whitman's attitude seems monstrous. It is monstrous because it pretends to persuade the soul while it slights the intellect; because it pretends to gratify the feelings while it outrages the taste. The point is that it does this *on theory*, wilfully, consciously, arrogantly. It is the little nursery game of "open your mouth and shut your eyes." Our hearts are often touched through a compromise with the artistic sense, but never in direct violation of it. Mr. Whitman sits down at the outset and counts out the intelligence. This were indeed a wise precaution on his part if the intelligence were only submissive! But when she is deliberately insulted, she takes her revenge by simply standing erect and open-eyed. This is assuredly the best she can do. And if she could find a voice she would probably address Mr. Whitman as follows:—

"You came to woo my sister, the human soul. Instead of giving me a kick as you approach, you should either greet me courteously, or, at least, steal in unobserved. But now you have me on your hands. Your chances are poor. What the human heart desires above all is sincerity, and you do not appear to me sincere. For a lover you talk entirely too much about yourself. In one place you threaten to absorb Kanada. In another you call upon the city of New York to incarnate you, as you have incarnated it. In another you inform us that neither youth pertains to you nor 'delicatesse,' that you are awkward in the parlour, that you do not dance, and that you have neither bearing, beauty, knowledge, nor fortune. In another place, by an allusion to your 'little songs,' you seem to identify yourself with the third person of the Trinity.

"For a poet who claims to sing 'the idea of all,' this is tolerably egotistical. We look in vain, however, through your book for a single idea. We find nothing but flashy imitations of ideas. We find a medley of extravagances and commonplaces. We find art, measure, grace, sense sneered at on every page, and nothing positive given us in their stead. To be positive one must have something to say; to be positive requires reason, labour, and art; and art requires, above all things, a suppression of one's self, a subordination of one's self to an idea. This will never do for you, whose plan is to adapt the scheme of the universe to your own limitations. You cannot entertain and exhibit ideas; but, as we have seen, you are prepared to incarnate them. It is for this reason, doubtless, that when once you have planted yourself squarely before the public, and in view of the great service you have done to the ideal, have become, as you say, 'accepted everywhere,' you can afford to deal exclusively in words. What would be bald nonsense and dreary platitudes in any one else becomes sublimity in you.

"But all this is a mistake. To become adopted as a national poet, it is not enough to discard everything in particular and to accept everything in general, to amass crudity upon crudity, to discharge the undigested contents of your blotting-book into the lap of the public. You must respect the public which you address; for it has taste, if you have not. It delights in the grand, the heroic, and the masculine; but it delights to see these conceptions cast into worthy form. It is indifferent to brute sublimity. It will never do for you to thrust your hands into your pockets and cry out that, as the research of form is an intolerable bore, the shortest and most economical way for the public to embrace its idols—for the nation to realize its genius—is in your own person.

"This democratic, liberty-loving, American populace, this stern and war-tried people, is a great civiliser. It is devoted to refinement. If it has sustained a monstrous war, and practised human nature's best in so many ways for the last five years, it is not to put up with spurious poetry afterwards. To sing aright our battles and our glories it is not enough to have served in a hospital (however praiseworthy the task in itself), to be aggressively careless, inelegant, and ignorant, and to be constantly preoccupied with yourself. It is not enough to be rude, lugubrious, and grim. You must also be serious. You must forget yourself in your ideas. Your personal qualities—the vigour of your temperament, the manly independence of your nature, the tenderness of your heart—these facts are impertinent. You must be *possessed*, and you must thrive to possess your possession. If in your striving you break into divine eloquence, then you are a poet. If the idea which possesses you is the idea of your country's greatness, then you are a national poet; and not otherwise."

1865. Here reprinted from *Views and Reviews* by Henry James, edited by LeRoy Phillips (1908).

*

THE LIMITATIONS OF DICKENS

Our Mutual Friend is, to our perception, the poorest of Mr. Dickens's works. And it is poor with the poverty not of momentary embarrassment, but of permanent exhaustion. It is wanting in inspiration. For the last ten years it has seemed to us that Mr. Dickens has been unmistakeably forcing himself. *Bleak House* was forced; *Little Dorrit* was laboured; the present work is dug out as with a spade and pickaxe.

Of course—to anticipate the usual argument—who but Dickens could have written it? Who, indeed? Who else would have established a lady in business in a novel on the admirably solid basis of her always putting on gloves and tying a handkerchief around her head in moments of grief, and of her habitually addressing her family with "Peace! hold!" It is needless to say that Mrs. Reginald Wilfer is first and last the occasion of considerable true humour. When, after conducting her daughter to Mrs. Boffin's carriage, in sight of all the envious neighbours, she is described as enjoying her triumph during the next quarter of an hour by airing herself on the doorstep "in a kind of splendidly serene trance," we laugh with as uncritical a laugh as could be desired of us. We pay the same tribute to her assertions, as she narrates the glories of the society she enjoyed at her father's table, that she has known as many as three copper-plate engravers exchanging the most exquisite sallies and retorts there at one time. But when to these we have added a dozen more happy examples of the humour which was exhaled from every line of Mr. Dickens's earlier writings, we shall have closed the list of the merits of the work before us.

To say that the conduct of the story, with all its complications, betrays a long-practised hand, is to pay no compliment worthy the author. If this were, indeed, a compliment, we should be inclined to carry it further, and congratulate him on his success in what we should call the manufacture of fiction; for in so doing we should express a feeling that has attended us throughout the book. Seldom, we reflected, had we read a book so intensely *written*, so little seen, known, or felt.

In all Mr. Dickens's works the fantastic has been his great resource; and while his fancy was lively and vigorous it accomplished great things. But the fantastic, when the fancy is dead, is a very poor business. The movement of Mr. Dickens's fancy in Mr. Wilfer and Mr. Boffin and Lady Tippins, and the Lammles and Miss Wren, and even in Eugene Wrayburn, is, to our mind, a movement lifeless, forced, mechanical. It is the letter of his old humour without the spirit. It is hardly too much to say that every character here put before us is a mere bundle of eccentricities, animated by no principle of nature whatever.

In former days there reigned in Mr. Dickens's extravagances a comparative consistency; they were exaggerated statements of types that really existed. We had, perhaps, never known a Newman Noggs, nor a Pecksniff, nor a Micawber; but we had known persons of whom these figures were but the strictly logical consummation. But among the grotesque creatures who occupy the pages before us, there is not one whom we can refer to as an existing type. In all Mr. Dickens's stories, indeed, the reader has been called upon, and has willingly consented, to accept a certain number of figures or creatures of pure fancy, for this was the author's poetry. He was, moreover, always repaid for his concession by a peculiar beauty or power in these exceptional characters. But he is now expected to make the same concession, with a very inadequate reward.

What do we get in return for accepting Miss Jenny Wren as a possible person? This young lady is the type of a certain class of characters of which Mr. Dickens has made a specialty, and with which he has been accustomed to draw alternate smiles and tears, according as he pressed one spring or another. But this is very cheap merriment and very cheap pathos. Miss Jenny Wren is a poor little dwarf, afflicted, as she constantly reiterates, with a "bad back" and "queer legs," who makes doll's dresses, and is for ever pricking at those with whom she converses in the air, with her needle, and assuring them that she knows their "tricks and their manners." Like all Mr. Dickens's pathetic characters, she is a little monster; she is deformed, unhealthy, unnatural; she belongs to the troop of hunchbacks, imbeciles, and precocious children who have carried on the sentimental business in all Mr. Dickens's novels; the little Nells, the Smikes, the Paul Dombeys.

Mr. Dickens goes as far out of the way for his wicked people as he does for his good ones. Rogue Riderhood, indeed, in the present story, is villainous with a sufficiently natural villainy; he belongs to that quarter of society in which the author is most at his ease. But was there ever such wickedness as that of the Lammles and Mr. Fledgeby? Not that people have not been as mischievous as they; but was any one ever mischievous in that singular fashion? Did a couple of elegant swindlers ever take such particular pains to be aggressively inhuman?—for we can find no other word for the gratuitous distortions to which they are subjected. The word *humanity* strikes us as strangely discordant, in the midst of these pages; for, let us boldly declare it, there is no humanity here.

Humanity is nearer home than the Boffins, and the Lammles, and the Wilfers, and the Veneerings. It is in what men have in common with each other, and not what they have in distinction. The people just named have nothing in common with each other, except the fact that they have nothing in common with mankind at large. What a world were this world if the world of *Our Mutual Friend* were an honest reflection of it! But a community of eccentrics is impossible. Rules alone are consistent with each other; exceptions are inconsistent. Society is maintained by natural sense and natural feeling. We cannot conceive a society in which these principles are not in some manner represented. Where in these pages are the depositaries of that intelligence without which the movement of life would cease? Who represents nature?

Accepting half of Mr. Dickens's persons as intentionally grotesque, where are those exemplars of sound humanity who should afford us the proper measure of their companions' variations? We ought not, in justice to the author, to seek them among his weaker—that is, his mere conventional—characters; in John Harmon, Lizzie Hexam, or Mortimer Lightwood; but we assuredly cannot find them among his stronger—that is, his artificial creations.

Suppose we take Eugene Wrayburn and Bradley Headstone. They occupy a half-way position between the habitual probable of nature and the habitual impossible of Mr. Dickens. A large portion of the story rests upon the enmity borne by Headstone to Wrayburn, both being in love with the same woman. Wrayburn is a gentleman, and Headstone is one of the people. Wrayburn is well-bred, careless, elegant, sceptical, and idle: Headstone is a high-tempered, hard-working, ambitious young schoolmaster. There lay in the opposition of these two characters a very good story. But the prime requisite was that they should *be* characters: Mr. Dickens, according to his usual plan, has made them simply figures, and between them the story that was to be, the story that should have been, has evaporated. Wrayburn lounges about with his hands in his pockets, smoking a cigar, and talking nonsense. Headstone strides about, clenching his fists and biting his lips and grasping his stick.

There is one scene in which Wrayburn chaffs the schoolmaster with easy insolence, while the latter writhes impotently under his well-bred sarcasm. This scene is very clever, but it is very insufficient. If the majority of readers were not so very timid in the use of words we should call it vulgar. By this we do not mean to indicate the conventional impropriety of two gentlemen exchanging lively personalities; we mean to emphasise the essentially small character of these personalities. In other words, the moment, dramatically, is great, while the author's conception is weak. The friction of two *men*, of two characters, of two passions, produces stronger sparks than Wrayburn's boyish repartees and Headstone's melodramatic commonplaces.

Such scenes as this are useful in fixing the limits of Mr. Dickens's insight. Insight is, perhaps, too strong a word; for we are convinced that it is one of the chief conditions of his genius not to see beneath the surface of things. If we might hazard a definition of his literary character, we should, accordingly, call him the greatest of superficial novelists. We are aware that this definition confines him to an inferior rank in the department of letters which he adorns; but we accept this consequence of our proposition. It were, in our opinion, an offence against humanity to place Mr. Dickens among the greatest novelists. For, to repeat what we have already intimated, he has created nothing but figure. He has added nothing to our understanding of human character. He is master of but two alternatives: he reconciles us to what is commonplace, and he reconciles us to what is odd. The value of the former service is questionable; and the manner in which Mr. Dickens performs it sometimes conveys a certain impression of charlatanism. The value of the latter service is incontestable, and here Mr. Dickens is an honest, an admirable artist.

But what is the condition of the truly great novelist? For him there are no alternatives, for him there are no oddities, for him there is nothing outside of humanity. He cannot shirk it; it imposes itself upon him. For him alone, therefore, there is a true and a false; for him alone, it is possible to be right, because it is possible to be wrong. Mr. Dickens is a great observer and a great humourist, but he is nothing of a philosopher.

Some people may hereupon say, so much the better; we say, so much the worse. For a novelist very soon has need of a little philosophy. In treating of Micawber, and Boffin, and Pickwick, *et hoc genus omne,* he can, indeed, dispense with it, for this—we say it with all deference—is not serious writing. But when he comes to tell the story of a passion, a story like that of Headstone and Wrayburn, he becomes a moralist as well as an artist. He must know *man* as well as *men,* and to know man is to be a philosopher.

The writer who knows men alone, if he have Mr. Dickens's humour and fancy, will give us figures and pictures for which we cannot be too grateful, for he will enlarge our knowledge of the world. But when he introduces men and women whose interest is preconceived to lie not in the poverty, the weakness, the drollery of their natures, but in their complete and unconscious subjection to ordinary and healthy human emotions, all his humour, all his fancy, will avail him nothing if, out of the fullness of his sympathy, he is unable to prosecute those generalisations in which alone consists the real greatness of a work of art.

This may sound like very subtle talk about a very simple matter. It is rather very simple talk about a very subtle matter. A story based upon those elementary passions in which alone we seek the true and final manifestation of character must be told in a spirit of intellectual superiority to those passions. That is, the author must understand what he is talking about. The perusal of a story so told is one of the most elevating experiences within the reach of the human mind. The perusal of a story which is not so told is infinitely depressing and unprofitable.

1865. From *Views and Reviews* (1908).

*

HAWTHORNE: *THE SCARLET LETTER*

His publisher, Mr. Fields, in a volume entitled *Yesterdays with Authors,* has related the circumstances in which Hawthorne's masterpiece came into the world. "In the winter of 1849, after he had been ejected from the Custom-house, I went down to Salem to see him and inquire after his health, for we heard he had been suffering from illness. He was then living in a modest wooden house. . . . I found him alone in a chamber over the sitting-room of the dwelling, and as the day was cold he was hovering near a stove. We fell into talk about his future prospects, and he was, as I feared I should find him, in a very desponding mood." His visitor urged him to bethink himself of publishing something, and Hawthorne replied by calling his attention to the small popularity his published productions had yet acquired, and declaring he had done nothing and had no spirit for doing anything. The narrator of the incident urged upon him the necessity of a more hopeful view of his situation, and proceeded to take leave. He had not reached the street, however, when Hawthorne hurried to overtake him, and, placing a roll of MS. in his hand, bade him take it to Boston, read it, and pronounce upon it. "It is either very good or very bad," said the author;

"I don't know which." "On my way back to Boston," says Mr. Fields, "I read the germ of *The Scarlet Letter;* before I slept that night I wrote him a note all aglow with admiration of the marvellous story he had put into my hands, and told him that I would come again to Salem the next day and arrange for its publication. I went on in such an amazing state of excitement, when we met again in the little house, that he would not believe I was really in earnest. He seemed to think I was beside myself, and laughed sadly at my enthusiasm." Hawthorne, however, went on with the book and finished it, but it appeared only a year later. His biographer quotes a passage from a letter which he wrote in February, 1850, to his friend Horatio Bridge. "I finished my book only yesterday; one end being in the press at Boston, while the other was in my head here at Salem, so that, as you see, my story is at least fourteen miles long. . . . My book, the publisher tells me, will not be out before April. He speaks of it in tremendous terms of approbation; so does Mrs. Hawthorne, to whom I read the conclusion last night. It broke her heart, and sent her to bed with a grievous headache—which I look upon as a triumphant success. Judging from the effect upon her and the publisher, I may calculate on what bowlers call a ten-strike. But I don't make any such calculation." And Mr. Lathrop calls attention, in regard to this passage, to an allusion in the *English Note-Books* (September 14, 1855). "Speaking of Thackeray, I cannot but wonder at his coolness in respect to his own pathos, and compare it to my emotions when I read the last scene of *The Scarlet Letter* to my wife, just after writing it—tried to read it rather, for my voice swelled and heaved as if I were tossed up and down on an ocean as it subsides after a storm. But I was in a very nervous state then, having gone through a great diversity of emotion while writing it, for many months."

The work has the tone of the circumstances in which it was produced. If Hawthorne was in a sombre mood, and if his future was painfully vague, *The Scarlet Letter* contains little enough of gaiety or of hopefulness. It is densely dark, with a single spot of vivid colour in it; and it will probably long remain the most consistently gloomy of English novels of the first order. But I just now called it the author's masterpiece, and I imagine it will continue to be, for other generations than ours, his most substantial title to fame. The subject had probably lain a long time in his mind, as his subjects were apt to do; so that he appears completely to possess it, to know it and feel it. It is simpler and more complete than his other novels; it achieves more perfectly what it attempts, and it has about it that charm, very hard to express, which we find in an artist's work the first time he has touched his highest mark—a sort of straightness and naturalness of execution, an unconsciousness of his public, and freshness of interest in his theme. It was a great success, and he immediately found himself famous. The writer of these lines, who was a child at the time, remembers dimly the sensation the book produced, and the little shudder with which people alluded to it, as if a peculiar horror were mixed with its attractions. He was too young to read it himself, but its title, upon which he fixed his eyes as the book lay upon the table, had a mysterious charm. He had a vague belief, indeed, that the "letter" in question was one of the documents that come by the post, and it was a source of perpetual wonderment to him that it should be of such an unaccustomed hue. Of course it was difficult to explain to a child the significance of poor Hester Prynne's blood-coloured A. But the mystery was at last partly dis-

pelled by his being taken to see a collection of pictures (the annual exhibition of the National Academy),
where he encountered a representation of a pale, handsome woman, in a quaint black dress and a white coif,
holding between her knees an elfish-looking little girl,
fantastically dressed, and crowned with flowers. Embroidered on the woman's breast was a great crimson *A*,
over which the child's fingers, as she glanced strangely
out of the picture, were maliciously playing. I was told
that this was Hester Prynne and little Pearl, and that
when I grew older I might read their interesting history.
But the picture remained vividly imprinted on my mind;
I had been vaguely frightened and made uneasy by it;
and when, years afterwards, I first read the novel, I
seemed to myself to have read it before, and to be familiar with its two strange heroines. I mention this
incident simply as an indication of the degree to
which the success of *The Scarlet Letter* had made the
book what is called an actuality. Hawthorne himself was
very modest about it; he wrote to his publisher, when
there was a question of his undertaking another novel,
that what had given the history of Hester Prynne its
"vogue" was simply the introductory chapter. In fact,
the publication of *The Scarlet Letter* was in the United
States a literary event of the first importance. The book
was the finest piece of imaginative writing yet put forth
in the country. There was a consciousness of this in the
welcome that was given it—a satisfaction in the idea of
America having produced a novel that belonged to
literature, and to the forefront of it. Something might at
last be sent to Europe as exquisite in quality as anything that had been received, and the best of it was
that the thing was absolutely American; it belonged to
the soil, to the air; it came out of the very heart of New
England.

It is beautiful, admirable, extraordinary; it has in the highest degree that merit which I have spoken of as the mark of Hawthorne's best things—an indefinable purity and lightness of conception, a quality which in a work of art affects one in the same way as the absence of grossness does in a human being. His fancy, as I just now said, had evidently brooded over the subject for a long time; the situation to be represented had disclosed itself to him in all its phases. When I say in all its phases, the sentence demands modification; for it is to be remembered that if Hawthorne laid his hand upon the well-worn theme, upon the familiar combination of the wife, the lover, and the husband, it was after all but to one period of the history of these three persons that he attached himself. The situation is the situation after the woman's fault has been committed, and the current of expiation and repentance has set in. In spite of the relation between Hester Prynne and Arthur Dimmesdale, no story of love was surely ever less of a "love story." To Hawthorne's imagination the fact that these two persons had loved each other too well was of an interest comparatively vulgar; what appealed to him was the idea of their moral situation in the long years that were to follow. The story, indeed, is in a secondary degree that of Hester Prynne; she becomes, really, after the first scene, an accessory figure; it is not upon her that the *dénoûment* depends. It is upon her guilty lover that the author projects most frequently the cold, thin rays of his fitfully-moving lantern, which makes here and there a little luminous circle, on the edge of which hovers the livid and sinister figure of the injured and retributive husband. The story goes on, for the most part, between the lover and the husband—the tormented young Puritan minister, who carries the secret of his own lapse from pastoral purity locked up beneath an exterior that commends itself to the reverence of his flock, while he sees the softer partner of his guilt standing in the full glare of exposure and humbling herself to the misery of atonement—between this more wretched and pitiable culprit, to whom dishonour would come as a comfort and the pillory as a relief, and the older, keener, wiser man, who, to obtain satisfaction for the wrong he has suffered, devises the infernally ingenious plan of conjoining himself with his wronger, living with him, living upon him, and while he pretends to minister to his hidden ailment and to sympathise with his pain, revels in his unsuspected knowledge of these things and stimulates them by malignant arts. The attitude of Roger Chillingworth, and the means he takes to compensate himself—these are the highly original elements in the situation that Hawthorne so ingeniously treats. None of his works are so impregnated with that after-sense of the old Puritan consciousness of life to which allusion has so often been made. If, as M. Montégut says, the qualities of his ancestors *filtered* down through generations into his composition, *The Scarlet Letter* was, as it were, the vessel that gathered up the last of the precious drops. And I say this not because the story happens to be of so-called historical cast, to be told of the early days of Massachusetts and of people in steeple-crowned hats and sad-coloured garments. The historical colouring is rather weak than otherwise; there is little elaboration of detail, of the modern realism of research; and the author has made no great point of causing his figures to speak the English of their period. Nevertheless, the book is full of the moral presence of the race that invented Hester's penance—diluted and complicated with other things, but still perfectly recognisable. Puritanism, in a word, is there, not only objectively, as

Hawthorne tried to place it there, but subjectively as well. Not, I mean, in his judgment of his characters, in any harshness of prejudice, or in the obtrusion of a moral lesson; but in the very quality of his own vision, in the tone of the picture, in a certain coldness and exclusiveness of treatment.

The faults of the book are, to my sense, a want of reality and an abuse of the fanciful element—of a certain superficial symbolism. The people strike me not as characters, but as representatives, very picturesquely arranged, of a single state of mind; and the interest of the story lies, not in them, but in the situation, which is insistently kept before us, with little progression, though with a great deal, as I have said, of a certain stable variation; and to which they, out of their reality, contribute little that helps it to live and move. I was made to feel this want of reality, this over-ingenuity, of *The Scarlet Letter*, by chancing not long since upon a novel which was read fifty years ago much more than to-day, but which is still worth reading—the story of *Adam Blair*, by John Gibson Lockhart. This interesting and powerful little tale has a great deal of analogy with Hawthorne's novel—quite enough, at least, to suggest a comparison between them; and the comparison is a very interesting one to make, for it speedily leads us to larger considerations than simple resemblances and divergences of plot.

Adam Blair, like Arthur Dimmesdale, is a Calvinistic minister who becomes the lover of a married woman, is overwhelmed with remorse at his misdeed, and makes a public confession of it; then expiates it by resigning his pastoral office and becoming a humble tiller of the soil, as his father had been. The two stories are of about the same length, and each is the masterpiece (putting aside of course, as far as Lockhart is concerned, the *Life of Scott*) of the author. They deal alike with the manners of a rigidly theological society, and even in certain details they correspond. In each of them, between the guilty pair, there is a charming little girl; though I hasten to say that Sarah Blair (who is not the daughter of the heroine, but the legitimate offspring of the hero, a widower) is far from being as brilliant and graceful an apparition as the admirable little Pearl of *The Scarlet Letter*. The main difference between the two tales is the fact that in the American story the husband plays an all-important part, and in the Scottish plays almost none at all. *Adam Blair* is the history of the passion, and *The Scarlet Letter* the history of its sequel; but nevertheless, if one has read the two books at a short interval, it is impossible to avoid confronting them. I confess that a large portion of the interest of *Adam Blair*, to my mind, when once I had perceived that it would repeat in a great measure the situation of *The Scarlet Letter*, lay in noting its difference of tone. It threw into relief the passionless quality of Hawthorne's novel, its element of cold and ingenious fantasy, its elaborate imaginative delicacy. These things do not precisely constitute a weakness in *The Scarlet Letter;* indeed, in a certain way they constitute a great strength; but the absence of a certain something warm and straightforward, a trifle more grossly human and vulgarly natural, which one finds in *Adam Blair*, will always make Hawthorne's tale less touching to a large number of even very intelligent readers, than a love-story told with the robust, synthetic pathos which served Lockhart so well. His novel is not of the first rank (I should call it an excellent second-rate one), but it borrows a charm from the fact that his vigorous, but not strongly imaginative, mind was impregnated with the reality of his subject. He did not always succeed in rendering this reality; the expression is sometimes awkward and poor. But the reader feels that his vision was clear, and his feeling about the matter very strong and rich. Hawthorne's imagination, on the other hand, plays with his theme so incessantly, leads it such a dance through the moon-lighted air of his intellect, that the thing cools off, as it were, hardens and stiffens, and, producing effects much more exquisite, leaves the reader with a sense of having handled a splendid piece of silversmith's work. Lockhart, by means much more vulgar, produces at moments a greater illusion, and satisfies our inevitable desire for something, in the people in whom it is sought to interest us, that shall be of the same pitch and the same continuity with ourselves. Above all, it is interesting to see how the same subject appears to two men of a thoroughly different cast of mind and of a different race. Lockhart was struck with the warmth of the subject that offered itself to him, and Hawthorne with its coldness; the one with its glow, its sentimental interest—the other with its shadow, its moral interest. Lockhart's story is as decent, as severely draped, as *The Scarlet Letter;* but the author has a more vivid sense than appears to have imposed itself upon Hawthorne, of some of the incidents of the situation he describes; his tempted man and tempting woman are more actual and personal; his heroine in especial, though not in the least a delicate or a subtle conception, has a sort of credible, visible, palpable property, a vulgar roundness and relief, which are lacking to the dim and chastened image of Hester Prynne. But I am going too far; I am comparing simplicity with subtlety, the usual with the refined. Each man wrote as his turn of mind impelled him, but each expressed something more than himself. Lockhart was a dense, substantial Briton, with a taste for the concrete, and Hawthorne was a thin New England, with a miasmatic conscience.

In *The Scarlet Letter* there is a great deal of symbolism; there is, I think, too much. It is overdone at times, and becomes mechanical; it ceases to be impressive, and grazes triviality. The idea of the mystic A which the young minister finds imprinted upon his breast and eating into his flesh, in sympathy with the embroidered badge that Hester is condemned to wear, appears to me to be a case in point. This suggestion should, I think, have been just made and dropped; to insist upon it and return to it, is to exaggerate the weak side of the subject. Hawthorne returns to it constantly, plays with it, and seems charmed by it; until at last the reader feels tempted to declare that his enjoyment of it is puerile. In the admirable scene, so superbly conceived and beautifully executed, in which Mr. Dimmesdale, in the stillness of the night, in the middle of the sleeping town, feels impelled to go and stand upon the scaffold where his mistress had formerly enacted her dreadful penance, and then, seeing Hester pass along the street, from watching at a sick-bed, with little Pearl at her side, calls them both to come and stand there beside him—in this masterly episode the effect is almost spoiled by the introduction of one of these superficial conceits. What leads up to it is very fine—so fine that I cannot do better than quote it as a specimen of one of the striking pages of the book.

But before Mr. Dimmesdale had done speaking, a light gleamed far and wide over all the muffled sky. It was doubtless caused by one of those meteors which the night-watcher may so often observe burning out to waste in the vacant regions of the atmosphere. So powerful was its radiance that it thoroughly illuminated the dense medium of cloud, betwixt the sky and earth. The great vault brightened, like the dome of an immense lamp. It showed the familiar scene of the street with the distinctness of mid-day, but also with the awfulness that is always imparted to familiar objects by an unaccustomed light. The wooden houses, with their jutting stories and quaint gable-peaks; the door-steps and thresholds, with the early grass springing up about them; the garden-plots, black with freshly-turned earth; the wheel-track, little worn, and, even in the market-place, margined with green on either side;—all were visible, but with a singularity of aspect that seemed to give another moral interpretation to the things of this world than they had ever borne before. And there stood the minister, with his hand over his heart; and Hester Prynne, with the embroidered letter glimmering on her bosom; and little Pearl, herself a symbol, and the connecting-link between these two. They stood in the noon of that strange and solemn splendour, as if it were the light that is to reveal all secrets, and the daybreak that shall unite all that belong to one another.

That is imaginative, impressive, poetic; but when, almost immediately afterwards, the author goes on to say that "the minister looking upward to the zenith, beheld there the appearance of an immense letter— the letter *A*—marked out in lines of dull red light," we feel that he goes too far and is in danger of crossing the line that separates the sublime from its intimate neighbour. We are tempted to say that this is not moral tragedy, but physical comedy. In the same way, too much is made of the intimation that Hester's badge had a scorching property, and that if one touched it one would immediately withdraw one's hand. Hawthorne is perpetually looking for images which shall place themselves in picturesque correspondence with the spiritual facts with which he is concerned, and of course the search is of the very essence of poetry. But in such a process discretion is everything, and when the image becomes importunate it is in danger of seeming to stand for nothing more serious than itself. When Hester meets the minister by appointment in the forest, and sits talking with him while little Pearl wanders away and plays by the edge of the brook, the child is represented as at last making her way over to the other side of the woodland stream, and disporting herself there in a manner which makes her mother feel herself "in some indistinct and tantalising manner, estranged from Pearl; as if the child, in her lonely ramble through the forest, had strayed out of the sphere in which she and her mother dwelt together, and was now vainly seeking to return to it." And Hawthorne devotes a chapter to this idea of the child's having, by putting the brook between Hester and herself, established a kind of spiritual gulf, on the verge of which her little fantastic person innocently mocks at her mother's sense of bereavement. This conception belongs, one would say, quite to the lighter order of a story-teller's devices, and the reader hardly goes with Hawthorne in the large development he gives to it. He hardly goes with him either, I think, in his extreme predilection for a small number of vague ideas which are represented by such terms as "sphere" and "sympathies." Hawthorne makes too liberal a use of these two substantives; it is the solitary defect of his style; and it counts as a defect partly because the words in question are a sort of specialty with certain writers immeasurably inferior to himself.

I had not meant, however, to expatiate upon his defects, which are of the slenderest and most venial kind. *The Scarlet Letter* has the beauty and harmony of all original and complete conceptions, and its weaker spots, whatever they are, are not of its essence; they are mere light flaws and inequalities of surface. One can often return to it; it supports familiarity and has the inexhaustible charm and mystery of great works of art. It is admirably written. Hawthorne afterwards polished his style to a still higher degree, but in his later productions—it is almost always the case in a writer's later productions—there is a touch of mannerism. In *The Scarlet Letter* there is a high degree of polish, and at the same time a charming freshness; his phrase is less conscious of itself. His biographer very justly calls attention to the fact that his style was excellent from the beginning; that he appeared to have passed through no phase of learning how to write, but was in possession of his means from the first of his handling a pen. His early tales, perhaps, were not of a character to subject his faculty of expression to a very severe test, but a man who had not Hawthorne's natural sense of language would certainly have contrived to write them less well. This natural sense of language—this turn for saying things lightly and yet touchingly, picturesquely yet simply, and for infusing a gently colloquial tone into matter of the most unfamiliar import, he had evidently cultivated with great assiduity. I have spoken of the anomalous character of his Note-Books—of his going to such pains often to make a record of incidents which either were not worth remembering or could be easily remembered without its aid. But it helps us to understand the Note-Books if we regard them as a literary exercise. They were compositions, as school-boys say, in which the subject was only the pretext, and the main point was to write a certain amount of excellent English. Hawthorne must at least have written a great many of these things for practice, and he must often have said to himself that it was better practice to write about trifles, because it was a greater tax upon one's skill to make them interesting. And his theory was just, for he has almost always made his trifles interesting. In his novels his art of saying things well is very positively tested, for here he treats of those matters among which it is very easy for a blundering writer to go wrong—the subtleties and mysteries of life, the moral and spiritual maze. In such a passage as one I have marked for quotation from *The Scarlet Letter*, there is the stamp of the genius of style.

Hester Prynne, gazing steadfastly at the clergyman, felt a dreary influence come over her, but wherefore or whence she knew not, unless that he seemed so remote from her own sphere and utterly beyond her reach. One glance of recognition she had imagined must needs pass between them. She thought of the dim forest with its little dell of solitude, and love, and anguish, and the mossy tree-trunk, where, sitting hand in hand, they had mingled their sad and passionate talk with the melancholy murmur of the brook. How deeply had they known each other then! And was this the man? She hardly knew him now! He, moving proudly past, enveloped as it were in the rich music, with the procession of majestic and venerable fathers; he, so unattainable in his worldly position, and still more so in that far vista in his unsympathising thoughts, through which she now beheld him! Her spirit sank with the idea that all must have been a delusion, and that vividly as she had dreamed it, there could be no real bond betwixt the clergyman and herself. And thus much of woman there was in Hester, that she could scarcely forgive him—least of all now, when the heavy footstep of their approaching fate might be heard, nearer, nearer, nearer!—for being able to withdraw himself so completely from their mutual world, while she groped darkly, and stretched forth her cold hands, and found him not!

From Chapter V of *Hawthorne* (1879).

*

IVAN TURGÉNIEFF
(1818-1883)

There is perhaps no novelist of alien race who more naturally than Ivan Turgénieff inherits a niche in a Library for English readers; and this not because of any advance or concession that in his peculiar artistic independence he ever made, or could dream of making, such readers, but because it was one of the effects of his peculiar genius to give him, even in his lifetime, a special place in the regard of foreign publics. His position is in this respect singular; for it is his Russian savor that as much as anything has helped generally to domesticate him.

Born in 1818, at Orel in the heart of Russia, and dying in 1883, at Bougival near Paris, he had spent in Germany and France the latter half of his life; and had incurred in his own country in some degree the reprobation that is apt to attach to the absent—the penalty they pay for such extension or such beguilement as they may have happened to find over the border. He belonged to the class of large rural proprietors of land and of serfs; and with his ample patrimony, offered one of the few examples of literary labor achieved in high independence of the question of gain—a character that he shares with his illustrious contemporary Tolstoy, who is of a type in other respects so different. It may give us an idea of his primary situation to imagine some large Virginian or Carolinian slaveholder, during the first half of the century, inclining to "Northern" views; and becoming (though not predominantly under pressure of these, but rather by the operation of an exquisite genius) the great American novelist—one of the great novelists of the world. Born under a social and political order sternly repressive, all Turgénieff's deep instincts, all his moral passion, placed him on the liberal side; with the consequence that early in life, after a period spent at a German university, he found himself, through the accident of a trifling public utterance, under such suspicion in high places as to be sentenced to a term of tempered exile—confinement to his own estate. It was partly under these circumstances perhaps that he gathered material for the work from the appearance of which his reputation dates—*A Sportsman's Sketches,* published in two volumes in 1852. This admirable collection of impressions of homely country life, as the old state of servitude had made it, is often spoken of as having borne to the great decree of Alexander II the relation borne by Mrs. Beecher Stowe's famous novel to the emancipation of the Southern slaves. Incontestably, at any rate, Turgénieff's rustic studies sounded, like *Uncle Tom's Cabin,* a particular hour: with the difference, however, of not having at the time produced an agitation—of having rather presented the case with an art too insidious for instant recognition, an art that stirred the depths more than the surface.

The author was designated promptly enough, at any rate, for such influence as might best be exercised at a distance: he travelled, he lived abroad; early in the sixties he was settled in Germany; he acquired property at Baden-Baden, and spent there the last years of the prosperous period—in the history of the place— of which the Franco-Prussian War was to mark the violent term. He cast in his lot after that event mainly with the victims of the lost cause; setting up a fresh home in Paris—near which city he had, on the Seine, a charming alternate residence—and passing in it, and in the country, save for brief revisitations, the remainder of his days. His friendships, his attachments, in the world of art and of letters, were numerous and distinguished; he never married; he produced, as the years went on, without precipitation or frequency; and these were the years during which his reputation gradually established itself as, according to the phrase, European—a phrase denoting in this case, perhaps, a public more alert in the United States even than elsewhere.

Tolstoy, his junior by ten years, had meanwhile come to fruition; though, as in fact happened, it was not till after Turgénieff's death that the greater fame of *War and Peace* and of *Anna Karénina* began to be blown about the world. One of the last acts of the elder writer, performed on his death-bed, was to address to the other (from whom for a considerable term he had been estranged by circumstances needless to reproduce) an appeal to return to the exercise of the genius that Tolstoy had already so lamentably, so monstrously forsworn. "I am on my death-bed; there is no possibility of my recovery. I write you expressly to tell you how happy I have been to be your contemporary, and to utter my last, my urgent prayer. Come back, my friend, to your literary labors. That gift came to you from the source from which all comes to us. Ah, how happy I should be could I think you would listen to my entreaty! My friend, great writer of our Russian land, respond to it, obey it!" These words, among the most touching surely ever addressed by one great spirit to another, throw an indirect light—perhaps I may even say a direct one—upon the nature and quality of Turgénieff's artistic temperament; so much so that I regret being without opportunity, in this place, to gather such aid for a portrait of him as might be supplied by following out the unlikeness between the pair. It would be too easy to say that Tolstoy was, from the Russian point of view, for home consumption, and Turgénieff for foreign: *War and Peace* has probably had more readers in Europe and America than *A House of Gentlefolk* or *On the Eve* or *Smoke*—a circumstance less detrimental than it may appear to my claim of our having, in the Western world, supremely adopted the author of the latter works. Turgénieff is in a peculiar degree what I may call the novelists' novelist—an artistic influence extraordinarily valuable and ineradicably established. The perusal of Tolstoy —a wonderful mass of life—is an immense event, a kind of splendid accident, for each of us: his name represents nevertheless no such eternal spell of method, no such quiet irresistibility of presentation, as shines, close to us and lighting our possible steps, in that of his precursor. Tolstoy is a reflector as vast as a natural lake; a monster harnessed to his great subject—all human life!—as an elephant might be harnessed, for purposes of traction, not to a carriage, but to a coach-house. His own case is prodigious, but his example for others dire: disciples not elephantine he can only mislead and betray.

One by one, for thirty years, with a firm, deliberate hand, with intervals and patiences and waits, Turgénieff pricked in his sharp outlines. His great external mark is probably his concision: an ideal he never threw over— it shines most perhaps even when he is least brief—and that he often applied with a rare felicity. He has masterpieces of a few pages; his perfect things are sometimes his least prolonged. He abounds in short tales, episodes clipped as by the scissors of Atropos; but for a direct translation of the whole we have still to wait—depending meanwhile upon the French and German versions, which have been, instead of the original text (thanks

to the paucity among us of readers of Russian), the
source of several published in English. For the novels
and *A Sportsman's Sketches* we depend upon the nine
volumes (1897) of Mrs. Garnett. We touch here upon
the remarkable side, to our vision, of the writer's fortune
—the anomaly of his having constrained to intimacy
even those who are shut out from the enjoyment of his
medium, for whom that question is positively prevented
from existing. Putting aside extrinsic intimations, it is
impossible to read him without the conviction of his
being, in the vividness of his own tongue, of the strong
type of those made to bring home to us the happy truth
of the unity, in a generous talent, of material and form
—of their being inevitable faces of the same medal; the
type of those, in a word, whose example deals death
to the perpetual clumsy assumption that subject and
style are—æsthetically speaking, or in the living work—
different and separable things. We are conscious, reading
him in a language not his own, of not being reached by
his personal tone, his individual accent.

It is a testimony therefore to the intensity of his presence, that so much of his particular charm does reach
us; that the mask turned to us has, even without his
expression, still so much beauty. It is the beauty (since
we must try to formulate) of the finest presentation of
the familiar. His vision is of the world of character and
feeling, the world of the relations life throws up at every
hour and on every spot; he deals little, on the whole,
in the miracles of chance—the hours and spots over the
edge of time and space; his air is that of the great central
region of passion and motive, of the usual, the inevitable,
the intimate—the intimate for weal or woe. No theme
that he ever chooses but strikes us as full; yet with all
have we the sense that their animation comes from
within, and is not pinned to their backs like the pricking

objects used of old in the horse-races of the Roman carnival, to make the animals run. Without a patch of "plot" to draw blood, the story he mainly tells us, the situation he mainly gives, runs as if for dear life. His first book was practically full evidence of what, if we have to specify, is finest in him—the effect, for the commonest truth, of an exquisite envelope of poetry. In this medium of feeling—full, as it were, of all the echoes and shocks of the universal danger and need—everything in him goes on; the sense of fate and folly and pity and wonder and beauty. The tenderness, the humor, the variety of *A Sportsman's Sketches* revealed on the spot an observer with a rare imagination. These faculties had attached themselves, together, to small things and to great: to the misery, the simplicity, the piety, the patience, of the unemancipated peasant; to all the natural wonderful life of earth and air and winter and summer and field and forest; to queer apparitions of country neighbors, of strange local eccentrics; to old-world practices and superstitions; to secrets gathered and types disinterred and impressions absorbed in the long, close contacts with man and nature involved in the passionate pursuit of game. Magnificent in stature and original vigor, Turgénieff, with his love of the chase, or rather perhaps of the inspiration he found in it, would have been the model of the mighty hunter, had not such an image been a little at variance with his natural mildness, the softness that often accompanies the sense of an extraordinary reach of limb and play of muscle. He was in person the model rather of the strong man at rest: massive and towering, with the voice of innocence and the smile almost of childhood. What seemed still more of a contradiction to so much of him, however, was that his work was all delicacy and fancy, penetration and compression.

If I add, in their order of succession, *Rudin, Fathers*

and Children, Spring Floods, and *Virgin Soil,* to the three novels I have (also in their relation of time) named above, I shall have indicated the larger blocks of the compact monument, with a base resting deep and interstices well filled, into which that work disposes itself. The list of his minor productions is too long to draw out: I can only mention, as a few of the most striking— "A Correspondence," "The Wayside Inn," "The Brigadier," "The Dog," "The Jew," "Visions," "Mumu," "Three Meetings," "A First Love," "The Forsaken," "Assia," "The Journal of a Superfluous Man," "The Story of Lieutenant Yergunov," "A King Lear of the Steppe." The first place among his novels would be difficult to assign: general opinion probably hesitates between *A House of Gentlefolk* and *Fathers and Children.* My own predilection is great for the exquisite *On the Eve;* though I admit that in such a company it draws no supremacy from being exquisite. What is less contestable is that *Virgin Soil*—published shortly before his death, and the longest of his fictions—has, although full of beauty, a minor perfection.

Character, character expressed and exposed, is in all these things what we inveterately find. Turgénieff's sense of it was the great light that artistically guided him; the simplest account of him is to say that the mere play of it constitutes in every case his sufficient drama. No one has had a closer vision, or a hand at once more ironic and more tender, for the individual figure. He sees it with its minutest signs and tricks—all its heredity of idiosyncrasies, all its particulars of weakness and strength, of ugliness and beauty, of oddity and charm; and yet it is of his essence that he sees it in the general flood of life, steeped in its relations and contacts, struggling or submerged, a hurried particle in the stream. This gives him, with his quiet method, his extraordinary breadth; dissociates his rare power to particularize from dryness or hardness, from any peril of caricature. He understands so much that we almost wonder he can express anything; and his expression is indeed wholly in absolute projection, in illustration, in giving of everything the unexplained and irresponsible specimen. He is of a spirit so human that we almost wonder at his control of his matter; of a pity so deep and so general that we almost wonder at his curiosity. The element of poetry in him is constant, and yet reality stares through it without the loss of a wrinkle. No one has more of that sign of the born novelist which resides in a respect unconditioned for the freedom and vitality, the absoluteness when summoned, of the creatures he invokes; or is more superior to the strange and second-rate policy of explaining or presenting them by reprobation or apology—of taking the short cuts and anticipating the emotions and judgments about them that should be left, at the best, to the perhaps not most intelligent reader. And yet his system, as it may summarily be called, of the mere particularized report, has a lucidity beyond the virtue of the cruder moralist.

If character, as I say, is what he gives us at every turn, I should speedily add that he offers it not in the least as a synonym, in our Western sense, of resolution and prosperity. It wears the form of the almost helpless detachment of the short-sighted individual soul; and the perfection of his exhibition of it is in truth too often but the intensity of what, for success, it just does not produce. What works in him most is the question of the will; and the most constant induction he suggests, bears upon the sad figure that principle seems mainly to make among his countrymen. He had seen—he suggests to us —its collapse in a thousand quarters; and the most general tragedy, to his view, is that of its desperate adventures and disasters, its inevitable abdication and defeat. But if the men, for the most part, let it go, it takes refuge in the other sex; many of the representatives of which, in his pages, are supremely strong—in wonderful addition, in various cases, to being otherwise admirable. This is true of such a number—the younger women, the girls, the "heroines" in especial—that they form in themselves, on the ground of moral beauty, of the finest distinction of soul, one of the most striking groups the modern novel has given us. They are heroines to the letter, and of a heroism obscure and undecorated: it is almost they alone who have the energy to determine and to act. Elena, Lisa, Tatyana, Gemma, Marianna—we can write their names and call up their images, but I lack space to take them in turn. It is by a succession of the finest and tenderest touches that they live; and this, in all Turgénieff's work, is the process by which he persuades and succeeds.

It was his own view of his main danger that he sacrificed too much to detail; was wanting in composition, in the gift that conduces to unity of impression. But no novelist is closer and more cumulative; in none does distinction spring from a quality of truth more independent of everything but the subject, but the idea itself. This idea, this subject, moreover—a spark kindled by the innermost friction of things—is always as interesting as an unopened telegram. The genial freedom—with its exquisite delicacy—of his approach to this "innermost" world, the world of our finer consciousness, has in short a side that I can only describe and commemorate as nobly disinterested; a side that makes too many of his rivals appear to hold us in comparison by violent means, and introduce us in comparison to vulgar things.

1897

*

HONORÉ DE BALZAC

Stronger than ever, even than under the spell of first
acquaintance and of the early time, is the sense—thanks
to a renewal of intimacy and, I am tempted to say, of
loyalty—that Balzac stands signally apart, that he is
the first and foremost member of his craft, and that
above all the Balzac-lover is in no position till he has
cleared the ground by saying so. The Balzac-lover alone,
for that matter, is worthy to have his word on so happy
an occasion as this[1] about the author of *La Comédie
Humaine,* and it is indeed not easy to see how the
amount of attention so inevitably induced could at the
worst have failed to find itself turning to an act of homage. I have been deeply affected, to be frank, by the
mere refreshment of memory, which has brought in its
train moreover consequences critical and sentimental
too numerous to figure here in their completeness. The
authors and the books that have, as we say, done something for us, become part of the answer to our curiosity
when our curiosity had the freshness of youth, these
particular agents exist for us, with the lapse of time,
as the substance itself of knowledge: they have been
intellectually so swallowed, digested and assimilated
that we take their general use and suggestion for

[1] The appearance of a translation of the *Deux Jeunes
Mariées* in A Century of French Romance. [This essay by
James on Balzac originally appeared as a critical introduction
to Balzac's novel *Deux Jeunes Mariées* when it appeared in
this series as *The Two Young Brides* in London in 1902.
Editor's note.]

granted, cease to be aware of them because they have passed out of sight. But they have passed out of sight simply by having passed into our lives. They have become a part of our personal history, a part of ourselves, very often, so far as we may have succeeded in best expressing ourselves. Endless, however, are the uses of great persons and great things, and it may easily happen in these cases that the connection, even as an "excitement"—the form mainly of the connections of youth— is never really broken. We have largely been living on our benefactor—which is the highest acknowledgment one can make; only, thanks to a blest law that operates in the long run to rekindle excitement, we are accessible to the sense of having neglected him. Even when we may not constantly have read him over the neglect is quite an illusion, but the illusion perhaps prepares us for the finest emotion we are to have owed to the acquaintance. Without having abandoned or denied our author we yet come expressly back to him, and if not quite in tatters and in penitence like the Prodigal Son, with something at all events of the tenderness with which we revert to the parental threshold and hearthstone, if not, more fortunately, to the parental presence. The beauty of this adventure, that of seeing the dust blown off a relation that had been put away as on a shelf, almost out of reach, at the back of one's mind, consists in finding the precious object not only fresh and intact, but with its firm lacquer still further figured, gilded and enriched. It is all overscored with traces and impressions —vivid, definite, almost as valuable as itself—of the recognitions and agitations it originally produced in us. Our old—that is our young—feelings are very nearly what page after page most gives us. The case has become a case of authority *plus* association. If Balzac in himself is indubitably wanting in the sufficiently common felicity we know as charm, it is this association that may on occasion contribute the grace.

The impression then, confirmed and brightened, is of the mass and weight of the figure and of the extent of ground it occupies; a tract on which we might all of us together quite pitch our little tents, open our little booths, deal in our little wares, and not materially either diminish the area or impede the circulation of the occupant. I seem to see him in such an image moving about as Gulliver among the pigmies, and not less good-natured than Gulliver for the exercise of any function, without exception, that can illustrate his larger life. The first and the last word about the author of *Les Contes Drolatiques* is that of all novelists he is the most serious —by which I am far from meaning that in the human comedy as he shows it the comic is an absent quantity. His sense of the comic was on the scale of his extraordinary senses in general, though his expression of it suffers perhaps exceptionally from that odd want of elbow-room —the penalty somehow of his close-packed, pressed-down contents—which reminds us of some designedly beautiful thing but half-disengaged from the clay or the marble. It is the scheme and the scope that are supreme in him, applying this moreover not to mere great intention, but to the concrete form, the proved case, in which we possess them. We most of us aspire to achieve at the best but a patch here and there, to pluck a sprig or a single branch, to break ground in a corner of the great garden of life. Balzac's plan was simply to do everything that could be done. He proposed to himself to "turn over" the great garden from north to south and from east to west; a task—immense, heroic, to this day immeasurable—that he bequeathed us the partial performance of, a prodigious ragged clod, in the twenty monstrous years representing his productive career, years of concentration and sacrifice the vision of which still makes us ache. He had indeed a striking good fortune, the only one he was to enjoy as an harassed and exasperated worker: the great garden of life presented itself to him absolutely and exactly in the guise of the great garden of France, a subject vast and comprehensive enough, yet with definite edges and corners. This identity of his universal with his local and national vision is the particular thing we should doubtless call his greatest strength were we preparing agreeably to speak of it also as his visible weakness. Of Balzac's weaknesses, however, it takes some assurance to talk; there is always plenty of time for them; they are the last signs we know him by—such things truly as in other painters of manners often come under the head of mere exuberance of energy. So little in short do they earn the invidious name even when we feel them as defects.

What he did above all was to read the universe, as hard and as loud as he could, *into* the France of his time; his own eyes regarding his work as at once the drama of man and a mirror of the mass of social phenomena the most rounded and registered, most organized and administered, and thereby most exposed to systematic observation and portrayal, that the world had seen. There are happily other interesting societies, but these are for schemes of such an order comparatively loose and incoherent, with more extent and perhaps more variety, but with less of the great enclosed and exhibited quality, less neatness and sharpness of arrangement, fewer categories, subdivisions, juxtapositions. Balzac's France was both inspiring enough for an immense prose epic and reducible enough for a report or a chart. To allow his achievement all its dignity we should doubtless say also treatable enough for a history, since it was as a patient historian, a Benedictine of the actual, the living painter of his living time, that he regarded himself and handled his material. All painters of manners and fashions, if we will, are historians, even when they least don the uniform: Fielding, Dickens, Thackeray, George Eliot, Hawthorne among ourselves. But the great difference between the great Frenchman and the eminent others is that, with an imagination of the highest power, an unequalled intensity of vision, he saw his subject in the light of science as well, in the light of the bearing of all its parts on each other, and under pressure of a passion for exactitude, an appetite, the appetite of an ogre, for *all* the kinds of facts. We find I think in the union here suggested something like the truth about his genius, the nearest approach to a final account of him. Of imagination on one side all compact, he was on the other an insatiable reporter of the immediate, the material, the current combination, and perpetually moved by the historian's impulse to fix, preserve and explain them. One asks one's self as one reads him what concern the poet has with so much arithmetic and so much criticism, so many statistics and documents, what concern the critic and the economist have with so many passions, characters and adventures. The contradiction is always before us; it springs from the inordinate scale of the author's two faces; it explains more than anything else his eccentricities and difficulties. It accounts for his want of grace, his want of the lightness associated with an amusing literary form, his bristling surface, his closeness of texture, so rough with richness, yet so productive of the effect we have in mind when we speak of not being able to see the wood for the trees.

A thorough-paced votary, for that matter, can easily afford to declare at once that this confounding duality of character does more things still, or does at least the most important of all—introduces us without mercy

(mercy for ourselves I mean) to the oddest truth we could have dreamed of meeting in such a connection. It was certainly *a priori* not to be expected we should feel it of him, but our hero is after all not in his magnificence totally an artist: which would be the strangest thing possible, one must hasten to add, were not the smallness of the practical difference so made even stranger. His endowment and his effect are each so great that the anomaly makes at the most a difference only by adding to his interest for the critic. The critic worth his salt is indiscreetly curious and wants ever to know how and why—whereby Balzac is thus a still rarer case for him, suggesting that exceptional curiosity may have exceptional rewards. The question of what makes the artist on a great scale is interesting enough; but we feel it in Balzac's company to be nothing to the question of what on an equal scale frustrates him. The scattered pieces, the *disjecta membra* of the character are here so numerous and so splendid that they prove misleading; we pile them together, and the heap assuredly is monumental; it forms an overtopping figure. The genius this figure stands for, none the less, is really such a lesson to the artist as perfection itself would be powerless to give; it carries him so much further into the special mystery. Where it carries him, at the same time, I must not in this scant space attempt to say—which would be a loss of the fine thread of my argument. I stick to our point in putting it, more concisely, that the artist of the *Comédie Humaine* is half smothered by the historian. Yet it belongs as well to the matter also to meet the question of whether the historian himself may not be an artist— in which case Balzac's catastrophe would seem to lose its excuse. The answer of course is that the reporter, however philosophic, has one law, and the originator, however substantially fed, has another; so that the two laws can with no sort of harmony or congruity make, for the finer sense, a common household. Balzac's catastrophe—so to name it once again—was in this perpetual conflict and final impossibility, an impossibility that explains his defeat on the classic side and extends so far at times as to make us think of his work as, from the point of view of beauty, a tragic waste of effort.

What it would come to, we judge, is that the irreconcilability of the two kinds of law is, more simply expressed, but the irreconcilability of two different ways of composing one's effect. The principle of composition that his free imagination would have, or certainly might have, handsomely imposed on him is perpetually dislocated by the quite opposite principle of the earnest seeker, the inquirer to a useful end, in whom nothing is free but a born antipathy to his yokefellow. Such a production as *Le Curé de Village*, the wonderful story of Madame Graslin, so nearly a masterpiece yet so ultimately not one, would be, in this connection, could I take due space for it, a perfect illustration. If, as I say, Madame Graslin's creator was confined by his doom to patches and pieces, no piece is finer than the first half of the book in question, the half in which the picture is determined by his unequalled power of putting people on their feet, planting them before us in their habit as they lived—a faculty nourished by observation as much as one will, but with the inner vision all the while wideawake, the vision for which ideas are as living as facts and assume an equal intensity. This intensity, greatest indeed in the facts, has in Balzac a force all its own, to which none other in any novelist I know can be likened. His touch communicates on the spot to the object, the creature evoked, the hardness and permanence that certain substances, some sorts of stone, acquire by exposure to the air. The hardening medium, for the image soaked in it, is the air of his mind. It would take but little more to make the peopled world of fiction as we know it elsewhere affect us by contrast as a world of rather gray pulp. This mixture of the solid and the vivid is Balzac at his best, and it prevails without a break, without a note not admirably true, in *Le Curé de Village*—since I have named that instance—up to the point at which Madame Graslin moves out from Limoges to Montégnac in her ardent passion of penitence, her determination to expiate her strange and undiscovered association with a dark misdeed by living and working for others. Her drama is a particularly inward one, interesting, and in the highest degree, so long as she herself, her nature, her behaviour, her personal history and the relations in which they place her, control the picture and feed our illusion. The firmness with which the author makes them play this part, the whole constitution of the scene and of its developments from the moment we cross the threshold of her dusky stuffy old-time birth-house, is a rare delight, producing in the reader that sense of local and material immersion which is one of Balzac's supreme secrets. What characteristically befalls, however, is that the spell accompanies us but part of the way—only until, at a given moment, his attention ruthlessly transfers itself from inside to outside, from the centre of his subject to its circumference.

This is Balzac caught in the very fact of his monstrous duality, caught in his most complete self-expression. He is clearly quite unwitting that in handing over his *data* to his twin-brother the impassioned economist and surveyor, the insatiate general inquirer and reporter, he is in any sort betraying our confidence, for his good conscience at such times, the spirit of edification in him, is a lesson even to the best of us, his rich robust temperament nowhere more striking, no more marked anywhere the great push of the shoulder with which he makes his theme move, overcharged though it may be like a carrier's van. It is not therefore assuredly that he loses either sincerity or power in putting before us to the last detail such a matter as, in this case, his heroine's management of her property, her tenantry, her economic opportunities and visions, for these are cases in which he never shrinks nor relents, in which positively he stiffens and terribly towers—to remind us again of M. Taine's simplifying word about his being an artist doubled with a man of business. Balzac was indeed doubled if ever a writer was, and to that extent that we almost as often, while we read, feel ourselves thinking of him as a man of business doubled with an artist. Whichever way we turn it the oddity never fails, nor the wonder of the ease with which either character bears the burden of the other. I use the word burden because, as the fusion is never complete—witness in the book before us the fatal break of "tone," the one unpardonable sin for the novelist—we are beset by the conviction that but for this strangest of dooms one or other of the two partners might, to our relief and to his own, have been disembarrassed. The disembarrassment, for each, by a more insidious fusion, would probably have conduced to the mastership of interest proceeding from form, or at all events to the search for it, that Balzac fails to embody. Perhaps the possibility of an artist constructed on such strong lines is one of those fine things that are not of this world, a mere dream of the fond critical spirit. Let these speculations and condonations at least pass as the amusement, as a result of the high spirits—if high spirits be the word—of the reader feeling himself again in touch. It was not of our author's difficulties—that is of his difficulty, the great one—that I proposed to speak, but of his immense clear action. Even that is not truly

an impression of ease, and it is strange and striking that
we are in fact so attached by his want of the unity that
keeps surfaces smooth and dangers down as scarce to
feel sure at any moment that we shall not come back
to it with most curiosity. We are never so curious about
successes as about interesting failures. The more reason
therefore to speak promptly, and once for all, of the scale
on which, in its own quarter of his genius, success
worked itself out for him.

It is to that I *should* come back—to the infinite reach
in him of the painter and the poet. We can never know
what might have become of him with less importunity
in his consciousness of the machinery of life, of its furniture and fittings, of all that, right and left, he causes
to assail us, sometimes almost to suffocation, under the
general rubric of *things.* Things, in this sense with him,
are at once our delight and our despair; we pass from
being inordinately beguiled and convinced by them to
feeling that his universe fairly smells too much of them,
that the larger ether, the diviner air, is in peril of finding
among them scarce room to circulate. His landscapes,
his "local colour"—thick in his pages at a time when
it was to be found in his pages almost alone—his towns,
his streets, his houses, his Saumurs, Angoulêmes, Gué-
randes, his great prose Turner-views of the land of the
Loire, his rooms, shops, interiors, details of domesticity
and traffic, are a short list of the terms into which he saw
the real as clamouring to be rendered and into which
he rendered it with unequalled authority. It would be
doubtless more to the point to make our profit of
this consummation than to try to reconstruct a Balzac
planted more in the open. We hardly, as the case stands,
know most whether to admire in such an example as the
short tale of "La Grenadière" the exquisite feeling for
"natural objects" with which it overflows like a brim-

ming wine-cup, the energy of perception and description which so multiplies them for beauty's sake and for the love of their beauty, or the general wealth of genius that can calculate, or at least count, so little and spend so joyously. The tale practically exists for the sake of the enchanting aspects involved—those of the embowered white house that nestles on its terraced hill above the great French river, and we can think, frankly, of no one else with an equal amount of business on his hands who would either have so put himself out for aspects or made them almost by themselves a living subject. A born son of Touraine, it must be said, he pictures his province, on every pretext and occasion, with filial passion and extraordinary breadth. The prime aspect in his scene all the while, it must be added, is the money aspect. The general money question so loads him up and weighs him down that he moves through the human comedy, from beginning to end, very much in the fashion of a camel, the ship of the desert, surmounted with a cargo. "Things" for him are francs and centimes more than any others, and I give up as inscrutable, unfathomable, the nature, the peculiar avidity of his interest in them. It makes us wonder again and again what then is the use on Balzac's scale of the divine faculty. The imagination, as we all know, may be employed up to a certain point in inventing uses for money; but its office beyond that point is surely to make us forget that anything so odious exists. This is what Balzac never forgot; his universe goes on expressing itself for him, to its furthest reaches, on its finest sides, in the terms of the market. To say these things, however, is after all to come out where we want, to suggest his extraordinary scale and his terrible completeness. I am not sure that he does not see character too, see passion, motive, personality, as quite in the order of the "things" we have spoken of. He makes them no less concrete and palpable, handles them no less directly and freely. It is the whole business in fine—that grand total to which he proposed to himself to do high justice—that gives him his place apart, makes him, among the novelists, the largest weightiest presence. There are some of his obsessions—that of the material, that of the financial, that of the "social," that of the technical, political, civil—for which I feel myself unable to judge him, judgment losing itself unexpectedly in a particular shade of pity. The way to judge him is to try to walk all round him—on which we see how remarkably far we have to go. He is the only member of his order really monumental, the sturdiest-seated mass that rises in our path.

1902. From "Honoré de Balzac," in *Notes on Novelists with Some Other Notes* (1914).

GUSTAVE FLAUBERT:
MADAME BOVARY

One of the things that make [Flaubert] most exhibitional and most describable, so that if we had invented him as an illustration or a character we would exactly so have arranged him, is that he was formed intellectually of two quite distinct compartments, a sense of the real and a sense of the romantic, and that his production, for our present cognizance, thus neatly and vividly divides itself. The divisions are as marked as the sections on the back of a scarab, though their distinctness is undoubtedly but the final expression of much inward strife.

M. Faguet[1] indeed, who is admirable on this question
of our author's duality, gives an account of the romanticism that found its way for him into the real and of the
reality that found its way into the romantic; but he none
the less strikes us as a curious splendid insect sustained
on wings of a different coloration, the right a vivid red,
say, and the left as frank a yellow. This duality has in
its sharp operation placed *Madame Bovary* and *L'Éducation* [*sentimentale*] on one side together and placed together on the other *Salammbô* and *La Tentation* [*de
Saint-Antoine*]. *Bouvard et Pécuchet* it can scarce be
spoken of, I think, as having placed anywhere or anyhow. If it was Flaubert's way to find his subject impossible there was none he saw so much in that light as
this last-named, but also none that he appears to have
held so important for that very reason to pursue to the
bitter end. Posterity agrees with him about the impossibility, but rather takes upon itself to break with the
rest of the logic. We may perhaps, however, for sym-
metry, let *Bouvard et Pécuchet* figure as the tail—if
scarabs ever have tails—of our analogous insect. Only
in that case we should also append as the very tip the
small volume of the *Trois Contes,* preponderantly of the
deepest imaginative hue.

His imagination was great and splendid; in spite of
which, strangely enough, his masterpiece is not his most
imaginative work. *Madame Bovary,* beyond question,
holds that first place, and *Madame Bovary* is concerned
with the career of a country doctor's wife in a petty

[1] M. Émile Faguet's book *Gustave Flaubert,* published in
Paris in 1898 in the series *Les Grands Écrivains français.* was
discussed in some detail by James when he wrote this essay
on Flaubert (here printed in part) as a critical introduction
for an English translation of *Madame Bovary* published in
London by William Heinemann in 1902. [*Editor's note.*]

Norman town. The elements of the picture are of the fewest, the situation of the heroine almost of the meanest, the material for interest, considering the interest yielded, of the most unpromising; but these facts only throw into relief one of those incalculable incidents that attend the proceedings of genius. *Madame Bovary* was doomed by circumstances and causes—the freshness of comparative youth and good faith on the author's part being perhaps the chief—definitely to take its position, even though its subject was fundamentally a negation of the remote, the splendid and the strange, the stuff of his fondest and most cultivated dreams. It would have seemed very nearly to exclude the free play of the imagination, and the way this faculty on the author's part nevertheless presides is one of those accidents, manœuvres, inspirations, we hardly know what to call them, by which masterpieces grow. He of course knew more or less what he was doing for his book in making Emma Bovary a victim of the imaginative habit, but he must have been far from designing or measuring the total effect which renders the work so general, so complete an expression of himself. His separate idiosyncrasies, his irritated sensibility to the life about him, with the power to catch it in the fact and hold it hard, and his hunger for style and history and poetry, for the rich and the rare, great reverberations, great adumbrations, are here represented together as they are not in his later writings. There is nothing of the near, of the directly observed, though there may be much of the directly perceived and the minutely detailed, either in *Salammbô* or in *Saint-Antoine*, and little enough of the extravagance of illusion in that indefinable last word of restrained evocation and cold execution *L'Éducation Sentimentale*. M. Faguet has of course excellently noted this—that the fortune and felicity of the book were assured by the stroke that made the central figure an embodiment of helpless romanticism. Flaubert himself but narrowly escaped being such an embodiment after all, and he is thus able to express the romantic mind with extraordinary truth. As to the rest of the matter he had the luck of having been in possession from the first, having begun so early to nurse and work up his plan that, familiarity and the native air, the native soil, aiding, he had finally made out to the last lurking shade the small sordid sunny dusty village picture, its emptiness constituted and peopled. It is in the background and the accessories that the real, the real of his theme, abides; and the romantic, the romantic of his theme, accordingly occupies the front. Emma Bovary's poor adventures are a tragedy for the very reason that in a world unsuspecting, unassisting, unconsoling, she has herself to distil the rich and the rare. Ignorant, unguided, undiverted, ridden by the very nature and mixture of her consciousness, she makes of the business an inordinate failure, a failure which in its turn makes for Flaubert the most pointed, the most *told* of anecdotes.

There are many things to say about *Madame Bovary,* but an old admirer of the book would be but half-hearted—so far as they represent reserves or puzzlements—were he not to note first of all the circumstances by which it is most endeared to him. To remember it from far back is to have been present all along at a process of singular interest to a literary mind, a case indeed full of comfort and cheer. The finest of Flaubert's novels is to-day, on the French shelf of fiction, one of the first of the classics; it has attained that position, slowly but steadily, before our eyes; and we seem so to follow the evolution of the fate of a classic. We see how the thing takes place; which we rarely can, for we mostly miss either the beginning or the end, especially in the case

of a consecration as complete as this. The consecrations
of the past are too far behind and those of the future too
far in front. That the production before us *should* have
come in for the heavenly crown may be a fact to offer
English and American readers a mystifying side; but
it is exactly our ground and a part moreover of the total
interest. The author of these remarks remembers, as with
a sense of the way such things happen, that when a very
young person in Paris he took up from the parental table
the latest number of the periodical in which Flaubert's
then duly unrecognized masterpiece was in course of
publication. The moment is not historic, but it was to
become in the light of history, as may be said, so unforgettable that every small feature of it yet again lives
for him: it rests there like the backward end of the span.
The cover of the old *Revue de Paris* was yellow, if I
mistake not, like that of the new, and *Madame Bovary:
Mœurs de Province,* on the inside of it, was already, on
the spot, as a title, mysteriously arresting, inscrutably
charged. I was ignorant of what had preceded and was
not to know till much later what followed; but present
to me still is the act of standing there before the fire,
my back against the low beplushed and begarnished
French chimney-piece and taking in what I might of
that instalment, taking it in with so surprised an interest,
and perhaps as well such a stir of faint foreknowledge,
that the sunny little salon, the autumn day, the window
ajar and the cheerful outside clatter of the Rue Mon-
taigne are all now for me more or less in the story and
the story more or less in them. The story, however, was
at that moment having a difficult life; its fortune was all
to make; its merit was so far from suspected that, as
Maxime Du Camp—though verily with no excess of
contrition—relates, its cloth of gold barely escaped the
editorial shears. This, with much more, contributes for

us to the course of things to come. The book, on its appearance as a volume, proved a shock to the high propriety of the guardians of public morals under the second Empire, and Flaubert was prosecuted as author of a work indecent to scandal. The prosecution in the event fell to the ground, but I should perhaps have mentioned this agitation as one of the very few, of any public order, in his short list. *Le Candidat* fell at the Vaudeville Theatre, several years later, with a violence indicated by its withdrawal after a performance of but two nights, the first of these marked by a deafening uproar; only if the comedy was not to recover from this accident the misprised lustre of the novel was entirely to reassert itself. It is strange enough at present—so far have we travelled since then—that *Madame Bovary* should in so comparatively recent a past have been to that extent a cause of reprobation; and suggestive above all, in such connections, as to the large unconsciousness of superior minds. The desire of the superior mind of the day—that is the governmental, official, legal—to distinguish a book with such a destiny before it is a case conceivable, but conception breaks down before its design of making the distinction purely invidious. We can imagine its knowing so little, however face to face with the object, what it had got hold of; but for it to have been so urged on by a blind inward spring to publish to posterity the extent of its ignorance, that would have been beyond imagination, beyond everything but pity.

And yet it is not after all that the place the book has taken is so overwhelmingly explained by its inherent dignity; for here comes in the curiosity of the matter. Here comes in especially its fund of admonition for alien readers. The dignity of its substance is the dignity of Madame Bovary herself as a vessel of experience—a question as to which, unmistakably, I judge, we can only

depart from the consensus of French critical opinion.
M. Faguet for example commends the character of the
heroine as one of the most living and discriminated figures of women in all literature, praises it as a field for the
display of the romantic spirit that leaves nothing to be
desired. Subject to an observation I shall presently make
and that bears heavily in general, I think, on Flaubert
as a painter of life, subject to this restriction he is right;[1]
which is a proof that a work of art may be markedly
open to objection and at the same time be rare in its
kind, and that when it is perfect to this point nothing
else particularly matters. *Madame Bovary* has a perfection that not only stamps it, but that makes it stand
almost alone; it holds itself with such a supreme un-
approachable assurance as both excites and defies judgment. For it deals not in the least, as to unapproach-
ability, with things exalted or refined; it only confers
on its sufficiently vulgar elements of exhibition a final
unsurpassable form. The form is in *itself* as interesting,
as active, as much of the essence of the subject as the
idea, and yet so close is its fit and so inseparable its life

[1] The "restriction" which James presently makes in this
essay comes in his discussion of *L'Éducation sentimentale*,
when he compares that novel's hero, Frédéric Moreau, with
Emma Bovary: "Our complaint is that Emma Bovary, in spite
of the nature of her consciousness and in spite of her reflect-
ing so much that of her creator, is really too small an affair.
. . . She associates herself with Frédéric Moreau in *L'Éducation* to suggest for us a question that can be answered, I hold,
only to Flaubert's detriment. . . . Why did Flaubert choose,
as special conduits of the life he proposed to depict, such
inferior and in the case of Frédéric such abject human specimens? I insist only in respect to the latter, the perfection of
Madame Bovary scarce leaving one much warrant for wishing
anything better. Even here, however, the general scale and
size of Emma, who is small even of her sort, should be a
warning to hyperbole." [*Editor's note.*]

that we catch it at no moment on any errand of its own. That verily is to *be* interesting—all round; that is to be genuine and whole. The work is a classic because the thing, such as it is, is ideally *done,* and because it shows that in such doing eternal beauty may dwell. A pretty young woman who lives, socially and morally speaking, in a hole, and who is ignorant, foolish, flimsy, unhappy, takes a pair of lovers by whom she is successively deserted; in the midst of the bewilderment of which, giving up her husband and her child, letting everything go, she sinks deeper into duplicity, debt, despair, and arrives on the spot, on the small scene itself of her poor depravities, at a pitiful tragic end. In especial she does these things while remaining absorbed in romantic intention and vision, and she remains absorbed in romantic intention and vision while fairly rolling in the dust. That is the triumph of the book as the triumph stands, that Emma interests us by the nature of her consciousness and the play of her mind, thanks to the reality and beauty with which those sources are invested. It is not only that they represent *her* state; they are so true, so observed and felt, and especially so shown, that they represent the state, actual or potential, of all persons like her, persons romantically determined. Then her setting, the medium in which she struggles, becomes in its way as important, becomes eminent with the eminence of art; the tiny world in which she revolves, the contracted cage in which she flutters, is hung out in space for her, and her companions in captivity there are as true as herself.

1902. From "Gustave Flaubert" in *Notes on Novelists with Some Other Notes* (1914).

*

HENRY JAMES TO H. G. WELLS

[H. G. Wells was, like Kipling, one of the new English
talents of the eighteen-nineties that Henry James—eager to
see the novel invigorated by fresh material and imagination,
even when these issued from an experience or sensibility unlike his own—saluted with special enthusiasm. A friendship
between the two men developed as early as 1898. James
told Wells in 1899 that the younger man's work filled him
"with wonder and admiration," and in the following years
he praised as "extraordinarily and unceasingly interesting"
such books of Wells's as *Anticipations, A Modern Utopia,
Kipps, Ann Veronica, The New Machiavelli, Tono-Bungay,
Marriage, The Passionate Friends.* He sometimes protested
against Wells's unbridled habits and all-inclusive verve; he
warned him against "that accurst autobiographical form
which puts a premium on the loose"; he expressed to Mrs.
Humphry Ward his uneasiness at seeing in Wells the combination of "so much talent with so little art, so much life
with (so to speak) so little living." But he stuck to his
original belief that Wells was a master of social materials
and comedy in the tradition of Balzac and Dickens, and
in 1912 he wrote him: "I have read you, as I always read
you, and as I read no one else, with a complete abdication
of all those 'principles of criticism,' canons of form, pre-
conceptions of felicity, references to the idea of method or
the sacred laws of composition, which I roam, which I totter,
through the pages of others attended in some degree by
the fond yet feeble theory of, but which I shake off, as I
advance under your spell, with the most cynical inconsist-
ency." In 1914 James summed up his delight and confidence in Wells's gifts in a passage of his essay "The New
Novel," in which Wells shared James's attention with Joseph

Conrad, Arnold Bennett, Edith Wharton, Gilbert Cannan, Hugh Walpole, Compton Mackenzie, and (briefly) D. H. Lawrence.

In the summer of 1915 Wells published a book with a long title—*Boon, the Mind of the Race, the Wild Asses of the Devil, and the Last Trump,* purportedly "Being a First Selection from the Literary Remains of George Boon, Appropriate to the Times, Prepared for Publication by Reginald Bliss . . . with An Ambiguous Introduction by H. G. Wells." This was a loose ragbag of a book on literary, social, political, and moral themes, and it included a lengthy attack on James and a parody of the kind of novel he wrote and represented. James was paired with George Moore: "In early life both these men poisoned their minds in studios. . . . But James has never discovered that a novel isn't a picture . . . that life isn't a studio." "James *begins* by taking it for granted that a novel is a work of art that must be judged by its oneness. . . . Some one gave him that idea in the beginning of things and he has never found it out. He doesn't find things out." "He is the culmination of the Superficial type." "He sets himself to pick the straws out of the hair of Life before he paints her. But without the straws she is no longer the mad woman we love." Wells went on to attack James's principle of "selection" as against his own ideal of "saturation." "In practice James's selection becomes just omission and nothing more." "The only living human motives left in the novels of Henry James are a certain avidity and an entirely superficial curiosity. . . . It is like a church lit but without a congregation to distract you, with every light and line focused on the high altar. And on the altar, very reverently placed, intensely there, is a dead kitten, an egg-shell, a bit of string." "Having first made sure that he has scarcely anything left to express, he then sets to work to express it, with an industry, a wealth of intellectual stuff that dwarfs Newton. . . . And all for tales of nothingness. . . . It is leviathan retrieving pebbles. It is a magnificent but painful hippopotamus resolved at any cost, even at the cost of its dignity, upon picking up a pea which has got into a corner of its den. Most things, it insists, are beyond it, but it can, at any rate, modestly, and with an artistic singleness of mind, pick up that pea. . . ."

Wells later admitted that *Boon* had been his retaliation for James's inclusion of him, in the essay on "The New Novel," in "a bundle with a company of young men of questionable quality as one of the Younger Reputations."

James, on receiving and reading *Boon*, wrote to Wells.]

> 21 Carlyle Mansions,
> Cheyne Walk, S.W.
> July 6th, 1915.

My dear Wells,

I was given yesterday at a club your volume "Boon, etc.," from a loose leaf in which I learn that you kindly sent it me and which yet appears to have lurked there for a considerable time undelivered. I have just been reading, to acknowledge it intelligently, a considerable number of its pages—though not all; for, to be perfectly frank, I have been in that respect beaten for the first time—or rather for the first time but one—by a book of yours; I haven't found the current of it draw me on and on this time—as, unfailingly and irresistibly, before (which I have repeatedly let you know). However, I shall try again—I hate to lose any scrap of you that *may* make for light or pleasure; and meanwhile I have more or less mastered your appreciation of H. J., which I have found very curious and interesting after a fashion— though it has naturally not filled me with a fond elation. It is difficult of course for a writer to put himself *fully* in the place of another writer who finds him extraordinarily futile and void, and who is moved to publish that to the world—and I think the case isn't easier when he happens to have enjoyed the other writer enormously from far back; because there has then grown up the habit of taking some common meeting-ground between them for granted, and the falling away of this is like the collapse of a bridge which made communication possible. But I am by nature more in dread of any fool's paradise, or at least of any bad misguidedness, than in love with the idea of a security proved, and the fact that a mind as brilliant as yours *can* resolve me into such an unmitigated mistake, can't enjoy me in anything like the degree in which I like to think I may be enjoyed, makes me greatly want to fix myself, for as long as my nerves will stand it, with such a pair of eyes. I am aware of certain things I have, and not less conscious, I believe, of various others that I am simply reduced to wish I did or could have; so I try, for possible light, to enter into the feelings of a critic for whom the deficiencies so preponderate. The difficulty about that effort, however, is that one can't keep it up—one *has* to fall back on one's sense of one's good parts—one's own sense; and I at least should have to do that, I think, even if your picture were painted with a more searching brush. For I should otherwise seem to forget what it is that my poetic and my appeal to experience rest upon. They rest upon *my* measure of fulness—fulness of life and of the projection of it, which seems to you such an emptiness of both. I don't mean to say I don't wish I could do twenty things I can't—many of which you do so livingly; but I confess I ask myself what would become in that case of some of those to which I am most addicted and by which interest seems to me most beautifully producible. I hold that interest may be, *must* be, exquisitely made and created, and that if we don't make it, we who undertake to, nobody and nothing will make it for us; though nothing is more possible, nothing may even be more certain, than that my quest of it, my constant wish to run it to earth, may entail the sacrifice of certain things that are not on the straight line of it. However, there are too many things to say, and I don't think your chapter is really inquiring enough to entitle you to expect all of them. The fine thing about the fictional form to me is that it opens such widely different windows of attention; but that is just why I like the window so to frame the play and the process!

Faithfully yours,

Henry James

[Wells answered the above letter in part as follows, on July 8, 1915: "There is of course a real and very fundamental difference in our innate and developed attitudes towards life and literature. To you literature like painting is an end, to me literature like architecture is a means, it has a use. Your view was, I felt, altogether too prominent in the world of criticism and I assailed it in lines of harsh antagonism. And writing that stuff about you was the first escape I had from the obsession of this war. *Boon* is just a waste-paper basket. Some of it was written before I left my home at Sandgate (1911), and it was while I was turning over some old papers that I came upon it, found it expressive, and went on with it last December. I had rather be called a journalist than an artist, that is the essence of it, and there was no other antagonist possible than yourself. But since it was printed I have regretted a hundred times that I did not express our profound and incurable difference and contrast with a better grace. . . ." Later, on July 13, after receiving James's second letter, printed below, Wells added: "I don't clearly understand your concluding phrases —which shews no doubt how completely they define our difference. When you say 'it is art that *makes* life, makes interest, makes importance,' I can only read sense into it by assuming that you are using 'art' for every conscious human activity. I use the word for a research and attainment that is technical and special. . . ."]

Dictated.

21 Carlyle Mansions,
Cheyne Walk, S.W.
July 10th, 1915.

My dear Wells,

I am bound to tell you that I don't think your letter makes out any sort of case for the bad manners of "Boon," as far as your indulgence in them at the expense of your poor old H. J. is concerned—I say "your" simply because he has *been* yours, in the most liberal, continual, sacrificial, the most admiring and abounding critical way, ever since he began to know your writings: as to which you have had copious testimony. Your comparison of the book to a waste-basket strikes me as the reverse of felicitous, for what one throws into that receptacle is exactly what one doesn't commit to publicity and make the affirmation of one's estimate of one's contemporaries by. I should liken it much rather to the preservative portfolio or drawer in which what is withheld from the basket is savingly laid away. Nor do I feel it anywhere evident that my "view of life and literature," or what you impute to me as such, is carrying everything before it and becoming a public menace—so unaware do I seem, on the contrary, that my products constitute an example in any measurable degree followed or a cause in any degree successfully pleaded: I can't but think that if this were the case I should find it somewhat attested in their circulation—which, alas, I have reached a very advanced age in the entirely defeated hope of. But I *have* no view of life and literature, I maintain, other than that our form of the latter in especial is admirable exactly by its range and variety, its plasticity and liberality, its fairly living on the sincere and shifting experience of the individual practitioner. That is why I have always so admired your so free and strong application of it, the particular rich receptacle of intelligences and impressions emptied out with an energy of its own, that your genius constitutes; and *that* is in particular why, in my letter of two or three days since, I pronounced it curious and interesting that you should find the case I constitute myself only ridiculous and vacuous to the extent of your having to proclaim your sense of it. The curiosity and the interest, however, in this latter connection are of course for my mind those of the break of perception (perception of the veracity of *my* variety) on the part of a talent so generally inquiring and apprehensive as yours. Of course for myself I live, live intensely and am fed by life, and my value, whatever it be, is in my own kind of expression of that. Therefore I am pulled up to wonder by the fact that for you my kind (my sort of sense of expression and sort of sense of life alike) doesn't exist; and that wonder is, I admit, a disconcerting comment on my idea of the various appreciability of our addiction to the novel and of all the personal and intellectual history, sympathy and curiosity, behind the given example of it. It is when that history and curiosity have been determined in the way most different from my own that I want to get at them—precisely *for* the extension of life, which is the novel's best gift. But that is another matter. Meanwhile I absolutely dissent from the claim that there are any differences whatever in the amenability to art of forms of literature aesthetically determined, and hold your distinction between a form that is (like) painting and a form that is (like) architecture for wholly null and void. There is no sense in which architecture is aesthetically "for use" that doesn't leave any other art whatever exactly as much so; and so far from that of literature being irrelevant to the literary report upon life, and to its being made as interesting as possible, I regard it as relevant in a degree that leaves everything else behind. It is art that *makes* life, makes interest, makes importance, for our consideration and application of these things, and I know of no substitute whatever for the force and beauty of its process. If I were Boon I should say that any pretence of such a substitute is helpless and hopeless humbug; but I wouldn't be Boon for the world, and am only yours faithfully,

Henry James

IV

PORTRAITS OF PLACES

FOUR CITIES

*

James lived in what today appears as the last great age of romantic travel. The cities and monuments of Europe still
stood secure in their appointed places; space had not yet
been annihilated by engines, wires, wireless, and air-flight;
the sanctity of time and tradition still blessed the holy places
of historical and literary pilgrimage; nations lived in comparative amity and mutual respect. James was, moreover, an
American in an age when it was one of the duties of every
civilized American to rediscover and explore, assess or criticize, his legacy of breed, culture, and tradition in the Old
World. Virtually every distinguished American writer—
Whitman and Thoreau are the only notable exceptions—
made his journey to Europe: Franklin, Adams, and Jefferson,
Irving, Cooper, and Emerson, Hawthorne, Melville, and
Mark Twain, Howells, Norton, and Henry Adams. James became the archetype of that company, our great exponent of
the era of philosophic travel, the explorer on whom almost
all his literary followers—Henry B. Fuller, Stephen Crane,
Edith Wharton, Willa Cather, Lewis, Dos Passos, Heming-
way, Fitzgerald, T. S. Eliot—in some degree modeled their
later conquests of Europe.

Europe became part of his life "antecedent to choice."

Long before he went there by preference, long before he became that curious combination of "innocent abroad" and critical cosmopolite who recorded his discoveries in essays and books, he went as a baby in the first year of his life, and presently as a schoolboy. It became, by his father's express design, James's appointed destiny to experience the classic American division between the New and Old Worlds in his own person. He encountered England and Europe in his chosen role of "passionate pilgrim," and he made the encounter, in all its complex and critical ramifications, a major fact in his career and of his work. His models in his travel writings were not only the Americans who preceded him to Europe, but the European masters of this genre— Goethe, Stendhal, Gautier, Heine, Taine, Fromentin, Browning. W. H. Auden has said that "of all possible subjects, travel is the most difficult for an artist, as it is the easiest for the journalist." James as a traveler remains, even at his most casual or journalistic, unmistakably the artist who, "deprived of his most treasured liberty, the freedom to invent," discovers that "successfully to extract importance from historical personal events without ever departing from them, free only to select and never to modify or add, calls for imagination of a very high order."

James published seven books of his travel writings, but a great quantity of his reports remains uncollected in journals and newspapers. The finest distillation of these experiences went into his novels and tales, from *Roderick Hudson, The American,* and *The Portrait of a Lady* to *The Wings of the Dove, The Ambassadors,* and *The Golden Bowl.* From this great sum of material I have chosen four passages on four great cities, three European and one American, as representative of the rest.

The title of this section is borrowed from James's book *Portraits of Places.* "The After-Season in Rome" was first printed in *The Nation* for June 12, 1873, later included in *Transatlantic Sketches* (1875), and revised for *Italian Hours* (1909), from which the present text is taken. "Occasional Paris" was first printed as "Paris Revisited" in *The Galaxy* for January 1878, and later included under its present title in *Portraits of Places* (1883). The picture of London is part of a long essay called "London," which first appeared in *The Century Magazine* for December 1888, later amplified in *Essays in London and Elsewhere* (1893) and in *English Hours* (1905), the text here being taken from the last-named book. The excerpt titled "New York Revisited" is part of a long essay that was written after James's return to America in 1904; it first appeared in *Harper's Magazine* for February, March, and May 1906, and became Chapter II of *The American Scene* (1907).

THE AFTER-SEASON IN ROME

One may at the blest end of May say without injustice to anybody that the state of mind of many a *forestiero* in Rome is one of intense impatience for the moment when all other *forestieri* shall have taken themselves off. One may confess to this state of mind and be no misanthrope. The place has passed so completely for the winter months into the hands of the barbarians that that estimable character the passionate pilgrim finds it constantly harder to keep his passion clear. He has a rueful sense of impressions perverted and adulterated; the all-venerable visage disconcerts us by a vain eagerness to see itself mirrored in English, American, German eyes. It isn't simply that you are never first or never alone at the classic or historic spots where you have dreamt of persuading the shy *genius loci* into confidential utterance; it isn't simply that St. Peter's, the Vatican, the Palatine, are for ever ringing with the false note of the languages without style: it is the general oppressive

feeling that the city of the soul has become for the time
a monstrous mixture of watering-place and curiosity-
shop and that its most ardent life is that of the tourists
who haggle over false intaglios and yawn through pal-
aces and temples. But you are told of a happy time when
these abuses begin to pass away, when Rome becomes
Rome again and you may have her all to yourself. "You
may like her more or less now," I was assured at the
height of the season; "but you must wait till the month
of May, when she'll give you *all* she has, to love her.
Then the foreigners, or the excess of them, are gone;
the galleries and ruins are empty, and the place," said
my informant, who was a happy Frenchman of the
Académie de France, "*renaît à elle-même.*" Indeed I was
haunted all winter by an irresistible prevision of what
Rome *must* be in declared spring. Certain charming
places seemed to murmur: "Ah, this is nothing! Come
back at the right weeks and see the sky above us almost
black with its excess of blue, and the new grass already
deep, but still vivid, and the white roses tumble in odorous spray and the warm radiant air distil gold for the
smelting-pot that the *genius loci* then dips his brush
into before making play with it, in his inimitable way,
for the general effect of complexion."

A month ago I spent a week in the country, and on
my return, the first time I approached the Corso, became
conscious of a change. Something delightful had happened, to which at first I couldn't give a name, but
which presently shone out as the fact that there were
but half as many people present and that these were
chiefly the natural or the naturalized. We had been
docked of half our irrelevance, our motley excess, and
now physically, morally, æsthetically there was elbow-
room. In the afternoon I went to the Pincio, and the
Pincio was almost dull. The band was playing to a dozen

ladies who lay in landaus poising their lace-fringed parasols; but they had scarce more than a light-gloved dandy
apiece hanging over their carriage doors. By the parapet
to the great terrace that sweeps the city stood but three
or four interlopers looking at the sunset and with their
Baedekers only just showing in their pockets—the sunsets not being down among the tariffed articles in these
precious volumes. I went so far as to hope for them that,
like myself, they were, under every precaution, taking
some amorous intellectual liberty with the scene.

Practically I violate thus the instinct of monopoly,
since it's a shame not to publish that Rome in May is
indeed exquisitely worth your patience. I have just been
so gratified at finding myself in undisturbed possession
for a couple of hours of the Museum of the Lateran that
I can afford to be magnanimous. It's almost as if the old
all-papal paradise had come back. The weather for a
month has been perfect, the sky an extravagance of
blue, the air lively enough, the nights cool, nippingly
cool, and the whole ancient greyness lighted with an
irresistible smile. Rome, which in some moods, especially
to new-comers, seems a place of almost sinister gloom,
has an occasional art, as one knows her better, of brushing away care by the grand gesture with which some
splendid impatient mourning matron—just the Niobe
of Nations, surviving, emerging and looking about her
again—might pull off and cast aside an oppression of
muffling crape. This admirable power still temperamen-
tally to react and take notice lurks in all her darkness
and dirt and decay—a something more careless and
hopeless than our thrifty northern cheer, and yet more
genial and urbane than the Parisian spirit of *blague*. The
collective Roman nature is a healthy and hearty one,
and you feel it abroad in the streets even when the
sirocco blows and the medium of life seems to proceed

more or less from the mouth of a furnace. But who shall analyse even the simplest Roman impression? It is compounded of so many things, it says so much, it involves so much, it so quickens the intelligence and so flatters the heart, that before we fairly grasp the case the imagination has marked it for her own and exposed us to a perilous likelihood of talking nonsense about it.

The smile of Rome, as I have called it, and its insidious message to those who incline to ramble irresponsibly and take things as they come, is ushered in with the first breath of spring, and then grows and grows with the advancing season till it wraps the whole place in its tenfold charm. As the process develops you can do few better things than go often to Villa Borghese and sit on the grass—on a stout bit of drapery—and watch its exquisite stages. It has a frankness and a sweetness beyond any relenting of *our* clumsy climates even when ours leave off their damnable faces and begin. Nature departs from every reserve with a confidence that leaves one at a loss where, as it were, to look—leaves one, as I say, nothing to do but to lay one's head among the anemones at the base of a high-stemmed pine and gaze up crestward and skyward along its slanting silvery column. You may watch the whole business from a dozen of these choice standpoints and have a different villa for it every day in the week. The Doria, the Ludovisi, the Medici, the Albani, the Wolkonski, the Chigi, the Mellini, the Massimo—there are more of them, with all their sights and sounds and odours and memories, than you have senses for. But I prefer none of them to the Borghese, which is free to all the world at all times and yet never crowded; for when the whirl of carriages is great in the middle regions you may find a hundred untrodden spots and silent corners, tenanted at the worst by a group of those long-skirted young Propagandists who stalk about with solemn angularity, each with a book under his arm, like silhouettes from a mediæval missal, and "compose" so extremely well with the still more processional cypresses and with stretches of golden-russet wall overtopped by ultramarine. And yet if the Borghese is good the Medici is strangely charming, and you may stand in the little belvedere which rises with such surpassing oddity out of the dusky heart of the Boschetto at the latter establishment—a miniature presentation of the wood of the Sleeping Beauty—and look across at the Ludovisi pines lifting their crooked parasols into a sky of what a painter would call the most morbid blue, and declare that the place where *they* grow is the most delightful in the world. Villa Ludovisi has been all winter the residence of the lady familiarly known in Roman society as "Rosina," Victor Emmanuel's morganatic wife, the only familiarity, it would seem, that she allows, for the grounds were rigidly closed, to the inconsolable regret of old Roman sojourners. Just as the nightingales began to sing, however, the quasi-august *padrona* departed, and the public, with certain restrictions, have been admitted to hear them. The place takes, where it lies, a princely ease, and there could be no better example of the expansive tendencies of ancient privilege than the fact that its whole vast extent is contained by the city walls. It has in this respect very much the same enviable air of having got up early that marks the great intramural demesne of Magdalen College at Oxford. The stern old ramparts of Rome form the outer enclosure of the villa, and hence a series of "striking scenic effects" which it would be unscrupulous flattery to say you can imagine. The grounds are laid out in the formal last-century manner; but nowhere do the straight black cypresses lead off the gaze into vistas of a melancholy more charged with associations—poetic, romantic, historic; nowhere are there grander, smoother walls of laurel and myrtle.

I recently spent an afternoon hour at the little Protestant cemetery close to St. Paul's Gate, where the ancient and the modern world are insidiously contrasted. They make between them one of the solemn places of Rome— although indeed when funereal things are so interfused it seems ungrateful to call them sad. Here is a mixture of tears and smiles, of stones and flowers, of mourning cypresses and radiant sky, which gives us the impression of our looking back at death from the brighter side of the grave. The cemetery nestles in an angle of the city wall, and the older graves are sheltered by a mass of ancient brickwork, through whose narrow loopholes you peep at the wide purple of the Campagna. Shelley's grave is here, buried in roses—a happy grave every way for the very type and figure of the Poet. Nothing could be more impenetrably tranquil than this little corner in the bend of the protecting rampart, where a cluster of modern ashes is held tenderly in the rugged hand of the Past. The past is tremendously embodied in the hoary pyramid of Caius Cestius, which rises hard by, half within the wall and half without, cutting solidly into the solid blue of the sky and casting its pagan shadow upon the grass of English graves—that of Keats, among them—with an effect of poetic justice. It is a wonderful confusion of mortality and a grim enough admonition of our helpless promiscuity in the crucible of time. But the most touching element of all is the appeal of the pious English inscriptions among all these Roman memories; touching because of their universal expression of that trouble within trouble, misfortune in a foreign land. Something special stirs the heart through the fine Scriptural language in which everything is recorded. The echoes of massive Latinity with which the atmosphere is charged suggest nothing more majestic and monumental. I may seem unduly to refine, but the injunction to the reader in the monument to Miss Bathurst, drowned in the Tiber in 1824, "If thou art young and lovely, build not thereon, for she who lies beneath thy feet in death was the loveliest flower ever cropt in its bloom," affects us irresistibly as a case for tears on the spot. The whole elaborate inscription indeed says something over and beyond all it does say. The English have the reputation of being the most reticent people in the world, and as there is no smoke without fire I suppose they have done something to deserve it; yet who can say that one doesn't constantly meet the most startling examples of the insular faculty to "gush"? In this instance the mother of the deceased takes the public into her confidence with surprising frankness and omits no detail, seizing the opportunity to mention by the way that she had already lost her husband by a most mysterious visitation. The appeal to one's attention and the confidence in it are withal most moving. The whole record has an old-fashioned gentility that makes its frankness tragic. You seem to hear the garrulity of passionate grief.

To be choosing these positive commonplaces of the Roman tone for a theme when there are matters of modern moment going on may seem none the less to require an apology. But I make no claim to your special correspondent's faculty for getting an "inside" view of things, and I have hardly more than a pictorial impression of the Pope's illness and of the discussion of the Law of the Convents. Indeed I am afraid to speak of the Pope's illness at all, lest I should say something egregiously heartless about it, recalling too forcibly that unnatural husband who was heard to wish that his wife would "either" get well—! He had his reasons, and Roman tourists have theirs in the shape of a vague longing for something spectacular at St. Peter's. If it takes the sacrifice of somebody to produce it let somebody then be sacrificed. Meanwhile we have been having a glimpse of the spectacular side of the Religious Corporations Bill. Hearing one morning a great hubbub in the Corso I stepped forth upon my balcony. A couple of hundred men were strolling slowly down the street with their hands in their pockets, shouting in unison "Abbasso il ministero!" and huzzaing in chorus. Just beneath my window they stopped and began to murmur "Al Quirinale, al Quirinale!" The crowd surged a moment gently and then drifted to the Quirinal, where it scuffled harmlessly with half-a-dozen of the king's soldiers. It ought to have been impressive, for what was it, strictly, unless the seeds of revolution? But its carriage was too gentle and its cries too musical to send the most timorous tourist to packing his trunk. As I began with saying: in Rome, in May, everything has an amiable side, even popular uprisings.

1873. From *Transatlantic Sketches* (1875) and, as here printed, *Italian Hours* (1909).

OCCASIONAL PARIS

It is hard to say exactly what is the profit of comparing one race with another, and weighing in opposed groups the manners and customs of neighbouring countries; but it is certain that as we move about the world we constantly indulge in this exercise. This is especially the case if we happen to be infected with the baleful spirit of the cosmopolite—that uncomfortable consequence of seeing many lands and feeling at home in none. To be a cosmopolite is not, I think, an ideal; the ideal should be to be a concentrated patriot. Being a cosmopolite is an accident, but one must make the best of it. If you have lived about, as the phrase is, you have lost that sense of the absoluteness and the sanctity of the habits of your fellow-patriots which once made you so happy in the midst of them. You have seen that there are a great many *patriæ* in the world, and that each of these is filled with excellent people for whom the local idiosyncrasies are the only thing that is not rather barbarous. There comes a time when one set of customs, wherever it may be found, grows to seem to you about as provincial as another; and then I suppose it may be said of you that you have become a cosmopolite. You have formed the habit of comparing, of looking for points of difference and of resemblance, for present and absent advantages, for the virtues that go with certain defects, and the defects that go with certain virtues. If this is poor work compared with the active practice, in the sphere to which a discriminating Providence has assigned you, of the duties of a tax-payer, an elector, a juryman or a diner-out, there is nevertheless something to be said for it. It is good to think well of mankind, and this, on the whole, a cosmopolite does. If you limit your generalisations to the sphere I mentioned just now, there is a danger that your occasional fits of pessimism may be too sweeping. When you are out of humour the whole country suffers, because at such moments one is never discriminating, and it costs you very little bad logic to lump your fellow-citizens together. But if you are living about, as I say, certain differences impose themselves. The worst you can say of the human race is, for instance, that the Germans are a detestable people. They do not represent the human race for you, as in your native town your fellow-citizens do, and your unflattering judgment has a flattering reverse. If the Germans are detestable, you are mentally saying, there are those admirable French, or those charming Americans, or those interesting English. (Of course it is simply by accident that I couple the German name here with the unfavourable adjective. The epithets may be transposed at will.) Nothing can well be more different from anything else than the English from the French, so that, if you are acquainted with both nations, it may be said that on any special point your agreeable impression of the one implies a censorious attitude toward the other, and *vice versâ*. This has rather a shocking sound; it makes the cosmopolite appear invidious and narrow-minded. But I hasten to add that there seems no real reason why even the most delicate conscience should take alarm. The consequence of the cosmopolite spirit is to initiate you into the merits of all peoples; to convince you that national virtues are numerous, though they may be very different, and to make downright preference really very hard. I have, for instance, every disposition to think better of the English race than of any other except my own. There are things which make it natural I should; there are inducements, provocations, temptations, almost bribes. There have been moments when I have almost burned my ships behind me, and declared that, as it simplified matters greatly to pin one's faith to a chosen people, I would henceforth cease to trouble my head about the lights and shades of the foreign character. I am convinced that if I had taken this reckless engagement, I should greatly have regretted it. You may find a room very comfortable to sit in with the window open, and not like it at all when the window has been shut. If one were to give up the privilege of comparing the

English with other people, one would very soon, in a moment of reaction, make once for all (and most unjustly) such a comparison as would leave the English nowhere. Compare then, I say, as often as the occasion presents itself. The result as regards any particular people, and as regards the human race at large, may be pronounced agreeable, and the process is both instructive and entertaining.

So the author of these observations finds it on returning to Paris after living for upwards of a year in London. He finds himself comparing, and the results of comparison are several disjointed reflections, of which it may be profitable to make a note. Certainly Paris is a very old story, and London is a still older one; and there is no great reason why a journey across the channel and back should quicken one's perspicacity to an unprecedented degree. I therefore will not pretend to have been looking at Paris with new eyes, or to have gathered on the banks of the Seine a harvest of extraordinary impressions. I will only pretend that a good many old impressions have recovered their freshness, and that there is a sort of renovated entertainment in looking at the most brilliant city in the world with eyes attuned to a different pitch. Never, in fact, have those qualities of brightness and gaiety that are half the stock-in-trade of the city by the Seine seemed to me more uncontestable. The autumn is but half over, and Paris is, in common parlance, empty. The private houses are closed, the lions have returned to the jungle, the Champs Elysées are not at all "mondains." But I have never seen Paris more Parisian, in the pleasantest sense of the word; better humoured, more open-windowed, more naturally entertaining. A radiant September helps the case; but doubtless the matter is, as I hinted above, in a large degree "subjective." For when one comes to the point there is nothing very particular just now for Paris to rub her hands about. The Exhibition of 1878 is looming up as large as a mighty mass of buildings on the Trocadéro can make it. These buildings are very magnificent and fantastical; they hang over the Seine, in their sudden immensity and glittering newness, like a palace in a fairy-tale. But the trouble is that most people appear to regard the Exhibition as in fact a fairy-tale. They speak of the wonderful structures on the Champ de Mars and the Trocadéro as a predestined monument to the folly of a group of gentlemen destitute of a sense of the opportune. The moment certainly does not seem very well chosen for inviting the world to come to Paris to amuse itself. The world is too much occupied with graver cares—with reciprocal cannonading and chopping, with cutting of throats and burning of homes, with murder of infants and mutilation of mothers, with warding off famine and civil war, with lamenting the failure of its resources, the dulness of trade, the emptiness of its pockets. Rome is burning altogether too fast for even its most irresponsible spirits to find any great satisfaction in fiddling. But even if there is (as there very well may be) a certain scepticism at headquarters as to the accomplishment of this graceful design, there is no apparent hesitation, and everything is going forward as rapidly as if mankind were breathless with expectation. That familiar figure, the Parisian *ouvrier*, with his white, chalky blouse, his attenuated person, his clever face, is more familiar than ever, and I suppose, finding plenty of work to his hand, is for the time in a comparatively rational state of mind. He swarms in thousands, not only in the region of the Exhibition, but along the great thoroughfare—the Avenue de l'Opéra —which has just been opened in the interior of Paris.

This is an extremely Parisian creation, and as it is

really a great convenience—it will save a great many steps and twists and turns—I suppose it should be spoken of with gratitude and admiration. But I confess that to my sense it belongs primarily to that order of benefits which during the twenty years of the Empire gradually deprived the streets of Paris of nine-tenths of their ancient individuality. The deadly monotony of the Paris that M. Haussmann called into being—its huge, blank, pompous, featureless sameness—sometimes comes over the wandering stranger with a force that leads him to devote the author of these miles of architectural commonplace to execration. The new street is quite on the imperial system; it must make the late Napoleon III. smile with beatific satisfaction as he looks down upon it from the Bonapartist corner of Paradise. It stretches straight away from the pompous façade of the Opéra to the doors of the Théâtre Français, and it must be admitted that there is something fine in the vista that is closed at one end by the great sculptured and gilded mass of the former building. But it smells of the modern asphalt; it is lined with great white houses that are adorned with machine-made arabesques, and each of which is so exact a copy of all the rest that even the little white porcelain number on a blue ground, which looks exactly like all the other numbers, hardly constitutes an identity. Presently there will be a long succession of milliners' and chocolate-makers' shops in the basement of this homogeneous row, and the pretty bonnets and bonbonnières in the shining windows will have their ribbons knotted with a *chic* that you must come to Paris to see. Then there will be little glazed sentry-boxes at regular intervals along the curbstone, in which churlish old women will sit selling half a dozen copies of each of the newspapers; and over the hardened bitumen the young Parisian of our day will constantly circulate, looking rather pallid and wearing very large shirt-cuffs. And the new avenue will be a great success, for it will place in symmetrical communication two of the most important establishments in France— the temple of French music and the temple of French comedy.

I said just now that no two things could well be more unlike than England and France; and though the remark is not original, I uttered it with the spontaneity that it must have on the lips of a traveller who, having left either country, has just disembarked in the other. It is of course by this time a very trite observation, but it will continue to be made so long as Boulogne remains the same lively antithesis of Folkestone. An American, conscious of the family-likeness diffused over his own huge continent, never quite unlearns his surprise at finding that so little of either of these two almost contiguous towns has rubbed off upon the other. He is surprised at certain English people feeling so far away from France, and at all French people feeling so far away from England. I travelled from Boulogne the other day in the same railway-carriage with a couple of amiable and ingenuous young Britons, who had come over to spend ten days in Paris. It was their first landing in France; they had never yet quitted their native island; and in the course of a little conversation that I had with them I was struck with the scantiness of their information in regard to French manners and customs. They were very intelligent lads; they were apparently fresh from a university; but in respect to the interesting country they were about to enter, their minds were almost a blank. If the conductor, appearing at the carriage door to ask for our tickets, had had the leg of a frog sticking out of his pocket, I think their only very definite preconception would have been confirmed. I parted

with them at the Paris station, and I have no doubt that
they very soon began to make precious discoveries;
and I have alluded to them not in the least to throw
ridicule upon their "insularity"—which indeed, being
accompanied with great modesty, I thought a very
pretty spectacle—but because having become, since
my last visit to France, a little insular myself, I was more
conscious of the emotions that attend on an arrival.

The brightness always seems to begin while you are
still out in the channel, when you fairly begin to see the
French coast. You pass into a region of intenser light—
a zone of clearness and colour. These properties brighten
and deepen as you approach the land, and when you
fairly stand upon that good Boulognese quay, among
the blue and red douaniers and soldiers, the small ugly
men in cerulean blouses, the charming fishwives, with
their folded kerchiefs and their crisp cap-frills, their
short striped petticoats, their tightly-drawn stockings,
and their little clicking sabots—when you look about
you at the smokeless air, at the pink and yellow houses,
at the white-fronted café, close at hand, with its bright
blue letters, its mirrors and marble-topped tables, its
white-aproned, alert, undignified waiter, grasping a
huge coffee-pot by a long handle—when you perceive
all these things you feel the additional savour that foreignness gives to the picturesque; or feel rather, I should
say, that simple foreignness may itself make the picturesque; for certainly the elements in the picture I have
just sketched are not especially exquisite. No matter;
you are amused, and your amusement continues—being sensibly stimulated by a visit to the buffet at the
railway-station, which is better than the refreshment-
room at Folkestone. It is a pleasure to have people offering you soup again, of their own movement; it is a
pleasure to find a little pint of Bordeaux standing natu-

rally before your plate; it is a pleasure to have a napkin; it is a pleasure, above all, to take up one of the good long sticks of French bread—as bread is called the staff of life, the French bake it literally in the shape of staves—and break off a loose, crisp, crusty morsel.

There are impressions, certainly, that imperil your good-humour. No honest Anglo-Saxon can like a French railway-station; and I was on the point of adding that no honest Anglo-Saxon can like a French railway-official. But I will not go so far as that; after all I cannot remember any great harm that such a functionary has ever done me—except in locking me up as a malefactor. It is necessary to say, however, that the honest Anglo-Saxon, in a French railway-station, is in a state of chronic irritation—an irritation arising from his sense of the injurious effect upon the genial French nature of the possession of an administrative uniform. I believe that the consciousness of brass buttons on his coat and stripes on his trousers has spoiled many a modest and amiable Frenchman, and the sight of these aggressive insignia always stirs within me a moral protest. I repeat that my aversion to them is partly theoretic, for I have found, as a general thing, that an inquiry civilly made extracts a civil answer from even the most official-looking personage. But I have also found that such a personage's measure of the civility due to him is inordinately large; if he places himself in any degree at your service, it is apparently from the sense that true greatness can afford to unbend. You are constantly reminded that you must not presume. In England these intimations never proceed from one's "inferiors." In France the "administration" is the first thing that touches you; in a little while you get used to it, but you feel somehow that, in the process, you have lost the flower of your self-respect. Of course you are under some obligation to it. It has taken you off the steamer at Boulogne;[1] made you tell your name to a gentleman with a sword, stationed at the farther end of the plank—not a drawn sword, it is true, but still, at the best, a very nasty weapon; marshalled you into the railway-station; assigned you to a carriage—I was going to say to a seat; transported you to Paris, marshalled you again out of the train, and under a sort of military surveillance, into an enclosure containing a number of human sheeppens, in one of which it has imprisoned you for some half-hour. I am always on the point, in these places, of asking one of my gaolers if I may not be allowed to walk about on parole. The administration at any rate has finally taken you out of your pen, and, through the medium of a functionary who "inscribes" you in a little book, transferred you to a cab selected by a logic of its own. In doing all this it has certainly done a great deal for you; but somehow its good offices have made you feel sombre and resentful. The other day, on arriving from London, while I was waiting for my luggage, I saw several of the porters who convey travellers' impedimenta to the cab come up and deliver over the coin they had just received for this service to a functionary posted *ad hoc* in a corner, and armed with a little book in which he noted down these remittances. The *pourboires* are apparently thrown into a common fund and divided among the guild of porters. The system is doubtless an excellent one, excellently carried out; but the sight of the poor round-shouldered man of burdens dropping his coin into the hand of the official arithmetician was to my fancy but another reminder that the

[1] James's text—*Portraits of Places* (Boston, [1883] 1884) —has "Folkestone" here; obviously it should be "Boulogne." [*Editor's note.*]

individual, as an individual, loses by all that the administration assumes.

After living a while in England you observe the individual in Paris with quickened attention; and I think it must be said that at first he makes an indifferent figure. You are struck with the race being physically and personally a poorer one than that great family of largely-modelled, fresh-coloured people you have left upon the other side of the channel. I remember that in going to England a year ago and disembarking of a dismal, sleety Sunday evening at Folkestone, the first thing that struck me was the good looks of the railway porters —their broad shoulders, their big brown beards, their well-cut features. In like manner, landing lately at Boulogne of a brilliant Sunday morning, it was impossible not to think the little men in numbered caps who were gesticulating and chattering in one's path, rather ugly fellows. In arriving from other countries one is struck with a certain want of dignity in the French face. I do not know, however, whether this is anything worse than the fact that the French face is expressive; for it may be said that, in a certain sense, to express anything is to compromise with one's dignity, which likes to be understood without taking trouble. As regards the lower classes, at any rate, the impression I speak of always passes away; you perceive that the good looks of the French working-people are to be found in their look of intelligence. These people, in Paris, strike me afresh as the cleverest, the most perceptive, and intellectually speaking, the most human of their kind. The Paris *ouvrier*, with his democratic blouse, his expressive, demonstrative, agreeable eye, his meagre limbs, his irregular, pointed features, his sallow complexion, his face at once fatigued and animated, his light, nervous organisation, is a figure that I always encounter again with pleasure. In some cases he looks depraved and perverted, but at his worst he looks refined; he is full of vivacity of perception, of something that one can appeal to.

It takes some courage to say this, perhaps, after reading *L'Assommoir;* but in M. Émile Zola's extraordinary novel one must make the part, as the French say, of the horrible uncleanness of the author's imagination. *L'Assommoir,* I have been told, has had great success in the lower walks of Parisian life; and if this fact is not creditable to the delicacy of M. Zola's humble readers, it proves a good deal in favour of their intelligence. With all its grossness the book in question is essentially a literary performance; you must be tolerably clever to appreciate it. It is highly appreciated, I believe, by the young ladies who live in the region of the Latin Quarter—those young ladies who thirty years ago were called grisettes, and now are called I don't know what. They know long passages by heart; they repeat them with infinite gusto. "Ce louchon d'Augustine"—the horrible little girl with a squint, who is always playing nasty tricks and dodging slaps and projectiles in Gervaise's shop, is their particular favourite; and it must be admitted that "ce louchon d'Augustine" is, as regards reality, a wonderful creation.

If Parisians, both small and great, have more of the intellectual stamp than the people one sees in London, it is striking, on the other hand, that the people of the better sort in Paris look very much less "respectable." I did not know till I came back to Paris how used I had grown to the English *cachet;* but I immediately found myself missing it. You miss it in the men much more than in the women; for the well-to-do Frenchwoman of the lower orders, as one sees her in public, in the streets and in shops, is always a delightfully comfortable and creditable person. I must confess to the highest admiration for her, an admiration that increases with acquaintance. She, at least, is essentially respectable; the neatness, compactness, and sobriety of her dress, the decision of her movement and accent suggest the civic and domestic virtues—order, thrift, frugality, the moral necessity of making a good appearance. It is, I think, an old story that to the stranger in France the women seem greatly superior to the men. Their superiority, in fact, appears to be conceded; for wherever you turn you meet them in the forefront of action. You meet them, indeed, too often; you pronounce them at times obtrusive. It is annoying when you go to order your boots or your shirts, to have to make known your desires to even the most neat-waisted female attendant; for the limitations to the feminine intellect are, though few in number, distinct, and women are not able to understand certain masculine needs. Mr. Worth makes ladies' dresses; but I am sure there will never be a fashionable tailoress. There are, however, points at which, from the commercial point of view, feminine assistance is invaluable. For insisting upon the merits of an article that has failed to satisfy you, talking you over, and making you take it; for defending a disputed bill, for paying the necessary compliments or supplying the necessary impertinence—for all these things the neat-waisted sex has peculiar and precious faculties. In the commercial class in Paris the man always appeals to the woman; the woman always steps forward. The woman always proposes the conditions of a bargain. Go about and look for furnished rooms, you always encounter a concierge and his wife. When you ask the price of the rooms, the woman takes the words out of her husband's mouth, if indeed he have not first turned to her with a questioning look. She takes you in hand; she proposes conditions; she thinks of things he would not have thought of.

What I meant just now by my allusion to the absence of the "respectable" in the appearance of the Parisian population was that the men do not look like gentlemen, as so many Englishmen do. The average Frenchman that one encounters in public is of so different a type from the average Englishman that you can easily believe that to the end of time the two will not understand each other. The Frenchman has always, comparatively speaking, a Bohemian, empirical look; the expression of his face, its colouring, its movement, have not been toned down to the neutral complexion of that breeding for which in English speech we reserve the epithet of "good." He is at once more artificial and more natural; the former where the Englishman is positive, the latter where the Englishman is negative. He takes off his hat with a flourish to a friend, but the Englishman never bows. He ties a knot in the end of a napkin and thrusts it into his shirt-collar, so that, as he sits at breakfast, the napkin may serve the office of a pinafore. Such an operation as that seems to the Englishman as *naïf* as the flourishing of one's hat is pretentious.

I sometimes go to breakfast at a café on the Boulevard, which I formerly used to frequent with considerable regularity. Coming back there the other day, I found exactly the same group of habitués at their little tables, and I mentally exclaimed as I looked at them over my newspaper, upon their unlikeness to the gentlemen who confront you in the same attitude at a London club. Who are they? what are they? On these points I have no information; but the stranger's imagination does not seem to see a majestic social order massing itself behind them as it usually does in London. He goes so far as to suspect that what is behind them is not adapted for exhibition; whereas your Englishmen, whatever may be the defects of their personal character, or the irregularities of their conduct, are pressed upon from the rear by an immense body of private proprieties and comforts, of domestic conventions and theological observances. But it is agreeable all the same to come back to a café of which you have formerly been an habitué. Adolphe or Édouard, in his long white apron and his large patent-leather slippers, has a perfect recollection of "les habitudes de Monsieur." He remembers the table you preferred, the wine you drank, the newspaper you read. He greets you with the friendliest of smiles, and remarks that it is a long time since he has had the pleasure of seeing Monsieur. There is something in this simple remark very touching to a heart that has suffered from that incorruptible dumbness of the British domestic. But in Paris such a heart finds consolation at every step; it is reminded of that most classic quality of the French nature—its sociability; a sociability which operates here as it never does in England, from below upward. Your waiter utters a greeting because, after all, something human within him prompts him; his instinct bids him say something, and his taste recommends that it be agreeable. The obvious reflection is that a waiter must not say too much, even for the sake of being human. But in France the people always like to make the little extra remark, to throw in something above the simple necessary. I stop before a little man who is selling newspapers at a street-corner, and ask him for the *Journal des Débats*. His answer deserves to be literally given: "Je ne l'ai plus, Monsieur; mais je pourrai vous donner quelquechose à peu près dans le même genre—la *République Française*." Even a person of his humble condition must have had a lurking sense of the comicality of offering anything as an equivalent for the "genre" of the venerable, classic, academic *Débats*. But my friend could not bear to give me a naked, monosyllabic refusal.

There are two things that the returning observer is likely to do with as little delay as possible. One is to dine at some *cabaret* of which he retains a friendly memory; another is to betake himself to the Théâtre Français. It is early in the season; there are no new pieces; but I have taken great pleasure in seeing some of the old ones. I lost no time in going to see Mademoiselle Sarah Bernhardt in *Andromaque*. *Andromaque* is not a novelty, but Mademoiselle Sarah Bernhardt has a perennial freshness. The play has been revived, to enable her to represent not the great part, the injured and passionate Hermione, but that of the doleful funereal widow of Hector. This part is a poor one; it is narrow and monotonous, and offers few brilliant opportunities. But the actress knows how to make opportunities, and she has here a very sufficient one for crossing her thin white arms over her nebulous black robes, and sighing forth in silver accents her dolorous rhymes. Her rendering of the part is one more proof of her singular intelligence—of the fineness of her artistic nature. As there is not a great deal to be done with it in the way of declamation, she has made the most of its plastic side. She understands the art of motion and attitude as no one else does, and her extraordinary personal grace never fails her. Her Andromaque has postures of the most poetic picturesqueness—something that suggests the broken stem and drooping head of a flower that had been rudely plucked. She bends over her classic confidant like the figure of Bereavement on a bas-relief, and she has a marvellous manner of lifting and throwing back her delicate arms, locking them together, and passing them behind her hanging head.

The *Demi-Monde* of M. Dumas *fils* is not a novelty either; but I quite agree with M. Francisque Sarcey that it is on the whole, in form, the first comedy of our day. I have seen it several times, but I never see it without being forcibly struck with its merits. For the drama of our time it must always remain the model. The interest of the story, the quiet art with which it is unfolded, the naturalness and soberness of the means that are used, and by which great effects are produced, the brilliancy and richness of the dialogue—all these things make it a singularly perfect and interesting work. Of course it is admirably well played at the Théâtre Français. Madame d'Ange was originally a part of too great amplitude for Mademoiselle Croizette; but she is gradually filling it out and taking possession of it; she begins to give a sense of the "calme infernal," which George Sand somewhere mentions as the leading attribute of the character. As for Delaunay, he does nothing better, more vividly and gallantly, than Olivier de Jalin. When I say gallantry I say it with qualification; for what a very queer fellow is this M. de Jalin! In seeing the *Demi-Monde* again I was more than ever struck with the oddity of its morality and with the way that the ideal of fine conduct differs in different nations. The *Demi-Monde* is the history of the eager, the almost heroic, effort of a clever and superior woman, who has been guilty of what the French call "faults," to pass from the irregular and equivocal circle to which these faults have consigned her into what is distinctively termed "good society." The only way in which the passage can be effected is by her marrying an honourable man; and to induce an honourable man to marry her, she must suppress the more discreditable facts of her career. Taking her for an honest woman, Raymond de Nanjac falls in love with her, and honestly proposes to make her his wife. But Raymond de Nanjac has contracted an intimate friendship with Olivier de Jalin, and the action of the play is more especially De Jalin's attempt—a successful one—to rescue his friend from the ignominy of a union with Suzanne d'Ange. Jalin knows a great deal about her, for the simple reason that he has been her lover. Their relations have been most harmonious, but from the moment that Suzanne sets her cap at Nanjac, Olivier declares war. Suzanne struggles hard to keep possession of her suitor, who is very much in love with her, and Olivier spares no pains to detach him. It is the means that Olivier uses that excite the wonderment of the Anglo-Saxon spectator. He takes the ground that in such a cause all means are fair, and when, at the climax of the play, he tells a thumping lie in order to make Madame d'Ange compromise herself, expose herself, he is pronounced by the author "le plus honnête homme que je connaisse." Madame d'Ange, as I have said, is a superior woman; the interest of the play is in her being a superior woman. Olivier has been her lover; he himself is one of the reasons why she may not marry Nanjac; he has given her a push along the downward path. But it is curious how little this is held by the author to disqualify him from fighting the battle in which she is so much the weaker combatant. An English-speaking audience is more "moral" than a French, more easily scandalised; and yet it is a singular fact that if the *Demi-Monde* were represented before an English-speaking audience, its sympathies would certainly not go with M. de Jalin. It would pronounce him rather a coward. Is it because such an audience, although it has not nearly such a pretty collection of pedestals to place under the feet of the charming sex, has, after all, in default of this degree of gallantry, a tenderness more fundamental? Madame d'Ange has stained herself, and it is doubtless not at all proper that such ladies should be led to the altar by honourable young men. The point is not that the English-speaking audience would be disposed to condone Madame d'Ange's irregularities, but that it would remain perfectly cold before the spectacle of her ex-lover's masterly campaign against her, and quite fail to think it positively admirable, or to regard the fib by which he finally clinches his victory as a proof of exceptional honesty. The ideal of our own audience would be expressed in some such words as, "I say, that's not fair game. Can't you let the poor woman alone?"

1877 (so dated by James). From *Portraits of Places* (1883).

LONDON

I

There is a certain evening that I count as virtually a first impression,—the end of a wet, black Sunday, twenty years ago, about the first of March. There had been an earlier vision, but it had turned to grey, like faded ink, and the occasion I speak of was a fresh beginning. No doubt I had mystic prescience of how fond of the murky modern Babylon I was one day to become; certain it is that as I look back I find every small circumstance of those hours of approach and arrival still as vivid as if the solemnity of an opening era had breathed upon it. The sense of approach was already almost intolerably strong at Liverpool, where, as I remember, the perception of the English character of everything was as acute as a surprise, though it could only be a surprise without a shock. It was expectation exquisitely gratified, super-abundantly confirmed. There was a kind of wonder indeed that England should be as English as, for my entertainment, she took the trouble to be; but the wonder would have been greater, and all the pleasure absent, if the sensation had not been violent. It seems to sit there again like a visiting presence, as it sat opposite to me at breakfast at a small table in a window of the old coffee-room of the Adelphi Hotel—the unextended (as it then was), the unimproved, the unblushingly local Adelphi. Liverpool is not a romantic city, but that smoky Saturday returns to me as a supreme success, measured by its association with the kind of emotion in the hope of which, for the most part, we betake ourselves to far countries.

It assumed this character at an early hour—or rather, indeed, twenty-four hours before—with the sight, as one looked across the wintry ocean, of the strange, dark, lonely freshness of the coast of Ireland. Better still, before we could come up to the city, were the black steamers knocking about in the yellow Mersey, under a sky so low that they seemed to touch it with their funnels, and in the thickest, windiest light. Spring was already in the air, in the town; there was no rain, but there was still less sun—one wondered what had become, on this side of the world, of the big white splotch in the heavens; and the grey mildness, shading away into black at every pretext, appeared in itself a promise. This was how it hung about me, between the window and the fire, in the coffee-room of the hotel—late in the morning for breakfast, as we had been long disembarking The other passengers had dispersed, knowingly catching trains for London (we had only been a handful); I had the place to myself, and I felt as if I had an exclusive property in the impression. I prolonged it, I sacrificed to it, and it is perfectly recoverable now, with the very taste of the national muffin, the creak of the waiter's shoes as he came and went (could anything be so English as his intensely professional back? it revealed a country of tradition), and the rustle of the newspaper I was too excited to read.

I continued to sacrifice for the rest of the day; it didn't seem to me a sentient thing, as yet, to enquire into the means of getting away. My curiosity must indeed have languished, for I found myself on the morrow in the slowest of Sunday trains, pottering up to London with an interruptedness which might have been tedious without the conversation of an old gentleman who shared the carriage with me and to whom my alien as well as comparatively youthful character had betrayed itself. He instructed me as to the sights of London and impressed upon me that nothing was more worthy of my attention than the great cathedral of St. Paul. "Have you seen St. Peter's in Rome? St. Peter's is more highly embellished, you know; but you may depend upon it that St. Paul's is the better building of the two." The impression I began with speaking of was, strictly, that of the drive from Euston, after dark, to Morley's Hotel in Trafalgar Square. It was not lovely—it was in fact rather horrible; but as I move again through dusky, tortuous miles, in the greasy four-wheeler to which my luggage had compelled me to commit myself, I recognise the first step in an initiation of which the subsequent stages were to abound in pleasant things. It is a kind of humiliation in a great city not to know where you are going, and Morley's Hotel was then, to my imagination, only a vague ruddy spot in the general immensity. The immensity was the great fact, and that was a charm; the miles of housetops and viaducts, the complication of junctions and signals through which the train made its way to the station had already given me the scale. The weather had turned to wet, and we went deeper and deeper into the Sunday night. The sheep in the fields, on the way from Liverpool, had shown in their demeanour a certain consciousness of the day; but this momentous cab-drive was an introduction to the rigidities of custom. The low black houses were as inanimate as so many rows of coal-scuttles, save where at frequent corners, from a gin-shop, there was a flare of light more brutal still than the darkness. The custom of gin—that was equally rigid, and in this first impression the public-houses counted for much.

Morley's Hotel proved indeed to be a ruddy spot; brilliant, in my recollection, is the coffee-room fire, the hospitable mohogany, the sense that in the stupendous city this, at any rate for the hour, was a shelter and a point of view. My remembrance of the rest of the evening—I was probably very tired—is mainly a remembrance of a vast four-poster. My little bedroom-candle, set in its deep basin, caused this monument to project a huge shadow and to make me think, I scarce knew why, of *The Ingoldsby Legends*. If at a tolerably early hour the next day I found myself approaching St. Paul's, it was not wholly in obedience to the old gentleman in the railway-carriage: I had an errand in the City, and the City was doubtless prodigious. But what I mainly recall is the romantic consciousness of passing under the Temple Bar, and the way two lines of *Henry Esmond* repeated themselves in my mind as I drew near the masterpiece of Sir Christopher Wren. "The stout, red-

faced woman" whom Esmond had seen tearing after the
stag-hounds over the slopes at Windsor was not a bit
like the effigy "which turns its stony back upon St. Paul's
and faces the coaches struggling up Ludgate Hill." As I
looked at Queen Anne over the apron of my hansom—
she struck me as very small and dirty, and the vehicle
ascended the mild incline without an effort—it was a
thrilling thought that the statue had been familiar to
the hero of the incomparable novel. All history appeared
to live again, and the continuity of things to vibrate
through my mind.

To this hour, as I pass along the Strand, I take again
the walk I took there that afternoon. I love the place
to-day, and that was the commencement of my passion.
It appeared to me to present phenomena, and to contain
objects of every kind, of an inexhaustible interest; in
particular it struck me as desirable and even indispensable that I should purchase most of the articles in most
of the shops. My eyes rest with a certain tenderness on
the places where I resisted and on those where I succumbed. The fragrance of Mr. Rimmel's establishment
is again in my nostrils; I see the slim young lady (I hear
her pronunciation) who waited upon me there. Sacred
to me to-day is the particular aroma of the hair-wash
that I bought of her. I pause before the granite portico
of Exeter Hall (it was unexpectedly narrow and
wedge-like), and it evokes a cloud of associations which
are none the less impressive because they are vague;
coming from I don't know where—from *Punch,* from
Thackeray, from volumes of the *Illustrated London
News* turned over in childhood; seeming connected
with Mrs. Beecher Stowe and *Uncle Tom's Cabin.* Memorable is a rush I made into a glover's at Charing Cross
—the one you pass, going eastward, just before you

turn into the station; that, however, now that I think of it, must have been in the morning, as soon as I issued from the hotel. Keen within me was a sense of the importance of deflowering, of despoiling the shop.

A day or two later, in the afternoon, I found myself staring at my fire, in a lodging of which I had taken possession on foreseeing that I should spend some weeks in London. I had just come in, and, having attended to the distribution of my luggage, sat down to consider my habitation. It was on the ground floor, and the fading daylight reached it in a sadly damaged condition. It struck me as stuffy and unsocial, with its mouldy smell and its decoration of lithographs and wax-flowers—an impersonal black hole in the huge general blackness. The uproar of Piccadilly hummed away at the end of the street, and the rattle of a heartless hansom passed close to my ears. A sudden horror of the whole place came over me, like a tiger-pounce of homesickness which had been watching its moment. London was hideous, vicious, cruel, and above all overwhelming; whether or no she was "careful of the type," she was as indifferent as Nature herself to the single life. In the course of an hour I should have to go out to my dinner, which was not supplied on the premises, and that effort assumed the form of a desperate and dangerous quest. It appeared to me that I would rather remain dinnerless, would rather even starve, than sally forth into the infernal town, where the natural fate of an obscure stranger would be to be trampled to death in Piccadilly and have his carcass thrown into the Thames. I did not starve, however, and I eventually attached myself by a hundred human links to the dreadful, delightful city. That momentary vision of its smeared face and stony heart has remained memorable to me, but I am happy to say that I can easily summon up others.

II

It is, no doubt, not the taste of every one, but for the real London-lover the mere immensity of the place is a large part of its savour. A small London would be an abomination, as it fortunately is an impossibility, for the idea and the name are beyond everything an expression of extent and number. Practically, of course, one lives in a quarter, in a plot; but in imagination and by a constant mental act of reference the accommodated haunter enjoys the whole—and it is only of him that I deem it worth while to speak. He fancies himself, as they say, for being a particle in so unequalled an aggregation; and its immeasurable circumference, even though unvisited and lost in smoke, gives him the sense of a social, an intellectual margin. There is a luxury in the knowledge that he may come and go without being noticed, even when his comings and goings have no nefarious end. I don't mean by this that the tongue of London is not a very active member; the tongue of London would indeed be worthy of a chapter by itself. But the eyes which at least in some measure feed its activity are fortunately for the common advantage solicited at any moment by a thousand different objects. If the place is big, everything it contains is certainly not so; but this may at least be said—that if small questions play a part there, they play it without illusions about its importance. There are too many questions, small or great; and each day, as it arrives, leads its children, like a kind of mendicant mother, by the hand. Therefore perhaps the most general characteristic is the absence of insistence. Habits and inclinations flourish and fall, but intensity is never one of them. The spirit of the great city is not analytic, and, as they come up, subjects rarely receive at its hands a treatment drearily earnest or tastelessly thorough. There are not many—of those of which London disposes with the assurance begotten of its large experience—that wouldn't lend themselves to a tenderer manipulation elsewhere. It takes a very great affair, a turn of the Irish screw or a divorce case lasting many days, to be fully threshed out. The mind of Mayfair, when it aspires to show what it really can do, lives in the hope of a new divorce case, and an indulgent providence—London is positively in certain ways the spoiled child of the world—abundantly recognises this particular aptitude and humours the whim.

The compensation is that material does arise; that there is a great variety, if not morbid subtlety; and that the whole of the procession of events and topics passes across your stage. For the moment I am speaking of the inspiration there may be in the sense of far frontiers; the London-lover loses himself in this swelling consciousness, delights in the idea that the town which encloses him is after all only a paved country, a state by itself. This is his condition of mind quite as much if he be an adoptive as if he be a matter-of-course son. I am by no means sure even that he need be of Anglo-Saxon race and have inherited the birthright of English speech; though, on the other hand, I make no doubt that these advantages minister greatly to closeness of allegiance. The great city spreads her dusky mantle over innumerable races and creeds, and I believe there is scarcely a known form of worship that has not some temple there (have I not attended at the Church of Humanity, in Lamb's Conduit, in company with an American lady, a vague old gentleman, and several seamstresses?) or any communion of men that has not some club or guild. London is indeed an epitome of the round world, and just as it is a commonplace to say that there is nothing one can't "get" there, so it is equally true that there is nothing one may not study at first hand.

One doesn't test these truths every day, but they form part of the air one breathes (and welcome, says the London-hater,—for there be such perverse reasoners,—to the pestilent compound). They colour the thick, dim distances which in my opinion are the most romantic town-vistas in the world; they mingle with the troubled light to which the straight, ungarnished aperture in one's dull, undistinctive house-front affords a passage and which makes an interior of friendly corners, mysterious tones, and unbetrayed ingenuities, as well as with the low, magnificent medium of the sky, where the smoke and fog and the weather in general, the strangely undefined hour of the day and season of the year, the emanations of industries and the reflection of furnaces, the red gleams and blurs that may or may not be of sunset—as you never see any *source* of radiance, you can't in the least tell—all hang together in a confusion, a complication, a shifting but irremoveable canopy. They form the undertone of the deep, perpetual voice of the place. One remembers them when one's loyalty is on the defensive; when it is a question of introducing as many striking features as possible into the list of fine reasons one has sometimes to draw up, that eloquent catalogue with which one confronts the hostile indictment—the array of *other* reasons which may easily be as long as one's arm. According to these other reasons it plausibly and conclusively stands that, as a place to be happy in, London will never do. I don't say it is necessary to meet so absurd an allegation except for one's personal complacency. If indifference, in so gorged an organism, is still livelier than curiosity, you may avail yourself of your own share in it simply to feel that since such and such a person doesn't care for real richness, so much the worse for such and such a person. But once in a while the best believer recognises the impulse to set his religion in order, to sweep the temple of his thoughts and trim the sacred lamp. It is at such hours as this that he reflects with elation that the British capital is the particular spot in the world which communicates the greatest sense of life.

III

The reader will perceive that I do not shrink even from the extreme concession of speaking of our capital as British, and this in a shameless connection with the question of loyalty on the part of an adoptive son. For I hasten to explain that if half the source of one's interest in it comes from feeling that it is the property and even the home of the human race,—Hawthorne, that best of Americans, says so somewhere, and places it in this sense side by side with Rome,—one's appreciation of it is really a large sympathy, a comprehensive love of humanity. For the sake of such a charity as this one may stretch one's allegiance; and the most alien of the cockneyfied, though he may bristle with every protest at the intimation that England has set its stamp upon him, is free to admit with conscious pride that he has submitted to Londonisation. It is a real stroke of luck for a particular country that the capital of the human race happens to be British. Surely every other people would have it theirs if they could. Whether the English deserve to hold it any longer might be an interesting field of enquiry; but as they have not yet let it slip, the writer of these lines professes without scruple that the arrangement is to his personal taste. For, after all, if the sense of life is greatest there, it is a sense of the life of people of our consecrated English speech. It is the headquarters of that strangely elastic tongue; and I make this remark with a full sense of the terrible way in which the idiom is misused by the populace in general, than whom it has been given to few races to impart to conversation less of the charm of tone. For a man of letters who endeavours to cultivate, however modestly, the medium of Shakespeare and Milton, of Hawthorne and Emerson, who cherishes the notion of what it has achieved and what it may even yet achieve, London must ever have a great illustrative and suggestive value, and indeed a kind of sanctity. It is the single place in which most readers, most possible lovers, are gathered together; it is the most inclusive public and the largest social incarnation of the language, of the tradition. Such a personage may well let it go for this, and leave the German and the Greek to speak for themselves, to express the grounds of *their* predilection, presumably very different.

When a social product is so vast and various, it may be approached on a thousand different sides, and liked and disliked for a thousand different reasons. The reasons of Piccadilly are not those of Camden Town, nor are the curiosities and discouragements of Kilburn the same as those of Westminster and Lambeth. The reasons of Piccadilly—I mean the friendly ones—are those of which, as a general thing, the rooted visitor remains most conscious; but it must be confessed that even these, for the most part, do not lie upon the surface. The absence of style, or rather of the intention of style, is certainly the most general characteristic of the face of London. To cross to Paris under this impression is to find one's self surrounded with far other standards. There everything reminds you that the idea of beautiful and stately arrangement has never been out of fashion, that the art of composition has always been at work or at play. Avenues and squares, gardens and quays, have been distributed for effect, and to-day the splendid city reaps the accumulation of all this ingenuity. The result is not in every quarter interesting, and there is a tiresome monotony of the "fine" and the symmetrical, above all, of the deathly passion for making things "to match." On the other hand the whole air of the place is architectural. On the banks of the Thames it is a tremendous chapter of accidents—the London-lover has to confess to the existence of miles upon miles of the dreariest, stodgiest commonness. Thousands of acres are covered by low black houses of the cheapest construction, without ornament, without grace, without character or even identity. In fact there are many, even in the best quarters, in all the region of Mayfair and Belgravia, of so paltry and inconvenient, especially of so diminutive a type (those that are let in lodgings—such poor lodgings as they make—may serve as an example), that you wonder what peculiarly limited domestic need they were constructed to meet. The great misfortune of London to the eye (it is true that this remark applies much less to the City), is the want of elevation. There is no architectural impression without a certain degree of height, and the London street-vista has none of that sort of pride.

All the same, if there be not the intention, there is at least the accident, of style, which, if one looks at it in a friendly way, appears to proceed from three sources. One of these is simply the general greatness, and the manner in which that makes a difference for the better in any particular spot; so that, though you may often perceive yourself to be in a shabby corner, it never occurs to you that this is the end of it. Another is the atmosphere, with its magnificent mystifications, which flatters and superfuses, makes everything brown, rich, dim, vague, magnifies distances and minimises details, confirms the inference of vastness by suggesting that, as the great city makes everything, it makes its own system of weather and its own optical laws. The last is the congregation of the parks, which constitute an ornament not esewhere to be matched, and give the place a superiority that none of its uglinesses overcome. They spread themselves with such a luxury of space in the centre of the town that they form a part of the impression of any walk, of almost any view, and, with an audacity altogether their own, make a pastoral landscape under the smoky sky. There is no mood of the rich London climate that is not becoming to them—I have seen them look delightfully romantic, like parks in novels, in the wettest winter—and there is scarcely a mood of the appreciative resident to which they have not something to say. The high things of London, which here and there peep over them, only make the spaces vaster by reminding you that you are, after all, not in Kent or Yorkshire; and these things, whatever they be—rows of "eligible" dwellings, towers of churches, domes of institutions—take such an effective grey-blue tint that a clever water-colourist would seem to have put them in for pictorial reasons.

The view from the bridge over the Serpentine has an extraordinary nobleness, and it has often seemed to me that the Londoner, twitted with his low standard, may point to it with every confidence. In all the town-scenery of Europe there can be few things so fine; the only reproach it is open to is that it begs the question by seeming—in spite of its being the pride of five millions of people—not to belong to a town at all. The towers of Notre Dame, as they rise in Paris from the island that divides the Seine, present themselves no more impressively than those of Westminster as you see

them looking doubly far beyond the shining stretch of
Hyde Park water. Equally delectable is the large river-
like manner in which the Serpentine opens away between its wooded shores. Just after you have crossed the
bridge (whose very banisters, old and ornamental, of
yellowish-brown stone, I am particularly fond of), you
enjoy on your left, through the gate of Kensington Gardens as you go towards Bayswater, an altogether enchanting vista—a foot-path over the grass, which loses
itself beneath the scattered oaks and elms exactly as if
the place were a "chase." There could be nothing less
like London in general than this particular morsel, and
yet it takes London, of all cities, to give you such an
impression of the country.

IV

It takes London to put you in the way of a purely rustic
walk from Notting Hill to Whitehall. You may traverse
this immense distance—a most comprehensive diagonal
—altogether on soft, fine turf, amid the song of birds,
the bleat of lambs, the ripple of ponds, the rustle of
admirable trees. Frequently have I wished that, for
the sake of such a daily luxury and of exercise made
romantic, I were a Government clerk living, in snug
domestic conditions, in a Pembridge villa,—let me suppose,—and having my matutinal desk in Westminster. I should turn into Kensington Gardens at their
northwest limit, and I should have my choice of a hundred pleasant paths to the gates of Hyde Park. In
Hyde Park I should follow the water-side, or the Row,
or any other fancy of the occasion; liking best, perhaps,
after all, the Row in its morning mood, with the mist
hanging over the dark-red course, and the scattered
early riders taking an identity as the soundless gallop
brings them nearer. I am free to admit that in the Sea-

son, at the conventional hours, the Row becomes a weariness (save perhaps just for a glimpse once a year, to remind one's self how much it is like Du Maurier); the preoccupied citizen eschews it and leaves it for the most part to the gaping barbarian. I speak of it now from the point of view of the pedestrian; but for the rider as well it is at its best when he passes either too early or too late. Then, if he be not bent on comparing it to its disadvantage with the bluer and boskier alleys of the Bois de Boulogne, it will not be spoiled by the fact that, with its surface that looks like tan, its barriers like those of the ring on which the clown stands to hold up the hoop to the young lady, its empty benches and chairs, its occasional orange-peel, its mounted policemen patrolling at intervals like expectant supernumeraries, it offers points of real contact with a circus whose lamps are out. The sky that bends over it is frequently not a bad imitation of the dingy tent of such an establishment. The ghosts of past cavalcades seem to haunt the foggy arena, and somehow they are better company than the mashers and elongated beauties of current seasons. It is not without interest to remember that most of the salient figures of English society during the present century—and English society means, or rather has hitherto meant, in a large degree, English history—have bobbed in the saddle between Apsley House and Queen's Gate. You may call the roll if you care to, and the air will be thick with dumb voices and dead names, like that of some Roman amphitheatre.

It is doubtless a signal proof of being a London-lover *quand même* that one should undertake an apology for so bungled an attempt at a great public place as Hyde Park Corner. It is certain that the improvements and embellishments recently enacted there have only served to call further attention to the poverty of the elements and to the fact that this poverty is terribly illustrative of general conditions. The place is the beating heart of the great West End, yet its main features are a shabby, stuccoed hospital, the low park-gates, in their neat but unimposing frame, the drawing-room windows of Apsley House and of the commonplace frontages on the little terrace beside it; to which must be added, of course, the only item in the whole prospect that is in the least monumental—the arch spanning the private road beside the gardens of Buckingham Palace. This structure is now bereaved of the rueful effigy which used to surmount it—the Iron Duke in the guise of a tin soldier— and has not been enriched by the transaction as much as might have been expected.[1] There is a fine view of Piccadilly and Knightsbridge, and of the noble mansions, as the house-agents call them, of Grosvenor Place, together with a sense of generous space beyond the vulgar little railing of the Green Park; but, except for the impression that there would be room for something better, there is nothing in all this that speaks to the imagination: almost as much as the grimy desert of Trafalgar Square the prospect conveys the idea of an opportunity wasted.

None the less has it on a fine day in spring an expressiveness of which I shall not pretend to explain the source further than by saying that the flood of life and luxury is immeasurably great there. The edifices are mean, but the social stream itself is monumental, and to an observer not purely stolid there is more excitement and suggestion than I can give a reason for in the long, distributed waves of traffic, with the steady policemen marking their rhythm, which roll together and apart for

[1] The monument in the middle of the square, with Sir Edgar Boehm's four fine soldiers, had not been set up when these words were written. [*James's note.*]

so many hours. Then the great, dim city becomes bright and kind, the pall of smoke turns into a veil of haze carelessly worn, the air is coloured and almost scented by the presence of the biggest society in the world, and most of the things that meet the eye—or perhaps I should say more of them, for the most in London is, no doubt, ever the realm of the dingy—present themselves as "well appointed." Everything shines more or less, from the window-panes to the dog-collars. So it all looks, with its myriad variations and qualifications, to one who surveys it over the apron of a hansom, while that vehicle of vantage, better than any box at the opera, spurts and slackens with the current.

It is not in a hansom, however, that we have figured our punctual young man, whom we must not desert as he fares to the southeast, and who has only to cross Hyde Park Corner to find his way all grassy again. I have a weakness for the convenient, familiar, treeless, or almost treeless, expanse of the Green Park and the friendly part it plays as a kind of encouragement to Piccadilly. I am so fond of Piccadilly that I am grateful to any one or anything that does it a service, and nothing is more worthy of appreciation than the southward look it is permitted to enjoy just after it passes Devonshire House—a sweep of horizon which it would be difficult to match among other haunts of men, and thanks to which, of a summer's day, you may spy, beyond the browsed pastures of the foreground and middle distance, beyond the cold chimneys of Buckingham Palace and the towers of Westminster and the swarming river-side and all the southern parishes, the hard modern twinkle of the roof of the Crystal Palace.

If the Green Park is familiar, there is still less of the exclusive in its pendant, as one may call it,—for it literally hangs from the other, down the hill,—the remnant of the former garden of the queer, shabby old palace whose black, inelegant face stares up St. James's Street. This popular resort has a great deal of character, but I am free to confess that much of its character comes from its nearness to the Westminster slums. It is a park of intimacy, and perhaps the most democratic corner of London, in spite of its being in the royal and military quarter and close to all kinds of stateliness. There are few hours of the day when a thousand smutty children are not sprawling over it, and the unemployed lie thick on the grass and cover the benches with a brotherhood of greasy corduroys. If the London parks are the drawing-rooms and clubs of the poor, —that is of those poor (I admit it cuts down the number) who live near enough to them to reach them,— these particular grass-plots and alleys may be said to constitute the very *salon* of the slums.

I know not why, being such a region of greatness,— great towers, great names, great memories; at the foot of the Abbey, the Parliament, the fine fragment of Whitehall, with the quarters of the sovereign right and left,—but the edge of Westminster evokes as many associations of misery as of empire. The neighbourhood has been much purified of late, but it still contains a collection of specimens—though it is far from unique in this—of the low, black element. The air always seems to me heavy and thick, and here more than elsewhere one hears old England—the panting, smoke-stained Titan of Matthew Arnold's fine poem—draw her deep breath with effort. In fact one is nearer to her heroic lungs, if those organs are figured by the great pinnacled and fretted talking-house on the edge of the river. But this same dense and conscious air plays such everlasting tricks to the eye that the Foreign Office, as you see it from the bridge, often looks romantic, and the sheet of water it overhangs poetic—suggests an Indian palace bathing its feet in the Ganges. If our pedestrian achieves such a comparison as this he has nothing left but to go on to his work—which he will find close at hand. He will have come the whole way from the far northwest on the green—which is what was to be demonstrated.

V

I feel as if I were taking a tone almost of boastfulness, and no doubt the best way to consider the matter is simply to say—without going into the treachery of reasons—that, for one's self, one likes this part or the other. Yet this course would not be unattended with danger, inasmuch as at the end of a few such professions we might find ourselves committed to a tolerance of much that is deplorable. London is so clumsy and so brutal, and has gathered together so many of the darkest sides of life, that it is almost ridiculous to talk of her as a lover talks of his mistress, and almost frivolous to appear to ignore her disfigurements and cruelties. She is like a mighty ogress who devours human flesh; but to me it is a mitigating circumstance—though it may not seem so to every one—that the ogress herself is human. It is not in wantonness that she fills her maw, but to keep herself alive and do her tremendous work. She has no time for fine discriminations, but after all she is as good-natured as she is huge, and the more you stand up to her, as the phrase is, the better she takes the joke of it. It is mainly when you fall on your face before her that she gobbles you up. She heeds little what she takes, so long as she has her stint, and the smallest push to the right or the left will divert her wavering bulk from one form of prey to another. It is not to be denied that the heart tends to grow hard in her company; but she is a capital antidote to the morbid, and to live with her successfully is an education of the temper, a consecration of one's private philosophy. She gives one a surface for which in a rough world one can never be too thankful. She may take away reputations, but she forms character. She teaches her victims not to "mind," and the great danger for them is perhaps that they shall learn the lesson too well. . . .

From "London" (1888) in *Essays in London and Elsewhere* (1893) and, as here printed, in *English Hours* (1905).

NEW YORK REVISITED

The single impression or particular vision most answering to the greatness of the subject would have been, I think, a certain hour of large circumnavigation that I found prescribed, in the fulness of the spring, as the almost immediate crown of a return from the Far West.[1] I had arrived at one of the transpontine stations of the Pennsylvania Railroad; the question was of proceeding to Boston, for the occasion, without pushing through the terrible town—why "terrible," to my sense, in many ways, I shall presently explain—and the easy and agreeable attainment of this great advantage was to embark on one of the mightiest (as appeared to me) of train-bearing barges and, descending the western waters, pass round the bottom of the city and remount the other current to Harlem; all without "losing touch" of the

[1] James is writing here of his travels during his return visit to the United States in 1904-1905. [*Editor's note.*]

Pullman that had brought me from Washington. This absence of the need of losing touch, this breadth of effect, as to the whole process, involved in the prompt floating of the huge concatenated cars not only without arrest or confusion, but as for positive prodigal beguilement of the artless traveller, had doubtless much to say to the ensuing state of mind, the happily-excited and amused view of the great face of New York. The extent, the ease, the energy, the quantity and number, all notes scattered about as if, in the whole business and in the splendid light, nature and science were joyously romping together, might have been taking on again, for their symbol, some collective presence of great circling and plunging, hovering and perching seabirds, white-winged images of the spirit, of the restless freedom of the Bay. The Bay had always, on other opportunities, seemed to blow its immense character straight into one's face—coming "at" you, so to speak, bearing down on you, with the full force of a thousand prows of steamers seen exactly on the line of their longitudinal axis; but I had never before been so conscious of its boundless cool assurance or seemed to see its genius so grandly at play. This was presumably indeed because I had never before enjoyed the remarkable adventure of taking in so much of the vast bristling promontory from the water, of ascending the East River, in especial, to its upper diminishing expanses.

Something of the air of the occasion and of the mood of the moment caused the whole picture to speak with its largest suggestion; which suggestion is irresistible when once it is sounded clear. It is all, absolutely, an expression of things lately and currently *done*, done on a large impersonal stage and on the basis of inordinate gain—it is not an expression of any other matters whatever; and yet the sense of the scene (which had at several previous junctures, as well, put forth to my imagination its power) was commanding and thrilling, was in certain lights almost charming. So it befell, exactly, that an element of mystery and wonder entered into the impression—the interest of trying to make out, in the absence of features of the sort usually supposed indispensable, the reason of the beauty and the joy. It is indubitably a "great" bay, a great harbour, but no one item of the romantic, or even of the picturesque, as commonly understood, contributes to its effect. The shores are low and for the most part depressingly furnished and prosaically peopled; the islands, though numerous, have not a grace to exhibit, and one thinks of the other, the real flowers of geography in this order, of Naples, of Capetown, of Sydney, of Seattle, of San Francisco, of Rio, asking how if *they* justify a reputation, New York should seem to justify one. Then, after all, we remember that there are reputations and reputations; we remember above all that the imaginative response to the conditions here presented may just happen to proceed from the intellectual extravagance of the given observer. When this personage is open to corruption by almost any large view of an intensity of life, his vibrations tend to become a matter difficult even for *him* to explain. He may have to confess that the group of evident facts fails to account by itself for the complacency of his appreciation. Therefore it is that I find myself rather backward with a perceived sanction, of an at all proportionate kind, for the fine exhilaration with which, in this free wayfaring relation to them, the wide waters of New York inspire me. There is the beauty of light and air, the great scale of space, and, seen far away to the west, the open gates of the Hudson, majestic in their degree, even at a distance, and announcing still nobler things. But the real appeal, unmistakably, is in that note of vehemence in the local life of which I have spoken, for it is the appeal of a particular type of dauntless power.

The aspect the power wears then is indescribable; it is the power of the most extravagant of cities, rejoicing, as with the voice of the morning, in its might, its fortune, its unsurpassable conditions, and imparting to every object and element, to the motion and expression of every floating, hurrying, panting thing, to the throb of ferries and tugs, to the plash of waves and the play of winds and the glint of lights and the shrill of whistles and the quality and authority of breeze-borne cries—all, practically, a diffused, wasted clamour of *detonations*—something of its sharp free accent and, above all, of its sovereign sense of being "backed" and able to back. The universal *applied* passion struck me as shining unprecedentedly out of the composition; in the bigness and bravery and insolence, especially, of everything that rushed and shrieked; in the air as of a great intricate frenzied dance, half merry, half desperate, or at least half defiant, performed on the huge watery floor. This appearance of the bold lacing-together, across the waters, of the scattered members of the monstrous organism —lacing as by the ceaseless play of an enormous system of steam-shuttles or electric bobbins (I scarce know what to call them), commensurate in form with their infinite work—does perhaps more than anything else to give the pitch of the vision of energy. One has the sense that the monster grows and grows, flinging abroad its loose limbs even as some unmannered young giant at his "larks," and that the binding stitches must for ever fly further and faster and draw harder; the future complexity of the web, all under the sky and over the sea, becoming thus that of some colossal set of clockworks, some steel-souled machine-room of brandished arms and hammering fists and opening and closing jaws. The immeasurable bridges are but as the horizontal sheaths of pistons working at high pressure, day and night, and subject, one apprehends with perhaps inconsistent gloom, to certain, to fantastic, to merciless multiplication. In the light of this apprehension indeed the breezy brightness of the Bay puts on the semblance of the vast white page that awaits beyond any other perhaps the black overscoring of science.

Let me hasten to add that its present whiteness is precisely its charming note, the frankest of the signs you recognize and remember it by. That is the distinction I was just feeling my way to name as the main ground of its doing so well, for effect, without technical scenery. There are great imposing ports—Glasgow and Liverpool and London—that have already their page blackened almost beyond redemption from any such light of the picturesque as can hope to irradiate fog and grime, and there are others, Marseilles and Constantinople say, or, for all I know to the contrary, New Orleans, that contrive to abound before everything else in colour, and so to make a rich and instant and obvious show. But memory and the actual impression keep investing New York with the tone, predominantly, of summer dawns and winter frosts, of sea-foam, of bleached sails and stretched awnings, of blanched hulls, of scoured decks, of new ropes, of polished brasses, of streamers clear in the blue air; and it is by this harmony, doubtless, that the projection of the individual character of the place, of the candour of its avidity and the freshness of its audacity, is most conveyed. The "tall buildings," which have so promptly usurped a glory that affects you as rather surprised, as yet, at itself, the multitudinous skyscrapers standing up to the view, from the water, like extravagant pins in a cushion already overplanted, and stuck in as in the dark, anywhere and anyhow, have at least the felicity of carrying out the fairness of tone, of taking the sun and the shade in the manner of towers of marble. They are not all of marble, I believe, by any means, even if some may be, but they are impudently new and still more impudently "novel"—this in common with so many other terrible things in America —and they are triumphant payers of dividends; all of which uncontested and unabashed pride, with flash of innumerable windows and flicker of subordinate gilt attributions, is like the flare, up and down their long, narrow faces, of the lamps of some general permanent "celebration."

. . . . . .

My recovery of impressions, after a short interval, yet with their flush a little faded, may have been judged to involve itself with excursions of memory—memory directed to the antecedent time—reckless almost to extravagance. But I recall them to-day, none the less, for that value in them which ministered, at happy moments, to an artful evasion of the actual. There was no escape from the ubiquitous alien into the future, or even into the present; there was an escape but into the past. I count as quite a triumph in this interest an unbroken ease of frequentation of that ancient end of Fifth Avenue to the whole neighbourhood of which one's earlier vibrations, a very far-away matter now, were attuned. The precious stretch of space between Washington Square and Fourteenth Street had a value, had even a charm, for the revisiting spirit—a mild and melancholy glamour which I am conscious of the difficulty of "rendering" for new and heedless generations. Here again the assault of suggestion is too great; too large, I mean, the number of hares started, before the pursuing imagination, the quickened memory, by this fact of the felt moral and social value of this comparatively unimpaired morsel of the Fifth Avenue heritage. Its reference to a pleasanter, easier, hazier past is absolutely comparative, just as the past in question itself enjoys as such the merest courtesy-title. It is all recent history enough, by the measure of the whole, and there are flaws and defacements enough, surely, even in its appearance of decency of duration. The tall building, grossly tall and grossly ugly, has failed of an admirable chance of distinguished consideration for it, and the dignity of many of its peaceful fronts has succumbed to the presence of those industries whose foremost need is to make "a good thing" of them. The good thing is doubtless being made, and yet this lower end of the once agreeable street still just escapes being a wholly bad thing. What held the fancy in thrall, however, as I say, was the admonition, proceeding from all the facts, that values of this romantic order are at best, anywhere, strangely relative. It was an extraordinary statement on the subject of New York that the space between Fourteenth Street and Washington Square *should* count for "tone," figure as the old ivory of an overscored tablet.

True wisdom, I found, was to let it, to make it, so count and figure as much as it would, and charming assistance came for this, I also found, from the young good-nature of May and June. There had been neither assistance nor good-nature during the grim weeks of mid-winter; there had been but the meagre fact of a discomfort and an ugliness less formidable here than elsewhere. When, toward the top of the town, circulation, alimentation, recreation, every art of existence, gave way before the full onset of winter, when the upper avenues had become as so many congested bottle-necks, through which the wine of life simply refused to be decanted, getting back to these latitudes resembled really a return from the North Pole to the Temperate Zone: it was as if the wine of life had been poured for you, in advance, into some pleasant old punch-bowl that would support you through the temporary stress. Your condition was not reduced to the endless vista of a clogged tube, of a thoroughfare occupied as to the narrow central ridge with trolley-cars stuffed to suffocation, and as to the mere margin, on either side, with snow-banks resulting from the cleared rails and offering themselves as a field for all remaining action. Free existence and good manners, in New York, are too much brought down to a bare rigour of marginal relation to the endless electric coil, the monstrous chain that winds round the general neck and body, the general middle and legs, very much as the boa-constrictor winds round the group of the Laocoön. It struck me that when these folds are tightened in the terrible stricture of the snow-smothered months of the year, the New York predicament leaves far behind the anguish represented in the Vatican figures. To come and go where East Eleventh Street, where West Tenth, opened their kind short arms was at least to keep clear of the awful hug of the serpent. And this was a grace that grew large, as I have hinted, with the approach of summer, and that made in the afternoons of May and of the first half of June, above all, an insidious appeal. There, I repeat, was the delicacy, there the mystery, there the wonder, in especial, of the unquenchable intensity of the impressions received in childhood. They are made then once for all, be their intrinsic beauty, interest, importance, small or great; the stamp is indelible and never wholly fades. This in fact gives it an importance when a lifetime has intervened. I found myself intimately recognizing every house my officious tenth year had, in the way of imagined adventure, introduced to me—incomparable master of ceremonies after all; the privilege had been offered since to millions of other objects that had made nothing of it, that had gone as they came; so that here were Fifth Avenue corners with which one's connection was fairly exquisite. The lowered light of the days' ends of early summer became them, moreover, exceedingly, and they fell, for the quiet northward perspective, into a dozen delicacies of composition and tone.

One could talk of "quietness" now, for the shrinkage of life so marked, in the higher latitudes of the town, after Easter, the visible early flight of that "society" which, by the old custom, used never to budge before June or July, had almost the effect of clearing some of the streets, and indeed of suggesting that a truly clear New York might have an unsuspected charm or two to put forth. An approach to peace and harmony might have been, in a manner, promised, and the sense of other days took advantage of it to steal abroad with a ghostly tread. It kept meeting, half the time, to its discomfiture, the lamentable little Arch of Triumph which bestrides these beginnings of Washington Square— lamentable because of its poor and lonely and unsupported and unaffiliated state. With this melancholy monument it could make no terms at all, but turned its back to the strange sight as often as possible, helping itself thereby, moreover, to do a little of the pretending required, no doubt, by the fond theory that nothing hereabouts was changed. Nothing *was,* it could occasionally appear to me—there was no new note in the picture, not one, for instance, when I paused before a low house in a small row on the south side of Waverley Place and lived again into the queer mediæval costume (preserved by the daguerreotypist's art) of the very little boy for whom the scene had once embodied the pangs and pleasures of a dame's small school. The dame must have been Irish, by her name, and the Irish tradition, only intensified and coarsened, seemed still to possess the place, the fact of the survival, the sturdy sameness, of which arrested me, again and again, to fascination. The shabby red house, with its mere two storeys, its lowly "stoop," its dislocated ironwork of the forties, the early fifties, the record, in its face, of blistering summers and of the long stages of the loss of self-respect, made it as consummate a morsel of the old liquor-scented, heated-looking city, the city of no pavements, but of such a plenty of politics, as I could have desired. And neighbouring Sixth Avenue, overstraddled though it might be with feats of engineering unknown to the primitive age that otherwise so persisted, wanted only, to carry off the illusion, the warm smell of the bakery on the corner of Eighth Street, a blessed repository of doughnuts, cookies, cream-cakes and pies, the slow passing by which, on returns from school, must have had much in common with the experience of the shipmen of old who came, in long voyages, while they tacked and hung back, upon those belts of ocean that are haunted with the balm and spice of tropic islands.

These were the felicities of the backward reach, which, however, had also its melancholy checks and snubs; nowhere quite so sharp as in presence, so to speak, of the rudely, the ruthlessly suppressed birth-house on the other side of the Square. That was where the pretence that nearly nothing was changed had most to come in; for a high, square, impersonal structure, proclaiming its lack of interest with a crudity all its own, so blocks, at the right moment for its own success, the view of the past, that the effect for me, in Washington Place, was of having been amputated of half my history. The grey and more or less "hallowed" University build-

ing—wasn't it somehow, with a desperate bravery, both
castellated and gabled?—has vanished from the earth,
and vanished with it the two or three adjacent houses,
of which the birthplace was one. This was the snub, for
the complacency of retrospect, that, whereas the inner
sense had positively erected there for its private contemplation a commemorative mural tablet, the very wall that
should have borne this inscription had been smashed
as for demonstration that tablets, in New York, are unthinkable. And I have had indeed to permit myself this
free fantasy of the hypothetic rescued identity of a given
house—taking the vanished number in Washington
Place as most pertinent—in order to invite the reader
to gasp properly with me before the fact that we not
only fail to remember, in the whole length of the city,
one of these frontal records of birth, sojourn, or death,
under a celebrated name, but that we have only to reflect an instant to see any such form of civic piety inevitably and for ever absent. The form is cultivated, to the
greatly quickened interest of street-scenery, in many
of the cities of Europe; and is it not verily bitter, for
those who feel a poetry in the noted passage, longer or
shorter, here and there, of great lost spirits, that the
institution, the profit, the glory of any such association is
denied in advance to communities tending, as the phrase
is, to "run" preponderantly to the sky-scraper? Where,
in fact, is the point of inserting a mural tablet, at any
legible height, in a building certain to be destroyed to
make room for a sky-scraper? And from where, on
the other hand, in a façade of fifty floors, does one "see"
the pious plate recording the honour attached to one
of the apartments look down on a responsive people?
We have but to ask the question to recognize our necessary failure to answer it as a supremely characteristic
local note—a note in the light of which the great city

is projected into its future as, practically, a huge, continuous fifty-floored conspiracy against the very idea
of the ancient graces, those that strike us as having flourished just in proportion as the parts of life and the signs
of character have *not* been lumped together, not been
indistinguishably sunk in the common fund of mere
economic convenience. So interesting, as object-lessons,
may the developments of the American gregarious ideal
become; so traceable, at every turn, to the restless ana-
lyst at least, are the heavy footprints, in the finer
texture of life, of a great commercial democracy seeking
to abound supremely in its own sense and having none
to gainsay it.

. . . .

Still, as I have already hinted, there was always the
case of the one other rescued identity and preserved
felicity, the happy accident of the elder day still ungrudged and finally legitimated. When I say ungrudged,
indeed, I seem to remember how I had heard that the
divine little City Hall had *been* grudged, at a critical
moment, to within an inch of its life; had but just escaped, in the event, the extremity of grudging. It lives
on securely, by the mercy of fate—lives on in the delicacy of its beauty, speaking volumes again (more volumes, distinctly, than are anywhere else spoken) for
the exquisite truth of the *conferred* value of interesting
objects, the value derived from the social, the civilizing
function for which they have happened to find their
opportunity. It is the opportunity that gives them their
price, and the luck of there being, round about them,
nothing greater than themselves to steal it away from
them. They strike thus, virtually, the supreme note, and
—such is the mysterious play of our finer sensibility!—
one takes this note, one is glad to work it, as the phrase

goes, for all it is worth. I so work the note of the City Hall, no doubt, in speaking of the spectacle there constituted as "divine"; but I do it precisely by reason of the spectacle taken *with* the delightful small facts of the building: largely by reason, in other words, of the elegant, the gallant little structure's situation and history, the way it has played, artistically, ornamentally, its part, has held out for the good cause, through the long years, alone and unprotected. The fact is it has been the very centre of that assault of vulgarity of which the innumerable mementos rise within view of it and tower, at a certain distance, over it; and yet it has never parted with a square inch of its character, it has forced them, in a manner, to stand off. I hasten to add that in expressing thus its uncompromised state I speak of its outward, its æsthetic character only. So, at all events, it has discharged the civilizing function I just named as inherent in such cases—that of representing, to the community possessed of it, all the Style the community is likely to get, and of making itself responsible for the same.

The consistency of this effort, under difficulties, has been the story that brings tears to the eyes of the hovering kindly critic, and it is through his tears, no doubt, that such a personage reads the best passages of the tale and makes out the proportions of the object. Mine, I recognize, didn't prevent my seeing that the pale yellow marble (or whatever it may be) of the City Hall has lost, by some late excoriation, the remembered charm of its old surface, the pleasant promiscuous patina of time; but the perfect taste and finish, the reduced yet ample scale, the harmony of parts, the just proportions, the modest classic grace, the living look of the type aimed at, these things, with gaiety of detail undiminished and "quaintness" of effect augmented, are all there; and I see them, as I write, in that glow of appreciation which made it

necessary, of a fine June morning, that I should somehow pay the whole place my respects. The simplest, in
fact the only way, was, obviously, to pass under the
charming portico and brave the consequences: this im-
punity of such audacities being, in America, one of the
last of the lessons the repatriated absentee finds himself
learning. The crushed spirit he brings back from European discipline never quite rises to the height of the
native argument, the brave sense that the public, the
civic building is his very own, for any honest use, so
that he may tread even its most expensive pavements
and staircases (and very expensive, for the American
citizen, these have lately become,) without a question
asked. This further and further unchallenged penetration
begets in the perverted person I speak of a really romantic thrill: it is like some assault of the dim seraglio, with
the guards bribed, the eunuchs drugged and one's life
carried in one's hand. The only drawback to such freedom is that penetralia it is so easy to penetrate fail a little
of a due impressiveness, and that if stationed sentinels
are bad for the temper of the freeman they are good
for the "prestige" of the building.

Never, in any case, it seemed to me, had any freeman
made so free with the majesty of things as I was to make
on this occasion with the mysteries of the City Hall—
even to the point of coming out into the presence of the
Representative of the highest office with which City
Halls are associated, and whose thoroughly gracious
condonation of my act set the seal of success upon the
whole adventure. Its dizziest intensity in fact sprang
precisely from the unexpected view opened into the old
official, the old so thick-peopled local, municipal world:
upper chambers of council and state, delightfully of
their nineteenth-century time, as to design and ornament, in spite of rank restoration; but replete, above all,

with portraits of past worthies, past celebrities and city fathers, Mayors, Bosses, Presidents, Governors, Statesmen at large, Generals and Commodores at large, florid ghosts, looking so unsophisticated now, of years not remarkable, municipally, for the absence of sophistication. Here were types, running mainly to ugliness and all bristling with the taste of their day and the quite touching provincialism of their conditions, as to many of which nothing would be more interesting than a study of New York annals in the light of their personal look, their very noses and mouths and complexions and heads of hair—to say nothing of their waistcoats and neckties; with such colour, such sound and movement would the thick stream of local history then be interfused. Wouldn't its thickness fairly become transparent? since to walk through the collection was not only to see and feel so much that had happened, but to understand, with the truth again and again inimitably pointed, why nothing could have happened otherwise; the whole array thus presenting itself as an unsurpassed demonstration of the real reasons of things. The florid ghosts look out from their exceedingly gilded frames—all that *that* can do is bravely done for them—with the frankest responsibility for everything; their collective presence becomes a kind of copious tell-tale document signed with a hundred names. There are few of these that at this hour, I think, we particularly desire to repeat; but the place where they may be read is, all the way from river to river and from the Battery to Harlem, the place in which there is most of the terrible town. . . .

1906. From Chapter II of *The American Scene* (1907).

V

PASSAGES OF AUTOBIOGRAPHY
AND A JOURNAL

EDITOR'S NOTE

James's three autobiographical memoirs were his major undertaking in the last five years of his life. His last book of tales, *The Finer Grain,* appeared in 1910, and he still had in hand two long-planned novels, *The Sense of the Past* and *The Ivory Tower,* but the completion of these was circumvented by illness, hesitation, and the distressing outbreak of the European war in 1914. Meanwhile his return to the United States in 1904-1905, and again in 1910-11 when he accompanied his ailing brother William back from Europe to New Hampshire and saw him die there, had awakened memories of his youth in New York, Europe, Newport, and Cambridge. After recovering from his grief and the nervous disability that had afflicted him in 1909-11, he saw himself as the last survivor of his immediate family, and he determined to set down his recollections of the events and influences that had shaped his personality and career. *A Small Boy and Others* (1913) deals with the first fifteen years of his life; *Notes of a Son and Brother* (1914) deals with the next ten and particularly with the companionship and shared discoveries of his closest brother, William; *The Middle Years* (unfinished, 1917) shows him in London in 1869 and the early seventies, making his adult entry on the scenes to which his parents had first introduced him in infancy and boyhood, and partaking of the "banquet of initiation" which was to make him a citizen of Europe and a professional author.

These three memoirs were, however, prepared for by the fifty years of growing self-awareness and critical self-assessment which had preceded them and which James recorded not only indirectly in his fiction and essays but more directly in his letters and journals. Of the letters a selection is given later in this book. His *Notebooks* are perhaps the richest and most systematic ever kept by an English-writing novelist. As published in 1947, they contain not only the plans and cogitations that went into the making of almost all his novels and tales but entries of a more intimate character— summings up of purpose and ambition in his art that show the conscious design James felt developing out of his experiences. The first three excerpts given here, all taken from the three above-named memoirs, record from the vantage-point of his old age three high moments in James's youth. The titles I have supplied for them derive from James's own text. "The Sense of Glory" is Chapter XXV of *A Small Boy and Others,* and tells of James's discovery, in the Louvre in Paris in 1856 or '57 and at the age of thirteen, of what art and the "sense of form" were to mean to him. The passage called "The End of the Civil War: The Mask of Lincoln" is taken from Chapter XII of *Notes of a Son and Brother,* and hints of the profound impact which that war, in which two of his brothers fought, and its national hero made on James. "The Banquet of Initiation" is Chapter V of *The Middle Years,* and recounts James's entry into the literary world of London in the 1870's and his meeting with the novelist George Eliot, whom he saw as the leading artist and moral intelligence in Victorian fiction and a model for him in his own chosen craft. I have particularly included this passage because I have not been able to include one of James's pieces on George Eliot among the critical writings in Part III of this book. "The Voice of Concord" is taken from Chapter VIII of *The American Scene* (1907). It is not strictly a work of

autobiography, but its basis and reference are personal and
it may serve both as a fragment of James's intimate history
and as a comment on what Concord and its presiding spirits,
Emerson, Thoreau, and Hawthorne, had meant to him in
youth and later life. Lastly, the "Journal" which James
began in the Brunswick Hotel in Boston in November 1881,
continued in Cambridge and London, and finished in Paris in
November 1882, is taken from *The Notebooks of Henry
James* as edited by F. O. Matthiessen and Kenneth B.
Murdock (1947). It is the most extended and significant
document of its kind among James's papers—a review of
his life at the age of thirty-eight, an assessment of his
personal and imaginative assets, and a forecast of the thirty-
four years that were to remain to him for the writing of his
books and the achievement of success and fame in his chosen
career.

THE SENSE OF GLORY

A MEMORY OF PARIS IN YOUTH: THE LOUVRE AND THE GALERIE D'APOLLON

That autumn[1] renewed, I make out, our long and beguiled walks, my own with W. J. in especial; at the same
time that I have somehow the sense of the whole more
broken appeal on the part of Paris, the scanter confi-

[1] The autumn to which Henry James here refers (in Chapter XXV of *A Small Boy and Others*) was that of 1856 or
1857. With his family he traveled and lived during the years
1855-58 in Switzerland, England, and France, attending
schools in Geneva, Paris (Institution Fezandié), and Boulogne. [*Editor's note.*]

dence and ease it inspired in us, the perhaps more numerous and composite, but obscurer and more baffled intimations. Not indeed—for all my brother's later vision of an accepted flatness in it—that there was not some joy and some grasp; why else were we forever (as I seem to conceive we were) measuring the great space that separated us from the gallery of the Luxembourg, every step of which, either way we took it, fed us with some interesting, some admirable image, kept us in relation to something nobly intended? That particular walk was not prescribed us, yet we appear to have hugged it, across the Champs-Elysées to the river, and so over the nearest bridge and the quays of the left bank to the Rue de Seine, as if it somehow held the secret of our future; to the extent even of my more or less sneaking off on occasion to take it by myself, to taste of it with a due undiverted intensity and the throb as of the finest, which *could* only mean the most Parisian, adventure. The further quays, with their innumerable old bookshops and print-shops, the long cases of each of these commodities, exposed on the parapets in especial, must have come to know us almost as well as we knew them; with plot thickening and emotion deepening steadily, however, as we mounted the long, black Rue de Seine—*such* a stretch of perspective, *such* an intensity of tone as it offered in those days; where every low-browed vitrine waylaid us and we moved in a world of which the dark message, expressed in we couldn't have said what sinister way too, might have been "Art, art, art, don't you see? Learn, little gaping pilgrims, what *that* is!" Oh we learned, that is we tried to, as hard as ever we could, and were fairly well at it, I always felt, even by the time we had passed up into that comparatively short but wider and finer vista of the Rue de Tournon, which in those days more abruptly crowned the more compressed

approach and served in a manner as a great outer vesti-
bule to the Palace. Style, dimly described, looked down
there, as with conscious encouragement, from the high
grey-headed, clear-faced, straight-standing old houses
—very much as if wishing to say "Yes, small staring
jeune homme, we are dignity and memory and measure,
we are conscience and proportion and taste, not to mention strong sense too: for all of which good things take
us—you won't find one of them when you find (as
you're going soon to begin to at such a rate) vulgarity."
This, I admit, was an abundance of remark to such
young ears; but it did all, I maintain, tremble in the air,
with the sense that the Rue de Tournon, cobbled and
a little grass-grown, might more or less have figured
some fine old street *de province:* I cherished in short its
very name and think I really hadn't to wait to prefer
the then, the unmenaced, the inviolate Café Foyot of the
left hand corner, the much-loved and so haunted Café
Foyot of the old Paris, to its—well, to its roaring successor. The wide mouth of the present Boulevard Saint-
Michel, a short way round the corner, had not yet been
forced open to the exhibition of more or less glittering
fangs; old Paris still pressed round the Palace and its
gardens, which formed the right, the sober social antithesis to the "elegant" Tuileries, and which in fine,
with these renewals of our young confidence, reinforced
both in a general and in a particular way one of the
fondest of our literary curiosities of that time, the conscientious study of *Les Français Peints par Eux-Mêmes,*
rich in wood-cuts of Gavarni, of Grandville, of Henri-
Monnier, which we held it rather our duty to admire
and W. J. even a little his opportunity to copy in pen-
and-ink. This gilt-edged and double-columned octavo
it was that first disclosed to me, forestalling a better
ground of acquaintance, the great name of Balzac, who,

in common with every other "light" writer of his day, contributed to its pages: hadn't I pored over his exposition there of the contrasted types of "L'Habituée des Tuileries" and "L'Habituée du Luxembourg"?—finding it very *serré*, in fact what I didn't then know enough to call very stodgy, but flavoured withal and a trifle lubricated by Gavarni's two drawings, which had somehow so much, in general, to say.

Let me not however dally by the way, when nothing, at those hours, I make out, so much spoke to us as the animated pictured halls within the Palace, primarily those of the Senate of the Empire, but then also forming, as with extensions they still and much more copiously form, the great Paris museum of contemporary art. This array was at that stage a comparatively (though only comparatively) small affair; in spite of which fact we supposed it vast and final—so that it would have shocked us to foreknow how in many a case, and of the most cherished cases, the finality was to break down. Most of the works of the modern schools that we most admired are begging their bread, I fear, from door to door—that is from one provincial museum or dim back seat to another; though we were on much-subsequent returns to draw a long breath for the saved state of some of the great things as to which our faith had been clearest. It had been clearer for none, I recover, than for Couture's *Romains de la Décadence*, recently acclaimed, at that time, as the last word of the grand manner, but of the grand manner modernised, humanised, philosophised, redeemed from academic death; so that it was to this master's school that the young American contemporary flutter taught its wings to fly straightest, and that I could never, in the long aftertime, face his masterpiece and all its old meanings and marvels without a rush of memories and a stir of ghosts. William Hunt, the New

Englander of genius, the "Boston painter" whose authority was greatest during the thirty years from 1857 or so, and with whom for a time in the early period W. J. was to work all devotedly, had prolonged his studies in Paris under the inspiration of Couture and of Édouard Frère; masters in a group completed by three or four of the so finely interesting landscapists of that and the directly previous age, Troyon, Rousseau, Daubigny, even Lambinet and others, and which summed up for the American collector and in the New York and Boston markets the idea of the modern in the masterly. It was a comfortable time—when appreciation could go so straight, could rise, and rise higher, without critical contortions; when we could, I mean, be both so intelligent and so "quiet." We were in our immediate circle to know Couture himself a little toward the end of his life, and I was somewhat to wonder then where he had picked up the æsthetic hint for the beautiful Page with a Falcon, if I have the designation right, his other great bid for style and capture of it—which we were long to continue to suppose perhaps the rarest of all modern pictures. The feasting Romans were conceivable enough, I mean *as* a conception; no mystery hung about them—in the sense of one's asking one's self whence they had come and by what romantic or roundabout or nobly-dangerous journey; which is that air of the poetic shaken out as from strong wings when great presences, in any one of the arts, appear to alight. What I remember, on the other hand, of the splendid fair youth in black velvet and satin or whatever who, while he mounts the marble staircase, shows off the great bird on his forefinger with a grace that shows *him* off, was that it failed to help us to divine, during that after-lapse of the glory of which I speak, by what rare chance, for the obscured old ex-celebrity we visited, the heavens had once opened.

Poetry had swooped down, breathed on him for an hour and fled. Such at any rate are the see-saws of reputations —which it contributes to the interest of any observational lingering on this planet to have caught so repeatedly in their weird motion; the question of what may happen, under one's eyes, in particular cases, before that motion sinks to rest, whether at the up or at the down end, being really a bribe to one's own non-departure. Especially great the interest of having noted all the rises and falls and of being able to compare the final point— so far as any certainty may go as to that—either with the greatest or the least previous altitudes; since it is only when there have been exaltations (which is what is not commonest), that our attention is most rewarded.

If the see-saw was to have operated indeed for Eugène Delacroix, our next young admiration, though much more intelligently my brother's than mine, that had already taken place and settled, for we were to go on seeing him, and to the end, in firm possession of his crown, and to take even, I think, a harmless pleasure in our sense of having from so far back been sure of it. I was sure of it, I must properly add, but as an effect of my brother's sureness; since I must, by what I remember, have been as sure of Paul Delaroche—for whom the pendulum was at last to be arrested at a very different point. I could see in a manner, for all the queerness, what W. J. meant by that beauty and, above all, that living interest in "La Barque du Dante," where the queerness, according to him, was perhaps what contributed most; see it doubtless in particular when he reproduced the work, at home, from a memory aided by a lithograph. Yet "Les Enfants d'Édouard" thrilled me to a different tune, and I couldn't doubt that the long-drawn odd face of the elder prince, sad and sore and sick, with his wide crimped sidelocks of fair hair and his violet legs

marked by the Garter and dangling from the bed, was
a reconstitution of far-off history of the subtlest and most
"last word" modern or psychologic kind. I had never
heard of psychology in art or anywhere else—scarcely
anyone then had; but I truly felt the nameless force at
play. Thus if I also in my way "subtly" admired, one's
noted practice of that virtue (mainly regarded indeed,
I judge, as a vice) would appear to have at the time
I refer to set in, under such encouragements, once for
all; and I can surely have enjoyed up to then no formal
exhibition of anything as I at one of those seasons enjoyed the commemorative show of Delaroche given,
soon after his death, in one of the rather bleak salles
of the École des Beaux-Arts to which access was had
from the quay. *There* was reconstituted history if one
would, in the straw-littered scaffold, the distracted ladies
with three-cornered coifs and those immense hanging
sleeves that made them look as if they had bath-towels
over their arms; in the block, the headsman, the band-
aged eyes and groping hands, of Lady Jane Grey—not
less than in the noble indifference of Charles the First,
compromised king but perfect gentleman, at his inscrutable ease in his chair and as if on his throne, while
the Puritan soldiers insult and badger him: the thrill
of which was all the greater from its pertaining to that
English lore which the good Robert Thompson had, to
my responsive delight, rubbed into us more than anything else and all from a fine old conservative and
monarchical point of view. Yet of these things W. J.
attempted no reproduction, though I remember his repeatedly laying his hand on Delacroix, whom he found
always and everywhere interesting—to the point of trying effects, with charcoal and crayon, in his manner; and
not less in the manner of Decamps, whom we regarded
as more or less of a genius of the same rare family. They

were touched with the ineffable, the inscrutable, and Delacroix in especial with the incalculable; categories these toward which we had even then, by a happy transition, begun to yearn and languish. We were not yet aware of style, though on the way to become so, but were aware of mystery, which indeed was one of its forms—while we saw all the others, without exception, exhibited at the Louvre, where at first they simply overwhelmed and bewildered me.

It was as if they had gathered there into a vast deafening chorus; I shall never forget how—speaking, that is, for my own sense—they filled those vast halls with the influence rather of some complicated sound, diffused and reverberant, than of such visibilities as one could directly deal with. To distinguish among these, in the charged and coloured and confounding air, was difficult —it discouraged and defied; which was doubtless why my impression originally best entertained was that of those magnificent parts of the great gallery simply not inviting us to distinguish. They only arched over us in the wonder of their endless golden riot and relief, figured and flourished in perpetual revolution, breaking into great high-hung circles and symmetries of squandered picture, opening into deep outward embrasures that threw off the rest of monumental Paris somehow as a told story, a sort of wrought effect or bold ambiguity for a vista, and yet held it there, at every point, as a vast bright gage, even at moments a felt adventure, of experience. This comes to saying that in those beginnings I felt myself most happily cross that bridge over to Style constituted by the wondrous Galerie d'Apollon, drawn out for me as a long but assured initiation and seeming to form with its supreme coved ceiling and inordinately shining parquet a prodigious tube or tunnel through which I inhaled little by little, that is again and again, a general sense of *glory*. The glory meant ever so many things at once, not only beauty and art and supreme design, but history and fame and power, the world in fine raised to the richest and noblest expression. The world there was at the same time, by an odd extension or intensification, the local present fact, to my small imagination, of the Second Empire, which was (for my notified consciousness) new and queer and perhaps even wrong, but on the spot so amply radiant and elegant that it took to itself, took under its protection with a splendour of insolence, the state and ancientry of the whole scene, profiting thus, to one's dim historic vision, confusedly though it might be, by the unparalleled luxury and variety of its heritage. But who shall count the sources at which an intense young fancy (when a young fancy *is* intense) capriciously, absurdly drinks?—so that the effect is, in twenty connections, that of a love-philtre or fear-philtre which fixes for the senses their supreme symbol of the fair or the strange. The Galerie d'Apollon became for years what I can only term a splendid scene of things, even of the quite irrelevant or, as might be, almost unworthy; and I recall to this hour, with the last vividness, what a precious part it played for me, and exactly by that continuity of honour, on my awaking, in a summer dawn many years later, to the fortunate, the instantaneous recovery and capture of the most appalling yet most admirable nightmare of my life. The climax of this extraordinary experience—which stands alone for me as a dream-adventure founded in the deepest, quickest, clearest act of cogitation and comparison act indeed of life-saving energy, as well as in unutterable fear—was the sudden pursuit, through an open door, along a huge high saloon, of a just dimly-descried figure that retreated in terror before my rush and dash (a glare of inspired reaction from irresistible but shameful dread,) out of the room I had a moment before been desperately, and all the more abjectly, defending by the push of my shoulder against hard pressure on lock and bar from the other side. The lucidity, not to say the sublimity, of the crisis had consisted of the great thought that I, in my appalled state, was probably still more appalling than the awful agent, creature or presence, whatever he was, whom I had guessed, in the suddenest wild start from sleep, the sleep within my sleep, to be making for my place of rest. The triumph of my impulse, perceived in a flash as I acted on it by myself at a bound, forcing the door outward, was the grand thing, but the great point of the whole was the wonder of my final recognition. Routed, dismayed, the tables turned upon him by my so surpassing him for straight aggression and dire intention, my visitant was already but a diminished spot in the long perspective, the tremendous, glorious hall, as I say, over the far-gleaming floor of which, cleared for the occasion of its great line of priceless vitrines down the middle, he sped for *his* life, while a great storm of thunder and lightning played through the deep embrasures of high windows at the right. The lightning that revealed the retreat revealed also the wondrous place and, by the same amazing play, my young imaginative life in it of long before, the sense of which, deep within me, had kept it whole, preserved it to this thrilling use; for what in the world were the deep embrasures and the so polished floor but those of the Galerie d'Apollon of my childhood? The "scene of something" I had vaguely then felt it? Well I might, since it was to be the scene of that immense hallucination.

Of what, at the same time, in those years, were the great rooms of the Louvre almost equally, above and below, not the scene, from the moment they so wrought, stage by stage, upon our perceptions?—literally on almost all of these, in one way and another; quite in such a manner, I more and more see, as to have been educative, formative, fertilising, in a degree which no other "intellectual experience" our youth was to know could pretend, as a comprehensive, conducive thing, to rival. The sharp and strange, the quite heart-shaking little prevision had come to me, for myself, I make out, on the occasion of our very first visit of all, my brother's and mine, under conduct of the good Jean Nadali, before-mentioned, trustfully deputed by our parents, in the Rue de la Paix, on the morrow of our first arrival in Paris (July 1855) and while they were otherwise concerned. I hang again, appalled but uplifted, on brave Nadali's arm—his professional acquaintance with the splendours about us added for me on the spot to the charm of his "European" character: I cling to him while I gape at Géricault's "Radeau de la Méduse," the sensation, for splendour and terror of interest, of that juncture to me, and ever afterwards to be associated, along with two or three other more or less contemporary products, Guérin's "Burial of Atala," Prudhon's "Cupid and Psyche," David's helmetted Romanisms, Madame Vigée-Lebrun's "ravishing" portrait of herself and her little girl, with how can I say what foretaste (as determined by that instant as if the hour had struck from a clock) of all the fun, confusedly speaking, that one was going to have, and the kind of life, always of the queer so-called inward sort, tremendously "sporting" in its way—though that description didn't then wait upon it, that one was going to lead. It came of itself, this almost awful apprehension in all the presences, under our courier's protection and in my brother's company—it came just there and so; there was alarm in it somehow as well as bliss. The bliss in fact I think scarce disengaged itself at all, but only the sense of a freedom of contact and appreciation really too big for one, and leaving such a mark on the very place, the pictures, the frames themselves, the figures within them, the particular parts and features of each, the look of the rich light, the smell of the massively enclosed air, that I have never since renewed the old exposure without renewing again the old emotion and taking up the small scared consciousness. *That*, with so many of the conditions repeated, is the charm—to feel afresh the beginning of so much that was to be. The beginning in short was with Géricault and David, but it went on and on and slowly spread; so that one's stretched, one's even strained, perceptions, one's discoveries and extensions piece by piece, come back, on the great premises, almost as so many explorations of the house of life, so many circlings and hoverings round the image of the world. I have dim reminiscences of permitted independent visits, uncorrectedly juvenile though I might still be, during which the house of life and the palace of art became so mixed and interchangeable— the Louvre being, under a general description, the most peopled of all scenes not less than the most hushed of all temples—that an excursion to look at pictures would have but half expressed my afternoon. I had looked at pictures, looked and looked again, at the vast Veronese, at Murillo's moon-borne Madonna, at Leonardo's almost unholy dame with the folded hands, treasures of the Salon Carré as that display was then composed; but I had also looked at France and looked at Europe, looked even at America as Europe itself might be conceived so to look, looked at history, as a still-felt past and a complacently personal future, at society, manners, types, characters, possibilities and prodigies and mysteries of fifty sorts; and all in the light of being splendidly "on my own," as I supposed it, though we hadn't then that perfection of slang, and of (in especial) going and coming along that interminable and incomparable Seine-side front of the Palace against which young sensibility felt itself almost rub, for endearment and consecration, as a cat invokes the friction of a protective piece of furniture. Such were at any rate some of the vague processes—I see for how utterly vague they must show—of picking up an education; and I was, in spite of the vagueness, so far from agreeing with my brother afterwards that we didn't pick one up and that that never *is* done, in any sense not negligible, and also that an education might, or should, in particular, have picked *us* up, and yet didn't—I was so far dissentient, I say, that I think I quite came to glorify such passages and see them as part of an order really fortunate. If we had been little asses, I seem to have reasoned, a higher intention driving us wouldn't have made us less so—to any point worth mentioning; and as we extracted such impressions, to put it at the worst, from redemptive accidents (to call Louvres and Luxembourgs nothing better) why we weren't little asses, but something wholly other: which appeared all I needed to contend for. Above all it would have been stupid and ignoble, an attested and lasting dishonour, not, with our chance, to have followed our straggling clues, as many as we could and disengaging as we happily did, I felt, the gold and the silver ones, whatever the others might have been—not to have followed them and not to have arrived by them, so far as we were to arrive. Instinctively, for any dim designs we might have nourished, we picked out the silver and the gold, attenuated threads though they must have been, and I positively feel that there were more of these, far more, casually interwoven, than will reward any present patience for my unravelling of the too fine tissue.

From *A Small Boy and Others* (1913), Chapter XXV

*

THE END OF THE CIVIL WAR

THE MASK OF LINCOLN

Wherever I dip, again, I pull out a plum from under the tooth of time—this at least so to my own rapt sense that had I more space I might pull both freely and at a venture. The strongest savour of the feast—with the fumes of a feast it comes back—was, I need scarce once more insist, the very taste of the War as ending and ended; through which blessing, more and more, the quantity of military life or at least the images of military experience seemed all about us, quite paradoxically, to grow greater. This I take to have been a result, first of the impending, and then of the effective, break-up of the vast veteran Army, swamping much of the scene as with the flow of a monster tide and bringing literally home to us, in bronzed, matured faces and even more in bronzed, matured characters, above all in the absolutely acquired and stored resource of overwhelming reference, reference usually of most substance the less it was immediately explicit, the more in fact it was faded and jaded to indifference, what was meant by having patiently served. The very smell of having so served was somehow, at least to my supersensitive nostril, in the larger and cooler air, where it might have been an emanation, the most masculine, the most communicative as to associated far-off things (according to the nature, ever, of elements vaguely exhaled), from the operation of the general huge gesture of relief—from worn toggery put off, from old army-cloth and other fittings at a discount, from swordbelts and buckles, from a myriad saturated articles now not even lying about but brushed away with an effect upon the passing breeze and all relegated to the dim state of some mere theoretic commemorative panoply that was never in the event to be objectively disposed. The generalisation grew richly or, as it were, quite adorably familiar, that life was ever so handsomely reinforced, and manners, not to say manner at large, refreshed, and personal aspects and types accented, and categories multiplied (no category, for the dreaming painter of things, could our scene afford not to grab at on the chance), just by the fact of the discharge upon society of such an amount of out-of-the-way experience, as it might roughly be termed—such a quantity and variety of possession and assimilation of unprecedented history. It had been unprecedented at least among ourselves, we had had it in our own highly original conditions—or "they," to be more exact, had had it admirably in theirs; and I think I was never to know a case in which his having been directly touched by it, or, in a word, having consistently "soldiered," learnt all about it and exhausted it, wasn't to count all the while on behalf of the happy man for one's own individual impression or attention; call it again, as everything came back to that, one's own need to interpret. The discharge upon "society" is moreover what I especially mean; it being the sense of how society in *our* image of the word was taking it all in that I was most concerned with; plenty of other images figured of course for other entertainers of such. The world immediately roundabout us at any rate bristled with more of the young, or the younger, cases I speak of, cases of "things seen" and felt, and a delectable difference in the man thereby made imputable, than I could begin here to name even had

I kept the record. I think I fairly cultivated the perceiving of it all, so that nothing of it, under some face or other, shouldn't brush my sense and add to my impression; yet my point is more particularly that the body social itself was for the time so permeated, in the light I glance at, that it became to its own consciousness more interesting. As so many existent parts of it, however unstoried yet, to their minor credit, various thrilled persons could inhale the interest to their fullest capacity and feel that they too had been pushed forward—and were even to find themselves by so much the more pushable yet.

I resort thus to the lift and the push as the most expressive figures for that immensely *remonté* state which coincided for us all with the great disconcerting irony of the hour, the unforgettable death of Lincoln. I think of the springtime of '65 as it breathed through Boston streets—my remembrance of all those days is a matter, strangely enough, of the out-of-door vision, of one's constantly dropping down from Beacon Hill, to the brave edge of which we clung, for appreciation of those premonitory gusts of April that one felt most perhaps where Park Street Church stood dominant, where the mouth of the Common itself uttered promises, more signs and portents than one could count, more prodigies than one could keep apart, and where further strange matters seemed to charge up out of the lower districts and of the "business world," generative as never before of news. The streets were restless, the meeting of the seasons couldn't but be inordinately so, and one's own poor pulses matched—at the supreme pitch of that fusion, for instance, which condensed itself to blackness roundabout the dawn of April 15th: I was fairly to go in shame of its being my birthday. These would have been the hours of the streets if none others had been—

when the huge general gasp filled them like a great earth-shudder and people's eyes met people's eyes without the vulgarity of speech. Even this was, all so strangely, part of the lift and the swell, as tragedy has but to be of a pure enough strain and a high enough connection to sow with its dark hand the seed of greater life. The collective sense of what had occurred was of a sadness too noble not somehow to inspire, and it was truly in the air that, whatever we had as a nation produced or failed to produce, we could at least gather round this perfection of a classic woe. True enough, as we were to see, the immediate harvest of our loss was almost too ugly to be borne—for nothing more sharply comes back to me than the tune to which the "esthetic sense," if one glanced but from *that* high window (which was after all one of many too), recoiled in dismay from the sight of Mr. Andrew Johnson perched on the stricken scene. We had given ourselves a figure-head, and the figure-head sat there in its habit as it lived, and we were to have it in our eyes for three or four years and to ask ourselves in horror what monstrous thing we had done. I speak but of aspects, those aspects which, under a certain turn of them, may be all but everything; gathered together they become a symbol of what is behind, and it was open to us to waver at shop-windows exposing the new photograph, exposing, that is, *the* photograph, and ask ourselves what we had been guilty of as a people, when all was said, to deserve the infliction of that form. It was vain to say that we had deliberately invoked the "common" in authority and must drink the wine we had drawn. No countenance, no salience of aspect nor composed symbol, could superficially have referred itself less than Lincoln's mould-smashing mask to any mere matter-of-course type of propriety; but his admirable unrelated head had itself revealed a type—as if by the very fact that what made in it for roughness of kind looked out only less than what made in it for splendid final stamp, in other words for commanding Style. The result thus determined had been precious for representation, and above all for fine suggestional function, in a degree that left behind every medal we had ever played at striking; whereas before the image now substituted representation veiled her head in silence and the element of the suggested was exactly the direst. What, however, on the further view, was to be more refreshing than to find that there were excesses of native habit which truly we couldn't bear? so that it was for the next two or three years fairly sustaining to consider that, let the reasons publicly given for the impeachment of the official in question be any that would serve, the grand inward logic or mystic law had been that we really couldn't go on offering each other before the nations the consciousness of such a presence. That was at any rate the style of reflection to which the humiliating case reduced me; just this withal now especially working, I feel, into that image of our generally quickened activity of spirit, our having by the turn of events more ideas to apply and even to play with, that I have tried to throw off. Everything I recover, I again risk repeating, fits into the vast miscellany —the detail of which I may well seem, however, too poorly to have handled.

From Chapter XII of *Notes of a Son and Brother* (1914)

*

THE BANQUET OF INITIATION

LONDON AND GEORGE ELIOT

Why, however, should I pick up so small a crumb from that mere brief first course at a banquet of initiation which was in the event to prolong itself through years and years?—unless indeed as a scrap of a specimen, chosen at hazard, of the prompt activity of a process by which my intelligence afterwards came to find itself more fed, I think, than from any other source at all, or, for that matter, from all other sources put together. A hundred more suchlike modest memories breathe upon me, each with its own dim little plea, as I turn to face them, but my idea is to deal somehow more conveniently with the whole gathered mass of my subsequent impressions in this order, a fruitage that I feel to have been only too abundantly stored. Half a dozen of those of a larger and more immediate dignity, incidents more particularly of the rather invidiously so-called social contact, pull my sleeve as I pass; but the long, backward-drawn train of the later life drags them along with it, lost and smothered in its spread—only one of them stands out or remains over, insisting on its place and hour, its felt distinguishability. To this day I feel again *that* roused emotion, my unsurpassably prized admission to the presence of the great George Eliot, whom I was taken to see, by one of the kind door-opening Norton ladies, by whom Mrs. Lewes's guarded portal at North Bank appeared especially penetrable, on a Sunday afternoon of April '69. Later occasions, after a considerable lapse, were not to overlay the absolute face-value, as I may call it, of all the appearances then and there presented me—which were taken home by a young spirit almost abjectly grateful, at any rate all devoutly prepared, for them. I find it idle even to wonder what "place" the author of *Silas Marner* and *Middlemarch* may be conceived to have in the pride of our literature —so settled and consecrated in the individual range of view is many such a case free at last to find itself, free after ups and down, after fluctuations of fame or whatever, which have divested judgment of any relevance that isn't most of all the relevance of a living and recorded *relation*. It has ceased then to know itself in any degree as an estimate, has shaken off the anxieties of circumspection and comparison and just grown happy to act as an attachment pure and simple, an effect of life's own logic, but in the ashes of which the wonted fires of youth need but to be blown upon for betrayal of a glow. Reflective appreciation may have originally been concerned; whether at its most or at its least, but it is well over, to our infinite relief—yes, to our immortal comfort, I think; the interval back cannot again be bridged. We simply sit with our enjoyed gain, our residual rounded possession in our lap; a safe old treasure, which has ceased to shrink, if indeed also perhaps greatly to swell, and all that further touches it is the fine vibration set up if the name we know it all by is called into question—perhaps however little.

It was by George Eliot's name that I was to go on knowing, was never to cease to know, a great treasure of beauty and humanity, of applied and achieved art, a testimony, historic as well as æsthetic, to the deeper interest of the intricate English aspects; and I now allow the vibration, as I have called it, all its play—quite as if I had been wronged even by my own hesitation as to whether to pick up my anecdote. That scruple wholly fades with the sense of how I must at the very time have foreseen that here was one of those associations that would determine in the far future an exquisite inability to revise it. *Middlemarch* had not then appeared—we of the faith were still to enjoy that *saturation*, and *Felix Holt* the radical was upwards of three years old; the impetus proceeding from this work, however, was still fresh enough in my pulses to have quickened the palpitation of my finding myself in presence. I had rejoiced without reserve in *Felix Holt*—the illusion of reading which, outstretched on my then too frequently inevitable bed at Swampscott during a couple of very hot days of the summer of 1866, comes back to me, followed by that in sooth of sitting up again, at no great ease, to indite with all promptness a review of the delightful thing, the place of appearance of which nothing could now induce me to name, shameless about the general fact as I may have been at the hour itself: over such a feast of fine rich natural tone did I feel myself earnestly bend. Quite unforgettable to me the art and truth with which the note of this tone was struck in the beautiful prologue and the bygone appearances, a hundred of the outward and visible signs of the author's own young rural and midmost England, made to hold us by their harmony. The book was not, if I rightly remember, altogether genially greeted, but I was to hold fast to the charm I had thankfully suffered it, I had been conscious of absolutely needing it, to work.

Exquisite the remembrance of how it wouldn't have "done" for me at all, in relation to other inward matters, not to strain from the case the last drop of its happiest sense. And I had even with the cooling of the first glow so little gone back upon it, as we have nowadays learned to say, had in fact so gone forward, floated by its wave of superlative intended benignity, that, once in the cool quiet drawing-room at North Bank I knew myself steeped in still deeper depths of the medium. G. H. Lewes was absent for the time on an urgent errand; one of his sons, on a visit at the house, had been suddenly taken with a violent attack of pain, the heritage of a bad accident not long before in the West Indies, a suffered onset from an angry bull, I seem to recall, who had tossed or otherwise mauled him, and, though beaten off, left him considerably compromised—these facts being promptly imparted to us, in no small flutter, by our distinguished lady, who came in to us from another room, where she had been with the hapless young man while his father appealed to the nearest good chemist for some known specific. It infinitely moved me to see so great a celebrity quite humanly and familiarly agitated—even with something clear and noble in it too, to which, as well as to the extraordinarily interesting dignity of her whole odd personal conformation, I remember thinking her black silk dress and the lace mantilla attached to her head and keeping company on either side with the low-falling thickness of her dark hair effectively contributed. I have found myself, my life long, attaching value to every noted thing in respect to a great person—and George Eliot struck me on the spot as somehow *illustratively* great; never at any rate has the impression of those troubled moments faded from me, nor that at once of a certain high grace in her anxiety and a frank immediate appreciation of our presence, modest embarrassed folk as we were. It took me no long time to thrill with the sense, sublime in its unexpectedness, that we were perhaps, or indeed quite clearly, helping her to pass the time till Mr. Lewes's return—after which he would again post off for Mr. Paget the pre-eminent surgeon; and I see involved with this the perfect amenity of her assisting us, as it were, to assist her, through unrelinquished proper talk, due responsible remark and report, in the last degree suggestive to me, on a short holiday taken with Mr. Lewes in the south of France, whence they had just returned. Yes indeed, the lightest words of great persons are so little as any words of others are that I catch myself again inordinately struck with her dropping it off-hand that the mistral, scourge of their excursion, had blown them into Avignon, where they had gone, I think, to see J. S. Mill, only to blow them straight out again—the figure put it so before us; as well as with the moral interest, the absence of the *banal,* in their having, on the whole scene, found pleasure further poisoned by the frequency in all those parts of "evil faces: oh the evil faces!" *That* recorded source of suffering enormously affected me—I felt it as beautifully characteristic: I had never heard an *impression de voyage* so little tainted with the superficial or the vulgar. I was myself at the time in the thick of impressions, and it was true that they would have seemed to me rather to fail of life, of their own doubtless inferior kind, if submitting beyond a certain point to be touched with that sad or, as who should say, that grey colour: Mrs. Lewes's were, it appeared, predominantly so touched, and I could at once admire it in them and wonder if they didn't pay for this by some lack of intensity on other sides. Why I didn't more impute to her, or to them, that possible lack is more than I can say, since under the law of moral earnestness the vulgar and the trivial would be then involved in the poor observations of my own making—a conclusion sufficiently depressing.

However, I didn't find myself depressed, and I didn't find the great mind that was so good as to shine upon us at that awkward moment however dimly anything but augumented; what was its sensibility to the evil faces but part of the large old tenderness which the occasion had caused to overflow and on which we were presently floated back into the room she had left?—where we might perhaps beguile a little the impatience of the sufferer waiting for relief. We ventured in our flutter to doubt whether we *should* beguile, we held back with a certain delicacy from this irruption, and if there was a momentary wonderful and beautiful conflict I remember how our yielding struck me as crowned with the finest grace it could possibly have, that of the prodigious privilege of humouring, yes literally humouring so renowned a spirit at a moment when we could really match our judgment with hers. For the injured young man, in the other and the larger room, simply lay stretched on his back on the floor, the posture apparently least painful to him—though painful enough at the best I easily saw on kneeling beside him, after my first dismay, to ask if I could in any way ease him. I see his face again, fair and young and flushed, with its vague little smile and its moist brow; I recover the moment or two during which we sought to make natural conversation in his presence, and my question as to what conversation *was* natural; and then as his father's return still failed my having the inspiration that at once terminated the strain of the scene and yet prolonged the sublime connection. Mightn't *I* then hurry off for Mr. Paget?—on whom, as fast as a cab could carry me, I would wait with the request that he would come at the first possible moment to the rescue. Mrs. Lewes's and our stricken companion's instant appreciation of this offer lent me wings on which I again feel myself borne very much as if suddenly acting as a messenger of the gods—surely I had never come so near to performing in that character. I shook off my fellow visitor for swifter cleaving of the air, and I recall still feeling that I cleft it even in the dull four-wheeler of other days which, on getting out of the house, I recognised as the only object animating, at a distance, the long blank Sunday vista beside the walled-out Regent's Park. I crawled to Hanover Square—or was it Cavendish? I let the question stand—and, after learning at the great man's door that though he was not at home he was soon expected back and would receive my message without delay, cherished for the rest of the day the particular quality of my vibration.

It was doubtless even excessive in proportion to its cause—yet in what else but that consisted the force and the use of vibrations? It was by their excess that one knew them for such, as one for that matter only knew things in general worth knowing. I didn't know what I had expected as an effect of our offered homage, but I had somehow not, at the best, expected a relation—and now a relation had been dramatically determined. It would exist for me if I should never again in all the world ask a feather's weight of it; for myself, that is, it would simply never be able not somehow to act. Its virtue was not in truth at all flagrantly to be put to the proof—any opportunity for that underwent at the best a considerable lapse; but why wasn't it intensely acting, none the less, during the time when, before being in London again for any length of stay, I found it intimately concerned in my perusal of *Middlemarch,* so soon then to appear, and even in that of *Deronda,* its intervention on behalf of which defied any chill of time? And to these references I can but subjoin that they obviously most illustrate the operation of a sense for drama. The process of appropriation of the two fictions was experience, in great intensity, and roundabout the field was drawn the distinguishable ring of something that belonged equally to this condition and that embraced and further vivified the imaged mass, playing in upon it lights of surpassing fineness. So it was, at any rate, that my "relation"—for I didn't go so far as to call it "ours"—helped me to squeeze further values from the intrinsic substance of the copious final productions I have named, a weight of variety, dignity and beauty of which I have never allowed my measure to shrink.

Even this example of a rage for connections, I may also remark, doesn't deter me from the mention here, somewhat out of its order of time, of another of those in which my whole privilege of reference to Mrs. Lewes, such as it remained, was to look to be preserved. I stretch over the years a little to overtake it, and it calls up at once another person, the ornament, or at least the diversion, of a society long since extinct to me, but who, in common with every bearer of a name I yield to the temptation of writing, insists on profiting promptly by the fact of inscription—very much as if first tricking me into it and then proving it upon me. The extinct societies that once were so sure of themselves, how can they *not* stir again if the right touch, that of a hand they actually knew, however little they may have happened to heed it, reaches tenderly back to them? The touch *is* the retrieval, so far as it goes, setting up as it does heaven knows what undefeated continuity. I must have been present among the faithful at North Bank during a Sunday afternoon or two of the winter of '77 and '78— I was to see the great lady alone but on a single occasion before her death; but those attestations are all but lost to me now in the livelier pitch of a scene, as I can only call it, of which I feel myself again, all amusedly, rather as sacrificed witness. I had driven over with Mrs. Greville from Milford Cottage, in Surrey, to the villa George Eliot and George Lewes had not long before built themselves, and which they much inhabited, at Witley—this indeed, I well remember, in no great flush of assurance that my own measure of our intended felicity would be quite that of my buoyant hostess. But here exactly comes, with my memory of Mrs. Greville, from which numberless by-memories dangle, the interesting question that makes for my recall why things happened, under her much-waved wing, not in any too coherent fashion—and this even though it was never once given her, I surmise, to guess that they anywhere fell short. So gently used, all round indeed, was this large, elegant, extremely near-sighted and extremely demonstrative lady, whose genius was all for friendship, admiration, declamation and expenditure, that one doubted whether in the whole course of her career she had ever once been brought up, as it were, against a recognised reality; other at least perhaps than the tiresome cost of the materially agreeable in life and the perverse appearance, at times, that though she "said" things, otherwise recited choice morceaux, whether French or English, with a marked oddity of manner, of "attack," a general incongruity of drawing-room art, the various contributive elements, hour, scene, persuaded patience and hushed attention, were perforce a precarious quantity.

It is in that bygone old grace of the unexploded factitious, the air of a thousand dimmed illusions and more or less early Victorian beatitudes on the part of the blandly idle and the supposedly accomplished, that Mrs. Greville, with her exquisite goodnature and her innocent fatuity, is embalmed for me; so that she becomes in that light a truly shining specimen, almost the image or compendium of a whole side of a social order. Just so she has happy suggestion; just so, whether or no by a twist of my mind toward the enviability of certain complacencies of faith and taste that we would yet neither live back into if we could, nor can catch again if we would, I see my forgotten friend of that moist autumn afternoon of our call, and of another, on the morrow, which I shall not pass over, as having rustled and gushed and protested and performed through her term under a kind of protection by the easy-going gods that is not of this fierce age. Amiabilities and absurdities, harmless serenities and vanities, pretensions and undertakings unashamed, still profited by the mildness of the critical air and the benignity of the social—on the right side at least of the social line. It had struck me from the first that nowhere so much as in England was it fortunate to *be* fortunate, and that against that condition, once it had somehow been handed down and determined, a number of the sharp truths that one might privately apprehend beat themselves beautifully in vain. I say beautifully for I confess without scruple to have found again and again at that time an attaching charm in the general exhibition of enjoyed immunity, paid for as it was almost always by the personal amenity, the practice of all sorts of pleasantness; if it kept the gods themselves for the time in goodhumour, one was willing enough, or at least I was, to be on the side of the gods. Unmistakeable too, as I seem to recover it, was the positive interest of watching and noting, roundabout one, for the turn, or rather for the blest continuity, of their benevolence: such an appeal proceeded, in this, that and the other particular case, from the fool's paradise really rounded and preserved, before one's eyes, for those who were so good as to animate it. There was always the question of how long they would be left to, and the growth of one's fine suspense, not to say one's frank little gratitude, as the miracle repeated itself.

All of which, I admit, dresses in many reflections the small circumstance that Milford Cottage, with its innumerable red candles and candle-shades, had affected me as the most embowered retreat for social innocence that it was possible to conceive, and as absolutely settling the question of whether the practice of pleasantness mightn't quite ideally pay for the fantastic protectedness. The red candles in the red shades have remained with me, inexplicably, as a vivid note of this pitch, shedding their rosy light, with the autumn gale, the averted reality, all shut out, upon such felicities of feminine helplessness as I couldn't have prefigured in advance and as exemplified, for further gathering in, the possibilities of the old tone. Nowhere had the evening curtains seemed so drawn, nowhere the copious service so soft, nowhere the second volume of the new novel, "half-uncut," so close to one's hand, nowhere the exquisite head and incomparable brush of the domesticated collie such an attestation of *that* standard at least, nowhere the harmonies of accident—of intention was more than one could say—so incapable of a wrong deflection. That society would lack the highest finish without some such distributed clusters of the thoroughly gentle, the mildly presumptuous and the inveterately mistaken, was brought home to me there, in fine, to a tune with which I had no quarrel, perverse enough as I had been from an early time to know but the impulse to egg on society to the fullest discharge of any material stirring within its breast and not making for cruelty or brutality, mere baseness or mere stupidity, that would fall into a picture or a scene. The quality of serene anxiety on the part for instance of exquisite Mrs. Thellusson, Mrs. Greville's mother, was by itself a plea for any privilege one should fancy her perched upon; and I scarce know if this be more or be less true because the anxiety

—at least as I culled its fragrance—was all about the most secondary and superfluous small matters alone. It struck me, I remember, as a new and unexpected form of the pathetic altogether; and there was no form of the pathetic, any more than of the tragic or the comic, that didn't serve as another pearl for one's lengthening string. And I pass over what was doubtless the happiest stroke in the composition, the fact of its involving, as all-distinguished husband of the other daughter, an illustrious soldier and servant of his sovereign, of his sovereigns that were successively to be, than against whose patient handsome bearded presence the whole complexus of femininities and futilities couldn't have been left in more tolerated and more contrasted relief; pass it over to remind myself of how, in my particular friend of the three, the comic and the tragic were presented in a confusion that made the least intended of them at any moment take effectively the place of the most. The impression, that is, was never that of the sentiment operating—save indeed perhaps when the dear lady applied her faculty for frank imitation of the ridiculous, which she then quite directly and remarkably achieved; but that she could be comic, that she *was* comic, was what least appeased her unrest, and there were reasons enough, in a word, why her failure of the grand manner or the penetrating note should evoke the idea of their opposites perfectly achieved. She sat, alike in adoration and emulation, at the feet of my admirable old friend Fanny Kemble, the goodnature of whose consent to "hear" her was equalled only by the immediately consequent action of the splendidly corrective spring on the part of that unsurpassed subject of the dramatic afflatus fairly, or, as I should perhaps above all say, contradictiously provoked. Then aspirant and auditor, rash adventurer and shy alarmist, were swept away together in the gust of magnificent rightness and beauty, no scrap of the far-scattered prime proposal being left to pick up.

Which detail of reminiscence has again stayed my course to the Witley Villa, when even on the way I quaked a little with my sense of what *generally* most awaited or overtook my companion's prime proposals. What had come most to characterise the Leweses to my apprehension was that there couldn't be a thing in the world about which they weren't, and on the most conceded and assured grounds, almost scientifically particular; which presumption, however, only added to the relevance of one's learning how such a matter as their relation with Mrs. Greville could in accordance with noble consistencies be carried on. I could trust *her* for it perfectly, as she knew no law but that of innocent and exquisite aberration, never wanting and never less than consecrating, and I fear I but took refuge for the rest in declining all responsibility. I remember trying to say to myself that, even such as we were, our visit couldn't but scatter a little the weight of cloud on the Olympus we scaled—given the dreadful drenching afternoon we were after all an imaginable short solace there; and this indeed would have borne me through to the end save for an incident which, with a quite ideal logic, left our adventure an approved ruin. I see again our bland, benign, commiserating hostess beside the fire in a chill desert of a room where the master of the house guarded the opposite hearthstone, and I catch once more the impression of no occurrence of anything at all appreciable but their liking us to have come, with our terribly trivial contribution, mainly from a prevision of how they should more devoutly like it when we departed. It is remarkable, but the occasion yields me no single echo of a remark on the part of any of us—nothing more than the sense that our great author herself peculiarly suffered from the fury of the elements, and that they had about them rather the minimum of the paraphernalia of reading and writing, not to speak of that of tea, a conceivable feature of the hour, but which was not provided for. Again I felt touched with privilege, but not, as in '69, with a form of it redeemed from barrenness by a motion of my own, and the taste of barrenness was in fact in my mouth under the effect of our taking leave. We did so with considerable flourish till we had passed out to the hall again, indeed to the door of the waiting carriage, toward which G. H. Lewes himself all sociably, *then* above all conversingly, wafted us —yet staying me by a sudden remembrance before I had entered the brougham and signing me to wait while he repaired his omission. I returned to the doorstep, whence I still see him reissue from the room we had just left and hurry toward me across the hall shaking high the pair of blue-bound volumes his allusion to the uninvited, the verily importunate loan of which by Mrs. Greville had lingered on the air after his dash in quest of them; "Ah those books—take them away, please, away, away!" I hear him unreservedly plead while he thrusts them again at me, and I scurry back into our conveyance, where, and where only, settled afresh with my companion, I venture to assure myself of the horrid truth that had squinted at me as I relieved our good friend of his superfluity. What indeed was this superfluity but the two volumes of my own precious "last"—we were still in the blest age of volumes—presented by its author to the lady of Milford Cottage, and by her, misguided votary, dropped with the best conscience in the world into the Witley abyss, out of which it had jumped with violence, under the touch of accident, straight up again into my own exposed face?

The bruise inflicted there I remember feeling for the moment only as sharp, such a mixture of delightful small questions at once salved it over and such a charm in particular for me to my recognising that this particular wrong—inflicted all unawares, which exactly made it sublime—was the only rightness of our visit. Our hosts hadn't so much as connected book with author, or author with visitor, or visitor with anything but the convenience of his ridding them of an unconsidered trifle; grudging as they so justifiedly did the impingement of such matters on their consciousness. The vivid demonstration of one's failure to penetrate there had been in the sweep of Lewes's gesture, which could scarce have been bettered by his actually wielding a broom. I think nothing passed between us in the brougham on revelation of the identity of the offered treat so emphatically declined—I see that I couldn't have laughed at it to the confusion of my gentle neighbour. But I quite recall my grasp of the *interest* of our distinguished friends' inaccessibility to the unattended plea, with the light it seemed to throw on what it was really to *be* attended. Never, never save as attended—by presumptions, that is, far other than any then hanging about one—would one so much as desire *not* to be pushed out of sight. I needn't attempt, however, to supply all the links in the chain of association which led to my finally just qualified beatitude: I had been served right enough in all conscience, but the pity was that Mrs. Greville had been. This I never wanted for her; and I may add, in the connection, that I discover now no grain of false humility in my having enjoyed in my own person adorning such a tale. There was positively a fine high thrill in thinking of persons—or at least of a person, for any fact about Lewes was but derivative—engaged in my own pursuit and yet detached, by what

I conceived, detached by a pitch of intellectual life, from all that made it actual to myself. *There* was the lift of contemplation, there the inspiring image and the big supporting truth; the pitch of intellectual life in the very fact of which we seemed, my hostess and I, to have caught our celebrities sitting in that queer bleak way wouldn't have bullied me in the least if it hadn't been the centre of such a circle of gorgeous creation. It was the fashion among the profane in short either to misdoubt, before George Eliot's canvas, the latter's backing of rich thought, or else to hold that this matter of philosophy, and even if but of the philosophic vocabulary, thrust itself through to the confounding of the picture. But with that thin criticism I wasn't, as I have already intimated, to have a moment's patience; I was to become, I was to remain—I take pleasure in repeating—even a very Derondist of Derondists, for my own wanton joy: which amounts to saying that I found the figured, coloured tapestry *always* vivid enough to brave no matter what complication of the stitch.

From *The Middle Years* (1917), Chapter V.

THE VOICE OF CONCORD

I felt myself, on the spot,[1] cast about a little for the right expression of it, and then lost any hesitation to say that, putting the three or four biggest cities aside, Con-

---

[1] James is writing of his return, after an absence of twenty-one years, to America and New England in the autumn of 1904. [*Editor's note.*]

cord, Massachusetts, had an identity more palpable to the mind, had nestled in other words more successfully beneath her narrow fold of the mantle of history, than any other American town. "Compare me with places of my size, you know," one seemed to hear her plead, with the modesty that, under the mild autumn sun, so well became her russet beauty; and this exactly it was that prompted the emphasis of one's reply, or, as it may even be called, of one's declaration.

"Ah, my dear, it isn't a question of places of your 'size,' since among places of your size you're too obviously and easily first: it's a question of places, so many of them, of fifty times your size, and which yet don't begin to have a fraction of your weight, or your character, or your intensity of presence and sweetness of tone, or your moral charm, or your pleasant appreciability, or, in short, of anything that is yours. Your 'size'? Why, you're the biggest little place in America—with only New York and Boston and Chicago, by what I make out, to surpass you; and the country is lucky indeed to have you, in your sole and single felicity, for if it hadn't, where in the world should we go, inane and unappeased, for the particular communication of which you have the secret? The country is colossal, and you but a microscopic speck on the hem of its garment; yet there's nothing else like you, take you all round, for we *see* you complacently, with the naked eye, whereas there are vast sprawling, bristling areas, great grey 'centres of population' that spread, on the map, like irremediable grease-spots, which fail utterly of any appeal to our vision or any control of it, leaving it to pass them by as if they were not. If you are so thoroughly the opposite of one of these I don't say it's all your superlative merit; it's rather, as I have put it, your felicity, your good fortune, the result of the half-dozen happy turns of the wheel

in your favour. Half-a-dozen such turns, you see, are, for
any mortal career, a handsome allowance; and your
merit is that, recognizing this, you have not fallen below
your state. But it's your fortune, above all, that's your
charm. One doesn't want to be patronizing, but you
didn't, thank goodness, make yours. That's what the
other places, the big ones that are as nothing to you,
are trying to do, the country over—to make theirs; and,
from the point of view of these remarks, all in vain.
Your luck is that you didn't have to; yours had been,
just as it shows in you to-day, made *for* you, and you at
the most but gratefully submitted to it. It must be said
for you, however, that you keep it; and it isn't every
place that would have been capable——! You keep the
look, you keep the feeling, you keep the air. Your great
trees arch over these possessions more protectingly,
covering them in as a cherished presence; and you have
settled to your tone and your type as to treasures that
can now never be taken. Show me the other places in
America (of the few that have *had* anything) from
which the best hasn't mainly been taken, or isn't in im-
minent danger of being. There is old Salem, there is old
Newport, which I am on my way to see again, and
which, if you will, are, by what I hear, still comparatively intact; but their having was never a having like
yours, and they adorn, precisely, my little tale of your
supremacy. No, I don't want to be patronizing, but your
only fault is your tendency to improve—I mean just by
your duration as you *are;* which indeed is the only sort
of improvement that is not questionable."

Such was the drift of the warm flood of appreciation,
of reflection, that Concord revisited could set rolling
over the field of a prepared sensibility; and I feel as if
I had quite made my point, such as it is, in asking
what other American village could have done anything

of the sort. I should have been at fault perhaps only in speaking of the interest in question as visible, on that large scale, to the "naked eye"; the truth being perhaps that one wouldn't have been so met half-way by one's impression unless one had rather particularly *known*, and that knowledge, in such a case, amounts to a pair of magnifying spectacles. I remember indeed putting it to myself on the November Sunday morning, tepid and bright and perfect for its use, through which I walked from the station under the constant archway of the elms, as yet but indulgently thinned: would one know, for one's self, what had formerly been the matter here, if one hadn't happened to be able to get round behind, in the past, as it were, and more or less understand? Would the operative elements of the past—little old Concord Fight, essentially, and Emerson and Hawthorne and Thoreau, with the rest of the historic animation and the rest of the figured and shifting "transcendental" company, to its last and loosest ramifications—would even these handsome quantities have so lingered to one's intelligent after-sense, if one had not brought with one some sign by which they too would know; dim, shy spectralities as, for themselves, they must, at the best, have become? Idle, however, such questions when, by the chance of the admirable day, everything, in its own way and order, unmistakably came *out*—every string sounded as if, for all the world, the loose New England town (and I apply the expression but to the relations of objects and places), were a lyre swept by the hand of Apollo. Apollo was the spirit of antique piety, looking about, pausing, remembering, as he moved to his music; and there were glimpses and reminders that of course kept him much longer than others.

Seated there at its ease, as if placidly familiar with pilgrims and quite taking their homage for granted, the place had the very aspect of some grave, refined New England matron of the "old school," the widow of a high celebrity, living on and on in possession of all his relics and properties, and, though not personally addicted to gossip or to journalism, having become, where the great company kept by her in the past is concerned, quite cheerful and modern and responsive. From her position, her high-backed chair by the window that commands most of the coming and going, she looks up intelligently, over her knitting, with no vision of any limit on her part as yet, to this attitude, and with nothing indeed to suggest the possibility of a limit save a hint of that loss of temporal perspective in which we recognize the mental effect of a great weight of years. I had formerly the acquaintance of a very interesting lady, of extreme age, whose early friends, in "literary circles," are now regarded as classics, and who, toward the end of her life, always said, "You know Charles Lamb has produced a play at Drury Lane," or "You know William Hazlitt has fallen in love with such a very odd woman." Her facts were perfectly correct; only death had beautifully passed out of her world—since I don't remember her mentioning to me the demise, which she might have made so contemporary, either of Byron or of Scott. When people were ill she admirably forebore to ask about them—she disapproved wholly of such conditions; and there were interesting invalids round about her, near to her, whose existence she for long years consummately ignored. It is some such quiet backward stride as those of my friend that I seem to hear the voice of old Concord take in reference to her annals, and it is not too much to say that where her soil is most sacred, I fairly caught, on the breeze, the mitigated perfect tense. "You know there has been a fight between our men and the King's"—one wouldn't have been surprised, that crystalline Sunday noon, where so little had changed, where the stream and the bridge, and all nature, and the *feeling*, above all, still so directly testify, at any fresh-sounding form of such an announcement.

I had forgotten, in all the years, with what thrilling clearness that supreme site speaks—though anciently, while so much of the course of the century was still to run, the distinctness might have seemed even greater. But to stand there again was to take home this foreshortened view, the gained nearness, to one's sensibility; to look straight over the heads of the "American Weimar" company at the inestimable hour that had so handsomely set up for them their background. The Fight had been the hinge—so one saw it—on which the large revolving future was to turn; or it had been better, perhaps, the large firm nail, ringingly driven in, from which the beautiful portrait-group, as we see it to-day, was to hang. Beautiful exceedingly the local Emerson and Thoreau and Hawthorne and (in a fainter way) *tutti quanti;* but beautiful largely because the fine old incident down in the valley had so seriously prepared their effect. That seriousness gave once for all the pitch, and it was verily as if, under such a value, even with the seed of a "literary circle" so freely scattered by an intervening hand, the vulgar note would in that air never be possible. As I had inevitably, in long absence, let the value, for immediate perception, rather waste itself, so, on the spot, it came back most instantly with the extraordinary sweetness of the river, which, under the autumn sun, like all the American rivers one had seen or was to see, straightway took the whole case straightway into its hands. "Oh, you shall tell me of your impression when you have felt what *I* can do for it: so hang over me well!"—that's what they all seem to say.

I hung over Concord River then as long as I could, and recalled how Thoreau, Hawthorne, Emerson himself, have expressed with due sympathy the sense of this full, slow, sleepy, meadowy flood, which sets its pace and takes its twists like some large obese benevolent person, scarce so frankly unsociable as to pass you at all. It had watched the Fight, it even now confesses, without a quickening of its current, and it draws along the woods and the orchards and the fields with the purr of a mild domesticated cat who rubs against the family and the furniture. Not to be recorded, at best, however, I think, never to emerge from the state of the inexpressible, in respect to the spot, by the bridge, where one most lingers, is the sharpest suggestion of the whole scene—the power diffused in it which makes it, after all these years, or perhaps indeed by reason of their number, so irresistibly touching. All the commemorative objects, the stone marking the burial-place of the three English soldiers, the animated image of the young belted American yeoman by Mr. Daniel French, the intimately associated element in the presence, not far off, of the old manse, interesting theme of Hawthorne's pen, speak to the spirit, no doubt, in one of the subtlest tones of which official history is capable, and yet somehow leave the exquisite melancholy of everything unuttered. It lies too deep, as it always so lies where the ground has borne the weight of the short, simple act, intense and unconscious, that was to determine the event, determine the future in the way we call immortally. For we read into the scene too little of what we may, unless this muffled touch in it somehow reaches us so that we feel the pity and the irony of the *precluded* relation on the part of the fallen defenders. The sense that was theirs and that moved them we know, but we seem to know better still the sense that wasn't and that couldn't, and that forms

our luxurious heritage as our eyes, across the gulf, seek
to meet their eyes; so that we are almost ashamed of taking so much, such colossal quantity and value, as the
equivalent of their dimly-seeing offer. The huge bargain
they made for us, in a word, made by the gift of the
little all they had—to the modesty of which amount the
homely rural facts grouped there together have appeared to go on testifying—this brilliant advantage
strikes the imagination that yearns over them as unfairly
enjoyed at their cost. Was it delicate, was it decent—
that is *would* it have been—to ask the embattled farm-
ers, simple-minded, unwitting folk, to make us so inordinate a present with so little of the conscious credit
of it? Which all comes indeed, perhaps, simply to the
most poignant of all those effects of disinterested sacrifice
that the toil and trouble of our forefathers produce for
us. The minute-men at the bridge were of course interested intensely, as they believed—but such, too,
was the artful manner in which we see *our* latent, lurking, waiting interest like, a Jew in a dusky back-shop,
providentially bait the trap.

Beyond even such broodings as these, and to another
purpose, moreover, the communicated spell falls, in its
degree, into that pathetic oddity of the small aspect, and
the rude and the lowly, the reduced and humiliated
above all, that sits on so many nooks and corners, objects
and appurtenances, old contemporary things—contemporary with the doings of our race; simplifying our antecedents, our annals, to within an inch of their life,
making us ask, in presence of the rude relics even of
greatness, mean retreats and receptacles, construction-
ally so poor, from what barbarians or from what pigmies we have sprung. There are certain rough black
mementos of the early monarchy, in England and Scotland, there are glimpses of the original humble homes

of other greatness as well, that strike in perfection this grim little note; which has the interest of our being free to take it, for curiosity, for luxury of thought, as that of the real or that of the romantic, and with which, again, the deep Concord rusticity, momentary medium of our national drama, essentially consorts. We remember the small hard facts of the Shakespeare house at Stratford; we remember the rude closet, in Edinburgh Castle, in which James VI of Scotland was born, or the other little black hole, at Holyrood, in which Mary Stuart "sat" and in which Rizzio was murdered. These, I confess, are odd memories at Concord; although the manse, near the spot where we last paused, and against the edge of whose acre or two the loitering river seeks friction in the manner I have mentioned, would now seem to have shaken itself a trifle disconcertingly free of the ornamental mosses scattered by Hawthorne's light hand; it stands there, beyond its gate, with every due similitude to the shrunken historic site in general. To which I must hasten to add, however, that I was much more struck with the way these particular places of visitation resist their pressure of reference than with their affecting us as below their fortune. Intrinsically they are as naught—deeply depressing, in fact, to any impulse to reconstitute, the house in which Hawthorne spent what remained to him of life after his return from the Italy of his Donatello and his Miriam. Yet, in common with everything else, this mild monument benefits by that something in the air which makes us tender, keeps us respectful; meets, in the general interest, waving it vaguely away, any closer assault of criticism.

It is odd, and it is also exquisite, that these witnessing ways should be the last ground on which we feel moved to ponderation of the "Concord school"—to use,

I admit, a futile expression; or rather, I should doubtless say, it *would* be odd if there were not inevitably something absolute in the fact of Emerson's all but lifelong connection with them. We may smile a little as we "drag in" Weimar, but I confess myself, for my part, much more satisfied than not by our happy equivalent, "in American money," for Goethe and Schiller. The money is a potful in the second case as in the first, and if Goethe, in the one, represents the gold and Schiller the silver, I find (and quite putting aside any bimetallic prejudice) the same good relation in the other between Emerson and Thoreau. I open Emerson for the same benefit for which I open Goethe, the sense of moving in large intellectual space, and that of the gush, here and there, out of the rock, of the crystalline cupful, in wisdom and poetry, in Wahrheit and Dichtung; and whatever I open Thoreau for (I needn't take space here for the good reasons) I open him oftener than I open Schiller. Which comes back to our feeling that the rarity of Emerson's genius, which has made him so, for the attentive peoples, the first, and the one really rare, American spirit in letters, couldn't have spent his career in a charming woody, watery place, for so long socially and typically and, above all, interestingly homogeneous, without an effect as of the communication to it of something ineffaceable. It was during his long span his immediate concrete, sufficient world; it gave him his nearest vision of life, and he drew half his images, we recognize, from the revolution of its seasons and the play of its manners. I don't speak of the other half, which he drew from elsewhere. It is admirably, to-day, as if we were still seeing these things *in* those images, which stir the air like birds, dim in the eventide, coming home to nest. If one had reached a "time of life" one had

thereby at least heard him lecture; and not a russet leaf
fell for me, while I was there, but fell with an Emerso-
nian drop.

From Chapter VIII of *The American Scene* (1907).

A JOURNAL

BOSTON——CAMBRIDGE——LONDON——PARIS
25 NOVEMBER 1881–11 NOVEMBER 1882

Brunswick Hotel, Boston, November 25th, 1881. If I
should write here all that I might write, I should speedily fill this as yet unspotted blank-book, bought in London six months ago, but hitherto unopened. It is so long
since I have kept any notes, taken any memoranda,
written down my current reflections, taken a sheet of
paper, as it were, into my confidence. Meanwhile so
much has come and gone, so much that it is now too late
to catch, to reproduce, to preserve. I have lost too much
by losing, or rather by not having acquired, the note-
taking habit. It might be of great profit to me; and now
that I am older, that I have more time, that the labour
of writing is less onerous to me, and I can work more at
my leisure, I ought to endeavour to keep, to a certain extent, a record of passing impressions, of all that comes,
that goes, that I see, and feel, and observe. To catch and
keep something of life—that's what I mean. Here I am
back in America, for instance, after six years of absence,
and likely while here to see and learn a great deal that
ought not to become mere waste material. Here I am, *da
vero,* and here I am likely to be for the next five months.

I am glad I have come—it was a wise thing to do. I needed to see again *les miens,* to revive my relations with them, and my sense of the consequences that these relations entail. Such relations, such consequences, are a part of one's life, and the best life, the most complete, is the one that takes full account of such things. One can only do this by seeing one's people from time to time, by being with them, by entering into their lives. Apart from this I hold it was not necessary I should come to this country. I am 37 [1] years old, I have made my choice, and God knows that I have now no time to waste. My choice is the old world—my choice, my need, my life. There is no need for me today to argue about this; it is an inestimable blessing to me, and a rare good fortune, that the problem was settled long ago, and that I have now nothing to do but to act on the settlement.— My impressions here are exactly what I expected they would be, and I scarcely see the place, and feel the manners, the race, the tone of things, now that I am on the spot, more vividly than I did while I was still in Europe. My work lies there—and with this vast new world, *je n'ai que faire.* One can't do both—one must choose. No European writer is called upon to assume that terrible burden, and it seems hard that I should be. The burden is necessarily greater for an American—for he *must* deal, more or less, even if only by implication, with Europe; whereas no European is obliged to deal in the least with America. No one dreams of calling him less complete for not doing so. (I speak of course of people who do the sort of work that I do; not of economists, of social science people.) The painter of manners who

---

[1] He was actually 38. [Footnote by F. O. Matthiessen and K. B. Murdock in *The Notebooks of Henry James.* The footnotes to this journal are all from this edition.—*Editor's note.*]

neglects America is not thereby incomplete as yet; but a hundred years hence—fifty years hence perhaps—he will doubtless be accounted so. My impressions of America, however, I shall, after all, not write here. I don't need to write them (at least not *à propos* of Boston); I know too well what they are. In many ways they are extremely pleasant; but, Heaven forgive me! I feel as if my time were terribly wasted here! . . .

It is too late to recover all those lost impressions—those of the last six years—that I spoke of in beginning; besides, they are not lost altogether, they are buried deep in my mind, they have become part of my life, of my nature. At the same time, if I had nothing better to do, I might indulge in a retrospect that would be interesting and even fruitful—look back over all that has befallen me since last I left my native shores. I could remember vividly, and I have little doubt I could express happily enough, if I made the effort. I could remember without effort with what an irresistible longing I turned to Europe, with what ardent yet timid hopes, with what indefinite yet inspiring intentions, I took leave of *les miens*. I recall perfectly the maturing of my little plan to get abroad again and remain for years, during the summer of 1875; the summer the latter part of which I spent in Cambridge. It came to me there on my return from New York where I had been spending a bright, cold, unremunerative, uninteresting winter, finishing *Roderick Hudson* and writing for the *Nation*. (It was these two tasks that kept me alive.) I had returned from Europe the year before that, the beginning of September, '74, sailing for Boston with Wendell Holmes and his wife as my fellow passengers. I had come back then to "try New York," thinking it my duty to attempt to live at home before I should grow older, and not take for granted too much that Europe alone was possible; especially as Europe for me then meant simply Italy, where I had had some very discouraged hours, and which, lovely and desirable though it was, didn't seem as a permanent residence, to lead to anything. I wanted something more active, and I came back and sought it in New York. I came back with a certain amount of scepticism, but with very loyal intentions, and extremely eager to be "interested." As I say, I was interested but imperfectly, and I very soon decided what was the real issue of my experiment. It was by no means equally soon, however, that I perceived how I should be able to cross the Atlantic again. But the opportunity came to me at last—it loomed before me one summer's day, in Quincy St. The best thing I could imagine then was to go and take up my abode in Paris. I went (sailing about October 20th, 1875) and I settled myself in Paris with the idea that I should spend several years there. This was not really what I wanted; what I wanted was London—and Paris was only a stopgap. But London appeared to me then impossible. I believed that I might arrive there in the fulness of years, but there were all sorts of obstacles to my attempting to live there then. I wonder greatly now, in the light of my present knowledge of England, that these obstacles should have seemed so large, so overwhelming and depressing as they did at that time. When a year later I came really to look them in the face, they absolutely melted away. But that year in Paris was not a lost year—on the contrary. On my way thither I spent something like a fortnight in London; lodging at Story's Hotel, in Dover St. It was November—dark, foggy, muddy, rainy—and I knew scarcely a creature in the place. I don't remember calling on anyone but Lady Rose and H. J. W. Coulson, with whom I went out to lunch at Petersham, near Richmond. And yet the great city seemed to me enchanting, and I would have given my little finger to remain there rather than go to Paris. But I went to Paris, and lived for a year at 29 Rue de Luxembourg (now Rue Cambon). I shall not attempt to write the history of that year—further than to say that it was time by no means misspent. I learned to know Paris and French affairs much better than before—I got a certain familiarity with Paris (added to what I had acquired before) which I shall never lose. I wrote letters to the *New York Tribune,* of which, though they were poor stuff, I may say that they were too good for the purpose (of course they didn't succeed). I saw a good deal of Charles Peirce that winter—as to whom his being a man of genius reconciled me to much that was intolerable in him.[1] In the spring, at Madame Turgénieff's, I made the acquaintance of Paul Joukowsky. *Non ragioniam di lui—ma guarda e passa.* I don't speak of Ivan Turgénieff, most delightful and lovable of men, nor of Gustave Flaubert, whom I shall always be so glad to have known; a powerful, serious, melancholy, manly, deeply corrupted, yet not corrupting, nature. There was something I greatly liked in him, and he was very kind to me. He was a head and shoulders above the others, the men I saw at his house on Sunday afternoons—Zola, Goncourt, Daudet,

---

[1] James' reaction to Peirce was summed up in a letter home at the time: "He is a very good fellow—when he is not in ill-humour; then he is intolerable. But, as William says, he is a man of genius. . . ." Peirce wrote to William: "Your brother is looking pretty well, but looks a little serious. . . . He is a splendid fellow. I admire him greatly and have only discovered two faults in him. One is that his digestion isn't quite that of an ostrich and the other is that he isn't as fond of turning over questions as I am, but likes to settle them and have done with them. A manly trait too, but not a philosophic one."

etc. (I mean as a man—not as a talker, etc.) I remember in especial one afternoon (a weekday) that I went to see him and found him alone. I sat with him a long time; something led him to repeat to me a little poem of Th. Gautier's—*Les Vieux Portraits* (what led him to repeat it was that we had been talking of French poets, and he had been expressing his preference for Théophile Gautier over Alfred de Musset—*il était plus français,* etc.). I went that winter a great deal to the Comédie Française—though not so much as when I was in Paris in '72. Then I went every night—or almost. And I have been a great deal since. I may say that I know the Comédie Française. Of course I saw a great deal of the little American "set"—the American village encamped *en plein Paris.* They were all very kind, very friendly, hospitable, etc; they knew up to a certain point their Paris. But ineffably tiresome and unprofitable. Their society had become a kind of obligation, and it had much to do with my suddenly deciding to abandon my plans of indefinite residence, take flight to London and settle there as best I could. I remember well what a crime Mrs. S. made of my doing so; and one or two other persons as to whom I was perfectly unconscious of having given them the right to judge my movements so intimately. Nothing is more characteristic of certain American women than the extraordinary promptitude with which they assume such a right. I remember how Paris had, in a hundred ways, come to weary and displease me; I couldn't get out of the detestable *American* Paris. Then I hated the Boulevards, the horrible monotony of the new quarters. I saw, moreover, that I should be an eternal outsider. I went to London in November, 1876. I should say that I had spent that summer chiefly in three places: at Étretat, at Varennes (with the Lee Childes), and at Biarritz—or rather at Bayonne, where I took refuge being unable to find quarters at Biarritz. Then late in September I spent a short time at St. Germain, at the Pavillon Louis XIV. I was finishing *The American.* The pleasantest episode (by far) of that summer was my visit to the Childes; to whom I had been introduced by dear Jane Norton; who had been very kind to me during the winter; and who have remained my very good friends. Varennes is a little moated *castel* of the most picturesque character, a few miles from Montargis, *au coeur de l'ancienne France.* I well recall the impression of my arrival—driving over from Montargis with Edward Childe—in the warm August evening and reaching the place in the vague twilight, which made it look precisely like a *décor d'opéra.* I have been back there since—and it was still delightful; but at that time I had not had my now very considerable experience of country visits in England; I had not seen all those other wonderful things. Varennes therefore was an exquisite sensation—a memory I shall never lose. I settled myself again in Paris—or attempted to do so (I like to linger over these details, and to recall them one by one); I had no intention of giving it up. But there were difficulties in the Rue de Luxembourg—I couldn't get back my old apartment, which I had given up during the Summer. I don't remember what suddenly brought me to the point of saying—"Go to; I will try London." I think a letter from William had a good deal to do with it, in which he said, "Why don't you?—That must be the place." A single word from outside often moves one (moves *me* at least) more than the same word infinitely multiplied as a simple voice from within. I *did* try it, and it has succeeded beyond my most ardent hopes. As I think I wrote just now, I have become passionately fond of it; it is an anchorage for life. Here I sit scribbling in my bedroom at a Boston hotel—on a marble-topped table!

—and conscious of a ferocious homesickness—a home-sickness which makes me think of the day when I shall next see the white cliffs of old England loom through their native fog, as one of the happiest of my life! The history of the five years I have spent in London—a pledge, I suppose, of many future years—is too long, and too full to write. I can only glance at it here. I took a lodging at 3 Bolton St., Piccadilly; and there I have remained till today—there I have left my few earthly possessions, to await my return. I have *lived* much there, felt much, thought much, learned much, produced much; the little shabby furnished apartment ought to be sacred to me. I came to London as a complete stranger, and today I know much too many people. *J'y suis absolument comme chez moi.* Such an experience is an education—it fortifies the character and embellishes the mind. It is difficult to speak adequately or justly of London. It is not a pleasant place; it is not agreeable, or cheerful, or easy, or exempt from reproach. It is only magnificent. You can draw up a tremendous list of reasons why it should be insupportable. The fogs, the smoke, the dirt, the darkness, the wet, the distances, the ugliness, the brutal size of the place, the horrible numerosity of society, the manner in which this senseless bigness is fatal to amenity, to convenience, to conversation, to good manners—all this and much more you may expatiate upon. You may call it dreary, heavy, stupid, dull, inhuman, vulgar at heart and tiresome in form. I have felt these things at times so strongly that I have said—"Ah London, you too then are impossible?" But these are occasional moods; and for one who takes it as I take it, London is on the whole the most possible form of life. I take it as an artist and as a bachelor; as one who has the passion of observation and whose business is the study of human life. It is the biggest aggregation of

human life—the most complete compendium of the
world. The human race is better represented there than
anywhere else, and if you learn to know your London
you learn a great many things. I felt all this in that autumn of 1876, when I first took up my abode in Bolton
St. I had very few friends, the season was of the darkest
and wettest; but I was in a state of deep delight. I had
complete liberty, and the prospect of profitable work;
I used to take long walks in the rain. I took possession of
London; I felt it to be the right place. I could get English books: I used to read in the evenings, before an
English fire. I can hardly say how it was, but little by
little I came to know people, to dine out, etc. I did, I
was able to do, nothing at all to bring this state of things
about; it came rather of itself. I had very few letters—
I was afraid of letters. Three or four from Henry Adams,
three or four from Mrs. Wister, of which I only, as I
think, presented one (to George Howard). Poor Motley, who died a few months later, and on whom I had
no claim of *any* kind, sent me an invitation to the Athe-
naeum, which was renewed for several months, and
which proved an unspeakable blessing. When once one
starts in the London world (and one cares enough about
it, as I did, to make one's self agreeable, as I did) *cela
va de soi;* it goes with constantly increasing velocity. I
remained in London all the following summer—till
Sept. 1st—and then went abroad and spent some six
weeks in Paris, which was rather empty and very lovely,
and went a good deal to the theatre. Then I went to
Italy, spending almost all my time in Rome (I had a little
apartment flooded with sun, in the Capo le Case). I
came back to England before Xmas and spent the following nine months or so in Bolton St. The club question had become serious and difficult; a club was indispensable, but I had of course none of my own. I went

through Gaskell's (and I think Locker's) kindness for some time to the Travellers'; then after that for a good while to the St. James's, where I could pay a monthly fee. At last, I forget exactly when, I was elected to the Reform; I think it was about April, 1878. (F. H. Hill had proposed, and C. H. Roberts had seconded, me: or vice versa.) This was an excellent piece of good fortune, and the Club has ever since been, to me, a convenience of the first order. I could not have remained in London without it, and I have become extremely fond of it; a deep local attachment. I can now only briefly enumerate the landmarks of the rest of my residence in London. In the autumn of 1878 I went to Scotland, chiefly to stay at Tillypronie. (I afterwards paid a short visit at Gillesbie, Mrs. Rogerson's, in Dumfriesshire.) This was my first visit to Scotland, which made a great impression on me. The following year, 1879, I went abroad again —but only to Paris. I stayed in London during all August, writing my little book on Hawthorne, and on September 1st crossed over to Paris and remained there till within a few days of Xmas. I lodged again in the Rue de Luxembourg, in another house, in a delightful little *entresol entre cour et jardin,* which I had to give up after a few weeks however, as it had been let over my head. Afterwards I went to a hotel in the Rue St. Augustin (de Choiseul et d'Égypte) where I was staying during the great snow-storm of that year, which will long be famous. It was in that October that I went again to Varennes; I had other plans for seeing a little of France which I was unable to carry out. But I did a good deal of work: finished the ill-fated little *Hawthorne,*[1] finished

---

[1] James's *Hawthorne,* printed in 1879, was "ill-fated" in the attacks it provoked. He wrote Elizabeth Boott on 22 February 1880: "The American press, with 2 or 3 exceptions, seems furious over my poor little Hawthorne. It is a melancholy

Confidence, began *Washington Square,* wrote a *Bundle of Letters.* I went that Christmas, as I had been, I think, the Xmas before, to Ch. Milnes Gaskell's (Thorne's). In the spring I went to Italy—partly to escape the "season," which had become a terror to me. I couldn't keep out of it—(I had become a highly-developed diner-out, etc.) and its interruptions, its repetitions, its fatigues, were horribly wearisome, and made work extremely difficult. I went to Florence and spent a couple of months, during which I took a short run down to Rome and to Naples, where I had not been since my first visit to Italy, in 1869. I spent three days with Paul Joukowsky at Posilipo, and a couple of days alone at Sorrento. Florence was divine, as usual, and I was a great deal with the Bootts. At that exquisite Bellosguardo at the Hotel de l'Arno, in a room in that deep recess, in the front, I began the *Portrait of a Lady*[1]—that is, I took up, and worked over, an old beginning, made long before. I returned to London to meet William, who came out in the early part of June, and spent a month with me in Bolton St., before going to the continent. That summer and autumn I worked, *tant bien que mal,* at my novel which began to appear in *Macmillan* in October (1880). I got away from London more or less—to Brighton, detestable in August, to Folkestone, Dover, St. Leonard's, etc. I tried to work hard, and I paid very

---

revelation of angry vanity, vulgarity and ignorance. I thought they would protest a good deal at my calling New England life unfurnished, but I didn't expect they would lose their heads and their manners at such a rate." A letter to Howells a month earlier refers to some critics of the book as "bloodhounds" eager to besplatter "the decent public" with its author's "gore."

[1] When he wrote the preface to *The Portrait of a Lady* James's memory betrayed him into misdating this visit to the spring of 1879.

few visits. I had a plan of coming to America for the winter and even took my passage; but I gave it up. William came back from abroad and was with me again for a few days, before sailing for home. I spent November and December quietly in London, getting on with the *Portrait,* which went steadily, but very slowly, every part being written twice. About Xmas I went down into Cornwall, to stay with the John Clarks, who were wintering there, and then to the Pakenhams', who were (and still are) in the Government House at Plymouth. (Xmas day, indeed, I spent at the Pakenhams'—a bright, military dinner at which I took in Elizabeth Thompson [Mrs. Butler], the military paintress: a gentle, pleasing woman, very deaf.) Cornwall was charming, and my dear Sir John drove me far away to Penzance, and then to the Land's End, where we spent the morning of New Year's day—a soft moist morning, with the great Atlantic heaving gently round the outermost point of old England. (I was wrong just above in saying that I went *first* to the Clarks'. I went on there from Devonport.) I came back to London for a few weeks, and then, again, I went abroad. I wished to get away from the London crowd, the London hubbub, all the entanglements and interruptions of London life; and to quietly bring my novel to a close. So I planned to betake myself to Venice. I started about February 10th and I came back in the middle of July following. I have always to pay toll in Paris—it's impossible to pass through. I was there for a fortnight, which I didn't much enjoy. Then I traveled down through France, to Avignon, Marseilles, Nice, Mentone and San Remo, in which latter place I spent three charming weeks, during most of which time I had the genial society of Mrs. Lombard and Fanny L. who came over from Nice for a fortnight. I worked there capitally, and it made me very happy. I used in the morning to take a walk among the olives, over the hills behind the queer little black, steep town. Those old paved roads that rise behind and above San Remo, and climb and wander through the dusky light of the olives, have an extraordinary sweetness. Below and beyond, were the deep ravines, on whose sides old villages were perched, and the blue sea, glittering through the grey foliage. Fanny L. used to go with me—enjoying it so much that it was a pleasure to take her. I went back to the inn to breakfast (that is, lunch), and scribbled for 3 or 4 hours in the afternoon. Then, in the fading light, I took another stroll, before dinner. We went to bed early, but I used to read late. I went with the Lombards, one lovely day, on an enchanting drive—to the strange little old mountain town of Ceriana. I shall never forget that; it was one of the things one remembers; the grand clear hills, among which we wound higher and higher; the long valley, swimming seaward, far away beneath; the bright Mediterranean, growing paler and paler as we rose above it; the splendid stillness, the infinite light, the clumps of olives, the brown villages, pierced by the carriage road, where the vehicle bumped against opposite doorposts. I spent ten days at Milan after that, working at my tale and scarcely speaking to a soul; Milan was cold, dull, and less attractive than it had been to me before. Thence I went straight to Venice, where I remained till the last of June—between three and four months. It would take long to go into that now; and yet I can't simply pass it by. It was a charming time; one of those things that don't repeat themselves; I seemed to myself to grow young again. The lovely Venetian spring came and went, and brought with it an infinitude of impressions, of delightful hours. I became passionately fond of the place, of the life, of the people, of the habits. I asked myself at times whether it wouldn't be a happy thought to take a little *pied-à-terre* there, which one might keep forever. I looked at unfurnished apart ments; I fancied myself coming back every year. I *shall* go back; but not every year. Herbert Pratt was there for a month, and I saw him tolerably often; he used to talk to me about Spain, about the East, about Tripoli, Persia, Damascus; till it seemed to me that life would be *manquée* altogether if one shouldn't have some of that knowledge. He was a most singular, most interesting type, and I shall certainly put him into a novel. I shall even make the portrait close and he won't mind. Seeing picturesque lands, simply for their own sake, and without making any use of it—that, with him, is a passion—a passion of which if one lives with him a lit- tle (a little, I say; not too much) one feels the conta- gion. He gave me the nostalgia of the sun, of the south, of colour, of freedom, of being one's own master, and doing absolutely what one pleases. He used to say, "I know such a sunny corner, under the south wall of old Toledo. There's a wild fig tree growing there; I have lain on the grass, with my guitar. There was a musical mule- teer, etc." I remember one evening when he took me to a queer little wineshop, haunted only by gondoliers and *facchini*, in an out of the way corner of Venice. We had some excellent muscat wine; he had discovered the place and made himself quite at home there. Another evening I went with him to his rooms—far down on the Grand Canal, overlooking the Rialto. It was a hot night; the cry of the gondoliers came up from the Canal. He took out a couple of Persian books and read me extracts from Firdousi and Saadi. A good deal might be done with Herbert Pratt. He, however, was but a small part of my Venice. I lodged on the Riva, 4161, *quarto piano*. The view from my windows was *una bellezza;* the far- shining lagoon, the pink walls of San Giorgio, the downward curve of the Riva, the distant islands, the movement of the quay, the gondolas in profile. Here I wrote, diligently every day and finished, or virtually finished, my novel. As I say, it was a charming life; it seemed to me, at times, too improbable, too festive. I went out in the morning—first to Florian's, to breakfast; then to my bath, at the Stabilimento Chitarin; then I wandered about, looking at pictures, street life, etc., till noon, when I went for my real breakfast to the Café Quadri. After this I went home and worked till six o'clock—or sometimes only till five. In this latter case I had time for an hour or two *en gondole* before dinner. The evenings I strolled about, went to Florian's, listened to the music in the Piazza, and two or three nights a week went to Mrs. Bronson's. That was a resource but the milieu was too American. Late in the spring came Mrs. V.R., from Rome, who was an even greater resource. I went with her one day to Torcello and Burano; where we took our lunch and ate it on a lovely canal at the former place. Toward the last of April I went down to Rome and spent a fortnight—during part of which I was laid up with one of those terrible attacks in my head. But Rome was very lovely; I saw a great deal of Mrs. V.R.; had (with her) several beautiful drives. One in particular I remember; out beyond the Ponte Nomentano, a splendid Sunday. We left the carriage and wandered into the fields, where we sat down for some time. The exquisite stillness, the divine horizon, brought back to me out of the buried past all that ineffable, incomparable impression of Rome (1869, 1873). I returned to Venice by Ancona and Rimini. From Ancona I drove to Loreto, and, on the same occasion, to Recanati, to see the house of Giacomo Leopardi, whose infinitely touching letters I had been reading while in Rome. The day was lovely and the excursion picturesque; but I was not allowed to enter Leopardi's house. I saw, however, the dreary little hill-town where he passed so much of his life, with its enchanting beauty of site, and its strange, bright loneliness. I saw the streets—I saw the views he looked upon . . . Very little can have changed. I spent only an evening at Rimini, where I made the acquaintance of a most obliging officer, who seemed delighted to converse with a *forestiero*, and who walked me (it was a Sunday evening) all over the place. I passed near *Urbino*: that is, I passed a station, where I might have descended to spend the night, to drive to Urbino the next day. But I didn't stop! If I had been told that a month before, I should have repelled the foul insinuation. But my reason was strong. I was so nervous about my interrupted work that every day I lost was a misery, and I hurried back to Venice and to my MS. But I made another short absence, in June—a 5 days' *giro* to Vicenza, Bassano, Padua. At Vicenza I spent 3 of these days—it was wonderfully sweet; old Italy, and the old feeling of it. Vivid in my memory is the afternoon I arrived, when I wandered into the Piazza and sat there in the warm shade, before a *caffe* with the smooth slabs of the old pavement around me, the big palace and the tall *campanile* opposite, etc. It was so soft, so mellow, so quiet, so genial, so Italian; very little movement, only the waning of the bright day, the approach of the summer night. Before I left Venice the heat became intense, the days and nights alike impossible. I left it at last, and closed a singularly happy episode; but I took much away with me. . . .

I went straight to the Lake of Como and over the Splügen; spent only a lovely evening (with the next morning) at Cadenabbia. I mounted the Splügen under a splendid sky, and I shall never forget the sensation of rising, as night came (I walked incessantly, after we began to ascend) into that cool pure Alpine air, out of the stifling *calidarium* of Italy. I shall always remember a certain glass of fresh milk which I drank that evening, in the gloaming, far up (a woman at a wayside hostel had it fetched from the cow), as the most heavenly draft that ever passed my lips. I went straight to Lucerne, to see Mrs. Kemble, who had already gone to Engelberg. I spent a day on the lake, making the *giro;* it was a splendid day, and Switzerland looked more sympathetic than I had ventured to hope. I went up to Engelberg, and spent nearly a week with Mrs. Kemble and Miss Butler, in that grim, ragged, rather vacuous, but by no means absolutely unbeautiful valley. I spent an enchanting day with Miss Butler—climbing up to the Trübsee, toward the Joch Pass. The Trübsee is a little steel grey tarn, in a high cool valley, at the foot of the Titlis, whose great silver-gleaming snows overhang it and light it up. The whole place was a wilderness of the alpine rose—and the alpine stillness, the splendour of the weather, the beauty of the place, made the whole impression immense. We had a man with us who carried a lunch; and we partook of it at the little cold inn. The whole thing brought back my old Swiss days; I hadn't believed they could revive even to that point. . . .

New York, 115 East 25th St., December 20th, 1881. I had to break off the other day in Boston—the interruptions in the *morning* here are intolerable. That period of the day has none of the social sanctity here that it [has] in England, and which keeps it singularly free from intrusion. People—by which I mean ladies—think nothing of asking you to come and see them before lunch. Of course one can decline, but when many propositions of that sort come, a certain number stick. Besides, I have had all sorts of things to do, chiefly not profitable to recall. I have been three weeks in New York, and all my time has slipped away in mere movement. I try as usual to console myself with the reflection that I am getting impressions. This is very true; I have got a great many. I did well to come over; it was well worth doing. I indulged in some reflections a few pages back which were partly the result of a melancholy mood. I *can* do something here—it is not a mere complication. But it is not of that I must speak first in taking up my pen again—I shall return to those things later. I should like to finish briefly the little retrospect of the past year's doings, which I left ragged on the opposite page. . . . I came back from Switzerland to meet Alice,[1] who had been a month in England, and whom I presently saw at the Star and Garter, at Richmond. I spent two or three days with her, and saw her afterwards at Kew; then I went down to Sevenoaks and to Canterbury for the same purpose, spending a night at each place. I paid during July and August several visits. One to Burford Lodge (Sir Trevor Lawrence's); memorable on which occasion was a certain walk we took (on a Sunday afternoon), through the grounds of the Deepdene, an artificial but to me a most enchanting and most suggestive English place—full of foreign reminiscences; the sort of place that an Englishman of 80 years ago, who had made the grand tour and lingered in Italy, would naturally construct. I went to Leatherhead, and I went twice to Mentmore. (On one of these occasions Mr. Gladstone was there.) I went to Fredk. Macmillan's at Walton-on-Thames, and had some charming moments on the river. Then I went down into Somerset and spent a week at Midelney Place, the Lady Trevilian's. It is the impression of this visit that I wish not wholly to fade

[1] Henry James' sister.

away. Very exquisite it was (not the visit, but the impression of the country); it kept me a-dreaming all the while I was there. It seemed to me very old England; there was a peculiarly mellow and ancient feeling in it all. Somerset is not especially beautiful; I have seen much better English scenery. But I think I have never been more *penetrated*—I have never more loved the land. It was the old houses that fetched me—Montacute, the admirable; Barrington, that superb Ford Abbey, and several smaller ones. Trevilian showed me them all; he has a great care for such things. These delicious old houses, in the long August days, in the sovth of England air, on the soil over which so much has passed and out of which so much has come, rose before me like a series of visions. I thought of a thousand things; what becomes of the things one thinks of at these times? They are not lost, we must hope; they drop back into the mind again, and they enrich and embellish it. I thought of stories, of dramas, of all the life of the past —of things one can hardly speak of; speak of, I mean, at the time. It is art that speaks of those things; and the idea makes me adore her more and more. Such a house as Montacute, so perfect, with its grey personality, its old-world gardens, its accumulations of expression, of tone—such a house is really, *au fond,* an ineffaceable image; it can be trusted to rise before the eyes in the future. But what we think of with a kind of *serrement de coeur* is the gone-and-left-behind-us emotion with which at the moment we stood and looked at it. The picture may live again; but *that* is part of the past. . . .

Cambridge, December 26th. I came here on the 23d, to spend Xmas, Wilky[1] having come from the West (the first time in several years), to meet me. Here I sit

[1] Henry James' younger brother Garth Wilkinson.

writing in the old back sitting room which William and I used to occupy and which I now occupy alone— or sometimes with poor Wilky, whom I have not seen in some eleven years, and who is wonderfully unchanged for a man with whom life has not gone easy. The long interval of years drops away, and the edges of the chasm "piece together" again, after a fashion. The feeling of that younger time comes back to me in which I sat here scribbling, dreaming, planning, gazing out upon the world in which my fortune was to seek, and suffering tortures from my damnable state of health. It was a time of suffering so keen that that fact might [claim?] to give its dark colour to the whole period; but this is not what I think of today. When the burden of pain has been lifted, as many memories and emotions start into being as the little insects that scramble about when, in the country, one displaces a flat stone. Ill-health, physical suffering, in one's younger years, is a grievous trial; but I am not sure that we do not bear it most easily then. In spite of it we feel the joy of youth; and that is what I think of today among the things that remind me of the past. The freshness of impression and desire, the hope, the curiosity, the vivacity, the sense of the richness and mystery of the world that lies before us—there is an enchantment in all that which it takes a heavy dose of pain to quench and which in later hours, even if *success* have come to us, touches us less nearly. Some of my doses of pain were very heavy; very weary were some of my months and years. But all that is sacred; it is idle to write of it today. . . .

What comes back to me freely, delightfully, is the vision of those untried years. Never did a poor fellow have more; never was an ingenuous youth more passionately and yet more patiently eager for what life might bring.

Now that life has brought something, brought a measurable part of what I dreamed of then, it is touching enough to look back. I knew at least what I wanted then —to see something of the world. I have seen a good deal of it, and I look at the past in the light of this knowledge. What strikes me is the definiteness, the unerringness of those longings. I wanted to do very much what I have done, and success, if I may say so, now stretches back a tender hand to its younger brother, desire. I remember the days, the hours, the books, the seasons, the winter skies and darkened rooms of summer. I remember the old walks, the old efforts, the old exaltations and depressions. I remember more than I can say here today. . . .

Again, in New York the other day, I had to break off: I was trying to finish the little history of the past year. There is not much more to be said about it. I came back from Midelney, to find Alice in London, and spent ten days with her there, very pleasantly, at the end of August. Delightful to me is London at that time, after the horrors of the season have spent themselves, and the long afternoons make a cool grey light in the empty West End. Delightful to me, too, it was to see how *she* enjoyed it—how interesting was the impression of the huge, mild city. London is mild then; that is the word. And then I went to Scotland—to Tillypronie, to Cortachy, to Dalmeny, to Laidlawstiel. I was to have wound up, on my way back, with Castle Howard; but I retracted, on account of Lord Airlie's death. I can't go into all this; there were some delightful moments, and Scotland made, as it had made before, a great impression. Perhaps what struck me as much as anything was my drive, in the gloaming, over from Kirriemuir to Cortachy; though, taking the road afterward by daylight, I saw it was commonplace. In the late Scotch twilight, and the keen air, it was romantic; at least it was romantic to ford the river at the entrance to Cortachy, to drive through the dim avenues and up to the great lighted pile of the castle, where Lady A., hearing my wheels on the gravel (I was late) put her handsome head from a window in the clock-tower, asked if it was I, and wished me a bonny good-evening. I was in a Waverly Novel.

Then my drive (with her) to Glamis; and my drive (with Miss Stanley) to Airlie Castle, enchanting spot! Dalmeny is delicious, a magnificent pile of wood beside the Forth, and the weather, while I was there, was the loveliest I have ever known in the British Isles. But the company was not interesting, and there was a good deal of dreariness in the ball we all went to at Hopetoun for the coming of age of the heir. A charming heir he was, however, and a very pretty picture of a young nobleman stepping into his place in society—handsome, well-mannered, gallant, graceful, with 40,000 £ a year and the world at his feet. Laidlawstiel, on a bare hill among hills, just above the Tweed, is in the midst of Walter Scott's country. Reay walked with me over to Ashestiel one lovely afternoon; it is only an hour away. The house has been greatly changed since the 'Sheriff's' day;[1] but the place, the country, are the same, and I found the thing deeply interesting. It took one back. While I was at the Reays' I took up one of Scott's novels—*Redgauntlet;* it was years since I had read one. They have always a charm for me—but I was amazed at the badness of R.: *l'enfance de l'art*. . . .

[1] The "Sheriff" was Walter Scott, appointed Sheriff of Selkirkshire in 1799. He rented the house of Ashestiel, on the south bank of the Tweed, near Selkirk, in 1804.

Now and here I have only one feeling—the desire to get at work again. It is nearly six months that I have been resting on my oars—letting the weeks go, with nothing to show for them but these famous "impressions"! Prolonged idleness exasperates and depresses me, and though now that I am here, it is a pity not to move about and (if the chance presents itself) see the country, the prospect of producing nothing for the rest of the winter is absolutely intolerable to me. If it comes to my having to choose between remaining stationary somewhere and getting at work, or making a journey during which I shall be able to do no work, I shall certainly elect for the former. But probably I shall be able to compromise: to see something of the country and yet work a little. My mind is full of plans, of ambitions; they crowd upon me, for these are the productive years of life. I have taken aboard by this time a tremendous quantity of material; I really have never taken stock of my cargo. After long years of waiting, of obstruction, I find myself able to put into execution the most cherished of all my projects—that of beginning to work for the stage. It was one of my earliest—I had it from the first. None has given me brighter hopes—none has given me sweeter emotions. It is strange nevertheless that I should never have done anything—and to a certain extent it is ominous. I wonder at times that the dream should not have faded away. It comes back to me now, however, and I ache with longing to settle down at last to a sustained attempt in this direction. I think there is really reason enough for my not having done so before: the little work at any time that I could do, the uninterrupted need of making money on the spot, the inability to do two things at once, the absence of opportunities, of openings. I may add to this the feeling that I could afford to wait, that, looked at as I look at it, the drama is the ripest of all the arts, the one to which one must bring most of the acquired as well as most of the natural, and that while I was waiting I was studying the art, and clearing off my field. I think I may now claim to have studied the art as well as it can be studied in the contemplative way. The French stage I have mastered; I say that without hesitation. I have it in my pocket, and it seems to me clear that this is the light by which one must work today. I have laid up treasures of wisdom about all that. What interesting hours it has given me—what endless consideration it has led to! Sometimes, as I say, it seems to me simply deplorable that I should not have got at work before. *But it was impossible at the time,* and I knew that my chance would come. Here it is; let me guard it sacredly now. Let nothing divert me from it; but now the loss of time, which has simply been a maturing process, will become an injurious one. *Je me résume,* as George Sand's heroes say. I remember certain occasions; several acute visitations of the purpose of which I write come back to me vividly. Some of them, the earliest, were brought on merely by visits to the theatre—by seeing great actors, etc.—at fortunate hours; or by reading a new piece of Alex. Dumas, of Sardou, of Augier. No, my dear friend, nothing of all that is lost. *Ces emotions-là ne se perdent pas; elles rentrent dans le fonds même de notre nature; elles font partie de notre volonté.* The *volonté* has not expired; it is only perfect today. Two or three of the later occasions of which I speak have been among the things that *count* in the formation of a purpose; they are worth making a note of here. What has always counted, of course, has been the Comédie Française; it is on that, as regards this long day-dream, that I have lived. But there was an evening there that I shall long remember; it was in September, 1877. I had come over from London; I was lodging in the Avenue d'Antin—the house with a *tir* behind it. I went to see *Jean Dacier,* with Coquelin as the hero; I shall certain[ly not] forget that impression. The piece is, on the whole, I suppose, bad; but it contains some very effective scenes, and the two principal parts gave Coquelin and Favart a magnificent chance. It is Coquelin's *great* chance, and he told me afterwards in London that it is the part he values most. He is everything in it by turns, and I don't think I ever followed an actor's creation more intently. It threw me into a great state of excitement; I thought seriously of writing to Coquelin, telling him I had been his school-mate, etc.[1] It held up a glowing light to me—seemed to point to my own path. If I could have sat down to work then I probably should not have stopped soon. But I didn't; I couldn't; I was writing things for which I needed to be paid from month to month. (I like to remind myself of these facts—to justify my innumerable postponements.) I remember how, on leaving the theatre—it was a lovely evening—I walked about a long time under the influence not so much of the piece as of Coquelin's

---

[1] James had been for a time Coquelin's schoolmate at the Collège Communal in Boulogne, as he tells us in *A Small Boy and Others* (1913). When he wrote that book he looked back on Coquelin as "the most interesting and many-sided comedian, or at least the most unsurpassed dramatic *diseur* of the time." As early as 1877, in his essay on "The Théâtre Français" in the *Galaxy* for April, he devoted several appreciative paragraphs to Coquelin, but it was the performance of Lomon's *Jean Dacier* in September that brought his enthusiasm to its peak. The experience proved indeed unforgettable, and ten years later, in his essay on Coquelin in the *Century* for January 1887, James described just as he does here in the notebook his emotional excitement and his late evening walk after leaving the theater. The play, a four-act tragedy in verse, he called Coquelin's "highest flight in the line of rhymed parts."

acting of it, which had made the thing so human, so brilliant, so valuable. I was agitated with what it said to me that I might do—what I ought to attempt; I walked about the Place de la Concorde, along the Seine, up the Champs Elysées. That was nothing, however, to the state I was thrown into by meeting Coquelin at breakfast at Andrew Lang's, when the Comédie Française came to London. The occasion, for obvious reasons, was unpropitious, but I had some talk with him which rekindled and revived all my latent ambitions. At that time, too, my hands were tied; I could do nothing, and the feeling passed away in smoke. But it stirred me to the depths. Coquelin's personality, his talk, the way the *artist* overflowed in him—all this was tremendously suggestive. I could say little to him there—not a tittle of what I wished; I could only listen, and translate to him what *they* said—an awkward task! But I listened to some purpose, and I have never lost what I gained. It excited me powerfully; I shall not forget my walk, afterwards, down from South Kensington to Westminster. I met Jack Gardner, and he walked with me to leave a card at the Speaker's House. All day, and for days afterward, I remained under the impression. It faded away in time, and I had to give myself to other things. But this brings it back to me; and I may say that those two little moments were landmarks. There was a smaller incident, later, which it gives me pleasure to recall, as it gave me extreme pleasure at the time. John Hare asked me (I met him at dinner at the Comyns Carrs')—urged me, I may say—to write a play, and offered me his services in the event of my doing so. I shall take him at his word. When I came back from Scotland in October last I was full of this work; my hands were free; my pocket lined; I would have given a £100 for the liberty to sit down and hammer away. I imagined such a capital winter of work. But I had to come hither instead. If that however involves a loss of part of my time, it needn't involve the loss of all!

February 9th, 1882, 102 Mt. Vernon St., Boston. When I began to make these rather ineffectual records I had no idea that I should have in a few weeks to write such a tale of sadness as today. I came back from Washington on the 30th of last month (reached Cambridge the next day), to find that I should never again see my dear mother. On Sunday, Jan. 29th, as Aunt Kate sat with her in the closing dusk (she had been ill with an attack of bronchial asthma, but was apparently recovering happily), she passed away. It makes a great difference to me! I knew that I loved her—but I didn't know how tenderly till I saw her lying in her shroud in that cold North Room, with a dreary snowstorm outside, and looking as sweet and tranquil and noble as in life. These are hours of exquisite pain; thank Heaven this particular pang comes to us but once. On Sunday evening (at 10 o'clock in Washington) I was dressing to go to Mrs. Robinson's—who has written me a very kind letter—when a telegram came in from Alice (William's): "Your mother exceedingly ill. Come at once." It was a great alarm, but it didn't suggest the loss of all hope; and I made the journey to New York with whatever hope seemed to present itself. In New York at 5 o'clock I went to Cousin H.P.'s—and there the telegram was translated to me. Eliza Ripley was there—and Katie Rodgers— and as I went out I met Lily Walsh. The rest was dreary enough. I went back to the Hoffman House, where I had engaged a room on my way up town and remained there till 9.30, when I took the night-train to Boston. I shall never pass that place in future without thinking of the wretched hours I spent there. At home the worst was

over; I found father and Alice and A.K.[1] extraordinarily
calm—almost happy. Mother seemed still to be there—
so beautiful, so full of all that we loved in her, she
looked in death. We buried her on Wednesday, Feb 1st;
Wilky arrived from Milwaukee a couple of hours before.
Bob[2] had been there for a month—he was devoted to
mother in her illness. It was a splendid winter's day—
the snow lay deep and high. We placed her, for the present, in a temporary vault in the Cambridge cemetery—
the part that lies near the river. When the spring comes
on we shall go and choose a burial place. I have often
walked there in the old years—in those long, lonely
rambles that I used to take about Cambridge, and I had,
I suppose, a vague idea that some of us would some day
lie there, but I didn't see just that scene. It is impossible
for me to say—to begin to say—all that has gone down
into the grave with her. She was our life, she was the
house, she was the keystone of the arch. She held us all
together, and without her we are scattered reeds. She
was patience, she was wisdom, she was exquisite mater-
nity. Her sweetness, her mildness, her great natural beneficence were unspeakable, and it is infinitely touching
to me to write about her here as one that *was*. When
I think of all that she had been, for years—when I think
of her hourly devotion to each and all of us—and that
when I went to Washington the last of December I gave
her my last kiss, I heard her voice for the last time—
there seems not to be enough tenderness in my being
to register the extinction of such a life. But I can reflect,
with perfect gladness, that her work was done—her
long patience had done its utmost. She had had heavy
cares and sorrows, which she had borne without a mur-

[1] "A.K." was "Aunt Kate"—James' mother's sister, Kath-
arine Walsh.
[2] Henry James' youngest brother, Robertson.

mur, and the weariness of age had come upon her. I
would rather have lost her forever than see her begin
to suffer as she would probably have been condemned
to suffer, and I can think with a kind of holy joy of her
being lifted now above all our pains and anxieties. Her
death has given me a passionate belief in certain tran-
scendent things—the immanence of being as nobly created as hers—the immortality of such a virtue as that—
the reunion of spirits in better conditions than these.
She is no more of an angel today than she had always
been; but I can't believe that by the accident of her
death all her unspeakable tenderness is lost to the beings
she so dearly loved. She is with us, she is of us—the
eternal stillness is but a form of her love. One can hear
her voice in it—one can feel, forever, the inextinguish-
able vibration of her devotion. I can't help feeling that
in those last weeks I was not tender enough with her—
that I was blind to her sweetness and beneficence. One
can't help wishing one had only known what was coming, so that one might have enveloped her with the soft-
est affection. When I came back from Europe I was
struck with her being worn and shrunken, and now I
know that she was very weary. She went about her usual
activities, but the burden of life had grown heavy for
her, and she needed rest. There is something inexpres-
sibly touching to me in the way in which, during these
last years, she went on from year to year without it. If
she could only have lived she should have had it, and
it would have been a delight to see her have it. But she
has it now, in the most complete perfection! Summer
after summer she never left Cambridge—it was impossible that father should leave his own house. The country, the sea, the change of air and scene, were an
exquisite enjoyment to her; but she bore with the deepest gentleness and patience the constant loss of such

opportunities. She passed her nights and her days in that dry, flat, hot, stale and odious Cambridge, and had never a thought while she did so but for father and Alice. It was a perfect mother's life—the life of a perfect wife. To bring her children into the world—to expend herself, for years, for their happiness and welfare—then, when they had reached a full maturity and were absorbed in the world and in their own interests—to lay herself down in her ebbing strength and yield up her pure soul to the celestial power that had given her this divine commission. Thank God one knows this loss but once; and thank God that certain supreme impressions remain! . . .

All my plans are altered—my return to England vanishes for the present. I must remain near father; his infirmities make it impossible I should leave him. This means an indefinite detention in this country—a prospect far enough removed from all my recent hopes of departure.

August 3d, 1882, 3 Bolton St. W. From time to time one feels the need of summing-up. I have done it little in the past, but it will be a good thing to do it more in the future. The prevision with which I closed my last entry in these pages was not verified. I sailed from America on the date I had in my mind when I went home— May 10th. Father was materially better and had the strongest wish that I should depart; he and Alice had moved into Boston and were settled very comfortably in a small, pretty house (101 Mt. Vernon St.). Besides, their cottage at Manchester was rapidly being finished; shortly before sailing I went down to see it. Very pretty —bating the American scragginess; with the sea close to the piazzas, and the smell of bayberries in the air.

Rest, coolness, peace, society enough, charming drives; they will have all that.—Very soon after I had got back here my American episode began to fade away, to seem like a dream; a very painful dream, much of it. While I was there, it was Europe, it was England, that was dreamlike—but now all this is real enough. The Season is over, thank God; I came in for as much of it as could crowd itself into June and July. I was out of the mood for it, preoccupied, uninterested, bored, eager to begin work again; but I was obliged, being on the spot, to accommodate myself to the things of the day, and always with my old salve to a perturbed spirit, the idea that I was seeing the world. It seemed to me on the whole a poor world this time; I saw and did very little that was interesting. I am extremely glad to be in London again; I am deeply attached to London; I always shall be; but decidedly I like it best when it is "empty," as during the period now beginning. I know too many people—I have gone in too much for society. . . .

Grand Hôtel, Paris, November 11th. Thanks to "society," which, in the shape of various surviving remnants of the season, and to a succession of transient Americans and to several country visits, continued to mark me for its own during the greater part of the month of August, I had not even time to finish that last sentence written more than three months ago. I can hardly take up at this date the history of these three months: a simple glance must suffice. I remained in England till the 12th of September. Bob, whom I had found reclining on my sofa in Bolton St. when I arrived from America toward the last of May—(I hadn't even time, above, to mention my little disembarkation in Ireland and the few days I spent there)—Bob, who as I say was awaiting me at my lodgings in London—greatly to my surprise, and in a very battered and depressed condition, thanks to his unhappy voyage to the Azores—sailed for home again in the last days of August, after having spent some weeks in London, at Malvern and at Llandudno, in Wales. The last days, before sailing, he spent with me. About the 10th of September William arrived from America, on his way to the Continent to pass the winter. After being with him for a couple of days, I came over to Paris via Folkestone (I came down there and slept, before crossing), while he crossed to Flushing, from Queenborough. All summer I had been trying to work, but my interruptions had been so numerous that it was only during the last weeks that I succeeded, even moderately, in doing something. My record of work for the whole past year is terribly small, and I opened this book, just now, with the intention of taking several solemn vows in reference to the future. But I don't even know whether I shall accomplish that. However, I am not sure that such solemnities are necessary, for God knows I am eager enough to work, and that I am deeply convinced of the need of it, both for fortune and for happiness. . . .

I scarcely even remember the three or four visits to which, in the summer, I succeeded in restricting my "social activity." A pleasant night at Loseley—Rhoda Broughton was there. Another day I went down there to lunch, to take Howells (who spent all August in London) and Bob. Two days at Mentmore; a Saturday-to-Monday episode (very dull) at Miss de Rothschild's, at Wimbledon; a very pleasant day at the Arthur Russells', at Shiere. This last was charming; I think I went nowhere else—having wriggled out of Midelney, from my promised visit to Mrs. Pakenham, and from pledges more or less given to Tillypronie. Toward the last, in

London, I had my time pretty well to myself, and I felt, as I have always felt before, the charm of those long, still days, in the empty time, when one can sit and scribble, without notes to answer or visits to pay. Shall I confess, however, that the evenings had become dull? . . .

I had meant to write some account of my last months in America, but I fear the chance for this has already passed away. I look back at them, however, with a great deal of tenderness. Boston is absolutely nothing to me— I don't even dislike it. I like it, on the contrary; I only dislike to live there. But all those weeks I spent there, after Mother's death, had an exquisite stillness and solemnity. My rooms in Mt. Vernon St. were bare and ugly; but they were comfortable—were, in a certain way, pleasant. I used to walk out, and across the Common, every morning, and take my breakfast at Parker's. Then I walked back to my lodgings and sat writing till four or five o'clock; after which I walked out to Cambridge over that dreary bridge whose length I had measured so often in the past, and, four or five days in the week, dined in Quincy St. with Father and Alice. In the evening, I walked back, in the clear, American starlight. —I got in this way plenty of exercise. It was a simple, serious, wholesome time. Mother's death appeared to have left behind it a soft beneficent hush in which we lived for weeks, for months, and which was full of rest and sweetness. I thought of her, constantly, as I walked to Boston at night along those dark vacant roads, where, in the winter air, one met nothing but the coloured lamps and the far-heard jingle of the Cambridge horse-cars. My work at this time interested me, too, and I look back upon the whole three months with a kind of religious veneration. My work interested me even more than the importance of it would explain—or than the success of it has justified. I tried to write a little play (D[*aisy*] M[*iller*]) and I wrote it; but my poor little play has not been an encouragement. I needn't enter into the tiresome history of my ridiculous negotiations with the people of the Madison Square Theatre, of which the Proprietors behaved like asses and sharpers combined; this episode, by itself, would make a brilliant chapter in a realistic novel. It interested me immensely to write the piece, and the work confirmed all my convictions as to the fascination of this sort of composition. But what it has brought [me] to know, both in New York and in London, about the manners and ideas of managers and actors and about the conditions of production on our unhappy English stage, is almost fatally disgusting and discouraging. I have learned, very vividly, that if one attempts to work for it one must be prepared for *disgust,* deep and unspeakable disgust. But though I am disgusted, I do not think I am discouraged. The reason of this latter is that I simply can't afford to be. I have determined to take a year—even two years, if need be— more, in experiments, in studies, in attempts. The dramatic form seems to me the most beautiful thing possible; the misery of the thing is that the baseness of the English-speaking stage affords no setting for it. How I am to reconcile this with the constant solicitation that presses upon me, both from within and from without, to get at work upon another novel, is more than I can say. It is surely the part of wisdom, however, not to begin another novel at once—not to commit myself to a work of *longue haleine.* I must do *short* things, in such measure as I need, which will leave me intervals for dramatic work. I say this rather glibly—and yet I sometimes feel a woeful hunger to sit down to another novel. If I can only *concentrate* myself: this is the great lesson of life. I have hours of unspeakable reaction against my smallness of production; my wretched habits of work—or of un-work; my levity, my vagueness of mind, my perpetual failure to focus my attention, to absorb myself, to look things in the face, to invent, to produce, in a word. I shall be 40 years old in April next: it's a horrible fact! I believe however that I have learned how to work and that it is in moments of forced idleness, almost alone, that these melancholy reflections seize me. When I am really at work, I'm happy, I feel strong, I see many opportunities ahead. It is the only thing that makes life endurable. I must make some great efforts during the next few years, however, if I wish not to have been on the whole a failure. I shall have been a failure unless I do something *great!* . . .

From *The Notebooks of Henry James* (1947).

VI

LETTERS

1869-1915

EDITOR'S NOTE

The Letters of Henry James, which Percy Lubbock edited in two volumes in 1920, is a selection from the immense correspondence of James's lifetime. It remains to the present day the amplest edition we have of his communications with his family, his friends, his professional associates and literary contemporaries. It has been supplemented by several shorter collections of his letters, the most important being: "A *Most Unholy Trade*": *Being Letters on the Drama by Henry James* (Cambridge, Mass.: Scarab Press, 1923); *Letters of Henry James to Walter Berry* (Paris: Black Sun Press, 1928); *Henry James: Letters to A. C. Benson and Auguste Monod,* edited by E. F. Benson (New York: Scribner's, 1930); *Theatre and Friendship: Some Henry James Letters,* by Elizabeth Robins (New York: Putnam's, 1932); *Henry James and Robert Louis Stevenson: A Record of Criticism and Friendship,* by Janet Adam Smith (New York: Macmillan, 1948); "Letters of Henry James to Mr. Justice Holmes," edited by M. A. DeWolfe Howe, *Yale Review,* XXXVI, No. 3 (March 1949), pp. 410-33; "Henry James's Letters to the LaFarges," edited by John LaFarge, Jr., *New England Quarterly,* XXII (June 1949), pp. 173-92; and Virginia Harlow's *Thomas Sergeant Perry: A Biography and Letters to Perry from William, Henry, and Garth Wilkinson James* (Durham, N.C.: Duke University Press, 1950)—the last especially valuable for containing the earliest extant letters of James, as well as his correspondence with a lifelong friend. I have taken all the letters in the following selection from Lubbock's volumes as published in New York by Charles Scribner's Sons.

They cover a space of forty-six years, from 1869, when James made his first adult trip to Europe, to June 1915, in the last year of his life, when he decided to become a British subject. They have been selected to show, however fragmentarily, the drama of his career in America, in Europe, and in literature. They touch on his discovery of England, his "siege of London," his wanderings in Italy and France, his meetings with the literary great in Paris and London, his determined conquest of English society, his fortunes in authorship, the keenly felt losses he suffered in the deaths of his father, mother, sister, and closest brother, his doomed effort to achieve success in the theater, which reached its climax in January 1895 when his *Guy Domville* was jeered by the British public, his discovery of Lamb House at Rye, which he made his last settled home in England, his return to America in 1904-1905, his sense of becoming a survivor of a passing generation, the honors he received on his seventieth birthday in 1913, the profound shock he felt on the coming of war in 1914, and his eventual decision to become a citizen of his adopted country eight months before his death.

His correspondents here are readily recognizable: his father, his mother, his brother William, who became the celebrated Harvard psychologist and philosopher, and his brilliant sister, Alice, who joined him in England in her last invalid years and died there in 1892; William Dean Howells, the American novelist, editor, and critic, foremost and longest-lasting of James's literary contemporaries in America; Grace Norton, his old friend of Cambridge, sister of Charles Eliot Norton of Harvard; Mrs. William James, his sister-in-law; Edmund Gosse, the English critic; Mrs. Henry White, a friend of New York and Paris; Thomas Sergeant Perry of Boston, a friend of James from the time they were youths together at Newport in 1860; Henry Adams, the American editor and historian, author of *The Education of Henry Adams* and *Mont-Saint-Michel and Chartres*, whom James knew in America and Europe over a space of forty years; Howard Sturgis, the American expatriate in England, author of *Belchamber* and other novels, also a friend of many years; Walter Van Rensselaer Berry, another American expatriate, of Paris, friend of James, Mrs. Wharton, and Proust; Edith Wharton, the American novelist and quasi-disciple of James, whom he knew in the last fifteen years of his life in Paris, America, and England; Mrs. W. K. Clifford and Rhoda Broughton, both late Victorian novelists and old friends in England; and his nephew, Henry James, Jr., oldest son of William James, who was eventually to become his uncle's as well as his father's literary executor. These are only a few of the friends and relatives whom James engaged in correspondence from the 1860's to his death.

Here James is glimpsed, writing in London, in Paris, in Italy, in America, in the night watches of Lamb House, in his last flat in London—writing the copious, confiding, lavish, and inimitable letters which, like his travel essays, belong to a different age from ours: pouring them forth in all the intervals of his incessant practice of his craft, until they become a running chronicle of his long life in the world and in his art.

"THE MAGNITUDE OF LONDON": TO MISS ALICE JAMES

[London]
7 Half Moon St., W.
March 10th [1869].

Ma sœur chérie,

I have half an hour before dinner-time: why shouldn't I begin a letter for Saturday's steamer? . . . I really feel as if I had lived—I don't say a lifetime—but a year in this murky metropolis. I actually believe that this feeling is owing to the singular permanence of the impressions of childhood, to which any present experience joins itself on, without a broken link in the chain of sensation. Nevertheless, I may say that up to this time I have been crushed under a sense of the mere magnitude of London—its inconceivable immensity—in such a way as to paralyse my mind for any appreciation of details. This is gradually subsiding; but what does it leave behind it? An extraordinary intellectual depression, as I may say, and an indefinable flatness of mind. The place sits on you, broods on you, stamps on you with the feet of its myriad bipeds and quadrupeds. In fine, it is anything but a cheerful or a charming city. Yet it is a very splendid one. It gives you here at the west end, and in the city proper, a vast impression of opulence and prosperity. But you don't want a dissertation of commonplaces on London and you would like me to touch on my own individual experience. Well, my dear, since last week it has been sufficient, altho' by no means immense. On Saturday I received a visit from Mr. Leslie Stephen (blessed man) who came unsolicited with the utmost civility in the world and invited me to dine with him the next day. This I did, in company with Miss Jane Norton. His wife made me very welcome and they both appear to much better effect in their own premises than they did in America. After dinner he conducted us by the underground railway to see the beasts in the Regent's Park, to which as a member of the Zoological Society he has admittance 'Sundays.' . . . In the evening I dined with the invaluable Nortons and went with Chas. and Madame, Miss S. and Miss Jane (via underground railway) to hear Ruskin lecture at University College on Greek Myths. I enjoyed it much in spite of

fatigue; but as I am to meet him some day through the
Nortons, I shall reserve comments. On Wednesday evening I dined at the N.'s (toujours Norton, you see) in
company with Miss Dickens—Dickens's only unmarried
daughter—plain-faced, ladylike (in black silk and black
lace,) and the image of her father. I exchanged but ten
words with her. But yesterday, my dear old sister, was
my crowning day—seeing as how I spent the greater
part of it in the house of Mr. Wm. Morris, Poet. Fitly to
tell the tale, I should need a fresh pen, paper and spirits.
A few hints must suffice. To begin with, I breakfasted,
by way of a change, with the Nortons, along with
Mr. Sam Ward, who has just arrived, and Mr. Aubrey
de Vere, *tu sais,* the Catholic poet, a pleasant honest old
man and very much less high-flown than his name. He
tells good stories in a light natural way. After a space
I came home and remained until 4½ p.m., when I had
given rendez-vous to C.N. and ladies at Mr. Morris's
door, they going by appointment to see his shop and C.
having written to say he would bring me. Morris lives
on the same premises as his shop, in Queen's Square,
Bloomsbury, an antiquated ex-fashionable region, smell-
ing strong of the last century, with a hoary effigy of
Queen Anne in the middle. Morris's poetry, you see,
is only his sub-trade. To begin with, he is a manufac-
turer of stained glass windows, tiles, ecclesiastical and
medieval tapestry, altar-cloths, and in fine everything
quaint, archaic, pre-Raphaelite—and I may add, exquisite. Of course his business is small and may be carried on in his house: the things he makes are so handsome, rich and expensive (besides being articles of the
very last luxury) that his *fabrique* can't be on a very
large scale. But everything he has and does is superb
and beautiful. But more curious than anything is himself.
He designs with his own head and hands all the figures

and patterns used in his glass and tapestry, and further-
more works the latter, stitch by stitch, with his own
fingers—aided by those of his wife and little girls. Oh,
ma chère, such a wife! *Je n'en reviens pas*—she haunts
me still. A figure cut out of a missal—out of one of
Rossetti's or Hunt's pictures—to say this gives but a
faint idea of her, because when such an image puts
on flesh and blood, it is an apparition of fearful and
wonderful intensity. It's hard to say whether she's a
grand synthesis of all the pre-Raphaelite pictures ever
made—or they a 'keen analysis' of her—whether she's
an original or a copy. In either case she is a wonder.
Imagine a tall lean woman in a long dress of some dead
purple stuff, guiltless of hoops (or of anything else, I
should say,) with a mass of crisp black hair heaped into
great wavy projections on each of her temples, a thin
pale face, a pair of strange sad, deep, dark Swinburnian
eyes, with great thick black oblique brows, joined in
the middle and tucking themselves away under her hair,
a mouth like the 'Oriana' in our illustrated Tennyson,
a long neck, without any collar, and in lieu thereof some
dozen strings of outlandish beads—in fine complete.
On the wall was a large nearly full-length portrait of her
by Rossetti, so strange and unreal that if you hadn't seen
her you'd pronounce it a distempered vision, but in fact
an extremely good likeness. After dinner (we stayed
to dinner, Miss Grace, Miss S. S. and I,) Morris read
us one of his unpublished poems, from the second series
of his un-'Earthly Paradise', and his wife having a bad
toothache, lay on the sofa, with her handkerchief to her
face. There was something very quaint and remote from
our actual life, it seemed to me, in the whole scene:
Morris reading in his flowing antique numbers a legend
of prodigies and terrors (the story of Bellerophon, it
was), around us all the picturesque bric-a-brac of the

apartment (every article of furniture literally a 'specimen' of something or other,) and in the corner this dark silent medieval woman with her medieval toothache. Morris himself is extremely pleasant and quite different from his wife. He impressed me most agreeably. He is short, burly, corpulent, very careless and unfinished in his dress, and looks a little like B. G. Hosmer, if you can imagine B. G. infinitely magnified and fortified. He has a very loud voice and a nervous restless manner and a perfectly unaffected and business-like address. His talk indeed is wonderfully to the point and remarkable for clear good sense. He said no one thing that I remember, but I was struck with the very good judgment shown in everything he uttered. He's an extraordinary example, in short, of a delicate sensitive genius and taste, saved by a perfectly healthy body and temper. All his designs are quite as good (or rather nearly so) as his poetry: altogether it was a long rich sort of visit, with a strong peculiar flavour of its own. . . . Ouf! what a repulsively long letter! This sort of thing won't do. A few general reflections, a burst of affection (say another sheet), and I must close . . . Farewell, dear girl, and dear incomparable all—

Your H.

"THIS WONDROUS ENGLAND":
TO HIS MOTHER

7 Half Moon St., W.
March 26, 1869.

My dearest Mother,

. . . This will have been my fifth weekly bundle since my arrival, and I can't promise—or rather I forbear to threaten—that it shall be as hugely copious as the others. But there's no telling where my pen may take me. You see I am still in what my old landlord never speaks of but as 'this great metropolis'; and I hope you will believe me when I add, moreover, that I am in the best of health and spirits. During the last week I have been knocking about in a quiet way and have deeply enjoyed my little adventures. The last few days in particular have been extremely pleasant. You have perhaps fancied that I have been rather stingy-minded towards this wondrous England, and that I was [not] taking things in quite the magnanimous intellectual manner that befits a youth of my birth and breeding. The truth is that the face of things here throws a sensitive American back on himself—back on his prejudices and national passions, and benumbs for a while the faculty of appreciation and the sense of justice. But with time, if he is worth a copper, the characteristic beauty of the land dawns upon him (just as certain vicious chilblains are now dawning upon my poor feet) and he feels that he would fain plant his restless feet into the rich old soil and absorb the burden of the misty air. If I were in anything like working order now, I should be very sorry to leave England. I should like to settle down for a year and expose my body to the English climate and my mind to English institutions. But a truce to this cheap discursive stuff. I date the moment from which my mind rose erect in impartial might to a little sail I took on the Thames the other day in one of the little penny steamers which shoot along its dirty bosom. It was a grey, raw English day, and the banks of the river, as far as I went, hideous. Nevertheless I enjoyed it. It was too cold to go up to Greenwich. (The weather, by the way, since my arrival has been horribly damp and bleak, and no more like spring than in a Boston

January). The next day I went with several of the
Nortons to dine at Ruskin's, out of town. This too was
extremely pleasant. Ruskin himself is a very simple
matter. In face, in manner, in talk, in mind, he is weakness pure and simple. I use the word, not invidiously,
but scientifically. He has the beauties of his defects;
but to see him only confirms the impression given by
his writing, that he has been scared back by the grim
face of reality into the world of unreason and illusion,
and that he wanders there without a compass and a
guide—or any light save the fitful flashes of his beautiful
genius. The dinner was very nice and easy, owing in
a great manner to Ruskin's two charming young nieces
who live with him—one a lovely young Irish girl with
a rich virginal brogue—a creature of a truly delightful
British maidenly simplicity—and the other a nice Scotch
lass, who keeps house for him. But I confess, cold-
blooded villain that I am, that what I most enjoyed was
a portrait by Titian—an old doge, a work of transcend-
ent beauty and elegance, such as to give one a new sense
of the meaning of art. . . . But, dearest mammy, I must
pull up. Pile in scraps of news. Osculate my sister most
passionately. Likewise my aunt. Be assured of my senti-
ments and present them to my father and brother.

Thy Henry jr.

THE AMERICAN IN EUROPE:
TO HIS MOTHER

Florence, Hôtel de l'Europe.
October 13th, 1869.

My darling Mammy,

   . . . For the past six weeks that I have been in Italy
I've hardly until within a day or two exchanged five

minutes' talk with any one but the servants in the hotels and the custodians in the churches. As far as meeting people is concerned, I've not as yet had in Europe a very brilliant record. Yesterday I met at the Uffizi Miss Anna Vernon of Newport and her friend Mrs. Carter, with whom I had some discourse; and on the same morning I fell in with a somewhat seedy and sickly American, who seemed to be doing the gallery with an awful minuteness, and who after some conversation proposed to come and see me. He called this morning and has just left; but he seems a vague and feeble brother and I anticipate no wondrous joy from his acquaintance. The 'hardly' in the clause above is meant to admit two or three Englishmen with whom I have been thrown for a few hours. . . . One especially, whom I met at Verona, won my affections so rapidly that I was really sad at losing him. But he has vanished, leaving only a delightful impression and not even a name—a man of about 38, with a sort of quiet perfection of English virtue about him, such as I have rarely found in another. Willy asked me in one of his recent letters for an 'opinion' of the English, which I haven't yet had time to give—tho' at times I have felt as if it were a theme on which I could write from a full mind. In fact, however, I have very little right to have any opinion on the matter. I've seen far too few specimens and those too superficially. The only thing I'm certain about is that I like them—like them heartily. W. asked if as individuals they 'kill' the individual American. To this I would say that the Englishmen I have met not only kill, but bury in unfathomable depths, the Americans I have met. A set of people less framed to provoke national self-complacency than the latter it would be hard to imagine. There is but one word to use in regard to them—vulgar, vulgar, vulgar. Their ignorance—their stingy, defiant, grudging attitude to-

wards everything European—their perpetual reference
of all things to some American standard or precedent
which exists only in their own unscrupulous wind-bags
—and then our unhappy poverty of voice, of speech
and of physiognomy—these things glare at you hideously. On the other hand, we seem a people of *character*,
we seem to have energy, capacity and intellectual stuff
in ample measure. What I have pointed at as our vices
are the elements of the modern man with *culture* quite
left out. It's the absolute and incredible lack of *culture*
that strikes you in common travelling Americans. The
pleasantness of the English, on the other side, comes
in a great measure from the fact of their each having
been dipped into the crucible, which gives them a sort
of coating of comely varnish and colour. They have been
smoothed and polished by mutual social attrition. They
have manners and a language. We lack both, but particularly the latter. I have seen very 'nasty' Britons, certainly, but as a rule they are such as to cause your heart
to warm to them. The women are at once better and
worse than the men. Occasionally they are hard, flat,
and greasy and dowdy to downright repulsiveness; but
frequently they have a modest, matronly charm which
is the perfection of womanishness and which makes
Italian and Frenchwomen—and to a certain extent even
our own—seem like a species of feverish highly-developed invalids. You see Englishmen, here in Italy, to a
particularly good advantage. In the midst of these false
and beautiful Italians they glow with the light of the
great fact, that after all they love a bath-tub and they
hate a lie.

16*th, Sunday.* I *have* seen some nice Americans and
I still love my country. I have called upon Mrs. Hunting-
ton and her two daughters—late of Cambridge—whom
I met in Switzerland and who have an apartment here.

The daughters more than reconcile me to the shrill-voiced sirens of New England's rock-bound coast. The youngest is delightfully beautiful and sweet—and the elder delightfully sweet and plain—with a plainness *qui vaut bien des beautés.* . . .

Maman de mon âme, farewell. I have kept my letter three days, hoping for news from home. I hope you are not paying me back for that silence of six weeks ago. Blessings on your universal heads.

> Thy lone and loving exile,
> H. J. jr.

SUNDAY AT MME. VIARDOT'S:
TO HIS FATHER

> [Paris]
> 29 Rue du Luxembourg.
> April 11th [1876].

Dear Father,

. . . The slender thread of my few personal relations hangs on, without snapping, but it doesn't grow very stout. You crave chiefly news, I suppose, about Ivan Sergeitch [Turgenev], whom I have lately seen several times. I spent a couple of hours with him at his room, some time since, and I have seen him otherwise at Mme. Viardot's. The latter has invited me to her musical parties (Thursdays) and to her Sundays *en famille. I* have been to a couple of the former and (as yet only) one of the latter. She herself is a most fascinating and interesting woman, ugly, yet also very handsome or, in the French sense, *très-belle.* Her musical parties are rigidly musical and to me, therefore, rigidly boresome, especially as she herself sings very little. I stood the other night on my legs for three hours (from 11 till 2) in a suffocating room, listening to an interminable fiddling, with the only consolation that Gustave Doré, standing beside me, seemed as bored as myself. But when Mme. Viardot does sing, it is superb. She sang last time a scene from Gluck's *Alcestis*, which was the finest piece of musical declamation, of a grandly tragic sort, that I can conceive. Her Sundays seem rather dingy and calculated to remind one of Concord 'historical games' etc. But it was both strange and sweet to see poor Turgenev acting charades of the most extravagant description, dressed out in old shawls and masks, going on all fours etc. The charades are their usual Sunday evening occupation and the good faith with which Turgenev, at his age and with his glories, can go into them is a striking example of that spontaneity which Europeans have and we have not. Fancy Longfellow, Lowell, or Charles Norton doing the like, and every Sunday evening! I am likewise gorged with music at Mme. de Blocqueville's, where I continue to meet Émile Montégut, whom I don't like so well as his writing, and don't forgive for having, à l'avenir, spoiled his writing a little for me. Calling the other day on Mme. de B. I found with her M. Caro, the philosopher, a man in the expression of whose mouth you would discover depths of dishonesty, but a most witty and agreeable personage. I had also the other day a very pleasant call upon Flaubert, whom I like personally more and more each time I see him. But I think I easily—more than easily—see all round him intellectually. There is something wonderfully simple, honest, kindly, and touchingly inarticulate about him. He talked of many things, of Théo. Gautier among others, who was his intimate friend. He said nothing new or rare about him, except that he thought him after the Père Hugo the greatest of French poets, much above

Alfred de Musset; but Gautier in his extreme perfection was unique. And he recited some of his sonnets in a way to make them seem the most beautiful things in the world. Find in especial (in the volume I left at home) one called *Les Portraits Ovales.* . . . I went down to Chartres the other day and had a charming time—but I won't speak of it as I have done it in the Tribune.[1] The American papers over here are *accablants,* and the vulgarity and repulsiveness of the Tribune, whenever I see it, strikes me so violently that I feel tempted to stop my letter. But I shall not, though of late there has been a painful dearth of topics to write about. But soon comes the *Salon.* . . . I am very glad indeed that Howells is pleased with my new tale; I am now actively at work upon it. I am well pleased that the *Atlantic* has obtained it. His own novel I have not read, but he is to send it to me.

Your home news has all been duly digested. Tell Willy that I will answer his most interesting letter specifically; and say to my dearest sister that if she will tell me which—black or white—she prefers I will send her gratis a fichu of écru lace, which I am told is the proper thing for her to have.

Ever, dearest daddy, your loving son,

H. James jr.

[1] James was at this time contributing a series of reports on French life and art to the *New York Tribune. [Editor's note.]*

ENGLISH SPLENDORS: TO HIS MOTHER

Mentmore, Leighton Buzzard,
November 28th, 1880.

Dearest mammy,

. . . This is a pleasant Sunday, and I have been spending it (from yesterday evening) in a very pleasant place. 'Pleasant' is indeed rather an odd term to apply to this gorgeous residence, and the manner of life which prevails in it; but it is that as well as other things beside. Lady Rosebery (it is her enviable dwelling) asked me down here a week ago, and I stop till tomorrow a.m. There are several people here, but no one very important, save John Bright and Lord Northbrook, the last Liberal Viceroy of India. Millais, the painter, has been here for a part of the day, and I took a walk [with him] this afternoon back from the stables, where we had been to see three winners of the Derby trotted out in succession. This will give you an idea of the scale of Mentmore, where everything is magnificent. The house is a huge modern palace, filled with wonderful objects accumulated by the late Sir Meyer de Rothschild, Lady R.'s father. All of them are precious and many are exquisite, and their general Rothschildish splendour is only equalled by their profusion. . . .

I have spent a good part of the time in listening to the conversation of John Bright, whom, though I constantly see him at the Reform Club, I had never met before. He has the repute of being often "grumpy"; but on this occasion he has been in extremely good form and has discoursed uninterruptedly and pleasantly. He gives one an impression of sturdy, honest, vigorous,

English middle-class liberalism, accompanied by a certain infusion of genius, which helps one to understand how his name has become the great rallying-point of that sentiment. He reminds me a good deal of a superior New Englander—with a fatter, damper nature, however, than theirs. . . . They are at afternoon tea downstairs in a vast, gorgeous hall, where an upper gallery looks down like the colonnade in Paul Veronese's pictures, and the chairs are all golden thrones, belonging to ancient Doges of Venice. I have retired from the glittering scene, to meditate by my bedroom fire on the fleeting character of earthly possessions, and to commune with my mammy, until a supreme being in the shape of a dumb footman arrives, to ventilate my shirt and turn my stockings inside out (the beautiful red ones imparted by Alice—which he must admire so much, though he doesn't venture to show it,) preparatory to my dressing for dinner. Tomorrow I return to London and to my personal occupation, always doubly valued after 48 hours passed among *ces gens-ci*, whose chief effect upon me is to sharpen my desire to distinguish myself by personal achievement, of however limited a character. It is the only answer one can make to their atrocious good fortune. Lord Rosebery, however, with youth, cleverness, a delightful face, a happy character, a Rothschild wife of numberless millions to distinguish and demoralize him, wears them with such tact and bonhomie that you almost forgive him. He is extremely nice with Bright, draws him out, defers to him etc., with a delicacy rare in an Englishman. But, after all, there is much to say—more than can be said in a letter—about one's relations with these people. You may be interested, by the way, to know that Lord R. said this morning at lunch that his ideal of the happy life was that of Cambridge, Mass., "living like Longfellow." You may imagine that at this the company looked awfully vague, and I thought of proposing to him to exchange Mentmore for 20 Quincy Street.

I have little other personal news than this, which I have given you in some detail, for entertainment's sake. . . . I embrace you, dearest mother, and also your two companions.

Ever your fondest
H. James, jr.

THE DEATH OF THE FATHER: TO WILLIAM JAMES

131 Mt. Vernon St.,
Boston.
Dec. 26th, '82.

My dear William—

You will already have heard the circumstances under which I arrived at New York on Thursday 21st, at noon, after a very rapid and prosperous, but painful passage. Letters from Alice and Katherine L. were awaiting me at the dock, telling me that dear father was to be buried that morning. I reached Boston at 11 that night; there was so much delay in getting up-town. I found Bob at the station here. He had come on for the funeral only, and returned to Milwaukee the next morning. Alice, who was in bed, was very quiet and A. K. was perfect. They told me everything—or at least they told me a great deal—before we parted that night, and what they told me was deeply touching, and yet not at all literally painful. Father had been so tranquil, so painless, had died so easily and, as it were, deliberately, and there had been none—not the least—of that anguish and confusion which we imagined in London. . . . He simply, after the "improvement" of which we were written before I sailed, had a sudden relapse—a series of swoons—after which he took to his bed not to rise again. He had no visible malady—strange as it may seem. The "softening of the brain" was simply a gradual refusal of food, because he *wished* to die. There was no dementia except a sort of exaltation of his belief that he had entered into "the spiritual life." Nothing could persuade him to eat, and yet he never suffered, or gave the least sign of suffering, from inanition. All this will seem strange and incredible to you, but told with all the details, as Aunt Kate has told it to me, it becomes real—taking father as he was—almost natural. He prayed and longed to die. He ebbed and faded away, though in spite of his strength becoming continually less, he was able to see people and talk. He wished to see as many people as he could, and he talked with them without effort. He saw F. Boott and talked much two or three days before he died. Alice says he said the most picturesque and humorous things. He knew I was coming and was glad, but not impatient. He was delighted when he was told that you would stay in my rooms in my absence, and seemed much interested in the idea. He had no belief apparently that he should live to see me, but was perfectly cheerful about it. He slept a great deal, and as A. K. says there was "so little of the sick-room" about him. He lay facing the windows, which he would never have darkened—never pained by the light. . . . 27th a.m. Will send this now and write again tonight. All our wish here is that you should remain abroad the next six months.

Ever your

H. James

"THE VOICE OF STOICISM"—"THE GIFT OF LIFE": TO GRACE NORTON

131 Mount Vernon St., Boston.
July 28th [1883].

My dear Grace,

Before the sufferings of others I am always utterly powerless, and your letter reveals such depths of suffering that I hardly know what to say to you. This indeed is not my last word—but it must be my first. You are not isolated, verily, in such states of feeling as this— that is, in the sense that you appear to make all the misery of all mankind your own; only I have a terrible sense that you give all and receive nothing—that there is no reciprocity in your sympathy—that you have all the affliction of it and none of the returns. However— I am determined not to speak to you except with the voice of stoicism. I don't know *why* we live—the gift of life comes to us from I don't know what source or for what purpose; but I believe we can go on living for the reason that (always of course up to a certain point) life is the most valuable thing we know anything about, and it is therefore presumptively a great mistake to surrender it while there is any yet left in the cup. In other words consciousness is an illimitable power, and though at times it may seem to be all consciousness of misery, yet in the way it propagates itself from wave to wave, so that we never cease to feel, and though at moments we appear to, try to, pray to, there is something that holds one in one's place, makes it a standpoint in the universe which it is probably good not to forsake. You are right in your consciousness that we are all echoes and reverberations of the *same,* and you are noble when your interest and pity as to everything that surrounds you, appears to have a sustaining and harmonizing power. Only don't, I beseech you, *generalize* too much in these sympathies and tendernesses—remember that every life is a special problem which is not yours but another's, and content yourself with the terrible algebra of your own. Don't melt too much into the universe, but be as solid and dense and fixed as you can. We all live together, and those of us who love and know, live so most. We help each other—even unconsciously, each in our own effort, we lighten the effort of others, we contribute to the sum of success, make it possible for others to live. Sorrow comes in great waves—no one can know that better than you—but it rolls over us, and though it may almost smother us it leaves us on the spot, and we know that if it is strong we are stronger, inasmuch as it passes and we remain. It wears us, uses us, but we wear it and use it in return; and it is blind, whereas we after a manner see. My dear Grace, you are passing through a darkness in which I myself in my ignorance see nothing but that you have been made wretchedly ill by it; but it is only a darkness, it is not an end, or *the* end. Don't think, don't feel, any more than you can help, don't conclude or decide—don't do anything but *wait.* Everything will pass, and serenity and *accepted* mysteries and disillusionments, and the tenderness of a few good people, and new opportunities and ever so much of life, in a word, will remain. You will do all sorts of things yet, and I will help you. The only thing is not to *melt* in the meanwhile. I insist upon the necessity of a sort of mechanical condensation—so that however fast the horse may run away there will, when he pulls up, be a somewhat agitated but perfectly identical G. N. left in the saddle. Try not to be ill—that is all; for in that there is a failure.

You are marked out for success, and you must not fail.
You have my tenderest affection and all my confidence.
Ever your faithful friend—

Henry James

AFTER *Guy Domville:*
TO WILLIAM JAMES

34 De Vere Gardens, W.
Jan 9th, 1895.

My dear William,

I never cabled to you on Sunday 6th (about the first
night of my play,)[1] because, as I daresay you will have
gathered from some despatches or newspapers (if there
have been any, and you have seen them,) the case was
too complicated. Even now it's a sore trial to me to have
to write about it—weary, bruised, sickened, disgusted
as one is left by the intense, the cruel ordeal of a first
night that—after the immense labour of preparation
and the unspeakable tension of suspense—has, in a few
brutal moments, not gone well. In three words the delicate, picturesque, extremely human and extremely ar-

---

[1] *Guy Domville* was the most ambitious of the plays James
wrote in the years 1890-95. It was produced by George
Alexander at St. James's Theatre, London, on January 5,
1895. James, in a great state of agitation and suspense, stayed
away from the opening night (he attended Oscar Wilde's
An Ideal Husband at the Haymarket instead). When he
went to St. James's to take the final curtain call he was
greated by the mingled applause of his admirers and the
noisy jeers of the gallery. A vivid account of this famous
disaster among London first nights is given by Leon Edel in
his edition of *The Complete Plays of Henry James* (1949),
pp. 465-83. [*Editor's note.*]

tistic little play was taken profanely by a brutal and ill-disposed gallery which had shown signs of malice prepense from the first and which, held in hand till the end, kicked up an infernal row at the fall of the curtain. There followed an abominable quarter of an hour during which all the forces of civilization in the house waged a battle of the most gallant, prolonged and sustained applause with the hoots and jeers and catcalls of the roughs, whose *roars* (like those of a cage of beasts at some infernal "zoo") were only exacerbated (as it were) by the conflict. It was a cheering scene, as you may imagine, for a nervous, sensitive, exhausted author to face—and you must spare my going over again the horrid hour, or those of disappointment and depression that have followed it; from which last, however, I am rapidly and resolutely, thank God, emerging. The "papers" have, into the bargain, been mainly ill-natured and densely stupid and vulgar; but the only two dramatic critics who count, W. Archer and Clement Scott, have done me more justice. Meanwhile all *private* opinion is apparently one of extreme admiration—I have been flooded with letters of the warmest protest and assurance. . . . Everyone who was there has either written to me or come to see me—I mean every one I know and many people I don't. Obviously the little play, which I strove to make as broad, as simple, as clear, as British, in a word, as possible, is over the heads of the *usual* vulgar theatre-going London public—and the chance of its going for a while (which it is too early to measure) will depend wholly on its holding on long enough to attract the *unusual*. I was there the second night (Monday, 7th) when, before a full house—a remarkably good "money" house, Alexander told me—it went singularly well. But it's soon to see or to say, and I'm prepared for the worst. The thing fills me with horror for the abysmal

vulgarity and brutality of the theatre and its regular
public, which God knows I have had intensely even
when working (from motives as "pure" as pecuniary
motives *can* be) against it; and I feel as if the simple
freedom of mind thus begotten to return to one's legitimate form would be simply by itself a divine solace for
everything. Don't worry about me: I'm a Rock. If the
play has no life on the stage I shall publish it; it's altogether the best thing I've done. You would understand
better the elements of the case if you had seen the thing
it followed (*The Masqueraders*) and the thing that is
now succeeding at the Haymarket—the thing of Oscar
Wilde's. On the basis of *their* being plays, or successes,
my thing is necessarily neither. Doubtless, moreover,
the want of a roaring actuality, simplified to a few big
familiar effects, in my subject—an episode in the history
of an old English Catholic family in the last century—
militates against it, with all usual theatrical people, who
don't want plays (from variety and nimbleness of fancy)
of different *kinds*, like books and stories, but only of one
kind, which their stiff, rudimentary, clumsily-working
vision recognizes as the kind they've had before. And
yet I had tried so to meet them! But you can't make
a sow's ear out of a silk purse.—I can't write more—
and don't ask for more details. This week will probably
determine the fate of the piece. If there is increased
advance-booking it will go on. If there isn't, it will be
withdrawn, and with it all my little hope of profit. The
time one has given to such an affair from the very first
to the very last represents in all—so inconceivably great,
to the uninitiated, is the amount—a pitiful, tragic bank-
ruptcy of hours that might have been rendered retro-
actively golden. But I am not plangent—one must take
the thick with the thin—and I have such possibilities
of another and better sort before me. I am only sorry

for your and Alice's having to be so sorry for yours forever,

Henry

"A GREAT CHANGE IN MY LIFE":
TO W. D. HOWELLS

34 De Vere Gardens, W.
January 22d, 1895.

My dear Howells,

. . . I am indebted to you for your most benignant letter of December last. It lies open before me and I read it again and am soothed and cheered and comforted again. You put your finger sympathetically on the place and spoke of what I wanted you to speak of. I *have* felt, for a long time past, that I have fallen upon evil days— every sign or symbol of one's being in the least *wanted*, anywhere or by any one, having so utterly failed. A new generation, that I know not, and mainly prize not, has taken universal possession. The sense of being utterly out of it weighed me down, and I asked myself what the future would be. All these melancholies were qualified indeed by one redeeming reflection—the sense of how little, for a good while past (for reasons very logical, but accidental and temporary,) I had been producing. I *did* say to myself "Produce again—produce; produce better than ever, and all will yet be well"; and there was sustenance in that so far as it went. But it has meant much more to me since *you* have said it—for it *is*, practically, what you admirably say. It is exactly, moreover, what I meant to admirably do—and have meant, all along, about this time to get into the motion of. The whole thing, however, represents a great change in my life, inasmuch as what is clear is that periodical publication is practically closed to me—I'm the last hand that the magazines, in this country or in the U.S., seem to want. I won't afflict you with the now accumulated (during all these past years) evidence on which this induction rests—and I have spoken of it to no creature till, at this late day, I speak of it to you. . . . All this, I needn't say, is for your segretissimo ear. What it means is that "production" for me, as aforesaid, means production of the little *book*, pure and simple—independent of any antecedent appearance; and, truth to tell, now that I wholly *see* that, and have at last accepted it, I am, incongruously, not at all sorry. I am indeed very serene. I have always hated the magazine form, magazine conditions and manners, and much of the magazine company. I hate the hurried little subordinate part that one plays in the catchpenny picture-book—and the negation of all literature that the insolence of the picture-book imposes. The money-difference will be great—but not so great after a bit as at first; and the other differences will be so all to the good that even from the economic point of view they will tend to make up for that and perhaps finally even completely do so. It is about the distinctness of one's *book-position* that you have so substantially reassured me; and I mean to do far better work than ever I have done before. I have, potentially, improved immensely and am bursting with ideas and subjects—though the act of composition is with me more and more slow, painful and difficult. I shall never again write a *long* novel; but I hope to write six immortal short ones—and some tales of the same quality. Forgive, my dear Howells, the cynical egotism of these remarks—the fault of which is in your own sympathy. Don't fail me this summer. I shall probably not, as usual, absent myself from these islands—

not be beyond the Alps as I was when you were here last. That way Boston lies, which is the deadliest form of madness. I sent you only last night messages of affection by dear little "Ned" Abbey, who presently sails for N.Y. laden with the beautiful work he has been doing for the new Boston public library. I hope you will see him—he will speak of me competently and kindly. I wish all power to your elbow. Let me hear as soon as there is a sound of packing. Tell Mildred I rejoice in the memory of her. Give my love to your wife, and believe me, my dear Howells, yours in all constancy,

Henry James

THE DISCOVERY OF LAMB HOUSE:
TO MRS. WILLIAM JAMES

Dictated.

34 De Vere Gardens, W.
1st December, 1897.

Dearest Alice,

It's too hideous and horrible, this long time that I have not written you and that your last beautiful letter, placed, for reminder, well within sight, has converted all my emotion on the subject into a constant, chronic blush. The reason has been that I have been driving very hard for another purpose this inestimable aid to expression, and that, as I have a greater loathing than ever for the mere manual act, I haven't, on the one side, seen my way to inflict on you a written letter, or on the other had the virtue to divert, till I should have finished my little book, to another stream any of the valued and expensive industry of my amanuensis. I *have*, at last, finished my little book—that is *a* little book, and so have

two or three mornings of breathing time before I begin
another. Le plus clair of this small interval "I consecrate
to thee!"

I am settled in London these several weeks and making the most of that part of the London year—the mild,
quiet, grey stretch from the mid-October to Christmas
—that I always find the pleasantest, with the single
defect of its only not being long enough. We are having,
moreover, a most creditable autumn; no cold to speak
of and almost no rain, and a morning-room window at
which, this December 1st, I sit with my scribe, admitting a radiance as adequate as that in which you must
be actually bathed, and probably more mildly golden.
I have no positive plan save that of just ticking the
winter swiftly away on this most secure basis. There are,
however, little doors ajar into a possible brief absence.
I fear I have just closed one of them rather ungraciously
indeed, in pleading a "non possumus" to a most genial
invitation from John Hay to accompany him and his
family, shortly after the new year, upon a run to Egypt
and a month up the Nile; he having a boat for that same
—I mean for the Nile part—in which he offers me the
said month's entertainment. It is a very charming opportunity, and I almost blush at not coming up to the
scratch; especially as I shall probably never have the like
again. But it isn't so simple as it sounds; one has on one's
hands the journey to Cairo and back, with whatever
seeing and doing by the way two or three irresistible
other things, to which one would feel one might never
again be so near, would amount to. (I mean, of course,
then or never, on the return, Athens, Corfu, Sicily the
never-seen, etc., etc.) It would all "amount" to too much
this year, by reason of a particular little complication—
most pleasant in itself, I hasten to add—that I haven't,
all this time, mentioned to you. Don't be scared—I

haven't accepted an "offer." I have only taken, a couple
of months ago, a little old house in the country—for the
rest of my days!—on which, this winter, though it is,
for such a commodity, in exceptionally good condition,
I shall have to spend money enough to make me quite
concentrate my resources. The little old house you will
at no distant day, I hope, see for yourself and inhabit
and even, I trust, temporarily and gratuitously possess
—for half the fun of it, in the coming years, will be
occasionally to lend it to you. I marked it for my own
two years ago at Rye—so perfectly did it, the first instant I beheld it, offer the solution of my long-
unassuaged desire for a calm retreat between May and
November. It is the very calmest and yet cheerfullest
that I could have dreamed—*in* the little old, cobble-
stoned, grass-grown, red-roofed town, on the summit
of its mildly pyramidal hill and close to its noble old
church—the chimes of which will sound sweet in my
goodly old red-walled garden.

The little place is so rural and tranquil, and yet dis-
creetly animated, that its being within the town is, for
convenience and immediate accessibility, purely to the
good; and the house itself, though modest and unelab-
orate, full of a charming little stamp and dignity of its
period (about 1705) without as well as within. The
next time I go down to see to its "doing up," I will try
to have a photograph taken of the pleasant little old-
world town-angle into which its nice old red-bricked
front, its high old Georgian doorway and a most delightful little old architectural garden-house, perched along-
side of it on its high brick garden-wall—into which all
these pleasant features together so happily "compose."
Two years ago, after I had lost my heart to it—walking
over from Point Hill to make sheep's eyes at it (the
more so that it is called Lamb House!)—there was no

appearance whatever that one could ever have it; either that its fond proprietor would give it up or that if he did it would come at all within one's means. So I simply sighed and renounced; tried to think no more about it; till at last, out of the blue, a note from the good local ironmonger, to whom I had whispered at the time my hopeless passion, informed me that by the sudden death of the owner and the preference (literal) of his son for Klondyke, it might perhaps drop into my lap. Well, to make a long story short, it *did* immediately drop and, more miraculous still to say, on terms, for a long lease, well within one's means—terms quite deliciously moderate. The result of these is, naturally, that they will "do" nothing to it: but, on the other hand, it has been so well lived in and taken care of that the doing —off one's own bat—is reduced mainly to sanitation and furnishing—which latter includes the peeling off of old papers from several roomfuls of pleasant old top-to-toe wood panelling. There are two rooms of complete old oak—one of them a delightful little parlour, opening by one side into the little vista, church-ward, of the small old-world street, where not one of the half-dozen wheeled vehicles of Rye ever passes; and on the other straight into the garden and the approach, from that quarter, to the garden-house aforesaid, which is simply the making of a most commodious and picturesque detached study and workroom. Ten days ago Alfred Parsons, best of men as well as best of landscape-painters-and-gardeners, went down with me and revealed to me the most charming possibilities for the treatment of the tiny out-of-door part—it amounts to about an acre of garden and lawn, all shut in by the peaceful old red wall aforesaid, on which the most flourishing old espaliers, apricots, pears, plums and figs, assiduously grow. It appears that it's a glorious little growing exposure, air, and soil—and all the things that were still flourishing out of doors (November 20th) were a joy to behold. There went with me also a good friend of mine, Edward Warren, a very distingué architect and loyal spirit, who is taking charge of whatever is to be done. So I hope to get in, comfortably enough, early in May. In the meantime one must "pick up" a sufficient quantity of ancient mahogany-and-brass odds and ends —a task really the more amusing, here, where the resources are great, for having to be thriftily and cannily performed. The house is really quite charming enough in its particular character, and as to the stamp of its period, not to do violence to by rash modernities; and I am developing, under its influence and its inspiration, the most avid and gluttonous eye and most infernal watching patience, in respect of lurking "occasions" in not too-delusive Chippendale and Sheraton. The "King's Room" will be especially treated with a preoccupation of the comfort and aesthetic sense of cherished sisters-in-law; King's Room so-called by reason of George Second having passed a couple of nights there and so stamped it for ever. (He was forced ashore, at Rye, on a progress somewhere with some of his ships, by a tempest, and accommodated at Lamb House as at the place in the town then most consonant with his grandeur. It would, for that matter, quite correspond to this description still. Likewise the Mayors of Rye have usually lived there! Or the persons usually living there have usually *become* mayors! That was conspicuously the case with the late handsome old Mr. Bellingham, whose son is my landlord. So you see the ineluctable dignity in store for me.) But enough of this swagger. I have been copious to copiously amuse you.

Your beautiful letter, which I have just read over again is full of interest about you all; causing me spe-

cial joy as to what it says of William's present and prospective easier conditions of work, relinquishment of
laboratory, refusal of outside lectures, etc., and of the
general fine performance, and promise, all round, of the
children. What you say of each makes me want to see
that particular one most. . . . I had a very great pleasure the other day in a visit, far too short—only six hours
—from dear old Howells, who did me a lot of good in
an illuminating professional (i.e. commercial) way, and
came, in fact, at quite a psychological moment. I hope
you may happen to see him soon enough to get from him
also some echo of *me*—such as it may be. But, my dear
Alice, I must be less interminable. Please tell William
that I have two Syracuse "advices," as yet gracelessly
unacknowledged—I mean to him—to thank him for. It's
a joy to find these particular months less barren than
they used to be. I embrace you tenderly all round and
am yours very constantly,

Henry James

AMERICA REVISITED: TO EDMUND GOSSE

The Mount,
Lenox, Mass.
October 27th, 1904.

My dear Gosse,

The weeks have been many and crowded since I received, not very many days after my arrival, your incisive letter from the depths of the so different world
(from this here;) but it's just because they have been so
animated, peopled and pervaded, that they have rushed
by like loud-puffing motor-cars, passing out of my sight
before I could step back out of the dust and the noise

long enough to dash you off such a response as I could
fling after them to be carried to you. And during my
first three or four here my postbag was enormously—
appallingly—heavy: I almost turned tail and re-em-
barked at the sight of it. And then I wanted above all,
before writing you, to make myself a notion of how, and
where, and even *what*, I was. I have turned round now
a good many times, though still, for two months, only in
this corner of a corner of a corner, that is round New
England; and the postbag has, happily, shrunken a good
bit (though with liabilities, I fear, of re-expanding,)
and this exquisite Indian summer day sleeps upon these
really admirable little Massachusetts mountains, lakes
and woods, in a way that lulls my perpetual sense of
precipitation. I have moved from my own fireside for
long years so little (have been abroad, till now, but
once, for ten years previous) that the mere quantity of
movement remains something of a terror and a paralysis
to me—though I am getting to brave it, and to like it,
as the sense of adventure, of holiday and romance, and
above all of the great so visible and observable world
that stretches before one more and more, comes through
and makes the tone of one's days and the counterpoise
of one's homesickness. I am, at the back of my head and
at the bottom of my heart, transcendently homesick, and
with a sustaining private reference, all the while (at
every moment, verily,) to the fact that I have a tight
anchorage, a definite little downward burrow, in the
ancient world—a secret consciousness that I chink in
my pocket as if it were a fortune in a handful of silver.
But, with this, I have a most charming and interesting
time, and [am] seeing, feeling, how agreeable it is, in
the maturity of age, to revisit the long neglected and
long unseen land of one's birth—especially when that
land affects one as such a living and breathing and feel-

ing and moving great monster as this one is. It is all very
interesting and quite unexpectedly and almost uncannily
delightful and sympathetic—partly, or largely from
my intense impression (all this glorious golden autumn,
with weather like tinkling crystal and colours like mol-
ten jewels) of the sweetness of the country itself, this
New England rural vastness, which is all that I've seen.
I've been only in the country—shamelessly visiting and
almost only old friends and scattered relations—but
have found it far more beautiful and amiable than I had
ever dreamed, or than I ventured to remember. I had
seen too little, in fact, of old, *to* have anything, to speak
of, to remember—so that seeing so many charming
things for the first time I quite thrill with the romance
of elderly and belated discovery. Of Boston I haven't
even had a full day—of N. Y. but three hours, and I
have seen nothing whatever, thank heaven, of the "lit-
tery' world. I have spent a few days at Cambridge,
Mass., with my brother, and have been greatly struck
with the way that in the last 25 years Harvard has come
to mass so much larger and to have gathered about her
such a swarm of distinguished specialists and such a big
organization of learning. This impression is increased
this year by the crowd of foreign experts of sorts
(mainly philosophic etc.) who have been at the St.
Louis congress and who appear to be turning up overwhelmingly under my brother's roof—but who will
have vanished, I hope, when I go to spend the month of
November with him—when I shall see something of
the goodly Boston. The blot on my vision and the
shadow on my path is that I have contracted to write
a book of Notes[1]—without which contraction I simply

---

[1] The book which James had contracted to write about his
trip to America appeared as *The American Scene* in 1907.
[*Editor's note.*]

couldn't have come; and that the conditions of life, time, space, movement etc. (really to *see*, to get one's material,) are such as to threaten utterly to frustrate for me any prospect of simultaneous work—which is the rock on which I may split altogether—wherefore my alarm is great and my project much disconcerted; for I have as yet scarce dipped into the great Basin at all. Only a large measure of Time can help me—to do anything as decent as I want: wherefore pray for me constantly; and all the more that if I can only arrive at a means of application (for I see, already, from here, my *Tone*) I shall do, verily, a lovely book. I am interested, up to my eyes—at least I think I am! But you will fear, at this rate, that I am trying the book on you already. I *may* have to return to England only as a saturated sponge and wring myself out there. I hope meanwhile that your own saturations, and Mrs. Nelly's, prosper, and that the Pyrenean, in particular, continued rich and ample. If you are having the easy part of your year now, I hope you are finding in it the lordliest, or rather the *un*lordliest leisure. . . . I commend you all to felicity and am, my dear Gosse, yours always,

Henry James

BROTHER TO BROTHER:
TO WILLIAM JAMES

Lamb House, Rye
November 23rd, 1905.

Dearest William,

. . . I mean (in response to what you write me of your having read the *Golden B[owl]*) to try to produce some uncanny form of thing, in fiction, that will gratify you, as Brother—but let me say, dear William, that I shall greatly be humiliated if you *do* like it, and thereby lump it, in your affection, with things, of the current age, that I have heard you express admiration for and that I would sooner descend to a dishonoured grave than have written. Still I *will* write you your book, on that two-and-two-make-four system on which all the awful truck that surrounds us is produced, and *then* descend to my dishonoured grave—taking up the art of the slate pencil instead of, longer, the art of the brush (vide my lecture on Balzac). But it is, seriously, too late at night, and I am too tired, for me to express myself on this question—beyond saying that I'm always sorry when I hear of your reading anything of mine, and always hope you won't—you seem to me so constitutionally unable to "enjoy" it, and so condemned to look at it from a point of view remotely alien to mine in writing it, and to the conditions out of which, *as* mine, it has inevitably sprung—so that all the intentions that have been its main reason for being (with *me*) appear never to have reached you at all—and you appear even to assume that the life, the elements forming its subject-matter, deviate from felicity in not having an impossible analogy with the life of Cambridge. I see nowhere about me done or dreamed of the things that alone for me constitute the *interest* of the doing of the novel—and yet it is in a sacrifice of them on their very own ground that the thing you suggest to me evidently consists. It shows how far apart and to what different ends we have had to work out (very naturally and properly!) our respective intellectual lives. And yet I can read *you* with rapture—having three weeks ago spent three or four days with Manton Marble at Brighton and found in his hands ever so many of your recent papers and discourses, which, having margin of mornings in my room, through both breakfasting and lunching there (by the habit of the house,) I found time to read several of— with the effect of asking you, earnestly, to address me some of those that I so often, in Irving St., saw you address to others who were not your brother. I had no time to read them there. Philosophically, in short, I am "with" you, almost completely, and you ought to take account of this and get me over altogether. . . .

But oh, fondly, good-night!

Ever your
Henry

WINTER MIDNIGHT AT LAMB HOUSE:
TO MRS. HENRY WHITE

Lamb House, Rye.
Dec. 29, 1908.

Dearest Margaret White,

I sit here to-night, I quite crouch by my homely little fireside, muffled in soundless snow—where the loud tick of the clock is the *only* sound—and give myself up to the charmed sense that in your complicated career, amid all the more immediate claims of the *bonne année,* you have been moved to this delightful sign of remembrance of an old friend who is on the whole, and has always been, condemned to lose so much more of you (through divergence of ways!) than he has been privileged to enjoy. Snatches, snatches, and happy and grateful moments—and then great empty yearning intervals only—and under all the great ebbing, melting, and irrecoverableness of life! But this is almost a happy and grateful moment—almost a *real* one, I mean— though again with bristling frontiers, long miles of land

and water, doing their best to make it vain and fruitless. You live on the crest of the wave, and I deep down in the hollow—and your waves seem to be all crests, just as mine are only concave formations! I feel at any rate very much in the hollow these winter months—when great adventures, like Paris, look far and formidable, and I see a domestic reason for sitting tight wherever I turn my eyes. That reads as if I had thirteen children—or thirty wives—instead of being so lone and lorn; but what it means is that I have, in profusion, modest, backward labours. We have been having here lately the great and glorious pendulum in person, Mrs. Wharton, on her return oscillation, spending several weeks in England, for almost the first time ever and having immense success—so that I think she might fairly fix herself here—if she could stand it! But she is to be at 58 Rue de Varenne again from the New Year and you will see her and she will give you details. *My* detail is that though she has kindly asked me to come to them again there this month or spring I have had to plead simple abject terror—terror of the pendulous life. I am a *stopped* clock—and I strike (that is I caper about) only when very much wound up. Now I don't have to be wound up at all to tell you what a yearning I have to see you all back *here*—and what a kind of sturdy faith that I absolutely shall. Then your crest will be much nearer my hollow, and vice versa, and you will be able to look down quite *straight* at me, and we shall be almost together again—as we really must manage to be for these interesting times to come. I don't want to miss any more Harry's freshness of return from the great country—with the golden apples of his impression still there on the tree. I have always only tasted them plucked by other hands and—baked! I want to munch these *with* you—en famille. Therefore I confidently await and evoke you. I delight in these proofs of strength of your own and am yours always and ever,

Henry James

THE DEATH OF WILLIAM JAMES:
TO THOMAS SERGEANT PERRY

[William James, in failing health, had gone to Nauheim in Germany in the spring of 1910 to seek a cure. Henry James, himself in ill health at the time, joined him there with Mrs. James, and in August returned with them to America, where William James died at his summer home in New Hampshire on August 26, 1910.—*Editor's note.*]

Chocorua, N.H.
Sept. 2nd, 1910.

My dear old Thomas,

I sit heavily stricken and in darkness—for from far back in dimmest childhood he had been my ideal Elder Brother, and I still, through all the years, saw in him, even as a small timorous boy yet, my protector, my backer, my authority and my pride. His extinction changes the face of life for me—besides the mere missing of his inexhaustible company and personality, originality, the whole unspeakably vivid and beautiful presence of him. And his noble intellectual vitality was still but at its climax—he had two or three ardent purposes and plans. He had cast them away, however, at the end —I mean that, dreadfully suffering, he wanted only to die. Alice and I had a bitter pilgrimage with him from far off—he sank here, on his threshold; and then it went horribly fast. I cling for the present to *them*—and so try to stay here through this month. After that I shall be with them in Cambridge for several more—we shall

cleave more together. I should like to come and see you
for a couple of days much, but it would have to be after
the 20th, or even October 1st, I think; and I fear you
may not then be still in villeggiatura. *If* so I *will* come.
You knew him—among those living now—from furthest
back with me. Yours and Lilla's all faithfully,

Henry James

THANKS FOR A GIFT:
TO WALTER V. R. BERRY

[H. J. never at any time received presents easily, and the
difficulty seems to have reached a climax over one recently
sent him by Mr. Berry. It may not be obvious that the gift
in question was a leather dressing-case.—*Note by Percy
Lubbock*.]

Lamb House, Rye.
February 8th, 1912.

Très-cher et très-grand ami!

How you must have wondered at my silence! But it
has been, alas, inevitable and now is but feebly and
dimly broken. Just after you passed through London—
or rather even *while* you were passing through it—I
began to fall upon evil days again; a deplorable bout of
unwellness which, making me fit for nothing, gave me a
sick struggle, first, in those awkward Pall Mall conditions, and then reduced me to scrambling back here as
best I might, where I have been these several days but
a poor ineffectual rag. I shall get better here if I can still
further draw on my sadly depleted store of time and
patience; but meanwhile I am capable but of this weak
and appealing grimace—so deeply discouraged am I
to feel that there are still, and after I have travelled so

far, such horrid little deep holes for me to tumble into. (This has been a deeper one than for many months, though I am, I believe, slowly scrambling out; and blest to me has been the resource of crawling to cover here— for better aid and comfort.) . . . The case has really and largely been, however, all the while, dearest Walter, that of my having had to yield, just after your glittering passage in town, to that simply overwhelming *coup de massue* of your—well, of your you know what. It was *that* that knocked me down—when I was just trembling for a fall; it was that that laid me flat.

February 14th. Well, dearest Walter, it laid me after all so flat that I broke down, a week ago, in the foregoing attempt to do you, and your ineffable procédé, some manner of faint justice; I wasn't then apt for any sort of right or worthy approach to you, and there was nothing for me but resignedly to intermit and *me recoucher.* You had done it with your own mailed fist— mailed in glittering gold, speciously glazed in polished, inconceivably and indescribably sublimated, leather, and I had rallied but too superficially from the stroke. It claimed its victim afresh, and I have lain the better part of a week just languidly heaving and groaning as a result *de vos œuvres*—and forced thereby quite to neglect and ignore all letters. I am a little more on my feet again, and if this continues shall presently be able to return to town (Saturday or Monday;) where, how- ever, the monstrous object will again confront me. That is the grand fact of the situation—that is the tawny lion, portentous creature, in my path. I can't get past him, I can't get round him, and on the other hand he stands glaring at me, refusing to give way and practically blocking all my future. I can't live with him, you see; be- cause I can't live *up* to him. His claims, his pretensions, his dimensions, his assumptions and consumptions,

above all the manner in which he causes every surrounding object (on my poor premises or within my
poor range) to tell a dingy or deplorable tale—all this
makes him the very scourge of my life, the very blot on
my scutcheon. He doesn't regild that rusty metal—he
simply takes up an attitude of gorgeous swagger, straight
in front of all the rust and the rubbish, which makes me
look as if I had stolen *somebody else's* (re-garnished
blason) and were trying to palm it off as my own. Cher
et bon Gaultier, I simply can't *afford* him, and that is the
sorry homely truth. *He is out of the picture*—out of
mine; and behold me condemned to live forever with
that canvas turned to the wall. Do you know what that
means?—to have to give up going about at all, lest
complications (of the most incalculable order) should
ensue from its being seen what I go about *with.* Bonne
renommée vaut mieux que sac-de-voyage doré, and
though I may have had weaknesses that have brought
me a little under public notice, my modest hold-all
(which has accompanied me in most of my voyage
through life) has at least, so far as I know, never *fait
jaser.* All this I have to think of—and I put it candidly
to you while yet there is time. That you shouldn't have
counted the cost—to yourself—that is after all perhaps
conceivable (quoiqu'à peine!) but that you shouldn't
have counted the cost to *me,* to whom it spells ruin:
that ranks you with those great lurid, though lovely,
romantic and historic figures and charmers who have
scattered their affections and lavished their favours
only (as it has presently appeared) to consume and
to destroy! More prosaically, dearest Walter (if one of
the most lyric acts recorded in history—and one of the
most finely aesthetic, and one stamped with the most
matchless grace, *has* a prosaic side,) I have been truly
overwhelmed by the princely munificence and generos-

ity of your procédé, and I have gasped under it while tossing on the bed of indisposition. For a beau geste, c'est le plus beau, by all odds, of any in all my life ever esquissé in my direction, and it *has*, as such, left me really and truly panting helplessly after—or rather quite intensely *before*—it! What is a poor man to do, mon prince, mon bon prince, mon grand prince, when so prodigiously practised upon? There is *nothing*, you see: for the proceeding itself swallows at a gulp, with its open crimson jaws (*such* a rosy mouth!) like Carlyle's Mirabeau, "all formulas." One doesn't "thank," I take it, when the heavens open—that is when the whale of Mr. Allen's-in-the-Strand celestial shopfront does—and discharge straight into one's lap the perfect compendium, the very burden of the song, of just what the Angels have been raving about ever since we first heard of them. Well *may* they have raved—but I can't, you see; I have to take the case (the incomparable suitcase) in abject silence and submission. Ah, Walter, Walter, why do you do these things? they're magnificent, but they're not—well, discussable or permissible or forgiveable. At least not all at once. It will take a long, long time. Only little by little and buckle-hole by buckle-hole, shall I be able to look, with you, even one strap in the face. As yet a sacred horror possesses me, and I must ask you to let me, please, though writing you at such length, not so much as mention the subject. It's better so. Perhaps your conscience will tell you why— tell you, I mean, that great supreme *gestes* are only fair when addressed to those who can themselves gesticulate. I can't—and it makes me feel so awkward and graceless and poor. I go about trying—so as to hurl it (something or other) back on you; but it doesn't come off— practice *doesn't* make perfect; you are victor, winner, master, oh irresistible one—you've done it, you've brought it off and got me down forever, and I must just feel your weight and bear your might to bless your name—even to the very end of the days of yours, dearest Walter, all too abjectly and too touchedly,

Henry James

ON HIS SEVENTIETH BIRTHDAY:
TO 270 FRIENDS

[On James's seventieth birthday—April 15, 1913—a group of 270 friends sent him a letter, a piece of plate ("a really splendid 'golden bowl' of the highest interest and most perfect taste"), and a request that he sit for his portrait to John Singer Sargent (the portrait is now in the National Portrait Gallery, London). This is James's letter of thanks; at the end he wrote the names of the friends who had offered him tribute.—*Editor's note*.]

21 Carlyle Mansions,
Cheyne Walk, S.W.
April 21st, 1913.

Dear Friends All,

Let me acknowledge with boundless pleasure the singularly generous and beautiful letter, signed by your great and dazzling array and reinforced by a correspondingly bright material gage, which reached me on my recent birthday, April 15th. It has moved me as brave gifts and benedictions can only do when they come as signal surprises. I seem to wake up to an air of breathing good will the full sweetness of which I had never yet tasted; though I ask myself now, as a second thought, how the large kindness and hospitality in which I have so long and so consciously lived among you could fail to act itself out according to its genial nature and by some inspired application. The perfect grace with which it has embraced the just-past occasion for its happy thought affects me, I ask you to believe, with an emotion too deep for stammering words. I was drawn to London long years ago as by the sense, felt from still earlier, of all the interest and association I should find here, and I now see how my faith was to sink deeper foundations than I could presume ever to measure—how my justification was both stoutly to grow and wisely to wait. It is so wonderful indeed to me as I count up your numerous and various, your dear and distinguished friendly names, taking in all they recall and represent, that I permit myself to feel at once highly successful and extremely proud. I had never in the least understood that I was the one or signified that I was the other, but you have made a great difference. You tell me together, making one rich tone of your many voices, almost the whole story of my social experience, which I have reached the right point for living over again, with all manner of old times and places renewed, old wonderments and pleasures reappeased and recaptured—so that there is scarce one of your ranged company but makes good the particular connection, quickens the excellent relation, lights some happy train and flushes with some individual colour. I pay you my very best respects while I receive from your two hundred and fifty pair of hands, and more, the admirable, the inestimable bowl, and while I engage to sit, with every accommodation, to the so markedly indicated "one of you," my illustrious friend Sargent. With every accommodation, I say, but with this one condition that you yourselves, in your strength and goodness, remain guardians of the result of his labour—even as I remain all faithfully and gratefully yours,

Henry James

P.S. And let me say over your names.

"WE ARE LONE SURVIVORS":
TO HENRY ADAMS

21 Carlyle Mansions
Cheyne Walk, S.W.
March 21, 1914.

My dear Henry,

I have your melancholy outpouring of the 7th, and I know not how better to acknowledge it than by the full recognition of its unmitigated blackness. *Of course* we are lone survivors, of course the past that was our lives is at the bottom of an abyss—if the abyss *has* any bottom; of course, too, there's no use talking unless one particularly *wants* to. But the purpose, almost, of my printed divagations was to show you that one *can,* strange to say, still want to—or at least can behave as if one did.[1] Behold me therefore so behaving—and apparently capable of continuing to do so. I still find my consciousness interesting—under *cultivation* of the interest. Cultivate it *with* me, dear Henry—that's what I hoped to make you do—to cultivate yours for all that it has in common with mine. *Why* mine yields an interest I don't know that I can tell you, but I don't challenge or quarrel with it—I encourage it with a ghastly grin. You see I still, in presence of life (or of what you deny to be such,) have reactions—as many as possible —and the book I sent you is a proof of them. It's, I suppose, because I am that queer monster, the artist, an obstinate finality, an inexhaustible sensibility. Hence

---

[1] James had sent Henry Adams a copy of his second autobiographical memoir, *Notes of a Son and Brother,* recently published. [*Editor's note.*]

the reactions—appearances, memories, many things, go on playing upon it with consequences that I note and "enjoy" (grim word!) noting. It all takes doing—and I *do*. I believe I shall do yet again—it is still an act of life. But you perform them still yourself—and I don't know what keeps me from calling your letter a charming one! There we are, and it's a blessing that you understand—I admit indeed alone—your all-faithful

Henry James

THE COMING OF THE WAR: 1914

TO HOWARD STURGIS

Lamb House, Rye.
[Continuing a letter of
August 4th, 1914.]

Dearly beloved Howard!

. . . *August 5th.* The taper went out last night, and I am afraid I now kindle it again to a very feeble ray—for it's vain to try to talk as if one weren't living in a nightmare of the deepest dye. How can what is going on not be to one as a huge horror of blackness? Of course that is what it is to you, dearest Howard, even as it is to your infinitely sickened inditer of these lines. The plunge of civilization into this abyss of blood and darkness by the wanton feat of those two infamous autocrats is a thing that so gives away the whole long age during which we have supposed the world to be, with whatever abatement, gradually bettering, that to have to take it all now for what the treacherous years were all the while really making for and *meaning* is too tragic for any words. But one's reflections don't really bear being uttered—at least we each make them enough for our individual selves and I didn't mean to smother you under mine in addition to your own. . . .

But good-night again—my lamp now is snuffed out. Have I mentioned to you that I am not here alone?— having with me my niece Peggy and her younger brother —both "caught" for the time, in a manner; though willing, even glad, as well as able, to bear their poor old appalled Uncle the kindest company—very much the same sort as William bears you. I embrace you, and him too, and am ever your faithfullest old

H. J.

TO MISS RHODA BROUGHTON

Lamb House, Rye.
August 10th, 1914.

Dearest Rhoda!

It is not a figure of speech but an absolute truth that even if I had not received your very welcome and sympathetic script I should be writing to you this day. I have been on the very edge of it for the last week—so had my desire to make you a sign of remembrance and participation come to a head; and verily I must—or may—almost claim that this all but "crosses" with your own. The only blot on our unanimity is that it's such an unanimity of woe. Black and hideous to me is the tragedy that gathers, and I'm sick beyond cure to have lived to see it. You and I, the ornaments of our generation, should have been spared this wreck of our belief that through the long years we had seen civilization grow and the worst become impossible. The tide that bore us along was then all the while moving to *this* as its grand Niagara—yet what a blessing we didn't know it. It seems to me to *undo* everything, everything that was ours, in the most horrible retroactive way—but I avert my face from the monstrous scene!—you can hate it and blush for it without my help; we can each do enough of that by ourselves. The country and the season here are of a beauty of peace, and loveliness of light, and summer grace, that make it inconceivable that just across the Channel, blue as *paint* today, the fields of France and Beligum are being, or about to be, given up to unthinkable massacre and misery. One is ashamed to admire, to enjoy, to take any of the normal pleasure, and the huge shining indifference of Nature strikes a chill to the heart and makes me wonder of what abysmal mystery, or villainy indeed, such a cruel smile is the expression. In the midst of it all at any rate we walked, this strange Sunday afternoon (9th), my niece Peggy, her youngest brother and I, about a mile out, across the blessed grass mostly, to see and have tea with a genial old Irish friend (Lady Mathew, who has a house here for the summer,) and came away an hour later bearing with us a substantial green volume, by an admirable eminent hand, which our hostess had just read with such a glow of satisfaction that she overflowed into easy lending. I congratulate you on having securely put it forth before this great distraction was upon us—for I am utterly pulled up in the midst of a rival effort by finding that my job won't at all consent to be done in the face of it. The picture of little private adventures simply fades away before the great public. I take great comfort in the presence of my two young companions, and above all in having caught my nephew by the coat-tail only *just* as he was blandly starting for the continent on Aug. 1st. Poor Margaret Payson is trapped somewhere in France—she *having* then started, though not for Germany, blessedly; and we remain wholly without news of her. Peggy and Aleck have four or five near maternal relatives lost in Germany—though as Americans they may fare a little less dreadfully there than if they were English. And I have numerous friends—we all have, haven't we?—inaccessible and unimaginable there; it's becoming an anguish to think of them. Nevertheless I do believe that we shall be again gathered into a blessed little Chelsea drawing-room—it will be like the reopening of the salons, so irrepressibly, after the French revolution. So only sit tight, and invoke your heroic soul, dear Rhoda, and believe me more than ever all-faithfully yours,

Henry James

TO MRS. W. K. CLIFFORD

Lamb House, Rye.
August 22nd, 1914.

Dearest Lucy,

I have, I know, been quite portentously silent—your brief card of distress to-night (Saturday p. m.—) makes me feel it—but you on your side will also have felt the inevitability of this absence of mere vain and vague remark in the presence of such prodigious realities. My overwhelmed sense of them has simply left me nothing to say—the rupture with all the blest old proportion of things has been so complete and utter, and I've felt as if most of my friends (from very few of whom I have heard at all) were so wrapped in gravities and dignities of silence that it wasn't fair to write to them simply to make *them* write. And so it has gone—the whole thing defying expression so that one has just stared at the horror and watched it grow. But I am not writing now, dearest old friend, to express either alarm or despair—and this mainly by reason of there being so high a decency in *not* doing so. I hate not to possess my soul—and oh I should like, while I am *about* that, to possess yours for you too. One doesn't possess one's soul unless one squares oneself a good deal, in fact very hard indeed, for the purpose; but in proportion as one succeeds that means preparation, and preparation means confidence, and confidence means force, and that is as far as we need go for the moment. Your few words express a bad apprehension which I don't share—and which even our straight outlook here over the blue channel of all these amazing days, toward the unthinkable horrors of its almost other edge, doesn't *make* me share. I don't in the least believe that the Germans will be "here"—with us generally—because I don't believe—I don't admit—that anything so abject as the allowance of it by our overwhelming Fleet, in conditions making it so tremendously difficult for them (the G.'s), is in the least conceivable. Things are not going to be so easy for them as that—however uneasy they may be for ourselves. I *insist* on a great confidence—I cultivate it as resolutely as I can, and if we were only nearer together I think I should be able to help you to some of the benefit of it. I have been very thankful to be on this spot all these days—I mean in this sympathetic little old house, which has somehow assuaged in a manner the nightmare. One invents *arts* for assuaging it—of which some work better than others. The great sore sense I find the futility of talk—*about* the cataclysm: this is so impossible that I can really almost talk about other things! . . . I am supposing you see a goodish many people—since one hears that there are so many in town, and I am glad for you of that: solitude in these

conditions being grim, even if society is bleak! I try to
read and I rather succeed, and also even to write, and
find the effort of it greatly pays. Lift up your heart,
dearest friend—I believe we shall meet to embrace and
look back and tell each other how appallingly interesting
the whole thing "was." I gather in all of you right affectionately and am yours, in particular, dearest Lucy, so
stoutly and tenderly,

Henry James

TO MRS. WHARTON

Lamb House, Rye.
September 21st, 1914.

Dearest Edith,

Rheims is the most unspeakable and immeasurable
horror and infamy—and what is appalling and heart-
breaking is that it's *"for ever and ever."* [1] But no words
fill the abyss of it—nor touch it, nor relieve one's heart
nor light by a spark the blackness; the ache of one's
howl and the anguish of one's execration aren't mitigated by a shade, even as one brands it as the most hideous crime ever perpetrated against the mind of man.
There it *was*—and now all the tears of rage of all the
bereft millions and all the crowding curses of all the
wondering ages will never bring a stone of it back! Yet
one tries—even now—tries to get something from saying that the measure is so full as to overflow at last in

---

[1] It will be remembered that the first news of the bombard-
ment of Rheims Cathedral suggested greater destruction than
was the fact at that time. The wreckage was of course carried much further before the end of the war. [*Note by Percy
Lubbock.*]

a sort of vindictive deluge (though for all the stones that *that* will replace!) and that the arm of final retributive justice becomes by it an engine really in some degree proportionate to the act. I positively do think it helps me a little, to think of how they can be made to wear the shame, in the pitiless glare of history, forever and ever—and not even to get rid of it when they are maddened, literally, by the weight. And for that the preparations must have already at this hour begun: how *can't* they be as a tremendous force fighting on the side, fighting in the very fibres, of France? I think too somehow—though I don't know *why*, practically—of how nothing conceivable could have so damned and dished them forever in our great art-loving country!

. . . All homage and affection to you, dearest Edith, from your desolate and devoted old

H. J.

"CIVIS BRITANNICUS SUM": TO HENRY JAMES, JUNIOR

[Henry James was to become naturalized as a British subject on July 26, 1915. On that day he wrote Edmund Gosse: "since 4.30 this afternoon I have been able to say Civis Britannicus sum!" The present letter to his nephew anticipated the event by a month.—*Editor's note*.]

Dictated

21 Carlyle Mansions,
Cheyne Walk, [London], S.W.
June 24th, 1915.

Dearest Harry,

I am writing to you in this fashion even although I am writing you "intimately"; because I am not at the present moment in very good form for any free play of hand, and this machinery helps me so much when there is any question of pressure and promptitude, or above all of particular clearness. That *is* the case at present— at least I feel I ought to lose no more time.

You will wonder what these rather portentous words refer to—but don't be too much alarmed! It is only that my feeling about my situation here has under the stress of events come so much to a head that, certain particular matters further contributing, I have arranged to seek technical (legal) advice no longer hence than this afternoon as to the exact modus operandi of my becoming naturalised in this country. This state of mind probably won't at all surprise you, however; and I think I can assure you that it certainly wouldn't if you were now on the scene here with me and had the near vision of all the circumstances. My sense of how everything more and more makes for it has been gathering force ever since the war broke out, and I have thus waited nearly a whole year; but my feeling has become acute with the information that I can only go down to Lamb House now on the footing of an Alien under Police supervision—an alien friend of course, which is a very different thing from an alien enemy, but still a definite technical outsider to the whole situation here, in which my affections and my loyalty are so intensely engaged. I feel that if I take this step I shall simply rectify a position that has become inconveniently and uncomfortably false, making my civil status merely agree not only with my moral, but with my material as well, in every kind of way. Hadn't it been for the War I should certainly have gone on as I was, taking it as the simplest and easiest and even friendliest thing: but the circumstances are utterly altered now, and to feel with the country and the cause as absolutely and ardently as I feel, and not offer them my moral support with a perfect consistency (my material is too small a matter), affects me as standing off or wandering loose in a detachment of no great dignity. I have spent here all the best years of my life—they practically have *been* my life: about a twelvemonth hence I shall have been domiciled uninterruptedly in England for forty years, and there is not the least possibility, at my age, and in my state of health, of my ever returning to the U. S. or taking up any relation with it as a country. My practical relation has been to this one for ever so long, and now my "spiritual" or "sentimental" quite ideally matches it. I am telling you all this because I can't not want exceedingly to take you into my confidence about it—but again I feel pretty certain that you will understand me too well for any great number of words more to be needed. The real truth is that in a matter of this kind, under such extraordinarily special circumstances, one's own intimate feeling must speak and determine the case. Well, without haste and without rest, mine has done so, and with the prospect of what I have called the rectification, a sense of great relief, a great lapse of awkwardness, supervenes.

I think that even if by chance your so judicious mind should be disposed to suggest any reserves—I think, I say, that I should then still ask you not to launch them at me unless they should seem to you so important as to balance against my own argument and, frankly speaking, my own absolute need and passion here; which the whole experience of the past year has made quite unspeakably final. I can't imagine at all what these objections should be, however—my whole long relation to the country having been what it is. Regard my proceeding as a simple act and offering of allegiance and devotion, recognition and gratitude (for long years and innumerable relations that have meant so much to me,) and it remains perfectly simple. Let me repeat that I feel sure I shouldn't in the least have come to it without this convulsion, but one is *in* the convulsion (I wouldn't be out of it either!) and one must act accordingly. I feel all the while too that the tide of American identity of consciousness with our own, about the whole matter, rises and rises, and will rise still more before it rests again—so that every day the difference of situation diminishes and the immense fund of common sentiment increases. However, I haven't really meant so much to expatiate. What I am doing this afternoon is, I think, simply to get exact information—though I am already sufficiently aware of the question to know that after my long existence here the process of naturalisation is very simple and short. . . . My last word about the matter, at any rate, has to be that my decision is absolutely tied up with my innermost personal feeling. I think that will only make you glad, however, and I add nothing more now but that I am your all-affectionate old Uncle,

Henry James

*

BIBLIOGRAPHY

I: THE FURTHER READING OF HENRY JAMES

James himself once gave advice on the reading of his novels. On September 14, 1913, he wrote his old friend Mrs. G. W. Prothero, who had appealed to him to supply her friend, a "young man from Texas," Mr. Stark Young, with guidance in the study of his books. James made two lists of his major novels, "all on the basis of the Scribner's (or [London] Macmillan's) collective and revised and prefaced edition" of his fiction. The first list contained *Roderick Hudson** (1876), *The Portrait of a Lady** (1881), *The Princess Casamassima** (1886), *The Wings of the Dove** (1902), *The Golden Bowl** (1904). The second list, which he called "the more 'advanced,'" also included five novels: *The American** (1877), *The Tragic Muse** (1890), *The Wings of the Dove** (1902), *The Ambassadors** (1903), and *The Golden Bowl** (1904).

These two lists are useful to readers wishing to trace James's progress as a novelist, but both of them lack certain novels of major importance which no serious reader will want to miss: *The Europeans* (1878), *Washington Square* (1881), *The Bostonians* (1886), *The Spoils of Poynton** (1897), *What Maisie Knew** (1897), *In the Cage** (1898), and *The Awkward Age** (1899). For more specialized readers there remain the early novels *Watch and Ward* (1878) and *Confidence* (1880); *The Other House* (1896) and *The Sacred Fount* (1901); and two unfinished novels, *The Ivory Tower* (1917) and *The Sense of the Past* (1917).

James's shorter fiction ranges from short stories to long tales or *nouvelles*. These run to over a hundred titles. As a supplement to the fiction included in this book I offer the following suggestions for reading. I list them under several convenient categories. I omit stories included in the present volume, and I asterisk titles revised by James in the New York Edition. The dates here are of first publication, usually in magazines, sometimes in book collections of his tales. The first book publication of all these tales is given in the *Chronology* on pages 29-36.

* Asterisks indicate that titles so marked were revised and included by James in the New York Edition of his fiction, 1907-1909, but the dates given are those of first book publication.

Beginnings: Early Tales. "The Story of a Year" (1865), "Poor Richard" (1867), "A Most Extraordinary Case" (1868)—these three dealing with the Civil War; "A Landscape Painter" (1866), "The Romance of Certain Old Clothes" (1868), "DeGrey: A Romance" (1868), "Gabrielle de Bergerac" (1869), "Travelling Companions" (1870).

The International Theme. "A Passionate Pilgrim" * (1871), "Madame de Mauves" * (1875), "An International Episode * (1878), *Daisy Miller** (1878), "A Bundle of Letters" * (1879), "The Pension Beaurepas" * (1879), "The Point of View" * (1882), "The Siege of London" * (1883), "A London Life" * (1888), *The Reverberator** (1888), " 'Europe' " * (1899), "Miss Gunton of Poughkeepsie" * (1900), "Fordham Castle" * (1904).

The Comedy and Tragedy of Society. "Eugene Pickering" (1874), "Lady Barbarina" * (1884), "Georgina's Reasons" (1885), "Louisa Pallant" * (1888), "The Liar" * (1888), "The Patagonia" * (1888), "Mrs. Temperley" (1889), "The Solution" (1889), "Brooksmith" * (1891), "The Chaperon" * (1891), "The Wheel of Time" (1892), "Lord Beaupré" (1893), "The Two Faces" * (1901), "The Beldonald Holbein" * (1901), "Mrs. Medwin" * (1901), "Flickerbridge" * (1902), "The Special Type" (1903), *Julia Bride** (1908), "Crapy Cornelia" (1909), "Mora Montravers" (1909).

Stories of Writers and Artists. "The Madonna of the Future" * (1873), "The Author of Beltraffio" * (1884), "The Aspern Papers" * (1888), "The Lesson of the Master" * (1888), "The Private Life" * (1892), "The Middle Years" * (1893), "Sir Dominick Ferrand" (1893), "The Death of the Lion" * (1894), "The Coxon Fund" * (1894), "The Next Time" * (1895), "The Figure in the Carpet" * (1896), "John Delavoy" (1898), "Broken Wings" * (1900), "The Abasement of the Northmores" * (1900), "The Tone of Time" (1900), "The Story in It" * (1903), "The Velvet Glove" (1909). A good collection of the tales on this theme is *Stories of Writers and Artists* by Henry James, edited by F. O. Matthiessen (1946).

Ghostly Tales. "Sir Edmund Orme" * (1892), "The Private Life" * (1892), "Owen Wingrave" * (1893), "The Altar of the Dead" * (1895), "The Friends of the Friends" * ([1896] 1909), "The Turn of the Screw" * (1898), "The Great Good Place" * (1900), "The Real Right Thing" * (1900), "Maud-Evelyn" (1900), "The Third Person" (1900), "The Jolly Corner" * (1908). For all of James's stories of this kind, see Leon Edel's excellent edition of *The Ghostly Tales of Henry James* (1948).

James's major writings in criticism are contained in the book collections he himself made of his critical essays. The little book on *Hawthorne* (1879) is of first importance. His other books of criticism and the essays of special importance in them are: *French Poets and Novelists* (1878)—"Théophile Gautier," "Charles Baudelaire," "Honoré de Balzac," "Balzac's Letters," "George Sand," "Ivan Turgénieff," "The Théâtre Français." *Partial Portraits* (1888)—"Emerson," "The Life of George Eliot," "Anthony Trollope," "Robert Louis Stevenson," "Alphonse Daudet," "Guy de Maupassant," "Ivan Turgénieff," "The Art of Fiction." *Essays in London and Elsewhere* (1893)—"James Russell Lowell," "Gustave Flaubert," "Pierre Loti," "Henrik Ibsen," "Criticism." *The Question of Our Speech / The Lesson of Balzac* (1905). *Notes on Novelists with Some Other Notes* (1914)—"Robert Louis Stevenson," "Émile Zola," "Gustave Flaubert," "Honoré de Balzac" (two essays), "George Sand" (three essays), "Gabriele D'Annunzio," "The New Novel, 1914," "The Novel in *The Ring and the Book*." Of the early criticisms collected by LeRoy Phillips in *Views and Reviews* (1908), those particularly interesting are "The Novels of George Eliot," "Swinburne's Essays," "Matthew Arnold's Essays," "Mr. Walt Whitman," "The Limitations of Dickens," "Tennyson's Drama," and "Mr. Kipling's Early Stories." Pierre de Chaignon la Rose's edition of other early *Notes and Reviews* (1921) shows James as a critic and reviewer of books from 1864 to 1886. James's single collection of his writings on art is *Picture and Text* (1893). His writings on drama, theater, and acting have been admirably collected by Allan Wade under the title *The Scenic Art* (1948). In all these fields of criticism of literature, art, and drama, James wrote much that remains uncollected; most of this work is listed in LeRoy Phillips's *Bibliography of the Writings of Henry James* (New York: Coward-McCann, 1930).

James's memoir of *William Wetmore Story and His Friends* (1903) is a book of great charm and fascination, and a major document on James's own relations with Europe.

His dramas may now be read in Leon Edel's definitive edition of *The Complete Plays of Henry James* (1949), with their copious biographical, textual, and critical annotations.

His writings on travel, cultures, societies, are best followed in the series of these he himself published in book form: *Transatlantic Sketches* (1875), *Foreign Parts* (1883), *Portraits of Places* (1883), *A Little Tour of France* (1885), the essay on "London" in *Essays in London and Elsewhere* (1893), *English Hours* (1905), *The American Scene* (1907)—his major work of this kind—and *Italian Hours* (1909). Here again a great quantity of James's writing remains uncollected and must be traced in Phillips's *Bibliography*.

Phillips gives the basic facts on the complex details of the editions and publishers of James's books in England and America (such details have not been included above), but his work is importantly supplemented by I. R. Brussel's *Anglo-American First Editions* (London and New York: Bowker Co., 1935-36), indispensable to students of James's bibliography.

II: BIOGRAPHY AND CRITICISM

Biography. No full biography of Henry James has yet appeared, but a life, detailed and authorized, is in preparation by Leon Edel. James' own three autobiographical memoirs are indispensable: *A Small Boy and Others* (1913), *Notes of a Son and Brother* (1914), and *The Middle Years* (1917). Percy Lubbock's edition of *The Letters of Henry James* (New York: Scribner's, 1920) contains a sketch of his life as well as the valuable letters themselves. For other collections of letters, see the Editor's Note to Part VI of this book. F. W. Dupee's *Henry James* in the American Men of Letters Series (New York: William Sloane Associates, 1951) gives an account of the life as well as critical interpretation of the works. Much additional material on Henry James is included in the records of his family:

James, Henry, Jr., *The Letters of William James* (Boston: Atlantic Monthly Press, 1920).

Grattan, C. Hartley, *The Three Jameses: A Family of Minds* (New York: Longmans, Green, 1932).

Warren, Austin, *The Elder Henry James* (New York: Macmillan, 1934).

Burr, Anna Robeson, *Alice James: Her Brothers, Her Journal* (New York: Dodd, Mead, 1934).

Perry, Ralph Barton, *The Thought and Character of William James* (Boston: Little, Brown & Co., 1935).

Matthiessen, F. O., *The James Family, Including Selections from the Writings of Henry James Senior, William, Henry, and Alice James* (New York: Alfred A. Knopf, 1947).

The personality and legend of Henry James are strikingly presented in:

Bosanquet, Theodora, *Henry James at Work* (London: Hogarth Press, 1924). An essay by his last secretary.

Nowell-Smith, Simon, *The Legend of the Master* (New York: Scribner's, 1948). A compilation of reports and anecdotes of H.J. by those who knew him; the best guide to the many contemporary memoirs and biographies which include accounts of James.

Fundamental to the study of James's life, as well as his art, are:
James, Henry, *The Art of the Novel: Critical Prefaces* (New

York: Scribner's, 1935), with a preface by R. P. Blackmur. James's prefaces for the New York Edition of his fiction.

Matthiessen, F. O., and Kenneth B. Murdock, editors, *The Notebooks of Henry James* (New York: Oxford University Press, 1947). This contains the plans, sketches, and "germs" of his fiction and includes much autobiographical material.

The crucial years that James spent writing for the theater are dealt with in the following books and editions, which contain much additional biographical material:

Edel, Leon, *Henry James: Les Années Dramatiques* (Paris: Jouve et Cie., 1931).

Robins, Elizabeth, *Theatre and Friendship: Some Henry James Letters* (New York: Putnam's, 1932).

Wade, Allan, ed., *The Scenic Art: Notes on Acting and the Drama, 1872-1901*, by Henry James (New Brunswick, N. J.: Rutgers University Press, 1948).

Edel, Leon, ed., *The Complete Plays of Henry James* (Philadelphia: J. B. Lippincott, 1949).

Criticism. Interpretation and evaluation of James's art is voluminous. Essays and discussions in books on fiction cannot be listed fully here. A lengthy bibliography up to 1941 is included in *Henry James: Representative Selections,* edited by Lyon P. Richardson (Cincinnati: American Book Co., 1941), and this is reproduced in *The Question of Henry James,* a symposium of Jamesian criticism, edited by F. W. Dupee (New York: Henry Holt, 1945). It has been extended to include the years 1941-48 by Eunice C. Hamilton in *American Literature,* XX (1948-49), pp. 424-35. The following are the principal books that have been written on James; titles of special value are indicated by an asterisk:

Andreas, Osborn, *Henry James and the Expanding Horizon* (Seattle: University of Washington Press, 1948).

* Beach, Joseph Warren, *The Method of Henry James* (New Haven: Yale University Press, 1918). An early study but still one of the soundest general treatments.

Brooks, Van Wyck, *The Pilgrimage of Henry James* (New York: E. P. Dutton and Co., 1925). Notable as an extreme argument against James's expatriation from America and its effect on his work.

Cary, Elizabeth Luther, *The Novels of Henry James* (New York: Putnam's, 1906). The earliest book on James.

* Dupee, F. W., *Henry James* (New York: William Sloane

Associates, 1951). A valuable work combining biography and criticism.

Edel, Leon, *The Prefaces of Henry James* (Paris: Jouve et Cie., 1931).

Edgar, Pelham, *Henry James: Man and Author* (London: Grant Richards; Boston: Houghton Mifflin, 1927). General and descriptive chiefly.

Garnier, Marie-Reine, *Henry James et la France* (Paris: Honoré Champion, 1927).

Hueffer [Ford], Ford Madox, *Henry James: A Critical Study* (New York: Dodd, Mead, 1916). Personal and eccentric, but stimulating as a study of craft and style.

* Kelly, Cornelia Pulsifer, *The Early Development of Henry James* (Urbana: University of Illinois, 1930). Documented, scrupulous, sound; especially valuable for its study of James's European literary affiliations.

* Matthiessen, F. O., *Henry James: The Major Phase* (New York: Oxford University Press, 1944). A study of the period 1895-1910.

Milano, Paolo, *Henry James: o Il Proscritto Volontario* (Milan: Arnoldo Mondadori, 1948).

* Roberts, Morris, *Henry James's Criticism* (Cambridge: Harvard University Press, 1929). The fullest study of James as critic.

Snell, Edwin Marion, *The Modern Fables of Henry James* (Cambridge: Harvard University Press, 1935). Short but perceptive.

* Stevenson, Elizabeth, *The Crooked Corridor: A Study of Henry James* (New York: Macmillan, 1949). A limited but sensitive introductory study of James.

West, Rebecca, *Henry James* (London: Nisbet and Co., 1916). A short early study; opinionated but stimulating.

No effort is made here to list recent reprints or collections of James's work, but the following should be mentioned because of the biographical or critical material they include:

Auden, W. H., ed., *The American Scene* by Henry James (New York: Scribner's, 1946).

Edel, Leon, ed., *The Ghostly Tales of Henry James* (New Brunswick, N. J.: Rutgers University Press, 1948).

Fadiman, Clifton, ed., *The Short Stories of Henry James* (New York: Random House, 1945).

Kenton, Edna, ed., *Eight Uncollected Tales of Henry James* (New Brunswick, N. J.: Rutgers University Press, 1950).

Matthiessen, F. O., ed., *Henry James: Stories of Writers and Artists* (New York: New Directions, 1946).

Matthiessen, F. O., ed., *The American Novels and Stories of Henry James* (New York: Alfred A. Knopf, 1947).

Rahv, Philip, ed., *The Great Short Novels of Henry James* (New York: Dial Press, 1944).

Richardson, Lyon P., ed., *Henry James: Representative Selections* (Cincinnati: American Book Company, 1941).

A number of critical symposia on Henry James have been published, the most notable being:

The Little Review, Henry James Number, Vol. V, No. 4 (August 1918), pp. 1-64. Prepared by Ezra Pound, with essays by Ethel Colburn Mayne, Ezra Pound, T. S. Eliot, John Rodker, Theodora Bosanquet.

The Hound and Horn, "Homage to Henry James," Vol. VII, No. 3 (April-June 1934), pp. 361-562. Edited by Lincoln Kirstein. With essays by Marianne Moore, Lawrence Leighton, Edmund Wilson, Francis Fergusson, Stephen Spender, Newton Arvin, R. P. Blackmur, Alice Boughton, John Wheelwright, Robert Cantwell, Edna Kenton, H. R. Hays, Glenway Wescott.

The New Republic, Memorial Issue on William and Henry James, Vol. CVIII, issue of February 15, 1943. With essays by Alfred Kazin, Jacques Barzun, Irwin Edman, William Troy, Philip Rahv.

The Kenyon Review, Henry James Number, Vol. V, No. 4 (Autumn 1943), pp. 481-617. Edited by Robert Penn Warren. With essays by Katherine Anne Porter, Francis Fergusson, Jacques Barzun, John L. Sweeney, F. O. Matthiessen, Austin Warren, David Daiches, Eliseo Vivas, R. P. Blackmur.

The Question of Henry James, edited by F. W. Dupee (New York: Henry Holt and Co., 1945). With essays by Thomas Wentworth Higginson, William Dean Howells, Frank Moore Colby, Herbert Croly, Max Beerbohm, Joseph Conrad, Ford Madox Ford, Percy Lubbock, Stuart P. Sherman, Joseph Warren Beach, Thomas Beer, T. S. Eliot, Van Wyck Brooks, Vernon Louis Parrington, Edna Kenton, Constance Rourke, Edmund Wilson, R. P. Blackmur, Morton Dauwen Zabel, F. O. Matthiessen, Stephen Spender, W. H. Auden, André Gide, Jacques Barzun, William Troy, Philip Rahv.

The books and critical collections previously listed will illustrate for the reader much of the best Jamesian criticism and the characteristic "approaches" of the past several decades. Certain other essays on James have special value in dealing with fundamental, sometimes controversial, aspects of his work. The following are some of the most important:

Anderson, Quentin, "Henry James and the New Jerusalem," *Kenyon Review*, VIII (Autumn 1946), pp. 515-66. An inquiry into the influence of his father's religious and philosophic ideas on James's art and thought.

Bewley, Marius, "James's Debt to Hawthorne," *Scrutiny* (Cambridge, England), XVI (September 1949), pp. 178-195, and (Winter 1949), pp. 301-317; XVII (Spring 1950), pp. 14-31. A detailed study of a major influence on James.

Bewley, Marius, "Appearance and Reality in Henry James," *Scrutiny*, XVII (Summer 1950), pp. 90-114.

Blackmur, Richard P., "Henry James," in *Literary History of the United States*, Vol. II (New York: Macmillan, 1948). A sound general account and estimation.

Eliot, T. S., "In Memory" and "The Hawthorne Aspect," *The Little Review*, V (August 1918), pp. 44-53. Reprinted in Edmund Wilson's anthology *The Shock of Recognition* (New York: Doubleday, 1943) and in F. W. Dupee's *The Question of Henry James* (New York: Holt, 1945). Eliot's most important writings on James; important as the view of a continuator.

Kenton, Edna, "Henry James to the Ruminant Reader: *The Turn of the Screw*," *The Arts*, VI (November 1924), pp. 245-55. A pioneer essay on psychological elements in James.

Leavis, F. R., "Henry James," in *The Great Tradition* (New York: George W. Stewart, 1949). Acute and essential; one of the most valuable among recent critical treatments.

Leavis, F. R., "James's *What Maisie Knew:* A Disagreement," *Scrutiny*, XVII (Summer 1950), pp. 115-27.

Lubbock, Percy, *The Craft of Fiction* (New York: Scribner's, 1921). Includes several analyses of James's novels by a disciple of his critical method.

Pound, Ezra, "Henry James," in *Make It New* (New Haven: Yale University Press, 1935). Program notes and commentary on the work in general.

Rahv, Philip, "The Heiress of All the Ages" and "Attitudes Toward Henry James," in *Image and Idea: Fourteen Essays on Literary Themes* (New York: New Directions, 1949).

Rosenzweig, Saul, "The Ghost of Henry James: A Study in Thematic Apperception," in *Character and Personality* (Duke University Press), XIII, No. 2 (December 1943); reprinted in *Partisan Review*, XI (Fall 1944), pp. 436-55. Perhaps the most notable psychological inquiry into James's personality and fiction.

Rourke, Constance, "The American," in *American Humor: A Study of the National Character* (New York: Harcourt, Brace, 1931). A brilliant essay on humor and native satire in James.

Spender, Stephen, "Part One: Henry James," in *The Destructive Element: A Study of Modern Writers and Beliefs* (Boston: Houghton Mifflin, 1935).

Trilling, Lionel, "Introduction" to *The Princess Casamassima* (New York: Macmillan, 1948); reprinted in *The Liberal Imagination* by Lionel Trilling (New York: Viking Press, 1950).

Wilson, Edmund, "The Ambiguity of Henry James," in *The Triple Thinkers* (New York: Harcourt, Brace, 1938; but revised and expanded: New York: Oxford University Press, 1948). A notable, Freudian, and provocative interpretation of *The Turn of the Screw*, but also a suggestive review of the whole body of James's work; one of the most stimulating of recent interpretations. The view it presents has been variously opposed or debated; see, for instance, Robert B. Heilman's "The Freudian Reading of *The Turn of the Screw*," *Modern Language Notes*, LXII (November 1947), pp. 433-45, and "*The Turn of the Screw* as Poem," *University of Kansas City Review*, XIV (Summer 1948), pp. 277-89; also A. J. A. Waldock's "Mr. Edmund Wilson and *The Turn of the Screw*," *Modern Language Notes*, LXII (May 1947), pp. 331-34; E. E. Stoll's "Symbolism in Coleridge," *Publications of the Modern Language Association*, LXIII (March 1948), pp. 214-33; Francis X. Roellinger's "Psychical Research and *The Turn of the Screw*," *American Literature*, XX (1948-49), pp. 401-412; Glenn A. Reed's "Another Turn on James's *Turn of the Screw*," *American Literature*, XX (1948-49), pp. 413-23; and further, "The 'Hallucination' Theory of *The Turn of the Screw*" in *A Treatise on the Novel* by Robert Liddell (London: Cape, 1947), pp. 138-145, and Leon Edel in his *Ghostly Tales of Henry James* (New Brunswick, N. J.: Rutgers University Press, 1948).

Winters, Yvor, "Maule's Well, or Henry James and the Relation of Morals to Manners," in *Maule's Curse: Seven Studies in the History of American Obscurantism* (Norfolk, Conn.: New Directions, 1938); now reprinted in Winters' *In Defense of Reason* (New York: Swallow Press and William Morrow, 1947; and University of Denver, Alan Swallow, 1950). A basic and radical study of moral and social elements in James.

It must finally be emphasized again that Henry James was an author who subjected much of his fiction to revision, not only for the 24 volumes of the New York Edition (Scribner's, 1907-1909), but even in earlier transitions from serialized to book form and frequently from edition to edition in book form (*The American* is a notable example of this). Sometimes such revision, of a more incidental kind, appeared in successive editions of his critical, travel, and other writings. The serious reader must consequently be aware of what version of a text he is reading.

The New York Edition [lately reissued] was published by Scribner in New York and by Macmillan in London; and to its 24 original volumes of novels and tales the unfinished novels *The Ivory Tower* and *The Sense of the Past* were added in 1917, the *Letters* in 1920. These are revised texts and sometimes reappear in recent reprintings or anthologies. (The present volume reproduces the texts of its fiction from the New York Edition.) Critical opinion as to the wisdom of James's revisions has naturally differed. In the 35 volumes of *The Novels and Stories of Henry James* which Macmillan published in London in 1921-23, the editor, Percy Lubbock, included, besides the texts and prefaces of the New York Edition, eleven further volumes of novels and tales which James did not have room for in the New York Edition or chose to omit from it; only a few works, like "Covering End," *The Other House,* and *The Outcry,* which James converted into or novelized from his plays, were omitted. This invaluable edition is also, regrettably, out of print at present. The nonfictional writing of James has never been collected in a uniform edition. Editions of his early uncollected work that have been made by various editors since his death are listed in the *Chronology* of the present volume. Current reprint editions of James's work should, but do not always, indicate which version of their text they employ. Phillips's *Bibliography* and I. R. Brussel's *Anglo-American First Editions,* both mentioned above, are basic equipment for investigating the complex conditions of James's texts and editions.

M.D.Z.

SUPPLEMENT, 1968

BY HENRY JAMES

Dupee, F. W., ed., *Henry James's Autobiography* (New York: Criterion Books, 1956).

Edel, Leon, ed., *American Essays* (New York: Knopf Vintage Books, 1956).

————, ed., *The Complete Tales of Henry James* (London: Rupert Hart-Davis, 1961–64; Philadelphia: Lippincott, 1962–65; 12 vols.).

————, ed., *The Future of the Novel* (New York: Knopf Vintage Books, 1956).

————, ed., *Selected Letters of Henry James* (New York: Farrar, Straus, and Cudahy, 1955).

Kenton, Edna, ed., *Eight Uncollected Tales of Henry James* (New Brunswick, N.J.: Rutgers University Press, 1950).

The Novels and Tales of Henry James, New York Edition (New York: Scribner's, 1907–17, reprinted 1962–65; · 26 vols.).

Sweeney, John L., ed., *The Painter's Eye: Notes and Essays on the Pictorial Art* (London: Rupert Hart-Davis; Cambridge, Mass.: Harvard University Press, 1956).

Zabel, Morton Dauwen, ed., *Major Critical Essays* (New York: Doubleday Anchor Books, 1956).

BIBLIOGRAPHY

Edel, Leon, and Dan H. Laurence, *A Bibliography of Henry James* (London: Rupert Hart-Davis, 1957; 2nd. ed., rev., 1961).

Modern Fiction Studies, XII (Spring 1966), 117–77.

Spiller, Robert E., "Henry James," in Floyd Stovall, ed., *Eight American Authors: A Review of Research and Criticism* (New York: Modern Language Association of America, 1956), pp. 367–418.

BIOGRAPHY

Bell, Millicent, *Edith Wharton and Henry James: The Story of a Friendship* (New York: George Braziller, 1965).

Borklund, Elmer, "Howard Sturgis, Henry James, and Belchamber," *Modern Philology,* LVIII (May 1961), 255–69.

Donovan, Alan B., "My Dear Pinker: The Correspondence of Henry James with His Literary Agent," *Yale University Library Gazette*, XXXVI (October 1961), 78–88.

Edel, Leon, *The Diary of Alice James* (New York: Dodd, Mead, 1964).

——, *Henry James: The Untried Years: 1843–1870* (Philadelphia and New York: Lippincott, 1953).

——, *Henry James: The Conquest of London: 1870–1881* (Philadelphia: Lippincott, 1962).

——, *Henry James: The Middle Years: 1882–1895* (Philadelphia: Lippincott, 1962). Edel's full biography is the most important of the new works on James.

——, and Lyall H. Powers, eds., "Henry James and the Bazar Letters," *Bulletin of the New York Public Library*, LXII (February 1958), 17–103.

——, and Gordon N. Ray, eds., *Henry James and H. G. Wells: A Record of Their Friendship, Their Debate on the Art of Fiction, and Their Quarrel* (Urbana, Ill.: University of Illinois Press, 1958).

Hyde, Montgomery H., *The Story of Lamb House, Rye: The Home of Henry James* (Rye, Sussex: Adams of Rye, Ltd., 1966). An excellent little history of James's English home.

LeClair, Robert C., *The Young Henry James* (New York: Bookman Associates, 1955).

Monteiro, George, *Henry James and John Hay: The Record of a Friendship* (Providence, R.I.: Brown University Press, 1965).

Rosenbaum, S. P., "Letters to the Pell-Clarkes from Their 'Old Cousin and Friend' Henry James," *American Literature*, XXXI (March 1959), 46–58.

Roughead, William, ed., *Tales of the Criminous* (London: Cassell, 1956).

Swan, Michael, "Henry James the Heroic Young Master," *The London Magazine*, II (May 1955), 78–86.

Weber, Carl J., and Burdett Gardner, "Letters of James to Vernon Lee (Violet Pagel)," *PMLA*, LXVIII (September 1953), 672–95.

CRITICISM

Anderson, Quentin, *The American Henry James: The Novelist as Moralist* (New Brunswick, N.J.: Rutgers University Press, 1956).

Beach, Joseph Warren, *The Method of Henry James* (Philadelphia: Albert Saifer, 1954).

Bewley, Marius, *The Complex Fate* (New York: The Grove Press, 1953).

Blackall, Jean Frantz, *Jamesian Ambiguity and* The Sacred Fount (Ithaca, N.Y.: Cornell University Press, 1965). A helpful study of one of James's most "difficult" novels.

Bowden, Edwin T., *The Themes of Henry James* (New Haven, Conn.: Yale University Press, 1956).

*Cargill, Oscar, *The Novels of Henry James* (New York: Macmillan, 1961). A very useful compendium, identifying sources and offering a thorough review of scholarship and criticism.

Clair, John A., *The Ironic Dimension in the Fiction of Henry James* (Pittsburgh: Duquesne University Press, 1965).

Cranfill, Thomas M., *An Anatomy of* The Turn of the Screw (Austin, Texas: University of Texas Press, 1965).

*Crews, Frederick C., *The Tragedy of Manners: Moral Drama in the Later Novels of Henry James* (New Haven, Conn.: Yale University Press, 1957). The best study of James's "major phase" since Matthiessen's classic work.

Dupee, F. W., *Henry James* (New York: Doubleday Anchor Books, 1956).

*Edel, Leon, ed., *Henry James: A Collection of Critical Essays,* Twentieth Century Views (Englewood Cliffs, N.J.: Prentice-Hall, 1963). Collection of "classic" essays.

Gale, Robert L., *The Caught Image: Figurative Language in the Fiction of Henry James* (Chapel Hill, N.C.: University of North Carolina Press, 1964).

Geismar, Maxwell, *Henry James and the Jacobites* (Boston: Houghton Mifflin, 1963). A rather cranky scolding of the Jamesian cultists; well aimed at a fair and vulnerable target, yet somewhat frustrated by its crankiness.

*Hoffman, Charles G., *The Short Novels of Henry James* (New York: Bookman Associates, 1957). Sensitive and intelligent criticism of James's work in the genre.

Holder-Barell, Alexander, *The Development of Imagery and Its Functional Significance in Henry James's Novels,* The Cooper Monographs, No. 3 (Bern: Francke Verlag, 1959).

*Holland, Laurence B., *The Expense of Vision: Essays on the Craft of Henry James* (Princeton, N.J.: Princeton University Press, 1964).

Horne, Helen, *Basic Ideas of James's Aesthetics as Expressed in the Short Stories Concerning Artists and Writers* (Marburg: Erich Mauersberger, 1960).

*Krook, Dorothea, *The Ordeal of Consciousness in Henry James* (New York: Cambridge University Press, 1962). Possibly the most illuminating criticism of James to appear in recent years.

Lebowitz, Naomi, *The Imagination of Loving: Henry James's*

* Critical works of special value.

Legacy to the Novel (Detroit, Mich.: Wayne State University Press, 1965).

Levy, Leo B., *Versions of Melodrama: A Study of the Fiction and Drama of Henry James, 1865–1897* (Berkeley, Calif.: University of California Press, 1957).

Matthiessen, F. O., *The American Novels and Stories of Henry James* (New York: Knopf, 1947).

McCarthy, Harold T., *Henry James: The Creative Process* (New York: Thomas Yoseloff, 1958).

Marks, Robert, *James's Later Novels: An Interpretation* (New York: William-Frederick Press, 1960).

Mordell, Albert, ed., *Discovery of a Genius: William Dean Howells and Henry James* (New York: Twayne Publications, 1961).

*Poirier, Richard, *The Comic Sense of Henry James: A Study of the Early Novels* (New York: Oxford University Press, 1960). Skillfully illuminates a neglected aspect of James's art; a sequel study of the later novels remains to be done.

Sharp, Sister M. Corona, *The "Confidante" in Henry James: Evolution and Moral Value of a Fictive Character* (Notre Dame, Ind.: University of Notre Dame Press, 1963).

Stone, Edward, *The Battle of the Books: Some Aspects of Henry James* (Athens, Ohio: Ohio University Press, 1964).

Swan, Michael, *Henry James* (London: Arthur Barker, Ltd., 1952).

Vaid, Krishna Baldev, *Technique in the Tales of Henry James* (Cambridge, Mass.: Harvard University Press, 1964).

*Ward, Joseph A., *The Imagination of Disaster: Evil in the Fiction of Henry James* (Lincoln, Neb.: University of Nebraska Press, 1961). Clarifies an important topic in James.

Wegelin, Christof, *Image of Europe in Henry James* (Dallas, Tex.: Southern Methodist University Press, 1958).

West, Muriel, *A Stormy Night with* The Turn of the Screw (Phoenix, Ariz.: Frye and Smith, 1964).

Wiesenfarth, Joseph, *Henry James and the Dramatic Analogy* (New York: Fordham University Press, 1963).

Wright, Walter F., *The Madness of Art: A Study of Henry James* (Lincoln, Neb.: University of Nebraska Press, 1962).

PAMPHLETS

Edel, Leon, *Henry James,* University of Minnesota Pamphlets on American Writers (Minneapolis, Minn.: University of Minnesota Press, 1960). Briefest but soundest of the lot.

Jefferson, D. W., *Henry James,* Writers and Critics Series (Edinburgh: Oliver and Boyd, 1960).

* Critical works of special value.

McElderry, Bruce R., Jr., *Henry James,* Twayne's United States Authors Series, No. 79 (New York: Twayne Publishers, 1965).

HANDBOOKS

Putt, S. Gorley, *A Reader's Guide to Henry James* (Ithaca, N.Y.: Cornell University Press, 1966).

L.H.P.